Monkey Trap

Nova sapiens Book I

By Lee Denning

Twilight Times Books
Kingsport, Tennessee

Monkey Trap

Twilight Times Books
POB 3340
Kingsport TN 37664
http://twilighttimesbooks.com/

First paperback printing, November 2004

Library of Congress Cataloging-in-Publication Data

Denning, Lee.
  Monkey trap / Lee Denning.
      p. cm. -- (Nova sapiens ; bk. 1)
   ISBN 1-931201-34-X (trade pbk: alk. paper)
   I. Title. II. Series: Denning, Lee. Nova sapiens ; bk. 1.
PS3604.E586M66 2004
813'.6--dc22

                    2004019347

Pastel sketches by Heather Rosenberry

Printed in the United States of America.

Dedication

In the sixteenth century, Copernicus departed from the accepted wisdom that the earth was the center of the universe. He had the good sense to die just as his work was being published. Almost a century later Galileo and Bruno espoused his ideas. They paid a price for departure from the dogma of their era, but in many ways established the basis for modern science. *Monkey Trap* is dedicated, with respect and admiration, to the growing number of present-day scientists and philosophers who are unencumbered by dogma and unafraid to apply science in its best use, to stretch the envelope of our understanding.

Acknowledgments

A number of people kindly provided thoughts and opinions on the various drafts of *Monkey Trap*: Ann Astarita, an environmental scientist and mother; Brett Anningson, a writer and minister; Kathi Chiaruzzi, a teacher and skeptic; Gail Gentle, a human resources consultant and farmer; Nick Harding, a Special Forces soldier and lawyer; Sam Rosenberg, a psychologist and manufacturing entrepreneur; Larry Pender, a writer and student. Malo Forde, tennis partner and friend, helped out with Irish authenticisms and irrepressible humor. Ginger James, cheerleader and confidante, kick-started the story-telling process and provided invaluable insights and feedback along the road. Lida Quillen at Twilight Times Books saw the potential in the novel, and adopted it. Dr. Bob Rich provided the kind of thoughtful editing that hones without losing essentials. Joe, Tim, Rich and Yev all picked up our slack so this venture could proceed.

Special thanks to Dr. Roger Nelson, an experimental cognitive psychologist and director of the Global Consciousness Project at Princeton--he smilingly endorsed co-option of his science into our fiction. We encourage readers visit the Project's website at *noosphere.princeton.edu*. The implications of Dr. Nelson's work to concepts of consciousness are truly fascinating.

We also deeply appreciate the current research of other like-minded scientists and philosophers, many of them affiliated with the Institute of Noetic Sciences. Seed concepts from the Institute's various publications underpin several of *Monkey Trap's* speculations. We have taken great liberties in extrapolating those concepts to fit our story, and apologize if some seem off the mark. Any errors, of course, are completely our own. We encourage readers to visit the Institute's website at *www.noetic.org* for enlightenment on the nature of consciousness and related subjects.

Chapter 1

The Assassin sat in the crotch of a tree awaiting the time his target would appear. He contemplated the full moon, cradling into the mountains to the west. To the east, the sun would be easing toward the treetop horizon, a fat glowing orange in the humid air. The artist in him admired the ethereal light of the approaching tropical dawn. Viewed from space, he was under the terminator: half the planet in darkness, half in light.

Like me, the Assassin smiled crookedly. The smile faded as his hard hands unfolded the delicate gossamer-winged angel of death. The morning birdsong of the jungle grew muted around him.

Creating the little killer drone had been complex, yet it operated so simply. He marveled again at the miniaturization and technology, proud of his part in its creation. Then he ran down the preflight checklist on his laptop computer screen.

The drone's soft feminine voice whispered confirmation in his ear:

"Wings configured.

"Power up.

"Control surfaces functional.

"Telemetry up, both directions.

"Global positioning engaged.

"Target acquisition up.

"Laser guidance operative.

"Darts armed."

The tiny laptop showed an all-green board. He disconnected the umbilical cord connecting his laptop to the killer drone and stepped out of his tree hammock onto the branch. With the foliage pushed down by his weight, the drug lord's compound became clearly visible, pocketed into a hillside over two miles away on the north side of the valley. The straight lines of the crop fields on the valley floor, and the clear fields of fire they allowed, defined the compound for what it truly was: a well-defended enclave.

The Assassin studied it carefully through his binoculars in the growing light, his soldier's training appreciating their thoroughness. He spoke into his headset microphone, ticking off key points:

"The file on security is quite accurate.

"Electronic surveillance and random roving patrols extend almost this far out.

"Physical barriers, landmines, concertina fences closer in.

"Not just your usual small arms; confirm Vulcan cannon on the Hummers.

"Armored vehicles, probably custom-built hybrids, under the camouflage netting; I can't ID.

"They have an array of heavy-caliber machine guns and rocket-grenade launchers, also under the netting.

"Both fixed and mobile antiaircraft platforms; I see four and two."

The Assassin thought back through the intelligence file he had memorized. Security run by ex-Israeli intelligence officers and former Legionnaires; criminals all, but nonetheless some of the most devious minds in their craft. Probably the latest and best technology drug money can buy, he admitted. They certainly had the best security operation in the entire drug trade, both people and equipment.

"Feeling pretty secure, are you?" he concluded the analysis. "Well, not *this* morning, and not from *me*." The threat slid out easily through his crooked smile.

The Assassin kissed the little killer drone, and pointed it toward the compound. Within seconds, it integrated its camera view with that of the high-altitude recon drone above them, solving out the global positioning equations, computing its flight path.

The drone whispered into his headset, "Object location acquired, release when ready."

"Fly true, angel," he blessed, and the drone slid from his hand. It lofted with delicate grace and eerie quiet eastward away from his treetop nest, taking a meandering course through the uppermost canopy of the jungle.

No one could pick up the little killer drone by instrument; even tuned radars would paint its composite materials as a small bird. No one would likely pick it up by eye; with its gossamer wings and pale colors it flew ghostlike through the skies, day or night. Even so, the Assassin guided it in from the east, keeping it in the dawn light at treetop level.

The intelligence profile said the target would appear on the balcony right at sunrise. He did—a huge, hulking, dark-skinned man, a barrel chest with a thick cover of black hair, on top of oddly short legs. The recon drone, hovering at 84,000 feet in the air ten miles east, picked him up immediately. Another marvel of technology, the recon drone was solar-powered; it could hold on-station in the stratosphere above the clouds for months or years. It had been watching the compound for the past two weeks, preparing for this moment. Now, the stereoscopic vision of its wingtip cameras transmitted an image of superb resolution to the Assassin's laptop. Diego Corrano, *el Jefe*, was unmistakable, right down to the wart on his ugly nose.

The target Corrano started his stretches and *tai chi* on the balcony outside his bedroom, slowly working into a rhythm. That balcony also served as the box seat from which he oversaw tortures and executions from time to time, if the reports were to be believed. The Assassin had studied them all carefully, and believed them.

"Stand up nice and straight, asshole," he smiled at the target so highly resolved on his laptop screen.

Corrano obliged, and the Assassin clicked the pointer on the image's hairy chest. The software limned an outline around him, and held it, no matter how the man moved. A brief pause followed while the codes in both the killer drone and the recon drone ran their preloaded subroutines. *Target Confirmed* flashed on his laptop screen, and almost simultaneously the killer drone's soft voice whispered in his ear.

"Target acquired, engage when ready."

The Assassin scrolled to the *Execute Auto* selection, clicked on it and sat forward in his tree nest, watching the screen intently. The little killer drone folded its wings back and accelerated. Now operating under its own logic scheme, it would react faster and more reliably than his ability to control it from a distance.

Diego Corrano, *el Jefe*, undisputed leader of the world's foremost cocaine and heroin conglomerate, stretched his arms to the tropical sky, a light sweat building on his skin. He turned east and squinted into the rising sun, unaware of the laser bead steadying down on his hairy chest. The dart followed immediately, burying itself in the hard fat and muscle under the rib cage. The strange warmth of the paralytic blanked out the minor sting of the dart almost before he could feel it. The recon drone showed his face clearly. The target stumbled, confused, as his left side went numb. A dark exultation flooded into the Assassin, hard-edged and cold. *El Jefe* screamed something into the bedroom behind him as he staggered and turned.

"Hit confirmed," the drone's soft whisper reported to the Assassin.

Corrano collapsed into the arms of a sunburned bald-headed man in jungle fatigues who ran from the bedroom out onto the balcony.

Aviram Glickman, the drug cartel's security chief, from the file photos, the Assassin thought, and laughed quietly.

"Ah, well, why not? Reinforce our message."

The little killer drone executed a steep climb away into a barrel roll for another pass. The genomic toxin, keyed to Corrano, probably wouldn't affect Glickman much, but the paralytic would be nasty while it lasted. The Assassin scrolled to *Backup Target* and clicked on the security chief's screen image. The software limned an outline. He bypassed the protective checks and clicked *Execute Manual*.

"No innocents in this place, Avi," he muttered as he headed the drone out of its roll and straight back toward the balcony.

The security chief pulled the dart out of a moaning Corrano, looking at it in amazement. With maybe a sense of motion in his peripheral vision, or maybe just primitive instinct, the man yanked over a table and crouched behind it, blindly firing his pistol sunward and screaming the alert into his lapel mike. It was little use: the targeting software compensated and the dart took him in the cheek.

"Manual execute hit confirmed on backup target," the drone's voice whispered. "Wing damage, implementing reverse course retrieval program."

The little killers had to be retrieved whenever possible; they were fiendishly difficult to replace. So the Assassin tracked it on his laptop, faithfully following its zig-zag programmed return path just above the treetops.

"Shit! It's only making half-speed," he muttered, "this is dangerous. Let's hope they can't see it."

His finger hovered over the *Self Destruct* command on the laptop. But he couldn't do it. The machine embodied both art and engineering of the highest order. It represented skill and knowledge and other things he once had lived for and still admired. And it was a friend, a fellow hunter, a comrade in arms, more than a machine. A predator, like him.

So he waited patiently, catching his damaged angel of death gently in his arms when it finally arrived. A message sounded instantly in his earphone, relayed from the recon drone above.

"Omega-One, Omega-One, you've been sighted. We have a scramble from the compound, three jeeps headin' south toward your position. And about one klick west we have movement toward you showin' on infrared. Maybe a foot patrol; three or four troops. Withdraw immediately. Repeat, withdraw immediately. Proceed to primary EZ and signal for rendezvous."

"Roger, understood," the Assassin replied. "Heading out. Setting angel to SDC."

He sighed and stuffed additional malleable plastique into the drone body and set it into the crotch of the tree, where its shredded wing material would be invitingly visible from the ground. He toggled the red internal microswitch labeled *Self-Destruct on Contact*. The drone would detonate thirty seconds after being moved.

With any luck at all, it would take out one or more of the security troops, and make them think twice about ambushes. That should slow them down a little. He slipped the laptop computer in his weapons harness, loaded his backpack, dropped the rope and rappelled to the ground.

He ran at hard lope southward through the jungle along one of the game trails picked out and memorized earlier from the recon graphics. They couldn't track him from their helicopters under the triple canopy, and they couldn't get jeeps down the trails. But the dogs would be a different story, and thinking of that he picked up his pace. He ran for nearly ten minutes before hearing the explosion, muffled through the heavy canopy. He said a brief requiem for his little killer drone.

Running hard now, out of the jungle through a clear area of low shrubs near a gorge, the Assassin finally heard the dogs. No problem, he thought, I'll go downstream and drop the pack on the bank, with a contact detonator. The dogs will go for it and chew it to pieces and blow themselves up for their troubles. That should buy me plenty of time to reach the extraction zone. He put the pack down and loosened the Kevlar vest that also served as a weapons harness. An explosive charge taken from his harness went quickly into the pack, wired with a detonator to fire on a broken circuit. He looked at his watch as he straightened up. Thirty minutes to work westward to the EZ. Plenty of time.

The Assassin was about to turn on his transponder and call in the extraction team when the rifle fire stitched across his partially unprotected back, knocking him into the gorge. As he fell, in what seemed like micro-slow motion, the analytical part of his mind put the shooter at over a quarter-mile. Another random roving patrol, he thought. Ah, shit, with those you just have to take your chances. A lucky shot from a distance. And me with my vest off. Life is all probabilities, isn't it?

John Jacob Connard, former Special Forces soldier, US Army. In the context of this mission, the Assassin. Uncertain professions, both. He had been shot before, and knew the numbness of shock would yield to pain. This time, though, he would be dead before he felt it. A blessing.

He watched the pack fall ahead of him. He saw the sheer drop to the river below, and admired the rising sun sparkling the top of the waterfall as he fell past. Colombia is a beautiful place to die, he thought. Then, as he turned in the air and his view rolled down the gorge, he dropped face-first through foliage growing out the side of the cliff and collided with an explosion of white feathers, a beak digging sharply into his cheek.

A dove's nest. The Assassin silently apologized for the unintended harm as his mind slid into shock. His falling motion seemed to slow to nothing and the cliff wall ballooned out to embrace him. The pain hit, unexpectedly, too early, in a brilliant flash of deep blue light. His vision tunneled down onto his watch, then faded out entirely. It was 0549.

Goddard Space Flight Center, Greenbelt, MD | Sunday 0540 EDT

A bit over 2,500 miles north of the Columbian jungle and its jagged cliffs, the night crew for the SDI exercises at Goddard Space Flight Center was just wrapping up, unaware of the Assassin or his activities.

Edwin Edwards, night-shift controller for the exercises, smiled broadly at his crew as he rose from the control chair, congratulating them.

"All right, ladies and gentlemen, that was a very good response, on a challenging exercise. This segment is hereby complete. Thank you so much for your hard work and focus. Shift change is coming up. So relax a moment, then get your notes together to brief your day-shift replacements, please.

"And speaking of the day shift... hey, good morning, Aaron. Can't sleep? Or are you just real anxious to get into it?"

Aaron O'Meara, a day-shift player for the exercises, rolled his wheelchair smoothly over the threshold into the big room as he spoke.

"Can I play with the system for a few minutes, sir? While there's a break? I'm wondering if it will still pick up those asteroids we were looking at yesterday afternoon."

"Sure, Aaron, why not? You're here early for your shift, and after all this *is* basic research." Edwards chuckled as he added "and maybe at some point we'll need to defend ourselves from space as well as from the surface. Disgruntled North Korean asteroid belt miners boosting a few into collision paths, that sort of thing...."

This pleasantly dissolved the remaining tension in the big room, the 'X-Room' at Goddard. The Center as well as each of the team members had a lot vested in the outcome. The two-week long, round-the-clock exercise had been designed to test the ability of satellite sensors to detect, and lasers to destroy, simulated ballistic missiles arcing up out of the atmosphere. The program was still called SDI, Strategic Defense Initiative, a throwback to the Reagan era. A game, here in this time and this place, but possible life and death in the future. Rogue governments. Terrorist groups. More of a concern every day. A brave new world.

The night crew smiled tired greetings at Aaron and stretched weary backs. The controller exited the X-Room and went to relieve the pressure of too much overnight coffee.

Aaron O'Meara, Ph.D, Goddard's most youthful astrophysicist, tapped the keyboard, and the gimbaled sensors on the satellite array swung spaceward. He admired the angled view of the earth's blue envelope on the big screen as the sensors traversed the southern horizon. But then, as the field of vision rotated away from the planet and outward into space, the impossibility appeared. Aaron's breath left his lungs in a whoosh of shock. His professional decorum deserted him.

"Holy shit!" he yelled, "Tracking on! Tracking on! Turn the fucking tracking on!"

But Jack Walton, the tactical tracking technician, had seen it too, and his hands already were flying over the control board. The sensor array on the satellite stopped its traverse.

"History! Plot it, for God's sake, Jack, plot it! Gimme the history! Amy! No, I mean Bill, go find Ed. If he's in the can, get him out of there quick!"

"History plotting, coming up, a few seconds," Walton yelled, fingers flying. Then, anticipating the next commands, "Recording all. Tac computer and mainframe both. Full archival engaged."

The big screen split into two displays. The top one showed double-stranded flaming interwoven spirals; erratic, disjointed motions flashing through space. They watched, fascinated. Jack Walton made the first coherent statement.

"I don't think the digitizer can keep up with those motions."

Aaron was thinking about that when the plot came up on the bottom display, the tactical computer displaying the object's trajectory.

"Jesus, Jack, you may be right. What the hell is that thing? It just came out of nowhere, south of the ecliptic, must be half the distance to the moon. Incredible delta-V's. And it's headed in... Omigod!"

On the top screen, the object bifurcated, a small part dancing with a bigger part, all crazy erratics and transverses and reverses, spiraling explosions of light and motion.

"It's a fucking dog-fight," Walton muttered, fingers flying with the afterthought of instructing the mainframe to increase the scan capture rate.

"Jack, the thing's gonna impact. Gimme a plot projection solved to the earth's surface, can you?"

"Aye sir," Walton said, his old Navy reflex kicking in even though now a civilian who outranked Aaron O'Meara by a huge margin in age and experience. "Coming up."

The team watched in rapt horror as the berserk dance ended in a flash of light and two separate objects hurtled earthward at high velocity.

"Entry coming up," Walton announced. "Larger object projected impact northwest South America, probably Columbia. Smaller object mid-Atlantic coast, US." The plot followed the trajectories, still erratic and spiraling, but now clearly separate. The projected impact points flickered around on the screen as the computer tried to update solutions to motions outpacing its software. Then probability algorithms kicked in, painting somewhat steadier crimson oval impact zones.

"Delmarva looking likely," Walton amended. "Jesus! Could be this area. At that speed if this thing's got any size to it, we're fucking toast! Brace yourselves!"

Aaron O'Meara slammed home the brake locks on his wheelchair and grabbed the edge of the control console. Tension streamed into the room. Adrenaline levels tracked the two plots on the bottom screen. The objects intersected the atmosphere. The top screen optical showed strangely distorted blue and green flaming patterns in the earth's envelope.

Random thoughts of imminent death ran through ten minds. My children; they *have* to live. I left dishes in the sink. I wish I had. I wish I hadn't. Now I'll never...

Then, a few seconds later, the patterns abruptly snapped off just as abruptly as they had snapped into being. The crimson ovals of ground-zero impact zones flickered out. The real-time clock above the big screen showed 05:48:01 EDT.

Dead silence filled the X-Room, except for the exhalations of held breath. A few signs of the cross. Then Amy McLaughlin's shaky voice: "Are we dead yet?"

A burst of nervous laughter erupted.

"Because if we're not, I gotta pee."

Edwin Edwards, exercise controller, ran back into the room into the midst of raucous hysteria.

"All right, what the hell is going on?"

Ten voices clamored as one. The controller calmed them.

"Okay, I think I've got it: incoming object, high speed, split in two, one of the projected impacts right here. But I didn't hear a boom. Anybody hear a boom? Feel anything shake? No? So that's good, right? We're all still here, right? So let's all calm down! Jack, can you show us a replay?"

They watched the replay, fascinated. The object just snapped into existence at 05:45:58 EDT, with no hint of any precursor motion. The ensuing division and crazy dance took two minutes and three seconds elapsed time to projected impact, then just as abruptly snapped out of existence. Chattering commentary from ten of the brightest minds in the business peppered the controller as they watched.

"Okay, I don't know what happened here any better than you," Edwards told them, "but we weren't annihilated. I guess we gotta report it. Aaron, come with me, please. The rest of you, please just try to calm down. Reset the satellite to the exercise scenario, and get ready to brief your shift replacements. Jack, would you carve this event out of the data file and tag it as Non-Exercise Anomaly or something? That way anybody interested can fool with it on the backup system down the hall and not interfere with the exercise. We've got a mission here, and it's costing the taxpayer big bucks, so we can't let ourselves get blown off course by this. Although it sure as hell is fascinating. C'mon, Aaron."

In his office, the controller took off his glasses and rubbed the bridge of his nose tiredly.

"Aaron, I've got to call this in. I don't even know to whom. But it's clearly something odd enough and seems real enough that I can't just write it off. Now, here's my problem," he enumerated the points on his fingers.

"One. You have this wonderful wacky sense of humor.

"Two. You're far too partial to practical jokes. And so's your buddy Jack Walton.

"Three. You came on shift a half-hour early, wanting to peer into space.

"And four. The next thing you know we've got an invasion of freaking flaming vortices that scares the shit out of everybody.

"So, Aaron, before I go making a public fool out of myself, and possibly even hurting our program here, this would be a good time to tell me it's one of your jokes. We'll all have a real good laugh. Talk for weeks about how O'Meara suckered us. Again. But there won't be any harm done. You understand?"

Amazement and consternation and hurt flashed in alternating patterns across Aaron's open countenance. He stuttered to get the words out.

"Ed…" he began, but the insistent buzz of a high priority call interrupted. The controller held up his hand.

"Hold it; I gotta take this, Aaron. It's the hot line."

"Sorry to bother you, sir," the Goddard duty officer said, "but we have a priority call from the Pentagon holding. A colonel in the Situation Room over there wants to know since we had the satellite active, did we track any atmospheric anomalies with our SDI arrays? They got a buncha ghosts on east coast radars and some visual sightings of strange stuff in the DC area. They're scrambling some F16s out of Andrews and choppers out of Quantico and Pax River. No ground impacts reported, but Homeland Security is antsy. Helluva whoop-ti-doo, sir, they want to know can we shed any light on it."

"Okay. Tell them we do have something. We'll send it over the secure defense net. Couple of gigabytes, probably. Take us about five minutes to prep it, maybe five to download. Tell them it's about two minutes of digital MPEG. That's m-p-e-g. Give me two minutes to get to the backup X-Room, F117. Patch them in there."

Then, hanging up, "Aaron, I'm sorry. It did seem like a logical question to ask, but unless you're so good a hacker you can also create real effects in the atmosphere, I have to apologize."

Aaron had already deduced the nature of the conversation.

"No impacts or explosions, I take it?"

"Apparently not."

"Ed, no offense taken. Hey, I'm fantastically flattered that you think I could manage to pull off a stunt like this. Wow! What a compliment! Come on, I'll help you set up the files for upload before I report for the exercise. Who wants them, anyway? Isn't this something? I haven't been this excited since I went too wide on the turn down the handicapped ramp in the parking garage...."

Aaron O'Meara's youthful exuberance played counterpoint to his precocious technological knowledge, and he chattered stream-of-consciousness ideas at the controller as he wheeled beside his boss down the hall to the backup X-Room.

C&O Canal Bike Trail, Washington, DC | Sunday 0547 EDT

Legs pumping, heart thumping, sweat rolling down her back, bike tires humming, Lara Picard was in a Zen-like state. Some distant part of her mind efficiently processed details: pace, gearing, braking, twists and turns and occasional discontinuities in the asphalt. The rest of her mind was totally immersed in the present moment: pulsing with the rhythm of her body, devoid of thinking, open to the universe. Fatigue was a distant thing, unimportant. She looked at her watch, realizing a personal best was imminent on this ride along her favorite bike training route. The time was 0548.

She encountered little traffic at this early hour, Washington DC sleeping off its Saturday night excesses on a Memorial Day weekend. A fat full moon illuminated the pre-dawn morning, giving plenty of light to see. The cool air bore a slight humidity. Wispy fog tendrils layered over the river, reminding her of her farm-girl roots. A young healthy organism riding flat out, her soul hummed in tune with the beauty of the river and the bike trail and the sun coming up over the horizon. She became one with the universe, a resonant frequency, on this fine early Sunday morning.

Head down, Lara barely sensed the eerie flashing ahead of her; the trees between the trail and the river mostly shielded it. She never saw the strange spiraling fire in the sky, nor the splash in the water. She only saw, speeding downhill a minute later, the bee's motion at the top of her peripheral vision. She had no time to react before it flew into her open mouth at full air intake. She tried to cough it out. In an instant of inattention, her front tire caught a rut off the asphalt, and she and the bike were airborne over an embankment. Her perceptions sped up and the world turned in slow motion, as if clicking through freeze-frame images. Impact with the ground came in a brilliant flash of green light as she blanked out.

Inert on a pebbled rocky shelf above a drainage swale, her breathing labored, her body broken and bleeding, Lara's mind sought another place....

God, he's a great lover, she thought, her body still sweating lightly from their exertions. She admired his body in the dim light, sinewy muscle over a bone structure that came as close as she'd ever seen to perfect aesthetic balance. Michelangelo's David, she mused. Or maybe more like those old movies of Bruce Lee when he's in motion. What a wonderful body.

Her lover slept on, a slight smile twitching the corner of his mouth as she knelt by the bed and ran her hand down from shoulder to hip. He gave a tiny moaned exhalation of contentment, but stayed sunk into post-coital relaxation, sound asleep. She nuzzled him gently in the small of the back, whispered how much she loved him, then pulled the sheet up and went to take her shower.

He woke and studied her as she came toweling herself out of the bathroom.

"You are looking exceptionally gorgeous this morning, my love."

"Now, I wonder why that is?" She laughed, toweling off unabashedly in front of him.

He patted the side of the bed.

"Sit down, I think I have an answer. It will make you even more gorgeous, if that's remotely possible...."

"Later, satyr." She laughed again. "I'm going for a bike ride."

"My God, woman, you should be way too tired for a bike ride! Am I not doing my job here? Please let me make amends. I'll really try to do better!"

His good intentions were punctuated by a rising under the sheet, which she studied interestedly.

"Nah, I'm not tired, I'm energized, and I'm going for a bike ride, before the traffic picks up. It's getting light enough outside. You put your head back down on your pillow and have a little snooze, and then you can massage my sore legs and buns when I get back. You know how much we both like that."

"Umm, that's all well and good, but how about a quickie to energize you some more, speed you on your way, make you nice and limber, keep you from getting saddle-sores or something?" He threw off the sheet to more expressively salute the idea.

She felt herself moistening.

"You've already given me saddle-sores, buster. So I'm going to wriggle into my biking shorts... unless... something should just happen to wriggle in before that," she said coyly. "So, hey, catch me if you can, big boy."

She grinned, flipped the towel over his face, and fled to her dressing closet on the other side of the bedroom....

Lara Ellen Picard, lawyer and mother and triathlete and lover, lay inert and bleeding on a shelf of rock between the C&O Canal and the Potomac River. As the morning sun and its heat rose over the tree line, her mind spiraled around and around that erotic event, struggling to pull up more detail. Did it take place this morning, or last Sunday morning?

She couldn't recall. Her mind seemed to have fuzzed into a state of hyperactive unspooling; remembrances and emotions flashed through it as if that most recent memory had been on the surface, and like the fastened end of a runaway ball of string it was now unwinding other memories. What a strange sensation, she thought. Almost like her consciousness was being unraveled from within her brain. Almost like it was being read into some kind of legal record. Ah, she recognized dimly, that must mean I'm dying.

But as if to counterpoint that thought and thus deny death, the unraveling suddenly reversed. The erotic memory flooded back. An overpowering sense of warmth and love ran alongside passion and spun into the forefront of her consciousness. She saw her lover in a vision so clear and acute it was almost painful.

Passion, she acknowledged fondly, oh yes; but love the far greater part of it. Even with a body in shock and pain, Lara moistened in reaction to her vision, validating once again those elemental forces that exist at the base of the brain and serve to drive life onward. Her mind, beckoned, fled toward those elemental forces. Toward survival.

Chapter 2

The Pentagon Situation Room duty officer, a crew-cut young Air Force officer in his shirt sleeves, looked sweaty and agitated on Goddard's closed-circuit defense net monitor screen.

"Okay, Dr. Edwards," the man said, "I understand you're the SDI exercise controller in charge today. We've looked at your video clips, and thank you for sending them over. But just what in hell are we looking at?"

"We haven't anything certain to offer you, I'm afraid," Edwards replied. "All we can say is that apparently it was a real phenomenon. It isn't anything that anyone here has ever seen before, or has even heard about. It originated too far out to be a magnetospheric effect, and there weren't any solar flares in progress, and it wasn't northern lights. Nothing was there, and then all of a sudden something *was* there. And it seemed like it had some mass."

"Did anything reach the ground, Dr. Edwards?"

"Apparently not. We checked for seismic events at the Naval Observatory, which is within our projected impact footprint for the East Coast object, but they show nothing, not a whisper. On the other hand, it seems unlikely that it was pure energy, it just held together too well. We have a call into the Near-Earth Asteroid Tracking Station on Maui. NEAT's run by NASA and the Jet Propulsion Lab, so maybe they can tell us if something burned up on entry. Now what can you tell us? And with whom am I speaking, by the way?"

"Sorry. I'm Jason Smith, Lieutenant Colonel, Air Force. I've got the duty slot this wonderful Sunday morning. I don't know how we're going to classify this, Dr. Edwards, but here's what we've got.

"Half the radars on the east coast painted some strange transients, looked like an incoming object at high speed, but it wasn't. The traces show down through the whole radar horizon, from high altitude right down to ground. Since our radars won't bounce off pure energy, the object either had mass, or it created some kind of atmospheric anomaly, or it emitted strongly in the microwave frequencies. We've also got reports from Metropolitan PD and Virginia State Police of sightings of meteorites or lightning or static discharges or spaceships or whatever, in the general area of Georgetown University, my old alma mater."

Past the control booth glass, across the room, Edwards saw Amy McLaughlin rating competing hypotheses on the whiteboard, with most of the team nodding 'yes' as she checked off points of agreement. Aaron O'Meara in his wheelchair also was nodding his head, but in the 'no' direction. Edwards squinted at the whiteboard, considering what to say.

"Ummm. Georgetown, huh? My alma mater, too. Say, Colonel, maybe the Jesuits have arranged some sort of divine inspiration for their basketball program. Lord knows they've done some strange things over the centuries. And they really want to move back to being the powerhouse in the Big East."

The colonel's jaw dropped, then he laughed.

Good, thought the controller, watching him on the screen; he's got a sense of humor under pressure. Maybe there's hope for him yet.

"Look, Dr. Edwards, I'm sorry if I'm agitated," Smith replied, "but I got maybe fifteen minutes before all the freaking brass in the world is gonna be honking our phones. We scrambled three F-16s for high cover, we got two Cobras at low altitude over the Potomac, and four Stallions headed there. They're all burning through taxpayer dollars at their usual atrocious rate. The brass will want some answers. What am I gonna tell 'em, I don't have a clue? Also, the press is going to be all over our ass, along with Homeland Security. Can you help me out? Please?"

The 'please' did it. The controller squinted harder at the whiteboard across the room.

"Okay, Colonel, I can tell you that the leading candidate hypothesis here at Goddard—and I'm not saying it's right or wrong, so you should cover anything you tell your brass with all the appropriate qualifiers—is that a small high-velocity asteroid from below the plane of the ecliptic collided with another asteroid or piece of space junk. Several of the pieces were deflected into a collision path with earth. The high energy of the impact and the speed through the magnetic fields and ionosphere created some phenomenal visual effects. But apparently nothing reached the surface in the DC area. No hazard to the public, so far as we can tell. I'll send you an email right away with the wording and terminology we prefer, and follow it up as we learn more."

The colonel smiled encouragingly across the video link.

"And in the meantime," Edwards continued, "my team here suggests you folks check the weather radars and see what they picked up on those wavelengths. Oh, and see what you can find out about the South American fragment. We projected an impact in southwest Colombia. That was a much bigger fragment, so some of it may actually have reached the ground. Bogota or Panama City or possibly Caracas might have picked up something if it hit the ground. There should be plenty of seismographs down there—it's a tectonically active region."

"Great!" Colonel Smith replied, yelling instructions to staff off-camera, "Anything else?"

"Nope, that's it for now. We'll see if NEAT has anything on the event; if they do, we'll send it over. Good luck with your brass."

Edwards clicked the video link into standby, and went out from the glassed control booth into the backup X-Room to observe the debate going on with his team. Although still good-natured and smiling, clearly Aaron O'Meara's Irish dander was up as he yelled at Amy McLaughlin.

"So what if nine of you think it's a high-velocity asteroid? That just means nine of you are wrong, and I'm right! Jesus, just look at those motions! Appearance out of nowhere! Incredible directional changes! Lateral spirals, retrograde! Way too much delta-V for any kind of natural Newtonian mass... it had to be controlled! And energy doesn't behave that way either! There is absolutely no question about it. Too much coherence. Too much order. It *had* to be controlled!"

"What are you saying, Aaron?" Edwards asked quietly.

Aaron beamed at him. "What I'm saying, Ed, is that this rogue asteroid idea is bullshit. What we've got here is... visitors!"

Jungle of Purace District, Colombia | Sunday 0621 EDT

The soft green light of dawn had given way to bright early morning as the sun angled up over the treetops on the opposite side of the gorge. A shaft of sunlight shone through the crevice in the cliff wall, into the cave beyond. The shaft moved slowly downward as the sun moved higher in the sky, and eventually lit the Assassin's scraped and bloody face. He sat upright, his back braced against the rear cave wall, legs out straight in front of him. He smiled faintly in reflex as the warmth of the light moved down over his eyelids, drawing his mind away from its death spiral. The unmistakable sharp crack of high explosives reverberated in the cave. He smiled more as he recognized the sound and intuited the price his pursuers had just paid for his backpack in the streambed. That brought him nearly awake, briefly.

I was airborne and fell through the trees into some damn bird nest, he remembered. *So how the hell did I end up in a cave? The last time I was in a cave, I'd broken my ankle and Dad had to get me out.*

The friendly sunbeam moved down on his neck and chest, soothing him with its warmth, fighting against the shutdown of blood loss and shock. As the Assassin's body warmed, his mind seemed to unwind, flashing through memories and emotions, unraveling them back into the past. Searching, as if looking for one key memory.

"Son of a bitch," he muttered to the empty cave, "they're right. Your life does flash before your eyes." Then his mind, beckoned, ran toward the memory of a different cave, in a better place and a better time. Toward warmth and love. And survival....

He was nine years old. He could have crawled out of that cave, he thought, even though his ankle throbbed mercilessly, but his flashlight showed just how effectively the rock slide had pinned his leg.

Two miles downhill, in the off-base housing complex favored by married senior noncoms, his mother shot straight up from a kitchen chair. Her lovely golden Eurasian complexion paled to white.

"Jake, John's in trouble. He's hurt," she said.

The soldier's heart skipped. He didn't argue; he had never known his wife's strange instincts to be wrong. He simply steadied her with his big hands on her shoulders.

"Any idea where?"

"No, no, I can't tell. Not too far, I think."

His mind raced. "Okay, you call his friends' houses, see where he might be. I'll drive around the complex, maybe I can spot him. Stay by the phone. I'll be back in ten minutes or so."

Jacob Connard had the combination of analytical mind and calm gravitas that had moved him rapidly within the Army, from a troubled young mixed-race recruit whose only distinguishing characteristic was his teal-colored eyes, to his present position as topkick in the 1st Special Forces Group at Fort Lewis, Washington. Sergeant Major Connard, a highly respected and decorated war hero with three tours in Vietnam, had seen it all. Although not prone to panic, concern for their only child grabbed at his heart more than any firefight in the jungle. He exhaled with relief when he saw Jimmy Shelton at the tennis courts.

"Jimmy, where's John, you have any idea?"

"I don't know, sir, he may be biking up on the back trails on the reservation. I haven't seen him since lunch."

Connard detected the temporizing note, and the glance away from eye contact.

"He's not up in those caves I told you boys to stay away from, is he? Jimmy! This is important! Did he say he was going up there?"

"Yessir," Jimmy replied, shuffling his feet, "he did."

"Do you know which cave he would be in?"

"Probably, sir."

"Okay, Jimmy, get in the car. I'm going to ask your momma if I can borrow you awhile."

Jimmy Shelton had found the cave with no problem, and Jacob Connard had crawled in and lifted the two-hundred pound rock off his son's leg like a feather. As that memory finished unwinding, John opened his eyes into the present, in a different cave, in the Colombian jungle....

"Hi, Dad." He smiled at the hallucination of his beloved father, who had been dead now for seven years.

"Thought I told you to stay the hell out of caves, John." His father smiled back. "If you weren't shot up so bad, I'd give you another whuppin'."

"I'm dying, Daddy," he whispered. Tears clouded John's vision as his father's huge strong hands held his face and tousled his hair, then eased him away from the cave wall and explored down to the entry wounds in his shoulder and back.

"My, my, my. You went and got yourself torn up as bad as I did on the Trail in Cambodia that time. Well, now, you just rest easy, son, and we'll see what we can do here."

John's wounds started to itch unmercifully as his consciousness collapsed into his father's gentle touch. His mind beckoned him backwards again, in a whispering chase to remember how the boy had become the man.

"When you were just a baby, boy," his father's image whispered at him, "your mama would put her hand in your crib when you were sleeping, and you would reach out and touch it, and never even wake up."

The memories seemed to have a will of their own as they played across the Assassin's consciousness, their clarity so sharp it was almost painful.

Goddard Space Flight Center, Greenbelt, MD | Sunday 0630 EDT

"Okay, okay, Aaron, we get your points," Edwin Edwards conceded. He held up his hands, exerting his authority as exercise controller and signaling a halt to the heated debate. "And they *are* pretty good ones. And maybe the rest of us *are* having a collective knee-jerk reaction. But, sheesh, Aaron, what you suggest is preposterous! It's just too damn tough to swallow! Aliens! Extra-terrestrials, ETs! Visitors from elsewhere, or maybe *elsewhen*, if I follow your logic! Good Lord, Aaron! Five of your good friends here think you've gone wacko, and four aren't so sure, but they think it's likely. And you *know* how much shit would hit the fan if this gets out! Think about it, man! For God's sake!"

Aaron smiled smugly back at his boss from his wheelchair, smoothing down the curly red hair he had theatrically pulled to express his sole dissenting opinion. Edwards studied the group, contemplating the dynamics. Nobody's really pissed, he thought. They're engaging the problem. Aaron's smart mouth isn't turning them off, it's making them reexamine their reasoning. This is a good healthy argument.

"Okay," he made the time-out sign with his hands to forestall more debate, "I haven't heard any new thoughts or significant variations in the past ten minutes. What I'm hearing is we have five strongly favoring a high velocity rogue asteroid, one strongly favoring ETs, and four saying either one is plausible given the facts we have before us, is that a fair assessment?"

Heads nodded around the table in front of the scribbled-over whiteboard. But the digital record of that extraordinary event kept respooling onto the big screen behind them, a metronomic questioning. A certain uneasiness in his team's eyes and expressions told the controller that this mystery wasn't quite resolved.

"All right," Edwards returned to practicality, "we absolutely *have* to get back to doing what we're paid to do, which is run this damn exercise. Aaron, your day-shift team awaits, you need to get over to the primary X-Room right now. We're almost an hour late starting this next segment of the exercise, and if we delay any more we'll lose the satellite window it needs. So hustle, please."

"Might I enquire as to what you're going to do with this split vote, Ed?" Aaron's crooked grin held him on its hook as he wheeled toward the door.

"Aaron, I'm going to advise the Pentagon exactly of our present 5-4-1 consensus, and take my lumps. My ridicule lumps. I'll urge them to make their own evaluation, and after that to get second, third and fourth opinions. That should spread the confusion through the bureaucracy far enough and wide enough to give our asses some serious cover."

"They'll stifle it, Ed," Aaron's expression turned sober as he spoke back through the doorway. "They'll drop a top-secret blanket on it, and just sit on it. Any kind of reaction we might have made to this event will be committee'd to death. By the time they get done with *that* dance, it'll be too late for any kind of intelligent reaction."

Having slipped in the final word, he wheeled off down the hall, frowning dissatisfaction but knowing his boss and mentor Dr. Edwin Edwards had no other realistic choice.

C&O Canal Bike Trail, Washington, DC | Sunday 0631 EDT

The thwack-thwack sound of the helicopter rotors registered dimly on Lara

Picard's consciousness, but did not raise her to awareness of her surroundings or condition. She lay still and unmoving on the rock shelf. Memories continued to unwind through her mind.

The bike lay on another ledge ten feet further down the escarpment, its front wheel bent, its rear wheel occasionally moving with the small breezes coming off the river and channeling up through the rock face. The sun crept up over the tree line to the east, casting direct light on the bike trail, but not yet on her inert form. Other early morning cyclists had passed by on the trail, along with a few joggers. None of them could see her on the shelf below, even if they had been looking that way.

A big crow swooped down, landing cautiously twenty feet away. He cocked his head and cawed, hopping toward her, drawn by the smell of blood and the prospect of a meal. Her bleeding had stopped, but her breathing remained ragged. It rasped once in her throat, loudly, and her fingers twitched. With a caw of reconsideration and disappointment, the crow flapped off to seek breakfast elsewhere.

I know that sound, some part of her mind said about the helicopter rotors, *I know that sound*. The recognition triggered the unspooling of another reel of memories. They cascaded on top of those running restlessly through her mind during the forty minutes since she crashed down onto the rocks....

Five years ago, she and the technical team from the EPA had ridden in on the support chopper over the woods and fields of New Hampshire, yelling last-minute communications over the thwack-thwack of the rotors. They caught the tanker red-handed, pumping its toxic load into the ground, in the most spectacular bust of environmental polluters in a decade. The other chopper with the armed FBI team had gone on ahead to land inside the plant security fence, where the agents served the warrants and made the arrests. A full RICO case, extraordinary in scope, it resulted in seventeen indictments, twelve guilty pleas, four convictions, long prison terms and penalties well into eight figures.

She remembered the grim satisfaction she had felt when they brought the plant manager, in handcuffs, out to her at the dump site.

"You!" he had exclaimed.

"Me," she agreed, a smile as cold as the north wind in their New Hampshire winters, implacable bleakness in her emerald eyes. "I told you your days were numbered, asshole."

Lying there on the ledge, her cold smile ran away into sadness as she remembered their stupidity, and the outcome of their arrogance. Those assholes thought they could just keep on doing it, pumping hazardous waste into the deep bedrock fractures, camouflaging the operation as a process water supply well.

Migration of contamination in bedrock aquifers is as erratic as the rock fractures themselves. It was unusual, but not totally improbable, for pollution to migrate a long distance. It bubbled out of a rock crevice, an artesian spring tucked into the side of a hill on her family's farm.

Lara knew enough environmental science to divine what the source had to be: the specialty plastics factory three miles up the road. There was nothing else around. But the factory claimed they didn't use the chemicals found in the spring, showed their proof of that, then stonewalled further inquiries, citing lack of evidence. They blew her off, and their attorneys won.

But their polite, oily, condescending attitudes as they wore her mother down financially and spiritually drove Lara into law school at night. She fell back on the trapper mentality bequeathed by her father, who had counseled patience and persistence in getting rid of farm vermin, not giving up, merely seeking a different means to her end.

Her mother died of liver cancer, particularly insidious and rapidly invasive. Long-term exposure to vinyl chloride was indicated. This chemical had been found in the farm's artesian spring, in concentrations far above the drinking water standards.

Lara put it all together afterwards, too late. The well water supply to the farmhouse tested clean. But her mother never liked the taste of water from their farmhouse well; it had a softener and iron removal system. So she must have trekked up to the spring, not realizing it was polluted, to fill up bottles of drinking water for the refrigerator; bottles that contained a slow and insidious poison.

The farm had gone from a break-even proposition to a slowly losing one. Their legal battle with the plastics factory had tipped it over the edge. She realized this when studying the records for the estate.

"Mom, why didn't you tell me? Why didn't you ever tell me," she had whispered, tears dripping onto the papers.

Lara had to sell the farm to avoid receivership; she had no other choice. Heartbroken, her resolve hardened into steel. They ruined my sacred spring. They killed my mom. They stole my farm. Her steel resolve became tempered, with a razor edge.

She transferred to the EPA Region 1 offices in Boston, so she could pick up the pieces of her life, and re-started law school at night. Four years of that, and then the bar exam, and suddenly Lara was a very hot commodity within the Agency. A bachelor's degree in chemistry, a master's in biochemistry, a law degree, some environmental forensics experience and a first-class mind for techno-legal strategy. She declined the suggested career track leading to management, preferring instead the excitement and moral fulfillment of the criminal chase. She transferred to EPA headquarters in Washington at the first opportunity, to work in the criminal enforcement program.

Lara found her niche there, an environmental scientist and attorney, working with the Justice Department and FBI on domestic environmental crimes, and sometimes with the CIA on crimes with overseas connections, Freon smuggling or exporting of hazardous wastes to illegal dumpsites in third-world countries. As she learned and grew, and honed her technical and legal skills, she never forgot for one second the pollution of her wooded retreat and her mother's untimely death. She looked for different angles, new technologies, fresh ways to trap those vermin, along with their oily, condescending legal counsel.

Jungle of Purace District, Colombia | Sunday 0633 EDT

In the fetal position now, unconscious, the Assassin's body twitched on the cave floor. Reflexively, his feet pushed into the pebbled sand, moving him forward, as a sleeping infant moves in a crib, as he might once have moved to touch his mother's hand. He inched gradually back into the shaft of light that had moved away from him as the sun rose higher. He pushed along until felt the sun again on the side of his face. Not waking, he turned his closed eyes into the warming brightness and saw his baby sister's sunny smile. Her image formed another loving, tugging sensation in his mind, unwinding more memories....

"Hi, John." The hallucination of his baby sister smiled shyly at him in the cave. "Remember when you taught me how to answer the telephone?"

He remembered. She'd been three years old, or maybe two, and couldn't articulate "l's"; they came out "w's". "Huwwo?" she would say, holding the receiver in both of her tiny hands. A tentative greeting, massive uncertainty in her voice about what the results would be. But she answered anyway, sometimes chattering as she gained confidence, and usually bringing the phone to the right person in the end.

Sunlight glistened on a tear that ran down the Assassin's cheek and vanished in the sand of the cave floor.

"Sure I do, kiddo. I remember everything about you."

She was a happy, inquisitive child. With their father frequently gone on missions, John became her confidante, her co-conspirator in practical jokes, her power broker and negotiator when she got in trouble. He read her stories, played her games, kissed her dirty stubbed toes, pulled out her splinters, wiped her tears.

They were soulmates in a happy, tight-knit little family, in the tight-knit culture of the Army Special Forces.

On graduation from high school, John enlisted in the Army, craving the challenge and excitement of his father's profession, sensing he had the same talent for it. When he left for basic training, he picked Jessica up and hugged her hard, and she clung to his neck just as hard, kissing his cheek, smiling an almost-seven-years-old-now brave smile, but crying all the same.

Jessica's smiling image in the cave did the very same now, her tears seeming to drip onto his riddled shoulder and side. The droplets caught the sunlight, and as they touched his body, they flared ever so briefly in a strange and beautiful six-pointed blue cross pattern, like the reflected light on a star sapphire. The Assassin stirred a little on the sand of the cave floor, and smiled. The itching in his wounds softened. More memories unwound in his mind.

Delta Charlie One, 6,000 ft over Potomac River | Sunday 0640 EDT

"Delta Charlie One reporting on-station, high and low assets in place, two and four, all in our designated positions, fuel nominal. All sensor pods up on all aircraft. We show a full data stream feed, with receipt at your end. Would you confirm that, Command-One?" The Marine Corps major in the lead Sea Stallion helicopter succinctly summarized the status. He thought to himself that flying around the nation's capital on a beautiful early Sunday morning definitely beat the losing poker hand he'd been playing out in the ready room.

A pause at the other end, while the computer parsed out the secure transmissions from six pods, verified their status and began to signify status verification on the monitors in the Command-One console abutting the Pentagon Situation Room.

"Ah, roger, Delta Charlie One. Working. Give us a moment." Then, "Affirmative, we have full data stream from each aircraft. All sensors operational—all green boards. You're looking good, gentlemen. How's the haze layer?"

"Not bad. Horizontal visibility about ten miles. A little steam fog over the river, but we can see through it. Looks like some low stratus northwest, maybe around Great Falls. Just what exactly are we looking for, Command-One?"

The pause was longer this time. The pilot of Delta Charlie One tapped his headset with a hand-signal query to his copilot, but the returned thumbs-up said the radio connection was still live. He waited impatiently for a response, feeling the sweat building on his palms.

Chapter 3

The Army was good to its soldier John Connard. The career track had been no surprise: early selection to the Special Forces, intensive training in reconnaissance, espionage, languages. He became a karate black belt, skilled with his hands and all manner of weapons, under the tutelage of a diminutive grand master named Duc Li.

He remembered his initial introduction: a tiny man with a shaved head and gray goatee sat in the lotus position on the center of the mat in the dojo at Camp Pendleton. The team of six trainees filed in cautiously, not knowing what to expect. They had been told only hype and jokes about the advanced martial arts training. But they'd heard the rumors, and were nervous.

"Sit," Duc Li had said, waving his hand to indicate the front of the mat. They sat, unconsciously attempting to emulate his lotus, some limber enough, some not. He studied them awhile, smiling. His eyes were intense and penetrating; they glinted with the humor of a recognized connection as he stared at John, and John stared back. Then with no windup or warning, Duc Li went from his relaxed sitting lotus through an improbable backflip to stand facing his new trainees.

"We get along," he predicted, smiling, "You just call me 'sensei', hokay?"

John smiled as he remembered their initial introduction, and unconsciously inched his body forward along the cave floor to keep under the warm sunbeam.

"So, John, what you been doing since we talk last time?" the hallucination of his sensei Duc Li asked. This triggered his memories to seemingly unravel both forward and backward at the same time, a dizzying complex melody of contrapuntal feelings and ideas.

His dark skin and dialect fluency made him a natural for covert drug interdictions in South America. The CIA and DEA shared with him their knowledge of how the drugs flowed, and taught him how to follow the money.

Then came the Gulf War, the first one. His Special Ops team, an early entrant, rapidly became a legend. Wraiths in the sand, they used evolving technological tools both to gather intelligence and to set up traps. He won a Silver Star for extracting the crew of a downed chopper under fire, against improbable odds. He had his father's talent for seeing the enemy flaws and weaknesses, for finding the way out. The legends grew. They took to calling him the Magician, like they had called his father in Vietnam.

The Army brought him home near the end of the war, when his father lay dying, an undiagnosed melanoma that he had stubbornly ignored until too late. Sergeant Major Jacob Alexander Connard died calmly, after pinning the lieutenant's bars on his son's collar. He died proud that the boy's accomplishments were exceeding his, and that the Army had a new Magician. The family grieved, cherished the tri-folded flag, closed ranks, carried on. A warrior family, that was their way.

The image of Duc Li nodded and smiled at him in the Colombian cave, encouraging him to continue his recollections. Again he felt the tugging sensation in his mind, an invitation. As his consciousness faded down to a deeper level, more scenes fled across his mind's eye....

— After the war, the Army posting him at Cal Tech to study control system dynamics, a plum assignment to a top graduate school.

— His professors there calling him the Magician, too.

— The later posting to the Defense Advanced Research Projects Agency, and the DARPA AeroVironment team in nearby Monrovia.

— The team creating the little DARPA surveillance device that later became the prototype for his killer drone.

An exploded computer-generated diagram of the device now rotated in the Magician's mind, and turned into an abstraction his mother the artist might have painted. Other scenes passed by, fleeting....

— His mother.

— Her quiet pride in her son.

— Her accidental death. No time to say goodbye

— His sister Jessica, desolate, bereft, crying.

They had consoled each other and edged past their mother's death, bonded yet further by grief. More scenes flashed into his mind, but slowing now, bringing more detail....

— Jessica in her senior year in the Psych program at San Diego State, smiling in the sunshine outside a classroom where they met for lunch one day.

— The two of them growing even closer, the short distance no barrier to frequent visits, with phone calls in between.

— His occasional stops at Camp Pendleton, en route to San Diego, to spar with Duc Li and keep his skills sharp.

— Jessica's laughter, regaining its tinkling resonance as she recovered from sadness; a sound like a brook running over stones, set to music....

Eyes shut and deeply entranced in those memories, the Magician smiled into the Colombian cave. The image of Duc Li smiled gently back at him.

Delta Charlie One, 6,000 ft over Potomac River | Sunday 0643 EDT

After a long pause, Command-One in the basement of the Pentagon responded to its airborne assets, telling them what they were seeking.

"Delta Charlie One, be advised we have reports of atmospheric tracks of some kind roughly over the Potomac southwest of Georgetown last hour, running up to the northwest. We may have an unanticipated entry event of space junk or some meteor fragments. On the other hand, it could have been a rocket track or some other projectile weapon launched from some point to the south. Homeland Security is thinking about bumping up from Condition Yellow, depending on what you report.

"You are to conduct visual recon for any kind of dispersed cloud of fine particulate matter in the air below 3,000 feet. Anything on land that looks like an impact zone. Any discolorations in the water, particularly in the reservoir. Maintain full scanning packages and uplinks on all aircraft. Full data feed, all channels. Do you copy?"

"Roger, Command-One." The Stallion pilot arched an eyebrow at his copilot, the silent question hanging between them as to whether this signaled the start of more terrorism.

"Okay, Tom, everybody heard that," he said to his copilot, "so advise our high cover in the Cobras to hold on-station at their altitude. Tell Air Traffic we got a situation here, clear all commercial traffic southward, freeze the private flights and especially the freakin' news choppers. Work it out. While we're focused on the ground, I don't want any mid-air collisions. You keep our airspace clear, I'll work the choppers." He broke off to switch to the secure tactical frequency and instruct the other helicopters.

"Okay, gentlemen, you all heard Command-One. I want a standard square-search pattern, tight grid. Delta Charlie Two, you take the area north of Chain Bridge up to Glen Echo. Delta Charlie Three, you take it from Chain Bridge southeast to the south end of the reservoir. Delta Charlie Four, you got it from there down over the island.

"Hold your levels at 3,500 feet. Delta Charlie One will hang at 6,000 feet, Cobras at 8,000, in case this *is* terrorism and any surprises come at you from the ground. We see anything needs a closer look, we'll tell you. Make sure your gamma counters are in alarm mode in case there's anything radioactive in the air out there.

Keep your canister samplers handy in case we see some airborne particulate stuff.

"I want all gunners acting as spotters, talking to your onboard recorders non-stop, separate channels, anything you see, any impressions you have, I don't care how weird it is. There could be one helluva debrief on this one, boys; so let's do it by the book."

Shortly into their search pattern, Delta Charlie Four reported a biker down and apparently injured, off the C&O Canal bike trail, and probably not visible from the trail due to the terrain. They advised DC Metro Dispatch of the precise coordinates.

Hours later, having seen nothing unusual but one downed biker, the recon operation stood down, its sole tangible result countless gigabytes of digital reconnaissance data showing nothing at all. The Homeland Security condition remained at Yellow. A certain amount of grumpiness in military and civilian brass for being awakened too early on a Sunday morning was tempered by a better-safe-than-sorry shrug of the shoulders.

The lack of any result provided a certain duty officer in the Pentagon Situation Room the latitude to downplay the Goddard 5-4-1 vote on the possibility of an extraterrestrial visitor. But though he downplayed it, he elected to pass it along through channels, not to stifle it as a cynical Aaron O'Meara had predicted.

Jungle of Purace District, Colombia | Sunday 0657 EDT

Inside the cave in Colombia, the Magician smiled again into the sunbeam's warmth, remembering his sister's infectious laughter. But then his thoughts came, too abruptly, up against that time of darkness in his soul where the melody of unwinding memories turned to a raw jangle and stopped altogether. The hallucination of Duc Li raised an eyebrow.

"You must face it," Duc Li whispered softly into his dream. "John, you must face it."

Eyes ground shut, John screamed into the sand of the cave floor: a primal, gut-wrenching wail of desolation echoing off the rock walls, echoing the sound torn from him six years ago when they unzipped the bag around his baby sister's body in the morgue.

He had lost his breakfast into the handwashing sink. The death and destruction in the Gulf War and other engagements he had seen and the horror he felt those times were as nothing. His father's death he had absorbed. His mother's accidental death was a shock, but he'd dealt with it. But this? So young. So smart. So pretty. So funny. At four years old, she had cuddled in his lap as he read to her, pointing inquisitively at the words as she learned how to read. This loss consumed him, cold black flames in his heart.

"Why?" he cried, "Why her, why not me? Why not anybody else? Oh, God, not her. Not her!"

"This *is* your younger sister, then? Jessica Connard?" Sturgeon asked for the record.

John walked slowly back to the body. He looked at her slashed neck, cut almost entirely through. He stared at the distinctive birthmark just above the slash, despairing. A question mark shape, a subject of dismay to her in her sensitive early teens, a subject of merriment for the rest of the family. Here, in this place and time, a mark that closed out all hope.

"Yes. It is," he whispered, acknowledgment a gasping sob that carried a part of him away forever. He reached out to stroke her cold cheek.

"Please don't touch her," the Medical Examiner said, firmly but kindly.

Inside the cave in Colombia, the gentle half-smile fled from Duc Li's image, and a tear ran down his cheek. John's memories continued to cascade outward, jagged and uneven.

"Come on, Mr. Connard, let's sit down in the other room for a bit," Sturgeon had said, "if you can give us some information to start with, maybe we can nail this creep real quick. What's your sister's middle name? Date of birth? Local address? Where was she last night? The ME needs to start the autopsy. The quicker we get on this, the better." As he guided the wobbly man out of the autopsy room, Sturgeon told him about the high percentage for closing out homicide cases when they got a handle on them right away.

In the waiting room, Sturgeon put his arm across John's heaving shoulders, handing him a glass of water, waiting for the questions. When they came, the detective's answers were forthright; they could not be framed gently. Jessica Connard had been severely beaten. Raped, too, by the look of the scene. Her throat had been cut. It looked like her assailant had tried to decapitate her.

Inside the cave, another tear ran down the cheek of Duc Li's image. Secondary memories cascaded outward from John's mind toward that image. These were fragmented and erratic; memories not directly experienced but rather pieced into the history that John gleaned from Sturgeon later in the investigation....

Seven months after Jessica's slaughter, LAPD had reconstructed the carjacking and abduction, and conclusively identified the murderer from semen DNA: one Duane Lee Smith, a crack user and sometime dealer. He was a huge, unkempt, red-bearded white man prone to violent rages, an unconvicted rapist, a true redneck, a sociopath. But even though LAPD knew exactly what he looked like with and without a beard, and had his full miserable criminal history on file, all their resources hadn't been able to find him. Seven months of vexation, and they still hadn't been able to nail the creep.

But somebody sure nailed him, Sturgeon had thought, admiring with clinical satisfaction the terror frozen in the wide open eyes. Smith's head had been messily impaled on the banister post inside the front door of the crackhouse. A warning to others? A message of terror? A definite statement, no matter how you slice it.

"Aw, shit, no," the detective had exclaimed, enlightenment immediate and over-powering. Jessica Connard had been beaten and raped and killed in this very same crackhouse. Her head had been nearly cut off. And she has a big brother: John Connard, Captain, U.S. Army, 1st Special Forces Group, a war hero, a combat vet-eran with a Silver Star, a soldier called the Magician by his buddies, a truly danger-ous man, likely one of the most accomplished killers on the face of the planet.

During his interviews on the case, the detective apparently had disclosed far too much information. John Connard, Sturgeon realized in retrospect as he stared at the head, had been an extremely subtle and clever interviewer himself; a Magician, for a fact.

They had spoken not a month ago. Captain Connard was still on detached duty, Cal Tech and DARPA, and still living in the LA area.

"Aw shit," Sturgeon repeated as he studied the impaled head, "I'm gonna have to talk to that boy. Hope to Christ he magicianed himself a fucking good alibi."

Inside the cave in Colombia, the somber image of Duc Li watched a soul turn to ashes. Out of those ashes an Assassin had been born. The image nodded in sad understanding.

C&O Canal Bike Trail, Washington, DC | Sunday 0701 EDT

Lara lay motionless in the early morning light, flat on the shelf of rock beneath the bike trail. Her fist slowly opened and closed spasmodically, in time with the rise and fall of the approaching siren. Her mind seized the association, and the search pattern unspooling her memories paused to consider this new memory path. Identified as a key event, her mind traveled obediently back to that first time a police siren had come to her....

Snow over glare ice. It can happen even to a careful man like Joshua Picard. Lara's father rode the big tractor, plowing the snow from that sudden heavy squall two days after Christmas, two months before her sixteenth birthday. He had de-cided to clear a path out of the paddock for the cows, let them move around a bit more. The tractor slipped backwards on the unseen ice and the big rear wheel, the left one, dropped over the edge of the rock wall, throwing him to the ground. He rolled in the snow, but not fast enough. Her mother saw it from the kitchen window and screamed. They both ran out. His upper body was pinned into the snow and ice, the tractor front wheel hub crushing his chest. Frothy blood bubbled from the side of his mouth. Lara analyzed the situation in an instant. They couldn't wait for help, the weight would suffocate him.

"Mom, grab his collar, pull him out," she screamed as she braced her back against the engine compartment, planting her boots in the snow, flexing her knees to work her small body under the massive weight. Slowly, grunting, she extended her legs, the strong quadriceps quivering. She ignored the hot engine exhaust manifold scorching its way through her jacket, sizzling an L-shaped memory of that terrible day forever into the flesh of her back. Her mother pulled him clear.

"Mom, call 911! Get his poncho! Get some blankets!" The commands snapped her mother out of her shock, and she sprinted back to the house.

Lara cried to him, "You're going to be okay, Dad, just hang on. You're going to be okay!" That drew him back to consciousness, briefly.

"I'm sorry, honey," he whispered, a frothy, raspy sound.

"Hush, Dad, it's okay. It's okay, these things happen. We're getting help, you're going to be okay. You're going to be okay!"

But he wasn't. He died there with his head cradled in her hands, bleeding to death from the rib fragments that had penetrated his heart and lungs, telling her in a moment of clarity and foreknowledge of his passing how much he loved her.

As Lara and her mother knelt there in the snow, the police and EMT radio dialog had crackled about them, punctuating their sobbing and the lowing of the cows and the whimpering of their dog. Yes, she knew those siren sounds; those are the sounds you never forget....

The DC Metro Police officer pulled off on the side of the canal towpath, shutting off his siren but leaving the lights flashing, and walked down to the bike path, speaking into his shoulder mike. The call had come in from Dispatch that Park Police rangers were all tied up with a military thing, and could he respond. Being just across the canal from the park, he did.

"Dispatch, this is 342, I'm at the scene, approaching the bike trail. Where is the victim again?"

"East of the trail, 342, toward the river. The Marine chopper reported an embankment, so there may be a drop-off. If it looks difficult, wait for backup, about two minutes out," the radio crackled in response.

"Okay, Dispatch, I see her. Access is okay."

He clambered down, thinking to himself, Jesus, what a beauty. Hope she's not hurt too bad. When she didn't respond, he assessed her as well as his training allowed, not moving her, reporting into his radio, listening to the crackling answers, looking over the scene for possible signs of a crime, waiting for his backup and the ambulance to arrive.

Jungle of Purace District, Colombia | Sunday 0702 EDT

In the cave in Colombia, the image of Duc Li nodded his acceptance of the Assassin. "An ancient code, John," the hallucination whispered. "An ancient code. A warrior's retribution for the killing of innocents."

The whisper tugged at other peripheral memories. Fragments of recollections obediently assembled and sequenced themselves in John's mind as his body lay unmoving in the sand. Inferences, gleaned in later conversations with Detective Sturgeon, flowed among the fragments, filling in blanks, integrating the history, bringing coherence....

The autopsy report on Duane Lee Smith carried more caveats than most, possibly because modern forensic science had little to evaluate; just a head, with testes in the throat and the penis peeking obscenely out of the mouth like a soggy cigar butt. The body was never found. The Army, although not willing to disclose the nature of the exercise, confirmed to LAPD that Captain Connard had been continuously camped in the California hills and canyons west of Camp Pendleton day and night, on a classified mission. Incontrovertibly, the Magician was accounted for, three days before and two days after the likely time of Smith's death as established by the ME.

Albeit pleased to log into the investigative record his conclusive elimination of Captain John Connard as a suspect in the Smith homicide, Sturgeon didn't believe it for a minute. He just wondered how John had managed to fool the ME.

The second and third heads were out of Sturgeon's jurisdiction, one in San Diego, one in Long Beach. But he was contacted to consult, re *modus operandi*. Their connections to Smith were gradually puzzled out. A drug and weapons dealer in San Diego had supplied Smith with a stolen pistol used in robberies. It might have been used in a kidnapping. Another, more upscale, drug dealer in Long Beach, specialized in cocktails of coke and designer drugs. One of his cocktails might have been the combination that sent Smith over the edge, a rush of chemical soup to his demented brain causing him to risk kidnapping a pretty girl who was just in the wrong place at the wrong time.

"So who's the next head gonna belong to, John?" Sturgeon queried him over an off-duty beer in the Pasadena bar near CalTech, two days after the third head was found. He added, thoughtfully, "You know, if it doesn't go down in LAPD jurisdiction, we have only an academic interest."

Captain John Connard, sipping his beer, savoring the nuances of the message he'd just been given, knowing this moment ultimately would come, edged around the question obliquely.

"Gene, I wish whoever is doing this the very best. These people are scum, vermin. And there's an exterminator out there. This is a good thing. A boon to society."

"The papers are picking it up, John. The public is getting concerned. Three heads, no bodies, for God's sake. They think there's a serial killer on the loose. The pressure on us is going to build."

"Gene, the public can discern the difference between vermin extermination and the murder of innocents. Frankly, I think they either don't care, or applaud it, so long as it's careful and targeted. Especially if it stays confined to the drug trade, and no innocents are hurt. Besides, your police motto is 'to serve and protect', and isn't that what's happening here?"

Sturgeon smiled at the touché in spite of himself. "But the heads, dammit, John, that's just too goddamn much. Disappearance, no trace, is one thing. These kinds of people do disappear sometimes. We do a little investigation, make a few routine reports, mention the possibility of foul play, and let it fade down into our big pile of administrivia. No problem-o. Heads, we have to do something. Yeah, maybe heads make a good strong message, but I've got to tell you the risk of something coming unraveled over time is pretty high."

John contemplated his beer without response, wondering if Sturgeon were wired, deciding he wasn't. Then he turned his head to study the tired, lined face that had seen too much sorrow in its time. The man truly cares about me, he thought.

"John, I've gotten to know you. I care about you," Sturgeon said, reflecting that very thought. "I look at the weight you've lost, the bags under your eyes. I'm worried. I had a talk with the Army; I know you declined counseling. John, you're worth more as a human being than hundreds of those drug-peddling sacks of shit out there. Thousands. Think about our conversation. Please." The detective finished his beer and patted the Assassin goodbye.

John remembered clearly how his shoulder muscles had been tense, banded steel under the detective's kind hand. Those muscles now tightened reflexively at the memory, pulling his outstretched arm back toward his body, leaving tracks of clawed fingers in the sand of the cave floor. As the sun rose higher over the Colombian jungle and the sunbeam moved away from the Assassin's body, the image of Duc Li nodded his understanding once again. But he frowned at the descent into darkness of his favorite pupil.

Chapter 4

Aaron O'Meara had the logistics support seat for this segment of the SDI exercise. As one of the less stressful assignments, he could handle it with only partial concentration. The rest of his mind replayed the morning's astonishing event, trying to work out the puzzle of the odd spiraling motions. They fit no conceivable model of energy behavior in an unconfined environment like space; at least no model of which he was aware.

Gravity, he thought. Inverse-square, two pieces rotating around a common center. Micro-sized black holes might do it. But that would have meant massive destruction down here. And how could they separate? How did they disappear? To elsewhere? Or elsewhen?

His mind ranged outward, seeking possibilities: nuclear strong forces, binding energies, gluons, gravitons. Probably a number of postulates that could fit the observations, but macro rather than subatomic? He realized he didn't know enough about particle physics. He mused briefly on some forgotten anthropologist's observation that, to a primitive culture, any technological development from more than a hundred years in their future would be perceived as magic.

"Well, this is magic, all right," he muttered to himself, absently fulfilling his SDI exercise duties without much conscious effort. Then an insight flashed into his questing mind. Ah, maybe the problem here is that there are more dimensions than my limited perspective can handle. String theory. Relativistic discontinuities. I need to read up on it. Make some calls. And quantum teleportation, didn't Bell Labs do something on that? The onset of intense curiosity and a driven need to figure out what it all meant produced a seductive tingle in his mind. Aaron smiled at the prospect of an upcoming three days off. He would have time to work on this puzzle.

Then, tangentially, he had a different thought: *consciousness.* If those actions were controlled, then maybe the minds directing them were strong enough to leave some kind of trace. Maybe they'd perturb the... what was it called... the *noosphere*? He thought idly of that outfit at Princeton, his alma mater. I had a really wild conversation with their project director at one of the post-doc reunion bashes last summer, he remembered. What was it? Oh, yeah, the Global Consciousness

Project. Maybe I'll give him a call. Or didn't he say they have a website now? Umm, he did. Next break, I'll sneak down to my office and have a look at it....

Google found the site for him easily, searching on 'global consciousness'. He browsed quickly through it, reading, refreshing his memory of last summer's fascinating and strange conversation, muttering to himself.

"Okay, yeah. A network of random event generators, computer algorithms that produce zeroes or ones randomly. Yup. Just like I remembered. A heads-or-tails coin flip, two hundred flips a second. Over time the probabilities are random, a fifty-fifty chance of either."

But human group consciousness, when sufficiently focused, caused non-random results. The effects were not huge, but were statistically significant, a proven phenomenon. The collective consciousness of a group of people could cause random event generators to go non-random. Such generators were placed at different locations in the world. They were called eggs, Aaron remembered as he flicked through the web pages.

Eggs. He smiled at the symbolism. Life yet to come, or life unrealized until fertilized by conscious action. The eggs now numbered over a hundred, he saw. Each computer in the network sent its results to a central computer, where they were processed and uploaded to the website server, with only a few minutes delay from data generation to availability to website visitors.

"Wow, neat", he observed, "nearly real-time! Pretty impressive!" He hurried on through the website, talking to his computer screen as if it were a partner in his inquiry.

"So let's see what we got here..." he clicked on the data access button, then the real-time display button, then the time-trend button, and was looking at tiny graphs of the current outputs of each of over a hundred random event generators, scattered across the world. Each graph showed an uncharacteristic and unmistakable loss of randomness, simultaneously, from 0546 to 0548, EDT.

"Sweet baby Jesus," he whispered, forgetting momentarily his cheerful agnosticism, absently reverting to his mother's expression as he studied the small charts intently. "Each egg. No exceptions. Same pattern. Sweet baby Jesus, bring me on home!"

Aaron was no statistician, but didn't have to be to realize that the odds against this were beyond calculation.

"Be like winning the lottery," he whistled, "and then winning it over and over every single day for the rest of your life, that's about what the odds are for this pattern appearing by itself." He shivered as he realized just how precisely the timing coincided with the two-minute event burned into his mind earlier in the morning.

C&O *Canal Bike Trail, Washington, DC | Sunday 0712 EDT*

A police sergeant arrived, rattling down onto the ledge to back up his patrolman. He found Lara Picard's ID card in the pocket of the biking jersey and called her name. She still didn't respond, but part of her consciousness tracked the arrival of a new entity, re-registering the crackling communication sounds burned in her memory. Thus triggered, her memories spun forward in her dream to the time when such communications had become commonplace in her professional life....

In the back of the utility van with the FBI surveillance team, Lara studied the warehouse, matching up in her mind the visual images with the hidden surveillance cameras they had positioned around the periphery of the loading docks. The radio communications sounds crackled around them. The van was camouflaged as a line locator service, and two technicians were indeed out on the sidewalk, looking at blueprints, using handheld detectors to locate buried pipes and electrical lines, spraying paint marks on the street and sidewalk to note the location. The watchers in the warehouse had observed for a while, and then seemed to relax as the technicians worked their way down the street past the warehouse.

"Okay, Lara, looks like you were right. Our buddy Romeo has himself a new sidelight, smuggling in Freon along with coke and heroin. Looks like the Bureau and EPA are going to do some business together on this one. But keep in mind these aren't your typical witless envirowussies, these assholes will actually shoot at you."

FBI Special Agent Thomas Charles Demuzzio, Lara remembered fondly, had been more than a bit worried about his new collaborator.

"Thanks, TC, that sounds like good advice for a raw recruit like me to keep in mind," she'd answered, "but I need to get a closer look inside that warehouse by the overhead door, see how they labeled those shipping containers with the Freon. Here's how we're going to do it. I promise I'll be careful."

They'd argued about the downside, her personal risk, them having to rescue her, thus making the arrests prematurely before all the spidery connections in this case had been traced out. But her logic was impeccable, the risk low, the information value high. As the van turned the corner, out of view of the watchers in the warehouse, she dropped out the side door and sprinted a circuitous route back to the staging area where she had parked her rental car. The support team, a San Diego police unit, helped her unscrew the tire valve just enough so that the tire would bleed flat by the time she got to the freeway exit ramp opposite the warehouse.

It worked like a charm. The right rear tire started to thump, and she controlled the car gently down the ramp, slewing it a little to make sure the watchers would pick it up. She went through the light, and ground to a halt just past the driveway in front of the overhead doors. The surveillance van was working its way back down the other side of the street, and she felt a little safer. All right, *show time*, she thought.

She got out of the rental car, walked around it, and bent over the right rear tire to give the watchers a good view of her gorgeous ass in the tight jeans. Lara knew the power of her beauty. If this doesn't get their attention, they're freaking zombies, she thought, bending over again as she wrestled the spare tire and jack out of the trunk and set them on the curb. She rummaged in the trunk some more, ran her hand through her hair, feigning confusion and frustration. Then she walked over to the overhead door, tempering the natural uninhibited grace of her walk with the slight trepidation that would be appropriate to the circumstances of a pretty lady with a flat tire in a not-so-good part of town.

"Hullo," she'd yelled, shielding her eyes from the sun with her hand so she could see inside the dimmer warehouse, "anybody got a phone I can use?"

"No hablo Ingles," the guard supervising the unloading said gruffly, waving the kid unloading the truck back to his work, not letting him ogle.

"No hablo Ingles," he repeated as he moved to block her view inside the warehouse door. But it was too late, she'd seen the markings on the containers carrying the Freon, and committed them to memory.

"Good morning, señorita," Romeo said cheerily as he tapped the guard out of his way and jumped lightly off the loading dock, "you need help with that tire?"

Aha, she thought, I knew our little Romeo couldn't resist that nice view of my ass. Her satisfaction level notched up.

"Oh, thank you, sir. I just need a phone, I don't think there's a handle for the jack in this rental. I probably should have stayed with Hertz or Avis."

"Ah, let us look, señorita. Often they put these things where you do not expect." He looked behind panels in the car trunk, moving her suitcase and carry-on. She saw him note the airline tag from O'Hare, just a quick passing glance, but knew he had it locked in his mind. He found the jack handle up front, under the engine hood, in clips on the strut above the radiator. She knew it was there, of course, not in the trunk where she had been rooting around. Her increasing frustration had been a good act, a way to get inside to use their phone. Romeo changed the tire for her, and advised her not to drive too far or too fast on the small donut spare.

"Oh, thank you so much, sir. I learned something about cars this morning," she simpered, reaching into her pocketbook and pulling out a ten dollar bill. He waved it off graciously.

"Well, then, thank you again. I have to be going, I'm going to be late for my job interview if I don't get back to the hotel and get changed," she said, holding out her hand.

He bowed slightly, and kissed her hand, rather than shaking it.

Now that's interesting, she thought as she drove away waving. A nice soft touch. Totally unexpected. Given his profile, no ring on my finger, he should have been all over me, wanting my hotel phone number, a meeting for a drink. If the profile is right, there's only two possibilities: he's got too many women right now and is just tuckered out, or he's on a short leash. She replayed her impressions. The guard kept too close an eye on him. Something's gone wrong. His papa's got him on a short leash. Ah, that's interesting, maybe an opening.

Jungle of Purace District, Colombia | Sunday 0713 EDT

In the cave in Colombia, John Connard's memories continued to unwind. The image of Duc Li nodded agreement with Detective Sturgeon's advice: forego the heads. But the Assassin was intent on his terrible retribution....

The last one had been difficult. The trail of those responsible for Jessica's death led to a palatial estate, home to one Dennis Corrin, a transplanted Panamanian drug wholesaler. High in the canyons overlooking Los Angeles, the estate sat in a neighborhood of explicit and unabashed wealth; a place light-years removed from the crackhouse where Jessica was killed. Carefully defended, it had guards both visible and concealed, electronic surveillance, and dogs. But those were useless against the Magician, and the target was no match for the Assassin.

Working Corrin's headless carcass through the meat processing plant, John whistled cheerfully as he pondered the information he had extracted from the dead man. Now he understood better the dynamics of the business and the player relationships at the wholesale drug level, and knew he would eventually puzzle out the Colombia connection. In the meantime, he found it entirely appropriate and satisfying that another of Jessica's killers was becoming an ingredient of dog and cat food.

The sole off-shift operator of the automated processing plant rested comfortably in a drugged sleep from which he would awake refreshed, remembering nothing out of the ordinary. But then suddenly there *was* something out of the ordinary, and a surge of adrenaline kicked John's senses to a higher level. He kept whistling, but casually picked the machine pistol out of the pack at his feet, holding it down behind his leg while he half-turned to face the sensed presence.

"Wondered how you did it!" The rotund face smiled at him beatifically from a few paces away.

A little over five feet tall, John thought, stocky, a definite paunch. And he's unarmed. How did he get in? How in hell did he get so close without me knowing it? And who the hell is he?

"Really nothing at all to running this line; the processing is totally automated," John replied, pretending to be the operator, thinking this odd little man was a screwball who had somehow wandered into the factory.

The man guffawed; an infectious, smiling laugh that made his belly bounce up and down.

"Oh, Jasus, John Connard, no, no, no. Not the machinery! I meant the *bodies*. A great puzzle to me it was, how you got rid of the *bodies*!"

He knows my name. He knows what I'm doing. That's truly amazing, John thought, shivering with a second burst of adrenaline. He thumbed the safety off the pistol, covering its mechanical click with a cough, keeping it behind his back. His trained eyes flickered over the platforms and catwalks and other areas of the factory, looking for the support team. No one. The place was empty but for the two of them and the sleeping operator.

Rather than acknowledging the implications of the intruder's statement, he parsed the lilt and cadence of Celtic overlaid by American, and said instead, "Ireland. In the south. Kerry, possibly?" Then, as an afterthought, with a disarmingly friendly grin, "You a leprechaun, come to America by some chance?"

"Ah, no, me lad. 'Tis a fine leprechaun might I make, but not quite yet. Maybe in me next life. Which, by the way, I wouldna want to be quite so imminent as the Glock behind your back might accidentally make it."

The Magician moved laterally, adrenaline-charged, the liquid speed and grace of a panther, and put a solid column behind his back. The muzzle of the pistol held rock-steady on the intruder's chest, while his dark blue eyes flickered around the deserted factory. *Nothing. No one.* This is surreal, he thought.

"If you're not a leprechaun, and don't want to be reincarnated as dog food, you may want to tell me why you're here."

The little man smiled broadly at him, as if the gun were irrelevant.

"A simple thing it is, John Connard, a simple thing. You are a supremely accomplished artist. Your brush strokes are pain and sufferin' and death. You use them boldly. Your canvas is retribution. I would like to commission you to do some pieces of your very fine art for me."

Art. An interesting way of looking at it, John thought. Then: aw shit, this loony-tune wants to hire me as a hit man! The Assassin stirred within, and almost pulled the trigger, but in seminal truth his efforts did have an element of art about them. And his mother had been a fine artist. He had inherited her artistic sensibilities if not her talent. The Assassin's finger tapped the trigger guard, but the Magician's curiosity controlled it.

"And what sort of art would you have in mind?"

"An art of morality, John Connard, an art of great and wonderful morality. Very much the same kind of art you engage in right here, this fine early mornin'. And no, you have not gone mad, at least not clinically. I am neither leprechaun nor devil. I am quite real, and I mean you no harm. So be a good lad, put down the gun. Find me another Tyvek suit so I don't get blood and gore all over me fresh clean shirt, and I'll help you tidy up this nasty lot, and we can quicker be off to discuss our mutual art over a fine wholesome Irish breakfast. What do you say, me lad? Hmmm?"

In the cave in Colombia, the image of Duc Li nodded his understanding of the strange events unwinding from John's memories, and of those events yet to occur....

Rashers, sausages, eggs, Irish porridge, juice. They sat in a booth in an Irish pub near UCLA, closed at that pre-dawn hour, but somehow not closed to his companion. The little man had pounded merrily on the rear door in the alley, yelling up at a second floor window, "God love you, Eileen! But only if you feed us, darlin'!"

They were greeted by a tiny smiling woman with flaming red hair, who called his companion Alexander, and engaged in non-stop repartee while setting the places and serving the breakfast.

"My father's middle name was Alexander," John offered, his belly full with breakfast, his tensions dissipated as much by the food as by his companion's cheerfully unrepentant engagement as an accomplice in a capital crime.

"And a fine name it is. From the Greek. Means 'helper of men'. Oh, terribly sorry. I'm Alexander Shaughnessy. Historian. Absurdist. Philosopher. Moralist. Art lover extraordinaire." He stuck his hand across the breakfast table.

John smiled at him, taking his hand, noting it had a fierce strength inconsistent with the man's size and appearance. "And I evidently don't need to introduce myself, Mr. Shaughnessy..." his voice tailed off, inviting explanation.

"Oh, call me Alex, please. And may I call you John, Captain John Jacob Connard?"

"Given the circumstances," John conceded wryly.

"And a fine name that is too, John. From the Hebrew. Means God is gracious, or God's grace. So here is my proposition, John of God's grace. It has three parts..."

John observed the change from banter to the sharp-edged logic of synopsis. This little man is accustomed the rigors of command, he realized. Their waitress had disappeared, taking with her the emptied plates but leaving a fresh pot of coffee, no sound of her anywhere.

"First, John, no head this time. Give it to me and I'll dispose of it appropriately. If you spike it onto the gatepost up at the mansion, that's in LAPD jurisdiction. Detective Lieutenant Sturgeon will be called in. He is just too smart. He likes you, even approves of what you're doin', but he'll soon run out of his own moral latitude, and have no choice. Given enough time and enough of his oddball thinkin', and enough application of Ockham's Razor by the Medical Examiner, they will figure out your preservation technique. They can get down to the sub-cellular level easily now, you know."

"Ockham's Razor won't play well off a grand jury, let alone a trial jury, Alex. It's too complex. And the MEs in this city are terribly overworked. It seems a reasonable risk."

"Ah, but John, John, me lad, to what end this risk? A statement that an avengin' angel is coming? Creation of a climate of terror in the drug trade? There is art in that, I grant you, no question. But there are more elegant brush strokes for a talent as great as yours. Much more effective strokes. And consider the downside of your head campaign. You put your good friend Detective Sturgeon in a moral box. You bring public discomfort, if not shame, to the Army, which has been your family. You may become a popular hero, but you don't give a tinker's damn about that, and the visibility would limit your mission. Now I ask you, is that the best art?"

The logic of the Magician danced with the rage of the Assassin in John's mind, but his face remained expressionless. Alex Shaughnessy patiently waited out the long silence.

"All right, Alex," John finally bowed to the Magician's logic, actually relieved by the release of his own growing uncertainty about the head campaign, "I'll consider that. And second?"

"Second, John. Finish your thesis. Get your degree. Suspend your huntin' for a time. We need the time to structure you into our program. Tell the Army you want the counselin' offered. We need that as a basis to set up the discharge and compassionate release from your present duties, and reassignment to our little artistic endeavor. Possibly we can get you brevetted to major in the process."

"You said 'we', Alex. I'm not going to ask who you work for. I know how compartmentalized black operations are. I also know how much power some of them have, but you're dealing with the Army bureaucracy here, are you sure you can do this?"

"Yes."

John marveled at the flat total conviction. It flew in the face of what he knew about his own extraordinary value to an evolving technological Army. He studied the little man, feeling the hidden power. No one has ever snuck up that close to me when my combat awareness is kicked in, he mused. Just how in hell did he do that? There was nothing there, and then he just appeared, smiling at me. I guess I do believe him. This odd little anomaly can actually do everything he says.

"Okay, Alex. I'll consider that. And third? What sort of art would we produce?"

"You and I will create a great and wonderful and moral work of art, me lad. Our canvas will embrace the world. We will study where the most damage and disruption can be caused inside the drug trade. We will identify candidate individuals. We will select the targets. You will have the freedom to decline any target, for any reason, without question. If you accept, you will be inserted into the area near the target.

"You will introduce a genomic toxin into the target, in whatever manner is appropriate. The toxin begins to change the target's body, with a disease that is quite strange and painful, and quite resistant to any known cure or palliative therapy. However, the mind remains fully lucid. At some point we will send an invitation to the target, offering relief and reversal of the disease in exchange for what we want, which is more information to shut down the drug trade.

"We believe a fair proportion of the targets will accept. We will also start a 'hand of God' myth, or rumors of ju-ju, or hexes, or faeries, or whatever superstitious or religious device works in a particular culture, to sow terror and the expectation of terrible and inevitable retribution, and to otherwise generally disrupt the drug business. Now that, me young friend, is *art*!"

"So this is still a theoretical program, Alex? You haven't actually done this yet?"

"We lack only an implementer on the ground, an infiltrator, a resourceful warrior of your caliber. The toxins are functional. We have samples from over a hundred potential targets, and have fully sequenced their genomes."

Gene research lay well out of John Connard's area of expertise, but he knew enough to find this frightening. He said so.

"Indeed it is frightenin', me lad," Alex said soberly, the smile running away from his face. "And 'tis a brave new world, a suddenly more dangerous world. We must hope and pray the human race has the moral depth and balance to avoid being subverted by its awful potential. I have studied you, Captain John Jacob Connard, and I believe you are a moral man, one who cannot be subverted. You are indeed the artist who must paint this canvas. You are the one."

John studied him, appreciating the power of the personality, the carefully understated plea, knowing instinctively that this man required a decision, right now, right here over the breakfast table. Solely on the basis of what had been said: in black operations there were no contracts, no letters of engagement, nothing written down. An incredible risk? Maybe, maybe not. And what difference was there, really; did not the Assassin's present campaign carry plenty of risk? This cheerful strange little man offered him an opportunity to extend his campaign, and add significant support. To trust or not to trust, he pondered, isn't that always the question in this business? The Magician set free the analytical part of his mind, and tuned to his other ways of knowing, the complex intuitions of his mother's heritage. The answer came to him instantly, without reservation.

"I accept," he said, and held out his hand.

The image of Duc Li again nodded his understanding of those unspooled memories, and John began to stir on the cave floor in Colombia. His mind swam slowly up through more recent memories toward the present. Four years and seventeen targets after first meeting Alexander Shaunnessy, he had traveled an odyssey of terror and retribution through the Philippines, Malaysia, Burma, Afghanistan, Mexico, and much of Central and South America. Finally, two hours ago, he had come to their latest target: Diego Corrano, *el Jefe*, sequestered in his protected enclave in southwest Colombia.

As consciousness gradually returned, John Connard, Magician and Assassin, acknowledged the morality and value of their campaign. He was truly proud of its success, and for the most part admired their growing artwork. But John Connard, soldier and human being, wondered—every time he painted another element—whether each target marked a redemption under his given name of God's grace, or whether each marked a further descent into the darkness and madness painted across their canvas.

Chapter 5

As Lara's mind chased on a blinding fast-forward through the satisfying memories of her early cases, the EMTs worked the ambulance over to the bike path and clambered down onto the rock ledge to make their assessment. Lara's body did not stir, but the medical terminology in their dialog reached down into her consciousness. This shifted the racing memories onto a different track; insidious and troublesome. She moaned, a raspy forlorn sound devoid of hope....

It had been a whirlwind courtship. Lara Ellen Picard at 26 years old was new to Washington, but clearly headed for stardom in government legal circles. She also was beautiful, sexy, single and lonely. Malcolm Sean O'Donnell, pushing 40, was a genius mathematician and analyst in the Department of Defense. Tall and lean, his Black Irish heritage handsomely graying, Lara was drawn in by his edgy humor and cynical observations of the human condition in that center of power, the capital of the nation. She didn't know of his madness until it spiraled past control.

"I do," she had said, not quite a year after they met, smiling at him in front of the justice of the peace in Alexandria, Virginia. Five months pregnant, she carried in front, definitely showing. The accidental conception might de-rail her career plans, but she would not abort. Her new husband humored her.

"I do," he had agreed. But she heard the temporizing note, and it frightened her.

Malcolm O'Donnell's emotional abuse of her started not long after, in the eighth month of her pregnancy. They were subtle unpleasant episodes that she wrote off to the growing pressures of incipient fatherhood for a middle-aged man. Lara found ways to understand and forgive, insulating herself with positive thoughts so that the child she carried would not sense her growing anxiety.

"Life has its ups and downs," she spoke to the baby inside her as she rocked in the chair near the end of her term, rubbing her belly, "you just have to roll with the bad times, Josh. Everything will work out okay."

Lara believed the baby heard her, felt her loving hand through the amniotic fluid. Joshua Sean O'Donnell was born on Valentine's Day, a healthy eight pound package who instinctively squirmed into nursing position and belched happily afterwards. Lara was happy, up until Easter.

Malcolm O'Donnell's physical abuse started that spring, just as the foliage shrugged off winter and the cherry blossoms burst out around Washington's Tidal Basin. The first time Lara wrote off as just rough sex, her husband a virile man who had gone too long without. And he did apologize, and clearly was sorry. But the episodes following got stranger and darker. Many days he behaved as a normal and considerate husband. But then something would send him into a dark mood, turning his brilliant mind in on itself, creating some gnawing horror at the core of his being. She discerned the pattern, studied it, researched it. It didn't fit any classical syndrome of mental distress. His attacks on her were too focused, too thoughtful, too controlled. Sadistically sexual, but they stopped cleverly short of visible damage.

"Mal, you've got to get help," Lara begged him.

But he wouldn't. In the autumn, she finally described the events to her friend, Karen Dunleavy, a forensic psychologist.

"Clearly there's a pathology here, Lara, and it sounds like he may be deteriorating. Fast. If the DOD isn't picking up on this—and it seems like they're not—they won't kick him into their Employee Assistance Program. So unless you want your husband arrested and charged, there isn't much the system can do. He has to acknowledge his problem and come in himself. And of course you need to protect yourself. I'm always here if it gets to the point where you need a safe place, just remember that."

Never in her life had Lara felt so alone and helpless. By Thanksgiving, it turned much worse. She could no longer deal with it, and slept alone, refusing sex, taking the abuse, managing to block most of the blows, begging him again and again to get help. Joshua would no longer go to his father, even when he was not having an episode, sensing that this was no longer a person he knew.

Early New Year's morning, she woke to Joshua's screams. He cowered in his crib, staring at his father through tears, terrified wails ripping from his throat. She grabbed the baby up in her arms, snarling, protecting him, backing away out the nursery door.

"What did you do to him, Malcolm?"

"I didn't touch him, Lara. We were just visiting. Can't I visit with my son?" A horrifying smile, death in it, distorted his face.

"Malcolm, Josh and I are leaving. You've got two hours. When we get back, I expect you to be gone to get yourself some help. If you're not, the police will be here. I'll show them my bruises, tell them you're threatening Josh.

"So, goddamn you, you can either go and get the help you need, or you can stay and I'll force it on you. And I will do that! Either way, you're going to get help! Do you understand that?"

Malcolm was over the edge somewhere, into his darkness.

"Do you understand?" she screamed.

He nodded, the awful smile frozen into place, blankness in his eyes. Terrified, Lara grabbed her coat and Joshua, bundling him quickly into the car. She drove to Karen Dunleavy's house and sobbed out her horror in her friend's arms.

She left Josh there, and against her friend's advice went back to the house. His car was still parked on the street.

"Malcolm?" she yelled from inside the front door. No answer. The house was quiet. Maybe he's gone, she thought. Thank God, maybe he did go for help. Trembling, she walked through the small house.

He lay on their bed, the pill bottle beside him, the clear plastic bag taped securely around his neck, his finger pointing at the torn-out journal page beside him by way of explanation.

Numb, her heart in her throat, she saw the empty eyes stare up at her through the plastic, unblinking. She ripped the plastic open, tilting back his head, ignoring the foul exhalation, trying to breathe life back into him as she alternately screamed her cry for help into the phone by the bedside.

The EMTs, two men and a woman, had pulled her off, and labored over Malcolm intensely but unsuccessfully. They declared him beyond resuscitation, dead at the scene. They were kind; a good team, an experienced one, and shifted their ministrations to her. Probably a massive overdose, they told her. Oxygen deficiency. Suffocation. Irreversible brain damage. Even if she'd gotten back earlier, there would have been nothing anyone could have done. The litany of their exculpatory medical terminology ran through her head in a repeating loop, but without lessening the guilt she felt. The police were thorough, but just as kind.

"Malcolm," Lara whispered as they loaded him onto the gurney, "I'm sorry. I'm so sorry. I wish I could have helped you. I love you, Malcolm."

Global Consciousness Project, Princeton University, NJ | Sunday 0720 EDT

"Thanks for the ride, Jeff," Adrienne Baxter said as she swung deftly off the back of his motorcycle. "C'mon in for a minute, I'll give you a quick tour."

She key-carded them into the building, the two of them alone on a campus deserted on a holiday weekend after exams. The tour of a nondescript and unremarkable office full of computers was not the object, she thought honestly, she just wanted to feel his lean soccer-player body pressed against her one last time before she went to work. And then she thought—seeing passion flare in his eyes—yes, Jeffrey, maybe your hands can have a quick tour of my body, like they were having last night. And then we will see, young man, how disciplined you are, what sort of long-term potential you may have.

Jeff listened attentively to Adrienne's explanations about the Global Consciousness Project. She told him about random event generators, the network spread over the globe; how the network responded in non-random fashion to major events that captured world-wide attention. She told him about the statistical evaluations and data display functions that were her job, and how much she loved it. She told him how happy she'd been when the Project had picked her—a mere undergraduate assistant—because of her programming skills. The young man listened attentively, but his eyes wandered down to the nipples pressing out against the fabric of her tank top. They were reacting to the coolness of the air-conditioned room rather than him, but he probably wouldn't know that. Well, this is as safe a time and place as any for the test, she thought.

"Okay, Jeffrey, that's it for the tour. Now you have to quit ogling my boobs, and I have to get to work. Thanks for the ride. So give me a nice kiss and be on your way."

He smiled into her eyes, hands on her bare shoulders, wondering how long he could stretch out this kiss, savoring what his young male perspective saw as an implied challenge. He dropped his hands down to her waist, sliding across the smooth skin of her back as they embraced in a long, lingering kiss.

C&O Canal Bike Trail, Washington, DC | Sunday 0721 EDT

The medical language that had been used by the EMTs at the scene of Malcolm O'Donnell's suicide scene eight years ago was some of the same terminology Lara now heard vaguely on the rock shelf below the bike trail. Except that the present tone of the language sounded more optimistic about her condition, and a lot more puzzled. Her mind dismissed those present EMT voices and retreated back into her dream memories....

"So tragic."

"Such a brilliant mind."

"So young."

"So unnecessary."

"Such a shame."

"So sorry for your loss."

During Malcolm's wake at the funeral home, Lara had stoically endured the parade of condolences and acknowledged the platitudes, giving a dim smile of thanks to those offering truly heartfelt tributes to her late husband.

Ahh, Malcolm, what could have been, what *should* have been, she cried into the bleakness in her soul. How did it go wrong? How could I let it? Guilt made her want to scream out her sins to the world. Eyes puffy, she looked over at ten-month old Joshua, nestled in Karen Dunleavy's arms. Ah, Josh. Thank God I have you. I have that much left of Mal, at least.

Dunleavy had tried to help Lara, both as friend and psychologist, during her agonizing articulation of guilt on New Year's Day, four days past.

"Lara, first of all, Malcolm surely died long before you walked into the bedroom. More important, *he* chose to. Not you. Him. He is responsible. Not you. You begged him to get help. He would not. He knew something was drastically wrong, but didn't act. He killed himself, period. Nothing to do with you."

On an intellectual plane, Lara knew that was correct. Still, the guilt flickered in and out of her mind, like some obscene serpent tongue.

The line of mourners at the wake wound down to one remaining; a short older man she didn't recognize. Probably one of Malcolm's DOD colleagues, she thought. He held her hand in both of his, and gave her a warm smile, full of understanding and compassion. His soft gray eyes looked through hers, seemingly into her soul, and he said softly "'Tis not your fault."

"I'm sorry," she replied, "I don't... I don't... understand, but thank you."

He put his hands on her shoulders, ignoring the dismissal, and repeated his statement, more softly but somehow with enormous power. "'Tis *not* your fault."

Tears flooded her eyes as the compassion of this total stranger flooded her soul. She collapsed into his arms, knowing on an emotional plane that he spoke certain truth. She felt guilt flow away like an ebbing tide over the sand, and sobbed into his shoulder. Those few mourners remaining looked away to hide their embarrassment or grief, but Karen Dunleavy smiled her approval through her own tears....

On the rock ledge below the bike trail, an EMT felt Lara's neck carefully and then gently removed the bike helmet. He listened to the rasping breath, and fished a dead bumblebee out of her throat. This almost brought her back, but the symphony of memories had not yet played out; the melodic peacefulness of the last movement drew her back into the dream....

After Lara had cried herself out, and the mourners had all left, she and the compassionate stranger went over to Karen Dunleavy, who was quietly instructing the funeral director about the cremation details in Malcolm O'Donnell's will.

As Karen and Joshua turned toward them, a remarkable thing happened: Joshua twisted in Karen's arms, smiled broadly, and with an inarticulate sound of joy tried to launch himself at the stranger.

"May I?"

She realized later his question might not have been verbal, maybe just a cocked eyebrow above those warm gray eyes.

"Josh is of an age he's very skittish around strangers, especially males," she started to explain, but by this time Joshua had locked his arms firmly around the stranger's neck and squeezed him with delight.

"Yes, yes, so I see," he replied, laughing, "therefore, I must not be a stranger. Hello, wee lad! Have we met before?"

He held Joshua out in front of his face, smiling broadly at him, and the baby warbled something back, inarticulate, but laughing. Then, remembering his manners, the stranger tucked the boy casually in the crook of his left arm, and offered his right hand to Lara.

"Oh, I'm sorry. Hamilton O'Donnell, Malcolm's uncle, twice or so removed. I'm sorry for your troubles, Lara. God knows I'll do anythin' I can to help you in this time of distress. If only I had been in the country, I might have been able to help Malcolm. Too late for that, but I can certainly help you, and this wee lad here, if you need it."

Lara studied him, evaluating, noting again the fundamental kindness in the crinkles around his eyes. Josh remained contentedly cradled in the man's arm, and started working out the handkerchief nestled in the breast pocket of his jacket. Well, Josh, obviously believes he's okay, she thought. He's never gone to anybody like that, except me and maybe Karen.

"Thank you, Mr. O'Donnell. I appreciate that very much. If there are some relatives of Malcolm that I need to contact, if you could get me a list... especially in Ireland, I understand he had some distant family members there. That would be very helpful. Oh... possibly you're from that branch of the family?"

"Indeed I am, the very branch. And would you please call me Ham, I much prefer the informality of my American persona."

"That's where I know you from!" Dunleavy interrupted, suddenly animated, "you're the Ham O'Donnell that put together that crisis intervention center for poor kids down in Southeast DC, aren't you?

"Lara, this man is a saint and a genius both," she enthused. "You wouldn't believe what he's gotten accomplished down there. It's incredible. He's made more of a difference than all the city government programs combined."

Lara studied the man again. He seemed mildly embarrassed.

"The very same Ham O'Donnell," he echoed, "but I'm afraid you overstate my role. I merely provided some seed money and attracted good people with good ideas. It took off on its own from there like a scalded cat."

Karen Dunleavy, Ph.D., psychologist, scholar and frequent caustic critic of governmental attempts at social engineering, snorted her disagreement with his understatement and offered her hand.

"Dr. O'Donnell, it is my very great pleasure to meet you personally. I've admired your work for years," she said formally.

"And I yours, Dr. Dunleavy. And please just call me Ham."

"And you please call me Karen," she said, releasing his hand with an extra squeeze of appreciation. "Come on, Ham, come on, Lara, we've had enough damn misery for one afternoon, how about if we all go back to my place for a good Italian supper! With a nice robust Chianti, and maybe a couple of stronger pops!"

Over supper, the conversation turned to the pragmatic, a respite for Lara, holding her emotions at bay. She made plans for scattering Malcolm's ashes, as he had wanted, onto the wild coastal waters off the Beare Peninsula in the south of Ireland. When her discomfort at reentering their small house on Devonshire Place became apparent, Ham immediately offered her the use of the vacant half of his duplex on Phoenix Court, a quiet location that backed up against Montrose Park, off R Street, north of Georgetown, not far away.

Umm, she thought, I can't impose on Karen much longer. Her kids come back next week. DC real estate is tight. Decent rentals are even worse in this town. The wine had blunted her pain, but paradoxically seemed to have dispelled the post-trauma fuzziness from her thoughts. She watched Hamilton O'Donnell across the table, bouncing a clearly delighted Joshua on his knee. She wondered about his motivation. She studied the lined face. He looked back at her calmly. There's love and laughter in that face, she thought, and not a little pain. And, God, doesn't it seem like there are just ages and ages of wisdom and compassion in those gray eyes. But a twinkle, too. She looked at her friend Karen Dunleavy, who gave a minute nod of agreement.

"Ham, that's so nice of you. I don't know what to say." Lara's sorrow and guilt slammed into her again like a freight train. Her eyes misted at the immeasurable kindness and compassion of a man who five hours ago was a total stranger who had just lost a nephew.

Global Consciousness Project, Princeton University, NJ | Sunday 0722 EDT

A soft computer chime sounded somewhere behind Adrienne Baxter. A part of her mind noted the chime, and tried to recall what it meant, but her attention dispersed into an enveloping passionate fog as Jeff broke off the long kiss and licked her neck. Then he kissed downward, nuzzling the tank top covering her small firm breasts, warming her nipples with hot breath through the fabric. She didn't really object to that, and her young body responded. More passion fogged her mind, her back arching, her hands in his hair.

The audible chime and a screen pop-up had been written into the code to flag the occurrence of an event above the Center's arbitrarily-programmed threshold for extreme cases of non-randomness. It would sound every five minutes until an operator responded, or until it timed out after ninety minutes. It had really been just a joke to write a six-sigma trigger into the code, but Adrienne had written it in anyway, and then promptly forgot about it.

The chime sounded one last time, while Jeff fumbled at the button on Adrienne's shorts. She was dazed with passion, but managed to say no. His hands continued to work the button, even though she was holding them tightly. He clearly had passed a certain threshold of insistence. This triggered her back to the present. Now she had to apply the test; the one that made sure she would never be hurt again. She shoved him forcibly away.

"Jeff! I said no! I mean no! Cool off! Okay?" She took her hands off his to adjust her tank top.

"Okay," he said, controlling a shiver of passion, and smiled at her. But then his hands lowered again to the button, and she caught and pushed them away. They returned, more insistent, and she twisted away and yelled no. He stopped, but it was a close thing; she could tell by the heat in his eyes. Her libido competed with the sadness that another one had failed her test. Adrienne sighed, and led the frustrated young man to the door and pushed him out, smiling weakly.

The computer chime that had sounded its odd warning was now off in some unimportant middle distance in her mind and headed toward oblivion, sunk into a strange mix of passion and sadness. She forgot it entirely.

MedStar Unit 9 Ambulance, Washington DC | Sunday 0728 EDT

Lying there on the rock ledge as the EMTs slipped the backboard underneath her and strapped her on, Lara gave the first indication that she might be swimming up toward consciousness. She smiled, remembering the good times that had followed her fortuitous encounter with Hamilton O'Donnell. What had started out as a temporary expedient for short-term lodging turned out to be one of the best decisions she had ever made. UncaHam, Joshua immediately started calling him with his unformed palate. The man embodied amazing kindness, humor, imagination, creativity, and intelligence. She and Josh had shared many fine times with him over the past eight years.

Those memories swam along the underside of her consciousness while the EMTs loaded her into the ambulance, MedStar Unit 9. She came to, briefly, when the attendant checked her pulse.

"Lara. Lara Picard. Do you hear me? That's your name, isn't it Lara?"

"Yes. Don't shout in my ear," she rasped, barely audible, her throat dry and irritated.

"Sorry. How many fingers?" He held up three.

"Three. What happened? I crash my bike?" She remembered then: flipping through the air, separating from the bike, trying to twist her feet underneath her, too late. A flash of brilliant green light and then oblivion... except... except... the dreams. They had been great dreams, she thought; full color, historically accurate, excruciatingly detailed. Just as if the memories had been played back on the high-est quality digital video. I would have made a wonderful witness, she thought. Wait... I was a witness once, wasn't I? She abandoned the ambulance to chase back into her mind and unspool that memory.

"Shit! We had her back, then she faded," the EMT spoke into the active comm link to the ER at Georgetown University Hospital. "Vitals still good. She's breath-ing cleanly now. Thought we had a collarbone, but now it looks okay, just a bruise, probably. We're inbound, five minutes. She's wired up, you should have telemetry."

"Lara. Lara Picard," he called her name again, getting no response.

"Okay, MedStar Niner. Doesn't sound like you can do much, just keep moni-toring her vitals," the ER coordinator told him out of the speaker above his head, "advise us of any changes."

"Roger. Hey, just for the record, as I'm sitting here, I'm seeing that bruise around her collarbone fading away..."

"Say again, MedStar Niner?"

"Georgetown, when we strapped her on the backboard it looked like a collar-bone fracture, and the area was bruised. I'm sitting here looking at a bruise that's fading into nothing as I watch it."

"Umm... ah... well, roger, MedStar Niner. Just keep monitoring her vitals. We see her BP, looks good. Pulse rate low, but regular. Typical athlete. Her breathing okay?"

"Yeah, twelve a minute. Great lungs," he answered the comm link, feeling mod-erately guilty for admiring the contents of the sports bra below the collarbone.

But Lara was deaf to this dialog, lost in a dizzying unwinding of memories from that time of her life when she had been a witness, but almost wasn't....

Julius Castagna was on trial. He was a drug importer, a major *jefe* in the west coast connection. His son, the junior Julius, a.k.a. Romeo for his undeniable good looks, was on trial with him. This was three years after her little flat tire act in front of Romeo and the Castagna family drug warehouse in San Diego. Her testimony only related to their Freon smuggling sideline. This had seemed like a minor EPA footnote to a major DEA drug case, but a skillful defense team had shredded the government's drug case to the point where now a conviction was far from certain. The prosecutors felt that her testimony on Freon smuggling, scheduled for the following morning, would tie it all back together for a confused jury. Romeo and his father obviously thought that too. They had her carjacked that evening.

The cokeheads had strung her hands to the rafters in a dilapidated garage in the wrong part of San Diego. They snorted lines as they worked her over, enjoying themselves. Lara took the slaps and punches and caresses, saying nothing, observing, watching their timing. She didn't waste her energy in despair, even knowing she was as good as dead. One chance, she thought, I've got just one chance to maybe take one of these assholes with me. When Asshole A turned to Asshole B to suggest a particularly humorous obscenity, she kicked her feet backward, brought up her knees, and lashed forward viciously with her right foot. She caught Asshole A under the chin and snapped back his head. He dropped to the floor like an empty sack.

Asshole B glared at her. Then a delayed coke rush hit him and he snickered. He walked over to the inert man, kicking him unceremoniously. He got halfway raised up from looking at his partner when the shotgun blast from the far window ripped into his head and shoulders. TC Demuzzio and a San Diego PD SWAT team stormed into the room on the heels of the sound.

"I'm okay, TC," she answered his unspoken question as he cut her down, "they were just getting started. How did you find me so fast?"

"You must have a guardian angel, Lara. A grandmother saw you get snatched in the hotel garage and wrote down the tag. Your rental car has a locator; they've been having problems lately with disappearing inventory."

Lara started a prayer of thanks to technology and serendipity, but then lost interest in conversation as the stress reaction set in. She ran to the corner and vomited on the floor. She made her statement later to the local police, over a three-martini room service dinner, preceded by an hour-long scrub in the hotel shower. Demuzzio recorded the statement and provided friendly support and that

Au Bon Pain
Au Bon Pain 069

Office Catering Specialists 800-765-4227

STORE #000069

QUESTIONS - CONCERNS?
Call us at 1 800 TALK ABP
Visit us at our website:
http://WWW.AUBONPAIN.COM

Ticket #919

2009-02-17   08:45:36
000069 3 15 919

SM ABP Coffee	1.59
FOR HERE	1.59
Tax	.10
Amount Due	$1.69
$5 CASH	$5.00
Change	$3.31

imposing federal presence he affected whenever he found it useful.

No charges would be filed against her assailants. Both were dead; one of a shotgun blast to the head, the other, a broken neck. This worried Demuzzio, and he said so.

"Lara, you're not in the Bureau, but you're part of the team; I can wangle counseling for you, our expense," he offered awkwardly. "If you're a little shaky on this, it's okay. A lot of us have been through it. Counseling helps sometimes."

"TC, I've never before in my life killed anything bigger than a fly or mosquito. Does killing a human being bother me? Probably it would, but not *that* asshole. Not a bit. I wouldn't even call him a human being. I was *trying* to kill him, just like he was going to kill me, after they finished playing with me. You get that, TC? I wasn't just trying to take him out of action, I was trying to *kill* him. The only thing that really shocks me is that I was successful."

"You absolutely sure you're okay with this, Lara?"

"I'm okay, TC. Really. And you know what else," she asked, her voice slowing into tight control over her emotions, "after I got done barfing my guts out, I just wanted to stand the asshole up and break his neck from the other direction!"

She reached out and patted the agent's big shoulder. "I'm okay. Just keep somebody posted here tonight in case our two Juliuses get word that their bozos weren't up to the job. They may have a backup plan. And when we're back in DC I want the name of that martial arts guy you fibbies use for training, the one that does private coaching on the side. I see I've been remiss in that aspect of my life."

The next day, Lara had limped onto the witness stand, her bruises covered with makeup, and smiled serenely at the discomfited Castagnas. She gave the clear and credible testimony that turned the jury back onto the right track. The prosecutors all agreed that it looked like the jury had made the intuitive leap between Freon smuggling and drug smuggling; it looked like Lara's testimony had moved them beyond reasonable doubt. The defense team evidently thought so, too. The two Castagnas, father and son, copped a plea the next morning. She heard it on the news, in a replacement rental car, spinning up the PCH just south of Long Beach. She whooped and pounded the steering wheel, chuckling all the way north to her spur-of-the-moment rendezvous and mini-vacation with Josh and Ham at Disneyland.

Chapter 6

Like a swimmer submerged too long, John Connard burst upwards through the surface of consciousness into the full light in the front of the cave. He inhaled deeply of the warm tropical air. Fragmented pieces of his memories seemed to drip off his mind, much as the sweat dripped off his body in the growing heat. Bare from the waist up, he somehow had removed his bloodied shirt; it lay tossed on a rock beside the crevice entrance. He stood up and stretched in the sun, taking a deeper breath, smiling at the memory fragments. Child. Man. Soldier. Magician. Then, finally, Assassin.

Puzzlement followed hard on the heels of awareness. A little pinkish flesh showed on his left side, left of and below the nipple, where the exit wound had been. A similar faded mark showed on his forearm where the slug had tumbled, chipping bone and gouging muscle. He felt up his back with his hand. No entry hole, just a mild warmth and tingling under his probing fingers. He mentally catalogued the sensations:

No pain.

Full range of motion.

Not stiff, not sore.

Strong.

Alert.

He spoke aloud to the cave, reaching the inescapable conclusion, feeling giddy.

"Well, it feels pretty good to be dead. Who would've thought? Okay! Guess I'm ready for the next step."

He stepped into the blazing tropical sun on the little shelf outside the cave entrance, throwing his arms open to it.

"I've done some good things. I've done some bad things. I'm ready for whatever happens next," he announced to the sun. He squinted out over the lush jungle foliage, thinking again that Colombia had been a beautiful place to die.

A dry humorous voice spoke to him from the back of his mind.

If you don't stop targeting yourself in broad daylight, you will be dead. They're still hunting you down on the valley floor, and all they have to do is look up through a break in the canopy.

Reacting to the voice, the Magician sprang backwards into the cave, instincts and training instantly engaging. He landed in a fighting crouch, feet spread, hands weaving through the classic blocking positions, eyes flickering around, scanning the cave. A sane mind cannot immediately accept such a voice within itself, and milliseconds later he wasn't even sure he'd heard anything. He re-catalogued his sensations:

Combat adrenaline.

Feel good.

Feel alive. In fact, more alive than I can ever remember feeling.

He pinched his forearm, hard. It stung.

I'm thirsty.

I'm hungry. In fact, famished.

A suddenly recalled analogy hooked John; it brought him in, let him readjust his perception of reality to include a voice in his mind beside his own.

He had been in the desert canyons of southern California, southeast of LA on one of the DARPA exercises, testing out experimental recon drones. Camped alone as a long-range patrol, his mission was to use the drone to assess and then penetrate a simulated secure enemy enclave without being detected.

An abandoned dog appeared, drawn by the smell of his warming MRE rations. Not long out of puppyhood, the wild and scraggly animal obviously survived in the wilderness by his wits and hunting skills. But he hadn't been born wild, he knew of people, and had come creeping in toward John. Skittish with approach-avoidance conflict, he wanted the food, but didn't like the danger.

John tore open another MRE kit, leaned over and set it on a rock.

"Come on, pooch, dinner is served," he said softly.

The dog whined, crawling forward on his belly. John kept talking to him, a light friendly banter, letting him know that here was a friend, a compassionate soul, not an enemy. Three rations later, carefully spaced, they had become fast friends. The dog licked his hands, and then finally his face; a little miracle of faith and trust in the California desert.

And that's a clear allegory for this not-so-little miracle in a cave in Colombia, John thought. I should have fallen to the bottom of the cliff, and instead I'm here inside a cave near the top. I was bleeding to death, and instead I don't have a scratch. In his mind, he played back the dry humor in the voice that had sent him springing backwards into the cave. It also had carried concern and compassion.

"Okay", he admitted to the cave, "three things. I'm not dead. I've got company in my head. The company seems friendly."

He picked up his bloody camouflage shirt, took one of the energy bars out of the pocket, and sat down to eat. Think of this as just a nice relaxed dinnertime conversation, John told himself. Breathing the calming routine taught by Duc Li, he set aside the impossibility of it all and gingerly opened the new door in his consciousness. He knew with the certainty of his mother's strange instincts that a different reality lay on the other side.

An image will make it easier to communicate, the voice spoke over his lowered barriers. *It will give you a nexus with me, a focal point for your thoughts. Think of an image you would like to communicate with.*

John shrugged away the natural reaction that this conversation could not be happening. "What is, is," he instructed himself aloud, "and what isn't, isn't."

His mother's image floated across the consciousness of his new reality. No, he thought, we're emotionally too close. His father's image. No, the same thing. My friend and mentor Alex Shaughnessy? No, we're also too close, in a different way.

Duc Li. My sensei, my coach. My philosopher-warrior friend.

An excellent choice, John Connard, the image of Duc Li said, forming out of the haze in his mind, becoming more than a simple visualization, becoming an image of depth and power. The metaphorical image somehow conveyed the truest nature of the man. It resonated with a vibrant energy, carrying implications of depths not normally seen with eyes or heard with ears.

John was blinded momentarily by the sheer beauty of the image, until there came a sensed adjustment of tuning this nexus down a notch. He breathed the calming routine again, remembering the pooch in the desert, relaxing himself into trust.

I could have grabbed that dog, John thought, but I let him make his own decisions, and approach me however he felt comfortable. I believe I trust this thing in my mind. It surely saved my life.

The last of his muscle tension slipped away as acceptance settled in. It felt strange, but very real. And he sensed no threat. John shrugged again, fatalistically. Then he stepped through the open door into his new consciousness.

The image of Duc Li floated in the space beyond, sitting cross-legged. It smiled appreciatively at John's display of mental control over his emotions. Then it smiled more broadly yet at his intuitive instant creation of a mind-space in which they could communicate, a multidimensional hologram inside his head.

"Who are you? Why are you in my mind? Did you heal me? And how? What's this about?" John asked his new nexus.

MedStar Unit 9 Ambulance, Washington, DC | Sunday 0730 EDT

Lara chuckled again in the ambulance, transitioning back into consciousness more easily this time, mentally synthesizing what should be in those blank areas in her memories of the recent past, reconstructing how she came to be in the ambulance.

"We're getting her back, Georgetown," her attendant announced to the comm link, "she just giggled."

"Say again, MedStar Niner?"

"She giggled, Georgetown. As in laughed."

"Ah... roger, MedStar Niner. Just keep monitoring her vitals, you'll be here in another minute."

"My head is cold, and I can't move it. What's that around it?" Lara looked straight at him.

"That's a set of cold packs, ma'am, and you're immobilized, you may have some head or neck injuries."

"I feel pretty good. I haven't felt this good in a long time. Maybe ever. You shoot me up with something?"

"No, Lara, we just strapped you onto the board, and now we're enroute to Georgetown Medical Center. They have a very nice ER."

"Thank you, I don't believe I need any emergency services right at the moment... I really am feeling very good. What's your name?"

"John. John Tompkins. What were you laughing at, Lara?"

"Nice dream, John. A funny dream. Made me laugh."

"Oh yeah? What was it about, Lara?"

Her brow furrowed. "I don't remember."

Something in their conversation triggered a recent memory, a very pleasant one. Her mind slid easily into its embrace. The ambulance siren and context and the conversation with an EMT named John Tompkins faded to a tiny dot on the horizon of her consciousness.

"Georgetown, she's drifted off again. We were talking, and she looked at me, and focused on me, and then faded out."

"Roger, MedStar Niner. Just uncouple the sensors, get her ready to transfer."

Lara smiled again in her dream state, at the memory of how she had limbered up for her morning bike ride. Not this morning, she now recalled, but the previous weekend....

"Catch me if you can, big boy," she'd hooted, flipping her wet towel over his face and running past him around the bed into her dressing closet.

Catch her he did, pausing with his hands on the closet doorjamb, flipping on the light to better admire her.

"Gotcha cornered now, babe. This is a closet!"

"I know. Why do you think I ran in here? Oh, I'm sorry! Now I remember. I have to get dressed." She bent over and faked an attempt to put a leg through her biking shorts, loving the vignette, wanting to keep the tease going, almost tasting the heat building in him.

"What you've got on is just fine for a ride with me," he laughed delightedly at her tease.

His hands caressed her; gentle, thoughtful, knowing. God, I'm a lucky woman, she thought, as his lips and tongue moved down her neck, pausing on a nipple, working in a slow arc down to her hip bone. She grabbed his head, pulling him upright to lick his ear, and whispered her need into it.

"Now, I want you now," she husked, emphasizing her welcome by parting her legs and pushing up onto her toes.

He smiled and leaned against her, sliding his hands down her back as he slid into her moist throbbing body. She moaned with pleasure, lifted herself off the floor with her arms around his neck, and hooked her heels around his legs. Just a few heartbeats later, muffling her gasps of ecstasy in his shoulder, they both spiraled into orgasm. In her dream, the moment seemed to go on and on, as if the pleasure had a life of its own and didn't want to let go.

Jungle of Purace District, Colombia | Sunday 0731 EDT

In the cave in the Colombian jungle, John's new nexus answered his questions with wordless conceptual communications of extraordinary depth and clarity, floated into his newly formed mind-space.

I am an observer, a delegate of sorts to your race. Your species is approaching a cusp, a turning point. Within a generation, or several, your minds will discern how to extend individual consciousness outward to embrace a greater consciousness. This is the first step toward development of incredible power. Some of your philosophers and scientists suspect that such a turning point is coming. They call it a macroshift.

That communication rotated around in John's new mind-space, displaying faceted complexities. He saw beauty in it, and danger too. The intuition and the question came to him simultaneously.

"Oh! So there *are* more advanced species out there! And there's a question of whether we may be joining them, isn't there?"

Yes. A question.

"Times of change, turning points," John continued with his intuition, "are usually unstable."

Yes. Delicate and unstable. Your race could make a quantum leap forward, or could regress into chaos, or take a terrible path to destruction. Or possibly nothing would happen, although that seems less likely.

John pondered that for a moment, tasting the honesty and concern underlying the communication. Belatedly, he realized that this nexus he had created was really a composite. The visual image, he thought, is certainly Duc Li. But the language is precise and exact, not at all Duc Li's fractured English; it's almost exactly that of Mr. Scanlon, my high school lit teacher.

With another flashing intuition, he asked, "You were observing, but now you're intervening? What happened?"

Ah, John Connard, Duc Li was correct, you do have the second sight. My reverie, my passive observation of your race, has been perturbed by an intruder, an Other.

The concept of *Other* shot a complex feeling of horror, distaste and sorrow into his mind-space. A Lucifer, a fallen angel, was the closest interpretation he could make.

Yes, there are rogue members of our species, just as there are of yours. This being is evil, and would develop your race into a tool to serve its foul ends. Your race is a potential source of incredible power. It is a magnet for those who would use it to serve their own ends. The Other is a renegade of my own species. It attacked me. I defended myself.

The spiraling energy battle flashed across John's mind-space as his nexus waved the images into being. The concepts behind the battle evaded the limits of his physical or mathematical comprehension, but he tasted the shock and horror of the sudden onslaught and the determined defense.

The intruder and I spent our vessel's resources and energies to exhaustion, a fierce battle. Neither clearly prevailed, and I believe it survived, like I did, but with its vessel destroyed. Then we intersected your plane of existence, your planet. Both our vessels were destroyed. I came to be in this place. The Other came to be in the country of your origin, the United States, somewhere on the east coast.

The concept of *came to be* projected across his mind-space with implications of dimensions of reality and transport through planes of reality that were totally arcane. They slid around the corners of his mind and he couldn't quite grasp them. But clearly his nexus existed in more dimensions than he did.

My physical form cannot exist for long on the surface of your planet, it needs to be protected by cellular interweaving with an organism. I needed you to survive. I apologize for the intrusion into your mind and your being, John Connard.

"Survival would have been assured in any body, yet you chose me..." He let the question hang in the dimensionless space between them.

I searched for the optimum being within my range of detection and limited mobility. You stood out clearly from the rest.

"But I was wounded."

Not at the time, but I... sensed... you would be.

"You saw it before it happened? Was it the bird?" John asked, making the connection.

Yes, I needed a means to reach you before you fell to the valley floor and the damage to your... physical aspect exceeded what could be repaired.

"You saved my life. You fixed my body," John said in wonderment.

Yes.

"How is that possible? There had to be fragments of vertebrae, ribs, collapsed lung, massive blood loss, a huge exit wound. I was a mess."

Your mind, John Connard, is a biological computer. The proper repair codes exist in your genetic structure, they merely need... expediting. Physically, what your researchers call stem cells are generated at an accelerated rate, moved to the wound location, and instructed to rebuild the type of bone or tissue that was damaged.

"Control at the cellular level," John marveled, the impossibility of it weighing on him.

Not impossible, the nexus Duc Li smiled; *after all, you are here, are you not? How long ago were organ transplants impossible? How long will it be before your scientists discover how to re-grow damaged organs?*

John pinched himself again. He squinted out of the cave mouth into the bright tropical morning, flexed his fingers and looked down at his side.

"Guess so," he agreed out loud, "guess I am here. But..." his thoughts trailed off into strange memories of the laying on of hands, against a backdrop of rhythmic chanting. The memories were odd and fragmented, but vibrant with power.

Some members of your species have been doing this sort of healing for millennia, although not with the focus and power I applied. Your western civilization has walked a different path, one of science and technology, so you practice healing from without rather than within. But there is a different tao; in fact there are many taos for healing within your species.

"It's been what," John looked at his watch, still struggling to absorb this, "a little over two hours to heal me?" Incredulity floated in his thoughts, inescapable.

Time and metabolic energy are for us just dimensions of reality to be managed, much as your species manages spatial dimensions and the forms of physical energy you employ. You have my same capability, latent within you. With sufficient practice, your mind can develop the skill to manage these dimensions. If the capability were not present, I could not have healed you. In fact, I truly did not heal you. You healed yourself. I acted as your guide, opening the gateway to the power of your greater consciousness. I showed your mind the way, expedited the process, focused it, made it more efficient.

John sensed within his mind and body the essential *rightness* of that statement. His intellectual resistance to the multiple impossibilities collapsed into acceptance. He didn't understand it, maybe couldn't. But it clearly had happened. Being a pragmatist, he accepted it.

"So what other dimensions of reality can you manage, and what can I manage, by myself and with your help, and what would you have me manage?" His mind jumped to the next intuition and he voiced it immediately. "Besides my latent capabilities, whatever they are, you picked me for my hunting skills, didn't you? Or at least my mindset. You need a soldier, don't you? You and I are going to hunt down your enemy, aren't we?"

I need your help, John Connard. Your species, your entire planet, your evolving greater consciousness, all need your help.

The directness and the honesty of the plea were overwhelming. The implications of not helping played out across the mind-space between him and his nexus. Power gone berserk. A young race turned to evil, sent screaming on a jihad of terror and conquest across the universe. Death and destruction. Indescribable suffering, for untold generations into the future. It had happened before, that much was clear.

We must stop the Other here and now, John Connard, before its evil takes root.

An extended recitation of all the evil that could come played through his mind-space, answering his questions, washing away his skepticism, until the mission resonated in his being. It's no different than what I'm already doing, he admitted. Eliminating evil, making the world a better place. It's just on a bigger scale. I have to do it. There's no real choice here.

Palpable relief floated out from his nexus and the image of Duc Li smiled gently. John now understood that the moral structure of this being required a willing participant, not a puppet. He truly was free to choose his own course.

"I have just one question. What happens if we get this monster tracked down and I decide maybe he's not really a bad guy after all?"

You are a moral being, John Connard. I am content that you decide.

"But you would be destroyed if I misjudge, or get fooled, or somehow screw up and get suborned, is that not correct?"

That is correct. We both would be destroyed.

"And you still trust me, my decisions?"

Your memories say you have been suborned in the past into an abuse of power, but you have learned from the experience. It is indeed possible that you could make a mistake, or an error in judgment, or be deceived. But you have balance; you are able to discern. You have your mother's second sight; you are unlikely to be fooled. I will take my chances with you, John Connard. I am content.

A soldier's code, John mused. You trust me, I trust you. Nobody knows what tomorrow's battle will bring, but we fight together, we look out for each other. Can't do any better than that. He smiled at the comfort in that thought. Clearly, his old comrades in arms would have to join them. Both the Magician and the Assassin would be called to this new mission.

Georgetown University Hospital, Washington, DC | Sunday 0734 EDT

MedStar Unit 9 pulled into the Reservoir Road Emergency Room entrance to Georgetown University Hospital, and they lifted Lara onto the waiting gurney. The change in state snapped her to full consciousness, with a complete and acute recollection of who she was, what had happened on the bike, and her recovery by police and EMTs. The brightness and sharpness of this recollection pained her, and she de-tuned it several notches, automatically, without thinking.

"Okay, Ms. Picard, I see you're back with us now," the young intern said cheerfully, walking alongside the gurney. "I'm Peter Arkanian, the ER physician this morning. We're just going to do a quick evaluation here and then pop you down to the MRI unit, see if there's any indication of damage to your noggin."

The thought of magnetic resonance imaging bothered Lara somehow.

"No, doctor, first we're going to talk. My 'noggin' is feeling quite well, thank you. Just unstrap me. I want to wiggle around better, assess myself. I think those kind souls in the ambulance over-reacted a little bit."

"Believe me, Ms. Picard, you're better off not moving. If you have cranial bleeding or a concussion, you can do more damage." He wheeled the gurney into an examining room.

"Doctor... Arkanian, look at me. I don't feel anything hurt, and I'd like to be unstrapped, please. Am I not fully alert?" Lara transfixed him with a cold emerald stare, fully aware and totally focused, reaching intuitively toward his mind, and feeling something click over as she touched it.

"Okay, Ms. Picard," the young physician looked surprised with himself as he reached for the straps. "You sure don't fit the profile the EMTs were transmitting. So let's try it by stages, very, very slowly. No sudden motions of your head, or any other part of your body. Let me move you. If you feel any dizziness or pain, or anything odd at all, let me know, okay?"

"Okay," she agreed, a smile returning warmth to her eyes.

As she lay there, following his instructions, letting him do his diagnostic tests, she reflected on her state. She actually did feel great. Maybe it's the psychological lift from being alive when she should be dead, she reasoned. But no, even with massive releases of endorphins into her bloodstream she would still have some sense of physical damage to her body. And there was none. None at all. It made no sense.

It obviously made no sense to young Dr. Peter Arkanian, either.

"Ms. Picard, there's dried blood on your shirt and shorts, and rips in both. But there are no contusions or abrasions on you that I can see," he said as his fingers gently and systematically probed the scalp under her short blond hair.

"I've always been a quick healer, Doctor."

"Not in an hour or two, you haven't." He smiled at her.

That's true, she thought, not in an hour or two. But now I'm different, somehow. I feel like a new person, a bigger person, expanded somehow, grown past my body outline, and it's like the usual rules don't apply anymore. And I just made a physician's decision for him, in some strange way. Maybe landing on my head rearranged something, changed me in some fundamental way? She tried to form an image of her new self, suddenly sensing that the answers lay within her mind. She needed a visualization; an image to anchor onto.

A blurry memory of the statue of Justice at the Supreme Court flittered across the back of her mind, and then obediently came into focus as she willed it to better resolution. No, that's not me, she thought, the nose is too Roman. We'll just give her my features, make her easier to relate to. Dump the scales and the blindfold, those would be for a judge. Let's just keep it simple: Justice in a white robe, open hands, my own face. But smiling, not stern. Warm, not cold.

While Lara responded to the physician's diagnostic questioning with her forebrain; with the new other part of her mind she played around with the image. She tried out different options, as she had when clothing dolls as a child, until she was content that her integration had the right feel. She turned the image around in her mind, examining the texture, the impressions. It felt comfortable. It felt like her. Satisfied, she clicked it on, and said hello.

In full accordance with what she somehow knew would happen, the image smiled gently at her, and replied.

Hello. Thank you for creating me, for giving me birth. I am a nexus, a link, to your broader consciousness. May I explore the dimensions of this reality, while you deal with our physician friend?

Lara would have been shocked and disconcerted had the contact not felt so natural, so... expected. The sensation likened to the warmth and comfort of an old friend. Sure, she thought, be my guest, and turned her attention to her examiner.

"Does this hurt?" Arkanian asked, pressing the areas around her collarbones.

"Nope," she said, sitting up.

"I said no sudden motion!" he exclaimed, visibly irritated.

"Doctor Arkanian. I'm not hurt. I feel great. My head's just fine. I don't think I banged it much at all. Thank God for bike helmets and ANSI standards, huh?" She got off the examining table and stood up, stretching her slim body, smiling at him. "Get me a release form and I'll sign out. I've got a busy day coming up."

"Sit down, Lara, you're not going anywhere. You need at least a twenty-four-hour observation period."

She noted the shift to her first name, an attempt to exert authority.

"Nonsense, Peter," she replied, "all you would be observing is a perfectly healthy woman with a lot to do, getting frustrated. There is absolutely no reason why I need to be observed."

"Actually," the physician said carefully, "there are two reasons. First, several types of brain damage can show up as delayed effects. Unless we eliminate that possibility, you could suddenly drop dead."

"I can see you don't believe that's the case," Lara stared at him intently, "so what's the second reason?"

"Second, you have bloodied, ripped clothing, but there's not a scratch on you. The only explanation is that you faked it. This means there is some psychological problem, Lara, and you need to be evaluated by a good psychiatrist. Fortunately, we have one on call, and she's very good. She can help you work your way out of whatever this problem is that you're trying to deal with."

Lara reflected on that for a moment. "Peter, that's a very interesting analysis, and from your point of view it's perfectly logical. But it's wrong. Now, please, get me a release form, or I'll just walk out of here and leave you with the ton of paperwork you'll need to do to cover the Hospital's butt properly. And, believe me, I know paperwork—I'm a lawyer."

She watched him waver between getting the form and having the ER security detail lock her down. Lara shook her head no, as if guessing his line of thinking. She smiled pleasantly, but felt her eyes literally flash at him, brilliant green flaring from the pupils. She sensed something in his mind click over sharply, dropping him into agreement. She could almost read his unspoken rationalization from the expressions chasing across his face: okay, if she is wacky, and she is a lawyer, who needs that kind of double misery?

"All right, Ms. Picard, if you're accepting total responsibility for your condition, and want to sign the release declining treatment, we can do that. I don't agree, and I'll note that on the form. Come on, let's walk down to the desk and do the details. If you fall over in the hallway, all bets are off. Do you have somebody we can call to pick you up?"

"I'll call," she said, thinking that Ham still ought to be home with Josh, "just point me to a phone."

She gave the desk her medical insurance information, signed the financial responsibility form, and used the phone while Dr. Peter Arkanian filled out the release form.

"Hi, Ham. I need a ride, are you busy?"

"Lara, we were just wonderin' about you," replied Hamilton O'Donnell. "Holdin' breakfast we were, Josh and I. Did you flat out again, out in the hinterlands? Surely we'll come get you. Where?"

"I'll be walking west on Reservoir Road from the GU Hospital, Ham, past the embassies. I'll probably be past the intersection at Foxhall by the time you get to me. Stay on Reservoir, it runs into Canal Road. I need to pick up my bike off the bike trail there."

"Hospital? Lara, are you okay? Were you in the hospital?"

"Yes, Ham, but I'm fine. I've been checked out by one of their handsome young interns," she said, smiling at Arkanian. He was busily writing an extensive note on the bottom of the release form.

"Lara, why don't you just hold your hoult, sit tight in the hospital and we'll pick you up there?"

"Ham, I'm fine, I really am. It's an absolutely beautiful morning, and I've just had a strange and wonderful experience of some kind, and I need to walk while I think about it. Reservoir Road. If you see me collapsed on the sidewalk, you'll know I was wrong, but I truly do feel wonderful. Okay?"

"Sure, and that's fine, Lara, if you say so. I'll gather up Joshua and we'll be along shortly. If you don't feel up to walkin', just sit down and wait. Please. Would you do that for me, *a gra*?"

"Yes, Ham. Thanks for your concern. Take your time. I really do need to reflect a little. See you in a few. Bye."

Chapter 7

"We will need weapons? Support? What?" Having made his decision, John Connard immediately moved to the practical combat perspective of the Magician.

Support we should avoid if at all possible. Your race is at a very delicate point in its macroshift, in its evolution. Best not to perturb that by involving others. Tiny effects that would normally be lost to entropy can be crucial at times like this. Chaos theory, your mathematicians call it.

"How about support from your people, then?"

My vessel is destroyed. I do not know if my warning escaped the attack, or when it might be received and recognized. If we wait, the outcome will likely be decided: the Other will prevail. Such an outcome would be difficult to undo, perhaps impossible without widespread destruction.

John shuddered at the scenes of destruction still vividly etched in his mind.

"Weapons, then?"

Your mind is your weapon, John Connard, and it has new capabilities. You are an accomplished physical fighter. We will extend those skills, drawing on non-physical realms.

Concepts floated across his mind-space. They felt reassuringly familiar to the Magician, and clearly had an internal logic, but his mind couldn't parse the meaning.

"Hmm? I'm sorry, I think you'll have to show me."

Turn your mind to the concept I set before you.

The blue-tinged Technicolor beauty entranced the artist in him as it expanded into his mind-space. "Good God, that's lovely."

Yes. The concept you see is what Duc Li would call your ki, *but now it is much more.*

"Yes, I sense that."

Your ki *is but the tip of an iceberg, it is connected to a spirit energy, to your greater consciousness. Dissolve into it now, become one with it.*

Several false attempts, but then the Magician found the path.

"Umm, like slipping into a hot tub when you're really cold."

Yes. Good. You have conjoined. Now visualize this ki *running through your being.*

"Ahh," he gasped as the warm joy of the spirit energy welcomed him like some cosmic womb. It was alive and aware, and it *knew* him.

Sit. Contemplate. Sense the essence of it. Resonate with it. Become it.

The Magician sat in the cave, in the lotus position, now in shadow, the sun having lifted above the entry crevice. He closed his eyes and tuned out the surroundings, letting himself feel the expanded reality, dimension, and purpose. Time hung suspended, or maybe had a different meaning. The resonance coursed through him. Joy ran with it, almost orgasmic. He struggled for control, but didn't get it. He collapsed into the spirit energy, and paradoxically had full control. The dimmed cave brightened with the aura forming about him. He opened his eyes, sensing without seeing a six-pointed dark blue star sapphire pattern pulsating gently in their pupils, in time with the rhythms of his heart.

Good, good. Now, there is a dimension in the universe of dark energy. You sense it; you have brushed against it. Your ki, *your greater self, can access it. You can direct it; control it, to the extent that the capabilities of your mind and body will permit. Reach your mind into that dimension.*

The symbology that floated into existence to point the way was largely imponderable, and his mind contained no useful metaphor, but the symbols instructed him clearly enough. Mentally, he severed the umbilical cords to his existing reality, his simplistic four-dimensional world, and reached his mind out along the symbolic pathway into the field of dark energy. A conjunction of his *ki* with the field took form, and he felt the strange tingle of energy coursing through his mind and body.

Ah, yes, John Connard. You have it. It will manifest differently in this reality. Now, slowly, slowly extend the energy from your hand.

He raised his open hand. As the thumb automatically tucked back and the calloused palm tightened, a plane of pure blue energy crackled into the air. An elongated oval line, it seemed to start on his hand and curve back into it. The oval projected outward as he willed it. Its edge line flickered with an ionizing flame, bright and deadly; its inner core carried a semi-transparent glow. He suddenly knew, without really understanding, how this could be. His mind stepped over an unseen edge as he rose smoothly from the lotus into the movements of a training kata, a defense against a four-cornered attack. He embraced the energy, became part of it. Like a dancer, he moved around the sandy floor of the cave, hands weaving, sweeps and blocks, planes of energy flowing outward, ionizing the air, crackling blue in the dim light.

The blue-bladed extension of his hand sheared through the rolled-up cuff of his shirt and carved a groove into the rock beneath it. He felt the jar of the contact, on several different levels, and laughed with the savage joy of a wild beast liberated from a cage. He carved the walls with sweeps and chops, blasted gouges into them with punches of blue lightning from his hands. Suffused with the joy of an elemental beast, his body flowed like liquid into the motions of the kata. Somehow, his mind remained calm and detached. The *eye of the storm*, Duc Li called it: the ultimate enlightenment of active meditation in the center of battle. Instinctively, almost absently, he wed the energy field to his muscle memory, and locked it in.

Enough! You will deplete your physical body's resources overly much. You must have food and water.

"Okay!" With a barely conscious mental motion, he turned down the energy draw to a barely sensed trickle.

"I'm not human anymore, am I?" he wondered.

On the contrary, you are more human. You see what it is to be one with a reality of which before you were barely aware.

As the energy tuned down, he felt fatigue. A strangely different fatigue, spiritual and mental as well as physical, it was clearly a withdrawal effect. I'll have to watch that, he thought absently, as he examined the scorched and chipped rocks. The air carried the heavy ozone smell of lightning.

He was famished. They conversed as he ate the rest of his energy bars, and drank from a trickle of groundwater running down the cave wall.

"Okay, that's certainly an eye-opener. Or better, a mind-opener. Tell me about it, if you can put it into terms I can comprehend," he asked his nexus.

You have different ways of comprehension, my young friend. The intellectual is probably the least of them. Your ki *knows innately how to use the energy field, how it may be caused to interact with this reality. I but point the way around some of your learned preconceptions of what can and cannot be in your reality.*

"And the source of the energy itself, is it this spirit *ki* of which I am a part?"

The ki *you sense yourself a part of? That is the spirit, the life-force, of your planet, and of life and consciousness in the universe. You have always been a part of it. It stands outside any physical continuum. It can control and direct the physical energies of the universe. The energies you just used are not spirit; they are physical, taken from a different dimension. The universe has more dimensions than your species can presently perceive. Some of your brightest theoretical mathematicians have made postulates that are not far from the truth.*

"That young post-doc I dated at Cal Tech? String theory, branes, N-dimensional space, maybe eleven dimensions? Maybe she wasn't as wacky as I thought?" Great sex, John recalled, but very, very difficult to talk to, her mind in a different zone most days.

Thirteen prime dimensions, and a number of derivatives, but it is likely your species will develop an intuitive understanding prior to the full intellectual understanding. We ourselves have not achieved a full understanding of the concepts. The universe has many mysteries and subtleties.

"So my *ki* can take physical energy from different dimensions, control it, use it? What about conservation of mass and energy?"

The principle in your mind is quaint and limited, but the more general concept is valid across many dimensions. Several of these dimensions are separated from your reality by less than the width of a proton. One of these is the dark energy field.

Complex symbols floated across John's view. He recognized few of them. But the totality had a resonance to it, and he knew without understanding that it truly revealed a multi-dimensional reality, expressed in mathematical terms.

"I sense that it's right, but I certainly don't comprehend," John said.

Given time, my young friend, you will. You will.

Georgetown University Hospital, Washington, DC | Sunday 0755 EDT

A dancer's grace, Dr. Peter Arkanian thought, watching Lara Picard walk away. Light on her feet. Obviously a superb athlete. Definitely a tough cookie. World-class actress, too, if she was faking her accident. And if she wasn't... his mind veered away from that medical impossibility....

"Hey there, new me," Lara sub-vocalized as soon as she passed out of earshot of the guards at the Emergency Room entrance, "tell me about it. *All* about it."

The image began to form within a sort of structured space in her mind at this invitation. Intuitively, she shaped that space, starting off with the metaphor of a movie screen, but then expanding it into multiple dimensions. It felt odd at first. She adjusted and tuned, then when it felt right, a new mind-space snapped fully into place, sharp and clear. It carried an intense familiarity, as if it had always been there, as much a part of her as her arms and legs. An older but unworn image of herself awaited in that space, robed in white.

Behind the image she sensed, as if in a hall of mirrors, a thousand generations of her predecessors. The evolution, the growth in the minds and spirits of those beings that had converged down to her, had a brightness and beauty almost over-whelming. Crying, she tuned it down to a bearable level. A chain of symbols, meaning unknown but somehow intuited, scrolled across the mind-space between her and the image. Comprehension rolled over a threshold: she was a new kind of child aborning from this chain of generations. She was an early arrival, a precursor, there were and would be others. Lara felt the connection with those possibilities, and was suffused with happiness. She cried some more.

So you see, Lara, so you see. The gentle voice sounded in her mind. A voice much like hers, it carried a touch of her mother's accent, a soothing cadence.

"I have always been this way?"

You have always been this way. You know that. Your physical world is not your entire world; it never has been.

"Ah! Those times at the pool," she remembered with a strong sense of *deja vu*, "my sacred little pool, on the farm. Lying in the sun, my feet in the water."

Yes, you have visited this realm before. Now you have fully entered it. This is your new reality, what your evolution has been striving toward.

"And you? Who are you?"

You know me, Lara. I am you. I am an image of your greater self, your being that exists in more than one reality and more than just physical dimensions. I represent, as your more spiritual martial arts instructors would say, your ki, your spiritual essence. This image we create together is merely a nexus, a link, to your greater consciousness.

"And this warm ocean of joy I'm sensing, this is part of my new reality?"

It is the field of consciousness of all things, greater than that of your singular mind. It is growing, evolving and changing, as humanity grows, evolves and changes.

"God?" she murmured the question.

A shrug, smiling. *As you understand that concept.*

"And these points I sense brightening and dimming nearby in this... field? These are other consciousnesses?"

These are likely a number of individual consciousnesses united in a common purpose, a church service, a prayer group, a meditation room. There are as yet no individual minds in the world that have achieved your level of receptivity and more fully entered this larger reality.

"So, I'm not human anymore?" Lara asked as she turned left out of the Hospital grounds and walked uphill on Reservoir Road.

You are more human. You are another step forward in evolution. There will be many more to follow. A cascade. Punctuated equilibrium is the evolutionary concept.

Lara's mind shied away that sudden enlightenment; the concept contained too complex a mix of beauty and danger as it expanded in her mind-space. She couldn't absorb it, and changed the subject.

"So, I'm a new kind of being? This is how I came to be healed? I was badly hurt, wasn't I? So I'm plugged into this greater consciousness? It wants me whole and intact?"

In your case, in our case, your brush with death released an ancient message coded in your genetic structure, and you became part of this larger reality, and it became a recognized part of you. This consciousness has great love, and love can heal. You are not the first to experience this. It is just not common in modern Western culture.

"It took," Lara objected, looked at her watch to confirm this, "a little over two hours to bring me back from nearly dead?" She was a scientist; incredulity floated in the mind-space between them. Then, in a moment of insight: "Did you heal me?"

In your new and greater reality, time and energy are merely dimensions that may be managed. I did not heal your body. I merely opened it to the power and love of your greater consciousness, and your body healed itself.

Lara sensed within her nexus some temporizing in that statement, some sense that the complexities of her *ki*, her greater self, would not be fully comprehensible until she developed her understanding further. The musing thought crossed her mind that *Ki* also was the name of the ancient Sumerian goddess of the earth. The white-robed figure smiled at the thought, and elucidated.

The proper repair codes exist in your genetic structure, they merely need to be enabled by your mind. Then your body generates undifferentiated cells at an accelerated rate, moves them to the injury, and rebuilds the damaged tissue.

"Control at the cellular level?" She rebelled, all her scientific training arguing the impossibility. Frogs do it, but not mammals. "Have other humans ever done this?"

It is rare. Mostly they are genetic anomalies, in whom talents are prematurely and incompletely expressed. But within several generations there will be a critical mass of individuals with true capabilities. They will have an ability to act in concert, to use the greater consciousness to manage other energies and dimensions. You are the first generation, a prototype of sorts, of this new human species. A messenger, perhaps.

Lara's innate scientific skepticism warred with the information from her new companion as they walked down Reservoir Road in the morning sunlight. But even the most resistant of skeptics must surrender to overwhelming evidence, and she felt herself sliding toward acceptance. Clearly, she now existed within a new reality.

Northwest Washington, DC | Sunday 0756 EDT

"Mom dump her bike?" Joshua O'Donnell asked, having overheard his Uncle

Hamilton's phone conversation with his mother Lara.

"Indeed and she did, Joshua. Indeed and she did. We are instructed to pick her up on Reservoir Road."

"She's not hurt?" The boy's question dangled in an anxious space between them. "You look worried."

"Ah, lad, 'tis it not me that's always worryin' about your mum? She presses the envelope of what's possible, God love her. On a bicycle, and on most everythin' else too. Worrisome to an old man, 'tis." Hamilton O'Donnell appeared lost in reverie for a moment, changing expressions chasing across his face.

"Uncle Ham?" Joshua's intense eyes studied his uncle.

"Go on now, boy, will you! Put the eggs back in the fridge, and I'll get the car out of the garage," Ham replied, deflecting Joshua back to the other side of the duplex. Damn, that one is just too smart, he thought. An IQ off the charts, so high it has no reliable measure. Nine years old chronologically and physically, but intellectually he's much, much older. And so hyper-aware that sometimes I think he can almost read my mind.

Ham backed the car out of the garage and up against the curb, and put the top down. It was a lovingly restored 1958 Edsel convertible. He used it as a working vehicle, and had none other. Most days, he walked or took the Metro.

"Ah, me lad, what a beautiful mornin'. We are to take our time, your mum instructed. Needed some time to reflect on her experiences, she said."

"What sort of experiences, Uncle Ham? She's dumped her bike before. She gets up, brushes off the dirt, and keeps on going. The only thing she ever thinks about is how not to fall off again."

"Dunno, me boy. That's just what she said. Take our time. She wanted to walk and reflect."

"You think she's out of it? Bumped her head?"

"Mmm, no. The emergency room would have kept her."

The two of them got into the car and drove out of Phoenix Court, turning west on R Street.

Jungle of Purace District, Colombia | Sunday 0757 EDT

"Speaking of time, I sense it's running. Shouldn't we be on our way?" John asked into the dust-laden air of the cave.

Yes, but several more things before we leave this refuge. First, we must establish the parameters of your control. You have a natural facility with the energy field as a fighting tool, but there are other tools. And we must establish what you can do safely.

Now, engage the energy field, and focus it in your fingertip.

John engaged it, surrendered to it, felt its warmth and... concurrence... was the only term he thought fit. His aura brightened and his index finger thrummed lightly, pulsating in time with his heartbeat.

Good! Now turn it, just so.

Another chain of symbols appeared in his mind-space. He interpreted the symbols to mean a portal, with his being as the key. Placing himself in the portal lock, he turned the key.

Yes! Excellent!

"And what do I have here," John wondered aloud. "It has a very precise structure; rigorous, almost... crystalline."

It is a manifestation of another dimension. Its expression in this reality is as a gravitational field.

Of course! The recognition slipped easily into his mind; he saw parts of the symbology as equivalent to the classical equations describing gravitational attraction between two masses.

Good! Now use the gravity field to pick up that rock, and hold it against the cave wall.

The intellectual part of John's mind briefly rebelled at that, but he squelched it firmly with the certainty of his new reality. Extending the field from his finger toward the rock, he visualized what he wanted to happen. The field reached out to the rock and enveloped it. He lifted it, slowly, somehow feeling its weight. He sensed the weight to be within his parameters, whatever those were. Pinning the rock to the wall, he held it there, evaluating the displacement until he understood the tensors required. Then he let it drop. The gravity field collapsed back into his finger.

His nexus was impressed. *John Connard, you are even deeper than your memories portray you. I am a fortunate being, to have been dealt such a champion in this reality.*

John smiled his appreciation. I did feel the finesse there, he thought. And now I understand, at least intuitively, the transform functions between the fields.

Good! Then next, this will be more of a challenge for you, I think. A field of the absence of energy, or more correctly, of the absence of coherence in this reality.

Some kind of entropic end-point, he mused. "A null state? Chaos? Nothingness?"

The mathematical concept in your mind of a null set, an empty set, most accurately defines that dimension. As you can manage dimensional energy, so can you manage its absence. Emptiness is merely another dimension. Open your hand, and hold your palm out in front of you.

He did, his hand glowing slightly, a pulsating pocket of blue energy cupped between his palm and fingers.

Now, replace the energy field in your palm with nothingness.

He visualized, but nothing happened. His nexus remained silent, expectant. He sank deeper into his new consciousness, his expanded *ki*, his greater reality. He surrendered himself to it, contemplating the Zen null state: lucid but detached and uninvolved.

A small black cloud formed off the end of his palm. His hand cooled palpably as some of the energy left it.

Excellent. Now cast it from you.

He opened his palm and shoved, a gentle wrist motion like tossing a wad of paper into a wastebasket. The cloud broke free of his hand, and drifted toward the cave wall on a straight-line trajectory. As it drifted, its blackness lessened. Just before it hit the rock, he could see the rock patterns through it.

It cannot sustain itself independently in this reality, his nexus answered his unspoken question, *a good thing, because it can be quite deadly.*

John walked over to the rock wall and rubbed off a trace of dust where the cloud had impacted.

"It disrupted the crystalline structure? How deep?"

One or two layers, several molecules, nanometers.

"And what effect on organic matter? Human bodies specifically?"

Approximately the same, depending on the field strength remaining at contact.

"So you'd lose some skin, and eyes could be a problem, but that's not very destructive, and certainly not deadly. It doesn't seem like much of a weapon."

On the contrary, my young friend, its deadliness is more subtle, and more dangerous. Like a matador's cape, it can conceal the sword coming in behind it. It also can be used as a shield, absorbing the energy used against it. Attuned differently, it may be used to envelop the being controlling it, bringing disguise and near-invisibility to those who see in limited dimensions. Hold out your palm again.

John did so, forming the small black cloud.

Now, thin it down to a sheet, with a thickness only slightly greater than zero.

The symbols floating across his mind-space showed him the way to another portal. He turned the mental key and it happened: a sheet of shimmering distortion appeared, strange and difficult to look at.

Good! Now draw it around you, like a loose set of clothes, or a cloak. It seems strange, but this null field is a part of you, it cannot harm you.

Shivering at the strangeness, John nonetheless made the mental motions the symbology indicated, drawing the null field around him like a cloak. He gazed astonished at his hands and feet. *Something* was there, he could tell, existing in an uncertain way the eye and mind could not grasp, but he could also see the cave floor and walls through the shimmering. The ultimate camouflage, his soldier's mind thought; if you didn't move, you would blend into almost any background.

"So how does it work? Does it bend light around it?"

No. Light energy, electromagnetic energy, in this reality loses its coherence when it encounters the null field. It becomes chaotic, obeys different rules. Some is reflected, some is refracted. Some speeds up, some slows down. Some is eliminated, some is created. The quantum hologram of your immediate locus is recast, with different rules.

John filed that arcane concept in the back of his mind for future study and focused on the immediate.

"So why is it dangerous?"

Your null field is keyed to your being, so it cannot harm you. But it can harm the minds of other beings who are not... resonating with you on the same... frequency. To them it is chaos, dissolution of mental form and substance.

"And the converse is true? I can be harmed by a null field not my own?"

Yes. Contact with the null has a psychic effect, confusion of reasoning, lapse of memory, dilution of purpose, loss of consciousness if the field applied is strong enough.

"Sounds like television," John smiled.

The effect may be only momentary, but you know as a warrior how long moments can be, and how much they can decide in a battle. The Other will fight with this weapon, John Connard, it is a favored weapon of darkness and deception. You understand well the metaphor of a cloak, but have not the natural skill level with the null that you have with control of energy. We must practice.

John heard him, but he also heard a distant dissonance in the consciousness field, a sense of perturbation. A tide of time pressure lapped up toward him. His nexus felt it too. Their enemy was alive, and stirring.

Georgetown, Washington, DC | Sunday 0759 EDT

Joshua O'Donnell remained silent for a few moments as the Edsel navigated westward on R Street into Georgetown. Then, "Uncle Ham, what was my father like? Am I like him?"

A quintessentially Joshua non-sequitur, thought Hamilton O'Donnell as he pondered the questions. The boy absorbs and analyzes and decides like lightning. Then he moves onto the next connection, which more often than not isn't apparent to anyone else. Disconcerting to us lesser mortals.

"God in heaven, Joshua," he exclaimed, "what's the connection there, to your mum spillin' off her bike?"

"Well, Mom told you she needed time to reflect, right? When she gets that way she's usually thinking about him. Sometimes she looks at me real close and then just sort of... fades. Her mind goes to another place; someplace sad, it looks like from her face. Especially around Christmas and New Year's."

"Well, Joshua, you do have your daddy's good looks—thick black hair, blue-green eyes, olive skin—definitely an Irish gypsy. You look very much like he did at your age, as I recall.

"And, Joshua, you have some of his mannerisms. That raised left eyebrow, for example. It must be genetic rather than learned from the environment, because you were still a wee babe when he died, not even a year old. Your mum sees those mannerisms, and it triggers memories, I think. She goes to her sad place to wonder what might have been, what should have been, had she been able to save the poor soul."

"So tell me what he was like," Joshua repeated.

"A bright wee *gossoon*, me lad, a child prodigy much like you. He grew up to be a world-class mathematical genius. Could have been a concert pianist, had he pursued his music. But he was proud, arrogant. He put himself above the rest of humanity. His childhood wasn't happy, or secure like yours. That turned his brilliant intellect down darker pathways. He lacked compassion. I think it possible that he could not bring himself to love."

"Is that why he committed suicide? He couldn't love Mom? He couldn't love me? I have his genes. Will I become like that?"

"Ah, Joshua, such questions! I cannot say what went on in Malcolm's mind. But you have your mum's genes as well as your dad's. You have happiness and love and security in your life. All your mum and I can give you. You have compassion for people and understandin' of life, as far beyond your nine years as is your intellect. You will never travel the path your father took, boy."

"But life is all probabilities, Uncle Ham, you told me so."

"Indeed I did, and indeed it is. And while no outcome is absolutely certain, the probabilities are all on your side, young man."

"Did you arrange that somehow, Uncle Ham? The genetic probabilities, I mean."

Hamilton O'Donnell was so shocked he almost missed the turn onto Reservoir Road. How in the name of God did he get *there*, he wondered. That's so close, it's uncanny. I've underestimated his wild card talents again.

"The morning my father committed suicide, he was going to kill me," Joshua continued, calmly, staring intently at his uncle. "I never want to be like that. He was a genetic mistake."

"I think you will always find within you the strength to love, Joshua, regardless of how your genes are arranged," Ham answered carefully. "Your mum has enormous capacity for love. She loved your father deeply. That's why she gets reflective at times, and goes off to her distant sad place. She still cannot fathom why she couldn't bring your dad out of his dark state, into the light of her love. She is reconciled to the reality, I believe, but it still saddens her, and she still feels guilt, eight years later."

"How can you feel guilt for something when you did your best, and had no other control over the outcome?"

"Oh, Joshua, guilt is such a subtle thing, and so easily placed upon yourself."

"But Mom is a pretty rational person, and she knows herself."

"That she does, me lad, that she does. But she is a strongly moral person. Part of her moral code includes carin' and nurturin'. She follows the instructions of Jesus and Mohammed and Buddha and Confucius and all the other great humanist philosophers in that regard.

"So she is askin' herself, especially around the holidays, 'what could I have done more, what could I have done differently'. She puts the guilt on herself. Rationally, she knows better, but emotionally..." Hamilton O'Donnell's voice tailed off into the uncertainty of trying to guess a complex person's innermost feelings.

Chapter 8

As Lara strode past the corner of Reservoir and Hoban Roads, a cloud came over the sun. A long emptiness in her new mind-space imparted some sense of a dropped curtain. Then a sudden exhalation of sorrow and horror came from her nexus, features twisting in disgust.

Ah! Lara, you are no longer the only one. There is another!

Dissonance shuddered through the new fabric in her mind, and she trembled at the sudden fear flowing through it.

Evil has been born this minute. A monster has evolved into this new reality. It seeks power. Absolute power. It will not abide our existence. It will come for us. As soon as it gathers strength, it will come.

She felt it, vaguely: a distant discord, a cold small darkness far down in her new consciousness. Palpably different than the friendly warm twinkles around her, it had an eerie glow behind its darkness, like the corona of a total solar eclipse. In her mind-space, the glow had a harsh blue tinge, an obscene, unnatural cast to it.

We will have to destroy this thing!

Resolve hardened in her nexus, and became her own. Intuition accompanied the resolve, sliding easily into her mind. She abruptly understood, with a profound certainty: things happen for a reason. I am here in this place at this time because I need to be. I need to protect this new evolutionary child within my mind, within all of our minds.

"Yes," she said, shivering with some cosmic sense of preordained conflict, "I know."

This evolutionary child must be in Josh's mind too, she thought; anything I have, my son probably has in spades. The fierce protective instinct of mothers everywhere flared within her.

We must preserve your self, your son, your evolving greater consciousness, your new species. This thing could turn human evolution from grace to evil. We must stop it. We must prepare you.

Lara could almost taste the sorrow in that plea. Visions on visions of horrible futures played out across the mind-space between her and her nexus. A new and promising evolutionary step turned to evil, its power unchecked, its goodness suborned, reverting to fundamentalism, then to savagery. A tidal wave of death and destruction and suffering would come crushing down, and last generations into the future.

We must trap and destroy this thing, *before its evil can take root.*

The mission resonated in Lara's new consciousness. It's no different than what I'm already doing, she thought; trapping criminals, making the world a better place. This is what I'm good at. And I have no real moral choice. I can't take Josh and run, with the evil I'm sensing, this thing would just get more powerful and hunt me down. No, we have to let it come for me, then trap it and attack. We have to take it down, and take it down fast and hard.

Relief floated out from her nexus and the image of her older self smiled gently. Lara realized that she could elect to run, that the ethos within her *ki* and its greater consciousness allowed her the freedom to pursue a course wholly of her own choosing. But the intuition of coming conflict made her purpose stark in her mind: she would stand and fight.

Strange, Lara reflected, that such a decision could be so clear and obvious, so immediate, but it resonated through her being like a clarion call of truth, inescapable. The being just born was evil incarnate. She would trap it and destroy it. And she would win. She had to.

Northwest Washington, DC | *Sunday 0808 EDT*

"Aha! And there's herself now!" Hamilton O'Donnell broke into his nephew's questioning.

"Mom!" Joshua yelled, leaping over the Edsel door onto the sidewalk before the car had stopped, running to hug her.

She caught his flying form up in her arms and grinned at him.

"Easy big boy, if you knock me over, I could be back in the hospital!" She smiled, hugging him tight and holding him off the ground like a feather.

"You feel different, Mom!" He grinned back at her as she put him down.

"Oh? What do I feel like? Am I missing some parts?"

"You feel like..." his mind sifted through his impressions, synthesizing, "like energy, I think."

Lara laughed. "Well honey, I never finished my ride, so maybe I didn't get all my energy properly dissipated."

"Uh huh. Right," the boy replied, raising an eyebrow and touching her arm to verify the sensation. Mom sidestepped, he thought, and that's not like her. This energy is like nothing I've ever felt; and it's just bubbling off her. And the phone call.

And the look on my uncle's face. Something's going on. For sure. Something big. Impressions and nuances began to coalesce around his thought process, feeding it.

"Hi, Ham. Thanks for the lift," Lara said, patting the man's shoulder as she pulled the seatback forward.

"Lara, there's no loss on you for someone just flown off a bicycle. But are you sure you wouldn't sooner go right home? Your shirt's ripped and bloodied, even if you didn't get skint like last time. Joshua and I can find the bike, I'm sure."

"No, Ham. That's an expensive bike. I think it must be down at the bottom of the gully. This should only take a few minutes. Besides," she said, turning to her son as he slid into the back seat, "I'm energized, right, Josh?" She ruffled his curly black head. He felt his hair tingle from the strange energy in her hand.

Joshua ruffled his mother's soft, short-cut blond hair in reply. Energy there, too, he realized, same as in her hand. It's not like a static charge, it's more like some kind of frequency resonance. Wonder if we could measure it?

His mind ran down the pathways of the possible, through his knowledge of electromagnetic fields, and came up empty. As they pulled away from the curb, he turned his mother's face toward him and stared deep into her emerald eyes, looking for the difference he sensed there. He had the briefest impression of a flaring six-pointed star before she smiled enigmatically at him, and leaning over the seatback, kissed his forehead. A star, he thought, entranced; a mythical symbol, a guide, a bringer of light. His mother *was* different, all right. *Very* different. Something *was* going on. Something big.

"You know, Lara," Ham remarked as they turned off Reservoir onto Canal Road, "sometimes events like this, a scare or a trauma, can change our perspective. *Satori*, the Japanese call it, instant enlightenment. Suddenly you have a different view of reality, a different sense of your place in the universe, of feelin' more plugged in. That reportedly can infuse you with a sense of well-bein' and energy. Lots of endorphins released into the bloodstream, that sort of thing. You may have a letdown later on."

Nice try, Uncle Ham, Josh thought, but my hands know what they're feeling, and it ain't endorphins.

"There's a parking area down on the right, Ham," Lara told him, "just pull in there and we can take the footbridge over the canal. The spot is further down the trail, maybe a hundred yards. The bike might be down in a gully, but it shouldn't take long to find."

Tire tracks and trampled weeds outlined the area for them.

"This is it," she said, walking to the edge and looking down at the rocky shelf.

"Okay, guys, it's got to be down there somewhere, see if you can spot anything shiny in all that undergrowth."

"There it is, Mom," her son pointed as they scanned the area, "it's jammed in that overhang down below."

"Yup, I see it, Josh," she replied, and without hesitation stepped casually into space. She landed on the narrower rock shelf below as easily as if she had stepped off a sidewalk curb.

"Mom!"

She looked up at him. "What?"

"Mom?" His mouth was open wide with surprise.

"What, Josh?"

The boy just shook his head. Behind him, Hamilton O'Donnell looked on with a quizzical expression. Lara pulled the bike out of the crevice and examined it.

"Not too bad. Fork looks okay. Needs a new front rim. Here, Ham, can you get this?" She handed the bike easily up toward him, right hand holding the saddle, the left stretched out to keep her balance on the narrow footing. As he hauled it up, she put her hands on the rock wall, flexed her knees slightly, and sprang effortlessly to the upper shelf alongside them.

"Mom!"

She looked down at him. "What?"

His mouth was opened but he couldn't speak for a moment.

"What, Josh?"

"Uncle Ham, did you see that?"

"Umm. Yes, Joshua, I did. Your mother obviously is quite fit. Tolerated her accident rather well, I would say," he observed dryly, "rather better than the bicycle."

"Fit?" Josh's voice squeaked up an octave, "Fit? Fit, my ass!"

"Joshua! Language!" Lara scolded.

"Mom! I saw it! I saw what you just did!"

"Well of course you saw it, Josh. What's the problem?"

"It's impossible," he squeaked.

"What's impossible?" she puzzled. "I jumped down, got the bike, handed it up, jumped back up."

"The way you did it, Mom! Like it took no effort!"

"Well, maybe all that martial arts training is paying off." She smiled, ruffling his hair. "And you said yourself I feel full of energy."

"Energy? Energy? What I just saw is... freaking magic!"

"Language, Josh, language," Lara reminded him, squeezing his shoulder.

Walking the bike back to the parking lot, Josh argued that the drop was ten feet, Lara countered more like six feet. Hamilton O'Donnell argued both sides, causing trouble. They all started to laugh as she loaded the bike into the back seat of the Edsel, the argument dissolving into the special relationship among the three of them, and they laughed some more as Ham turned the car toward home.

"But Mom," Joshua persisted, "you're *different* this morning! Really! You seem bigger, somehow, like you're some kind of expanded version of yourself. The energy I feel is just a part of it. You're *different*. You just don't drop ten feet and barely flex your knees. I calculated the force. It doesn't happen at six feet either. Something else absorbed the force, or it wasn't there to be absorbed. Either way you're *different*." He turned to his uncle with an earnest look. "Isn't that right, Uncle Ham?"

"Why, Joshua, me bucko! I never take issue with your analyses, you know that," he responded slyly. That was so blatantly untrue it broke them all into renewed laughter.

"Okay, Josh," Lara relented, "okay. I'll tell you what I can about how I feel."

"You're right, I *am* different. When I went off the bike and hit my head, I think some sort of metaphysical connection kicked in and tied me into a greater consciousness. I'm aware now of a different reality, one with more dimensions, of which our reality is just a part. I'm standing in its gateway, exploring it a little, cautiously. That's why I wanted time to walk and reflect.

"And it healed my injuries. Or, maybe more correctly, being part of this greater consciousness allowed me to manage the dimensions of this new reality to heal myself. I understand it very little, but somehow I know that's truly what happened.

"And now... now, well, I'm part of something bigger. I don't know whether this is temporary or not, but there is great energy to it, and a warmth about it, a feeling of connectedness. I've had instants like this in my life, but never anything sustained. I guess I'm not surprised you can feel the energy," she concluded.

"Uncle Ham!" Josh exclaimed excitedly, "Yes! Yes! Remember that book you gave me for my sixth birthday? 'Flatland'? Mom, did you read that, about two-dimensional beings in a planar reality, and one of them finds out about a third dimension?"

"No, Josh, I didn't read it, but you sure told me all about it. I remember being impressed by your wild extrapolations from that story to our own reality."

"But they weren't so wild, were they, Uncle Ham," Josh said, his laser stare trying to pin his uncle's mind onto the dissection mat.

Hamilton O'Donnell turned his face away, focusing on the upcoming left turn, the edge of a smile not quite hidden.

But Josh had already turned to his mother, the questions spilling from his mind almost faster than his mouth could say them.

"How many dimensions do you sense, Mom?

"Is time a dimension?

"Is energy a dimension?

"What kinds of energy are there?

"Are they each a separate dimension?

"How are the dimensions separated?

"Do we exist in all of them, or just some?

"Is that greater consciousness a dimension itself, or something different?

"Is it like a field, I mean like an electromagnetic field?

"What kind of energy is it?

"How come I can feel it coming off of you?

His mind outran his speech and he fell silent as they pulled up at the house. Lara hugged him tight, smiling over his curly head at his uncle.

"Tell you what, sport," she said, getting out of the car and lifting her bicycle from the rear seat, "you go collaborate with your uncle on one of those famous omelettos. And put about six eggs in mine, please, I'm starved. I'm going to have a shower and think about your questions. We'll talk over breakfast, okay?"

Jungle of Purace District, Colombia | Sunday 0839 EDT

In the cave in Colombia, instruction by his nexus in expanded reality continued for John Connard.

One more thing, and we will be on our way. Movement through space: you must be able to control your locus in your spacetime framework, to move more freely about, not constrained by what you call Newtonian physics.

He pondered that. "Inertia? Gravity? F equals ma? You mean levitate? Fly?"

I know not what form will suit you. Sit, and contemplate with me what may be.

John sat again in the lotus position, and engaged the greater reality. Its energy coursed through him, along with its welcoming joy, and he collapsed into it. The cave brightened with his pale blue aura.

Good, now lift from your sitting position without moving.

He did, and felt the pressure of the cave floor depart his legs. His nexus Duc Li contemplated the effort, gauging it.

This is not your natural mode. It is too linear for you, I see. Too fine a control is required. You could learn to be a flyer, but for you it is not efficient. Look at the end of the cave. Focus on it.

John let himself settle back onto the floor, surprised; he thought it had felt natural enough.

Feel the energy of this greater reality around you. It has many dimensions you can manage. You can use them to step in and out of your space, holding your time dimension constant. It is the equivalent of a mathematical transposition, or rather two transpositions. The first takes the holographic matrix of your being into another place, and the second takes your matrix out of it. The components of your reality matrix are transposed, so to speak, into other-dimensional coordinates, and then switched back again. You can be where you choose to be. All that is required is that you choose to be there. Look at the end of the cave. Focus on it.

He sensed energy building, anticipatory.

Now, John Connard, the end of the cave. Just be there.

He collapsed himself into the field, and suddenly, effortlessly, he *was* there: still in the lotus position, his face not a foot from the rear wall of the cave. There had been no sense of time passing, no feeling of muscle movement, only a mild disorientation that had quickly faded. How did he do it? He catalogued the actions in his mind, locking them to the field of his new reality. He stood and turned, looking back at the undisturbed imprint of his buttocks and legs in the sand near the cave entrance.

Ah, yes, my friend, this is the nature of your gift. Your mind has much more talent for this than levitating or flying. Do it again. Look at the front of the cave. Focus on it. Now, be there.

He did, and he was. This time he heard behind him the inrush of air into the place his body had left, and felt the brief pressure on his face as he displaced the air at his arrival point.

"Do I need to look at where I'm going to get there? Can I just visualize a transposition point?"

Your mind does not yet have sufficient visualization power required to transpose without sight of your objective.

"Could I make a mistake and end up planted inside a tree?"

No, two bodies cannot coexist in the same spacetime in this reality. If the object at your arrival locus cannot be easily displaced, you will be reflected back to your origin locus, but since no time passed it will be as if nothing happened. A failed transposition, that is all.

Questions ran through his mind, but he dismissed them until later. For now, he felt the time pressure of the uncertain future on him. He was a skilled soldier and assassin; difficult to imagine his adversary would be equally qualified for battle. But that could change. The more time that passed, the more likely it was to change. He recalled a proven maxim of war: the side that arrives 'the firstest with the mostest' wins. He felt the growing urge within himself and his greater consciousness to move on, to engage the enemy now, while he and his new nexus surely held a decisive advantage.

Yes, it is time to go. The other battle skills you may need we can develop en route.

John trembled with the realization of strange forces converging into this time and place. In his mind's eye he saw many possible pathways to disaster. But he was a soldier.

"Best get on with it then," he murmured to himself and the guest in his mind.

Chapter 9

On his next break from the SDI exercise, Aaron scrolled back through the Global Consciousness Project website data. The graphs were interactive Java portrayals that wouldn't print, but he found the tabular data and printed out the statistics for the 15-minute period encompassing the event. Then he printed out the periods before and after that. He studied the pages on his lap as he wheeled back to the exercise. Seeing that it hadn't picked up and judging he had a few minutes yet, he continued down the hall to the Backup X-Room, where as expected he found his boss Ed Edwards.

"Aaron," the controller said, glancing at his watch "you on break? Well, I'm glad you're here. The duty officer from NEAT called, pretty much confirmed the rogue asteroid hypothesis. The event was low to their horizon, but they caught enough to confirm it. I've advised the Pentagon."

"They're wrong, Ed."

The flat authoritative tone of Aaron's statement caught Edwards by surprise. He smiled. "Okay, Aaron, I know how stubborn you can be, and you actually had me coming around to your point of view, but I think it's time you gave this one up. NEAT had a totally different shot of it, sideways and down low; we saw it nearly head-on, and you know how that distorts things. Too bad, I was just getting more enamored with the possibility of our first real ET."

"And what did they say about those controlled spiral motions, Ed?"

"Energy pulses. The thing showed up with enormous kinetic energy, a total rogue from outside the solar system. It must have been spinning like a top. Iron core, probably highly magnetized. The collision and subsequent breakup transferred some of this to energy pulses, some of it in the visible spectrum. NEAT says it was very pretty. We just saw the pulses as spiral motions from our perspective."

Aaron considered this. "Not bad, Ed. Takes care of some of the facts. But they're wrong." The flat tone was back.

"Man, I gotta go home, get some sleep!" The controller yawned, stretched, and patted Aaron on the shoulder.

Aaron stopped him as he stood up. "Ed, I know you're tired. But here, before you make up your mind on the wrong side of this issue, just look at this."

He spread the printouts from the Global Consciousness Project website over the table, explaining: the quantitative, measurable, statistically significant effects caused by applied consciousness, the clear step-change from random to non-random during the event, the incalculable odds against it occurring by chance. But halfway through, he could tell he wasn't delivering sufficient proof for Edwin Edwards, Ph.D., consummate engineer, scientist and skeptic.

"I've actually looked at that website, Aaron; I'm as curious as anybody else. I believe the data are credible. The statistics are solid. The interpretation is reasonable. Human consciousness can have an effect on the randomness of computerized coin-flips; I'm willing to concede that as a working hypothesis. But you're leaping way too far when you extrapolate. Extra-terrestrial consciousnesses affecting random event generators? How do we know they would even operate on the same wavelength or field or whatever carries the effect? So the effect coincides exactly with the timing of our event this morning, so what? How about a purely physical explanation? The event generators are inside computers—maybe they were affected by the magnetic effects this event created? Or maybe, since a lot of people evidently saw it, maybe some sort of profound spiritual experience in global human consciousness caused the effect? There are a lot of hypotheses that seem to me like they would fit better. Ockham's Razor, Aaron."

"Ed, I think you're wrong. If you step outside of your preconceptions, you can see that my explanation fits more of the facts and requires fewer assumptions. I'm gonna talk to the people at Princeton, see what they think, okay?"

"Aaron, *please* don't let this consume any more of your attention today. Just play out this exercise segment. Be a good government worker bee. At six PM this evening you're a private citizen with three days off to do whatever you want. Fool with it then.

"But do not, repeat do not, send anybody this event record. The Pentagon hasn't classified it yet, and probably won't, given what the public and media interest will be, but we could look bad if we preempt anything the DOD feels is their turf. If you see it showing up on TV, at that point it's public information and you can send it out.

"Prior to that, I guess you can talk to Princeton about it, though, if they want to try to figure out what the magnetic effects might have done to their equipment. Be interesting to hear their views. Good luck in raising anybody on a Memorial Day weekend; probably be Tuesday before you find a live person to talk to up there."

"Okay, Ed, I got it. Yassuh, boss," Aaron said contritely.

Though contrite, Aaron O'Meara stole an extra few minutes from the exercise, wheeling down the hall to his office, composing the questions as he went. He sent a quick email to the GCP website.

Northwest Washington, DC | Sunday 0857 EDT

Lara showered, the water and steamy mist luxuriant to her heightened senses. She felt the sensations pass over into her greater consciousness. They resonated there, becoming magnified and integrated within that realm. Integration, she sensed, that's what's going on here. The longer I'm in this new reality, the more I become it.

Her nexus agreed. *You will become the next step, and your son after you, and many others after that. It is natural. It is in your genetic code. It is the evolutionary plan.*

And what do I tell Josh, she thought, hanging the question in the space between them.

He is too bright; you cannot deceive him for long. So tell him what you will. He will discern much anyway. Just do not tell him anything that would bring him to aid you in our struggle. He cannot help, and it would be dangerous. He is not ready.

Lara probed for the dark presence in her mind as she stepped out of the shower. It still lingered there, distant and vague. Not very active yet, she judged, realizing that when it stirred more she would sense it. She dressed and went downstairs, inhaling the cooking smells as she walked into the kitchen.

"Oh, my, that smells good," she said, ruffling Joshua's hair. "I'm starved!"

As the three of them ate breakfast, she dealt with her son's questions as well as she could.

"Josh, I don't know how many dimensions there are, I just sense there are several more than our usual three. Or four, if you count time. I don't think consciousness is a dimension, at least in any way I can conceive it. I somehow see dimensions as the hardware and consciousness as the software; that's the closest I can get with an analogy that makes any sense to me."

"Can I go there, Mom? Can you take me?"

Typical nine-year old, she thought, always up for an adventure.

"I don't think so, Josh. Not yet, anyway. Something has to switch over in your mind, first."

She watched him test that, mentally setting up switches, turning them on and off, making up combinations of switches as he continued the inquiry.

"So when, Mom? When will it happen in my mind? Will it ever happen?"

"I don't know, dear. I think probably it will, but I don't know."

"What does it feel like, this consciousness, is it a field, like a magnetic field?"

"Umm, yep, sort of, but I'd say it's more like being in a fluid, with a feeling of contact, connectedness. Remember that time we went snorkeling down in the Caymans? The clear water, the warm sun on your back, how those beautiful fish swam all around you, and it all seemed so natural and you seemed such a part of it? That's sort of what it feels like."

"Can you move around in this consciousness fluid, Mom? How do you know you won't get lost? Do you have a guide?"

"You know, Josh, I don't think I have the words to explain it. You can certainly move around, although motion isn't really a concept that fits well. You can't get lost, there's nothing to lose, because you're part of it—actually, you're it and it's you. I have a presence in the consciousness, a bigger me, a more-dimensional me, but she's not a guide, she's just me. She is more aware of the larger reality and the other dimensions. She's part of them, but she isn't separate from me. She knows a lot more than I know. It might be more accurate to say that I'm just a more limited manifestation of her in our four dimensions."

"Is she the energy I feel when I touch you, Mom?"

"I don't know, honey," Lara said reflectively, "she's intellectual energy... no, spiritual energy would be a better term, if there is one. It's possible, I guess, but I suspect the energy you're feeling is some sort of manifestation of one of the dimensions of energy in that reality. Maybe I'm leaking?"

They all chortled at the thought of her leaking energy.

"But maybe that's true, Mom," Joshua reflected. "You just ate three times what you normally do, so maybe you are leaking energy."

Yeah, Lara thought, I did. And I'm still pretty hungry. Then aloud: "Come on, you two, let's clean up this mess. I need to take a cup of tea and go meditate on my new condition. I really do need some time and solitude to digest it all."

Lara kissed her son's head, smiled at his uncle Hamilton, and took her tea upstairs to the bedroom. The faintest hint of flickering energy enveloped her in the dimmer light of the stairwell, not so much visible as sensed.

Global Consciousness Project, Princeton University, NJ | Sunday 0910 EDT

At the GCP Data Center, Adrienne struggled over the dichotomy of erotic stimulation and emotional disappointment. Jeffrey Ruiz, clearly, was history, but thoughts of him and other unsuccessful relationships buzzed through her mind irritatingly, like mosquitoes in a swamp.

"Bummer," she finally exclaimed, "I really need to forget Jeff, or I'll never write this damn algorithm!"

Getting the code to come together, she thought, felt like trying to connect her two thumbs with eyes shut. Close, but just missing. I'd better walk around, get a drink of water, do something else for a bit and get my mind off Jeffrey, she told herself. Looking for diversions, Adrienne opened GCP email.

Who's Aaron O'Meara, Ph.D., and what's *gsfc.gov*, she wondered, and then laughed out loud as she read the questions.

"What a nut case! We get some wackos sending in stuff, but this! Oh, this is a classic! Wonder what the government's smoking down there! Wait'll the boss sees this one," she laughed more while printing it off. She dropped it on the desk in the Director's office, scrawling a humorous note.

Still chuckling, she went back to coding with a clearer head. The algorithm eased gracefully out of her mind and ran down through her fingers onto the keyboard and into her computer, almost autonomously.

"Okay," Adrienne patted her computer, "that's more like it! Now let's see what this solution does with live data."

Her new algorithm's graphing output plotted the past three days of data on the screen. The display looked like a grassy field in a light breeze: gentle undulations in the surface, but overall reasonably flat, like it should be. But then... outliers popped up, caught by her programmed significance criterion, standing well above the green field, turning to yellow. There. There. There... six, maybe seven.

"Hot diggity dog!" she yelped, "by God there is some bias in those puppies, who would have thought? And it's gotta be real, three days is plenty long enough for a baseline!"

Adrienne switched over to a data table view, studying strings of statistics to determine why those outliers had triggered. Something nagged at the back of her mind as she scanned the data: the variability in the mean is way too high, what the hell is going on here?

Keying into the algorithm's individual 15-minute data segments, she watched as the monitor scrolled forward through them.

"Jeesh, what the hell is this?" The data period from 0545 to 0600 stood out starkly from those before and those after. All the generators, over a hundred of them, simultaneously in that period, showed a consistent, almost uniform, non-random characteristic. It was as if they froze on either zero or one, a head or a tail, and stayed there, for a portion of that 15-minute period. Too preposterous, she thought; something happened in the mainframe, a virus, maybe, and it replaced the data. Or maybe somebody hacked the system. This cannot be real. *Nothing* has that kind of effect on random event generators spread all over the world, nothing. *Nothing!*

But then... "Omigod," she squeaked, running to the Director's desk and grabbing the email she had so laughingly dismissed.

"Wow! Wow-wee! I take it back, maybe the government's not smoking strange stuff!" She picked up the phone to call her boss, the Project director, but put it down. She reread the email. She picked up the phone again, then put it down, her entire body quivering with excitement and indecision.

"Maybe I should find out exactly what the hell is going on before I bother the boss," she talked her flying emotions down a notch, "so calm down, girl, get ahold of yourself. It's just another problem. Study it. Analyze it. What's the first step?"

Adrienne checked the raw data stream coming into the mainframe. The anomaly was there, no question. So the mainframe didn't do it, and the website didn't do it, and it wasn't hacked, and it wasn't a virus. Hardware? No, the hundred plus sites came in on different communications protocols, across different servers, over different modem lines, at least three, sometimes as many as six.

"Okay, I'm out of possible hardware explanations," she conceded, sitting down at the keyboard. As she typed an email response to one Aaron O'Meara at the Goddard Space Flight Center, Adrienne silently repented her recent smart-ass remarks, hoping the man would be able to enlighten her with the reasons behind his suddenly all-too-relevant questions.

Jungle of Purace District, Colombia | Sunday 0911 EDT

"Best get on with it," John repeated, "but first let's leave Corrano's boys a little memento."

The Assassin dug the laser tripwire unit out of his weapons harness, along with the remaining plastic explosive, and rigged it with a detonator in the rock rubble on the cave wall. Setting the reflector on the opposite wall, in a crevice where they wouldn't see it until too late, he verified on the tiny unit that it would detonate on the fifth break of the invisible laser beam. Satisfied, he ripped a piece of loose fabric from his bloody shirt and tossed the shirt on the floor in the back of the cave, where it would be barely visible from the entrance. Picking up his machine pistol and weapons harness, he moved cautiously to the cave opening and looked out.

Use your consciousness, John Connard, not just your eyes.

He smiled at the remonstrative tone. His father had used it. Duc Li had used it.

"Of course," he acknowledged, and half shut his eyes to call into his new mind-space a perception of the consciousness field around him. He vaguely sensed the minds of his hunters, deployed below him in the valley. A common goal, he intuited; that's what connects them together out of this diffuse pattern.

Indeed. The hunt. You are their goal.

"Well, we have to put this in a more usable context," John objected, "I can't work with it. How about a radar screen as a metaphor?"

A sense of shifting, a changing of the point of view, and a radar screen painted itself into his mind-space. He studied the pattern, and decided that the top of the screen would always be the direction in which he faced. The image obliged, dim dots of consciousness rotating around as he looked in different directions. Okay, he thought, this should work. The consciousnesses seem to be stronger closer in and weaker further out, but this may be my perception rather than their signal strength.

That is basically correct.

The image trimmed itself a little as John looked horizontally eastward across the gorge, and then southeastward downriver. The screen gimbaled in his mind-space to match the vision. Repeating it several times made the dizziness clear. The perception began to seem natural, an integration of the visual world with the new consciousness radar in his mind.

"Okay, I've got them. They're all on the valley floor, under the canopy on the other side of the river. I don't sense any others up above on the top of the cliff. Should be okay. Let's get out of here, shall we? See if I can avoid getting shot this time."

Please. We have no time to waste on wounds.

A medical miracle was only wasted time? The dry humor made him smile.

The Assassin tucked the piece of torn shirt into a crevice in the face of the cliff, where it would be visible from below and lure searchers into the cave. Looking upward, he saw just sheer rock wall, with few handholds. Without pitons, he couldn't climb it, but now there were other ways, weren't there? Grimacing at the thought of such an acid test, he prepared his mind to engage his new transposition skill. A tree limb overhung the gorge, fifty feet above and a hundred feet north. He focused on it. Magic, he thought; you're the Magician.

Just be there, John Connard, just be there.

The Magician collapsed into his *ki*, willed the transposition, and instantly materialized on the limb, windmilling his arms to stay balanced. Instinctively looking inward toward the trunk of the tree, he instantly stood there beside it, on solid ground. His exhalation of relief was cut short: a tree snake dropped from the limb above, its jaws gaping, fangs striking at him. Without conscious thought and with blinding speed, John sidestepped the striking head and struck with his open hand. Blue energy flamed out. The snake's fangs closed on the tree trunk and suspended the head there, but the headless body hung thrashing in the foliage, pumping blood in all directions.

Stepping behind the trunk to avoid being bathed in blood, the Magician silently apologized to the snake for his unthinking reaction.

Yes, you have coupled the energy field to your ki *very tightly, and you will use it instinctively. Training and practice will improve your discernment of conditions where its use is inappropriate.*

So I'm pretty dangerous right now, he thought, his concern floating in the mind-space between them.

Yes. But you have been dangerous since you became a soldier. Access to other dimensions merely provides you with more powerful weapons. A better sword. A better shield.

Then I need to practice, before we return to civilization. The thought evolved from a request into a demand. Better weapons demand more care. I cannot endanger innocents. I must have tighter control.

Of course.

We will practice on our enemy of the moment, John thought, before I go to the backup extraction zone. The troops are out searching. The compound will be lightly guarded. I can close out some loose ends. The Assassin stirred within him at the idea.

John Connard held the radar screen metaphor in his mind as he ran down the game trails, locking it in tightly to operate in the background, almost like his autonomic nervous system. He transposed across open spaces, where he had a good line of sight, in instantaneous leaps. Points and clusters of consciousnesses flickered on the mental screen and updated their positions as he moved. It quickly began to feel very natural. The Magician smiled at how fast his new talents were developing. The Assassin exulted in the power they represented.

Chapter 10

Lara sat crosslegged on the throw rug in front of the open balcony doors of her bedroom, the soft light from the woods outside diffusing around her. She closed her eyes, cradled her tea mug, and sought balance for her mind.

"All right," she said to herself and her nexus, speaking aloud to better sequence her thoughts, "let's work it out:

"Where is this monster?

"When is it coming?

"What sort of trap do I set?

"Will I need help?

"How do I track its approach?

"Can it conceal itself from me?

"Who is it?

"Male or female?

"What does he or she look like?

"Can it sense me like I sense it?"

Her nexus waved a partial structure of responses into being.

Observe.

Colorful symbology appeared in her mind-space. It seemed to integrate her questions, and then an image spread out, taking a form familiar to her experience: concentric rings, radial lines. A radar screen metaphor, she realized, and I'm at the center. Now, that's a lot better, she thought, an analogy I can relate to. In response to her unspoken query, the screen expanded outward, slowing and stopping after it picked up the small malevolent blue-glowing blip on its far periphery.

"Almost due south, 2,500 miles. Where would that be, the Caribbean? No, further south. Okay, I can look it up in the atlas. So how does it move? Is it going to suddenly appear in my closet? Or does it have to take planes and boats and trains and cars like the rest of us?"

Teleportation over great distances is likely a number of generations away. It requires acquisition and practice of a number of different predecessor skills. I believe our enemy will need some time to reach us. If it is confident in its abilities, it will try to reach us quickly, before we can fully develop your abilities; if not, it will wait and train, and gather its strength. Locally, possibly, it may teleport. Or it may fly, as you do.

"Fly? You mean without an airplane or other device?"

You have already flown, you have this ability.

"So Josh was right?"

Indeed. He is an astute observer.

At a more fundamental level of knowing, below that of conscious thought, she wasn't surprised.

"Hmm. Guess I knew that."

Her nexus smiled at her. *Guess you did.*

"I'll have to practice flying, I guess?"

Yes, you know that too. It should not take long; your latent ability is very high. And it is a survival skill, you must develop it.

Wow, she thought, I'm looking forward to this. I used to dream about flying with those hawks over the farm all the time.

The trap, her nexus continued, shifting the structure of responses to a new image. It showed her as bait at the center, but the nature of the trap was just a fuzzy outline.

The trap may not need to be particularly elegant. This kind of evil can abide no other competing power. Its means are direct, brutal, overpowering. This is a cunning Beast, but it will enter the trap, even knowing it is there, if it perceives its abilities and power will allow it to prevail.

"So, I'll call TC, get him and the Bureau to help," she muttered out loud, but then stopped abruptly at the obvious problem. FBI Special Agent TC Demuzzio, her long-time friend and colleague, could supply many resources, but... he also was the government.

"Oh! I can't tell him the whole story, can I? If I do, he can't possibly accept it, it's just too far out. And if I demonstrate, somehow prove that it's true... then he'll know about this evolutionary leap. And if he knows, then the government will know. I don't believe I want that. It may be dangerous. This new species of human would be better born quietly. Our government may be more restrained than most others in the world, but this change is going to upset a lot of applecarts. What's your perspective? Can you see the future?"

Forces from many dimensions converge in this present time. I sense many futures possible from this convergence. I do not know which one will prevail, but caution is surely advisable. The first children born to this new species may well be seen as fulcrums, like the bastard sons of kings in past times. Power may seek them for its own

purposes, good or evil. Anonymity is their best protection, until they come of age. The prudent course is circumspect. You will need a plausible story for TC Demuzzio.
That shouldn't be too difficult, she thought. TC may be a cynic and a skeptic, but he trusts my instincts. If I tell him I think there's going to be a third attempt on my life, he'll listen. She tucked that thought into the back of her mind, and considered the outline of her trap.

"I will see this Beast move, on my consciousness radar screen?"

Yes.

"Does it see me on its screen, or whatever similar tool it has?"

Yes, but I believe your sensing ability may be more acute at a distance.

Lara flexed the strange muscles of her new sensing ability, feeling them ripple outward through her new perceptions. She looked at her consciousness radar, and delicately reached out her mind to probe the darkness on its southern periphery, just outside the 2,500 mile ring. The spot sharpened in her view and became a black blotchy mass, an uneven changing outline with a forbidding blue glow around it, an ugly amoeba, primeval. As she tried to move her perception yet closer, the image fuzzed, losing all resolution. But the inimical sense of evil remained, pulsating darkly.

Fear rose, with gorge in her throat. She paused to recite a calming mantra, willing herself back into control, and then laid a tiny mental touch on the Beast. There! It was moving! Westward, but with a slight vector north. An insidious tickling rose into the base of her brain, giving a sense of something familiar, something she should recognize, and all the more horrifying for it. It knows me. It knows I'm here, she realized.

"I can tell by the prickle of my thumbs, something wicked this way comes," Lara quoted shakily, probing around the monster, taking its measure.

Jungle of Purace District, Colombia | Sunday 0942 EDT

Alternating running with transposing where he had sight lines, the Magician angled toward the ridge overlooking the north boundary of the compound. Standing on a tree limb on the ridge, he paused to study the activity. A jeep with three soldiers roared through the gate and drove eastward across the outer fields. Good, he thought, checking his radar screen; the place is pretty well emptied out. He held the picture of the compound in his mind while he mapped out the best transpositions and planned his attack.

Warehouse first, he thought, that's where the drug inventory will be. I'll take that out as a diversion. He transposed to a doorway inset into a corner of that building, and looked through the glass down an empty hall. The door had a key-card reader beside it. Standard equipment, he noted, not difficult to beat. But he hadn't the time or equipment.

Matter in this dimension is not relevant to transposition.

His nexus provided the answer before he even framed the question. That's cool, he thought, and transposed himself into the hall inside the building, verifying that material walls were no barrier so long as he could see his objective. He looked around warily. Surveillance cameras? If so they were well hidden. Keeping a null field lightly wrapped around him, he ran down the hallway to the door he thought would lead to the drug processing and packaging bays. He glanced through the door glass and saw two guards, no one else visible.

The Magician transposed himself behind the guards, and the puff of displaced air made them turn. He struck the nearer one with a twisting inward punch to the kidney, his left hand intentionally suppressing the energy field. The other guard barely opened his mouth to cry out when the Assassin's back-handed plane of curling blue energy decapitated him. His head wobbled eerily on his neck for a moment before the pumping blood dislodged it and it fell to the floor ahead of the collapsing body. The head rolled across the floor, bouncing off the other guard, who lay on the floor retching dry heaves from the pain of the kidney punch. His wide eyes looked up, terrified, bouncing frantically between the severed head and the blue-flamed apparition above him.

"*Ira de Dios! La mano de Dios!*" the guard retched. His feet frantically pushed on the floor, scrabbling away.

Ah, good, another success! The '*Hand of God*' mythos, the Magician thought. Alex's psych-war program has been very effective, I'll have to let him know.

He stalked the scrabbling guard slowly, letting the terror build. Eyes frozen on the apparition, the guard pushed back into the piled pallets of bagged cocaine and could go no further. Extending a gravity field from his left hand, the Magician dragged the guard erect and snapped him up against the stacked bags, knocking his hat off in the process.

Jesus, he thought, a kid. These assholes are truly disgusting, using children like this.

"How many soldiers?" he asked the boy, using the local dialect.

"Thirty," the boy babbled.

"How many guard chiefs?"

"Five."

"Cameras, are there cameras in this warehouse?"

"No cameras."

"The electrical generator, where is that?"

The boy tried to gesture, but couldn't move his hand against the gravity force. The Magician lightened and refocused the field, allowing some arm movement and letting more air into the lungs. The boy pointed back over his shoulder, and off to the right.

"In this warehouse?"

"Yes."

"Where are the weapons?"

The boy pointed back over his shoulder, and off to the left.

"In the warehouse?"

"Yes."

The Magician collapsed the energy plane pulsating in his right hand down to a minute bubble, and used it to sever the chain holding a small gold cross around the boy's neck. He caught it in ghostly fingers and held it up in front of his helpless prey's wide eyes.

"You have sinned," the Magician told him, "it is a sin to deal in *la cocaina*."

"I have sinned," the boy agreed, retching.

"The hand of God will strike all those who sin with *la cocaina*," the Magician intoned.

"You are the Hand of God?" Terror crescendoed in the boy's eyes.

"I am the angel of death, the Hand of God," the Magician agreed, making the null field grow blue-rimmed wings out of his shoulders. He took the boy's hand, putting the gold cross in it, and closed the small fist tight around it.

The boy trembled uncontrollably and soiled his pants as he looked on imminent death.

"Child," said the Magician, "you will sin no more. Tell me you will sin no more."

"Sss... sin no more," the boy stuttered paralyzed agreement and acceptance, closing his eyes, tightening his fist on his cross.

Quickly, and not without sympathy, John Connard waved chaos down through the boy's head, withdrawing the gravity field and letting him collapse on the floor.

"How about that," he asked aloud, probing the consciousness level of the inert body, "did I get the null field about right?"

Physiologically, he will sleep for about an hour, the intensity of your field was appropriate. You wish him to awake with a clear memory of his terror, recognizing that he must redeem himself, so that he will return to farming or other more wholesome enterprise. The configuration of your null field was appropriate to that. And so he will awake, and realize he remains alive. He will relate his story. By this, your Hand of God mythos will be further leavened, serving your objectives. But, John Connard, once he does this, he is in danger... the drug lords will interrogate him, probably by torture, then likely kill him to keep the myth from spreading further.

The thought from his nexus carried an ineffable sadness about those aspects of human nature that would so degrade children.

It might be kinder to kill him now.

He's a child, an innocent. I cannot do it.

He is a soldier. He would kill you. Innocence is relative.

I cannot do it.

Conflicted emotions passed across the mind-space between them.

Ah, yes, John Connard, I understand. A delicate moral balance, is it not? The acknowledgment from his nexus carried sympathy and sorrow and humor and joy all at the same time.

The Magician pondered that balance as he ran through the warehouse looking for the generator room. The hum led him to the right door. The big generator ran smoothly, coasting along on a fraction of its power.

He wiped his finger over the oil filter housing and smelled it, confirming diesel fuel and not gasoline, which was more volatile. He pulled the fire hose from its wall reel out into the warehouse, into the middle of the palletized drug bales, and sliced off its nozzle. He walked back along the hose, squeezing it into a round cross-section. As he did this, the Magician looked upward and studied the high ceiling. Roof vent fans, but no fire suppression system. Good!

Back in the generator room, he slashed a tight plane of energy through the fire hose, and then through the soft copper of the diesel fuel return line. He quickly worked the hose up onto the cut fuel line. The capacity of the pump would assure that the excess fuel not being used by the engine would now run out into the warehouse instead of back into the supply tank. Pulling the hose up as far as he could on the copper line, he wiped his hands and watched to be sure the engine vibration wouldn't work it off. The hose stayed in place, and he could see diesel fuel beginning to pool under the pallets in the warehouse.

"Perfect!" And now, me lad," he mimicked Alex's Irish brogue, "on to the next wee bit of mischief!"

He ran to the door the boy guard had indicated as the weapons room, and blew off its lock with a burst of energy. Sudden activity on his consciousness radar told him that opening the door had raised a warning. He had, he judged, maybe two minutes before guards would converge on the warehouse. The sudden demands from the communicator on the belt of the headless senior guard echoed in the warehouse. Adrenalin kicked the Magician to a higher level, and time seemed to slow down.

He scanned the weapons room quickly, his eyes flickering over the assorted boxes. Ah, hand grenades, RPGs, incendiaries, just what the doctor ordered, he thought. He stuffed grenades in his pants pockets, piled boxes of incendiaries onto a flatbed cart and wheeled them out into the center of the warehouse, shoving the cart hard so that it ran into the growing puddle of diesel fuel under the stacked drug pallets. He grabbed two loose incendiaries, tossed the inert child guard over his shoulder, and ran out the far door of the warehouse. A jeep was parked in the shade of an outbuilding by the fence perimeter. The keys were in it, and the jeep's hood was warm. The gate in the fence, not fifty meters away, was wide open. No one in this immediate locus, his consciousness radar told him. He dropped the boy into the back seat, tearing off his communicator and clipping it to his own shoulder harness. Crouching behind the vehicle, he studied the warehouse.

Then his mental radar screen brightened, and a pattern appeared, linking its dots of consciousness. They came, as he knew they must, in teams of two, to the doors on the four corners of the warehouse. Four soldiers entered the warehouse, leaving four to cover each door. Their radio chatter on the communicator told him they smelled diesel fuel.

When the last soldier had entered, the Magician looked up at the roof of the warehouse and transposed there, crouching behind the cupola of the roof exhaust fan, directly over the center of the diesel fuel puddle. He wedged open one side of the butterfly cover, and set the incendiaries on the other. Looking down through the fan housing, he saw the entry team discover the headless torso, and heard them call out for Ramon, who must be the boy guard. Their shock as they came upon the cart of explosives in the middle of their cocaine hoard was palpable. He would have felt it, he thought, even absent the exquisitely tuned radar screen in his mind.

"Come on, now," the Assassin murmured, "easy, boys, easy, just check it out, verify no surprises waiting for you, and then move on in and get the cart, come on, just do it."

As if they heard his bidding, the big one barked orders, and two soldiers shouldered their weapons and moved in on the cart, wading through the puddle of diesel fuel. More barked orders, and the third guard moved around the pile toward the hose.

"Okay, that's about right," the Assassin murmured cheerfully. He pulled the tabs on the incendiaries and dropped them along with the boy's communicator down through the fan housing. The big guard caught the motion out of the corner of his eye, and instinctively fired a burst up at the fan. The bullets punched through the light steel roof.

"Nice reaction time," the Magician acknowledged from a safe distance. He had transposed across the compound to the roof of the mansion instantly as he dropped the incendiaries. The explosion bulged the roof of the warehouse and the fan housing blew off. Black smoke jetted up through the hole. On his mental radar screen, dots of consciousness winked out.

Global Consciousness Project, Princeton University, NJ | Sunday 0959 EDT

Adrienne Baxter sat in front of the computer monitor, fingers poised on the keyboard, contemplating the third draft of her email response to the fascinating inquiry of one Aaron O'Meara at the Goddard Space Flight Center in Maryland.

I've got to tone this down, she thought, it sounds way too excited. It needs to be more professional, more scientific. This could be huge for the Project. For me, too. The scientific community will go berserk! She fought down the excitement. Methodical, she thought. Be methodical, that's the key. Be succinct, that's another key. Above all, be logical. She moved the cursor, rearranging text sections until she felt pleased.

To: aaron.omeara@gsfc.gov

From: arbaxter@princeton.edu

Subject: GCD Anomaly & Your Inquiry

Dear Dr. O'Meara:

I read your email an hour ago. Thank you for bringing this anomaly to our attention. I am continuing to evaluate and analyze our global consciousness detector (GCD) data. I have a call in to our Director to get his views on the anomaly. He hasn't called back yet, but I believe I can share with you my findings thus far:

(1) Of 117 GCDs (aka eggs or REGs), 110 were operational and reporting during the anomaly.

(2) All 110 exhibited the same behavior. Each GCD froze on a 0 or a 1.

(3) I have methodically eliminated all the possible explanations that have occurred to me so far (mainframe hardware or software problem, virus, hacker, server protocols, modems, our website software).

(4) On this basis I conclude that the raw data appear to be valid, the

system conveyed them properly, and they were evaluated correctly.

(5) Since that anomaly, and up until now, most of the network has returned to its normal state, but there are two localized exceptions. Six detectors in your general area (Washington-Baltimore-Richmond) have shown a pattern inconsistent with anything we've ever seen before. One detector in Bogota, and possibly also those in Panama City and Quito, show a similar pattern.

(6) The pattern is periodic excursions from the random to the non-random, almost cyclical. Although these GCDs don't lock onto o's or 1's, they clearly move from random to non-random and back.

(7) There is some variability in the frequency of these oscillations as well as their amplitude. (Amplitude may be the wrong term, but I use it here as meaning the strength (time-duration) of the departure from random—not having seen this effect before we haven't established any terminology.)

(8) The six GCDs in your area have continued this novel behavior in frequency and amplitude consistently over the five-hour period since the initial event.

(9) The GCD in Bogota, and to a lesser extent the GCDs in Panama City and Quito, show a similar consistency for the first two hours, but then the oscillations get more frequent and more pronounced for the next three hours.

(10) If you could share with us the basis for your inquiry, that might help focus our efforts...

Thank you for bringing this to our attention.

Adrienne Baxter, Analyst, Global Consciousness Project

There, she thought, re-reading it; that sounds suitably stuffy! It's very dispassionate, very scientific. He'll think I'm about a hundred years old. Hope the boss won't mind that I gave myself a title. I wonder what he's like, this Aaron O'Meara. Got a sharp mind, that's for sure. Hope it's not classified and he can tell us what it's all about.

Adrienne added her phone number as an afterthought, and hit *Send*.

Jungle of Purace District, Colombia | Sunday 1001 EDT

No more threat from the warehouse, the Assassin decided; those left alive would be trying to fight the fire. He expanded the reach of his consciousness, zooming the metaphorical radar screen out from its tightly focused locus to as far as his mind could reach. He sat quietly on the mansion roof for a moment, in the protected nook of a small cooling tower, invisible from ground or air. While the warehouse turned into a roaring inferno punctuated by blasts of exploding ordnance, he tracked foot patrol and helicopter movements on his consciousness radar, computing distance, guessing at the command-and-control protocols, assessing the time he had before the field forces would be recalled to the compound and his mission made more difficult.

"Fifteen minutes, twenty at the outside," he muttered, not liking his own analysis. Running to the east edge of the roof, he dropped the short distance to the balcony where Diego Corrano had taken the toxic dart in his side a few hours ago. *El Jefe* lay inside on the bed, attended by a physician. His security chief, Avi Glickman, slouched in a loveseat, the left side of his face still obscenely drooped from the paralytic dart.

"Hello, Avi," said the Assassin, transposing himself beside the loveseat. The three occupants of the room snapped around in shock at the voice and appearance of an indecipherable wraith in their midst. Glickman's attention was short-lived; he had barely reached for his machine pistol when the Assassin's backhanded slash removed his head. He caught the head by the ear and tossed it onto Corrano's bed, where it rolled forward in an obscene bloody path to stare at *El Jefe*, its teeth chattering in a death reflex. The physician's hand dove toward his black bag as the Assassin strode forward, but a punching motion separated the physician from the pistol. The flash of blue energy knocked the man over the bed and out onto the balcony, his chest crushed.

"Sorry I can't stop and chat, Diego," the Magician said brusquely in the colloquial dialect as he leaned over the terrified drug lord. "But don't worry, you'll be hearing from us shortly. The toxin is working inside you, and you actually will be pleased to hear from us."

Let him agonize over that, he thought, as he waved a chaos field down over *El Jefe*, dropping him into unconsciousness. He picked up Glickman's machine pistol and stood in the center of the room, rotating a slow complete turn. Six minds remaining in the mansion, his consciousness radar told him. Three, down 15 feet from me. That puts them on the ground floor: three guards, one at each entrance. Okay. The other three are down 25 feet, so there must be a basement. And they're clustered, so it's probably one room. Ah, a center of some sort, a command bunker, maybe, or communications, or computers. That's what I want!

A rear stairwell off the bedroom led down four flights to an unlocked door. Three heads looked up from their computer monitors in consternation as the door burst open and a vision of optical madness wreathed in blue flames landed among them. Three heads snapped back as punches broke bone and cartilage.

With quick slashes of an energy plane, the Magician excised the hard drive from the computer labeled 'Server'. He tucked it in his pants pocket, removing grenades to make room. Then he pulled all the other computers into a pile on the floor and dragged the unconscious technicians out of the room.

He pulled the pins on three grenades, tossed them back into the computer room toward the piled computers, and took the stairs four at a time up to the ground floor. The sound was muffled, but the concussions shook the building. He ran down the hall toward the rear entrance. As he turned the corner, he tossed his last grenade around the corner of the hall behind him, and fired a burst from his machine pistol ahead down the hall, full into the chest of the surprised guard.

He paused briefly in the doorway, oriented himself on the jeep where he'd left the boy, and transposed to it. He drove the jeep through the open gate and westward down the jungle trail. The canopy closed over the trail within a few hundred meters, keeping them shielded from the helicopters rapidly approaching over the treetops to the east.

The Magician whistled cheerfully as he bumped westward toward his backup EZ, his secondary extraction zone, reflecting on what he had learned in his self-imposed practice session. Quite satisfactory, he decided. More control was needed, but control over his new skills was developing very quickly. His nexus agreed, the image of Duc Li smiling enigmatically.

Yes, John Connard, the Magician always was a good student.

No blips on my screen in the west direction, he noted; they all went east looking for me, and now they're all converging back to the compound. This trail, he recalled from studying the satellite photos, would intersect what passed for a major highway in Colombia in about seven kilometers. The backup EZ was a high rock outcrop a kilometer north of that point.

The Magician computed the probable time it would take to work his way there. Ah, better call for my ride now, he realized. He stopped the jeep and pulled the small transponder out of his weapon harness, entering the authentication code, hitting the *Send* button. A microburst transmission shot up to the recon drone circling above him at 84,000 feet.

I'll leave the boy with the jeep at the intersection, John decided. If the kid takes my message to heart, he can drive the jeep westward into the mountains, away from his past. Just possibly the boy may follow my instruction, since he saw the hand of God. Maybe he'll find redemption in a better life. He has a chance. That's all I can give him.

Northwest Washington, DC | Sunday 1002 EDT

Downstairs, Hamilton O'Donnell sat motionless, pretending to read the Sunday New York Times, but actually studying his nephew. Joshua worked industriously on a diagram sketched out on a large piece of paper on the dining room table. Such diagrams, Ham knew, were reserved for special situations, where the boy needed to better visualize the patterns unfolding in his prodigious intellect.

And this situation would definitely be one of those, wouldn't it, laddie, he thought.

The old man smiled as he recalled their conversation at the bike trail. The boy's spatial perception was spot-on, the distance down to the ledge to which his mother had so casually dropped was almost exactly ten feet. And Lara's knees had barely flexed on landing; that was accurate, too, as were the boy's lightning calculations of the forces involved.

Remembering their conversation on the ride back to the house made Ham smile even more. The boy had such a wide-eyed innocence about his questioning. The contrast was entrancing: a mind of incredible power, but like any child's, curious, edgy and fun-loving.

Flatland, for God's sake, Ham thought. How neatly the boy skewered me with that classic little story about perception of unseen dimensions, all the while watching my face. A laser straight to the heart of the matter, and I never saw it coming. With the slightest edge of sarcasm, too, his cunning little subtext playing underneath that innocent earnest look. Ha! The boy is telling me he's onto something, and won't let go.

Well, he reminded himself as he lifted up the newspaper to conceal his smile, don't lose sight for a moment that he's probably smarter than you. He is, after all, the result of countless generations of selective breeding.

Flatland! God, I love that child.

Chapter 11

Aaron O'Meara, back in the Goddard X-Room, dutifully played his role in the SDI exercise, his analysis of the astonishing event five hours ago temporarily at a standstill. He had checked his email on the last break, but found nothing from Princeton or the Global Consciousness Project. Probably nobody home there, he thought morosely. Well, what the hell; it's Sunday morning on a holiday weekend and exams are over. What do I expect?

As the morning exercise segment tapered down, the day-shift Exercise Controller called a halt to their activities for a brunch break. Aaron cleared his monitor screen for the next set-up, waved the obligatory hi-fives at his exercise team, and rolled his wheelchair quickly down the hall to his office.

The message indicator on his office computer blinked an email from GCP.

"Hot damn! Somebody is awake up there! Hope it's not just the janitor," he said as he opened the email. He read the message three times, quickly, then folded his hands under his chin and stared at his keyboard. Well, he reflected, it sure as shit wasn't the janitor. The message was sharp, succinct. It implied an on-the-fly analysis and troubleshooting of the raw data. That's not a trivial exercise, and this woman did it in what... an hour? This was a high-level mind, the very best he could have hoped for.

"Adrienne Baxter, I love you," he shouted at the message on his monitor screen. He read the message again. Then the subtlety struck him, and smiling, he talked to his monitor.

"Ah, Adrienne, you start off by '*sharing* your findings' with me. And possibly there may be some risk in that for you, since you evidently couldn't contact your Director to get his approval before you responded. And you close by inviting me to '*share* with you the basis for my inquiry'. Oh, Adrienne, my dear, such an exquisite *quid pro quo*." He pondered that for a moment.

"Adrienne Baxter, I love you," he repeated, leaning over and kissing the monitor. "I'm putty in your hands, my dear. Of course I'll spill my guts. Or all I can spill, given the constraints the boss laid on me. Don't go away, dear, I've just got to get some food and I'll be right back."

The astrophysicist patted the monitor affectionately and wheeled off down the hall to the backup X-Room where the caterer had laid out brunch for the exercise team. As he propelled the wheelchair down the hall with his well-developed arms, his mind played back the communications allowed by his boss. Okay, Ed said three things: 'you *may* talk to them about the event and what the magnetic effects might have been on their GCDs; you *may not* send them the video clip of the event; but if the Pentagon has released the clip to the media, you *may* send it'. He had to think through what he was going to say, and phrase his response very carefully.

Aaron smiled at his colleagues, grabbed a bagel sandwich and juice from the lunch table and wheeled back out the door, pleading the need for solitude and a few moments for reflection.

Global Consciousness Project, Princeton University, NJ | Sunday 1120 EDT

Adrienne Baxter sat in front of her computer monitor, chin on hand, scrolling through the GCD data, contemplating. This is very, very different, she thought. I've never even heard anybody speculate about something like this. Greater consciousness is a generalized field. It's non-local, affecting all detectors simultaneously. Okay, we *maybe* see some slight indications of local effects, like the attention of people focused on a solar eclipse shadow moving across a country, but that's pretty inferential. And we've never seen any indication of consciousness or whatever aspect we're measuring being diminished by distance. All the effects we've ever seen have been general but weak. They're definitely discernible statistically, and they probably truly exist, but they're just a tiny bit of order imposed on a huge field of randomness.

These localized oscillating patterns since the anomaly are truly different, she thought. This is no statistical chasing of inferred relationships; this is purely deterministic! Freaking cause-and-effect! The coherence and repeatability just jump right off the screen at you. Her thoughts chased off into a different region of her mind as the transients in the scrolling data itched maddeningly around the edge of some pattern she could not quite see. She took a deep breath and let it out.

"Ho, Adrienne," the Director boomed, smiling and laughing through the doorway. "Got your message. I put the heart attack it caused on hold so I can see this for myself!"

"Doctor Rodgers! I'm so glad you're here. I'm either going insane or we have a couple of actual anomalies here that are completely off the charts! If this is real, I might be better off insane!"

As he lowered himself into the chair opposite, she launched into a stream-of-consciousness waterfall of words and emotions, getting it all out as fast as she could, a catharsis of excitement. She watched, absently, light beads of sweat begin to build above his eyebrows, defying the air-conditioned coolness of the Data Center.

"Jesus, Adrienne. I don't know what to say. If this is real..." his voiced tapered off and he wiped his brow. Then he led her through it again, more slowly, asking questions and taking notes.

"Adrienne, everything you've done this morning has been absolutely perfect," he said as she concluded. "I couldn't have done better myself. And you know, I think I might actually have talked to this O'Meara fellow at a post-doc picnic or some sort of gathering not too long ago. Interesting young man, if it's who I remember. He's an aerospace engineer or something. A Princeton alumnus, actually. He's got a big shock of curly red hair. Goes around in a wheelchair, some kind of spinal injury, I think. Incredible mind. We had a fascinating discussion about the nature of consciousness. He gave me some ideas, different ways to look at it, well outside my own little box. Maybe he's even a closet mystic underneath all that brainpower.

"Okay, Adrienne, off the top of my head, I can't add anything useful to what you've already done, so where are we now?"

Paradoxically, watching the excitement rising in this imperturbable academic let Adrienne get better control of her own, and she launched into a thoughtful explanation of what she was doing and what she had planned.

"Okay, Doctor Rodgers, I'm screening the raw data, eyeballing it, looking for the strength of the departures from random. I think I've got a threshold of sorts I can use for a... noise... filter. Any excursions above that I'll transform into an... amplitude... function. We'll look at the oscillations, and see what that tells us. There's some kind of pattern or signature there, I just know there is, but I don't know what." She paused a moment to collect her thoughts. "I'll set up the solution so we can watch what's happening online with GCDs on the screen, almost as fast as it happens. I'll code the Washington DC area first, since that's the one that's clearly defined in the raw data. Depending on how that works out, I'll code a similar algorithm for the South America area. How does that sound?"

"Perfect," the Director agreed. "And while you're doing that, I'll send some emails and make some calls to our GCD host volunteers in the Washington area and in South America and the Caribbean. I'll ask them to set up their computers to update and download the data as fast as possible, continuously if they have DSL or broadband."

Their mutual roles understood and agreed upon, Adrienne Baxter and Nathan Rodgers turned with fascination and not a little trepidation to the tasks at hand.

Pacific Coastal Plain, Colombia | Sunday 1125 EDT

The extraction team sat on old ammunition crates in the tree-shaded area off to the side of the small landing strip near the Pacific coast of Colombia. The three of them were playing desultory poker, the traditional escape from the tension of waiting for an overdue contact. George, the pilot, got the message first in his ear-piece. The chirping of the laptop on the fourth crate, where the Magician sat last night for dinner, confirmed it seconds later.

"It's pretty late, well outside the profile," the pilot said, reminding them of the realities of this kind of work, that the transponder might have fallen into enemy hands.

"Nope, it's him, all right, got the right security code," answered Jake, the copilot, squinting at the laptop screen and then shielding it from the daylight with his bush hat. "He wants the backup EZ. That's good. It's closer. Easier to get to. We can stay under the hacienda's radar. What a guy!" Their tension released into action and they ran for the helicopter.

"Good thing for you he called," laughed the pilot as he flipped toggles and the turbines started to wind up, "my last hand was gonna clean you gents out of your last few shekels. Jake, soon as we're airborne, acknowledge the message and ask him to reconfirm with the backup security code. Art, unlimber us some Armalites, we're off profile a little and might as well be cautious. And just in case, prep the launcher and queue up a few of those smart rockets. The intel says these bozos got choppers. They show up we're gonna hafta punch their dance ticket."

"Aye, sir," they both acknowledged, a reaction which belied the supposedly civilian status of the crew and the helicopter's marking with an oil company logo. The chopper and its armed crew arrowed swiftly east and a little north, following the terrain as it lifted from the terrace of the coastal plain into the hill country.

Several hundred kilometers east of them, the Magician loped easily northward up the jungle trail, his directional sense working him unerringly toward his hilltop objective. The alert sensor in his wristwatch tickled, and a split second later he felt the silent vibration of the transponder/communicator on his weapons harness. He paused to punch in the backup code as requested and silently counseled them: relax, boys, just stay below the radar horizon and they won't even know you're here, they've got way too many other things on their minds this morning.

As he moved along the trail with surefooted grace, he cast his consciousness radar outward periodically, playing with it, tuning it, checking its sensitivity, analyzing the results. He practiced more, until the facility became innate, until it ran automatically in the background of his mental awareness. Now it would function as an automatic early warning system, periodically reaching out to the extent of its range, and warn him of any danger before it could get close enough for harm. He concentrated his thoughts on the approaching helicopter, envisioning it, visualizing the crew, trying to sense their collective consciousness. It didn't work. Still too far out, he thought. And yet, I have some undefined perception of our mutual enemy, who is thousands of miles away, how can that be?

Minds in this reality obey the rules of this reality for consciousness, John Connard. You will sense other human minds in a manner consistent with your metaphors for this reality. But the Other, and its human host, are not totally of this reality, and now, neither are you. Your mind partially resides and operates in other dimensions and realities. The rules are different. In time you will understand.

As if triggered by those thoughts, some vaguely sensed and undefined aspect of his distant adversary seemed to beckon, a dark teasing pull just outside his comprehension. Strangely, insidiously familiar, with sexual overtones, it slithered away from his mind's grasp. Before he could fasten onto it better, a more understandable signal edged it out of his mind: his extraction team had penetrated the outer limits of his consciousness radar and was moving perceptibly inward.

Thirty minutes later, George flew a skillful approach to the rock crag, circling around it, looking for their man. No visual, even though the transponder dot on the computer screen showed him very close.

"Well, GPS says he's here. Maybe he's under the ledge. It's a long climb up," Jake said, "you want to set me down and I'll go look?"

The Magician, tucked safely into the crotch of a tree below the summit, tracked and verified the aircraft, sensing the connected consciousnesses aboard, tasting the clustering effect of their common mission. When the aircraft headed out for another pass, he looked up at the rock outcrop, transposed, and appeared there.

"Sonofabitch, there he is!" Jake was astonished; he hadn't taken his eye off the hilltop for more than a split second. "Man, I just blinked, and there he was!"

"Well hey," laughed Art, "ain't that why they call him the Magician?" He slid open the door and extended his safety tether so he could assist the Magician's entry if needed.

But John needed no help, vaulting easily into the hovering chopper before it even touched down. Sweat glistened on his bare chest and dripped to the floor of the cabin as he shucked off his weapons harness. He smiled at Art and gave them all the thumbs-up sign for a successful mission. Art blinked at the transient impression he had of dark blue stars flashing from the Magician's eyes, but dismissed it as a trick of lighting as the chopper banked into the sun.

"Home, James," John ordered the pilot, slapping him on the shoulder.

"It's George today, not James," George answered, "and what's that pillar of black smoke out to the east? You gonna fill us in, or do we hafta catch it tonight on CNN?"

"Looks like the hacienda may be off in that direction," the Magician observed dryly, "possibly they had an accident." The chopper crew hooted as one.

The Magician just smiled a quiet smile. He only debriefed to one person, Alex Shaughnessy. He accepted the usual celebratory beer from Art and used it to wash down three energy bars. Then he wrapped a blanket around his cooling shoulders, reclined back and closed his eyes for the ride back to the coast.

"He ain't gonna tell us jack shit," George advised Jake, "just like he never does." Jake nodded his agreement, with the meaning if not the syntax.

The Magician relaxed in the warm cocooning effect of the three protective consciousnesses around him. His body calmed, his pulse rate dropped, and his mind disengaged and turned inward. He reviewed what he had learned, looked at it from different angles, synthesizing the experiences with his new powers into a more cohesive pattern. There were many questions for the calm image of Duc Li sitting in his mind:

I can feel the consciousness of other beings.

I can pull energy from an adjacent dimension.

I can control gravity, in a localized area.

I can pull a null field around me for camouflage, or use it as a shield or a weapon.

I can transpose myself to any location I can see.

Are there limits to these powers?

What are they?

His nexus contemplated him somberly, obviously weighing how to answer. Symbology floated across the mind-space between them, a tentative and indecisive rendering.

My young friend, all powers have limits. Your powers are impressive in one just born to them, but they are childlike in comparison to those your species will have when fully developed in future generations. Presuming it survives, of course. The limits to any of your powers derive mainly from how you perceive and interact with other dimensions. Fundamentally, you are constrained both by how your brain is physiologically formed, and how your mind has been taught.

My brain is the hardware, my mind is the software?

A valid analogy. Transposition as an example: in N-space, in all the dimensions in which your ki *exists, you are a probability function, a varying equation of state, controlled by your consciousness. Transposing is a phase shift in the probability function, made possible because other dimensions are now recognized by your consciousness, whereas they were not before. So you can will your probability function to move, just as you can will your arm to move. Your body ends up at the locus to which you willed your probability function, and the accoutrements along with it—clothing, weapons, whatever comprises your probability function at the instant.*

Bell Labs and the University of... Innsbruck, I think, demonstrated photon teleportation, or rather the states of the photons, several years ago. I remember reading about it in a physics journal. Is that the basis for this kind of ability?

His nexus smiled. *You are a curious and creative young species. Your thirst for discovery is enormous.*

John yawned, stretched and shifted around in his reclined seat, but didn't open his eyes. Art looked at him carefully, checking again for any visible damage, especially to the head. Seeing none, he let the Magician sleep on.

At one level of his expanded consciousness, John felt the kind intent of his three transient warrior colleagues and wrapped himself in its comfort, his body sleeping on. At another level, he worked methodically through his newfound talents with his nexus, understanding what he could, accepting the rest.

Northwest Washington, DC | Sunday 1205 EDT

Lara rose smoothly from her lotus position on the rug, and walked onto the small balcony outside the bedroom. She stretched toward the noonday sun, enjoying the flex of her muscles, the extraordinary acuteness of her senses, the soft warm air caressing her face.

"Wow, I'm hungry again. I had a huge breakfast, but it feels like I haven't eaten all day," she told the blue jay contemplating her from his perch in the adjacent tree. The jay squawked and flew off, a blue bullet through green foliage.

Yes, your energy intake requirements have increased. Your new existence is mostly mental and spiritual, but makes great demands on the body. You frequently will find yourself in need of food and drink.

I'll blow up like a balloon, she thought.

Unlikely. You will be fortunate not to lose weight. You must eat and drink frequently. You cannot afford to be physically depleted in the coming battle.

"Okay, so we'll eat. Let's see what my boys want," she said aloud, stretching again and walking downstairs. She found the two of them huddled over the dining room table, a big sketch pad full of arcane diagrams in front of them. The only thing missing from this picture is my third musketeer, she thought fleetingly. She leaned in between them, her arms around their shoulders, and looked at the diagrams.

"Hmm?" she enquired.

"Mom, we're trying to figure out how many dimensions there are, or at least how many you're in," Joshua said excitedly.

The science section of the Sunday New York Times lay beside the sketch pad, opened to an article about a new cosmological theory of the universe. The article was heavily marked up with Joshua's careless scrawl, with a few notations in Hamilton O'Donnell's more precise lettering. "This article on M-theory says ten dimensions, eleven if you include time, but Uncle Ham and I think there may be more. We're just trying to work it out."

Sure, and why not, she thought humorously as she studied the diagram for even a remote clue as to what it might mean. My nine-year old genius here is certainly not above pressing the status quo in the scientific community. Lord, what would I do if he didn't have his Uncle Ham to talk to?

"Okay, guys," she said aloud, "I know you're headed out for your usual Sunday afternoon adventure with your buddies down at the Smithsonian, but how about a quick lunch before you go?"

A few minutes later, Joshua watched his mother's food intake in astonishment.

"Wow, Mom, I guess you haven't eaten in a long time. As long ago as breakfast, maybe."

"I think operating in additional dimensions makes me hungrier than normal, Josh. I evidently have to feed my other selves, too. So remind me, what is the discussion subject at the Smithsonian this afternoon?"

"Black holes, Mom. Conceptual models for what happens. Event horizons. A guest lecturer from MIT."

"The woman is brilliant," Ham added. "She's modeled a precise correlation between black holes and government suction of taxpayer dollars. Took the EPA Superfund Program as an example, she did."

"Uh huh. Now Ham, I'm not feeling nearly feisty enough to take your bait." Lara smiled easily back at him. "So just tell me what else is on your agenda, and when you'll be back."

"After the lecture, and after Joshua has thoroughly pestered the poor woman with alternative conceptual models, we will strike out for the tennis courts. Our lad here needs more work on his topspin backhand. A slightly longer stroke for his two-handed swing, I believe. P'raps you would join us?"

"Umm. No thanks, Ham. Without our usual fourth, I think you and Josh would have a better time with just the two of you. And I have some more reflection to do. More things to sort out in my head."

Ham nodded his acceptance. "Well, all right then, me lad, be about gettin' dressed and getting' your tennis gear. We leave in three minutes. Not that I've ever known a Sunday Smithsonian gatherin' to start on time, mind you...."

Dressed in a polo shirt and slacks, carrying a packed his tennis bag, Joshua kissed Lara's cheek on the way out the door. She saw from his eyes that he still could feel her strange energy resonate at the contact. As the door closed behind her son and his uncle, her newly-acute hearing picked up his question: "Okay, Uncle Ham, what's *really* going on with Mom?"

Chapter 12

On the SDI Exercise lunch break, Aaron sat in his office and chewed contemplatively on a catered sandwich as he constructed a reply to Adrienne Baxter's email. His initial inquiry had been intended to eliminate machine electronic effects as an explanation for the response of the GCD network. Her email response had pretty much confirmed that. But... knowledge of the atmospheric anomalies might change her perspective a little, he thought. Best be fair to the rogue asteroid hypothesis.

And, he thought, I should make the communication a little less formal. He started typing:

To: arbaxter@princeton.edu
From: aaron.omeara@gsfc.gov
Subject: GCD Anomaly
Dear Adrienne,

Thanks so much for your quick response; I didn't think my email would find anyone there on a Sunday morning. I really appreciate the time you spent checking the data flow and developing your statistical checks.

This is a very strange event, both DOD and Homeland Security are involved, and nobody knows what to make of it yet. I don't know whether it's going to be classified or not. Here's what I can tell you as of now:

(1) At 0546-0548 this morning, objects appeared at about half the distance to the moon, about 20 degrees south of the ecliptic (the plane in which most of the planets and asteroids reside). We're running an exercise here at Goddard, and happened to have a satellite array looking in that direction. The objects had high velocities toward earth, and discharged incredible amounts of energy. I think they had some motions that are unexplainable by all the normal rules of astrophysics. We projected impact of the smaller object in the DC area, and the larger object somewhere in Colombia, south of Bogota.

(2) Then the objects disappeared. No impacts. Nothing on seismographs. The Pentagon had fighter jets and reconnaissance helicopters scanning the ground in the DC area for four hours this morning. They saw nothing at all.

(3) The consensus here at Goddard is that a high-velocity rogue asteroid from outside the solar system hit a small asteroid or piece of space junk and fragmented, and everything burned up on entry. NEAT (the asteroid tracking station on Maui) saw part of the action and came to the same conclusion. I think that consensus is wrong—too many of the observations just don't fit collision mechanics.

Good, Aaron thought, I've been up front with her, let her know it could be sensitive, and validated myself as an ethical scientist. There's some implied risk there for me, that's a good payback for her risk. He continued typing:

If you could think about several other things, and get back to me, that would be a great help:

(1) Are there any known purely physical phenomena (i.e., not consciousness-related) that would cause the effects noted for the initial event at 0546-0548? (I'm thinking of things like solar flares or neutrino wavefronts that might affect the electronics of your detectors.)

(2) Did any of the GCDs on the far side of the globe respond differently in any way than those from, say, Europe to Hawaii? (Presumably any physical effect might be modified by shielding from the planetary mass, or some timing difference induced.)

(3) For the post-event localized oscillations in the GCD network, is there any way to apply an algorithm that would relate amplitude—I don't know of any better term for this kind of phenomenon—at each GCD somehow to distance from the source of the oscillations? (I'm thinking that since Bogota was a clear effect and Quito and Panama City were weak effects, that may have some sort of meaning.) Could this concept be tested for the DC area, where the GCD array is denser?

Thanks for your phone number. I can't call you now, we're right in the middle of an exercise, but I'll try on the next break, probably around 3:15 or 3:30. Adrienne, we may be onto something so incredible we can scarcely comprehend it, so any outside-the-box thinking or speculation is fine with me. Thanks for all your hard work and for sharing your insights!

Aaron, GSFC astrophysicist and possible incipient nutcase.

"There, that takes care of a few interpersonal issues, and gets things off on a nice friendly basis. I hope she's got a sense of humor," he told his monitor as he pushed the *Send* button.

"Love you, Adrienne!" Aaron blew a kiss back toward the computer as he left his office and rolled back down the hall to the exercise.

As he wheeled past the backup X-Room, lunch stragglers were just catching the end of the noon news, in which a Pentagon spokesman outlined the events of the morning and showed pieces of the Goddard video clip to the public.

Pacific Coast of Columbia | Sunday 1245 EDT

"Wake up, sir, your next ride has arrived," Art announced to the sleeping Magician as the chopper flared to a neat landing beside the Harrier jump jet. John awoke, stretched and accepted the clean shirt Art handed him. He handed back the hard drive excised from the mansion's server, along with his own miniaturized laptop.

"Thanks, gentlemen, I appreciate your help," he said. "This hardware gets bubble-wrapped, please, in the diplomatic pouch, the usual protocol, okay?" He jumped lithely out of the chopper and waved them on their way.

"Good morning, sir," the Harrier pilot greeted him over the noise of the departing helicopter, "I understand you're familiar with our mode of transport here, can you confirm that for me, please?"

"I am," John smiled at the Marine officer, accepting the helmet. "You topped off enough for Panama City, direct?"

"Yes, sir, no problem."

"Let's do it then, Captain..." he looked at the name tag stitched on the flight suit, "Jarvis. And *toute suite*, a posse may be coming."

The pilot's cocked eyebrow told John that he had seen the recon aerials of the fire and doubted the posse. But the man just shrugged and followed John into the aircraft; he was only a taxi driver this morning.

"Any specific landing point, sir?" Jarvis enquired as he verified his passenger was strapped in. "Amador? Tocumen? If it's someplace else we may have to do some bureaucratic rigamarole."

"Tocumen's convenient, thank you. I've got a commercial flight stateside from there."

The Harrier's engines wound up and it rolled a short distance down the landing strip then clawed its way into the tropical sky.

"I had a tough morning, and I need to catch a few winks, if you'll excuse me?" John spoke into the intercom channel.

"Yes sir, that's fine. The trip will be slightly over an hour, depending on the routing we get around Panama City. It's usually pretty quiet at Tocumen. I'll wake you when we get there."

"Thanks, Captain." John promptly dismissed his present reality, closed his eyes, and dropped into consideration of his new and expanded skills. The contemplative image of Duc Li greeted him in his mind-space. His question floated between them: I sprouted wings of energy, back there in the warehouse, to simulate an angel of death and scare the boy. They were sort of thin and ephemeral, but the shape was right and the detail wasn't bad. Can I create images that are more concrete? Make illusions to confuse the enemy?

The Other would not be confused, John Connard... however, its human allies might be, at least momentarily. The concept is good, and possibly useful in creating a diversion... There is a spider inside your shirt, at the right front hem. Take hold of it, calm it with the slightest touch of the null field, let your ki embrace it. It is a living thing, part of your biosphere in this reality. Its consciousness is limited, but you will understand it.

The Magician flipped up the corner of his shirt, and the spider scuttled downward. His hand reached out in a lightning reflex and cupped the creature, simultaneously applying the tiniest trickle of a null field. He opened his palm, righted the quiescent spider, and looked at it closely with a slight sense of distaste. Hairy little beast, he thought. His training on flora and fauna indigenous to South America categorized it from the markings and structure. A dwarf tarantula, probably, not a banana spider or any of the really poisonous arachnids. Still, the question floated in his mind-space: will it bite? The image of Duc Li was amused.

Even the most toxic venom cannot harm you now; your body would neutralize it quickly. And if you are its friend, it will not bite—you are too big for it to eat. The spider is part of your world, and so it is in that sense part of you. Embrace it with your ki, now, and study how you may borrow its image.

And just exactly how the hell do I embrace a freaking spider, he wondered. But in the instant of wondering the answer came from within, and he narrowed the focus of his consciousness down to the twitching beast in his hand.

Hunger. Pain. Fear. Overwhelming need to copulate. The sensations arrowed into him, sharp and acute, primeval. He jerked and twitched, and felt his penis engorge. The creature roused from the ennui induced by the null field, and its tiny blip of consciousness brightened. The smallest hint of an aura formed around his hand and the spider. He studied the arachnid, letting it walk over his hand, admiring the way its eight limbs worked together. Good engineering, he thought appreciatively, letting all the observations flow into his consciousness, tucking them into a pocket of memory.

Good. Now place it on your leg and create an image beside it. You must use the energy field and the null field at the same time. I cannot describe to you how; you have not the terminology. But I believe you can intuit the method.

The Magician stilled the spider with a slight null field and placed it carefully on his leg. He exhaled slowly, rhythmically, reducing his pulse rate, integrating his awareness with the inert spider. He submersed his mind in the field of greater consciousness, seeking the inner peace he intuited would be required for creation. He sensed the dimension of the energy field, adjacent to his reality, not a proton's width away. The null field lay nested in an inexplicable dimension behind it, or possibly beside it or inside it. His mind tugged tentatively at both dimensions.

Yes, John Connard, you are on the right track.

In the mind-space between himself and the image of Duc Li, he built a hologram of the spider, drawing on forces that were complementary within the matrix of his greater consciousness. Then he opened his eyes and saw a second spider on his leg. Duc Li smiled along with him.

You have intuited the method. The capability is very strong in you. If reason and logic should forsake you in the coming battle, John Connard, you must remember that you have those other ways of knowing, a bequest from your parents.

The Magician made his spider simulacrum crawl forward, backward and sideways. Its motions were rough and tentative under his control, but smoothed out as he learned and adjusted. In a short time, the image-spider looked very real, and moved with a passable imitation of the motions in his memory. He passed his finger through it. It had no solidity, and shimmered out of existence when it contacted the residual fields in his finger. He created another, much faster. Moving it, practicing with it, he worked out the leg motions until they were identical with those in his memory. The image obediently scuttled down his leg, and up the seat back, then leaped gracefully back onto his knee. He wondered if it could be scaled up.

Scaling should not be a problem. The energy field and null field requirements are proportionate to the size of your creation.

Feeding more of each field into his creation, he swelled it to the size of his fist. He increased the feed, judiciously, and blew its body up to basketball size. Its multi-jointed legs were now almost as long as his arms. Then, in a perverse fit of humor, he made it stand on fully extended legs, like stilts, to peer out the plexiglass canopy.

At that instant, the Harrier, descending from cruising altitude, passed into the shadow of a thunderhead. The pilot glanced to his right and behind him and saw the fanged image reflected in the darkened plastic. The gut-wrenching fear of a totally unexpected monster temporarily overrode his training. His visceral reaction sent the jet into a screaming rolling dive, as if to run from the fanged monstrosity.

"Sir," he yelled, "there's a spider in the cockpit!" But as soon as he spoke, the image winked out.

The Magician realized what had happened, and suppressed a smile, feigning a yawning sleepy reply instead.

"Yeah, I see him. He's sitting on my knee. Cute little thing. Pretty markings. What's the matter, you think he may bite me?"

"How big is it, sir?" The pilot enquired with a note of urgency, leveling off the aircraft and trying to level off his thudding pulse.

"Oh, maybe a half-inch body. Legs are about an inch. Why?"

"Ah... nothing, sir. Must have been a reflection. Looked bigger."

Smiling, John sent the question into his mind-space. So how was that?

An effective diversion, my young friend. You have considerable latent artistic talent, too. The image was quite realistic.

"Tocumen slipped us right into the approach, sir, we'll be on the ground shortly." The pilot's voice quavered as he brought himself under control. "The helipad off the end of the terminal okay? I can refuel there."

"Sure, that's fine, Captain," the Magician acknowledged absently. He was starved again, he suddenly realized. He'd get a meal on the flight to Miami, and another on the flight to Washington. In first class, they would both be decent, but he couldn't wait. He had to eat, and eat now. His stomach growled agreement.

Yes, your energy intake requirements are much greater. You now exist in a broader reality. Though the primary aspects of your new existence are mental and spiritual, the demands on your physical body are greater. You frequently will find yourself in need of food and drink.

The jump jet vectored neatly down the runway and juked into position over the landing pad. It wafted down gently onto the concrete and taxied off to the side for refueling, its engines whining down.

"Thanks for the lift, Captain," the Magician said, shaking his pilot's hand. "I removed our other passenger for you." He opened his left hand to show him the spider sitting there comfortably.

"Ah, yes, well..." Jarvis was temporarily at a loss for words, "thank you, sir. The Corps is always happy to help out. And your insect control efforts are certainly appreciated. Sir."

The Magician waved at him and strode off toward the Military Liaison Office. But before he reached its door, he detoured to the manicured garden beside the building and gently ushered the spider from his hand into the shrubbery.

Northwest Washington, DC | Sunday 1257 EDT

Lara Picard had waved off her son and his uncle from the front porch of the brownstone on Phoenix Court. She now sat quietly at the dining room table, cradling a cup of tea while her modified metabolism literally sucked energy out of her lunch.

I need more information, she thought. I need to find out as much as I can about this new reality. Especially, *especially*, how to use it to defend myself and fight, and how I can use it to trap this monster. She opened her consciousness, and the image of her greater self waiting there smiled across the mind-space between them.

Yes. Ask.

You said—or I said, or we said, I'm not exactly sure how to think of us as one entity or two—that my trauma triggered a genetic key that opened my mind to you, my *ki*, and in turn we opened into our greater consciousness. I sense this is a truly unlimited consciousness, unconstrained by distance or other physical factors. But why, particularly, has it happened now, why not earlier? Why not later? Is the timing somehow part of a plan? Why do I sense there must there be a battle? Why must I live and the Beast die? Why wouldn't the nature and warmth of this greater consciousness I feel neutralize the Beast?

We will become integrated more as time goes on. The timing? There is no good answer. When a child is ready, it will be born. As to the whys... there is no answer that we may understand. We move inevitably toward love, but not without being tested in the fire of its opposites. Particular destinies may require strife and challenge. As to neutralization of the Beast by love, consider your own experiences: would the greed for money and power in those criminals you prosecuted have been turned aside by love?

But—Lara rejected the thought—most people aren't like that. They're fundamentally good, they nurture, they care. They do not have an inordinate love of money or power; they just want enough of both to have a happy existence.

Physically, the species is still mostly animal, with perceptions limited to the five senses, and fear and survival are still the most powerful drivers for many people.

Lara abruptly remembered the psych retrospectives, the classic *Einsatzgruppen* studies of pre-war Germany, devastating revelations about the human capacity to murder and destroy. But that was then, this is now, she objected. Now there's CNN, the internet, widespread exposure to public opinion, peacekeeping forces, war crime tribunals.

Sixty years is not even a blink in evolutionary terms. And there is a continuing litany up to the present, is there not? Russia. Cambodia. Sub-Saharan Africa. Iraq under Hussein. Afghanistan under the Taliban. The excuse is always the same: to protect the survival of our people, to preserve our own way, which is the right way, the only way.

But those are other places, other cultures, poorly educated, insular, not exposed to our philosophies of individual freedom and choice, diametric opposites to what this country represents. How could we be subverted?

We have a tradition of tolerance in this culture. Acceptance of other philosophies, of religions, of ways of life. This is a great strength, but it allows many subcultures to survive at the margin. People are all too easily drawn into power in these subcultures, into the natural tendency from our animal heritage. Fundamentalists of many religious sects. American Nazis. Skinheads. Survivalists. Street gangs. Theirs is a direct expression of power. Their way is the right way, the only way. Always with plausible reasons that have their real basis in the animal need to dominate and thus survive. The mind of the Beast, in all of them.

But could subcultures get enough of a following, combine together, be effective throughout the entire social fabric? Lara reviewed her knowledge of history again, glumly. Yes, a certain application of power by the Nazis in Germany, at just a few crucial turning points. And just a few men were enough.

And the same pattern clearly held through many more recent examples. So there is fundamentally no reason why it could not happen again. Her *ki* was correct: it *was* all about power.

Her enemy, the Beast, was almost certainly a man, she realized. The historical statistics did not include many females in such roles.

Within several generations, more minds will discern how to extend individual consciousness outward to embrace greater consciousness. This is the first step toward development of incredible power. Several philosophers and scientists are suspecting that such a turning point is coming—they call it a macroshift. *The human race could make a quantum leap forward, or could regress into a cycle of brutality and suffering. This Beast we must trap and destroy is most likely a man. Given the chance, he will subvert human evolution back to animal dominance, so he can control this incredible power for his own ends.*

We are more enlightened today, but that probably just means the Beast's means of subversion would need to be more subtle, Lara conceded sadly.

Yes. Humanity's macroshift hangs in the balance, and it is a delicate balance. This Beast must be destroyed.

Chapter 13

Nathan Rodgers, Nate to his friends and colleagues, Doctor Rodgers to his students, was a quiet and patient man, used to student excitability. He had seen immediately that he needed to let Adrienne unload it all before he could ask any questions. But as her story had unfolded, his own excitement became difficult to contain. Now, as he traced out the diagnostic work of his favorite undergraduate assistant, a light bead of sweat re-formed above his eyebrows. There were no errors in Adrienne's logic, not one. The huge anomaly early this morning—all GCDs going non-random at once—had to be a real event. It followed by the same logic that the later, more localized anomalies occurring in GCDs around Washington, DC—clear oscillations out of random into high states of order—also must be real. The network is seeing what the network is seeing, he thought. It doesn't matter that we have never observed anything like this before, it's as real as real can be. So accept that, Nate, and move on. Let's see if we can figure out what it means.

He walked out of his office into the main computer area. Adrienne's fingers flew over the keyboard, and she talked out loud to the data, coaxing them to yield their secrets. Nathan liked that, found the enthusiasm endearingly child-like. The technique worked for her, he reminded himself; he'd seen its success more than once.

"Okay," Adrienne muttered, oblivious to his presence, "now I've got your integrals proportioned to your degree of departure from random, you puppies. You're all nicely thresholded just above average background noise. So, let's just see how you plot out!"

She waved her forefinger in a triumphal downward curlicue motion like an orchestra conductor signaling the end of a movement, and jabbed the *Enter* button, turning her head and smiling over her shoulder as she finally sensed Nathan.

The SAS software screen came up and obediently plotted out a timeline from 0600 to 1200 along the horizontal axis. Then, one by one, it traced the history of the six Washington-area GCDs for that time period. Adrienne's breathing seemed attuned to the displays as they plotted. Flatline, *blip*, flatline, *blip*, flatline, *bigger blip*, flatline, *smaller blip*, flatline, oooh, some *really big blips* there coming up on 0800, no more flatline after those, just an elevated oscillating baseline.

Nathan, looking over her shoulder, saw at once the simple elegance of the analysis, and admired the six colored plots as they traced out. The flatline obviously represented her selection of a threshold for non-randomness. The blips above it were different sizes for each GCD, but coincident in time, and maintained about the same proportions with respect to each other. Of the six, the GCD in Georgetown always produced the highest blips. The one in Richmond always produced the lowest, sometimes barely showing. The others were in between.

As they studied the results of her handiwork, incoming email pinged on her computer. They both smiled when they saw it came from their new friend Aaron O'Meara, and quickly scanned the first paragraph. Then they gasped simultaneously, shocked at the content:

At 0546-0548 this morning, objects appeared... half the distance to the moon... running an exercise here at Goddard... satellite array looking... objects had high velocities toward earth... projected impact of the smaller object in the DC area... larger object somewhere in Colombia...

Adrienne paled. Nathan flushed. They stared at each other as the implications sank in.

"Omigod! Omigod! Omigod!" The rest of her thoughts knotted up, somewhere between mind and mouth.

"Adrienne," Nathan said slowly, "if it's what we're thinking... there's no indication this is a bad thing. It's way too early to guess at that. Our job is just to track what's happening, contribute what we can, okay? Okay?"

She looked searchingly at him. Some color returned to her cheeks. She smiled tentatively as her mind parsed the probabilities and concluded that advanced lifeforms were more likely to be benign than not. After all, was that not the direction of human evolution?

Scrolling down through the rest of Aaron O'Meara's email message, her tension dropped a little; that man apparently had managed to remain composed and thoughtful.

"Pretty smart, isn't he," she asked rhetorically.

"I'll say," the Director agreed. "Listen, I can take care of his first two questions. I think your time is better spent on analysis and his third question. Is that reasonable?"

"Oh sure, Doctor Rodgers. And he must have read my mind—I was about a millisecond away from that thought when his email came in! It's pretty easy to do, I'll just take the areas under each blip—each of my 1-minute integrals—and convert them to a string of numbers...." As her words tapered off into contemplation of the approach, Nathan absently wondered how this news would be greeted by the world at large. He wasn't at all sure he liked the implications. *Maybe I should* move my funds and stocks into a cash position, he thought irreverently. The market will go wacky, sure as hell, but which way? Then he shrugged it off, and patted his young colleague on the shoulder.

"Great, Adrienne, crunch your numbers. I'll work on the first two questions. Holler if you need me. Let's make this Aaron O'Meara just as impressed with us as we are with him."

Northwest Washington, DC | Sunday 1315 EDT

Lara removed her sandals and walked downstairs to the basement dojo. Running through karate katas always served to detach her mind and help her focus. She needed to fashion a subtle trap for the Beast.

The dojo was a bright, well-lit room with high ceilings, unusual for an old brownstone. Ham had knocked down the basement interior wall between the two duplexes, and replaced it with a steel support beam. French doors opened onto a little barbecue patio at ground level that abutted the woods of Montrose Park. A rubberized mat with good traction for bare feet covered much of the floor.

Lara draped her blouse over a chair and bowed to the body bag hanging from a ceiling hook above the center of the mat. She danced around the bag, in supple, fluid motions, loosening her muscles and tendons. She detached her mind from analytical thought, leaving only the image of her *ki*, who looked on approvingly. Amazing, she thought. It's so much easier now, more natural. I just dropped right into my zone. It's *never* been so easy.

A green aura began to take shape around her as she danced through the warmup of the first kata. She watched it in the floor-to-ceiling mirror panels that covered the south wall of the room. As she spun around the bag, the aura flickered around her in the room's fluorescent lights. It moved with her, an extension of herself, but yet with a certain seemingly independent fluidity all its own. Ah, she realized, from a depth of knowing much more basic than the analytical part of her brain, that's my *ki*, my greater self! She danced past the wall switch for the overhead lights and flicked it off with her toe. The room dimmed to the natural light coming in the French doors, a friendly soft hue from the shaded overhung patio and dappled sunlight on the green springtime foliage beyond.

Lara closed her eyes but somehow unerringly continued her whirling dance. On the other side of the bag, she opened them to look in the mirror. Her aura was more clearly apparent in the dimmed light, a living entity in constant motion.

"God, that's beautiful," she breathed aloud to her green-tinged Technicolor shadow as she danced.

Yes, we are. I am your ki, *I am you. But we are only the tip of an iceberg, a part of the energy of the greater consciousness. Dissolve into it now, become one.*

"Umm. That's warm. Cozy. Homey," Lara murmured, relaxing into the embrace.

Yes. Good, you have conjoined. Now visualize this consciousness running through your being.

"Ahh," she gasped as the joy enveloped her. It bloomed, alive and aware, and it *knew* her. She realized then that it was welcoming her back. She had visited that place this morning for her body to be healed, she saw. And before that, she had visited as a child, sitting beside her sacred pool on the farm where she grew up.

Yes, a homecoming, a jubilee. Dance. Meditate. Savor the essence. Resonate with it. Become it.

As Lara danced onward into the combat phases of the kata, she opened her mind into the expanded reality, dimensions and purpose of this greater consciousness. Time hung suspended, or had no meaning. Joy resonated through her being. As she passed the mirrors, emerald-hued six-pointed star patterns flared in her eyes, their pulsations tuned precisely to her rhythmic movements.

She slammed punches and kicks into the water-filled cushioned body bag, spinning and sometimes somersaulting away, her motions blurring with speed, her feet seeming to barely touch the mat. The heavy bag swung wildly from its ceiling anchor.

Wow, a remote part of her mind told her, I've never, ever been this zoned, not even in a sparring match. My God, the power! The incredible power!

Lara laughed aloud with uninhibited animal joy. With her laughter came an astringent odor, the smell of lightning around a thunderstorm, and her eyes flared more brightly.

She sailed across the mat, five feet in the air, and kicked the top of the bag with her right foot as she shoved off its middle with her left foot. Flipping over backwards, she came smoothly out of her landing crouch and swept her right arm out across her body, leaning all her explosive speed into that ingrained backup defensive motion. A planar closed loop of pure green energy arced out from her rigid open hand and sliced the bag in half, exploding it in a mist of droplets. The bottom of the bag dropped three feet to the floor, and geysered its water onto the mat.

Lara crouched, frozen, and stared in astonishment at the emptied half-bag lying on its side, water cascading from it. Then she stared at the top half, still swinging from its ceiling hook, dripping. Her nose took in the odd mixed odors of ozone and burnt rubber and vinyl.

Tightening her right hand into strike rigidity, she watched the plane of energy arc out several feet. It pulsed vibrantly, expectantly, a sword unsheathed, wanting to be blooded. She did the same with her left hand, with the same effect. Intuitively, she knew how she formed them. They were extensions of her hand, the energy driving out and then curling back under the influence of some kind of mental control field, closing the circuit back in her hand.

The planes flickered a blazing emerald-green light around a more translucent core. Planes of energy, Lara sensed, turning her hands. As mathematical functions, they had no thickness. But they clearly had a hunger, a desire for combat. Her intellectual taste for courtroom combat paled to insignificance beside the more primal hungers that urgently fed back into her mind from the blazing swords grown out of her hands. The swords hummed and crackled as she turned her hands and contemplated them.

You have found the energy field. Excellent. And you have tied it to a sword metaphor. You have a natural affinity for its use.

"Good Lord, you might have warned me!" Lara panted, struggling to control the strange new vibrations that coursed through her physical and metaphysical being. "How the hell did that happen? By itself? I certainly wasn't trying to find any energy field!"

Other dimensions are not necessarily ones you can find by looking for them. Sometimes they just present themselves, given the proper manner of invitation.

Symbology scrolled across the mind-space between her and her nexus, and she intuited the meaning without grasping all the symbols. She had indeed, she saw, invited the energy field to transition to her dimension, to serve her use, with a sword as its mental metaphor. The dimension is so close, she marveled; that's less than... less than the diameter of a proton. Is this the energy Josh felt in me? She floated the silent question into her mind-space.

Partially. He is sensitive. He will become adept, in his time. He feels the spiritual energy of your ki *and its connection to the greater consciousness, and he also feels the fields of physical energy you have commandeered. He may not as yet be able to distinguish between the two.*

Her *ki* smiled gently at her, allaying the concern before she could fully voice it. *And no, you could not have hurt him; the field cannot harm those you do not intend to harm, no more than could your own hands.*

Lara looked at those hands again, and consciously relaxed their tension as she opened her mind to accept the experience, and the power. Paradoxically, acceptance immediately delivered to her full control over the energy resonating in her body.

Yes. Acceptance. That is the way, is it not?

Global Consciousness Project, Princeton University, NJ | Sunday 1412 EDT

Totally absorbed in the new programming challenge, Adrienne's thoughts drove her fingers flying across the keyboard. Yes! 1-minute integrals as the new raw data, and I'll set the averaging time as a specified variable. Fifteen minutes first—that's as good a guess as any at this point. Given the strength of these signals, we shouldn't lose too much. And, yes, let's compute a circle as a confidence band around each location, that's easy enough....

She worked diligently, totally zoned into her chase, and two things became clear: the source originated near the Georgetown GCD, and the best predictor of field intensity was the inverse of distance to the negative 1.6 power. She didn't necessarily believe it, she realized, because it had no real world analog she knew of. But it still made a decent working hypothesis; all the data fit neatly. No matter the individual 15-minute time period to which she applied her algorithm, it drew a neat location circle every time. When the signals were weaker, the circles were larger; when the signals were stronger, the circles were smaller. That seemed right: the stronger the signal, the less the doubt about where it was coming from.

"Okay, you puppies, this makes sense," she murmured to the data, and as an afterthought she added crosshairs through the center of the circles, labeling them with latitude and longitude. She clicked through each 15-minute period again, checking for consistency. Yes, she thought, but there's a little location shift two hours in, and another maybe an hour later, and then stationary since. Had the thing moved?

Then, with a sudden instinct for what the next operational question would be, she downloaded a digital map of the northwest Washington area. She scaled her circles to fit, displaying them sequentially on top of the map, each circle fading into the next as a time clock played out on the bottom of the screen: digital footprints.

"Aha! Bingo! Sure as shit looks like an alien is walking around Georgetown," she giggled nervously, a whistling-in-the-dark giggle as she hit *Enter* again. The display marched automatically through the 15-minute solutions from 0600 to 1400, plotting one cross-haired circle for each 15-minute period, and holding each on the screen for three seconds before it faded into the next.

"Wow! Will you look at that," she exclaimed, contemplating the three solutions for the 15-minute periods ending 1330 through 1445. "No change in location, but the circles are really tightened down. So signal strength must be up! *Way* up! Wow!"

Northwest Washington, DC | Sunday 1502 EDT

Lara Picard, squeegeeing the water off the rubber mat and out onto the patio, had no inkling that her activity and location had shown up so precisely on a computer screen over a hundred miles away. She turned on the floor fan to drive off the remaining moisture, and tested her foot traction on the drying mat. That will do, she thought absently. Right now, I need to lock this power into my muscle memory, make it automatic.

It is automatic. It has already happened. Your natural talent with the energy field is extraordinarily high. What you may need is some practice against what your opponent may do. I will create in your mind a simulacrum of our enemy in the hanging remains of the body bag. We must attack him.

Dread built in her as the bag shifted its shape into the outline of the Beast. It had two hands and two legs and a head, but with no detail. The black emptiness of its body revealed an eerie transparency; she could see right through it. Somehow there and not there at the same time, it presented a constantly shifting obscenity to the eye and mind. An aura crackled, outlining the emptiness in a deep blue, almost purple haze. Blades of blue energy arced from its hands, hollow planes of no thickness. A sharp crackling electricity conveyed their deadliness.

She controlled her fear as she stalked around the mat, circling her enemy, watching the weaving hands and feet. Shit, she thought, there's a lot of training behind those motions, they look like mine. I hope the real thing isn't trained like that.

We must plan for the worst. Our enemy may be better trained than you. You cannot defeat this simulacrum; it is of your mind. But you will gain experience and finesse in your control of the energy field. Attack it!

She saw the slightest of openings, feinted a slash with her right hand and punched in with her left, a burst of green energy. The simulated Beast howled, only partially deflecting her direct thrust with the sweep of a blue energy plane formed on its forearm. Coruscating light resulted from the contact, accompanied by the harsh sound of a dissonance in the fabric of the energy field, a sound like broken glass combined with a thousand fingernails across a thousand blackboards. Score one for the home team, she thought, dancing away, parrying the counterpunches and jabs and scything sweeps with her own, but only narrowly blocking the unexpected bladed foot that flashed up between her legs. For the better part of an hour they sparred. The metaphor of sword and shield, she thought fleetingly, would never describe the deeper complexities of fighting with energy fields.

Enough! You have achieved sufficient control. You can trust your instincts now. Your metaphors will suffice.

The simulacrum of the Beast winked out as her nexus smiled into her mind-space.

Well, thank you, thought Lara, her body dripping with sweat, the energy still crackling around her, I'm reasonably pleased myself. She floated questions into the mind-space between them. Is that what the monster will look like? What's the nature of the center, the part that you can't really see, but somehow can see though? Is that part of the Beast, or did you put it there because we don't know what he looks like yet?

Our enemy may not have a discernible appearance. The center that you saw is chaos, a null field taken from a dimension beyond that of the energy dimension. The Beast will have some control of this dimension, most likely. It is a total absence of energy, or coherence, in this reality.

As Lara wiped herself down with one of the big terrycloth towels on the dojo wall, she poured her intuition—as well as a confident and humorous thought about her ability as a lawyer to create chaos—into the mind-space between them. Her nexus smiled.

Possibly so. We will see. Open your hand, and hold your palm out in front of you.

She did, her cupped hand glowing slightly with pulsating green-hued energy.

Now, replace the energy field in your palm with nothingness from the null dimension.

Symbols marched across her mind space, showing the location of that dimension, but she didn't need direction. She knew instinctively how to draw it to her. This instinct came, she realized, from her enlightenment about how the energy field had come to her, with the proper invitation, rather than her having to search it out. Her *ki* could invite these other dimensions, including the null. The chaos metaphor obediently moved forward in her mind-space, and a small black nothingness formed over her open palm. She felt her hand cool as some of its heat diffused into the nothingness above it.

Excellent. Now cast it from you.

With a flip of her wrist, Lara flung the chaos cloud at the remnants of the body bag hanging from the ceiling. She ordered it in her mind to envelop the bag, cling to it, make it disappear. The bag obediently shimmered and became transparent; she could see the wall behind it. The bag is no longer fully in this reality? She floated the question toward her nexus in the mind-space.

Not exactly, but that is a reasonable metaphor for the modified dimensions.

Actually, you perturb the hologram of the bag's existence. You have a great natural talent with nullity. You are a power to be reckoned with.

The expression sat somber on the face of her *ki*, her greater self.

Told you, Lara thought back at her smugly; it's all that legal training. She created another blackness in her hand, and instinctively thinned it down to a sheet, with a thickness only marginally greater than zero. She drew it around herself, laughing.

"This is how it's done, isn't it," she asked her image in the mirrored wall. But the answer was self-evident: a shifting center of nothingness limned by an emerald aura of energy looked back at her from the mirror. She played with the energy field and the null field in tandem, and realized how she could make herself almost, but not quite, invisible. In any case, she thought, I'll be able to blend into a background better than any chameleon. Offensive uses were not quite so apparent. She framed the questions in her mind, sequencing them. The answers reflected back instantly.

A chaos cloud is a terrifying offensive weapon. It absorbs psychic energy. A strong null field cast upon an enemy will cause prompt neural death. A weak field will cause unconsciousness or at the least a confusion of reasoning, a loss of memory, a dilution of purpose. You are capable of projecting a very strong field, although the strength drops off with both time and distance. All null fields neutralize each other, and that is the best defense. Our enemy will use this dimension, but I think it is unlikely he will have your great natural facility.

The null field would be her more subtle, more deadly weapon, Lara decided. And her facility with it would be underplayed until time for the trap to be sprung.

"Okay," she said, "I think I've got that down. Now let's talk about gravity, and flying."

Sit, and let us contemplate the energy field.

More symbols flowed into her mind-space. The dimension of gravity nestled into, or maybe behind, the energy dimension, she saw. As soon as she saw it, she understood how it could be unlocked and called under her control. She smiled, and her nexus smiled with her.

You appear to know what to do. Go ahead.

Effortlessly, she floated into the air. Tilting the field ever so slightly, she moved herself over the mat, hovering in front of the mirror. She grinned widely at herself.

"Hot damn, I've always, always, *always* wanted to do this!"

Carefree for a moment, she shoved off the mirror with her feet, flying across the room but misjudging her speed. Her intuitive control of the gravity field flared her neatly into a foot-down landing, but momentum she hadn't bled off enough stumbled her into the wall and she bumped her nose.

"Ouch! Maybe I'd better move this outdoors, until I get the technique down a little better."

But out on the patio she thought twice: too much light, best wait until dusk. Besides, Josh and Ham would be back soon, and she needed to clean up the dojo. Also, she had to eat something, and shower before they got home, so she wouldn't display for them again at dinner what a bottomless pit she had become for food.

Suddenly she realized that her entire focus for the past four hours had been inward. She sent her consciousness radar horizon shooting southward to its outer range, and saw immediately that the Beast had moved, this time more north than west, and about 400 miles closer to her. I'll check the position on the globe upstairs, she thought. But he's pretty resourceful, given that part of the world, catching a rides west and then north. She presumed both rides had been aircraft, given the distance he'd covered. She pondered what that might mean as she used her new skill to float up the stairs to the kitchen to feed her suddenly ravening hunger.

Chapter 14

"Hot diggety dog!" Adrienne Baxter approved her programming handiwork as she slouched back in her chair and studied the bright green circles plotting sequentially onto the underlying map. Then, reflecting more on the operational aspects of her construct as a possible tracking program, she added *Pause, Continue, Exit* and *Restart* buttons on the bottom of the plot screen beside the date/time box, and changed the display rate to one plot every five seconds. She sat back and watched it run again, grinning her satisfaction at the elegance of six hours of raw data synthesized down into 24 circles, each representing an average location for one 15-minute time period. The circles and their crosshair coordinates plotted onto the screen every five seconds, one after the other, digital footprints of an alien on earth. Six hours of movement had been condensed down to two minutes of run time, just lovely, she admitted.

Nathan Rodgers, coming out of his office into the data center, watched the code cycle through its plotted displays, and grinned himself.

"Adrienne, that's incredible! Is that saying what I think it's saying?"

"Yessir, Doctor Rodgers, it's a sequential plot of the best-fit 15-minute average locations of the source that's affecting these six GCDs."

"And the circles represent what, Adrienne?"

"A two-sigma uncertainty envelope—there's about 95 percent statistical confidence that the source is within the circle." She smiled at him nervously. "This assumes a normal distribution, and some other things we have no physical knowledge about. I wouldn't want to defend it in my senior thesis class. But I think it's good enough for our purposes right now."

"Wow! I agree, Adrienne, it's plenty good enough for now. Why are the circles different sizes?"

"Well, weaker signals during a 15-minute time block make the circles bigger. Physically this makes sense—if you're less confident about the position of the source, you have to draw a bigger circle to be 95 percent sure the source is within the circle.

"The second factor is movement. If the source is moving around rather than staying stationary during the 15-minute time block, the position fluctuates, and you have to expand the circle to accommodate the movement. This also makes sense physically. But I'm pretty sure my code is giving a good approximation for the average location within each 15-minute period."

The circles sequentially appearing and disappearing on the screen varied from about three miles to less than a mile across, by the scale at the bottom of the map. Nathan watched them for a moment.

"Adrienne, is there any way to tighten down the uncertainty statistic to try to get smaller circles, a more precise location?"

"Maybe, sir, but I'd need to know a lot more about the nature of the effect, I think." She smiled nervously again. "And what would we do if we knew the exact location? Drive down and ring the doorbell?"

Nathan smiled back at his assistant, but shivered a little at the question.

"This is plenty good enough, Adrienne," he repeated. "Can you put this display up on the website, so our new friend at Goddard can look at it? Then if the thing starts moving, he'll have its digital footprints. Consciousness footprints. Whatever that means." He shivered some more.

"Yessir, I can do that. I'll automate the solution code to upload the display to our website a few minutes after the end of each 15-minute time block. So every time he logs in and accesses the page, he'll be looking at a display that includes the most recent time period." And won't that just blow his socks right off, she thought excitedly, warmed by the idea of the gift she was about to deliver to a man she'd never met but already liked enormously.

"Okay, Adrienne, great! But before you do that, can we look at what's happened since noontime? We should be able to get up to almost..." he looked at his watch, "three o'clock?"

"No problem, Doctor Rodgers. She checked to verify her code continued to execute automatically, then hit *Enter*. The display obediently cycled through its 15-minute circular plots, one every five seconds. For the first eight plots, the crosshairs indicating the solved position didn't move much, and the green circles stayed about the same size they had been in the late morning. Then, the 1400 plot showed a sharply decreased circle, slightly under half a mile. They both inhaled sharply, noting that the crosshairs for the solved position hadn't shifted much at all. The green circle stayed small through the next three plots, the crosshairs changing very little. This brought them right up to the present time.

"Well, I guess that from noon to now," Adrienne offered, "the source isn't moving; it's just sitting there in one spot. Then about an hour ago, the signal must have gotten a lot stronger, but the position stayed stationary. So, it looks right now like the thing is still sitting in one spot, but putting out a lot more... more... juice... more consciousness activity... whatever that may mean." She paused the cycle on the last 15-minute time block.

"Looks like it may be in a park," Nathan observed, squinting at the underlying map through his bifocals. "What's that say, Montrose Park? Probably a residential area around it, wouldn't you say?"

Adrienne eyed the map speculatively. "I don't know, sir. I visited Georgetown University last year and walked around Georgetown, and a lot of that was old brownstone houses. But Georgetown itself is further south, I think. I don't know if I've ever been in this part of DC."

"Well, Adrienne, we're just speculating at this point. If you upload your plotting output to the website, I'll email our friend Aaron. He's tied into the government more than we are, so we'll lay it on him and he can take it from there." He smiled at her and walked back into his office to compose his thoughts. Then he typed:

From: nrrodgers@princeton.edu

To: aaron.omeara@gsfc.gov

Subject: Further re GCD Anomaly

Dear Aaron,

Thanks for your very informative and forthcoming response. Adrienne called me in, and I've independently verified everything she's done to evaluate the anomaly. We both believe the data are real, and reflect a real event. Of course, we didn't have any idea what that event might be until we heard from you.

In response to your specific questions:

(1) No known physical phenomena could cause the effects noted for the initial event. Solar flares or subatomic wavefronts may cause an occasional bit to flip in a computer, but nothing in a GCD should be affected. We've never seen any anomalies in the network traceable to magnetic storms or northern lights or anything else like that.

(2) All of the GCDs produced identical effects at the same time, irrespective of which side of the planet they were on. The slight timing differences are all attributable to minor discrepancies in GCD computer clock settings. I ran an exhaustive check on this.

(3) On your amplitude-to-distance question, Adrienne is working up something for you. When you next log onto our homepage, just add /psblet.htm. We've decided to call the parameter signal strength rather than amplitude, because that's a more general term for a phenomenon

we don't really understand at this point. I gather you are busy with your exercise, but hope you can find a few minutes to give us a call after you look at this. Adrienne can probably explain it better over the phone than I can in an email. It's pretty complex, and more than a little intuitive, but I believe it's scientifically and mathematically sound. We would like your feedback. In view of possible security issues, while this page has been added to our website, it is not otherwise disclosed or indexed for public access. So, its existence will not be known to anyone but you and us, for the time being.

Thanks again for sharing your information with us. Hope to hear from you soon.

Nathan Rodgers

PS. I believe we met at a post-doc reunion several years ago, and you had some very enlightening ideas on global consciousness? Big shock of curly red hair? Are you that O'Meara?

"The new page is online, Doctor Rodgers," Adrienne yelled from the other room.

"Perfect timing," he yelled back. Then he added their direct phone line numbers and hit *Send* on his email panel.

Goddard Space Flight Center, Greenbelt, MD | Sunday 1526 EDT

Aaron O'Meara, on a mid-afternoon break from the SDI exercise, wheeled excitedly down to his office, hoping for some response from the Global Consciousness Project. The incoming email icon blinked at him on his computer monitor.

"Hot off the press," he noted, "only 4 minutes ago! Eeehahh! And this one is from the main man himself."

Aaron paused to gather his composure, then double-clicked on the incoming message. He studied the message thoughtfully for the several seconds, then smiled broadly.

"Well, Doctor Nathan Rodgers, sir, aren't you just the very thing! And yes, I am that O'Meara. And yes, we did meet, and I busted your balls pretty good, but you seem to have taken that in a more positive light than maybe I intended, so I'm not complaining. Let's see what my babe Adrienne has ginned up for me!"

He keyed in as instructed and his reward was a webpage titled *Washington DC Area Anomaly*. It had a brief instruction set, date and time entry boxes for begin and end times, and an explanation that the circle represented a 95 per cent probability the source was inside it. He noted the 15-minute time block arrangement and its 5-second display rate.

"Jesus," he said to his empty office, truly startled, "is this gonna be what I think it's gonna be?"

He typed in 0600 in the *Start Time* box and, checking his watch, *1515* in the *End Time* box, then hit *Enter*. The entry webpage yielded to a map of the DC area that covered the northwest quadrant of the city and a small slice of Virginia across the Potomac. He watched the display cycle through once from start time to end time, and then watched it again.

"Wow! Wowee! What more could I want?" He pondered the shifting positions of the crosshairs, and the changing sizes of the circles. Okay, he thought, she's obviously triangulating source location somehow from the different signals at the six devices, but she's also carrying some sort of error band estimator along with the locations. So we can't necessarily tell from this whether the thing is moving or just generating signals of different... signal strength. Besides, it's a 15-minute average position and confidence interval.

Then it dawned on him why she did it that way. It was the best tradeoff: intelligibility of the display versus the complexity of the analysis. Laughing with pure delight at the mathematical elegance coupled to common sense, he grabbed his phone and punched the number offered in the email.

"Good afternoon. Global Consciousness Project. This is Nathan Rodgers."

"Hi, Nate, this is *that* Aaron O'Meara, and I'm so glad we met that time, because that made me think about whether your network might have had some response to the event this morning, and I'm so pleased to talk to you again, because you're giving me some world-class analysis here, and I gotta tell you, that Adrienne Baxter is an absolute genius," the stream-of-consciousness words piled hurriedly from his mouth, "which is a really good thing because I have a suspicion we're gonna need all the genius we can get to deal with this event we got cookin' here, whaddya think?"

"Hello, Aaron. We were hoping you'd find time to call. Hang on, let me patch in Adrienne...

"Adrienne, meet Aaron O'Meara, Princeton alumnus and government astrophysicist. Aaron, meet Adrienne Baxter, Princeton undergraduate and part-time GCP analyst."

Aaron was dumbfounded. An *under*graduate? With that sort of analysis capability? Holy shit, she had to be way, way off the charts!

"Hi, Aaron," she said in a soft contralto. Then, more softly, tentatively, "I love your mind."

"And... and..." Aaron stuttered, "I love yours, Adrienne... I can't believe you're an undergraduate. From the level of the stuff you've done here, I figured you were a Ph.D. candidate or maybe a post-doc."

Silence from Adrienne, but he heard Nathan chuckle. His reaction evidently was not unusual.

"Listen, folks," Aaron collected himself, saying, "I've only got a minute or two, then I have to get back to the exercise. I'm off around six this evening and after that I'll have three days available.

"Adrienne, your plotting routine is superb. The statistics you carried along to estimate the 95 per cent confidence circles must be pretty intuitive, but I trust them completely. I understand the tradeoffs you made to come up with a simple and understandable display, and I think it was exactly the right choice. Exactly!

"Now, I've got just a couple of questions. Can we look at the South America event with the same method? You probably don't have the same density in your GCD array down there, so it may not work at all. But maybe you could coax something out of it by changing the control parameters? Maybe relaxing the confidence interval?

"And, can you set something up where we can pick on a particular 15-minute time period of interest, and go back to its raw or intermediate data, and separate the source position changes from the signal strength changes? That might help to pinpoint locations better, if we should ever need to do that.

"And, last, can you generalize the code to be independent of the geographic location, so we could track these things if they start to move?" Aaron smiled at the silence on the other end of the line, visualizing their minds working out the implications.

Finally, Nathan Rodgers spoke. "I guess we could get to the point of needing that sort of information, couldn't we? I mean we as a country, or the government? DOD or the FBI or Homeland Security?"

"Mmm, guess we could," Aaron agreed noncommittally, keeping his voice neutral.

"I like the FBI for this one," Adrienne observed, "after all, it's clearly an X-File... Aaron, the answer to your first two questions is yes.

"I'll take a shot at South America, see what I can come up with. That's pretty easy, but it may not produce anything useful. There isn't much of an array down that way, and so the error bands will be high.

"I've already started thinking about signal strength versus position movement, and there's a way to do that, I think.

"But your third question, generalizing our little locator system into a tracking system for mobile sources? That will take a fair amount of thought and probably an awful lot of trial-and-error, and isn't going to happen very quickly. But I think maybe I can do it."

"Adrienne, that's great! You truly are a wizard! Listen, folks, I gotta go, they're hollering at me to come back to the exercise. I'll call you around six, or maybe a little before. Bye, Nathan. Bye, Adrienne." Aaron O'Meara hung up his phone, and wheeled off hurriedly down the hall, yelling that he was on his way.

Global Consciousness Project, Princeton University, NJ | Sunday 1540 EDT

Adrienne still felt the warm blush at Aaron O'Meara's compliments as she hung up the phone, and wondered why. *All sorts of people have been telling me about my talent for years. I'm always complimented, but it really doesn't mean much. Like telling an athlete they've got nice muscles. I mean, it's a so what, it's just who I am. But somehow it's wonderfully nice to hear it from Aaron. That's really weird!*

"Well, Adrienne, a fascinating conversation, huh?" Nathan Rodgers interrupted her reflection by walking out into the computer center, "and it brings up an interesting dilemma, doesn't it?"

"*A* dilemma," she responded, laughing. "*A* dilemma? Just *which* dilemma did you have in mind, Doctor Rodgers?"

He laughed with her. "Well, my immediate one is that I told our GCD operator volunteers I'd keep them posted on our analysis results. I for sure can't tell them we think two ETs have landed, and show them your locator plots. That would go public in about 30 seconds and likely pre-empt anything the government might need to do. But if I don't tell them something pretty quick, we're going to get buried by emails and then the phones will start to ring off the hook, even if it is Sunday and a holiday weekend."

"Oh, Doctor Rodgers, that's easy, I think. Look, here are the 1-minute integrals of departure from random," she keyed back several screens and gestured at her monitor, "these are the building blocks for the 15-minute averages that I used to plot the location circles." The monitor screen showed a time-trend plot of the six DC area GCDs, six jagged lines connecting the 1-minute data across a 15-minute time span.

"We could give them these graphs, or maybe bar-chart equivalents, along with the 1-minute integrals in a little numeric table underneath it that they could download. Without any information on the external event to connect it to, they'd probably stay occupied just trying to figure out what's going on with the GCDs.

How about that?" She tapped keys, advancing through several 15-minute time blocks to show her Director how it might look on a web page.

"Oh, and I need to do a variation of this anyway, to answer Aaron's first question," she added, "so I could kill two birds with one stone."

"I like that." Nathan deepened his voice, "Make it so, Data!"

"Aye, Captain," she replied, giggling but at the same time thinking that Hollywood might not be too far off the mark after all.

"And what dilemmas are at the top of *your* list, Adrienne," Nathan asked.

"Oh," she said, pausing thoughtfully, looking into the monitor as if the answer were inside, "maybe not dilemmas at this point, because we don't have any decisions to make just yet. Maybe more like questions. Why are they here? Have they been here before? Why are there two of them? When will they come together, and why?"

The Director's bushy eyebrows notched up over his bifocals.

"Adrienne? What makes you think they're going to get together?"

She looked at him owlishly, a dreamy smile counterpointing her wide eyes.

"They will come together. I know they will. I don't know what makes me think that. But I just know it somehow. I'm absolutely positive. It's very strange... but I know."

Georgetown University, Washington, DC | Sunday 1610 EDT

The light titanium-Kevlar racquet whipped upward through the tennis ball, driving it over the net and down the line, where its topspin dropped it neatly just inside the baseline.

"That's it, me lad, that's it! The very thing! Crouch down. Get the racquet head way low. Bring it up through the ball with the face perpendicular, nice and vertical. Follow through high. Yes! Do it again! Here!" Hamilton O'Donnell hit another ball to Joshua's backhand side. Repeating the same motions, Joshua drove the ball hard, coming up from a crouch, stepping into his two-handed swing, putting his legs and body into it, swinging from low to high. He smiled slightly as the hard-hit ball dropped sharply from its topspin, marking the clay of the court within a foot of the previous mark. Sweat saturated his shirt. When you practiced with Uncle Ham, you *worked*, he thought. But then, his uncle's Zen-ish training methods worked, so that made it all worthwhile.

"And that's a bit of alright, now, isn't it, Joshua? Now that you're good and tired, and a proper match for an old man, why, we'll play a few sets!"

Joshua laughed and drank some water, and then they got into it, a wonderful glorious dance of a game, as fine as any they'd ever played. His uncle, agile and fit to a degree completely belying his apparent age, had the skill and finesse that comes from years of playing the game. But Joshua was young and flexible and blindingly fast; on a clay court he could run down impossible shots. The boy won in a third-set tie-breaker, 11-9, one of just a handful of times he'd beaten his teacher. His uncle dropped his racquet and applauded the winning shot, a blazing two-handed backhand down the line.

"Ah, Joshua, me lad, a great game. You had me hoppin' out there like a herrin' on a griddle! Your topspin off the backhand is nigh onto perfection, now!"

As they walked off the court and down to the locker room, Joshua picked up the thread of the conversation they'd had leaving the Smithsonian.

"Talking about spin, Uncle Ham, and the negative social consequences around disclosure of a new species... and what Mom said about keeping things under wraps? About being cautious?"

"Yes, me lad," Hamilton said, tousling the boy's sweaty hair, "consequences. Definitely. But God in heaven, what do they have to do with the spin on a tennis ball?"

"Maybe if you could put the right kind of spin on the disclosure, the bad consequences could be eliminated? Or at least minimized to some acceptable level?" Joshua's mind hadn't stopped trying to work out how the variables in this puzzle might be modified to increase the probability of a good outcome, the outcome he really wanted—acceptance of his mother's new kind of humanity, with no one seeking gain or power from the evolutionary leap. Spin was a wild-card variable he had neglected in his earlier analyses. The insight came suddenly as he admired how effectively and consistently his topspin dropped the ball inside the baseline. Properly applied, the spin worked every time. That was just elementary physics and aerodynamics, foolproof. Maybe there was a social analog, he thought.

"Oh, Joshua, such a question! I swear to God this town runs on spin. Good PR practitioners make a fortune here. Whether even the best of them could spin a solution that would avoid the consequences of disclosure, I do not know. But I suspect it is not possible. The issue of emergence of a new species, a *Nova sapiens*, simply would be too big, too new, too threatenin' to the establishment. The temptation to control this power would be just too great. Your mom is dead-on right to be cautious."

Joshua processed his uncle's input, and as the hot water of the shower washed congealing sweat and clay dust off his young body, his logic washed disclosure down the drain along with them. It just wasn't a good option. In the adjacent stall, his uncle belted out *The Rose of Tralee* in a passable baritone, singing into the shower like a man without a care in the world.

Global Consciousness Project, Princeton University, NJ | Sunday 1647 EDT

"Doctor Rodgers," Adrienne called out to her boss, "the analysis for 1-minute deviations from randomness is uploaded. If you don't like it, holler. I'm gonna work on South America next."

Nathan Rodgers waved acknowledgment from his office desk and called up her new webpage. A bar chart format, he saw. Date and time down the left margin, starting with this morning at 0600 EDT at the top of the page. Horizontal bars, one per minute, representing signal strength, a measure of the degree of departure from randomness. Numeric values were tagged on the ends of the bars. Only six GCDs were presented on a display, but that's about all a website format would fit on a typical monitor and still be intelligible, he thought. The big flat-screen monitor in the computer room would fit ten, maybe more. He changed the GCD identifiers in the entry menu to look at the South America anomaly.

Aha! Where there had been only three GCDs responding, now there appeared a fourth, in Costa Rica. The bars were flat on the zero margin up until 1355, and then they started to build, an increasing but fluctuating pattern up until the last datum listed, at 1630. Was it just signal strength increasing, or actual movement toward Costa Rica, he wondered.

"Well, let's see," he muttered, adding in the plot for the Bogota GCD. That signal was continually present from 0600 to 1630, with some big spikes in the late morning. He added in the plot for Quito. It was a less pronounced version of Bogota. It had the same spiking pattern in the late morning... but then, was that a trend downward, starting around 1400? Maybe. But definitely downward after 1600. So what does all that tell me, he wondered, adding in the plot for Panama City in the Canal Zone.

"Oh, yeah! Yeah! Now you're giving me something," he exclaimed. The Panama City display showed the same late-morning spiking pattern, but then a clear increasing trend to a high level, steadying out around 1430 and holding there until it started to drop off after 1600.

Nathan walked over to the big map covering the inside wall of his office, showing the location of every GCD in the world-wide network of his Global Consciousness Project. He studied the geography, the four GCD locations in Central and South America, the distances between them.

He walked back to his desk and printed out the display of the four sites, the bar charts for the ten and one-half hours since 0600 that morning. He cut the four bar charts out of the printout, long skinny paper strips, and taped each onto the map next to its GCD location.

Nathan studied the map and the bar charts alternately, until there was no doubt left. Then he yelled out his office door, "Hey, Adrienne, the ET in South America is moving out!"

She came into his office and stood beside him, studying the map and the four small bar charts he'd taped to it.

"I know, Doctor Rodgers," she replied, giggling nervously, "I know. I told you so. They're going to come together!"

Chapter 15

"Sir, would you like dinner," the flight attendant repeated. She bent down to touch passenger John Connard's muscled forearm, drawing him out of his meditative state. He blinked at her and smiled.

"I'm sorry to disturb you, sir, but if you would like dinner, here in first class we offer chicken cordon bleu, or filet mignon. Both are excellent today, I'm told."

"Thank you. I'll have one of each, if you have extra," he said, smiling more at her, "I had a busy day, didn't get enough to eat."

The Magician dropped back into his reverie, trying to diagnose the intermittent sense of being probed. It had been a feathery touch on his consciousness, barely perceptible, but definitely real. Pulling those sensations now to the forefront of his consciousness, to the analytical part of his mind, he tried to dissect them, to infer the power and intelligence behind them, to benchmark their implied capabilities against his own.

It is good to reflect, when there is opportunity. The Other is cunning, John Connard, and appears to have picked a host with a subtle and formidable mind. That much we can deduce from the nature of the contact.

The Magician struggled to strip the camouflage off the image that had touched his consciousness. A hologram took shape in his mind-space: a brilliant green aura around an interior darkness. When he tried to examine it, the darkness became a shifting, impenetrable, unknowable black emptiness. It pulsated and changed shape like some primeval organism, some all-devouring amoeba. It defeated attempts by his mental eye to pin it down or see into it. It shifted and slid around the edges of his mind, much as the null field had shifted and slid around the edges of his physical eyes.

The darkness in the picture is a true representation: the absence of a connection between the personality and the soul. In your species, as in ours, this is a sure sign of the criminally insane. It is a force running rampant, unable to find its frame of reference; it is schizophrenic, sociopathic, amoral. There is no light, no goodness, in this thing.

John pondered the meaning of such a missing connection, feeling how terrifying it must be, sensing the danger in it. He wondered if he were the same kind of being.

This is a monster, a creature totally unlike you, John Connard. You have a dark side, but are fundamentally good. You do not hurt children, even if they are enemy soldiers, and you free them for a second chance. You have such a reverence for life you give even a lowly spider a chance to survive. You have a connection to your ki, your soul, and through that, to the essence of all creatures and all creation.

Strange in a soldier, he thought, tempered by battle, skilled in methods of destruction. Strange that I care so much.

No, not strange at all. You act from love. Even as the soldier, or the Magician, or the Assassin, you act from love.

"Hah!" John snorted aloud, rejecting the implausibility of the Assassin acting from love. But then the concept caught him: if the Assassin were an instrument, and not an entity? He chewed over that possibility as he chewed his steak.

Dinnertime in the Connard household of his youth had always been a time for philosophical discussions, a raucous and at times hilarious exchange of views, frequently argumentative but always loving. His father Jacob played the soldier-philosopher. His mother Arabel played the scholar-artist. Both were open-minded and nurturing to his young mind, as well as to Jessica's. The parents took their children's views seriously, respected them, questioned them. Made *him* question them, he suddenly realized. With a tidal wave of sadness rolling over him, he realized how much he missed those discussions, how much he had loved his family, how much he had lost. And how different he had become... especially as the Assassin.

I do *not* act from love, he postulated into the mind-space between him and his nexus. I act from vengeance. I act from justice. I am the beast you claim I'm not.

In response, the image of Duc Li smiled: gently, inscrutably, not judging, much the way his parents had smiled at him. Probably the same way he sometimes had smiled at Jessica: the wisdom of more years.

Ah, John Connard! You evaluate potential targets to paint on your growing canvas of death. You judge them. You select them. And yes, you believe that what you deliver to those you select is vengeance and justice. But vengeance and justice are moral constructs, human creations, useful social tools for an evolving species that has only limited knowledge of their greater selves. The greater consciousness does not judge; it delivers neither vengeance nor justice. It delivers balance. You are its instrument; you act from a deeper place than vengeance, or even justice. You act from love, to redress balance. You are far, far above the level of the beast.

Well, if I ever needed a good rationalization to keep myself sane in our little drug war, John thought, there it is: I'm acting from love.

A rationalization? Gentle amusement played across his mind-space. *Your St.*

Augustine said a similar thing: 'War is love's response to a neighbor threatened by force.' I believe you act from love.

Distracted, he murmured the obvious question aloud into the aircraft cabin. "If love is at stake here, then instead of destruction why not offer the Other love and redemption?"

"I'm sorry, sir, I missed what you just said," the flight attendant asked, coming up the aisle behind him.

"I said I loved the steak," he ad-libbed, smiling at her. She smiled back uncertainly and took away his empty plate, delivering the chicken cordon blue and another beer.

The Other is beyond redemption. It would turn any such offer to its own advantage, and use it against you. The Other would subvert your entire race, and bring down disaster on the known universe.

"Umm." The Magician pondered, tasting the hot chicken and cheese acutely with his heightened senses, savoring the offsetting tang of the cold beer, its bubbles seeming to explode on his palate in tiny detonations of pleasure. *How many of God's creatures truly are beyond redemption, I wonder?*

After you eat, you should rest, John Connard. It has been a long and wearying day. Seek that empty space Duc Li has shown you, your eye of the storm, and be one with it. That will help me also, since we are organically as well as psychically interwoven. I too am weary and need rest to regain my strength.

The concept of what his nexus considered to be *rest* floated into the Magician's mind-space. The edges of it faded off into dimensions he didn't grasp, but the center was clear enough: regrowth.

Ah, John thought into his mind-space, so this is not really natural for you. In fact it's quite difficult. You are not omnipotent beings. I had no idea!

Of course you didn't. I go, but I remain here with you also. The image of Duc Li, palpably exhausted, faded into those other dimensions, condensing down to a warm dot of diffuse white light in John's mind-space, but somehow leaving an impression of that gentle smile behind to keep him company.

Flight 152 flew northward through darkening azure skies, carrying the Magician, the Assassin, onward to his encounter with the enemy.

Global Consciousness Project, Princeton University, NJ | Sunday 1725 EDT

Walking back into the computer room at the Global Consciousness Project, Adrienne Baxter studied her adaptation of the code. The algorithms that had worked so flawlessly for the signal source in the Washington area did not convert well to the source in South America. The location crosshairs jumped around radically between sequential 15-minute time blocks, some of them moving over water off the coast of Colombia and then back again. The probability circles were so large they covered enormous expanses of land and water.

"Hmpf," she addressed the unhelpful data, "I need to look at you puppies a little differently, I think... well, maybe... hmm. Sure doesn't look like these signal strengths drop off nearly as sharply with distance, so there's a hypothesis. That ought to be easy enough to test...."

She keyed back into her code, did a *Save As* and renamed it, and changed the negative exponent in the distance-strength equation from 1.6 to 1.0. Then she reran the 15-minute location solutions. The sequence of circled crosshairs marched obediently out in time, one plot every five seconds. But the crosshairs no longer danced erratically all over the geography of that part of the world, and the circles had shrunk considerably.

"Aha," she breathed out, honoring intuition.

Nathan Rodgers, in his adjacent office, simultaneously let out a deep breath, composing an email:

To: aaron.omeara@gsfc.gov

From: nrrrodgers@princeton.edu

Subject: Status Update

Aaron,

(1) Please take a look at the 1-minute integrals that Adrienne loaded onto our website—just hit /anomaly from the main page. This gets at your question of separating movement from signal strength, in a way. She will no doubt come up with a more elegant method, but this is pretty good for now. It's a little subjective—you have to study the trends and look at them together, and draw your own inferences, but it works for me.

(2) I'm convinced our visitor from South America is on the move, headed northward. When you get to the anomaly page, just use the popup to select the GCD locations you want, and enter the date/times for the period you want to look at, and you'll see a display of the 1-minute signal strengths. Look at the data strings for Bogota in Colombia, Quito in Ecuador, San Jose in Costa Rica, and Panama City in the Canal Zone. Study them at the same time you're looking at a map of that part of the world and you'll see what I mean!

(3) Adrienne believes the two signal sources are going to get together somehow. She can't say why, but she's got a strong intuition about it. What

them getting together would mean, of course, we have no idea.
Call us when you're free, we'll be here.

Nathan

As the Director clicked the *Send* button on his email screen, Adrienne Baxter leaned back in her chair and rubbed her head. Momentarily at a loss on how best to deal with the tracking issue once the signal sources started to get closer together, the hiatus finally allowed her hunger pangs to be recognized.

"Doctor Rodgers", she called, "I'm starved. I just realized I haven't had anything since breakfast. Could we send out for a pizza or grinders or something?"

"Oh, Adrienne! Of course," he smiled as he walked out of the office. "Jeez, I shouldn't get so absorbed in the battle I forget to feed the troops! And I'm hungry myself, now that you remind me. How 'bout a quick walk to the deli? Clear our minds a bit before our next conversation with Aaron?"

Goddard Space Flight Center, Greenbelt, MD | Sunday 1730 EDT

Aaron O'Meara rolled down the hall, pleased that he'd performed so well on the SDI exercise when his mind really had been elsewhere. He mentally reviewed the final summation of his intended briefing to his boss. Lord knows what he's going to do with it, he thought. I don't know what the hell I would do in his shoes. The evidence is all there, sure as flies on a cow flop. But the trouble is, hits on consciousness detectors is not classic scientific analysis. I see it, clear as a bell, but he may not.

"Aaron!" Edwin Edwards yelled out as he entered the far end of the long hallway. "Okay, I'm here early, I got ten minutes for you, like you asked. So let's hear it!"

Uh-oh, thought Aaron, the man sounds irascible, pressure from the exercise, not much sleep, and then I dump this on him. He reversed his wheelchair and turned through the doorway to the backup X-Room, silently waving Edwards to follow.

"Aaron, my wife told me our video of this morning's event was on the noon news. I called the Pentagon on my way in, and they told me it's public; they're not gonna classify it. So if you want to send the video to Princeton, be my guest. Just keep in mind that the official story is a rogue asteroid breaking up, so Goddard's name doesn't need to be associated with any alternative theories. Not any. Okay? Now, what have you got?"

"It's all here for you, Ed, the whole story. I made a copy of everything, and put it in this folder." Aaron briefly recapped the event, his thought processes about consciousness and its anomalous effects on the GCD network, his emails and phone conversation with Nathan Rodgers and Adrienne Baxter. He spread out the consecutive printouts, one 15-minute position plot per page, the green circles and crosshairs superimposed on a map of northwest Washington. Edwin Edwards listened attentively, nodding his appreciation.

"Jeesh, Aaron, an undergraduate? This is a kid? She did this from scratch? In SAS? And then dumped it as a display on a web page? Holy shit! She's some kind of serious programming talent! You think maybe we could recruit her for Goddard?"

"Maybe. When I talk to her again I'll just mention what a great place this is to work," Aaron nodded agreement with his boss's assessment. "But what do you conclude, Ed, when you look at this stuff? Do we have disintegrating rocks here, or do we have ETs?"

Edwin Edwards, Ph.D., astrophysicist, a respected senior member of a rarified strata of the scientific community, stood above the conference table, shuffling the printouts around as he pondered. Aaron watched him struggle, and manfully refrained from saying anything. The man surprised him.

"Aaron, I think you're right. Fundamental scientific method. William of Ockham. I just can't escape the old bugger's razor."

"Okay, Ed," Aaron rejoiced in his new convert but carefully kept his voice neutral, "so what do we do about it?"

"Nothing."

"Nothing?" Aaron's jaw dropped. "Nothing?"

"Oh, I'll bundle up your package here in an email and send it off to the Pentagon as a possibility they may want to pursue. That will keep Goddard's ass covered. But I'm not inclined to press it. I mean, if these ETs are going to get together here on the planet, then maybe it's some kind of rescue mission. Would we want to intervene? Should we? Think about it. There are lots of possibilities here, besides your dogfight in space. Not all of them necessarily are bad. And there wasn't any damage done when they came down, was there?"

"Mmm," Aaron acknowledged, "I hadn't thought about it that way." Edwards certainly offered a plausible alternative.

"You cool with that approach, Aaron?"

"I guess so, Ed. It covers us, anyway. It passes the buck along. Whether anybody will stop the buck or not is a crapshoot."

"Aaron, for the next three days, you're on break. Just a plain old pure civilian, on your own. DOD elected not to classify the event, and they showed the tapes publicly, and the information is out. So work with the consciousness project folks at Princeton all you want. Have a blast. But if you wouldn't mind, just keep your cell phone handy. If shit hits the fan we may need to call you. And if something interesting starts to happen up at Princeton, please, *please* keep me updated with a call or an email. Unofficially. Okay?"

"Yessir," Aaron smiled at the compromise solution, and wheeled back to his office to make another phone call to his new friends and ET detectives, Nathan and Adrienne.

American Airlines Flight 152 Enroute to Miami | Sunday 1740 EDT

A smile and love and white light, thought the Magician, now there's a lesson for me. He thought of his lover, the only person still alive in this world who represented those things to him. He created a vision of her in his mind, radiantly happy, smiling at him. During a mission, he forced such memories out of his mind. The Magician and the Assassin could not be encumbered by distracting emotions: to be other than totally focused is to be dead.

But for now... for now I'm just John Connard, ex-soldier, he thought. I'm between missions. I have—he glanced at his watch—an hour, almost two, of peace and safety until we land in Miami. I can be myself. I can think about her, about the love and light she's brought into my life.

He shaped the pillow under his neck, reclined his seat, smiled at the flight attendant, and followed the lesson of his nexus into his own meditative state, seeking his *eye of the storm*. Yes, the storm is coming, he thought, no doubt about that at all. He visualized a hurricane, as viewed from an orbiting weather satellite, and formed the icon in his mind-space. Bands spiraled at the periphery, and dark wall clouds spun tightly around the center. But the eye upwelled warm moist air, a lightness and clarity to it, a place of serenity and calm in the middle of turbulence and destruction. There, there is my peace, he thought, there in the eye. He dropped toward it, making his mind-space empty, visualizing it as a blank piece of antique writing slate.

Memories of her smiles and light and love chalked a large heart on the slate. He fell alongside it, down into the calm eye of his storm. The rough slate surface faded into the lightly-tanned, smooth skin of her back as he remembered precisely how his finger once had traced a smiling heart upon it.

That loving and erotic memory welcomed him deeper into the eye of his storm, and he embraced it. This airplane would be over the Caymans right about now, a distant part of his consciousness noted. Ah, that had been a wonderful interlude, all smiles and love and that astonishing tropical island light. The shoal water green, the outer water deep blue, the sand and coral brilliant white. His mind spun back, dropping unerringly into those memories.

They had rented a two-person sea kayak and paddled it around the less-traveled areas of Grand Cayman, packing snorkeling gear and lunch. As they shipped their paddles and coasted into a deserted lagoon, he had traced a smiling heart in the sweat of her back, below the bikini strap. She laughed with delight and smiled back at him over her shoulder.

"On the way back, bub, you get to sit in front so I can do that to you. And so I can admire how your sweaty muscles slide over your ribs when you paddle," she added. "It's just such a delicious, primitive sight. Now I know how those Polynesian women felt on those long canoe rides. Makes me horny as hell."

For three days that February, not two months after they met, they had paddled and played and made love all around the island. Neither of them had ever been in a relationship that, almost instantly, seemed so natural. Neither of them was sure how it had happened or why. But clearly it was magical.

Relaxed into a meditative state on Flight 152, John fell deeper into his metaphorical eye of the storm. The rotating clouds at the storm's edge spun themselves into soft cotton and cocooned his soul in warmth as his thoughts drifted back to the time when they first met.

Chapter 16

Adrienne and Nathan were munching on their deli sandwiches in the computer room when she belatedly recognized the subtle difference in the data displaying on the big monitor screen.

"Aw, wow! Look, Doctor Rodgers," she yelled, "the South America signal dropped off at Ecuador, and picked up at Jamaica. For the signal to drop off that quick, and get picked up by another GCD like that, it's just gotta be in an airplane. We weren't gone that long getting sandwiches, we just missed it when we came back! It's on the move again, north!"

"Ah! So your instincts are right, Adrienne!" Rodgers swallowed hard to get the last bite of sandwich past the sudden lump in his throat. "Okay! Get the best positions you can on it, and I'll put stickies on the wall map. When we've got it near an airport, I'll check what airlines service it and when the flights leave, and see if there's a match for time and direction. I can pull that kind of information off the internet, I think."

"Yeah! That's a great idea! For starters, let's go back and see what happens when we first start to pick it up on more detectors!" She looked at her boss for agreement. He nodded, and her fingers flew across the keyboard.

"Look at this, sir, it hung around..." she continued, squinting at the geographic outline on the screen, "...Panama... for a couple of hours, it looks like. Then it started moving again. The average direction would be about due north. So I'd look for departures to the states, between say three o'clock and five o'clock this afternoon, our time, out of Panama."

"Yup," Nathan agreed, "and we're probably in the same time zone—about the same longitude. Maybe an hour different; I can check. Okay, Adrienne, you keep plugging away on your scheme to generalize the tracking algorithm. I've got to take a bathroom break, and then I'll track down the flights out of Panama. That will tell us something about our South American ET, won't it?"

Yeah, that's right, Adrienne thought, it *will* tell us something. Like our ET is pretty resourceful. Got money. Got power. Got the ability to move about without any difficulty in an alien land. But maybe it's not an alien land? So does this signal source have a human persona? An identity? A social security number? A passport?

Just as she abandoned that speculation to begin logging the 15-minute positions, the phone rang.

"GCP Center, this is Adrienne," she answered excitedly.

American Airlines Flight 152 Enroute to Miami | Sunday 1801 EDT

John Connard's spirit felt cocooned in warmth as his dreams spun back through a vortex of memories to when he first met his lover....

New Year's Eve, three and a half years ago, had been unseasonably mild for Washington. He was laying over, staying at the small apartment connected to Alex Shaughnessy's office condo on Water Street, debriefing on the Somalia mission, his third that year. The two men spent the afternoon tracing through financial connections to the drug harvest operations in Burma, plotting and analyzing their mistakes, learning and optimizing for the next mission.

Alex had wanted to drag him along to a formal New Year's Eve dinner party with some of the Georgetown faculty, but John declined. He remained tightly wound, antsy from the mission and the number of troops that died when he had to shoot his way out. The Assassin, not yet fully caged in the back of John's mind, gloated at the destruction, uncaring of the misery or the loss of innocents. The Magician, in the front of his mind, whispered that there should have been a better way, fewer casualties, less collateral damage. Unsettled, John knew he would be poor company at a black-tie, civilized affair.

Alex left, and the Magician studied the financial picture more, looking at the diagrams they'd drawn. He cross-referenced data on the growing computer database, finally isolating the operation's likely paymaster down to one particular Burmese banker. He entered the man's name on their list of candidates for the genomic toxin. Alex would do the detailed research later, using his marvelous shadow network of black ops sources and international intelligence contacts.

John finally pushed himself up from the conference table on which they'd spread their diagrams and work notes. He stretched and walked over to look out the window. The Washington Monument and Jefferson Memorial were visible, brightly lit up against the night. He contemplated them, curiously. That's why I do it, I guess. My little sister Jessica. And all those other innocents, hurt or killed, directly or indirectly, by the disease of drugs. I don't like the collateral casualties when they happen, but it's a decent tradeoff, I guess. It has to be.

The moral questions danced across his conscience, making him even more restless. The thermometer outside the window read 52 degrees and it wasn't dropping. The TV weather channel showed a blocking high parked over Bermuda, with strong advection of a Gulf Coast air mass. The warm front had pushed well north, past New York City into New England. The quixotic weather mirrored his frame of mind.

Ahh, shit, he thought, I'm okay. Alex wouldn't have left me alone if he thought I wasn't. I just need to blow off some steam, have a few beers. Talk to some normal human beings. Maybe find some sweet young thing and get laid. Getting shot at sure does make you horny.

Laughing derisively at himself, he crossed out of the office into the small adjoining apartment. Donning lightweight running shoes, shorts and a jersey with reflective markers, he put the condo key in his pocket and ran lightly out of the building, turning northward on 33rd Street.

He would drive the Assassin's restlessness from his mind, he thought, by running hard up to Tenleytown and back. He would shower, grab a beer and a sandwich in one of the pubs in Georgetown, then come back and watch the fireworks shoot off behind the Monument. And he would do it alone, he decided; his mood was far too foul for company.

Running past the Georgetown Recreation Center, coming up on the parking area behind the shops on Wisconsin Avenue, John caught a brief glimpse through the hedges of three men converging on a woman and child getting out of a sports car. Something furtive about those men, the Magician thought, and picked up his pace to a sprint. She must have heard the men approaching and turned, opening her mouth. The first attacker's fist caught her high on the head and knocked her down, stunned. The second man grabbed the child from behind, covering its mouth. The third was bringing back his foot to kick the woman when the Assassin launched himself over the low-slung car at a dead run and chopped him in the jaw. The assailant spun backwards, bounced off a dumpster and sat down hard on the pavement. Still in play, the Assassin saw, so he stamped on the man's knee, dislocating it, as he moved in on the first attacker. This has to be fast, he thought: just take him out and get to the third one before he can hurt the child.

Adrenaline spiked, and he seemed to float in a slow motion dance as he faked a punch and kicked the attacker in his rib cage. He heard the coughing whoosh of air his kick had displaced from lungs, and rolled smoothly out of the attack, altering his momentum to carry him toward the man holding the child. The assailant with the dislocated knee and broken jaw started to gasp.

As the freeze-frame view of his adrenalined state clicked forward, the Magician saw the tiny preliminary arm movements that presaged a broken neck for the child, and despaired that even his incredible speed might not be enough. But then the child bit down hard on the hand holding him, creating just enough of a distraction. A lightning kick to the man's knee, a driving heel of the hand under his chin, and the child was in John's arms, his captor falling away, unconscious or dead. He set the child down. A boy, he noted.

Then, the Magician's peripheral vision picked up more motion and the hazard it implied before he actually saw it. Instinctively, he moved between the boy and the pistol as it came out from under the first attacker's jacket. He charged forward, sensing it would be too late, hoping only that the combination of small caliber and silencer would preclude anything immediately disabling. The weapon swung upward to his midriff as the man's trigger finger contracted. But the woman, recovering, jammed her elbow in the man's side.

The silenced pistol huffed, and the shot pulled wide, just ticking the Assassin's right hip at the beltline, and the last thing the shooter saw was the sole of a running shoe exploding the cartilage of his nose. The back of his skull slammed into the pavement.

John let the rebound from the kick flip him over backward, and landed in front of the boy. His eyes flickered reflexively over the scene, scanning for other threats. He saw none. The time elapsed had been but seven or eight seconds, he thought. He calmed his breathing.

"You okay, kid?" he asked, turning toward him. The boy nodded yes, speechless.

"You okay, ma'am?" he asked, turning to the woman. She'd rolled to sit up, breathing hard, but held the silenced pistol rock-steady on his chest.

Good presence of mind, John noted, go for the weapon. And she obviously knows how to use it. What have we got here? She's police, probably, or an agency.

"Ah, you won't need that with me, ma'am, I'm really a peaceable soul." He smiled carefully at her and spread his arms, hoping the adrenaline had depleted sufficiently to return his facial expression to more or less normal, and not display the Assassin.

The boy stepped up beside him, taking his hand trustingly. The woman thumbed the safety on, and put the pistol down carefully on the asphalt. She held out her arms for the boy, trembling, and he ran into them. They clung to each other and rocked together.

John looked around at the deserted parking area. This is insane, he thought. Washington, DC, New Year's Eve and nobody around. He quickly checked the attackers. None conscious. One dead or close to it. All showing the pallor of shock, even in the poor lighting.

"Ma'am," he said gently, "we need to get you out of here, you and the boy. You took a pretty good blow to the head; you should have it looked at. You might have a concussion. I'll go out front, call 911. Or do you have a cell phone in your car?" She shook her head no.

Sirens sounded in the distance. Well, somebody heard or saw something and had the presence of mind to call it in, John thought.

The sound galvanized her. She picked up her pocketbook and car keys and the pistol.

"Come on," she told him, "get in the car. Your shorts are about to fall off, and you're bleeding." He looked down and felt around it gingerly.

"It's a graze," he told her, "no penetration." The shot had barely nicked the skin over his hipbone, but the elastic waistband of his shorts had been ripped through by the slug and hung by a thread.

"We should wait for the police," he observed.

"Please no," she responded, "No! I don't know why this happened. Or how it could have. We were supposed to be protected! I need to call into the Bureau, find out what got screwed up. I don't know whether Metro PD is compromised or not. I'm not trusting anybody until I find out what's going on."

Interesting woman, John thought. A government agent? Maybe. Definitely a warrior mentality, anyway. And the Metro Police compromised? So what's going on?

He climbed in the car after the boy, who squirmed into the miniscule rear seat. She floored the Porsche in first gear and drove right across the sidewalk, bouncing down into the alleyway and turning the corner onto Wisconsin Avenue before the cruisers converging on the parking lot could see her. This, he reflected wryly, was far more interesting that what he had planned for New Year's Eve.

"Sorry," she said, turning more sedately east onto R Street as she checked her rear view mirror. "You sure you're not hurt? I'll take you to the hospital if you want."

"A scratch, that's all. Some disinfecting ointment, and a gauze pad and some tape, that's all I need, I believe," he replied, now thinking it was just as well they hadn't hung around. The more anonymous he stayed, the better. Alex could damp out any police or agency interest in him pretty quickly, but newspapers were a different matter. John didn't need a picture of himself in the Washington Post as a New Year's Eve hero. Too many of the wrong people knew his face already. The Magician and the Assassin had made some serious enemies.

She turned into a driveway off a secluded side street a few blocks away, and thumbed the garage door opener clipped on the visor.

"Honey," she said to the boy as they entered the house through the kitchen, "run up to the bathroom, please, and get the first aid box, the big one with all the bandaids and the gauze pads. And there should be a bottle of peroxide in the cabinet somewhere."

"I have to make a phone call, and I guess I owe you a little more explanation," she said, looking into his eyes, a direct and open gaze, "but first come over here more under the light and pull up your shirt. I want to see the damage, make sure you don't need to be in the hospital."

The boy came running into the kitchen with the first aid kit under his arm and a peroxide bottle in his hand. That was fast, John thought.

"Smart kid, huh?" he asked her, smiling down at the boy.

"Oh, yes. Very. Here," she said, "hold these paper towels under the cut."

He did, and she poured peroxide liberally on it, dabbing with a gauze pad to blot it, her touch extraordinarily gentle on the raw tissue.

"I think maybe that should be sutured," she said, "I can see a little white there, looks like bone."

"Ah, no, ma'am, it's just a scratch. Bone's right under the skin there. Slug must have just barely nicked me. Couple of butterflies to pull the skin together and I'll be good as new in the morning."

"What are these other scars here," she asked, lightly touching the white marks higher on his side.

"Various things. Shrapnel. Hot phosphorus."

"You a soldier?"

"Used to be. Prior incarnation."

"So what do you do now, besides flying through the air and kicking in heads?" the woman asked, continuing to dab the blood away with dry sterile gauze pads.

"Now? Now I do market research. Overseas mainly. Third-world countries. Emerging economies."

"Umm," she said thoughtfully, dabbing away, "you get shot at much in that line of work? Shrapnel? Phosphorus? Anything like that?"

She's not sure about me, John realized. She's considering the possibility that this was some sort of staged event. Well, that's okay, I guess. It was pretty wild. And she obviously has a child to protect. I'd be cautious too.

"Not much, no," he answered, "but it's always a possibility. Many of the places I research are pretty much like the Wild West used to be. So people with some military background and capabilities are the preferred employees for my kind of job."

"Capabilities. Ah, yes." She cocked an eloquent eyebrow at him and continued to dab the oozing wound, but the pressure and frequency of the dabs changed ever so slightly.

Shit, she's not buying it, he thought. She's a smart cookie. Good interrogator. Definitely police or legal background. Here she's the one that picked up evidence, hauled ass away from a crime scene, taking two material witnesses along with her, and she's asking *me* all the questions. He smiled, almost laughed.

The boy had been watching the interplay, interested but silent. But then he put his hand on her arm.

"Mom!" the boy exclaimed, "Mom, he stepped between me and a gun! On purpose!"

She looked stricken.

"Oh, God. I'm sorry. I didn't realize that. You should be asking *me* the questions! So go ahead. Where would you like to start?"

The Magician smiled at her, realizing suddenly in the warm kitchen light how truly beautiful she was. And a mother, defending her child. So where do you start, with a woman like this, he wondered. He stuck out his hand.

"Hi. I'm John Connard."

Her eyes locked fully onto his, mesmerizing. Incredible life in those eyes, he saw. A connection with something very basic. A Druid priestess. An earth-mother. He knew the smile on his face had to be totally silly, a vacuous grin.

She found his hand without taking those incredible emerald eyes off his face.

"Hello, John Connard," she said softly, "I'm Lara Picard."

Their contact was electric. Reality shimmered, like some cosmic gong had sounded. They stood rooted in place in her kitchen, holding hands, just looking in each other's eyes, smiling.

Chapter 17

Fourteen miles west of Goddard Space Flight Center and fourteen hundred miles north of Flight 152, the old Edsel eased into a parking spot on the street. The boy and his uncle pulled out their tennis gear and walked down the sidewalk toward the house, conversing.

"Uncle Ham, when do you think Mom and John will get married?"

Not *if*, Hamilton O'Donnell noted, but *when*. So the boy has some sense of the cosmic inevitability, too. And the magic.

"Ah, me lad, I can assist in your inquiries on social and psychological issues, on government, on philosophy, possibly even on mathematics and science to some degree. But this is a matter of love you ask about. Romance. Amore. Quite beyond my ken, I'm afraid."

"The very first time Mom met John," Joshua continued, unwilling to have his question dismissed, "there in the kitchen, something happened. There was this light... that... sort of... engulfed them. And then it reached out, and included me. And it's still there around us. You can't see it, you can't smell it or taste it, but it's there. And with this new energy inside Mom... Mom and John have some purpose together, I think. Does this mean evolution is contagious and John will get it next?"

"Joshua, me lad, love does not necessarily mean marriage. For a union such as exists between your mum and John Connard—and yes, I sense the purpose too—marriage is a mere cultural formality. I believe they will choose to formalize their love, but such things are frequently determined by external events. Evolution may be such an event, I'm not sure. But such things always happen when the time is right."

"So when will the time be right, Uncle Ham?" Joshua asked as they walked into the house.

"Ah, yes. Time. When will it be right? Ecclesiastes, young Joshua, Ecclesiastes. A time to every purpose under heaven."

Wonderful soft voice, Aaron O'Meara thought as Adrienne answered the phone, I wonder if she looks as good as she sounds. God, that would be scary now, wouldn't it?

"Hi, Adrienne, this is Aaron. I got Nathan's email, and I see what he means. It looks like the source in DC is just sitting there, and the one from South America is heading north. My boss down here just came up with a theory on that; we should talk about it."

"Aaron," the soft voice told him, "why don't you hold that thought. Doctor Rodgers just stepped out for a moment; he should be back shortly. How are you coming with your exercise? It sounds fascinating. Are we going to be able to see that video clip you made of the event this morning?"

"Adrienne, I'm sending it this very instant. I had to knock the resolution way down so it doesn't choke our email program, but you should be able to see it just fine in a small video window on your browser. The Pentagon showed pieces of it on the noon news, so it's not classified. The official position in Washington is that it was a rogue asteroid collision and breakup. Ed—my boss—is sending my ET evaluation along to the Pentagon, but I doubt if they'll act. They may pass it along, so you guys may get some questions from some agency or the other, but my guess is probably not."

"Good grief, Aaron, this is huge! Are you sure?"

"It's huge, alright, but it's also way outside the box. I think there's a fifty-fifty chance of any reaction. And if there is one, it probably will be after the fact. Whatever the fact turns out to be."

Silence came from Adrienne's end of the line. Probably disbelief, he thought; she hasn't been around government much. He changed the subject brightly.

"Say, Adrienne, I can't even begin to tell you how amazed I am at your analysis and display codes. Have you given any thought to how you're going to separate the effects when they get closer together? How about coding them with different colors? And is there one characteristic difference, something you could use to distinguish their signals from each other when they come together?"

"Aaron, that's a good suggestion," she answered, "I'll code the South American source blue, I think. Bright blue and bright green are the colors that show up best on top of the map background. I'll go back and do that right away. Oh, Doctor Rodgers is back. Hang on, Aaron, he's going to pick up."

"Nathan," Aaron greeted him, "here's where we stand at Goddard. My boss, Ed Edwards, has gotten a full briefing from me on what we've found out today right up until now. He'll pass it along to the Pentagon. He's going to cast it as a hypothetical, a possibility consistent with the scientific observations, and let them decide. Privately, he agrees with us that ETs have landed, but he can't very well go screaming that out. He's got to play it as a straight scientific question that *may* bear examination, and let it go at that."

Nathan laughed. "I guess I see his point, Aaron. And there doesn't appear to be any damage caused so far. So maybe that's a good sign. After all, intelligent beings presumably would be careful not to cause harm, you would think."

"God, I hope so," Adrienne added.

"Well, you guys may or may not get some calls from the military, or the FBI," Aaron continued. "In the meantime, I think the best thing we can do is just do what we're doing; try to keep track of these things, monitor them, see what happens.

"Nathan, Adrienne, I downloaded a small version of our two-minute video to you. It's an MPEG file, you should be able to play it in your internet browser. I see this thing as a dogfight, with two flaming wrecks falling to earth, even though there wasn't anything physical detected on the surface. But Ed says he also can see this thing as an accident, a transport vessel being blown apart, and two pieces coming down. And now the big piece is just trying to get to the little piece in a rescue mission, not to continue a fight. Would you give this some thought as the things move closer together, please? And how long are you and Adrienne gonna hang out there? Can I give you a call later?"

"We'll think about it, for sure, Aaron. I'll be here for awhile. Adrienne's been here since early this morning, and I suspect she may be running out of gas, so I'll probably send her back to her dorm to get some rest..." Aaron heard the muffling sound of a hand going over the mouthpiece. "...but I guess from the way she's looking at me we're going to have a debate on that."

"We've got the South American source on a track north, since noon, with a probable stopover in Panama. If it's on a commercial flight, we can probably find it on an airline website and see where it's headed. If it's military or private, maybe you've got some government contacts down there you can ask? Anyway, you be thinking about that, and call us when you get to your house. You're going there now, right?"

"Yeah," Aaron agreed, but as he toggled through the plots for the DC source on his computer, he had another thought. "Be about 7:15 or 7:30 this evening before I make it home," he said with sudden excitement, "because by God I'm gonna detour through that part of Georgetown, where the signal is coming from. I'll call you from my cell phone in the van when I get there. You can look at your maps and talk me around the streets where it looks like the source is holed up. That sound like a plan?"

"Aaron, be careful, please," Adrienne's voice held concern. "There's a park there. Looks like it's part of Rock Creek Park from the aerials on the street map program, and pretty heavily wooded. There's an old cemetery there, too. Stay in your van, okay?"

Aaron smiled appreciatively. "You better believe I'll be careful! But damn, I just gotta nose around, Adrienne. Wouldn't you if you were close by?"

He visualized them looking at each other and shrugging agreement.

"Well, of course you would!" Aaron took their silence for acceptance. "So I'll hop in my van and do a little recon mission. I'll call you when I'm coming up on the area. Be about seven, maybe a little before. Talk to you then." He clicked off to forestall further debate, laughing at the absurdity of hunting for ETs in a handicap van in prosaic old Georgetown.

But because he knew himself well enough to realize that part of his laughter derived from nervousness, he left a brief note for Ed Edwards, updating all the information, outlining his reconnaissance plan.

Northwest Washington, DC | Sunday 1812 EDT

"Hi, Mom! We're home!" Joshua yelled into the house as they came through the front door.

Lara heard him from her upstairs bedroom, where she was toweling off and contemplating the way her reconfigured metabolism had magically processed the turkey, ham and bread slices she'd wolfed down when passing through the kitchen.

"I'm coming, Josh," she yelled downstairs. "Set the table, would you please? And take the pot of spaghetti sauce out of the fridge and put it on medium heat on the stove. We're having leftovers tonight. Thanks!"

Now how did I know they wouldn't need to shower first, she asked herself. Sometimes they shower there, sometimes they come back here to shower. The answer was astonishing. An open front door, a breeze behind them, and the ceiling fan upstairs had moved the air toward her. She had smelled the tiniest effluvium from the shampoo that was in the dispensers at the showers in the alumni locker rooms. She'd smelled it before on Josh's hair after tennis. That tiny a trace, she marveled, in just a waft of air blown upstairs. But then she also realized her ears were picking up their footsteps a floor below, and that she could discriminate between Ham's tread and Joshua's, even with the soft susurrus of the ceiling fan for background. My smell is more acute. My hearing is more acute. My entire mind and body feels more integrated. She pondered that as she walked downstairs to help prepare dinner.

The spaghetti is a symphony of good smells, Lara thought as they ate, but this dinner conversation is clearly at odds with it; I can actually smell the resistance coming off Josh. My fault, I guess. I need him and Ham out of the house, out of this area, safely tucked away under the wings of a couple of good FBI watchdogs. I need the decks cleared of non-combatants, and most definitely those two. If I have to worry about them, it could distract me, perhaps fatally. But how to tell my son, persuade him to stay clear, without terrifying him about the very real possibility I could lose the battle and be killed? Especially since he's determined to help out, and isn't buying my arguments.

"Mom," Joshua pressed his case, "this sense you have of an impending threat, it just doesn't make any sense it's that old threat coming back. Those idiots—papa Julius and junior Julius—died in jail, you said, three years ago. That means this sense you have that there's gonna be a fight, that somebody's coming after you, has to be related to your new state. Maybe even your new state was created as a response to the threat."

Lara gazed at her son thoughtfully.

"Mom?" Joshua repeated.

Dammit, she thought. My child is too smart for me. Most times he lets those little motherly dissimulations slide by. But not this time, the danger is too real. He senses it. He probably can read it all over me, with that hyper-awareness of his. He's not going to let me pull the mother rank on him, not this time.

She looked at him across the table, evaluating.

He looked back at her, his analyzing look.

She chose her words carefully. "Josh, I do not know. I just don't. What you say makes sense. But the source of the threat, or the timing, matters less than dealing with it. And that's what I'm going to do, dammit, I'm going to deal with it. In order to do that, I need you and Ham out of the way, and I need to know you're safe and sound."

"Mom, I want to stay with you. I'm pretty smart. I can help."

"Oh, honey! Thank you! But the best way you can help is for you to stay with your uncle Hamilton, out of the way, and safe and sound. I can't get distracted or have to worry about you. So, you've got to go, honey. That's it. I've made up my mind. I want you and your Uncle Ham parked in a hotel somewhere, well away from me, and heavily guarded. I've got to know you're safe. Okay? That's the best help you can give me. Please?"

Joshua looked at his uncle Hamilton for support.

"A mother's instincts, me lad, are always to be respected," his uncle said with a neutral expression. And then looking at the boy's rebellious face, he smiled at him and added firmly, "absolutely respected."

Lara watched her son look at his uncle across the table, analyzing, analyzing. Emotion and reason played a conflicted game across his face. He studied her again. Then he suddenly smiled and shrugged, surprising them both.

"Okay, Mom. You're the boss. But get John back here to help you, if you won't let me. He's pretty smart too. And he can be pretty nasty when he needs to be. He'll be a help if I can't."

Yeah, Josh, that's what I think too, she thought. He's a one-man army. And I sure need him now if I ever did.

"Ham?" she asked, "it's one of your market research projects he ran off on. Think you could track him down, get a message to him?"

Hamilton O'Donnell consulted his watch.

"Certainly," he answered, "but I don't know what his timin' would be for getting' back here. Let me go see if I can find out exactly where he is now, and get a message to him. Satellite systems tend not to have good phone coverage in that part of the world. I'll pack an overnight bag and be back directly."

"And Joshua, you go pack one too, please," Lara ordered as Ham exited into his half of the duplex.

"John must be in central Africa, Mom; equator or below. You notice Uncle Ham didn't say where he was?"

"Yes, Josh, I noticed. I expect he'll say what he can, when he can. Why do you think central Africa?"

"Bad satellite coverage. Not enough demand yet. Their economies are too poor to justify the cost. I read it in a stock prospectus for a new communications IPO."

Jesus, she thought, talk about eclectic tastes. Is there nothing this kid doesn't read? Out loud, she said, "Thanks for the insider scoop, honey, now get your butt upstairs, brush your teeth, pack your bag and get back down here in five minutes. I've got a couple of phone calls to make. Okay?"

She hugged him hard and tousled his hair, then strode purposefully into her small study behind the dining room, closing the door behind her.

The Bureau's duty officer picked up the call immediately.

"Recording. State your identity and go ahead," the gruff voice on the other end said.

"Lara Picard," she answered, adding the code that established her identity, "I want encryption, please."

Might as well be safe, she thought. TC will ream me out if I don't keep to procedure.

"Encryption, roger." A brief pause, then she heard the tone change. "Ready on our end, Ms. Picard, go ahead."

Lara punched the button on the small black box between her phone and the wall jack, and watched the red flicker through yellow and change to green as the electronic handshake routine completed.

"Encryption confirmed. Say again your identity and code." The gruff voice had gone tinny under the encryption.

"This is Lara Picard," she repeated slowly and distinctly, adding her code. "I have a Category 4 message for Special Agent Thomas Demuzzio."

From the brief pause at the other end, Lara knew that the duty officer was scrolling down through the database to the personalized protocol TC Demuzzio had set up after the third attempt on her life, three and a half years ago.

"Category 4 confirmed," the voice came back after another pause, "do you require local police support immediately at your location?"

Okay, she thought, they realize I'm legitimate. The tinniness of the encryption couldn't entirely remove the heightened adrenaline level from the voice. They know it's not an exercise. Good!

"Negative. No locals. Here's the message. I'll rendezvous with Agent Demuzzio and a team at the Irving Street safehouse at..." she looked at her watch, "...2100. I believe he's in town this weekend. Tell him three strikes, but they're still not out. He'll know what that means. And tell him my son and his uncle need protection, too. I'm going to tell them to get a suite in some hotel and then call in to you."

Okay, she thought, now the protective response protocols would be kicked in for the three of them, no questions asked. Except of course by TC, who was a professional skeptic and cynic. Answering his questions without sharing the basis for her need for protection, and keeping the lies to a minimum, that would require some delicacy. But what choice did she have? She needed to take out this monster quickly and cleanly. And to do that she needed TC's help.

"Please verify no protection required prior to 2100, ma'am," the tinny voice requested.

"No protection. Threat possibility only after midnight," she replied, mentally extrapolating in her other-dimensioned perception the approach speed of the blue-tinged black blotch in the corner of her mind.

"Tell TC I'm wearing my emergency transponder. Rendezvous 2100, at the Irving Street safehouse," Lara repeated, and hung up.

She pulled the transponder out of her desk, slipped in a fresh set of batteries, strapped it to her wrist and turned it on. The small LED indicated the device was operational and was being picked up by the GPS satellite. Now they could track her location to within a few meters, from headquarters or any field office, or—with an uplinked laptop—from almost anywhere in the world.

Ham and Josh were waiting for her in the living room, their bags beside them. Lara smiled at them, a commanding smile. Josh smiled back, tentatively.

"Okay, guys, here's the drill," she said. "Ham, pick a hotel. It's a holiday weekend and school's out at Congress, so you should be able to get in any place you pick. I don't want to know where it is, that's the security protocol. Get a suite, or connecting rooms, so bodyguards can be with you. Once you're in the room, call this number. Call from the room phone, not your cell phone. Tell the duty officer at the Bureau who you are, and tell him where you are. Then wait until the agents show up, and follow their directions."

She handed him the slip of paper with the phone number.

"I love you both," she said, hugging Hamilton O'Donnell's compact form, then picking up her son for a tighter squeeze. He squeezed his mother back just as tight, and she felt the undercurrents of her strange energy wrap around them both.

"Go now," she added, holding open the front door. "This should all be over in a day or so. I'll stay in touch, as best I can."

"Take care of yourself, Mom," Joshua said, struggling for control of his voice.

"I will, honey, I will. I promise. You, too." She watched them walk toward the old Edsel, blinking through her tears.

Chapter 18

Just as Lara turned back into her house, Aaron O'Meara turned his van off R Street onto the small cul-de-sac marked Phoenix Court. Needing both hands to operate the handicapped van, he used the cell phone earpiece and mike to let Adrienne navigate him through the streets around the signal source. Although the signal strength had dropped off, the location remained relatively stable; it appeared to be in Montrose Park north of R Street.

Which puts it on the west side of Phoenix Court just behind this short row of old brownstone duplexes, Aaron estimated. Classy neighborhood, he thought: older, understated, probably lots of money. A man and a boy tossed luggage into the back seat of a vintage convertible as he drove past. The street turned left but dead-ended twenty feet in, with a barricade across a dirt road into the park. He backed out and swung around, heading back to R Street, keeping up his running description of the short street to Adrienne.

The man stepped away from the car, a short, semi-rotund man with a friendly smile. No reason to be spooked here, Aaron thought, slowing to a stop as the man waved him down.

"Ah, 'tis directions you'll be needin', will ye now?" The man's quizzical gray eyes immediately took in the cell phone headset, and then the Goddard parking sticker on his windshield. "Well, that's all right, half the people in this town be needin' direction. Where is it you'll be wantin' to go, lad?"

An Irishman, he'd make a pretty unlikely alien, Aaron thought.

"Is this Montrose Park, sir?"

"That it is, lad, on your right, behind the houses. But the entrance is up further. Take a right onto R Street, and park right there. Or there's a spot in front of the turnoff for the walkin' path further down on the right." The man's quizzical expression changed to sympathy as he took in the handicapped tag hanging from the rear-view mirror. "Not real handicapped parkin' but I doubt they'd chase you out."

Aaron smiled his thanks at the man, and at the boy, whose eyes watched him intently. The kid, he wouldn't likely be an ET either, Aaron chuckled on the phone to Adrienne as he turned back onto R Street.

Northwest Washington, DC | Sunday 1901 EDT

As Aaron drove off, Lara stood on the opposite side of the house, looking out the French doors of the basement dojo into the darkening woods of Montrose Park. She went through a mental checklist: keys, money, credit card, license, all in one pocket of the shorts, cellphone in the other pocket, critical numbers programmed into memory. Velcro flaps over both pockets. Watch on her left wrist; the multipurpose job Ham had given her last Christmas. GPS transponder on her right wrist. Okay. It all checked.

No fannypack or backpack; anything else she might need would be kept at the safehouse. She'd had a tour of the house one time when she was contemplating keeping one of her witnesses there for protection. As good a place as any to set a trap, she reasoned. And it's got a bolthole in case things get really futzed up, a subsurface tunnel that will let you blow out of there in nothing flat. She picked the form-fitting windbreaker off the hook by the hanging bikes and snugged into it.

Minimize the wind resistance, and keep yourself warm, her *ki* agreed, sending that thought into her mind-space. Other instructions on aerodynamics followed, along with a reminder to mask herself with the null field before she took flight. Lara stepped outside and locked the door behind her.

Reaching into the null dimension, she withdrew the chaos required for concealment and willed it to cloak her body, gauging it to blend with the shadows and colors of the twilit woods. When she judged herself nearly invisible, she danced into a run and dove down the hillside, threading through the trees, following the terrain, staying three or four feet aloft. Pure joy and delight flooded her being. Her aura flared a bright emerald lightning around her; laughing, she bought it back under control.

Montrose Park, Washington, DC | Sunday 1902 EDT

A few hundred yards south and west of Lara's passage through the trees, having just pulled into the turnoff, Aaron watched a pulsating green glow flick through woods in the dimming light. Excitement and fear roiled his intestines as realizations tumbled through his mind.

Omigod!

I was right!

We do have visitors!

The sheer magnitude of discovery rendered him speechless. If he could have spoken out of his suddenly dry mouth, he would have confirmed to Adrienne that the average signal source position her algorithms had predicted was almost exactly the same location as that eerie green light. The light danced through the trees, moving quickly to the northeast, then it faded into the brighter light of the westering sun on thinner woods.

An indefinable part of Aaron's mind sensed a strange fleeting contact, not unpleasant at all. Excruciatingly intense curiosity pounded through him, countering his fear.

Rock Creek Park, Washington, DC | Sunday 1902 EDT

A partial adept, 200 yards rear left. Her *ki* did not seem surprised, and smiled enigmatically into their mind-space. The concept of a partial adept played across that space.

Most of Lara's mind stayed focused on navigation, letting her thread through the trees. She knew the purpose of the practice: work on it until it becomes automatic, until there is no conscious thought between perception and reaction. That's how birds do it, she realized. They don't stop to think 'branch coming up, dip left wing, flap right', they just do it. *I must practice until it becomes just that instinctual. Doesn't seem like it will take too long. I evidently don't need to concentrate on it exclusively; it's more like I just need to let it happen?* She floated the question in her mind-space.

The learning process is partitioned, a separate channel. Your mind has different parts, it can deal with multiple channels at the same time.

She saw the truth of that: another channel of her mind was simultaneously contemplating the concept of a partial adept. *I felt it,* she thought. *Him,* she amended, the contact clearly male. And he had a much sharper, more focused consciousness than the meditation groups impinging on her radar screen earlier. This contact displayed as a more singular point of light than those warm fuzzy glows. She decoded the light, and laughed. A formidable intellect, she saw. Its defining characteristic was curiosity: intense, raging curiosity, much like Joshua.

I cut the contact when I reined in my aura, she realized. *Maybe I should go back to Montrose Park and introduce us properly? Pity to let such curiosity go unrequited.*

But no, she decided, it was a whimsy for which there was no time. Lara dismissed that contact, cleared that channel from her mind, and opened herself totally to the experience of flying.

Global Consciousness Project, Princeton University, NJ | Sunday 1903 EDT

"Aaron," Adrienne repeated into her telephone, "there's a ramp-up in the activity level on our 1-minute integrals, it looks like. Do you hear me?" Then, with a pang of anxiety, "do you hear me? Aaron? Are you okay? Aaron!"

"Adrienne," Aaron gathered his wits and gasped into his cell phone, "...yes. Yes. I'm here." He paused to swallow, trying to get his dry throat to function. "Adrienne, I saw it. I saw it! There is by God an alien on this earth, and it was here and I saw it! Adrienne, I saw it! I even felt its mind, I think!"

Adrienne gestured wildly at Nathan to pick up the phone.

"Aaron, are you okay?" she repeated.

"Yes, I'm okay." His voice strengthened from a whisper into a croak. "I'm okay, Adrienne."

"I'm on the line, Aaron," Nathan announced. "What happened? Talk to us. Where are you, exactly, first of all?"

They heard Aaron take deep breaths and let them out, then his voice returned to normal, if a little hoarse.

"I'm partway down a maintenance road in Montrose Park, Nathan. Just north of R Street. I'm looking northeast, more or less. Off to the east, across a field, I saw this green glow in the trees. It flickered and shimmered and moved north real quick. When it got into a less dense part of the woods ahead of me and into more daylight, I lost it. Or it faded out or moved away, I can't tell which."

"What exactly did it look like, Aaron? Did it have a human shape, or something different? And how fast did it move?"

"I didn't actually see anything tangible, Nathan, just this green flickering glow in the trees, no shape to it. The distance from where it started to where it faded out looks like maybe a couple hundred yards. It covered that in... twenty-five or thirty seconds? That's a pretty good clip. Considering these are wooded areas, it's probably as fast as a person could run," Aaron replied. Then, calculating some more, "no, probably faster than anybody's gonna run through woods in dim light, realistically. I guess I really don't think it was a human on foot. A big cat, maybe, like a cheetah. You'd need four paws and real good cornering ability and reflexes to zip through the trees that fast, unless there's an open trail, and I don't see one from here."

"A bird, maybe?" Adrienne wondered. "Something that flies?"

"That's probably the closest natural possibility for what I saw, or think I saw. Birds can zip in and out of trees pretty neatly, and easily hit that speed. Adrienne, yes; that's a good possibility! Of course, if the entity is non-material, none of that may matter anyway."

"You said you felt its mind, Aaron?" Adrienne asked.

"I definitely felt a mind contact. Now that I think about it I know I've never felt anything like it before. Its contact... acknowledged me... if that's the right word. Realized I was there, watching. The contact had some overtones: a little surprise, some amusement, some sympathy. Or empathy. Empathy is a better descriptor, I think."

"So, Aaron, it wasn't unfriendly? This is probably the key question for us, for the human race, wouldn't you think?"

The urgency in Nathan's voice was abetted by Adienne's half-whispered "Amen to that!"

"No, it wasn't unfriendly. I'm definite on that. Maybe even friendly, given the empathy, but at least neutral. But here's the most important thing, I think. It had a sense of urgency about it, like it was going somewhere."

"Maybe you spooked it," Nathan wondered, "and it cleared out?"

"I don't think so, Nathan. I don't think it's easily spooked. The sense I got was that there was a job to be done; a sense of mission or purpose."

"For sure it's going somewhere, Aaron," Adrienne laughed in relief, "it's going to someplace where it can get ready for the rendezvous, that's what's happening here. The positions for the past three 1-minute integrals show it tracking just about northeast. These aren't real precise individually, of course, but my guess is it's moving up through Rock Creek Park, getting ready to connect up with the source from South America. Based on the contact you felt, the rescue mission hypothesis seems to fit a little better now than the battle hypothesis."

"Folks, I'm not exactly equipped to track it through the woods at night," Aaron replied, a certain regret apparent in his still-trembling voice, "so I'm heading home to grab some dinner. I'll check in when I'm sitting at my computer. Okay?"

Hanging up her phone, Adrienne stared at Nathan. He stared back, and spoke first.

"Contact! Finally, irrefutably, clearly demonstrated contact! A consciousness that shows up on detectors and clearly isn't human. Along with a physical presence, even if it is only light. Hard evidence! That's what I like best about this whole thing," Nathan Rodgers decided. He was a scientist, and a skeptic.

"What I like best," Adrienne Baxter responded, "is the touching of their minds. The existence of another sense, a conduit between two consciousnesses, a more direct way of communicating." She was a mathematician, and a dreamer.

Rock Creek Park, Washington, DC | Sunday 1904 EDT

Lara saw Rock Creek Park's old bridle path coming up, a long straight section

with no one was visible on it. No points of light showed nearby on her consciousness radar. She accelerated out of the trees and flew along the path, three feet
above. Then she stopped as hard as she could, tucking and flipping over to land
feet-first, running. Her toe caught a tree root and she would have fallen, but instead chose to fly back into the air, kill more momentum, and float down gently.
Looking back, the stopping distance was not great, perhaps twenty yards, but some
distance was clearly required. She willed the conscious memory of what she'd just
done down to that deeper level, wedding it to the flight controls in the base of
her mind. She adjusted them for momentum considerations, both in velocity and
direction.

As she practiced, and as control of flight became more automatic within the
primitive part of her mind, another channel opened to the memory of her first
flight together with her lover John Connard; an airplane flight.

Not two months after they met, he'd come back from a research trip in southern
Russia looking awful. Not so much physically, but spiritually. He seemed drawn
and strung out, even tormented. Her mothering instincts took over. When he said
all he wanted to do was sleep for five days curled up in her arms, she had cleared
her calendar for a long weekend and booked them on the early morning flight out
of Dulles to the Caymans. She'd fed him those island rum drinks and held him and
cuddled him and coddled him and pretty soon that torment just flushed right out
of his soul. The loving and erotic memory of that tropical interlude took her into
its warm embrace. God, what a wonderful time we had, she remembered....

He traced a heart in the sweat of my back, as we paddled the kayak into that
deserted cove. And then he lifted up the bikini and tickled my nipples and licked
behind my ear. We were so anxious to get to shore and make love we almost
dumped the kayak on the reef. Then on the next leg of the trip I made him sit in
front and did the same thing to him. Ah, the sweat running down those rippling
muscles, his little nipples under my fingers, what delicious sensations those were.

God, that was a great time. Magical. But we've been magical from the time we
first met, haven't we? I cleaned his graze wound, and we shook hands, standing
there in my kitchen, on New Year's Eve. I invited him to stay and clean up and
have dinner, but he said he'd finish his run and change his clothes and be back. And
he did come back, with a bottle of champagne and some of the best tenderloin I've
ever tasted. Josh went to bed right after the midnight fireworks at the monument.
An hour after that John and I had our own fireworks. To this day, neither of us is
sure how this happened or why. But it was much, much more than just escalated
libido from escaping danger. Our love was instantly magical, just absolutely

natural, like the sun rising and setting or the tides moving in and out.

Lara banked sharply around a turn in the path in Rock Creek Park, and paused to assess her newly-learned flying skills, but in a separate channel her memories ran on....

When we smelled Ham's Irish breakfast cooking that New Year's Day, we somehow didn't feel at all unnatural about strolling downstairs and into his half of the brownstone duplex, hand in hand. Ham was totally astonished, for sure. And when John called him Alex, that was enlightening. I never knew until that moment his full name was Alexander Hamilton Shaughnessy O'Donnell, or that they actually had known each other for years.

"*Anaim cairdi*," Ham had said in the Gaelic of his ancestors, when they told him about the encounter and the rescue the previous evening. "Lara, you and John are *anaim cairdi*, soulmates. You are destined always to be at the proper place, at the proper time, to take the proper course for each other. You were called, John, to that appointed instant. I thought it too early, but I was wrong."

She and John had looked at each other astonished, and laughed giddily. They demanded that Ham enlighten them. What sort of connection did he have with the Almighty—or other font of wisdom or knowing—that would tell him what might be an appointed instant? Or whether that instant might be too early, or too late? Ham wouldn't answer. He only smiled like the Sphinx and launched off into one of his complex Irish absurdities as he poured them more coffee and laughed along with them.

Chapter 19

Hamilton O'Donnell could feel his nephew's changed mood as they drove off. Yes, he thought, the boy's mind reached a turning point there back at the house, when he gave up his argument and smiled at his mum. Or maybe it wasn't his mind at all. Maybe it came from some deeper level. He somehow suddenly just let go.

"Well, me lad," he launched the opening gambit of their mind-dance, "you changed quite abruptly there, as if you sensed your mum was right. Suddenly developed a sixth sense, have ye?"

"Sixth? I only have five, Uncle Ham." Joshua's typical nine-year-old riposte to a mind-dance invitation was to play dumb.

"Ah, Joshua, well then, here's an allegory about senses, and the mind's interpretation of senses, this one from my old friend Plato...

"Prisoners have been chained inside a cave since birth, in such a way that they can only see shadows cast on the cave wall. They believe the shadows are reality, because they have no other frame of reference. Because of that belief, they never try to escape. One of them finally does escape, and discovers things of substance rather than just shadows. He is a person of courage and moral conviction, and feels he has to come back to the cave and free his fellow prisoners. When he comes back and tells them of his new reality, they think he's gone mad, and won't go with him outside the cave."

"So, Uncle Ham, what's your point?"

"Ah, me lad, you tell me."

"This is serious?"

"Ah, yes."

"Okay. The shadow is not the object casting it."

"Go on."

"Your reality is what you believe it to be."

"Very good! Go on."

"Your senses that lead to your beliefs can maybe come up a little short of the truer reality."

"Aha! And?"

"People's minds become conditioned to sensing the reality they expect, and they think anything else is wacky."

"Excellent! And the extrapolation would be?"

"A culture, or a civilization, is conditioned to a certain reality. A sense-based reality, in most cultures."

"Wonderful! Anythin' more?"

Joshua hesitated a moment, nervously, then asked, "Uncle Ham, am I going to leave the cave?"

"Joshua, me lad, I would say that's a distinct possibility. In fact, I think you did that just now, when you kissed your mum and left the house. Wouldn't you agree?"

Joshua studied his uncle carefully in the waning evening light in the open convertible, now driving north on Connecticut Avenue.

"Possibly," he answered, smiling.

The child is honest with himself, the old man thought, smiling back. When uncertain, he admits it. And now, if our little mind-dance follows its usual course, he's going to turn the tables, and ask his questions. God, how I love this boy.

He was right. Joshua posed the next question.

"And if I do leave the cave, will I come back to free the other prisoners from their shadows?" he asked.

"Well now, me lad, that would be up to you, would it not? Was it not Gandhi who said 'Be the change you want to see in the world'?"

"I don't know, Uncle Ham, should I read him?"

"Couldn't hurt. If you're interested we'll rent the movie sometime. Beautifully acted. Portrayal is not quite faithful to the man, but of course they didn't know him like I did."

Joshua giggled. "Uncle Ham, how is it that you have such a personal acquaintance with all these historical characters?"

Hamilton O'Donnell just smiled enigmatically, and winked at the boy.

Rock Creek Park, Washington, DC | Sunday 1913 EDT

In her present reality in Rock Creek Park, thoughts of John her *anam cara* melded, in Lara's mind, with an ethereal interlocking sense of cosmic acknowledgment and blessing. The intense physicality of mastering her new flying skills evidently had triggered more subtle changes, so that the sweat of training and the fullness of adrenaline-laden blood in her muscles now felt strangely inseparable from the restless love in her soul. New neural pathways opening, she thought. Her *ki* agreed, smiling at her, then reverted to the practical.

More practice is desirable, around manmade objects rather than trees. Versatility in movement, being comfortable flying in many different settings, including tight spaces, that is a useful combat skill. Her greater self displayed concepts of exactly how useful, diagramming them in her mind-space, rotating them to different perspectives. Lara nodded her understanding.

She had already passed under the Connecticut Avenue Bridge, but the Calvert Street Bridge—spanning Rock Creek and much of the park width—lay straight ahead. The light had dimmed, the sun below the horizon, the dusk in the woods turning a soft gray-green. She checked the chaos cloak formed around her body. Her aura was under control, tucked inside the cloak, only the hint of a vague emerald flicker that fit in somehow with the park's lush spring vegetation.

Lara gathered her new energies to her and whooped aloud into the growing dusk with the pure joy of freedom from gravity. Three dancing steps launched her northward along the path and upward into the sky. A coven of crows took flight with startled squawking as she burst through the upper canopy of the trees and arrowed toward the looming structure of the Calvert Street Bridge.

Her flight might have been visible to acute observers on either bridge. But they likely would have rubbed their eyes, and let their minds interpret otherwise: the movement of the leaves carved by her passage would be explained by the erratic breezes that sometimes kick up around sunset; the occasional emerald flash above the treetops would be explained as just a visual vagary, a trick of the twilight. Lara Picard was a wraith in the air.

Global Consciousness Project, Princeton University, NJ | Sunday 2032 EDT

"American Airlines, Flight 152, Adrienne," Nathan announced triumphantly, "the other candidates just don't match up anywhere near as closely." He had spent the past hour checking airplane schedules on the internet. The colored stickies tracking Flight 152 on his big wall map overlapped the 15-minute location circles plotted by Adrienne's algorithm. He sat back and surveyed his handiwork with satisfaction. Considering that he knew nothing about what the wind speed and direction currently were at 40,000 feet, and knew little about flight navigation corridors, he found the agreement extraordinary.

"That's really remarkable, Doctor Rodgers," Adrienne echoed his thoughts as she entered his office. "The stickies are where you estimate the position based on flying time to what, the middle of each 15-minute period?"

"Yes, exactly," he replied, "and see how a lot of them fall inside your 95 per cent probability circles?"

"Wow! So that flight took off at 1640 from, what's that, Tocumento? In Panama?

And it's landing at Miami at 2030? So it probably just landed?"

"I'd put serious money on it, Adrienne; nothing else comes close at all. Of course, some private or military flights might fit the same flight pattern. But this is an awfully, awfully good match."

They studied the map together. Then Adrienne voiced her thoughts.

"Okay," she said, "now we know it can move by standard transport. That says something."

"So it's either human or a stowaway," he added.

"And if it's just light, or energy, or something else immaterial, why would it need an airplane to travel in, anyway?"

"And the airplane wasn't delayed, so there wasn't any big security flap before takeoff."

"And therefore it's probably human, or somehow has attached itself to a person or to their baggage," she concluded.

"Yup," he agreed. "That seems the most likely scenario."

"Well, Doctor Rodgers, if it departs Miami and heads up this way, like I'm absolutely positive it will, and stays on commercial flights, what would they be?"

"Ah, Adrienne, for once I'm a little ahead of you. American leaving Miami at 2120, into DC National at 2359. Southwest leaving at 2140, into Dulles at 0125. A couple of later ones."

Kensington, MD | Sunday 2035 EDT

Aaron slid across the bench seat in the shower of his Kensington home, toweling off his lower body. His heavily muscled arms reflexively kneaded the muscles in his much weaker legs, stimulating the blood circulation. With efficient, practiced motions he worked into his sweatpants and slippers, and pulled on a tee shirt. He rolled in his wheelchair across the burnished wood floor to his computer workstation. There he paused to compose his roiling thoughts.

Did his ET sighting really change anything? What would any responsible government official in their right mind make of his story? A green glow moving through the trees in dim light, a transient mental contact he could barely describe? They'd ask what he'd been smoking. And that would be a perfectly legitimate question, he admitted.

Moreover, where could he find someone to listen? The Pentagon had his interpretation of the morning's event, but had chosen the asteroid theory instead. His boss believed him, but viewed Goddard solely as a generator of information, not a decision-maker. So who were the decision-makers in Washington? Politicians.

Even the executives of bureaucracies were politicians, or politically appointed. Forget that, he admitted, you just can't get a quick decision out of them; be like dragging an alligator by the tail out of a swamp full of molasses. There were much faster decision-makers in DOD, to be sure, but would they act? Could they act? This wasn't a war, at least not in any sense understood in the past.

Aaron sighed, and came out the same place as before. Absent any indication of an imminent threat, his obligation was to pass the information along through channels; specifically, through his boss at Goddard. His fingers flew over the keyboard, composing the email.

"There ya go, Ed," he told his computer monitor as he finished up, "it's all there, lock, stock and barrel." Plus eye of newt and hair of wolf and touch of *cannabis*, the back of his mind laughed sardonically. "And it's all properly scientific, with proper detachment. Hey, I'm just a disinterested observer, perfectly neutral, watching the experiment. No involvement, no hysteria, just nice calm rational reporting."

As a last thought, Aaron added Nathan's email address as a copy recipient, thinking, well, Ed, you told me I was free to work with them and share information. So let's get it fully on the record for everybody involved. That's probably the safest course. He hit the *Send* button, then logged onto the Global Consciousness Project website, studied the updated GCD data for a moment, and picked up the telephone.

Rock Creek Park, Washington, DC | Sunday 2038 EDT

Lara felt like tiny pixie against the massive stonework of the Calvert Street Bridge. She flew under the arches and around the columns, an aerial ballet with the bridge as her stage. She adapted her flying skill and ran upside-down under one arch of the bridge, laughing her pleasure out loud. Cloaked in chaos drawn from the null-field, she was virtually undetectable in the dusk, except that occasional flickers of emerald light escaped the outline of the field when she laughed. Those flickers appeared much like the sun's corona shining around the moon at full solar eclipse: a glow around the edges of an arcane emptiness. The emptiness flashed at impossible speeds and angles around the bridgework. Pigeons squawked and took flight, but no observers were present on the ground below to detect this wonder.

She was detectable, however, by the FBI team in the van driving up Connecticut Avenue. Their GPS receiver was set to the coded signal of the transponder strapped to her wrist.

The technician sitting in the back of the van with Special Agent T.C. Demuzzio slapped his equipment in irritation.

"What the fuck is the matter with this thing?" In the minute since he'd turned it on and confirmed the coded signal, the position had been dancing erratically.

"Some problem, Chuck?"

The technician looked out of the mirrored glass and saw they were driving over the Connecticut Avenue Bridge.

"Signal's flaky. It's strong enough, but no way can she be moving around like that. The bridge must be screwing things up. I don't think it's atmospherics."

"Show me!" Demuzzio's concern for his friend and protégé Lara Picard ratcheted suddenly upward.

"Oops, there it goes, TC. Smoothed out now. Looks like she's coming out from under Calvert Street. Okay, we've got a good lock. She's headed north, paralleling the Parkway. There's a trail or something down there, if I remember right."

TC Demuzzio relaxed back into his seat.

The technician squinted at the moving dot on the street map displayed on the computer screen, doing an eyeball estimate of her progress.

"She may be jogging, or on a bike," he guessed, "seems like she's going a little too fast for walking. But it looks like she's pretty much on track for the safehouse at 2100. We gonna drive down into the park and pick her up?"

"No. She called this shot. I'm assuming she knows what she's doing. We'll meet her there at the safehouse on Irving Street. Open the place up, check it out, get it ready. You stay in the van and track her, Chuck," Demuzzio instructed, "and when she gets here I want you to wand her, check her over good. The standard protocol, in case somebody tagged her with electronics somehow."

Lara flew a meandering path through the trees, navigating almost absently. Four times, she thought into her mind-space, I felt its contact four times, I think. I'm not counting the contact in the parking lot, the one you called a partial adept; that had an entirely different feel. These four contacts felt enticing, seductive. It wasn't unpleasant, and there even was an attraction to it. But it came from our enemy, I'm sure of it. I sensed a darkness in the contacts.

The darkness is a true representation of our enemy; it bespeaks the absence of a connection between the personality and the soul. This is a sign of a force running rampant, unable to find its frame of reference, its soul. It is psychopathic, amoral. The darkness you sense represents that absence of connection—an absence of light, an absence of goodness.

She pondered the meaning of such a missing connection, feeling its terror, sensing the danger in it. The place where the human condition has died, and all that is left is the beast.

Yes, this is a Beast, Lara Picard; it is the worst nightmare of an animal past. It is an evolutionary mistake, totally different from you. You are fully a human, evolving into the next stage. You have a fundamental connection to your ki, your soul, and through that, to the essence of all creatures and all creation. Unlike the Beast, you have a great love and reverence for life. He senses that. He will try to mimic it to entice you, to seduce you into his darkness.

She felt the repugnance of such a seduction permeate her mind-space, and floated her query into the morass. But such an evolved being! How? How could this happen?

Insane minds can evolve, too, from a trauma or other triggering event similar to yours. Evolution has no filter for good and evil; these are moral constructs of consciousness.

The attraction I felt did not seem necessarily evil.

Your two minds have evolved almost simultaneously. This means they must be alike in many ways. The Beast's mind is clever. He obviously can project affection, probably even love. What is more horrible, he can even mean love. But his is love in the sense of a good meal: you are a soul to be devoured. The path to darkness is always thus. He will devour you if he can, and try to kill you if he can't.

Jesus and the devil in the desert.

Precisely.

I must kill this Beast.

There is no other choice.

Chapter 20

The location plots for the South American source, Adrienne decided, were clearly converging on southern Florida.

"Well, my friend," she told the data "now with nine GCDs to triangulate from, if you just sit tight in Miami International for awhile, we should get a pretty damn good lock on you. And when you take off again, we should be able to bracket that pretty well, too. Do you know you're being watched? Do you know we're tracking you? We mean you no harm. I sure hope you feel the same way about us...."

The blue-circled crosshairs on her work station monitor stared back at her, unblinking. On the bigger flat-screen monitor at the central station, miniature timeline plots of the 1-minute integrals she was using as raw data marched forward, nine jagged blue lines fluctuating in response to both the signal strength and the varying distances between the source and each of the nine GCDs. Adrienne glanced over at Nathan Rodgers, in his office. Their computers simultaneously pinged receipt of email, and seconds later the phone rang.

"GCP Center, this is Nathan," she heard him answer, and then "Hi, Aaron," as he hit the conference button and waved her to pick up.

"Hello, Adrienne," Aaron said, "I see our South American source is now over south Florida, and your 1-minute raw data are steadying down. Does that mean a landing at Miami or Lauderdale, you think?"

"Aaron, here's what the data imply," Nathan interjected, describing how the GCP detector data fit a flight path for American 152 from Tocumeno to Miami, and none other. "Of course," he added, "it could be private or military on the same flight path, we can't really count that out."

"But if we're right," Adrienne added excitedly, "the locator algorithm will stabilize on Miami for awhile. At least until it hops another flight, or leaves the airport."

"Hmm. So when are the next flights out of Miami to DC, and will they have any passenger from Flight 152?" Aaron asked.

"Yeah, those would be the logical questions," Nathan replied, "but if we call American Airlines and start asking them about who got off the Panama flight that's getting onto a DC flight... that's sure to set off all sorts of security bells and whistles, and how would we explain it? 'We think one of your passengers is really an ET?' We'd probably all get arrested for perpetrating a hoax!"

"What I wonder about," Adrienne changed the subject, "is why they're getting together. Aaron, your initial hypothesis was so they could continue to fight. Your boss thinks maybe a rescue mission. That seems more plausible; unless it's maybe some kind of reunion or rejoining of separated parts..."

"Like maybe they're lovers?" Aaron chuckled.

"Yes, Aaron!" A dreamy tone entered Adrienne's soft voice. "Like maybe they desperately need to get together."

As she said that, she felt a melodic ripple up her backbone, a delicate fingering, full of resonance. She shivered with sudden pleasure, and wondered if Aaron had felt it too.

Northwest Washington, DC | Sunday 2050 EDT

Lara floated delicately, invisibly, through the trees on the east side of Rock Creek Park. Her flying had slowed as she pondered the strange ways of evolution. Having to destroy any mind just born into this new and glorious reality was troubling in a very visceral way. But clearly she had no other choice. She had to kill the Beast.

She flared to a landing, now practiced and sure, just inside the tree line at Adams Mill Road. A twisting motion in her mind released her hold on the null-field; the chaos cloak left her body and the green aura followed it. Visible again, just another rangy young woman out for a jog in the evening gloaming, she loped easily up the sidewalk toward the corner of Irving. She saw the rear of the house as she jogged by. Lights were on, movement inside. It did not surprise her at all when a man stepped out of the back of a white van and called her name.

"Ms. Picard, in here first, please."

As she stepped past him, he spoke into his communicator. "Client is onboard, sir."

"Is that TC?" she asked.

"Yes, ma'am. Agent Demuzzio. He said I should check you for bugs."

"Okay," she shrugged, "go ahead, I know the drill."

He ran the equipment over her body and reported into his communicator. "She's clean, sir."

Lara smiled at the technician and backed out of the van. Okay, she thought, this has to be quick. I've got to get TC on my side right away: Best to make him deny his own suspicions out loud. That's psychologically sound. Once he's said it, he won't want to back down.

"TC!" she exclaimed, hugging him as he reached the sidewalk, "thanks for coming after me." She stood back, hands still on his shoulders, and looked at him quizzically. "You think I'm crazy, don't you?"

"No, no, Lara, I don't think you're crazy. You've never been crazy. And I can't remember that I've ever seen you panic. So come on inside and tell me about it." He smiled as he held the door for her.

"Lara Picard, Agent Dave Ditka, Agent Tom Black," Demuzzio said, making the introductions as they went inside.

Lara shook their hands, assessing them as they assessed her. Good size beef, she noted. My age. Old enough to know a thing or two. Young enough to have good reflexes.

"Protocol calls for three, doesn't it, TC? You going to stick around?"

"No, Lara. Your third will be Mary Lovelock. She'll be here shortly, she's stopping to pick up some more firepower. She's about your size, so I asked her to bring some extra clothes."

I've met Mary, Lara remembered, and except for more red in her blond hair she could pass for me at a distance. So she makes a reasonable decoy. Ah, TC, you've taken me seriously. You've thought this through. Good!

"Ham and Josh?" she asked him.

"Yup. They're all settled in a nice suite, being guarded by Agents Socrates and..." he consulted his notebook, "Schmidt."

Lara exhaled her relief. "Thanks, TC."

TC Demuzzio stared at her intently. "Now, Lara, tell me what it's all about, your Category 4. This is a lot of government resources we're putting out here. Shit's gonna hit the fan Tuesday morning when the brass gets back and hears about it. You need something to drink while we talk?"

"Actually, TC, I'm starved. You keep this place stocked with any food?"

"Naw, just junk snacks. Ditka, buzz Lovelock, tell her to find an open supermarket with a deli and get a bunch of sandwiches. Thanks.

"Okay, Lara, let's go sit in the living room and talk."

The living room of the safehouse expanded into the dining area and kitchen, a great room, really, with no interior walls. They sat on opposite ends of a sofa, and Demuzzio shrugged an invitation with his outspread hands and raised eyebrows.

"TC, here it is in a nutshell," she responded. "An assassin is coming for me. I know it, absolutely. I'll get into that in a minute. The reason I wanted this safehouse is because I've seen it before, and it makes a good trap. My own home doesn't make a good trap. If I go into more secure custody, like Quantico or the Farm, the assassin might put off making an attempt. And I can't spend the rest of my life looking over my shoulder, or being worried about Josh."

Lara contemplated the big agent, knowing he was recalling past events. This would be the fourth attempt in... how many years? She watched his expression change, conceding her point: she shouldn't have to keep looking over her shoulder.

"TC, the reason I said I'd meet you here at the safehouse is that I needed some time to think. Alone. So I zigged and zagged my way up here for a couple of hours through the Park, letting the the woods free up my thinking. In those two hours, my mind confirmed everything that led me to make that Category 4 call."

"Umm. I've seen how that mind of yours works, Lara. So I'm listening."

"Okay, TC, let me take it from the top. Something's been bothering me for awhile, and it was just like the sensations I had before, when the two Juliuses were on my case. Looking back, for each attempt they made to kill me, there was a series of little somethings beforehand. These added up, and added up, until they triggered a warning bell. Each something by itself was pretty small, like somebody looking at me a trifle too long, or looking away, or fading into the surroundings just a little too well. Some hang-ups on phone calls to the house. Some crosstalk or static on the cell phone. No one big thing by itself, just a... confluence... of many little things. And it's happening again. I'm a scientist, TC. I think intuition is probably just your brain connecting dots you recognize at some other level of consciousness. Maybe down at the animal level, where your senses are tuned for survival."

Demuzzio rubbed his chin. "Okay, Lara, so you have this animal intuition. I can understand that, and accept it. I've had the feeling myself: in 'Nam way back when; on a few Bureau missions since then. You're being hunted, you're in the crosshairs, somehow you just know."

That's good, TC, that's really good, Lara thought to herself. You're halfway there. Just keep persuading yourself.

"The problem for me, Lara," he said finally, "is exactly how do I write this up? You called in a Category 4. You did it on the basis of adding up a lot of little signs, and animal intuition. We responded. You're protected. Your son and uncle are protected. But this chews up a lot of Bureau resources, which are so damn tight these days I almost gotta get papal dispensation to spend an extra minute in the can. So gimme some of your reasoning, and I'll see if I can spin it into a plausible tale the bean-counters will go for. Those unimaginative bastards can't understand animal intuition." He took out his notebook and started making notations in his inscrutable personal shorthand.

Bless you, TC, she thought. You're a good man and a dear friend, and now just buy into this last little bit, which is the only piece of real deception, and please forgive me for it. But if it all works out you'll never know. And that really is for the best.

Indeed, that is best. The thought was confirmed in Lara's mind-space. *Disclosing of evolving consciousness to third parties, especially official agencies, introduces other variables, wild cards. Chaos theory indicates many possible outcomes, some of which are unfavorable to successful evolution. Explanations that fit into this reality's current belief systems are much preferred.*

"Here's my theory, TC," Lara said, drawing on years of interrogation skills to control her facial expressions, "and it's based on meetings I sat in with your staff and the DEA guys, and some research of my own. So, this isn't solely my animal intuition.

"I think we're doing too much damage to the drug cartels. In addition, there's some sort of power struggle going on internally among the cartels; they're killing each other off. I get those interagency reports from DEA, and it's pretty clear that one of the cartels has got themselves some kind of super-assassin. Interpol code-named him *Warlock*, because they can't get any sort of handle on him. He's more elusive than the Jackal was. He's running a really nasty terror campaign. There are all sorts of rumors and myths, and they seem psychologically designed to drive people out of the drug business. And the myths are reinforced by very specific assassinations or disappearances. This has been going on for three or four years now, so far as DEA can tell. You know all this, probably better than I do."

"Yeah, sure, Lara, I've read some of the briefs. There's even a *sub rosa* betting pool at the Bureau on who *Warlock* tags next. So what?"

"So, TC, my theory is that whichever cartel is sponsoring *Warlock* is thinking that they have all the power just about consolidated, and now they're planning to remove the next thorn in their side. Which would be us—the enforcement community. They're going to terrorize us. Why they picked me first, I don't know. Maybe the Juliuses were part of their family or something. Their ultimate objective is probably to get to some kind of Mexican standoff, paralyze us with assassinations, so they can run a stable business operation again, bring their profit margins back up. Is this making any sense to you, TC?"

"Yeah, Lara, I've read the reports, heard the stories. What you say makes sense. I can spin a decent write-up off it. But... you want to trap this super-assassin, this *Warlock*, how's he gonna find you? And if he knows you're protected, why wouldn't he just wait it out, go work on another target for awhile?"

"That's the tough part, TC," she agreed. "I don't know why he wouldn't just be patient. Why take a risk? Why not whack me from a distance with a rifle, or with a bomb, in an ambush or in my car? Maybe that's less terrorizing, but it still works. All I can say is if you study the profile, he doesn't work that way. He likes to work close in. He must need the challenge. He must get off on it. And he's very surgical: only the target, not much collateral damage, no innocent bystanders killed. The profile says he's probably a psychopath, but with some kind of weird moral code not to hurt innocent bystanders.

"How's he going to find me? I don't know. Maybe he's got hacker resources that can crack your communications security. I actually think maybe he can smell me. That sounds strange, but when I came up through the park, I made sure I left plenty of scent on trees and bushes. Anyway, TC, he's coming. I can sense it. You probably think I'm crazy, but I'm telling you, I can sense it."

"All right, kiddo," he replied with some resignation, "this is pretty goddamn weird, but we're going with your animal intuition and screw the cost of the operation. You gotta know that if it gets toward the end of the week and there hasn't been any action, the bean-counters at the Bureau are gonna hoist my sorry ass so far up in the air the FAA'll want strobe lights on it. Just so you know, Lara."

She took a big weathered hand in both of hers and squeezed it affectionately, sighing her relief that he trusted her enough to ignore the elements that didn't quite fit together.

"Thanks, TC."

"Okay, Lara, you're welcome. Now let's walk around the place until Lovelock gets here with the sandwiches. I guess you probably remember all the security features from that time we boarded your environmental witness, but I want to make sure you've got the layout firmly in mind."

She catalogued the security features of the house in her mind as he gave her the tour.

"Here's the first panic chute, Lara," he said, pulling open the tall narrow closet door beside the fireplace. You just step in it, that's all you have to do. The pressure of your weight will trigger it off. The door will snap shut automatically. The whole thing is titanium, take an armor-piercing shell to get through it.

"After the door shuts, grab the two side handles, because the whole pod, with you in it, will drop like a shot down the chute, and level out in the tunnel. You end up in a subsurface vault on the park side of Adams Mill Road. You can stay there and wait for PD to arrive, or you can pop the top hatch to the surface and climb out into some bushes. Or you can exit the side hatch and climb down into the big storm culvert that dumps into Rock Creek, if you don't mind getting your feet wet.

"Everything is automatic, Lara. Once the system is triggered, all sorts of alarms go off. The drop tunnel is trip-wired so if anybody is foolish enough to chase you down through it they get a dose of anesthetic gas. It's on a UPS system so everything still works even if power is cut off.

"Yeah, TC, thanks. I remember it now."

They walked over the rest of the house, and he pointed out the hardened doors and walls, the retinal scanning required for entry, the armorplast windows with Kevlar draperies, the automated alarm functions that would bring a Metro SWAT team response within minutes. He waved out the windows, describing the perimeter detectors in the small yard outside.

Yes, Lara thought to herself, this will do nicely. Confidence flooded into her. The Beast can't possibly know what we've got here. And if he gets inside and I can't kill him, I've at least got a way out.

Just then Special Agent Mary Lovelock arrived, and they all got a thorough briefing by TC Demuzzio over sandwiches. Astonishment over Lara's appetite and humorous comments about her hollow leg accompanied the briefing. She smiled at them and blamed it on a strenuous workout in the park.

Northwest Washington, DC | Sunday 2101 EDT

Hamilton O'Donnell had put up many out-of-town visitors in the Embassy Row Hotel, and its staff cheerfully accommodated him with a suite of connecting rooms. He booked three nights, and then called the FBI number Lara provided. Now he stood, hand on Joshua's wiry young shoulder, on their fifth floor balcony. They contemplated the skyline, gazing southeast over the downtown area and the center of government. The Washington Monument penetrated the dusk off to their right, a shining obelisk in the middle distance. Venus showed clearly, higher in the sky. A full moon had risen above the eastern horizon off to their left, its lambent glow competing with the alabaster whiteness of the flood-lit monument.

"The moon is the mark of the High Priestess, young Joshua," the old man mused thoughtfully, "the card numbered two in the tarot deck. A fascinatin' juxtaposition of the moon with the monument, is it not?"

Joshua cocked an eyebrow at his uncle. "Tarot? I didn't know you were superstitious, Uncle Ham. And what's the juxtaposition? I'm not following you."

"Ah, me lad, have not all superstitions some element of truth, were we able to appreciate their full context? The juxtaposition? The moon and the monument?

The comparison is one of symbols, not the objects themselves. The monument, I believe, could easily be a sword—a sword such as carried by Justice, the card numbered eleven in tarot. Or the monument could represent a one, which would be the Magician. There may be a symbolic message here, could we but fathom it."

The old man watched Joshua being drawn into their mind-dance. He could almost read, on that expressive young face, the thoughts that went flashing like lightning down branched pathways, then converged.

"Uncle Ham, is Mom a High Priestess?" Joshua asked.

The boy truly is uncanny, his uncle thought. His nine-year old mind is so unencumbered by preconceptions that it can process even non-mathematical symbolism, concepts to which he has no previous exposure.

"Quite likely, me lad. Symbolically speakin'."

"And the danger that is coming for her, is that a Magician?"

"Quite possibly. Symbolically speakin'. In Roman mythos, Mercury with his winged sandals carries messages through the heavens. He is the god of magicians. But also of healers, writers, swindlers and thieves. A complex god, that one."

"Then could their juxtaposition be Justice?"

Ah, interesting question, the old man thought. The boy intentionally bypassed the obvious question about danger to his mother, and asked one of great subtlety. So... he intuits the allegory, he feels the symbolism. He actually feels it.

"Joshua," he answered obliquely, as befitted their mind-dance, "Justice is the twelfth tarot archetype. The astrological sign is the constellation Libra, the balanced scales. But the image of Justice on the tarot card carries a sword along with her scales. Symbolically speakin', the scales represent the balance between inner self and outer self. Or between necessity and choice. Or between other competin' aspects of the human condition. The sword represents the ability to reason, to choose, to act. And of course the sword has two edges. Justice, the restoration of balance, frequently requires cuttin' both ways."

"Uncle Ham?"

"Yes, me lad?"

The boy giggled. "I have no idea what you mean."

Hamilton O'Donnell slid his hand down Joshua's arm and hugged the child to him tightly, staring at the full moon rising, opposite the Monument.

"Ah, but you do, boy. Yes, you do."

Chapter 21

Passenger John Connard had passed uneventfully through customs at Miami International. He had nothing to declare, aside from the still-quiescent companion in his mind, and suppressed a humorous urge to list import of an extraterrestrial being onto U.S. soil. After re-stoking his hyperactive metabolism with sandwiches in the domestic concourse, he headed toward the gate for the connecting flight to Washington National.

Now, with the plane not quite an hour out of Miami, he closed his eyes and quieted his mind. The image of Duc Li remained only a passive warm dot of light in his new mind-space; his nexus remained in some other dimension, rejuvenating, regaining strength. John returned to his earlier reverie, contemplating the light and love that Lara Picard had brought into his life from the first moment they touched hands, there in her kitchen, three and a half years ago....

"And this is my son, Joshua," Lara had said, almost shyly, as if the child were a wondrous work of art freshly created in that very instant.

I crouched down to eye level to shake Josh's hand, and felt again that powerful and insistent connection. It carried different tones than with Lara, but somehow the same imperative. I remembered feeling that connection sometimes when I held my baby sister's hand.

In acknowledgment, Joshua brought his left hand onto mine, and squeezed my big hand in his two smaller ones, and I became a new friend. Looking down at us, Lara beamed happiness, moisture in her eyes. How very odd it was, almost like I'd been waiting my whole life for that very moment.

Reluctantly, almost as an afterthought, I stood up to ask her the pro forma questions, and to tell her my preference to remain anonymous. I watched her conflicted expressions as she struggled with how to answer a total stranger. Those emerald eyes danced and shimmered in the light, and I watched trust win out over caution.

"It's Ms. Picard," she answered my most important question first, even though I didn't explicitly ask it. "Josh's father died four years ago. And, given the circumstances, I wish you would just call me Lara."

How my heart lifted! I'd just fallen in love, and she wasn't married.

"And I'm just John," I agreed. We laughed together at the absurdity of our unacknowledged circumstance: two strangers instinctively, instantly in love. The rightness of the instinct needed no words—the cosmic connection reverberated through the kitchen, magnified with each small motion of a hand, each sideways glance, each little smile.

She answered the rest of my questions in order, ending with her suspicions about the Castagnas being the driving force behind the team that had just assaulted her.

Well, we can't have that, I decided. The Assassin would be pleased to provide a severed head to the organization, make sure they get the message to leave her alone. The Castagnas in prison? A bit more of a challenge, but the Magician can handle it. Alex will help. This woman and her son will not need to be looking over their shoulders any longer.

Pinning the waistband of my running shorts back together, I talked with Joshua while Lara made her phone call to the FBI.

"Well of course you can come back later, John," she said as I left. No hint of hesitation in her reply to my question. "We have a lot to talk about, I think. And thank you for saving us tonight." She smiled and kissed me full on the lips as we stood in her doorway.

And that's when I felt it again, that inescapable resonance. Her lips were incredibly soft, but overlaid an intense heat, almost volcanic. Waves of love and passion chased me like tongues of burbling lava down the steps of her house as I ran toward R Street....

In his mind, John Connard retraced the streets he'd traveled back to Georgetown, running at the easy rhythmic lope Duc Li advised him to use when seeking contemplation. He suddenly had a lot to contemplate.

Northwest Washington, DC | Sunday 2126 EDT

"I understand the symbolic sword well enough, Uncle Ham," Joshua said, putting his arm around his uncle's waist and hugging him in return, "and okay, I guess I get why Justice would carry scales in one hand and a sword in the other."

"And, me lad?" Hamilton O'Donnell stared off into the middle distance, letting the boy work on it.

"But I don't understand—I mean, I accept the symbolism and all—but how does it relate to Mom? Or to her new consciousness, or to an evolving new species? It's just too fuzzy, there are too many possibilities."

That there are, boy, he mentally acknowledged, that there are. And not all of them are good, either. But you're about to ask me that, are you not?

"Uncle Ham," Joshua surprised him with a tangential approach, "you go to church regularly, early Mass every Sunday morning, right?"

"That I do, me little *gossoon*, that I do. Keep the faith with me friends the Jesuits in the Georgetown Chapel. A fine Catholic Irishman I am. Every Sunday, six AM sharp. Haven't missed in twenty years. Longer, probably."

"And yet you're telling me about the tarot. Isn't that superstition? Isn't that a conflict with your religion?" Joshua cocked an eyebrow at his uncle who laughed with delight.

"Oh, Joshua, me lad, the Irish have a quite complex spiritual heritage. The Celts. The Norse. The Druids. And leprechauns, wizards, pooka, earth mothers. And then ould Saint Pat comes along to drive out the snakes and save our poor benighted souls from hell and damnation. We are a humble and thankful people. Accept salvation in any form, we will. There is no conflict in any of this. None at all!"

"Religion doesn't conflict with superstition?"

"Joshua, me Joshua! What is religion, but superstition with better marketin'?"

"Uncle Ham," Joshua asked, when the mirth subsided, "ever since I touched Mom this morning, and felt the energy in her, I have this sense that I'm like a... magnetometer, in a field that's shifting around me continually. Then you talk to me about the tarot, or about religion, or mysticism, and that sharpens my magnetometer focus somehow. I feel like there are threads of electrical current, weaving themselves, converging into a common time and place, right here, right now. I can almost see them."

"Threads comin' together in the here and now? Ah, 'tis a feelin' familiar at many times to many people, me lad. Many stories and myths revolve around it. Norse traditions have the Norns: the giantess of the past, the elf of the present, the dwarf of the future. Their names mean 'that which has become, that which is becoming, that which should become'."

"And in the Bible, Joshua, Ecclesiastes puts it a different way: 'That which has been, is now; and that which is to be has already been.' The same message, me lad."

"And the threads weave events together, Uncle Ham? So that they make a tapestry? Tell a story? What about the threads into the future? Is that story already told? What does your tarot say about that?"

"The tarot itself says nothin', young Joshua. You read into it what you will. Tarot is just a means to insight, a toolkit of symbols for the mystic, a toolkit that teaches."

"And what does it teach about the future, Uncle Ham?"

"Choices, boy. It teaches choices."

Global Consciousness Project, Princeton University, NJ | Sunday 2127 EDT

"Doctor Rodgers," Adrienne summarized, "I've got the crosshairs for the 2045, the 2100 and the 2115 time periods sitting practically on top of each other, five or six miles west of downtown Miami, and a little north. That's exactly where the map shows the airport. These locations have very tight probability circles, under a half-mile diameter, even with low signal strength." She studied the time-trend graph and the accompanying string of numbers winding across the monitor. "Except for three or four little blips, the signal stayed low right through the airport, and onto the DC flight, and just came up a few minutes ago."

Nathan spoke succinct notes into his digital recorder, summarizing. "South America signal source approximately stationary for time periods 2030-2115 at location MIA. Source departed MIA around 2115. Now moving north-northeast at a rate consistent with jet airplane speed, for time periods 2115-2215. Present location is off the coast of South Carolina at 2215. Source departure time from MIA and subsequent positions are consistent with expected flight path of American Airlines Flight 59 MIA to DCA."

He paused to draw a breath and peered over Adrienne's shoulder at the coordinate tracking display. The recorder had been a belated thought, but a good one. Increasingly, these events cried out to be documented in every detail possible, Nathan thought. He studied the tracking display, trying to draw more insight from it, his thumb poised over the Record button.

Northwest Washington, DC | Sunday 2128 EDT

"So the tarot teaches choices. And the sword symbolizes our ability to reason through a choice, and to act on our choice? But what do choices have to do with Mom? What do they have to do with her new... evolutionary state?" Joshua spoke uncertainly into the soft night air.

"Ah well, now why don't you tell your poor ould uncle, me lad? *You* tell me what *you* think. Did you ever read Darwin, like I suggested?"

The boy's expression turned serious as he accepted the clue to their mind-dance. "I always read what you suggest, Uncle Ham, I studied *Origin of Species* two years ago. And after that I read some of his revisionists, like Stephen Jay Gould. I tend to like punctuated equilibrium. Sudden changes in response to a species' context make a lot of sense. From a survival perspective, I mean. And now Mom may be a living example of that..."

"Ah, yes! And would the choices the punctuated organism makes be important for species survival? For evolution? What have you sopped up on that, my young sponge?"

"Not enough, Uncle Ham. You'll have to help me here." The boy looked at him helplessly.

Ah, thought the old man, so exquisitely plaintive. He tries to wheedle the answer out of me. God, I love you, boy, but what if I don't know? What if I'm the wrong oracle? What if the answer is in you, not in me? What if you have to come to it yourself?

"Uncle Ham?" Joshua wheedled again, affecting the sweetness of nine-year-old innocence.

Hamilton O'Donnell roared his mirth into the night. Oh, that look, he thought, it's just too much to bear. A forty-year old manipulator behind a nine-year old face! And that eyebrow over the smile! Mephistopheles on top of L'il Abner! Oh, it's just too much!

Northwest Washington, DC | Sunday 2130 EDT

"All right, people," Demuzzio concluded as he climbed into the van, "be very, very careful. Stay alert. This is one smart, dangerous psychopath."

The three agents nodded acceptance of those parting instructions, and looked at Lara protectively.

She swallowed hard as she looked back at them. They didn't understand, of course. They had no inkling of how deadly a monster was closing in. They didn't know that her main defense would be herself, not them. They didn't know that all the high-tech accoutrements of the house were just a trap, with the sole purpose of slowing or perturbing the Beast's attack, giving her enough offensive edge to kill him. They didn't know they were only the front-line troops, expendable; that chances were good one or all would be expended. She fully understood for the first time what John had told her about the rigors of command as a soldier: sometimes you must send people to their death. It tore at her heart.

This is the best way.

I know that, she projected sadly back into her mind-space, but it doesn't make it any easier.

She excused herself and went upstairs to the bedroom, claiming fatigue and the need to try to rest. She managed not to cry until the bedroom door shut behind her.

Ah, who I really need here with me is John, she told herself, stretching out on the bed. He's probably the best at this sort of soldiering, even though he's surely so highly classified he can never admit it. But he's out in the African bush somewhere, so face it, Lara, you're not going to get him back anytime soon.

She tried to review her strategy for the trap once more, but instead her mind took its own path and strayed back to the love of her life and his many talents. She visualized their first meeting, when he had rescued her and Josh from the Castagna thugs. Her thoughts drifted back, three years and five months, to that time in her kitchen when John had introduced himself....

"And this is my son, Joshua," I'd responded, pulling myself out of that roaring cosmic connection and regaining some presence of mind.

"Hello, Joshua," John had said gravely, crouching down to eye level and holding out his hand. "I'm pleased to meet you."

And Josh took John's hand with no hesitation at all, and smiled broadly and grabbed it with both of his. And then my heart was surely lost to this man.

"You said you need to make a phone call, I believe?" John asked. "Something about the DC police possibly being compromised? Were they supposed to be watching over you? And you need to check with the Bureau? I presume that's the FBI? Is your... situation... something you would care to share with me, Mrs. Picard?"

Ah, the expressions that must have run across my face! The uncertainty, the conflict, the desire to trust. And he read them all, I could see it in his eyes.

"And... well," John added gently, "now that I appreciate the complexities of your situation, I believe I would rather stay anonymous myself. If, of course, that's not too troublesome to you. My, um, business, is better served by keeping a low profile, Mrs. Picard."

He was testing me. And right then I realized his mind was as quick as his body. But also I somehow realized from that one touch that he really is a gentle soul, even though he could obviously kill with either hand or foot. The enormity of our encounter reverberated right down to my core. I looked at the light in his eyes, and the whole kitchen seemed to shimmer. Nothing in my life ever felt so right, so instantly, except Joshua. So I cast away caution.

"It's Ms. Picard. Josh's father died four years ago," I told him. "And, given the circumstances, I wish you would just call me Lara."

"And I'm just John."

Devastating, that smile. It invited trust, and I gave it. Totally.

"John, to answer your questions—briefly, and then I really do have to make a call—Metro PD was supposed to be keeping an eye on me. I had this hunch I was being targeted, like other hunches in the past that have been right, and I told the

Bureau about it. They set up a modest protection protocol. Supposedly Metro has me covered over the holidays. I'm under remote surveillance; there's a transponder on me, and one in my car. But they didn't work, or somebody's gotten lazy, or it's New Year's Eve and Metro is too shorthanded or too busy. Somebody just screwed up; that's the most logical explanation. But it's also remotely possible that somebody was bought off, or told to look the other way. Until the Bureau chases that one down, I'm not taking any chances. I don't want to involve the police in this if I don't know they're solid. I'm going to talk to my friend TC at the Bureau and have him sort it out."

"Targeted by...?"

Amazing, how the answers continued to just roll right out of me.

"I'm pretty sure it's a couple of drug cartel bozos. The Castagnas, Julius senior and Julius junior. I helped put them away ten years ago. They just can't seem to forgive me for that. This is their third attempt, if it's them. They're still in prison, but their organization apparently rolls on."

His eyes went cold and his face hardened as he processed that information.

"And now I really should make that call, if you'll excuse me for just a minute. And yes, of course I'll keep you anonymous, John, if you like."

From the phone in the living room, out of earshot, I watched him pin the waistband of his shorts back together and talk to Josh. I could almost see the connection forming between them.

And when John left, he knew exactly what to ask. And I knew exactly what to answer. I didn't even have to think about it.

"Well of course you can, John! Josh and I would be delighted to have you join us for our little New Year's Eve celebration."

Then, in the cosmic certainty of that moment, I slipped my arms around him and kissed him full on the lips.

"And thank you for saving us tonight, John."

His kiss was gentle and caring; but, God, the power beneath it, the intense effort at control. I was still trembling as I watched him run off down the street....

The memories of the volcanic passion smoldering and burbling so merrily underneath their first kiss released her only reluctantly back to the present. They left her, bereft, on the bed in the safehouse on Irving Street, trembling and forsaken at the absence of her lover and protector.

Lara Picard wiped her eyes on the sheets, stilled her trembling and forced herself to face reality. It was unlikely that John would return soon enough to help her this time. She was on her own.

Chapter 22

Adrienne teetered on the edge of the solution; she could just about taste it.

"C'mon, c'mon," she urged the lines of coding on her monitor screen, feeling in her mind the tickle of incipient discovery. She spoke softly, trying to coax the idea out like she'd tried to coax her mother's new kitten out from under the sofa last week. But, like the kitten, the idea wanted to play its own game with her.

The code on the screen showed her pattern recognition algorithm as fully functional, but it still needed to be keyed off some distinct difference in the two signals. She'd written the code in the blind faith that such a difference existed, and that she would be able to find it. Without it, her code would be useless: as the signal source now moving northward on Flight 59 came closer, it would overlap the DC source. Then they wouldn't be able to tell the two sources apart. But her intuition was very strong, and always on target when that strong. So the difference just *had* to be there, staring her in the face. All she had to do was recognize it. Frustrated, she slouched back in the chair, rubbed her tired eyes, put her feet up on the table, and rested her chin on her hands.

Something Aaron had said, the last time they talked, jokingly... "Maybe they're lovers", he'd said. The answer was hiding in that phrase, she thought, just like the kitten under the sofa. She tugged, and suddenly it leaped out at her.

"Aaron! Thank you! You did it," she yelped, making Nathan jump. "Doctor Rodgers, I know how to discriminate the signals! He gave me an idea! Now let's see if I'm right," she muttered, going back into the incoming GCD data, "zeroes and ones. Let's see if there truly is a preference...."

And there it was: the Washington source biased the GCD outcomes consistently toward zeroes, the South American source consistently toward ones. The observation had been there all along, buried in the back of her memory. Well, chalk up another one for intuition, Adrienne thought; sometimes it's downright scary. Hot diggety!

She dismissed her fatigue, and rapidly coded the discriminator as a front-end preprocessor of the incoming data. Now, the output of any detector within the influence of a signal source would be tagged with the code 'B' for blue or 'G' for green. Whooping aloud, she re-coded her 1-minute integrals of signal strength to run off the discriminated GCD data. When both sources affected a detector, the code now partitioned the two components. Sure, she admitted, there would be some canceling effects when the signals neutralized each other, but unless they were on exactly the same frequency all the time, it should work well enough....

Taking a deep breath, Adrienne ran the revised code on the Richmond GCD, which was now in between the two sources. It worked! Two components, separate outputs, neatly discriminated. The source in DC showed in bright green; the source moving up the coast in bright blue.

"Doctor Rodgers! I got it," she whooped again, "I got it!"

"Jesus, watching you program is like watching Mozart compose," Nathan said, looking at what had become a blue and green two-parameter plot. He patted congratulations on her shoulder.

Intensely absorbed, Adrienne Baxter neither heard the compliment nor felt the pat, thinking, while I'm on a roll here, just a few more little tweaks of the code. Then, I'm going to have pretty little blue crosshairs and circles, and pretty little green crosshairs and circles, and I'm going to get to watch you puppies come together and isn't this going to be super! She wondered briefly if she were being voyeuristic, but decided not. After all, this was science.

Northwest Washington, DC | Sunday 2133 EDT

"So, me lad," Hamilton O'Donnell said, levering himself into a more comfortable position and picking up the thread of their conversation, "evolutionary quantum leaps by Doctor Gould, rest his soul, are fine and dandy. But they do beg bigger questions. If such leaps are buried in our genetic structure, and are triggered when the time is right... well, how did they get there in the first place? Accident or design? And what determines when the time is right? Is it all a random, accidental Darwinian favorin' of better adaptations? Or is there a plan, a genetic blueprint? And if so, who made the plan, hmm? What does your keen young mind think of those issues?"

Joshua worked his feet up higher on the balcony rail, and tilted further back in his chair, contemplating his uncle's profile.

"Uncle Ham, I sorta like the idea that organisms or systems under stress, or exposed to a new ecological niche, can pop out an authorization triggering a new sequence in their genome. Chaos theory fits here, I think, better than Darwin."

The old man smiled off into the deepening night and kept probing. "So the sequence already exists in the genome? Like a successful adaptation to a new niche, or even a new species? All it awaits is a trigger?"

"Yeah. And when you have an endpoint, and a genetic code to get to it, and specific choices that can trigger the code... hard to say that's purely an accident," Joshua concluded.

"You truly believe the individual organism carries the code for its genetic future within it, young Joshua?"

"Yeah. Not hardwired, Uncle Ham, just possible genetic futures. But I do think some kind of opportunistic code for advancement is present in the human genome, and I guess it's purposeful." The boy smiled tentatively at his uncle, nine-year-old uncertainty belying the sophisticated opinion just offered.

"Umm. Fascinatin'." Hamilton O'Donnell unconsciously worked his feet up on the balcony rail, and angled his chair back, the better to mirror his nephew's position.

"And possible futures are determined by choices," the boy added.

Goddard Space Flight Center, Greenbelt, MD | Sunday 2137 EDT

Edwin Edwards, SDI Exercise Controller, was on the first break he'd been able to call since the exercise segment started at 1800 hours. He drank coffee while he read Aaron's email, fascinated. *The boy is onto something, and it could be huge*, he realized. *The question is what the hell do we do about it.* He studied the email's language and smiled. The words conveyed none of the excitement Aaron must be feeling. It was just calm, detached reporting of factual matters and observations, like reporting on a lab experiment. He noted a copy had gone to Nathan Rodgers.

"Well, Aaron," he addressed his empty office, "I did tell you that you could share the information, and that's obviously a crackerjack programmer at Princeton making sense out of this stuff. But what's conspicuously lacking in your report is any kind of opinion or recommendation or call to action...."

Aha! The boy's being cagey! Edwards grinned at the realization. *He's standing off from it, telling me I've got the ball. Beautifully understated, Aaron. We just might make a government bureaucrat out of you yet!*

He pondered sending a reply, but then decided, *no, maybe I really don't want to have seen this email just yet. I'll have to think about this whole crazy event some more. Maybe a lot more.*

Northwest Washington, DC | Sunday 2138 EDT

"So, my young geneticist, the concept of a genomic code for evolution has a good feel to it for you, eh? With a trigger to set it off?" Hamilton O'Donnell stretched his arms up above the hotel balcony and smiled hugely into the starry sky.

"Yeah! Some kind of code trigger, Uncle Ham," Joshua replied. "That's the simplest thing. Like buying software—you load it on your machine, and it's physically there, but you can't run it until you enter the activation or license number."

"Oh, goodness, me lad," his uncle roared with amusement, "so now we're all just biological computers, slouchin' toward some evolutionary horizon, waitin' for our codes to be activated? Do I see at the end of the tunnel in an aura of light a smilin' Bill Gates instead of the Pearly Gates?"

"Uh huh. Why not? The logic would be pretty much the same for biological codes as computer codes. And I think maybe simple viruses or retroviruses can carry pieces of genetic material for code triggers, Uncle Ham."

"Ah, Joshua! So we are merely biological machines, run by codes, by blueprints? The proper ones embedded? Activated at the proper evolutionary time? The creationists will be quite pleased with you. The fundamentalists will not. Always difficult to guess where the Pope will weigh in. The Dalai Lama will say this is nothing new."

The boy giggled a further argument. "But we're machines anyway, Uncle Ham; we're full of operating codes. Our autonomic nervous system, our immune system, they're all run by codes. You know that!"

"Well, yes. And that, my young friend, is all biological, which is perfectly fine for the animals. But what of us humans? What of our intellect? Our art? Our science? Our pursuit of enlightenment? Our screaming desire 'to boldly go where no man has gone before'? Is there no greater blueprint that encompasses our spirit? No creator of all this? No God? What say you to that, my young philosopher?"

"Hmm. Yeah. I guess I think there's a bigger blueprint, Uncle Ham. But the counter is that are plenty of evolutionary false starts and dead ends and only a fraction of one percent of the species that have existed on earth in the past still exist today. Why would God go to that much fuss? Just to allow choices?"

"Well, maybe God is a humorist, me lad, just havin' some fun along the evolutionary road. Have you ever seen a gooney bird matin' dance?"

American Airlines Flight 59 Enroute to Washington | Sunday 2139 EDT

The quiescent warm dot of diffuse white light expanded in John's mind-space and the smiling image of Duc Li re-formed. It pulled him out of his memories and back into the reality of the airplane cabin. He recognized regrowth and rejuvenation in his nexus as the image expanded fully into his consciousness.

Four times, he reported into his mind-space. I felt a contact four times while you were resting. I'm pretty sure about that. The feel of the contacts was very light, enticing, seductive. It wasn't intrusive or unpleasant, and it even felt nice, like a rub on the back. But it had an underlying darkness about it. It came from the Other, I'm sure of it. He shivered.

The image of Duc Li examined his memory of the four contacts, somberly, sadly.

The darkness you sense is true, the rest is deception. The human host selected appears to have a very powerful mind. The Other may have picked a host like itself, psychopathic and amoral. If not, it is proceeding by deception while it eats away the core beliefs of its host. In either case, the result is the same: a human being with no connection to its soul. The Other's contact may feel pleasurable, but that is an insidious superficial overlay. What lies beneath is the darkness you felt, an absence of light or goodness. That is the true nature of the Other.

John pondered the terror he would feel, the monster he would become, without a connection to his soul.

Yes, the Other truly is a monster, John Connard; it has regressed to the worst nightmare of the primitive past of our species. It has regressed to a time when the sole path to survival was power. It is totally different than you. Unlike the Other, you have a great love and reverence for life. The Other has lost touch with its soul and believes it will never regain it. It hates your species, your rapidly developing connection to evolving greater consciousness, your imminent turn toward the light. It will try to distort that connection, to seduce your evolving race into its darkness, to turn your growing power to its own use.

He felt the repugnance permeate his mind-space, and floated his query against it. How? How could this happen to such an advanced species as yours? The answer came slowly, painfully, the concepts unclear, occluded by a gray morass of sorrow and loss. Out of these depths a more familiar metaphor arose to clarify the murkiness: Lucifer.

Yes, John Connard, your species has its own stories, similar across many cultures. The literal translation of Lucifer from your Latin is bearer of light. And yet Lucifer fell from the light. He was brought down by his own pride, and remains constrained by his own pride from returning. Such stories carry the essential truth of how such things happen, and why they continue to happen, in your species and ours, and in all others throughout time and space. Pride. Putting the self ahead of the whole. That is the case here, with the Other.

The attraction I felt in these contacts seemed good; only the underlying darkness seemed evil, John objected.

Your mind and the mind of the Other's human host must be at a similar level of incipient evolution. This means your two minds must be alike in many ways. The Other is clever, and accustomed to manipulating feelings and emotions. It can project affection, even love, through its host's mind. But this is bait, like the scent from the flower that attracts its prey. It is a path to darkness. The Other wants to devour your soul if it can, and kill you if it can't.

So I must kill the Other. And to do that I must kill its human host.

There is no other choice.

Are there alternatives, a different interpretation of the Lucifer mythos? He floated the half-conceived question into his mind-space. Lucifer is a story with elemental truths about human nature, but after all, it's a story from more primitive times. So why would it necessarily still apply when human nature is changing for the better?

You remain troubled about the moral basis of our mission, John Connard. The image of Duc Li smiled gently in his mind-space, but with the sense of sadness still in his eyes.

No, the Other I can dispatch cheerfully, John thought back at him. But the host may be an innocent. I have never intentionally killed an innocent.

If the host once were innocent, it is no longer. The seduction into darkness cannot be resisted for long, even by the strongest human mind. The Other and its host are now inextricably woven together, at a cellular level, just as you and I. They cannot be separated unless the Other wills it. The Other cannot be forced to will the separation, by any means or subterfuge I can devise. And with the power growing in such a strong host mind, the Other cannot effectively be imprisoned or isolated. So they must both be destroyed.

Enlightenment, is that a possibility? John floated the spiritual concept his sensei Duc Li often had shared with him. Lucifer once bore the light, why not again?

The Other has lost contact with its soul, and cannot conceive of being connected with anything it cannot control, that it cannot manipulate. It cannot see that sharing the self is not losing the self. Sharing in the greater consciousness, one that it does not totally control... to the Other, that is a truly fearsome thing. So it cannot seek enlightenment, the price is too high.

The price is overcoming fear, that's all.

It covers over its fear with pride. It cannot admit to fear.

Pride. Putting the self ahead of the whole. All that malevolence. Destruction of an entire world, and an entire race? From fear? From pride?

It has happened before, on your world and on others. It will happen again. Here, if we do not prevent it.

Visions of destruction played out across his mind-space, reprising earlier visions in the cave. Ah, he thought, if Hitler had been a better artist, and hadn't been rejected by the Vienna Academy of Art... The pathways from that fateful convergence point eighty years ago had been complex, the outcomes uncertain at the time. But hindsight was clear and bleak, and the lesson apt for the damage that could be done by the Other, especially at this present point of convergence, this evolution of a new species. Power would go berserk. A young and frightfully talented race would be turned to evil, sent screaming on a jihad of terror and conquest across the universe. There would be death and destruction, and suffering untold, for generations into the future. The image of Duc Li painted more symbols to assist understanding, flowing them into his mind-space, cascades of torment.

John sighed, conceding, and glanced at his watch. A little more than an hour remained before their midnight arrival in Washington, DC.

Chapter 23

An authoritative knock on the hotel room door interrupted Joshua's whimsical response about the possible cosmic significance of the gooney bird's mating dance.

"Ah, Joshua, this must be our keepers." His uncle left the balcony and walked across the hotel room to open the door.

"Doctor O'Donnell? I'm Special Agent Jack Socrates." Brilliant white teeth smiled out of the big black man's face as he held up his ID for inspection. "Agent Schmidt is setting some electronics up in the suite next door, he'll be joining us shortly."

"Come in, come in, Agent Socrates," Hamilton O'Donnell said as he shook the man's hand. "My goodness, I feel safer already. And this is my nephew Joshua."

Joshua shook the agent's huge hand and admired his height and breadth of shoulder. His uncle spoke truly; there was in the big man's hand a sense of peace and security.

"If you don't mind, just go back to whatever you and Joshua were doing, sir," the agent said, "and I'll walk around and spot some of our new high-tech hardware here and there."

"Come, me lad, let's leave Mr. Socrates to his business, and return to our business. Which as I recall was ferretin' out the basis for human evolution. Or somethin' like that, was it not?"

They went back onto the balcony to pick up their conversation. Agent Socrates followed them out, inspecting it. He looked over the adjacent balconies on the hotel, and checked the sight lines to other buildings, evaluating.

"Uncle Ham," Joshua said, settling back in his chair and putting his feet up on the rail, "you've been asking me all the questions about what I think. Now I need to know what you think. You spoke of de Chardin, for example. Tell me more about him."

"Ah, Pierre Teilhard. Another old friend, me lad. Ancient French pedigree, and a Jesuit to boot, but I forgave him for both. He was a biologist, a paleontologist, a philosopher, quite an interesting mind; trained as a scientist, but he trusted intuition. He believed in a spirit of the earth, an evolving global consciousness.

He named it the *noosphere*. Forecast it, more than 50 years ago. He postulated an *omega point*, where consciousness coalesces into a new state of peace and unity over the globe. So, he was a mystic, a visionary. The dear man tried his best to reconcile his belief with Christian theology. Had difficulty there, but he made a plausible case, over the course of several books."

"Sounds a lot like what Mom was talking about this morning, Uncle Ham," Joshua ventured. "It sounds like what's happening, right here, right now, doesn't it? Except maybe there's a biological component to it—human evolution running alongside the evolution of global consciousness? Doesn't this feel sort of like a feedback loop to you?"

"Indubitably, me lad, indubitably."

Joshua jumped on that excitedly; his uncle rarely used words that were not conditioned by probability. "And if there *indubitably* is a feedback loop, Uncle Ham, that means you think it's some kind of active circuitry for consciousness, some kind of signal recognition and handling at both ends? At the individual end, and the global end?"

"Umm. Yes, me lad. But that thought would not be mine, exclusively, or even Pierre's. It goes back to pre-scientific cosmologies, to ancient wisdom, old beliefs. Me ould friend Aristotle, for example, articulated the concept of *entelechy*—the quality that causes matter to become what it should. Other philosophers and scientists over the years have proposed similar concepts, an *élan vital*, for example, an embedded creative force. Their view is that not enough can really be explained by accident, by evolution from random mutations in DNA followed by Darwinian selection. They say accidental evolution is statistically implausible, that it requires consciousness, and yes, resonance. Like the feedback loop you feel."

"Implausible," Joshua echoed, looking out over the night sky.

"Consciousness, resonance, feedback," the old man repeated. "None of these can be accidents; they require design, young Joshua, design. Or so these philosophies claim."

"Thanks, Uncle Ham," Joshua yawned hugely, "That makes sense. But I can't absorb any more of this right now. I'm going to hit the sack, I think."

"Fine, me lad, that's fine," his uncle replied absently, staring off in the direction of the Washington monument. "Just be brushin' your teeth properly, like your mum told you, there's a good lad."

Shortly after ten PM, Joshua lay in bed, thinking about biological and spiritual evolution as he dropped into sleep in the darkened room. Descending into dream state, his inner eye saw threads begin to wind around each other: a casual weaving together of two evolutions, a sketched beginning, a subtle sense of some pattern forming, like a tapestry.

American Airlines Flight 59 Enroute to Washington | Sunday 2221 EDT

John Connard sighed, reflecting on how much war and destruction was caused by fear and stupidity. But not this time, he resolved. This time he and the Magician and the Assassin would stop it before it got started.

Reclining back in his seat, he pushed those thoughts aside and instead filled his mind with their opposites. He contemplated his memories of Lara on Sunday morning a week ago, three days before he left for the Purace mission, calling them back now into the perfect acuity of his new consciousness...

A part of him sensed her vaguely as she knelt by the bed and ran her hand down his shoulder to his hip. He felt her nuzzle the small of his back, and moaned contentment vaguely through post-coital sleep. Later, as she came out of the shower, he woke to an appreciation of her finely honed muscles and tight sweet curves toweling off in front of him. I really love this woman, he thought for the millionth time. I love the way she walks: half exquisite femininity and half NFL linebacker. But somehow it's so wonderfully integrated. And she's such an incredible athlete, she may end up a better martial artist than me.

"You are looking exceptionally gorgeous this morning, my love."

"Now, I wonder why that is?" She grinned innocently as she toweled off in front of him.

He patted the side of the bed in invitation. "And I have something that will make you even more gorgeous, if that's even remotely possible...."

In the airplane, John smiled at the memory of that teasing, erotic, loving encounter that had ended up in her dressing closet. He imagined the memory flowing out of the airplane ahead of him, a mental telegram to the love of his life, telling her he would be back in her arms shortly. A little business first, then he would be back in her arms. He dropped out of the memory reluctantly; at 38,000 feet over the Atlantic off of South Carolina, John Connard was not nearly as high as he had been in the pre-dawn hours of Sunday morning a week ago.

Northwest Washington, DC | Sunday 2222 EDT

As the digital clock beside his bed flipped to 10:22 PM, Joshua felt a sudden strong sense of connection in his conceptual tapestry. It evaporated his dream, and sat him straight up. Wow, he thought, that was weird! It felt like standing on a Metro platform and having a subway zip by a window. You know there's an ad painted on the side of the train, but it goes by too fast for you to read it.

He recognized that the image had fit neatly within his dream-metaphor: more intertwining threads for his tapestry, connecting with the threads already there. His mind couldn't retrieve the image; it had been too fleeting. But it sure felt like a message, he thought. And those particular threads were probably about evolution, either biological or spiritual, since that's what I was thinking about when I fell asleep.

The experience held a strong sense of connection, and an important message, but he couldn't deduce the meaning of either. His inability rankled him. Frustration reduced the normally coherent contemplation of his powerful mind into ineffectual fragments. It dumped him unceremoniously back into the mental state more typical of a nine-year-old boy. Joshua O'Donnell tossed uncertainly on his bed, trying to return to sleep.

Global Consciousness Project, Princeton University, NJ | Sunday 2222 EDT

"Jeepers! Look at that!" Adrienne exclaimed, making Nathan jump. "That's about the strongest blip we've seen since the initial event!"

She pointed to the second monitor, off to the side, tracking the 1-minute integrals from their visitor from South America. They waited impatiently for the next minute to display. It did, but the spike had fallen back toward its steady baseline. Seven bright blue lines, representing seven GCDs in the Carolinas and Virginia, showed a strong spike at 2222. They stared at each other.

"Yeah!" Adrienne pointed at Nathan, as if he had actually spoken their simultaneous thought. "Let's look!" She spun her chair around to the worktable where the third monitor tracked the DC signal. Fingers flying over the keyboard, she toggled it back into display mode. Six bright green lines plotted across the screen, representing the six GCDs in the Washington area. Each showed a strong spike at 2222.

"Some kind of contact!" The words whooshed out of her.

"Some kind of *something* mutual, anyway," Nathan added, the heat of discovery raising the hair off the nape of his neck and bringing a flush to his ears.

The phone rang. Adrienne picked it up.

"Yes, Aaron, we did see that...."

She listened intently, and then nodded, grinning as she responded.

"Ooh, great idea, Aaron. If you're dealing with just one time period and you don't have to worry about a moving coordinate system, it should work, sure. You can pick the latitude and longitude of all the GCDs on the east coast off the website. Let us know if you pull anything out of it, okay?"

Kensington, MD / Sunday 2230 EDT

Aaron O'Meara didn't have Adrienne Baxter's programming skills, but he knew his way around a number of software applications for the physical sciences. Many of them were loaded on his home computer system. He opened one now, an isopleth plotting program he sometimes used for visualizing gravity fields in space, and input the GCD locations for the east coast. Then he picked off the signal intensities for those locations.

Using the 2222 time, plus two minutes on either side, he entered the data into the input screen of the plotting program, methodically checking his entries as he went along. Satisfied, he selected the 2220 data column and clicked the *Plot* button.

"Okay," he talked to the monitor as the plot came up on the screen, "that looks about right, sort of what I expected." The results screen showed the two signals as separate sources. It looked like a simplistic topographic map, plotting the signal strengths as one hill over the DC area, and another hill off the coast of South Carolina. He clicked the *Plot Next* button, unconsciously holding his breath as the 2221 time period plotted out.

"Well, now," Aaron said as his breath let out, "isn't that fascinating!" The hills showed the beginnings of a distortion. The isopleth pattern around the DC source elongated to the south-southwest. The pattern around the South Carolina source elongated to the north-northeast.

I've seen plots of this sort of thing before, he thought, or the inverse of it, anyway. It looks like two gravity wells interacting, or like two weather systems getting ready to merge. He instructed himself to keep an open mind; there were probably many other ways to look at this. He hit the *Plot Next* button for the 2222 time period, the spike that had captured their attention.

"Bingo!" he hooted, a whooshing exhalation, "son of a bitch, I knew it, I knew it!"

The plotting routine had changed the two hills into a single long ridge, connecting the sources into one unit, running up the coast from Georgia to Maryland. He hit the *Plot Next* button; the ridge disappeared and the two separate hills re-formed at 2223, and at 2224.

"Well, it was pretty quick, whatever it was," he told his monitor. He output the five plots to transmittable graphics, and emailed them to Adrienne Baxter, copying Edwin Edwards at Goddard.

Global Consciousness Project, Princeton University, NJ | Sunday 2241 EDT

The email alert chirped in the background as Nathan Rodgers stared at his annotated map of the east coast.

"I'll get it, Adrienne," he said, "you keep on what you're doing."

She stood up anyway, stretched and walked into his office.

"I'm stymied at the moment, Doctor Rodgers. That Aaron? What's he got to say?"

"He says 'Hi. See attached. Four earlier instances like this occurred, less pronounced, I'm examining. More later.'"

Nathan hit the button to download the graphics, labeled 2220 through 2224. He clicked them open in sequence as Adrienne looked over his shoulder.

"The 2220 time period looks like a topo map with two hills," he said.

"Umm," she said, "hills of consciousness."

"And 2221 looks like the consciousness hills are ridging toward each other a little bit," he said.

"Pseudopods," she said.

He smiled up at her to acknowledge the metaphor, and clicked the next graphic, the 2222 spike in the data that had grabbed their attention.

"Wow! The hills came together in a ridge!" he exclaimed. "Contact between the two consciousnesses, a bridge of some kind?"

"They're mating," she said.

He smiled at her again, and clicked the next graphic.

"Pretty quick mating, if that's what it was, Adrienne!" He laughed and clicked onto the last of the five. "Hardly any time at all. A minute later we're back to the separate hills of consciousness."

"Who knows what time means to them? It was a mating of their consciousnesses, Doctor Rodgers, a merging of some kind. I know it was." Her voice was polite, but certain.

She's instructing me, Nathan realized, even I'm three times her age. He laughed delightedly.

"Well then, Adrienne, a consciousness mating it is," he agreed, smiling up at her.

Kensington, MD / Sunday 2250 EDT

Jarred out of intense concentration by the cell phone ring, Aaron O'Meara jerked in his wheelchair, banging his knee against the bracket that mounted the computer under his big worktable. He massaged the knee absently, thinking sometimes it was good his legs didn't have too much feeling. He picked up the phone and saw the Princeton number displayed.

"Hi, folks," Aaron said, "what'd you think of the 2222 happening?"

"Fascinating, Aaron," Nathan Rodgers replied. "If we get some breathing room, I might try to go back and look at the raw data, see how much of the minute it actually took. But right now we're concentrating on how to track both sources when they get closer together. And they're getting closer as we speak."

"Yeah, I know. Is Adrienne having any luck with partitioning the two signals, Nathan? Anything I can do to help her out?"

"Actually, I think you already did, Aaron. I don't know exactly what you said, but a little over an hour ago Adrienne hollered your name and went tearing back into her software coding. She's been able to key off some bias of the South American source for producing more ones, and the DC source for producing more zeroes. That's statistical, not deterministic, of course, and offhand I wouldn't expect the separation to be razor-sharp. But the signal discriminator she coded to preprocess the data seems to give pretty clean results, from what we've seen so far."

"She's got some kind of true instinct for what's going on here, I think," Aaron replied. "Listen, when she gets done with her display coding, and she's happy with it, and you both have a few minutes, give me a call. I'll be right here, trying to generate some ideas. We need to talk about some philosophical issues, I think."

"Like what we tell the government?" Nathan Rodgers chuckled acknowledgment of that interesting question.

"Exactly that, Nathan. Call when you can. Bye now."

Northwest Washington, DC | Sunday 2301 EDT

Joshua tossed on his bed for forty minutes after feeling that strong but fleeting sense of connection. Unable to fall asleep, or even to process his impressions coherently, he finally pulled on a sweatsuit and went back out on the balcony to commune with his uncle.

"Ah, Joshua, *a gra*, cannot sleep, can we? Deep thought, deep mysteries, they do that, do they not?" Hamilton O'Donnell studied his nephew compassionately.

"I was thinking about biological and spiritual evolution while falling asleep,

Uncle Ham. But then I got this sudden sense of some kind of connection between the two. It flashed right through my mind, but seemed totally outside me somehow. It woke me up. It was really weird. I spent forty minutes trying to figure out what it was, and I just don't have a clue." Joshua looked imploringly at his uncle. "I was hoping maybe you could help me with it."

"Well, young lad, first things first, I suppose. I can tell you little about your... sense of connection, of course. But I can give you my ideas on the current debate about evolution—biological or spiritual—for what they're worth."

Joshua scrunched back in the chair on the balcony, hugging himself against the cooling air, waiting.

"Punctuated equilibria, me lad... let us start there. If such truly exist in biological evolution, then why not also in intellectual or social development, in spiritual evolution? On the biological side there are some decent data from paleontology and genome research. On the social side the evidence is a lot fuzzier, but still... there's the Golden Age of Greece, the Renaissance, periods of clear advancement in other cultures. It seems to me, Joshua, that any social constructs advancing the quality of the individual's condition and chances of success tend to succeed. Those that don't, tend to fail. Social developments that allow individuals to control their own fate, tend to succeed. Those that try too much to direct their fate, tend to fail. Ultimately."

"Some examples, Uncle Ham?"

"Well, lad, say almost any group of people who consciously and collectively make up their minds to make a social construct or development happen. A great example is the 'We the people...' statement from the foundin' fathers of this very country."

"Ah, I see, Uncle Ham. But why do such things happen? Would Aristotle's *entelechy* apply to social developments?"

"Oh, Joshua! You have such a fine ability to remember and extrapolate. Your concept is quite elegant, the *entelechy*, the within of things, applying to society. Why, I believe you may be right. And it may happen because a critical mass of people articulates its collective mindset, and that mindset's values, views, and ethics represent a simple and fundamental truth that resonates through the social fabric. Or at least resonates within enough individuals attuned to it."

"Thank you, Uncle Ham. But now that makes me wonder if maybe our spiritual evolution is somehow directly tied to our species' biological evolution; like there's some sort of feedback loop between the two. In any case, it sure looks like—or maybe feels like—some kind of interaction there."

"Ah, now you must give me an example, young man."

"Well, for an individual, the mind and the immune system connection is an example. The mental perception that something is funny, and physical laughter, with release of endorphins. And the feedback loop is—endorphins make you feel good and disposed to be amused. I mean, that's all biological, sure, and within a single body, but why couldn't there be a larger parallel?

"Whoa-ho, my young mystic, an intuitive leap of fascinatin' dimensions! Laughin' our way into enlightenment! Ah, what a fine idea!

Chapter 24

"Hot diggety-dog, Doctor Rodgers, it really works!"

Nathan observed, with a touch of envy, how the rush of success had banished fatigue from Adrienne's eyes. I wouldn't mind being that age again, he thought, able to bounce back like that. And her new algorithm really does work. Amazing!

The big flat-screen monitor showed the entire picture clearly. Green crosshairs with their tiny circles stayed stationary in Washington while the blue crosshairs with their bigger circles moved steadily up the east coast. The plots showed locations for each 15-minute period, latitude and longitude out to four decimal places neatly labeled on the crosshairs. The chronological sequence played out as a running slide show, then looped to repeat.

"Adrienne, I'm going to nominate you for the programming Olympics," Nathan breathed as he watched the slides clicked forward. "This is just amazing! And there, on your small screen! Green just moved into, what's that again..." He squinted at the background map, "ah, Rock Creek Park, around 1915. Okay, go ahead."

Adrienne toggled forward through the slides.

"Okay, looks like it's been pretty stationary since 2115, near the east edge of the Park..." she squinted in turn at the background map, "at the... at the Washington Zoo? Aw, Doctor Rodgers, this is too much! At the Zoo? I can't believe it! Green is gonna wait for Blue at the Zoo? Now this is really getting weird!"

"Adrienne, that might not be so strange," he said thoughtfully, "because, after all, it waited until dusk to move. And it stayed inside the Park. A lot of trees in there, if I remember correctly."

"Concealment," she agreed, nodding.

"And it took its time getting across Calvert Street," he added.

"Maybe waiting for a break in the traffic," she nodded again, "didn't want to be seen."

"And maybe it's got a chameleon act, or some kind of protective coloration that would work better in the Zoo than on city streets?"

"Maybe. Yeah, that's all very logical, but... oh, I don't know. And after all, it doesn't really have to be inside the Zoo, it could be on any of those streets close to it, the probability circles are a half-mile across. Oh, good, let's see what Aaron thinks," she concluded as the phone rang.

Aaron O'Meara, it turned out, had been asking himself exactly the same questions. The three of them talked about it at length, but with no resolution. The Zoo location might be significant, or might not. It was all speculation. They did agree that the next big thing would be the meeting of the two sources.

"Aaron," Adrienne announced, sensing that the Zoo location debate had wound down inconclusively, "I managed to separate the two signals. You gave me the idea, last time we talked. It turns out Blue—the South American source—produces a predominance of ones in the raw data. Green—here in DC—has a bias toward producing zeroes. It's not perfect, because sometimes the signals cancel each other out, but it's consistent enough. So I wrote a preprocessor to discriminate. I'm pretty sure it will work even when they get close together."

There was a pause, and Nathan could visualize Aaron contemplating the intuition and genius behind her simple statement.

"Adrienne," he replied, finally, "congratulations! That's great! Jeez, you have an absolutely uncanny ability with this stuff. When can I get a look at your results?"

Nathan watched his analyst's ears go pink at the compliment. Well I'm a monkey's uncle, he thought, she's falling for him over the freaking telephone.

"Thank you, Aaron. When you log onto our homepage, just add *psblet2.htm*. I'm going to delete the old set-up you've been using; I'm pretty sure it will be useless once Blue lands in Washington."

"Aaron, it seems like we've drifted off into the shorthand of Blue and Green for the two signal sources, are you following that?" Nathan added.

"I like that, Nathan. That's fine with me. As good a designation as any, since that's the way you've got them color-coded. And... Adrienne?"

"Yes, Aaron?"

She was a little breathless, Nathan noted. He felt a fatherly rush of affection for his young protege.

"You're gonna think this is... crazy," Aaron said tentatively, "but when you talk about discriminating the signals, I get this sense of yin and yang for the ones and zeroes. I think Blue is male and Green is female. Isn't that weird?"

Adrienne whooped out loud, a joyful laugh that bounced around the walls of the GCP Data Center.

"Aaron, you are absolutely right on!" Her laughter continued. "Of course that's true! It just sounds so weird when it's said out loud. Thank you! I didn't want to say it myself. But I believe you are absolutely right. Here we have a male, or some kind of essential male characteristic, homing in on a female or female characteristic. Oh, I'm so glad you said that, and not me!" Her laughter wound down into soft chuckling.

Nathan tried to sense the yin and yang that they were sensing, without success. He felt mildly put out and changed the subject.

"Well now, that brings another dimension to the problem, I guess," he said, "not that we needed it. I mean, what do we tell the government? Aaron, can we talk about that a bit? I'm getting a little nervous here, about what exactly our obligations are. It's clearly gone past the point of speculation. We've got solid evidence linking your initial event to the arrival of two consciousnesses who clearly have space travel, and likely have many other capabilities well beyond ours. We're tracking them. Presumably they're going to get together soon. What should we do?"

"Okay, Nathan, Adrienne, I've actually been thinking about this a lot," Aaron replied. "The way I see it, we do what our collective conscience and wisdom tell us is best, after we have a good debate. So we'll all have a say in the outcome.

"I see three possibilities here," Aaron continued, "only one of which morally demands that we take some kind of decisive action."

Good! He's been worrying about it as well as thinking about it, Nathan thought.

"The first," Aaron said, "is the idea of war, a battle, going on. It got started in space and ended up here on earth. If there's gonna be a battle here on the surface of the planet, then anybody caught between Blue and Green might get creamed by collateral damage. In this case, we've clearly got a moral obligation to disclose what's going on, and try our best to get some protection put in place, even though we have no idea what to protect against. Or maybe at least evacuate the battle zone.

"The second possibility," Aaron continued, "is that this is a rescue mission. The space event was an accident, and two ET's got separated and Blue is trying to get to Green. Assuming the rescue wouldn't hurt anybody on earth, the only moral obligation we have here is to try to help out the ET's if we're needed. We don't really know whether we have an obligation to the government, because we don't know whether capturing these things would be good or bad for the country, or the human race.

"And third," he went on, "maybe this is some sort of cosmic romance. Maybe this is what ETs do. Maybe Earth is one of their honeymoon spots, and their car broke down just outside, so they had to walk in, and got separated and took different routes, and Blue is coming to get Green. Or something like that. In which case our moral obligation is probably to mind our own business. Any other possibilities come to mind?"

"Nooo," Nathan said contemplatively.

"Just derivatives," Adrienne added, "I think you nailed the basic three, Aaron."

"Okay, Adrienne, Nathan, here's what I want to do. I'll argue the battle possibility. I'm not as solid on it as I used to be, but I still think it's plausible, because it sure as shit looked like a dogfight out there in space this morning. You weren't there, and you didn't see it on the big screen, but I did, and I'm still a little scared from what I saw, the incredible power it implied. So I'll argue that possibility, and you guys do your best to shoot down my arguments.

"Then, Nathan," he continued, "you argue the rescue possibility, and Adrienne and I will try to shoot that down. Then, Adrienne, you argue the romance possibility, and Nathan and I will try to shoot that down. Okay?"

The debate was both heated and humorous. It started out following the rules Aaron laid down, but by the end they had all switched viewpoints at least three times, and defended as well as attacked them. Finally, they subsided into mirth when Nathan said he finally understood why Congress could never agree on what to do about Social Security.

"Okay, okay, folks. Here's what we'll do," Aaron said, stepping into his *ex officio* role as government representative, taking charge of their consensus decision. "Any significant new data, any significant idea or insight we develop, any useful analysis we make or tool we develop, we'll not only share with each other, we'll document in an email, and make sure Ed at Goddard gets a copy. That way we'll build a good strong paper and electronic trail, and all the information can be kept current in one file so it can be transmitted electronically. Any agency that needs to come up to speed will be able to do it fast. It may seem like passing the buck, and maybe it is, but at least we've disclosed everything. We're protected: nobody's gonna be able to say we didn't get the word out. Your project is protected. Goddard is protected. We'll just keep cranking along until the event comes to its conclusion, processing info as we go, and passing it all along. If things change, we'll maybe rethink this. Okay?"

They all agreed, and hung up.

American Airlines Flight 59 Enroute to Washington | Sunday 2317EDT

John Connard, now over the coast of Virginia, chased back into his eye of the storm, to pick up the thread of his memories. With his acute new perception, he recalled exactly how Alex had looked, when he appeared with Lara that New Year's Day morning three and a half years ago. They had walked into Alex's kitchen, their arms around each other. He remembered the color of Alex's shirt, the buttons, the tanned face with its gunmetal gray eyes and bushy eyebrows. Shock and surprise passed across that weathered face, followed by consternation, followed by understanding, and then acceptance; the expressions marching in quick-step order. They were too quick for Lara to see, and too quick for him to see at the time. But he captured them now in his new and exquisitely detailed memory.

As John played those facial expressions, frame by frame, across his mind-space, he recalled his own consternation at discovering Alex's dual existence. As Alex Shaughnessy, the man collaborated with him as an artist on the canvas of death and destruction they painted for the drug trade. But he also was Hamilton O'Donnell, a philanthropist, a friend to Lara Picard, a great-uncle, friend and mentor to her son Josh. A strange development, John thought, but somehow—given his new perception—not really unexpected. Nor, in retrospect, was their hilarious discussion over breakfast. They all laughed about the possibility about having been together in prior incarnations.

"*Anam cara*," Alex had said, using the Gaelic of his ancestors. "Lara, you are John's *anam cara*, his soulmate, and he yours. You are destined always to be at the proper place, at the proper time, to take the proper course for each other. You were called, John, to that appointed instant last night, to protect Lara from harm. I thought it too early, but I was wrong. *Anaim cairdi* are always together when love requires it.

Lara had looked at John, astonished, and they both laughed in unison while demanding that Alex tell them what sort of information he possibly could have. What might be an appointed instant? How might that instant be too early, or too late? But Alexander Hamilton Shaughnessy O'Donnell wouldn't answer. He just smiled and diverted them adroitly into one of his absurd Irish parables as he poured more coffee and laughed merrily along with them.

Kensington, MD / Sunday 2320 EDT

Aaron struggled with the tone of his email, then decided on just straight, simple reporting of the facts. Let any agency interested make up its own mind. Just stick with cool dispassionate recitation of what we've found out, that's the ticket, he thought; Ed is certainly bright enough to read my intent. The government probably has the resources to check out airplane passenger manifests, and surely can get transponder data to compare to the GCD location plots. He typed quickly, accurately, synopsizing their timeline and discoveries so far, starting with the suspected American Airlines flight numbers and departure and arrival times.

He added the URL for the Global Consciousness Project public website page showing the 1-minute integrals for any GCD, then the URL for the private page displaying the 15-minute average locations of Blue and Green. He added the email addresses for Nathan Rodgers and Adrienne Baxter as cc's. Then he exhaled softly, and hit the *Send* button.

"So, Ed, my friend," Aaron addressed his soliloquy to the flickering computer screen, "you're certainly one of the sanest human beings I know. What will you do? Will you call me? Or will you heave this in the trash? Or sit on it for a while? Or will you send it on to the Pentagon or some other agency? And if you do that... will anyone react?"

He smiled at the unresponsive monitor. "I don't know, Ed. There's a country song with a pretty good line: 'If your phone don't ring, you'll know it's me.' That's my best guess as to what reaction this stuff is gonna get from our government. Let's just hope that's a good thing and not a bad thing."

American Airlines Flight 59 Enroute to Washington | *Sunday 2321 EDT*

Our lives are a tapestry, John realized as he came out of his memories, focused on the weave in the fabric of the airplane seat in front of him. And Alexander Hamilton Shaughnessy O'Donnell is one of the threads. The pattern, the weave, the art of that tapestry; I know it somehow. Familiarity itched at the back of his consciousness, but no enlightenment followed.

He pushed aside the question and tried to look into the future, past the conflict and death inexorably approaching. Wistfully, he re-painted across his mind-space the love and the light embodied by Lara Picard. She stood, nude, on a deserted beach on Grand Cayman Island, Venus on the half-shell. He felt the aching desire in his heart flood through the rest of his being.

The briefest sensation of a divergent thought from his nexus passed across his mind-space, an acknowledgment from some distant place. Then the image of Duc Li added a gossamer thread to the tapestry, almost wistfully: *The tao to the soul runs through the heart, John Connard.*

Goddard Space Flight Center, Greenbelt, MD | *Sunday 2329 EDT*

Ed Edwards, on a midnight break from the SDI exercise, munched on a sandwich while he scanned Aaron O'Meara's fascinating email messages. He smiled at the underlying tone of disinterested factual reporting and scientific detachment. The clever bastard is putting it square on me, and giving me all the latitude I need to go whichever way I want with this.

"Well, you know, Aaron," he reflected aloud, "I've got just exactly the same dilemma you have, only I'm a lot less persuaded there's a fight brewing. I think it's much more like a rescue. So, maybe I'll pass this along to the Pentagon, or maybe I won't.

"Or maybe," he said, unwrapping the other half of the sandwich, "I'll just happen not to have seen it yet, being so busy with the exercise and everything. And if I'm reading properly between your lines, Aaron, maybe that's what you really think is right anyway. Non-intervention."

He chewed some more of the sandwich and swallowed it, still contemplating. Forward the emails? To the Pentagon? His chain of command at NASA? FBI? CIA? NSC? Shit! What do I do here? Act or not? He couldn't decide. The parameters cascaded down through his mind: global consciousness; detectors that flip electronic coins; zeros or ones; heads or tails. Ah, heads or tails.

"Well, what the hell, that's good enough for me," he decided aloud, pulling a quarter out of his pocket. He flipped it in the air, caught it and slapped it down on monitor. Tails. No action. At least not for the moment. He walked away whistling, back to the SDI exercise, unaccountably pleased with his whimsical decision.

Northwest Washington, DC | Sunday 2349 EDT

"Relax yourself, me lad," Hamilton O'Donnell told his nephew as they sat companionably on the hotel balcony. "Calm those troubled waters of your mind, and tell your ould uncle about that sense of connection. It's evadin' your comprehension, you said. Start at the beginnin'. When did you first see that first thread?"

Joshua squirmed into a lotus in the chair and took calming breaths, as he'd been taught.

"I guess I've sensed threads as far back as I can remember, Uncle Ham," he said, struggling to refine his recall of fuzzy and half-buried intimations. "But there was never any weave, any pattern, that drew my attention. Or if there was, I looked at it and didn't really see it."

"Umm. Joshua, you need not feel badly, we all miss things that haven't sufficient context around them. Ask any thankful chameleon. What is the first thread that had enough context, the first one that you didn't dismiss?"

"When Mom got in the car this morning, Uncle Ham. I felt the energy inside her, and coming off her. And I saw a thread, some kind of connection to elsewhere. And now that I think about it, maybe a connection to elsewhen. Like it came from the past and ran into the future. That makes a weird kind of sense, I guess, in dimensions where time isn't relevant. But there's no way I can get my mind around these threads. I don't have any basis in experience, or science, or even in mathematical abstractions, that would help me out at all."

"Well, me lad, not all mysteries may be resolvable by science or mathematics. Rational thought may not be the final arbiter."

As Joshua's mind and thoughts circled around his in their warm and friendly mind-dance, he noted in the distance the landing lights of an aircraft switched on five miles to the south of their hotel balcony. The lights brightened as it lined up for landing at Ronald Reagan Washington National Airport. The old man sighed deeply, rubbing the back of his neck, letting a comfortable silence build between them while the boy backed away from rationality toward intuition.

"Thank you, Uncle Ham," Joshua finally said. "I don't know how you got me to see it, or what it means, but the threads are a little clearer now. There's a thread of danger winding around one of hope. They're pulling in other threads, and telling a story. Or maybe they're creating the story. And each of those threads has a sense of purpose, I think. Every single one."

The bright landing lights dropped below the tree line, out of their view, as the aircraft came onto final approach. At 2359 Sunday night, the wheels gently kissed the concrete runway at Washington National. American Airlines Flight 59 had brought John Connard, the Magician, the Assassin, home to meet the most subtle and dangerous enemy on any field of battle in human existence.

Alexander Hamilton Shaughnessy O'Donnell felt a teardrop form in his left eye.

"...and the hunter, home from the hill," he murmured.

Chapter 25

John stood quietly in the darkened window of the small office condo on Water Street, contemplating the moonlit sword of the Washington monument spearing the night sky. He had just finished dictating a brief synopsis of the Purace mission into the secure computer that would encrypt it. He made no mention of the visitor in his mind.

Alex would see the recording on Tuesday morning, probably, so he added a personal afterthought to please not tell Lara and Josh he'd returned. He said he was taking the car, would spend a couple of days in the country, and be back toward the end of the week. Alex wouldn't think anything of it. After a mission John frequently took a few days alone in the quiet hillside cabin in the Shenandoahs, west of Washington. He used the time to equilibrate his conscience, to fully shed his mission personae of Magician and Assassin. His mentor would likewise shed his Alexander Shaughnessy persona, then Ham and he and Lara and Josh would become again tightly-knit friends and family. The desire for a return to normality flooded through him. The four of them would play some tennis, go on a hike, have a picnic. He smiled into the moonlit night.

But the prospect of imminent battle pushed those thoughts abruptly out of the way. That's for later, John disciplined himself, so forget it. For now, just scope out the field of battle, then attack suddenly with brutal overwhelming force before the enemy can get better prepared. He saw the mental shrug from his nexus.

No plan survives first contact with the enemy. Simplest is best.

He smiled acknowledgment into his mind-space. If anyone had that military maxim tattooed on his brain, it would be a former combat soldier. As if to reinforce the reminder, the green-tinged black blot on his consciousness radar screen flickered seductively. Five klicks north, the Magician thought, and it knows I'm coming. It has set a trap, certainly. He focused his mind down to his cold, rational, singular objective: eliminate the Other.

Northwest Washington, DC | *Monday 0052 EDT*

Lara lay wide-awake in the second-story bedroom of the FBI witness protection program safehouse on Irving Street, still dressed in her workout clothes. She really wanted to shower, but with the Beast so near it would seem obscene, and she would somehow feel too vulnerable naked. Instead, she lay quietly on the bed, shaping the trap in her mind, and turning it around and re-shaping it. Her thoughts were bloody, but cold, sharp, rational. She visualized herself a predatory, ruthless spider, waiting patiently in her web.

Her *ki* observed these thoughts attentively as they danced and intertwined, and agreed. *We must focus full mind and will on destruction of the Beast.*

Lara examined her metaphorical web again: three agents in the safehouse. No, it would never hold the Beast; it wasn't strong enough. But it should be enough to entangle him, to throw off his balance, to present her with an opening. She would kill him quickly, without compunction, and would allow no thoughts of mercy to intervene or confuse her.

As if in response to her hardening resolve, the blue-tinged black blot on her radar screen flickered derisively. Three miles south, she thought, and he knows where I am, and he's coming for me. The depths of obscenity and depravity in that flickering blot stabbed fear into the core of her being. But the fear triggered a reflex, the same sense of outrage she had felt when the chemical company had polluted her sacred pool on the farm. This is no different, she thought. This is a sacred pool of nascent humanity, the next generation of evolution. It's a baby: innocent and sacred and pure and clean. This unspeakable Beast would defile it. Anger took her, and she allowed it the free run of her mind and soul, welcoming its metallic hardness.

Global Consciousness Project, Princeton University, NJ | Monday 0123 EDT

"Resting, gathering strength, planning? What?" Aaron's question came over the speakerphone into the workstation where Adrienne and Nathan had been contemplating that very question. The strength for both signals had ramped down even further on Blue's arrival at Washington National.

"Good question, Aaron," Nathan sighed, feeling the weariness of waiting. "Maybe all of the above. Or maybe, just because they're closer, they can make contact with a lower signal."

"Well, anyway, the signal strength didn't drop down far enough to affect the algorithms, Aaron," Adrienne's somewhat hoarse voice added, "so we're still getting a pretty tight lock on the locations. Green is stationary near the east side of the Zoo. Blue transited the airport and now it looks like it's stationary in the south of Georgetown, close to the river."

She sounds totally beat, Nathan noted. She's got to rest, especially if nothing's going to happen for a while.

"You think we still don't need to do anything, Aaron?" Adrienne asked, "I mean, other than keep your boss at Goddard posted?"

"Well, nothing much has happened that we didn't anticipate. Blue made it to Washington, like we figured. Green is hanging around, like we figured. Ed's got all this in my emails. I told him to call if he had any questions, or wanted me to do something else by way of evaluation. Haven't heard a peep from him. What I think we ought to do is take a hint from the ETs, and rest up ourselves, so long as nothing much is going on."

"Good idea, Aaron," Nathan agreed. "I slept in late this morning, until Adrienne phoned. I'm probably the freshest, so why don't I stand watch, and you can nap for a bit. I'm going to send Adrienne off to her dorm before she falls off her chair and starts snoring. I figure you guys both have been up almost 24 hours now, and under non-stop stress...."

Georgetown, Washington, DC | Monday 0144 EDT

John methodically worked his way through the sandwiches he'd made from supplies in Alex's well-stocked refrigerator. As he chewed, the green-limned black blot pulsed in his mind. It reminded him of the primal energy he had felt in the spider, his uninvited guest in the cockpit of the Harrier flight. That's probably not a bad analogy, he thought; it clearly is a trap.

The Magician reviewed the possible attack scenarios running through his mind. Let's just see what the weather's going to be like, see if that could be a factor. He turned on the television in the wall of the apartment's small sitting room.

CNN was interviewing a NASA spokeswoman, and absently he flicked to another channel, searching for the weather forecast. But then the few words he'd heard suddenly registered and he flicked back to hear the NASA woman's voiceover description of the strange event early Sunday morning. The graphic showed a colorful video of spiraling bands of light, captured by a satellite camera looking outward and down into space south of the ecliptic. The voice described it as a small high-velocity rogue asteroid collision, breaking apart in the atmosphere. He thumbed the volume up a bit.

"One piece tracked toward northwest South America, and one piece tracked into the Washington DC area," the NASA woman offered. "The Washington piece gave everybody a scare, but nothing actually hit the ground. It was pretty colorful, and there were some sightings, and a number of calls, but no damage."

"And that caused the helicopter activity over the Potomac this morning?" The newscaster was trying to knit it together for the audience.

"Well, there was some concern initially, because of radar anomalies, that this might be a terrorist attack of some sort." She smiled at her interviewer and continued smoothly. "My understanding is that some military resources were scrambled and did reconnaissance in the possible impact area for a few hours as a safety precaution. But they found nothing on the ground, and nothing floating in the air. We definitely established that it came from space, so it burned up completely on entry."

"And no ET's knocked on the White House door this morning?" The interviewer seemed pleased by his sly humor.

"Well, none that we know of," she deadpanned back.

The image of Duc Li answered the Magician's unspoken question.

Yes, that is the Other, John Connard. We must move quickly to prevent it from subverting the power structure here.

Ah, but maybe it already has, maybe that's part of the trap, thought the Magician. The green-limned black blot seemed to pulsate that thought back to him.

Northwest Washington, DC | Monday 0145 EDT

It hasn't moved, Lara directed the thought into her mind-space, for over an hour now.

The Beast gathers itself for the assault.

When will it come?

When it is ready. It is a powerful mind, but cautious, and cunning.

I think I need more of an edge.

Your mind is an edge. Your extraordinary intuitive skill with the null field, especially, is an edge.

I want to be as savage as it. Vicious.

Her *ki* pondered that, somberly.

That is truly dangerous. The racial memories are there, encoded deep in the brain. The primitive survival urges of the hunting animal to dominate with power, to kill and feed. The mother instinct to protect the young, to nurture and preserve. It is a delicate balance. It can so easily go wrong. You may destroy one beast only to replace it with another.

Myself?

Yes. Observe. Her *ki* formed a picture of her brain in her mind-space, drawing the images out of Lara's long-forgotten anatomy courses. Evolutionary layers peeled back to reveal what she was seeking. There they were, structures down deep, close to the brain stem: the pons, the limbic system, the hippocampus.

Yes. There. You must will it to happen.

Lara Picard took a deep breath, and directed her will into the depths of her brain.

As if a trigger had been pulled, or a dam burst, primal energies flowed into her, a roaring coalescence of blood and fury, inchoate and mindless, save for one purpose. Dominance: a vicious savagery that would assure survival and protect offspring. Conflicted emotions flowed into her mind-space, washing back over her nexus. The emotions carried with them back into her higher brain a fear of herself, or rather of the power she held as an instrument of destruction. She struggled to release the trigger and the emotions ramped down; but slowly, stubbornly, as if they had a life of their own. Her need to avoid being entrapped by her power clearly conflicted with her need to use it.

So you see. The acknowledgment carried sympathy and sorrow, but strangely leavened with humor and joy, all at the same time. *It is indeed a delicate balance, to use the power without becoming it. It puts you in a truly dangerous place.*

I will use this primal power, but I will not become it. I will keep the balance, she instructed her *ki.*

As you will.

Lara Picard sighed deeply, and reconciled her mind and soul to the viciousness and savagery likely needed to kill this Beast.

Global Consciousness Project, Princeton University, NJ | Monday 0208 EDT

Adrienne departed the GCP Center for her dorm room, as her boss directed, even though she wasn't sure she could rest. The brisk five-minute walk helped clear her head of the fatigue brought on by 20 hours of intense concentration and computer programming. She showered and brushed and flossed, focusing on those prosaic mechanical motions to disengage her mind. Then she turned off the lights and dropped into bed.

Shoot, I'll never be able to rest, she thought. But thirty seconds later her breathing pattern slowed, and a minute after that she dropped like a rock into deep sleep.

As Adrienne fell asleep, Nathan badgered his other colleague over the phone. "Look, Aaron," he repeated, "you've been up since when? Four or five AM Sunday? The 0200 Blue and Green locations haven't changed, and we've run out of ideas. So why the hell don't you catch a few winks too? I'll stand watch, and call you if anything changes. I'm a lot fresher, I slept in late on Sunday morning."

Aaron reluctantly agreed, and hung up the phone. He rubbed his eyes tiredly and pushed his wheelchair away from the computer workstation. Nathan's right, he thought. I need some rest. He wheeled into the bathroom, brushed his teeth, and rolled back to the massage chair opposite the workstation. He swung himself onto it and set the controls for low heat and gentle kneading. All 22 hours of mental multitasking abruptly caught up with him, and a minute later Aaron snored his way downward into deep sleep.

Nathan stared at the blue and green plots on his computer monitor, but the updates showed no change. I need to shift my position, he thought; if I don't, my spine's going to tighten up like a pretzel. He got up and stretched, and walked out of his office, circling the big computer room a few times, rubbing the small of his back. Then he picked up Adrienne's printouts of the 1-minute timeline plots and went back to his office. I'll take two aspirin and one of those muscle relaxants the orthopedist gave me for back spasms, he told himself. That should do the trick. Then I'll just sit in my recliner and study these printouts, let my back muscles unkink for a bit. He swallowed the pills, swung the recliner so he could see his computer screen, and adjusted the reading light over the chair. He sat down with the printouts, feeling alert and energized. Forty minutes later he was fast asleep.

Northwest Washington, DC | Monday 0447 EDT

Two guards outside, one inside with the target, the Magician saw from his consciousness radar. He sat cloaked in his null field, invisible in the crotch of a tree on the opposite side of Irving Street. He studied the nearly invisible guard fifty yards away, a smallish form dressed in matte black, blending into the shrubs and shadows at the front of the house. Periodically, the guard made tiny, economical motions, just enough to keep muscles from tightening up too much.

Excellent discipline, the Magician thought approvingly; if I didn't have my consciousness radar, I easily could have missed you. He looked at his watch. An hour before dawn. Their biorhythms would be depressed, their reflexes just infinitesimally slower. As good a time as any, he thought. Now. It's got to be fast. Don't give them time to react. Get it done. Fast.

He transposed to the small ornamental ledge over the front entrance of the house, five feet above the guard's head. The guard whirled at the whuff of displaced air, but too late. A formless patch of chaos snapped downward.

Shit! It's a woman, he realized, crouching over the inert body. Hope I didn't get the field too strong and do permanent damage. He tossed her machine pistol quietly onto the soil underneath a bush, then unzipped her vest to find the microphone. He sliced the wire with a tiny flare of energy from his finger. Streetlight reflected on the plastic identity card hung around the woman's neck. A few blue flickers escaped his null field as the realization hit him.

Not good, he told himself as he transposed to the roof of the house. The afterimage played across his mind for confirmation. The card had read Mary M. Lovelock, Special Agent, FBI. You're right about the Other subverting the power structure, he told his nexus as he sprinted lightly across the flat roof. And on a Sunday, too. The Other must have found a host within the law enforcement community, or connected to it. Otherwise there's no way it could happen so fast. The connections implied by that accomplishment fleeted through his mind in the few seconds it took him to run across the roof and transpose down onto the second guard in the rear of the house.

"Lovelock? Did you say something? Answer please!" Special Agent Toman Black whispered into his lapel mike as the phantom shape dropped in behind him. The Magician smelled the sudden fear on the man, the instinctive knowledge that his enemy had him. Then the agent collapsed under the neural paralysis of the chaos applied.

One last guard, inside, the Magician saw on the consciousness radar within his mind-space; the target upstairs, coming down fast.

Okay, there's no other way, he thought. Sometimes you have to accept collateral damage. I can't take a chance. I'm sorry.

He pushed aside his fear of a trap. He pushed aside the subtlety and finesse of the Magician. He pushed aside the humanity of the soldier John Connard. The hard, cold, focused primal rage that was the Assassin snapped into his mind and soul, overriding all else. Eyes glittered back at him from the window reflection, their starcross pattern bright with hellish blue intensity. The Assassin transposed past the window into the kitchen.

The last guard, crouched in the living room, caught the flickering blue phantom emptiness in his peripheral vision, and swung up his machine pistol with blinding speed.

Northwest Washington, DC | Monday 0447 EDT

Lara Picard sensed that the presence had stopped circling, and now waited, watching. The pulsating throb of its energy in her mind echoed the drumbeat of jungle drums: primitive, compelling, seeming to come from everywhere and nowhere. That made it impossible to discern the Beast's distance and direction.

But it was close, very close; she knew that. Now, she realized instinctively; now, it will attack.

"He's here!" she whispered into her lapel mike, to warn her keepers. Even as she said the words, she sensed the departure of one friendly consciousness, and then, seconds later, another. The departures nearly were lost in the insistent throbbing mental drumbeat, trivial notes drowned out by an orchestral cacophony.

Oh, God, I hope they died quick and clean, Lara thought. A wave of fear rose high in her mind, crested with the foam of implacable terror, driven by that insistent obscene drumbeat. It demanded that she leave her trap, turn and run. She nearly did. But then the primal rage came to her beckoning, and she held it in front of her, a sword, hard and sharp-edged, a dominant force of flickering green energy. The fear wave split into two around her, and she flew downstairs to battle the Beast.

"He's here!" she yelled, flaring to a landing crouch beside Dave Ditka. But the acknowledged fastest hands in the FBI were already firing.

Lara briefly glimpsed the formlessness in the shadows as it dove behind the island in the kitchen, the tracery of bullets riding too high, lodging in the hardened plastic of the armored windows.

In the next fraction of a second, she gathered the chaos of the null field into her right hand, all that she could gather without destroying herself. She backhanded it spinning into the kitchen to the left of the island, where she knew the Beast's momentum would carry it.

An unearthly coruscation of blue light around an emptiness impossible to comprehend erupted where the two fields collided. From within that collision came a primal scream of agony and hate.

A big cat, or a crocodile, they make noises like that when they're hurt, she remembered. She gathered her strength to cast the null field again.

Agent Ditka emptied his clip at the sound, then shoved Lara into the escape chute and slapped the control. The door slammed shut and her enclosure instantly dropped into the tunnel, taking her away from the danger.

"Ditka, you asshole!" Lara screamed to the tunnel walls, "we had him! We had him! And now you're dead, you stupid asshole!"

Ditka heard the scream, but it was dim and incoherent, and faded fast as she dropped to safety. He slammed another clip into his machine pistol and dove across the room, firing, taking cover behind the sofa with specially-reinforced titanium panels. A rasping, choking sound came from the kitchen, then a keening wail, an inhuman cry of torment and agony.

Jesus! Now I know what hell sounds like, he thought.

"Metro," he said to the lapel mike, "we got two casualties, front and rear of the house, outside. Got penetration of the house. The perp is in the kitchen. I think I hit him. Picard threw something at him, I don't know what. I think he's fucked up pretty good. But I don't know. Advise caution in your approach. I'm gonna drop a full clip on him right now, and come in behind it, so you better come in the front door or the north side windows, not the back. Oh, and I'm the one with the big white letters on the back of my jacket. Eff. Bee. Eye. Okay?"

Ditka vaguely heard the response. He stitched a full load from the pistol across the kitchen, totally demolishing what remained of the island. Then he reloaded and walked in a crouch toward the smoking pile of rubble.

"If you're not dead, cocksucker, you gonna wish you were," he muttered. "Those people were my friends."

Northwest Washington, DC | Monday 0449 EDT

The Assassin hung in the frame of the large recessed skylight over the kitchen, trying to shake off the residual effects of contact with the Other's thrown chaos. He had transposed there instinctively after neutralizing the null field, just before a hail of bullets blew apart the kitchen island. He remembered the searing pain and his guttural scream, the agonizing effort to dismiss the chaos back to its own null dimension. His mind ran on rapidly, fueled by the adrenaline of combat, taking stock of his condition in a fraction of a second:

My mind-space and consciousness radar are just a jumble of pixels and static.

They will gradually reorder into coherence. No image of his nexus Duc Li appeared, but the thought pattern was vaguely recognizable.

My null field is gone, so I'm visible. Can I get it back?

Yes, but it may take some time; the dimensional perturbations must equilibrate first.

Splinters of plastic and wood in my shoulder, blood starting to trickle down into my sweatshirt.

Not serious. But you should endeavor not to leave DNA in your wake.

One thing seemed clear enough at least; the dark presence of the Other was now moving away.

Yes. We are safe for the moment.

The Assassin receded into the background and John became the Magician.

It had me. Why did it run?

Good question.

The Magician looked up through the skylight as he felt some of his powers creep back. He had a sightline to an overhanging tree limb, he could transpose to safety. But he needed information first.

The agent walked unsuspecting beneath him and kicked at the smoking rubble. The Magician dropped lightly down, and in the absence of a working null field, simply clubbed the man on the back of his neck, dropping him onto the pile of rubble.

From that radio conversation, I've got maybe thirty seconds, the Magician thought. He ran into the living room, to the only position he'd seen the Other. A tall panel beside the fireplace hearth was opened slightly. Ah, he saw, a shaft, an escape route. Should I follow? Is it a trap? He dropped a fireplace log into the shaft. The boiling cloud of gas that erupted from below answered his question. Time to go!

The Magician started up the stairs so he could exit from the second floor, but then changed his mind. The gas might be poison. The agent's only doing his job; probably just following orders, or hoodwinked somehow. He's a soldier, like me. I've got to get him out. The gas began to billow out of the panel; it chased him into the kitchen. Holding his breath, he picked up the agent, grabbing a handful of the vest with his left hand. With his right hand, he tried to draw the null field down over himself, but it fragmented and fell away.

He shrugged and improvised. Using a partially restored gravity field to help hold the agent upright, he lifted him backward out the door. The letters on the back of the vest should be visible enough, he hoped.

"Hold your fire! Hold your fire! Coming out!" the Magician yelled in what he hoped was a passable imitation of the agent's voice. "Gas inside the house! Gas inside!"

Three steps and they cleared the small rear porch. A sightline to the roof of the house next door and the Magician disappeared, leaving the SWAT team to wonder what the hell it was they really had seen. The unconscious body of Agent Ditka, no longer held erect, tumbled backwards into the waist-high evergreen bushes, flipping over them to end up face down in a planting of pachysandra. A white mist of gas bled through the screen of the door, clearly visible in the sudden illumination of the spotlight from the SWAT van.

"Gas in the house," the SWAT commander yelled, "get those bodies down here to the sidewalk. Masks! Pull back from the house. Get your goddamn masks!"

Lights began to come on in the surrounding houses.

Global Consciousness Project, Princeton University, NJ | Monday 0450 EDT

The cacophony on the quiet residential streets of northwest Washington DC was mirrored in the lesser noises of the pings and other alarm sounds Adrienne Baxter had programmed into her tracking algorithms. The computers all made different sounds, but from their tinny small built-in speakers, not from external speakers which might have been much louder. Nathan Rodgers snorted uneasily in his sleep, but didn't wake up. His body only squirmed deeper into the chair, reflexively trying to give his sensitive back a more comfortable resting position. He dreamed he was a Navy fighter pilot downed at sea. A bevy of friendly dolphins surrounded him, helping to keep him afloat until the rescue choppers could get close enough to spot his dye marker.

On Aaron O'Meara's computer monitor in Kensington, Maryland, across the room from his slumbering form, blue and green trend lines spiked repeatedly, completely off-scale. Aaron's eyes were closed, but his body twitched in the massage chair, in time to the spikes on the monitor. He dreamed of explosions in space and spiraling bands of energy. He felt the pain and agony of separation, and the disorienting effect of sudden displacement into a foreign environment. He was a stranger in a strange land, and hunted.

Adrienne Baxter slept quietly and deeply in her dormitory bed in Princeton, New Jersey. The computer on the desk across the room was turned off. Her cell phone remained silent. She smiled as she slept, not exactly dreaming. But then she twitched and frowned, as her consciousness rose into dream state. Her mouth turned downward with a half-cry, half-snarl.

"No, oh God, no," she moaned in her sleep, "you fools! This isn't the way! Can't you see? This isn't the way it's supposed to be!"

Chapter 26

Lara screamed again at Agent David Ditka as the pod dropped down the escape chute, carrying her away from the Irving Street safehouse. A ten-second trip, it seemed more like ten hours to her adrenaline-laced senses. The pod hit the friction pads at the end of the chute and dumped her unceremoniously out into the subsurface vault. She slapped the button on the red panel marked *Arm Tunnel* and the pneumatic door sealed behind her.

Okay, she thought, if he comes down the tunnel after me he's in for a nasty surprise. She glanced up at the manhole to the surface, but decided she might be too vulnerable on exit, with her consciousness radar a jumble of white noise. So she spun the wheel on the hatch leading down into the storm drain, and dropped through when it opened. A minor odor of decay hit her nostrils, but she wouldn't be in the drain pipe long enough to worry about that, or any oxygen deficiency. She waved a beam of green energy from her hand for light. Left is down, she saw, and in two running steps was airborne, arrowing swiftly down the center of the 72-inch diameter storm drain under the Parkway, westward toward its discharge into Rock Creek.

As Lara flew out of the culvert, she simultaneously damped down her aura, collapsed the blade of green energy and drew her null field around her. But the field fragmented, and slipped away from her control.

Your control will return in a few moments. The interfaces between dimensions were distorted by the power of the null exchange. The picture in her mind space of her *ki* appeared similarly fragmented, portions briefly visible then gone in a wisp of broken smoke. But the thought and the calm inner voice came through clearly enough.

You drew an enormous amount of chaos from the null field and threw it at the Beast. Your chaos collided with his own null field, which he instinctively reinforced. The interfaces in this locus are still resonating with the force of the collision.

As Lara heard those thoughts, the fractured image of her *ki* began to re-cohere in her mind-space. She found that comforting, but it suddenly begged other questions. Can the interfaces be damaged or destroyed? Can we inadvertently loose destruction from the energy field or the null field in this world? The thought scared her.

Interfaces between dimensions are resilient, elastic, dynamic; they are conditions, not things. They have no physical existence, so cannot be destroyed. When you draw from other dimensions, you manipulate the interface to allow your will to happen, but the amount you can withdraw is limited to what your being can manage. You do not control these interfaces, except in a local sense. Damage may occur, but only localized.

The transfer of these thoughts, though still fragmented, took place in the split second it took Lara to bank sharply and follow Rock Creek downstream. She glanced up to her left and behind her. Blue lightning flashed in the safehouse window.

Northwest Washington, DC | Monday 0451 EDT

A quickly glanced sightline to the roof of the house next door, and the Magician transposed. The fleeting glimpse of his form vanished from the view of the SWAT team outside in the street as if it had never been.

The transposition seemed choppy, uncertain. As he hit the roof, he stumbled, and had the sensation of incompleteness, of no longer being quite as much a part of this reality as he had been. It almost felt like some small portion of him remained in the null dimension.

The feeling will pass. That was a formidable content of chaos to neutralize; very nearly too much. The image of a worried Duc Li tried to re-establish itself in his mind-space, flickering, struggling toward a coherent whole.

As the Magician looked down on the street activity from his vantage point on the roof, he conceded that the resources commanded by the Other were impressive. Three federal agents had been provided for protection; experienced ones, not the rookies that usually pulled weekend duty. A full Metro PD SWAT team had shown up within minutes; that meant they'd been pre-positioned. And this all happened on a holiday weekend, Memorial Day, in the early morning hours. *So, the Other has taken a human host with extraordinary connections in the Washington law enforcement community. It almost had to be an insider, and high-ranking. Or somebody politically connected.*

The image of his nexus, still trying to cohere its fragments, advised him accordingly. *This battle is over, for now. You need to rest, John Connard; eat, then rest.*

No, he objected, I flushed the Other out, and escaped its trap. It's unprotected now, and running. It's probably as depleted as I am. I will pursue.

The Magician recalled the assault, playing it through in slow motion in his mind-space, trying to infer data where he had no direct observations, trying to discern his misjudgments. There! Just before the agent fired, the shadow on the stairwell wall, moving down fast. He froze the image in his mind, turning it over, parsing out the distortions from different light sources and the various angles of the stairwell walls. The realization came slowly, but clearly.

"It's a woman! Jesus Christ! The Other took a woman host." Dismay flooded through him.

The fractured image of Duc Li finally knitted itself whole, and together they contemplated the image of the shadow on the stairs. Sober agreement from his nexus floated into John's mind-space alongside the image.

Indeed it seems to be a female of your species. If so, there is even more danger. The females—the child-bearers—in most young species like yours are more subtle than males. The trap this one set implies a highly developed capacity for guile and ambush. You must bear that in mind.

I have never intentionally hurt a woman or child, even in combat.

Your father did.

I know. In Cambodia. But they were maniacs. He had no choice.

As you have no choice, here. For the same reason.

His fragmented consciousness radar formed more fully into coherence then, and he sensed a position for the pulsating black blip. Outlined in a dim green haze, signal damped way down, she obviously was trying to conceal herself. She moved obliquely away, behind and to his left as he lay on the roof. Headed northwest, he judged, maybe a half-kilometer out.

Another gray government sedan with a flashing dashboard strobe skidded around the corner into the street below, and he heard a chopper in the distance. His null field ability still fragmented, he realized he couldn't conceal himself on the roof. Dismissing the weariness of his depleted state, the Magician transposed along sightlines through the trees into Rock Creek Park, and gave chase to the fleeing obscenity tracking away from him on his mental radar screen.

National Zoo, Washington, DC | Monday 0451 EDT

The white static on Lara's consciousness radar thinned out to show disconnected fragments of a picture as she flew downstream just over the surface of Rock Creek. She could not sense her three Bureau protectors in the inchoate mess, and choked down hard on her guilt and misery. The Beast, on the other hand, clearly was still alive. Evidently not in pursuit, so maybe he was temporarily trapped or disabled.

She landed in a crouch on the small stone bridge crossing the creek, the lower entrance to the Smithsonian's National Zoo.

I'll zip through here, she told herself. Probably nobody's around this early, and maybe I can confuse my signal with the animals. Or better yet... she gave the wild card idea a moment to gel in her mind-space. Her nexus considered it.

That may be possible, the thought came back. Symbolic constructs scrolled across her mind-space, showing her how.

A big African cat wakened, hissing and spitting at Lara as she flew past the Servals compound. Without the chaos from the null field cloaking her, she remained clearly visible even in the dim light before dawn. The nearby glows on her returning consciousness radar drew her northward to the Great Apes compound, and she flipped over to land gracefully in its outdoor yard. The lock on the access door to the building cages yielded to the green energy lanced from her fingertip, and she ran inside. The apes were sleeping in their cages.

Your intuition is correct. So long as the null field is fragmented, you may adhere fragments to the animals.

Will it hurt them?

No. Temporary confusion.

Will it slow down the Beast's pursuit?

He will sense the fragments of the field. He will associate them with you. He probably cannot leave such an anomaly uninvestigated.

Okay. Sorry ladies. Or gentlemen. She silently apologized as she ran to touch the four apes, roused suddenly from their group somnolence by the unknown presence. A roar of rage sounded behind her as she flew out the door of their cage.

"Oops, alpha male," Lara said as he slammed into the bars between the two cages. She lanced the lock on the big ape's cage door to the outdoor yard, and threw it open. As the huge creature boiled through it roaring, she hung in the air upside down and pinned a large fragment of the null field on his broad head. The big male spun and rolled in the dirt and grass of the outdoor compound, trying to throw off this unexpected and strange attachment. The smaller females exited their cages and rolled on the ground along with him, hooting their fear as they tried to escape their own chaos cloaks. Lara looked at their now-indecipherable forms, cloaked in flickering blackness, and barely evaded a leaping tackle from the alpha male. That will do nicely for a diversion, she thought, and flew over the building roof into the deserted Zoo grounds.

Her radar screen composed itself into coherence as Lara exited the ape compound, and she sensed the ugly blue-tinged black blotch start to move. She felt the fatigue, the soul-numbing weariness that manipulating chaos had cost her, both at the safehouse and here. It left her with a sensation of incompleteness, of no longer being totally in this reality. The Beast was coming, and the edge that her greater skill with the null field gave her was gone for now. Her mind ran down through the possibilities, and decided.

"Time to get outta Dodge," she muttered. Damping her aura as much as she could, Lara sprinted northwestward along the deserted Zoo drive, angling toward Connecticut Avenue.

National Zoo, Washington, DC | Monday 0454 EDT

The Magician transposed erratically through the trees in pursuit of his quarry, moving west and uphill into the National Zoo. He moved cautiously, because the signal on his consciousness radar had gone stationary, smoky, diffused. The blot no longer seemed an empty blackness, but more amorphous and gray, nearly translucent. The green hue flickered in and around the blotch. He wondered how she did that.

I do not know.

And why? Is she hurt?

Probably not.

Erecting some camouflage? Trying to hide?

Possibly.

It's another trap.

Likely.

Crouched in a gnarled oak tree overhanging an access drive, he recognized the Great Apes compound from his visits with Josh. She's in with the apes, he thought. She may not be hurt, but she's got to be depleted of energy or something, so she has to improvise, use other resources. Okay. So it's a trap, but the apes aren't likely to have automatic weapons. I can handle this, even weakened as I am.

As he considered it more, the hard edge of the Assassin crowded out other thoughts, entraining his mind in its flow of cold rage. Her trap failed. Now she's trapped herself. No place to go. It's an endgame. My game. The exultation he'd felt 24 hours ago while sighting the killer drone on Diego Corrano washed over him again.

Careful, John Connard. His nexus floated Plato's caution into his mind-space as a counterbalance. *Seeing something and judging its nature are different activities.*

The caution rolled off the Assassin. He transposed to the roof of the building and looked down into the outdoor yard of the compound. The pulsating amorphous mass on his consciousness radar resolved itself into multiple flickering forms on the far side of the yard, and a single form on the near side. All seemed apelike, but constantly shifted and distorted, as if moving in and out of reality.

She's hiding herself. In the group, probably. In the instant that thought ran through his mind he acted, materializing in front of the huddled mass with energy flaming from his hands.

The animals howled and four fields of blackness flew instantly from them toward his hands as if drawn by a supermagnet. Coruscating fragments of blue and green energy and pieces of gray nothingness spiraled around him.

Even though staggered by the force of the impact, the Assassin's primitive instincts felt the pounding approach behind him. Spinning, he instinctively swept outward across his back with his left hand, a shield of blue energy crackling from it.

The enormous drain of the contact—the pure coherent energy of his flaming shield meeting the pure incoherence of a large chaos fragment—hit him a millisecond before the physical body of the enraged alpha male slammed him through the huddled mass of shrieking females and into the hard concrete wall of the compound. He fell back stunned, wind knocked out, head ringing from the contact. The alpha male raged at him, then picked him up like a five-pound sack of potatoes and tossed him twenty feet into the dirt in the center of the compound.

The ape roared his challenge and bounded stiff-legged over to the wheezing form. He raised a mighty arm and began to swing it downward.

Even though on his hands and knees, trying to suck air back into his lungs, the Assassin sensed it. Instinct and years of training triggered a survival reaction, and now new skills were wedded to it.

A lance of blue energy swept upward with his backhand block, slicing off the ape's arm under the shoulder, continuing on to sever its head. Blood spurted out as the big animal dropped, spraying all over John Connard and the dirt floor. The arm bounced off his chest and sent him staggering back.

The four small females cowered and whimpered in the corner of the cage as the Assassin limped toward them. The light from the energy sword flickered in their wide dark terrified eyes.

"Ahh, I'm sorry," he told them. There clearly was no human form among them. The crackling energy around him flickered off and he limped across the bloody dirt to kneel beside the twitching body of the big male.

"I'm sorry, big fella," John murmured, putting his hand on the hairy back, "it was a reflex. Automatic reaction. I wish I could undo it." A hot tear dripped into the blood and fur.

Favoring his left ankle, hunched over bruised ribs, troubled in his soul, John Connard transposed through the trees northeastward toward his parked car, retreating from a conflict he now was surely too depleted to win. He paused briefly to let the cool running water of Rock Creek wash off the blood and dirt, a baptism for the next encounter.

Northwest Washington, DC | Monday 0458EDT

Joshua's small form tossed restlessly on his hotel bed, sheets twisting around him like the intertwining threads visualized by his sleeping mind. Immersed in a fitful dream of terrified animals and the gore of a predator, the nightmare setting seemed somehow familiar. He had been there. The threads in his dream ran red with blood, and the boy thrashed on the bed, sweat beading out on his young body. His right arm swept up from his hip and across his torso, the classic blocking motion for a downward strike. Droplets of sweat flew off his fingers to speckle the ceiling and wall.

National Zoo, Washington, DC | Monday 0500 EDT

Running up toward the Bird House, Lara sensed her pursuer's engagement in the Great Ape compound by the bright flare of blue on her now-functional consciousness radar. *Good,* she thought, *while he's not paying attention, I'll gain some ground on him.* Her running steps launched her into flight down a hiking trail through the woods of Rock Creek Park, behind the buildings on the east side of Connecticut Avenue.

When she saw a clearing in the brush and trees, she flew over the park's chain-link fence and flipped smoothly into a running landing in the alley behind a large apartment complex. A paper boy, delivering the morning's Washington Post, was just exiting the rear service entrance of the building. He regarded her athletic endeavor with his mouth agape.

"Shhh," she whispered, running past him, "we're filming!"

The boy nodded understanding as she passed, looking around for the cameras and grinning uncertainly.

In front of the apartment building, a taxi had returned a load of late-party carousers, and was just pulling out onto Connecticut Avenue when Lara ran out of the alley. She whistled it to a stop and climbed in. The driver looked at her suspiciously.

"Got a page," she explained, "have to cut my run short. Take a left up here on

Cathedral, I'll tell you where in a minute. And step on it."

He looked at her eyes carefully in the rear view mirror, and decided she was all right. As the cab turned onto Cathedral Avenue and headed west, Lara pulled out her cell phone.

"This is Lara Picard. I'm on a cell phone, unsecure."

"Yes, ma'am. Where are you now? Are you in danger? Are you injured?"

Am I in danger, Lara wondered. Well, I guess that's all relative. She checked her consciousness radar. The obscene black blot with its blue outline was falling behind her. She studied it.

"Ms. Picard? Are you there?"

"Yes. I'm in a cab, headed west on Cathedral Avenue, just passing..." she peered out the window, "29th Street."

She studied her consciousness radar. She was moving west, and the Beast was moving east. So he's had enough for now, she thought. He's as depleted as I am. This one was a standoff.

"No imminent danger, I think," she added, dropping her voice. "And I'm okay, no injuries. But you have casualties at the safehouse." The sob escaped her throat and wrapped itself around those words before she could clamp down on it.

"Yes, ma'am, we're aware of that," the duty officer replied stoically. "Ms. Picard, we're diverting the helicopter to pick you up at the Naval Observatory. We're showing your transponder position on Cathedral coming up on 34th, is that correct?"

"Yes, that's right," Lara replied. As she listened to the directions that followed, she let herself slide into weariness and grief, then clicked off the cell phone.

"Turn left on 34th," she instructed the driver, "and take me down to the Naval Observatory."

Northwest Washington, DC | Monday 0520 EDT

Special Agent Thomas Charles Demuzzio had been rousted out of bed by the phone call, and tasted the sourness around his unbrushed teeth as he yelled into the headset. It complemented the sourness in his soul. Thank God she's all right, he thought. I should have been smarter. I should have listened closer to what she was really trying to tell me. I should have trusted her instincts totally, forgotten about the goddamn bean counters and the cost of protection. I should have had a fucking Delta Force platoon around that house!

He sped into Washington from the southeast, from his home in Clinton, talking to the duty officer on his mobile phone.

The flasher he'd put on the roof ran a metronomic counterpoint to his staccato thoughts as he sped down the sparsely-trafficked highway into the city. *Warlock,* he told himself, I'm gonna nail your ass. I'm gonna pin it right to the fucking barn door. Count on it! He swung abruptly left through a flashing yellow light at the bottom of the off-ramp.

"Tell the chopper crew to pick me up at the OP helipad, after they pick up Picard," he continued yelling instructions, "and tell the Marines to sit on that cabbie until we get somebody over there to debrief him, okay?"

Demuzzio listened to the instructions being relayed to the Marine guard duty officer at the Naval Observatory. The sentries apparently had the cab in sight.

"All right, good. Now tell Quantico we're coming," he added, and then thought for a moment. He rattled off the commands as the logic of the next moves unfolded in his mind.

"Roust the Quantico sawbones outta bed.

"And roust up our consulting shrink, Sam Rosen, put him on standby.

"Then tell the security detail at Quantico we want the Bureau compound buttoned up tight as soon as we arrive.

"And wake up the Deputy, fill him in on what's gone down, tell him I'll report from the chopper after I talk to Picard.

"Now patch me into the SWAT commander. Please."

Demuzzio drove rapidly toward the government Outer Perimeter helipad in southeast DC while he conferred with the DC Metro SWAT commander, a Lieutenant Paquin.

"Lieutenant, if you've got the combo canisters with HEPA and organic vapor on your masks, you're okay. Even if your people get a whiff, it's no big thing. What's in the safehouse is a new variety of tear gas, mixed with a happy gas that fucks up your mobility. No permanent damage. You just sit in one place and cough and laugh and don't give a shit."

He listened to the SWAT commander's reply; his description of Agent Ditka's sudden ejection from the rear door, and the apparently instantaneous disappearance of the shadowy form propelling it, probably back into the house.

"Somehow I think the house is gonna be empty, but, yeah, I want you to go in. Just put a man on the roof first.

"There's a vault manhole in the bushes between Adams Mill Road and Rock Creek Parkway, just north of Quarry Road. It's a steel cover, got the phone company mark. Put a man on that. Tell him to shoot anything coming out. That manhole cover pops, don't even think, just hose it down."

"And there's a culvert for a big storm sewer main on the east side of Rock Creek, maybe a hundred yards north of the bridge into the Zoo. Put two men on that. Anything moves outta that culvert, just drop it.

"Tell all your people not to touch anything in the house, we're gonna have forensics in there. Don't let anybody enter the vault or culvert, either, just stand off and watch. Okay?"

He listened to the SWAT commander repeat his instructions, dispatching his personnel, and then got his second shock of the early morning.

"Say that again," he ordered. "They're alive? All three of 'em? Talk to me!"

Demuzzio ran that astonishing information through his head over and over as he approached the helipad. They're alive! Palpable relief flooded through him, along with a certain measure of reluctant thanksgiving for their benefactor.

Mary Lovelock and Toman Black had no sign of any physical damage, no holes or other obvious marks, no anesthetic darts stuck in them anywhere. Their vital signs were perfect. But they couldn't be roused, and were on the way to the hospital.

Gas, he thought, it has to be some kind of gas. But how the hell did he deliver it? From the roof, maybe?

My third agent, the big D, Big David Ditka, no gas for him. He's bruised at the nape of his neck, maybe a concussion. Got some other scrapes and bruises, but he's sitting up and talking, identifying all the right number of fingers.

And him a fucking black belt. Tae kwon do, third degree. He competes in tournaments to keep his edge. Got the fastest hands in the Bureau. He empties four clips out into some furniture, and then gets taken out like some fucking snot-nosed rookie! Demuzzio's wonderment notched up further.

"So this *Warlock* lives up to his reputation," he muttered to himself. "And he really *is* a goddamn magician! He only whacks the target. Only what he's paid to hit. Jesus! This isn't making any sense at all. This is one weird dude. Gotta be some high-level spook gone goofy. Probably ours. Who else would have the training, the resources? The Brits? The Israelis, maybe? Anzacs or Russkis, they're a longshot."

Grudgingly, he patched back into the SWAT control net and belayed the shoot-on-sight order, telling the team commander to capture the perp alive if at all possible.

Chapter 27

Lara heard the chopper first, and then saw it in the brightening sky to the east as the Marine jeep took her from the main gate of the Naval Observatory to its helipad. The aircraft flared to a neat landing and a black-vested figure jumped out to help her board.

She was barely buckled in when the helicopter lifted hard and banked left over tree-lined Massachusetts Avenue, quartering toward the southeast, with the dim light of dawn off to the port side. She felt the soothing sensation of escape through her fatigue, and almost dozed off while her custodian checked her pulse and looked her over for injuries.

"Tell TC I'm okay," she muttered. Then she withdrew into her mind. Struggling against its growing fuzziness, she tried to force some coherence into her thoughts. TC would be full of questions, she knew. But the truth held dangerous and unpredictable consequences. She would have to stay with the *Warlock* story.

That would be the lesser of the two evils. Her nexus floated agreement into her mind-space. The blue-tinged black blot receding on her consciousness radar pulsated eerily, reinforcing her decision.

On the ground four miles away, Special Agent TC Demuzzio clicked his cell phone off the helicopter contact and clicked back on to the SWAT team contact.

"Okay, Lieutenant, you cleared the house. I got that. So now, just open all the windows. There's an attic fan in the second floor hall. The switch is right underneath it, on the wall. Turn it on and leave it running. Pull your people out of the house. And don't disturb anything. I've got forensics on the way."

He listened to the SWAT team commander's questions, approvingly. Sharp boy, this one, he thought.

"Okay. Tell your press officer to spin a story about a terrorist attempt on a diplomat, say sorry we can't tell 'em any more right now. Cite national security. Say this is an FBI matter, and we'll have a briefing when we can, later in the morning or maybe around noon. That should get 'em off your back."

They worked out the logistics and communications a little more, then the chopper landed on the helipad and TC Demuzzio ended the phone conversation and ran to the opening cabin door.

"Lara, I'm sorry," he said, sliding onto the seat beside her and enfolding her in his big arms, "I should've had a freaking platoon out there."

She looked at him wanly.

"You didn't get him, did you, TC? The *Warlock*."

"No, Lara, we didn't. Sonuvabitch is still loose. Jesus, you're cold," he added. "Cooper, grab me a blanket!"

And just how did she know that, he wondered, that we didn't get him. Oh, the scramble to pick her up, get her safely out of the area. Yeah, that would tell her. He wrapped the insulating blanket around her as she shivered down into the seat.

"Three good people dead, TC."

It wasn't an accusation, Demuzzio saw, just a statement of mourning. She wasn't blaming him for his misjudgment. A tear formed in her left eye. He blinked his own eyes and lowered his head, and made a difficult decision. If she thought the agents were killed, it would force her to be more cautious, and might heighten even more her intuitive ability to detect impending harm. She might need an edge, for survival. *Warlock* was a formidable adversary.

"I'm sorry, Lara," he replied. A simple statement. Not a lie, exactly, it could mean a lot of things. But she took it as he intended. It confirmed her fears: the loss of those three entrusted to protect her. Three agents dead. He looked into her eyes sympathetically. She collapsed into him, sobbing.

Northwest Washington, DC | Monday 0550 EDT

The Magician worked his way slowly and patiently northward along the edge of the woods, ignoring the pain in his ankle, dismissing the chill that set in after he'd washed off the blood into Rock Creek. He could see and hear the activity behind him, and moved like a silent shadow out of the woods and down an alley to the 19th Street location where he'd parked his car under a burned-out streetlight. He eased it away from the curb, watching for police but not seeing any. The ring around the house had collapsed inward. He reflected on the experience as he drove away eastward.

Helluva trap she set up, with lots of resources. Helluva special house, too. And she pulled it all together on a Sunday. That means big time support for the next go-round. He felt the seeds of doubt.

But you are the Magician. The visage of Duc Li floated in his mind-space, gently chastising.

He smiled wryly. And almost a dead one, he sent the thought back into his mind-space. The power of that null field was enormous, like an elephant sat on me. I could almost feel my mind dissolving. And how the hell did she leave pieces of the null field on the apes? They had her... signal... her echo... her hologram? It could have been her; I thought it was. But she wasn't even in the compound.

The Other is a master of deception, John Connard. And it has found a human host, a female of like mind, full of cunning and deceit, and highly intelligent. The other has chosen well. An impression of begrudging acknowledgment formed in his mind-space.

The Magician turned south, working his way back to Alex's office condo. The fuzziness in his mind suggested more than fatigue from letdown after combat, he thought, more like a piece of him got carried off into the null dimension and didn't make it back. He parked the car in the garage under the office complex, and trudged wearily up the stairs.

Eggs, bacon, fruit, bagels, and juice were plentiful in the condo. He blessed Alex again for keeping a full pantry, and made himself a huge breakfast. The fuzziness in his mind receded somewhat. As he ate he played back how the black blot of the Other had receded on his consciousness radar. He dug back into his memory and pulled up locations and time. Flying or transposing would be dangerous in daylight, so she's in a chopper, he diagnosed. It picked her up west of the Zoo somewhere. A chopper means serious resources. That was bad news. Then, a stopover in southeast DC somewhere, and then they headed... south-southwest, roughly.

He got out a road atlas.

Flew right down the Potomac, he decided. Past Mount Vernon. Ah, Quantico, that had to be it; the Marine Corps base. The position stayed steady on his consciousness radar, confirming his guess. Quantico. That was worse news. They would have ramped up security as soon as the chopper set down. So, he would mount no attack today, not in the daylight. Tonight, maybe.

John shrugged, took a shower, toweled off, yawned hugely, and dropped into bed. As he slipped toward sleep, the Magician pondered the disturbing implications of the Other's rapid and complete access to power: a Marine base, a lot of protection, high-tech support. He wondered why—with so much power at its disposal, and knowing where he was—the Other didn't simply drop a battalion on him. Ah, it can't, he realized. It hasn't subverted the system that far yet. It can't take a chance; there would be too many questions. It still needs secrecy and guile to achieve its ends. A warm fuzziness crept back into his mind, enveloping it, preventing further thought. But he knew, as he fell asleep, that the next trap would be more dangerous.

National Zoo, Washington, DC | *Monday 0600 EDT*

Lieutenant James Paquin, SWAT team commander, verified that the gas was cleared from the safehouse, and was preparing for the Bureau's forensics team when the call came in from the duty desk.

"Say what?" he yelled into his head set, "An ape? Over in the Zoo? Yeah, I'll go. No, I'll go myself. Sure it's related! It's gotta be. I'll go take a look at the scene."

Breaking that contact, he yelled to his team, "Ramon, you're in charge here. Bob, get the van and drive me over to the Zoo for a few minutes, some kinda action went down over there, probably related."

Two minutes later, they were at the outdoor compound of the Great Ape building. He whistled as he saw the three parts of the big corpse, its blood pooled and splattered in the dirt. He looked at his watch. The Zoo had just opened for walking, and would open its exhibits in three hours. But this one obviously would have to be barricaded off as a crime scene. Well, it wasn't a Metro SWAT operation. Just get some facts, he told himself, then lay it on the Bureau and the Park Police.

"Any witnesses, by any chance?" he asked an obviously shaken Park Police officer.

"No, sir," the man said, "I heard this ruckus, and come running, but Mongo was down when I got here. I coulda swore I saw something crouched over him when I came around the corner, but probably it was a shadow or lighting, because nothing left the compound. And it's electrified, anyway. We didn't touch anything, just a keeper came and got the females back in their cages."

"Any web cams on this outdoor part?"

"No, sir, I don't believe so. I could check with Admin. The Director's on her way in, she should know for sure."

"Thanks, do that, please," Paquin said, and walked over to the wall to study the corpse. His analytical mind started working on it.

The head and arm were neatly severed. Lots of bone and gristle and muscle mass there, so that means phenomenal strength. It also means a helluva blade, sharp as a razor, long and heavy, a two-handed weapon. And a big animal like this isn't likely to sit still long enough for it to be so clean. Unless it was sleeping. Or maybe it was shot first, and I can't see the wound. Jesus, this sort of shit only happens in Hollywood, not in real life!

Then he thought back to the scene at the safehouse. The big FBI agent had been propelled backwards out of the door. There'd been the briefest vision of something shadowy behind him, vanished almost before it could register. When we get back to the ready room, we'll look at the videotape from the van, he decided. Maybe that had enough of an angle to pick something up. Maybe if we're lucky we can get a digital frame or two with a face. Maybe if we're real lucky we can figure out his fucking disappearing act.

Warlock, he mused. Well, he sure as shit was all of that. The action at the house and the action at the Zoo absolutely had to be connected, somehow. He only disabled three agents at the house, but then he dismembered an ape at the Zoo. What the fuck did that mean? A message of some kind? And then the perp disappeared, like a ghost.

Lieutenant James Paquin shivered slightly as he toggled into his communications net. He got a patch to FBI Special Agent TC Demuzzio, and filled him in on this strange new development.

FBI Special Operations Center, Quantico, VA | Monday 0610 EDT

Lara's semiconscious head nestled into TC Demuzzio's shoulder, and he could feel her twitch and shiver under the blanket as the helicopter dropped toward the landing pad at Quantico. He spoke softly into his communicator.

"An ape. Yeah. Okay. Thanks. Listen, *Warlock* is obviously outta there; you can pull your people off the culvert and the vault. Get all your troops back to your shop. Our debrief team is on the way, so make sure everybody hangs around." Demuzzio paused to collect his thoughts. "And leave the Zoo scene alone, that's mostly outta Metro's jurisdiction anyway. We'll get a Bureau team in there, work it out with the Park Police. Thanks." Then he switched channels and relayed his specific instructions down the control network.

"Ape? Zoo? What happened? Are the apes okay?" Lara struggled upright and spoke groggily.

Demuzzio squeezed her shoulder. "No, Lara. An ape was killed in the Zoo. A big male, name of Mongo. His head was chopped off. His arm too. It had to be *Warlock*. Probably pissed you got away. Sending us a message, maybe."

"Ah, Jesus, TC," Lara groaned, folding over as if she'd been hit in the stomach, "this is too much. This is too horrible."

Demuzzio grimaced and hugged her again. "C'mon, kid, we're setting down. A doctor's standing by to look at you, and then we gotta debrief you, at least for as long as you can stay awake. I think you're in some kinda shock, post-trauma thing. The doc will know."

"TC..." she started.

No, you must not! This event changes nothing! He will not understand. And if he finally does, and accepts the preposterous, you will become a tool of the government.

The consequences are too likely to be fatal to successful evolution. The visage of her nexus, her *ki*, her greater self, hardened into a formidable abjuration in her mind-space, the mouth a straight line, the planes of the cheeks hard and angular. It mirrored exactly how she herself looked, she realized, when refusing to negotiate a plea bargain. The previous logic of non-disclosure repeated itself, symbology flooding across her mind-space.

Yeah, that's right, she sighed, surrendering acknowledgment into her mind-space in return. I can't tell TC what's really going on. He's a good friend, but I can't give in to that weakness. The hard lines softened on the expression of her nexus, reflecting encouragement back at her.

"Yes, Lara?" TC prompted.

"TC, you're a true friend. Thanks for helping me." She wiped her face on the blanket, forced herself upright, and kissed his cheek. "Okay, let's go see the doc. And I desperately need something to eat." She leaned heavily on the agent as they walked into the building.

"Your blood electrolyte balance is probably all screwed up, Ms. Picard," the physician told her minutes later, withdrawing the blood sample. "We can fix that with an intravenous solution pretty quickly. But you're obviously an athlete, and you're not diabetic, so if we just give you something to eat nature should take its course. What's your preference? IV or food?"

"Food, please, I need food. Get me some high pulp orange juice, lots of it. And put some honey in it. And I want about six cheese and veggie omelets, and a bunch of bagels or a loaf of brown bread. Butter, not margarine. And coffee. Decaf."

The room's wired, Lara realized, when breakfast materialized on a wheeled cart. She dug in with a passion.

"TC, Doctor Agnozzi, have some," she gestured, pushing the cart over to the table. "You, too," she mumbled around a mouthful of omelet to the tall stranger who just entered.

"Ms. Picard," Agnozzi asked, "you want to slow down a little bit? You're making me nervous. I'm not sure your stomach is going to accept food at that rate."

"Have you ever been bulimic, Ms. Picard?" The tall stranger asked, as he watched her intake in astonishment.

"Nope," she replied, washing down the omelet with orange juice, "and who are you?"

"Sam Rosen, Ms. Picard. I'm a psychiatrist. I do some contract work for the Bureau from time to time. I happened to be available on this beautiful holiday morning. I'd like to help, if I can. If you need me to."

Lara contemplated him as she buttered a bagel, and then wiped her hand on a napkin and stuck it out over the table. He's a psych trauma guy, she decided.

"Thanks, Doctor," she said, shaking his hand, "it's good of TC to think of that, and it's good of you to come here on a holiday morning. Yeah, I've been through a lot, but I really think I'm going to be okay. Now, you couldn't possibly have had any breakfast, so here, have a bagel. Have some omelet. Plenty of plates and silverware. And don't worry about me. I'm not bulimic, never have been. I'm just a fast eater."

Demuzzio's left eyebrow went up.

Oops, Lara thought, there's an inconsistency; I used to lecture him about eating too fast, told him how I chewed everything twenty-five times.

The agent's cell phone distracted him, and he walked across the room to take the call.

"Demuzzio. Yeah. Talk to me. Okay. Agency place, isn't it? No, that's fine. Thanks, Jack. I'll let her know." He folded his phone back onto his belt. "Lara, that was Jack Socrates. He's on the road with your son and your uncle. We're taking them to a safehouse in New York. It belongs to CIA, a nice secure setup. Just a precaution."

"Thanks, TC," Lara smiled at him around a bagel, "you don't know what a relief that is."

She washed the mouthful down with more juice, as her three attendants watched her intently. Yes, gentlemen, she thought, you're seeing what you're seeing. I can feel it myself. My color's coming back. My fatigue lines are fading. I am indeed rebuilding myself right in front of you. And I know just as well as you do that's a metabolic impossibility. Well, you'll just have to live with it. Maybe I can explain later, when this crisis is over.

"Oh, this food hits the spot. Debrief me quick, TC, before I fall asleep," Lara told him, "and order me some more orange juice, would you please?" She continued working through the omelets and bagels, but at a slower pace.

Demuzzio walked over to the door, opened it and spoke into the hall. A technician, a short Asian woman, pushed in a cart with a video camera, placed it where she could pick up TC in profile and Lara in full face, turned it on, turned on the connected computer and watched the digital image form on the screen. She gave a friendly smile to Lara and gave Demuzzio the thumbs-up signal.

The agent spoke the time, date, place and identity of all present, and the purpose of the debriefing session. He announced it would be an initial session, limited in scope, because the witness needed to rest and recover from her experience.

Then he smiled at Lara, and invited her to tell the story of the safehouse, in her own way, in her own time, as best she could recall it.

Northwest Washington, DC | Monday 0740 EDT

John's lean hard body lay face down on the bed. His breaths were deep and slow, his pulse steady and powerful. The scrapes on his shoulder slowly turned pinkish, and then disappeared. The bruising and swelling around his ankle receded to nothing.

The fingers of his left hand hung off the edge of the bed. They twitched, but not with random firing of a synapse. They twitched in a pattern, as if enumerating, or conveying a coded message, or, possibly, working an instrument or a machine of some kind. His Magician mind dreamed of patterns, spiraling threads in a helix, streaming by him. He stepped into his mind-space and touched the threads with his fingers. They responded to his touch, giving off colors and hues, shadings that wove into the fabric of his reality. A part of him sensed their potential for being woven into other realities.

The threads were changing constantly. Some threads went on. Some stopped. Some had warmth and fullness. Some were cold and cutting. Some left his view but then returned to weave themselves back in with other threads. Some left and never returned. He marveled at the complexity, but the artist in him recognized the common intent of the underlying patterns: the threads were weaving toward a purpose. They wanted to create a tapestry, tell a story.

The Magician's body tossed fitfully on the bed. He couldn't see the story intended for the tapestry. Too much uncertainty intruded.

FBI Special Operations Center, Quantico, VA | Monday 0743 EDT

"Damn she's good, isn't she?" TC Demuzzio studied the digital video and admired the way his favorite protégé succinctly summarized her experience. She delivered facts first, cool, dry and unemotional, with occasional pauses to collect her thoughts and take in more food. Then, she wove in impressions about the battle, her sense of the enemy. It made an articulate, rational, coherent package. You'd never know she was milliseconds away from death just a few hours ago. Lara Picard was a better witness than any of the experts she had ever cross-examined in court, Demuzzio realized. She gave the clearest possible impression of honesty and forthrightness. A jury would love her. A judge would eat out of her hand.

"But she's lying, isn't she, Doc?"

"Yes, she is, TC," psychiatrist Sam Rosen agreed. He held up his hand to forestall conversation while he studied a key segment of the recorded video. "But it's not at all clear about what, or why. And it's more subterfuge than outright lying; it's a pattern of concealment. I'd say she's trying to keep you at a distance from questions she doesn't want to have to deal with."

The FBI's premier consultant on witness truthfulness shrugged, with a quizzical look at Demuzzio.

"And, by the way," Rosen continued, "I can also tell you with some certainty that she has a very good moral reason for doing what she's doing. She's your good friend, TC. She obviously respects you enormously. She loves you. Not in a romantic sense, but in a spiritual sense. That's all pretty clear. So her deception—if that's indeed what it is—has a very strong purpose behind it. She may be trying to protect you, or somebody else she cares about."

"Protect me?" Demuzzio was incredulous. "Shit, doc. I don't need protection. I'm Attila the fucking Hun. I'm about the last person on earth who needs to be protected."

"Umm. I wasn't necessarily thinking about physical protection." Rosen got a distant look on his face.

"Protection from what, then?"

"Knowledge, maybe."

"Knowledge? Bullshit! That doesn't make any sense at all!"

"Hmm. You sure?"

The agent stared back at Rosen, irritated. The psychiatrist looked calmly back, patiently waiting.

"So, maybe my name is Adam," Demuzzio finally asked, "and I'm standing here in the Garden, and Eve is trying to keep the apple of knowledge away from me, is that it? The apple's too dangerous for a dumb fuck like me to bite, is that it? I couldn't handle the knowledge? Is that what you're trying to tell me?"

"Why, TC, my old friend! There may be hope for you yet! What a wonderful analogy! Something like that, maybe. Or maybe it's what she thinks you would do with the knowledge. Now, whether this dilemma is real or just in her mind, that's a different question..." he paused as his attention shifted back to the video monitor.

"But the more I watch this tape, the more I think maybe her dilemma *is* real, TC," Rosen continued. "Just look at this sequence! Something totally abnormal is going on with her physiology. You saw how that food brought her back from nearly total exhaustion. It just can't happen that fast, so far as my medical background can tell me. Let's go down the hall and talk to Jim Agnozzi; he has to be more current on physical medicine than I am. Maybe he's gotten some of the blood work back. And she let him wire her up with those new mini-transmitters. Yeah, let's go talk to Jim, and watch her vitals and brainwaves while she sleeps. Maybe that will tell us something. This is all very strange. Extraordinary. And... TC?"

"Yeah, Doc?"

"I'm a little scared."

Chapter 28

Aaron O'Meara groaned in his sleep in the massage chair, rising slowly up toward wakefulness. He turned his head to the left, into the shaft of sunlight that had just cleared the dense junipers in the east yard and now slanted in through his workroom window. It snapped him fully awake.

"Jeez, sun's high, gotta be eight o'clock," he muttered, "I slept like a log. Things must be quiet, or Nathan would have buzzed me." He squinted across the room at the big flat-screen monitor. The 1-minute integrals seemed as level and steady as fields of blue and green corn for the two-hour period immediately past.

"So, our visitors haven't gotten together yet," Aaron yawned acknowledgement at the monitor. He stretched his muscular arms and upper body, threw the cover off and rolled smoothly into his wheelchair.

I'll have some yogurt and fruit and coffee, he decided, and then tell Nathan to go home and get some sleep. I can stand watch for a bit, and maybe talk to Adrienne. The sunlight flooding the room grew brighter with that cheerful thought.

Rolling back to the big computer workbench with his insulated mug of coffee, he looked at the two-hour window, then started scrolling backwards in time. A swallow of coffee met a gasp of astonishment that pushed the hot liquid partway up his sinus cavity. He sputtered and coughed and snorted coffee onto his sweatshirt.

"Jesus, Nathan," he roared, "why the hell didn't you wake me up?" He swallowed convulsively and wiped his sleeve across his nose and mouth. The period from 0545 back to 0445 showed spikes that were totally off-scale. He stared in amazement. "Shit hit the fan there, for sure."

Aaron's fingers trembled as he toggled over to look at the 15-minute location plots, starting with the 0200 period when he'd gone to bed.

"Nice and quiet, two or three miles apart," he told his computer screen, "then at 0400 Blue starts moving toward green, and at 0500 to 0545 we got pure craziness. The location solutions don't make any sense. It looks like they're right on top of each other, but the probability circles are totally blown out. Adrienne's algorithms can't handle it. Inputs are probably out of range or something. And then..." His voice trailed off as his consternation increased.

And then, he thought, by o6oo they're clearly moving apart. But they're both still in existence, so it wasn't a fight. Or if it was, it must have been a standoff. He toggled back to the 1-minute integrals of signal strength, and scrolled forward and backward through those, trying to glean some insight. Belatedly, the question hit him.

Nathan! All sorts of Adrienne's alarms should have gone off! Jesus, I hope he's okay.

Aaron picked up his cell phone and hit the speed-dial number for the Global Consciousness Project.

I-95 Southwest of Havre de Grace, MD | Monday 0745 EDT

Havre de Grace, read the sign for the upcoming exit.

"Haven of grace," Special Agent Jack Socrates translated from the French. "I always like driving through here, sir. A man can't hardly get enough grace, these days." The agent glanced down at the machine pistol arrayed neatly with extra clips on the front passenger seat, and smiled at Hamilton O'Donnell in the rearview mirror. The boy Joshua nestled into his shoulder, sleeping soundly.

"Doctor O'Donnell, how about if we pull off the road next exit, and wake our boy up for a little breakfast. He probably likes Egg McMuffins, right?"

"Ah, a treat that would be for the lad, to be sure. We must stay in the car, I presume?"

"Yes, sir, that would be best. Eat on the road. This vehicle is pretty good protection." Jack Socrates patted the dashboard, saying how the SUV had been hardened; special glass and Kevlar side panels, and how he enjoyed driving it.

Joshua visualized their conversation, but distantly; he was dreaming again of the interweaving threads of light he'd seen flash by his consciousness shortly after 10 PM last night. He stirred briefly against his uncle's shoulder as the threads became connected to the concepts on evolution being constructed in his mind. In his sleep, he reached out with mental fingers to catch those fleeting threads, to unfold their riddles.

The boy's physical fingers twitched in empathy as the spiraling threads resonated under his mental touch. In his dream, the threads shifted to become instrument strings, then morphed into the vibrations coming off the strings: the music itself. Different melodies within the music wove the multiplicity of spiraling threads into his reality, and into other realities.

Joshua studied the music metaphor, fascinated. He recognized it was not the thing itself, but rather an image, or hologram, that his mind had created. The melodies interacted, changed and shifted constantly, making a subtle, rich, complex music. The music had a purpose, he realized in wonderment, and the manifold melodies were weaving toward it. His hands warmed with energy as he fingered the strings, fascinated, and insight followed.

Oh, so *that's* the purpose, he thought. It's an evolutionary symphony. The threads of light became DNA melodies, spiraling through his hands. Retroviruses and fragmentary pieces of genome played contrapuntally within the melodies. When their time came, the boy saw, they would contribute to the music. A genetic change might bring a spiritual change. A spiritual change might bring a genetic change. They're tied together by interweaving melodies, or possibilities of melodies. The music is moving us all forward.

Joshua sensed that this present moment of time was a harmonic node. Biological and spiritual melodies were going to come together, in a moment of macroshift. A double macroshift: biological and spiritual. Would the music play well, or would it play poorly? Symphony or cacophony?

The uncertainty roused him. The hands that had metaphorically fingered the melodic genetic threads of the past and future of the human race now contained a warm Egg McMuffin. He laughed delightedly, along with his uncle and Special Agent Jack Socrates. His young laughter itself was a melody.

Global Consciousness Project, Princeton University, NJ | Monday 0805 EDT

The ringing phone finally succeeded in waking Nathan from a deep sleep. About five hours, he saw, looking at his watch. And my back loosened up, too, he thought. Well, isn't that a wonder. He swung his legs out of the recliner and stretched as he walked to the phone. The display showed Aaron O'Meara's cell phone number. The realization hit him: he'd fallen asleep on watch.

He picked up the phone. "Helluva watchdog I am, huh, Aaron?"

"You okay, Nathan?" Aaron's voice held concern. "Didn't any alarms go off? Why didn't you call? Is Adrienne there? What does she make of this?"

"Oh, oh. Something happen? Talk to me, Aaron. I took a muscle relaxant for my back spasms and it must have zonked me out pretty good. It's never done that before. Your phone woke me up just now."

Silence on the phone, and then Aaron laughed raucously.

"Nathan," he said, regaining control, "I don't know exactly how to tell you this, but you may have snoozed through the seminal event of the twenty-first century."

"Aw, shit! When, Aaron, when?" Nathan moved the phone, sat in front of his computer monitor and scrolled backward in time through the display of 1-minute integrals. He whistled when he saw the graphics for early morning, before dawn. Yup, he'd slept right through it.

"Oh, man! Look at that! Aaron, I'm sorry! I was feeling wide awake. I never expected to fall asleep. Jesus! Will you look at that! That's incredible! Totally off-scale. Maybe it's the same sort of thing that happened with the initial event yesterday. Aaron? Aaron, you there?"

Nathan started laughing himself, then roared as the absurdity fully sunk in. Both men were still chuckling, minutes later, as they discussed what to do.

"Okay, Nathan," Aaron said, "we agree there's probably some time before the next event, since Blue and Green have separated and they're both pretty quiet. I'm sending an email update to Goddard, and I'll send it to Ed's home too. He just got off shift, so he's probably in bed, but I'll call and let his wife know we've got an update for him.

"And Nathan, Green's been stable about 30 miles south-southwest since 0630; the location plots out on Quantico, Virginia. There's a big Marine Corps base there. So maybe there is some government action on this after all. If things stay quiet, I'm gonna drive down to the Zoo, see if there's any sign of what went on down there. I'm curious as hell."

Nathan agreed that was a reasonable idea, hung up, and dialed Adrienne's cell phone number.

"Hello," she yawned into her cell phone, finally picking it up on the eleventh ring, "Doctor Rodgers, what time is it? I was having the nicest dream; thought the phone was in my dream."

"It's after eight, Adrienne. Sorry to wake you, but there was an event, and we believe your talents are called for," he understated it. "So if you can drag yourself out of bed, come on over."

"An event? What sort of event?" Her voice came fully alert.

"Oh, it's probably best you see it yourself, Adrienne. And stop at the deli on your way here and get me an egg and ham and cheese on a bagel, would you please? And an extra-large coffee and juice. And get yourself whatever you want for breakfast. My treat, please."

"Oh, Lord, wait until she sees this," he chuckled as he hung up the phone. "She'll probably rip my fool head off; falling asleep right through all the bells and whistles she programmed! Human factors. They'll screw you every time!" For some reason that thought made him unaccountably cheerful, and he started laughing again.

I-95 West of Havre de Grace, MD | Monday 0817 EDT

The armored SUV turned back onto I-95 and arrowed northeastward, with Agent Schmidt in the backup car tight behind. Joshua chewed his Egg McMuffin slowly and thoroughly, as his mom had taught him. But now he enjoyed the different tastes in a new way, relating them to the nutrient balances his body unconsciously sought. He swallowed a sip of orange juice, and traced out how it would be metabolized. Then, realizing that feeding the body somehow related to feeding the spirit, his facile mind arabesqued into the end point of his waking dream: coincident cycles of biological and spiritual evolution, macroshifts. He swallowed another bite, and described his dream and its music metaphor to his uncle.

Hamilton O'Donnell studied the boy, smiling. "So, young lad, you had this fascinatin' intuitive leap, two macroshifts comin' together at the same time—a grand evolution of body together with a grand evolution of spirit. Well, I can see that. Musical cycles—frequencies—must coincide, for harmony, or a symphony, to exist. It seems a fair metaphor for evolution. So would your next question be 'how', or 'why'?"

Joshua grinned at how astutely his uncle had guessed his thoughts.

"It's not so much about cycles coming together at the same time, Uncle Ham, it's their relationship. Which is the cause and which is the effect, or does it work both ways? And is it an accident, with enough chances over time? Or is there a blueprint?"

"Ah, now there's an interestin' term, lad, a blueprint. Technology marches on, much like evolution, and blueprints are obsolete, but I take your meanin'. So, does spiritual enlightenment cause a change in your body? Is that what you mean? But that's pretty straightforward. Many measurements have demonstrated physiological effects during meditation or prayer."

"Sure, Uncle Ham, but I'm thinking maybe it goes deeper than that. Would a spiritual change in individuals feed back to trigger something in their genetic structure, the code we were speculating about? Or maybe it works in reverse? The code gets triggered and the spirit changes? If not in a specific individual, then maybe over several generations?"

"Ah yes, me young philosopher, the chicken or the egg, an age-old problem. But would not the bigger question be how the change is communicated and propagated among individuals, so that the species changes? When the critical mass we were speakin' about communicates its collective mindset, you would expect the concepts to resonate through like minds; but that's purely intellectual, is it not? A simple appreciation of common values? Where is the method for physical propagation in that, lad?"

"I dunno, Uncle Ham," Joshua said, talking excitedly and chewing at the same time, "but maybe that resonance of ideas and concepts can actually create some sort of physical or biological effect! What do you think?"

Joshua finished the last of the Egg McMuffin and wiped his fingers on the napkin. He smiled with contentment, his stomach full, his mind full, his spirit making progress.

"Thanks for feeding me, Uncle Ham," he said, knowing that his uncle, in their mind-dance, would take the broader meaning.

National Zoo, Washington, DC | Monday 0930 EDT

Aaron O'Meara drove southward on Connecticut Avenue, heading into Washington toward the National Zoo. Making coffee in the kitchen, he'd chanced to turn on the small television and watched a reporter holding forth in front of the crime scene tape at a house on Irving Street. As soon as he heard the reporter describe the setting, he pinned it as the location where Blue and Green had intersected so briefly but emphatically in the pre-dawn hour. He listened intently. The police were being tight-lipped, saying only that it was an FBI matter and there would be a press briefing in a few hours. There also had been some unspecified trouble at the Zoo, possibly connected, but the entrances were sealed off. Aaron had confirmed the action locations as well as he could from the badly overloaded location-plotting algorithms, and looked at a small-scale map of the area. It was definite, the locations were a clear match. But he wanted to see the physical scenes for himself.

Now, as the van crossed over the line into DC, he listened on his headset to the humorous aftermath of Adrienne's lecture to Nathan about falling asleep. His hands absently worked the van's handicapped driver controls with precise and skillful movements as he chimed into the discussion.

"I guess where I come out on this, Nathan," he said into the headset microphone, "is even though we were, ahem, snoozing, somebody in government must have paid attention. At least they did after that Blue and Green encounter, because we now have Green sitting at a federal facility in Virginia, and we know the FBI is involved at the Irving Street scene."

"But there's nothing special in the area where Blue's signal is located right now, Aaron," Adrienne's soft voice told him, "I've been in that part of Georgetown. It's not government stuff, Aaron, it's just private sector office buildings and expensive housing. It overlooks the river, but that's the only significant feature I can think of."

They speculated on the possibilities as Aaron drove southward toward the Zoo.

"Oops! Hey, guys," Aaron said excitedly, "the Zoo gates are closed on Connecticut Avenue. They've got barricades up. Traffic cops are waving people along. I'm going down to the next block and turn around, see if I can talk to what looks like a little command cluster there at the gate. Be back to you shortly." He clicked off as he saw an opportune empty driveway in front of an apartment complex, and turned the van around.

New Jersey Turnpike, East of Princeton, NJ | Monday 1002 EDT

"Music is a path," Joshua said suddenly, engaging the mind-dance with his uncle. "That's why I see the spiral helix as music. Musicians in an orchestra, or a band, have their own instruments, their own scores, they each play their own parts, but it all comes together. It's a path to togetherness."

"Mmm, Joshua?" Hamilton O'Donnell raised an eyebrow at his nephew's tangential leap.

"When you put that warm McMuffin in my hands, Uncle Ham, I dreamed that warm DNA threads were sliding through my fingers. My mind didn't know exactly what to make of that, probably, so it showed it as music. The different threads of DNA became melodies, different players, different instruments, but all weaving together into the music. It was very rich, very complex, a symphony. The separate melodies all had the same purpose, to combine, to become the whole."

"Mmm. Fascinatin', me lad. Truly fascinatin'. 'Tis an interestin' metaphor for your mind to choose. Music has always been a path to enlightenment. There are many others, of course, but I suppose your analytical mind may understand music best because of the physics of it."

"Uncle Ham, and I can't even adequately describe how fascinating it is. In my dream, there were feedback loops in the DNA, and feedforward loops, too. All filled with light. And control points, like musical codas. And things that tell an instrument when to play. And it all goes around and around in a big cycle of evolutionary music. And I think the more complex we get, the fuller and richer the music gets."

As Joshua reflected on how far back the music ran in time, and just how old some of the simpler DNA melodies were, the symphony in the back of his mind crescendoed and ended. He felt a profound sense of peace, a zone both within and without, where it seemed the warmth and light of countless generations past surrounded and enveloped him, and cherished his youth and exuberance.

Global Consciousness Project, Princeton University, NJ | *Monday 1017 EDT*

"Adrienne?" Nathan queried, "Adrienne, you in there?"

But Adrienne didn't look at him. She looked elsewhere, eastward, into the middle distance, trying to visualize her sudden sense of contact. Something had moved into the periphery of her consciousness. She glanced at the monitors, astonished. Blue hadn't moved. Green hadn't moved. But she definitely sensed a warm something in her mind, not herself, clearly another entity.

"Shhh, Dr. Rodgers. I think I'm being contacted!"

He stared at her, dumbfounded.

Adrienne continued to stare into the middle distance, entranced. The fleeting contact caressed her mind once more, then withdrew. Her analytical side parsed the surface impressions: warm, friendly, curious. And then there were the more subtle impressions: young, vibrant, even exuberant. It's not Aaron, she thought. Many of the same characteristics I believe he has. But this? No, this was a child, definitely. She smiled in wonderment.

National Zoo, Washington, DC | *Monday 1059 EDT*

Aaron O'Meara certainly got their attention when he pulled his handicap van up to the cones in front of the Zoo and announced he had information related to the recent events. The traffic officer made a pull-over spot for him. Now, Aaron was attempting to explain to a skeptical young detective sitting in the van's passenger seat exactly how the GCP tracking program worked.

"Mr. O'Meara. Doctor O'Meara," Detective Lucien Safire corrected himself, looking again at Aaron's Goddard ID card, driver's license and the tracking printouts. "You're telling me that you've been tracking things you think are alien minds, and they came together in this area early this morning, and they're connected with this situation we've got here?"

"In a nutshell, yes." Aaron went over it again, patiently. "Here, look again at the time plots since midnight. Blue gets into town around midnight. Starts moving toward Green around four AM. Then look what happened after that. Now, you tell me whether or not that's consistent with what you're investigating here. Which, by the way, you haven't told me about yet, and it hasn't been on the news, so I've got no way of knowing, right?"

Safire sighed, and leaned back into the van's passenger seat. Shit, he thought. I can't just blow him off. He may not be a nut case, after all. These goddamn plots hang together way too well with our timeline. And he's right; he's got no way of knowing about this, unless of course he's involved in the crime. But he sure doesn't fit the profile of a whacko who would be involved in something like this.

"Detective Safire, I know how crazy this sounds," Aaron continued, "but I'm a scientist. A Ph.D. astrophysicist, a good one. I work for the Goddard Space Flight Center. You can verify my employment. I'm not a nut case, and I don't go around perpetrating hoaxes."

"Okay, sir. May I have these sheets? I'll pass them up the chain of command, they'll get over to the FBI, probably. They're the lead on this."

Safire thumbed through the printouts some more, studying the blue and green crosshaired circles overlaid on a digital map of the DC area. There was one printout for every 15-minute period from midnight to 0930 this morning. Yup. It hung together. His detective intuition told him to trust the man. He sighed again.

"Okay, Doctor O'Meara. Thank you for coming forward. To answer your question about what happened here—and you can't tell this to the press, the Bureau is citing national security—three FBI agents were guarding a witness, in a house over on the east side of the Zoo. They got taken out by a terrorist. The witness escaped somehow. An ape got killed in the Zoo. We don't know why."

"An ape and three people killed?" Aaron was aghast.

"No, only the ape was killed. The agents are okay. They're all in the hospital, but it doesn't seem like they're seriously hurt." Safire's communicator sounded, requesting he report to the forensics team at incident command. He didn't answer it, staring alternately at Aaron and the printouts in his hand. "Okay, thanks, Doctor O'Meara. I gotta go. You available the rest of the day?"

"Sure," Aaron replied, "my cell phone is best. Number's on the card."

Safire climbed out of the van and told the traffic cop to work Aaron out into the congested traffic on Connecticut Avenue. He waved off the reporter who wanted to know who he'd been talking to and what he'd been given. He strode briskly through the Zoo gate, slapping the printouts in his hand, talking into his communicator, heading toward the mobile incident command center.

Aaron drove north on Connecticut Avenue, toward his Kensington home. The information from Detective Safire tumbled thoughts and emotions around in his mind, like a load of laundry in a dryer.

Had it been a rescue? No, unless a failed one.

Had it been a battle? Maybe, but if so a careful one, with collateral damage limited to one ape.

Had it been a mating? There might have been some contact, the crosshairs had come pretty close together. Hmm. Maybe Adrienne would have some thoughts about that.

Aaron pulled on the headset and hit the speed-dial button on his car phone, calling the Global Consciousness Project.

Chapter 29

TC Demuzzio, FBI Special Operations team leader, and Doctor Sam Rosen, FBI psychological consultant, discussed the video of Lara Picard as they walked down the hall. Both agreed that something very strange was going on. But what? Both agreed that Lara was concealing it. But why? The riddle evaded them.

"So, Jim, what's going on with our patient? You got it figured it out yet?" Rosen asked as they walked in the door of the small observation room.

Doctor James Agnozzi, FBI medical consultant and the on-call physician for the holiday weekend, raised an expressive eyebrow and shrugged in response. He handed Rosen the lab results.

"Ha! You tell me, Sam. I'm looking at some blood results that are just flatly impossible. I told the lab to re-run them, but I doubt if they made a mistake."

Rosen studied the first sheet handed to him.

"Well, Jim, this one's consistent with how she looked when TC brought her in, extreme electrolyte imbalance, nasty levels of metabolites. Looks sort of like she just finished a triathlon."

"Okay, Sam. I agree that's what it looks like. But it wasn't a triathlon, it was a mile run, maybe a mile and a half. And this is a superbly conditioned woman. She shouldn't even have been breathing hard, let alone have blood results like this. But okay, there's a lot of stress when you're attacked, so let's just take these results for what they are—data when she arrived here.

"Now look at the second sheet, Sam, just before we tucked her into bed. It's two hours later, about an hour after she polished off all that breakfast."

"Wow!" Rosen whistled. "Helluva recovery. You sure the lab didn't mix her sample up with somebody else's?"

"I asked, Sam, and they're checking. But it's totally unlikely. The lab is right up the road. It's a good lab. Does contract work for the Bureau. I sent the samples up with an agent, hand-delivered, chain of custody, all that. They ran 'em right away, faxed me the results."

Rosen studied the lab reports, holding them side-by-side.

"What we have here, my friends," he said to Demuzzio and Agnozzi, "assuming the lab didn't screw up, and assuming I'm remembering my medical training accurately, is the fastest freaking human metabolism on the face of the earth. Or some other kind of medical miracle."

"Exactly," Agnozzi agreed.

"You could see the juice coming back into her while she ate," Demuzzio said.

"Exactly, TC," said Rosen, "and all of us saw it. So in a way, these results don't surprise me; they're consistent with our observations. The trouble is, they're flatly impossible. You agree, Jim?"

"Yeah. I made some calls, managed to roust a couple of my colleagues. They just laughed, Sam. Said that sort of recovery is well outside the range, including hyperthyroid kids. Said mammalian mechanisms and biochemistry just can't work that fast. Not even gerbils."

"Superwoman?" Demuzzio's brow furrowed as he voiced the thought. The two medical practitioners didn't answer.

"Alright, Sam, now that you're blown out of the water, here's another anomaly," Agnozzi continued, gesturing toward the monitor screen. "Look at the EEG trace she's putting out. It's crazy, lots of beta, like what you would see in a waking state, with intense concentration or dialog, but it's not quite that, either. Atypical, but I don't know enough about it to say what the hell it is."

Rosen walked over to study the monitor, and nodded agreement.

"There's not any of the typical sleep cycle progression to it," Agnozzi went on, "there's no cycling down through alpha into theta and delta. She just dropped into this pattern you see on the monitor, bam, as soon as she hit the bed, and it hasn't changed. And the same pattern for two hours now. I've never heard of anything like this. It's like her mind is disconnected from her body."

"Yup. I've seen it; just one time, I think," Rosen said as he alternately studied the image of the sleeping woman, and her brain wave display, on their separate monitors. "A Zen master in meditation, if I recall right. Jim, I think what we've got here is a beta pattern superimposed on top of a theta or delta wave. Can you download this? I might have some pattern analysis software that could pick these waveforms apart."

"So, what does all that mumbo-jumbo mean, Sam?" TC Demuzzio rubbed his beefy hand tiredly over cropped hair. "She a superwoman, or what?"

Rosen stared at him thoughtfully, and then looked at Agnozzi. A tiny begrudging nod of acknowledgment passed between them.

Northwest Washington, DC | Monday 1206 EDT

Thirty miles north-northeast, in the south part of Georgetown, John's body lay inert on the bed of the small apartment. His accelerated metabolism finished the repairs, converting the raw materials of breakfast to biochemical building blocks, fabricating from them the required tissue. Although his body didn't move, one part of John's mind dreamed, and another part communed restlessly with his nexus, plotting and planning.

The Other has secured significant resources. That thought permeated his mind-space. A Quantico penetration would be very difficult. They would have high security, guards, infrared alarms, possibly high altitude or satellite scanning.

All those things. His nexus agreed with that assessment. *But you are the Magician.*

I'm not a suicidal Magician. If I'm killed completing the mission, okay, that's a reasonable tradeoff. But I can't get killed in the attempt, because then the Other survives, the monster wins, and humanity regresses to its darkest past. Or maybe gets wiped out.

Your actions at the Corrano compound in Purace were not suicidal. And you suspect there may be a way to complete the mission at Quantico, even in the face of unfavorable odds.

I do. There is a way. There always is a way. But I don't like it. Too many in-nocents would die. I might even know some of those people. So I can't go straight in with brute force, mowing everything down between me and the Other, even though that has a fair chance of success. Purace was different. In the Corrano com-pound, they all were legitimate targets.

The Other will grow stronger, surround itself with more layers of protection. That may force you to act in a situation not of your choosing. There may be more innocents killed later, if we delay.

The Magician sighed his understanding, thrashed on the bed, and rolled over.

FBI Special Operations Center, Quantico, VA | Monday 1303 EDT

Lara lay unmoving on the bed in the witness protective holding quarters at Quantico. Her inert body continued to belie the restless mind communing with her *ki*, which plotted and planned. When her mind had traced out and worked through the manifold possibilities until exhausted, her consciousness slanted side-ways, and she dreamed.

In the highly instrumented observation room a hundred feet away, Doctor James Agnozzi continued to watch the two monitors, still bewildered. One screen showed the sleeping woman, the other showed the output of the electroencepha-lograph sensor on her head and the vital sign sensor on her wrist. A subtle shift in the EEG pattern drew his attention. It marked the first change since she dropped onto the bed four hours ago.

"Well, that's something," Agnozzi murmured into the audio recording channel, "and if Sam is right about the waveforms, we've still got the underlying delta component, a nice deep slow beat tied to her pulse rate. And the motor neurons are still inhibited because she hasn't even twitched, so that fits.

"But the high-frequency beta riding on top of it, if Sam is right about that..." he paused to squint at the monitor, "then that beta just shifted into an alpha state. So, it looks like that part of her mind may be relaxing a bit."

The sideways slant of Lara's consciousness did indeed shift the frequency of one set of brainwaves, but the shift related less to a relaxation of her mind than to a shift out of its analytical state. It moved into a method of analysis more dependent on symbolism, metaphor, intuition, art—a method much more subtle. She dreamed of unfolding patterns, of interweaving melodies, elements of some great symphony. They danced through her mind-space, helical spiraling threads of light. The image of her nexus faded into the background as she reached out to the threads and let them play through her fingers.

Pretty, Lara thought, they're really pretty. And look how the threads all weave together into melodies! The musician in her appreciated the artistry. The scientist in her appreciated the symmetry, and then came to the abrupt realization that the threads represented patterns of DNA. And they had a common underlying pattern: some sort of hologram, with an evolutionary feedback loop. Retroviruses and other genomic snippets played into the DNA melodies running through her mental fingers, moving within the pattern toward their time. Some would be expressed as the tiny pure tones of tubular bells. Some would be expressed as a loud crash of cymbals. She sensed this present moment of time was a node within the pattern. And it was a major node, a confluence of harmonics, a moment of macroshift. Probably the cymbals for this one, she thought, uneasily.

Northwest Washington, DC | Monday 1400 EDT

The direction of John's thoughts turned away from battle planning, and into his earlier dreams. The artful weaving of threads through different realities re-formed, becoming a tapestry. He stepped into his mind-space and let the metaphor of the tapestry weave around him. Like life, he thought; it's like life. Random chance plays a role, for sure, but there are underlying patterns, too. He commanded the tapestry to show his own thread, and watched its light brighten against the others. His thirty-some years of existence formed a tiny whisper at the end of a long, long confluence of threads. He focused down on his thread, and that made it glow more brightly. Lara's thread spiraled in with his, and his hands reached to touch hers lovingly. Possibilities erupted from the contact. The future held many, it seemed. In some futures, his thread stopped. In some, her thread stopped. In some, both their threads stopped. In others the threads went on, weaving an especially bright and vivid scene on the tapestry. He tried to discern the story it told, but his tapestry metaphor would not yield it up.

John's body tossed again on the bed, as symbolic visions of those possible futures woke him up. Suddenly fully conscious, he shivered with the knowledge that life is never certain.

He rolled out of the bed, his determination fixed on the brighter outcome, the weaving of his thread with Lara's. That's the outcome I have to make happen, he thought. Then he put her out of his mind, and, as he ate, focused on the challenge of reconnoitering Quantico. The green-tinged black blot on his consciousness radar pulsated with evil intent, acknowledging the challenge.

FBI Special Operations Center, Quantico, VA | Monday 1457 EDT

The three men stood in the instrumented observation room, watching Lara Picard stir uneasily on the bed.

"She started twitching..." Doctor Jim Agnozzi checked his watch, "about an hour ago. This is a pretty classic REM-stage sleep pattern. Then she just snapped into this stage, Sam, no sleep spindles, no K-complexes, no apparent transition on the EEG at all. Here, look at this." Agnozzi scrolled the electroencephalograph trace backward in time on the monitor screen. The time hack in the center of the display read 1401 hours. Psychiatrist Sam Rosen, a veteran of many strange personality cases, studied it for a moment and laughed in disbelief.

"Yeah, Sam," Agnozzi answered, "I thought she was going to wake up maybe a couple of minutes after the transition, but she didn't. Just stayed in that REM-stage, twitching. But her pulse and blood pressure and temp are back up, too."

As the three men looked their different question marks at each other, Lara suddenly sat up on the bed and threw off the blanket. She looked straight at the concealed camera, and spoke to them.

"Hi, guys. I'm going into the bathroom. Turn the camera off in there, please. And order me lunch, if you wouldn't mind. I'm hungry again."

TC Demuzzio chuckled. "You looked around at the cameras while you were putting the sensors on her, didn't you, Doc?"

"You know, TC, I may have. I probably did. And that would be enough of a hint for her to figure it out, you think?" Agnozzi was impressed.

"Oh, sure," Demuzzio answered. "She's sharp as a tack with little tipoff signals, and logic would do the rest."

"Well, that's good," Rosen observed, "at least we don't have to add telepathy to the list of anomalies... at least, I don't think we do...."

The three men considered that statement as the EEG and vital sign graphics on the monitors went flat. Lara, in the bathroom, had removed the sensors.

Agnozzi shrugged, cut the sensor circuits and turned off the camera, and the three men walked down the hall.

"Thanks, TC, give me a minute." Lara smiled at the three men through the cracked door. As she dressed, she noted her running shoes had been vacuumed clean. Ah, TC, you clever devil, she thought, you know something odd is going on here, but you're not doing your usual straight-line approach. You're working around the margins, aren't you? Forensics has my clothes, and they taped or vacuumed off my shoes, I'll bet. I hope this run of uncharacteristic subtlety doesn't cramp you up too much.

She smiled faintly when she opened the door and announced again that she was starving.

Quantico Marine Corp Base, VA | Monday 1458 EDT

A slight breeze off the Potomac River blew across the municipal park in the town of Quantico, Virginia. It caressed the Magician's face as he looked westward over the Marine Corps base. The small town had a sleepy feel in the warm afternoon sun. Only the sounds of children's laughter and ball games in the park competed with the whispers of river waves slapping the rocks. The peace and tranquility of these natural rhythms played a strange counterpoint to bleak pulsations of the green-tinged dark blot in his mind-space. Those pulsations caressed him, too, but in a subtly evil way, a siren's song calling to him to approach, to fall into the snare. He shook off the uneasy feeling and walked back to his car to reconnoiter the roads around the perimeter of the base, pick out landmarks, and etch the possible field of battle in his mind.

The base was not a high-security area. The non-descript government building where his consciousness radar plotted the target, however, was a different story. The government-issue, standard block architecture showed nothing visible in the way of additional sentries. But it had a roof full of microwave dishes and other antenna arrays. One of them moved slightly as he looked at it. Satellite tracker, he thought. Or maybe it's following some airborne platform.

The scene seemed vaguely familiar, and his memory chased back to the few times in his Army career that he'd been on the base. Ah, the building was an FBI facility, he finally recalled. Some kind of advanced training center, or think tank. Special operations, maybe. Well, that made sense. The Other had either gotten very lucky, or in some other way had managed to select a human host with access to significant government resources. Difficult, he decided, but not impossible.

The Magician climbed back into his car, and drove westward around the base perimeter.

FBI Special Operations Center, Quantico, VA | Monday 1503 EDT

"Starving, huh? What's the matter, Lara, did three breakfasts only fill up one of your hollow legs?" TC Demuzzio smiled as she opened the door.

"If I could, Ms. Picard," Agnozzi added, "another quick blood sample before you eat? You look like you're feeling pretty good, but there's something strange going on with your metabolism, and I want to make sure nothing's going to sneak up on you and cause a problem later."

Lara looked at him skeptically, but elected not to argue. Agnozzi was quick and efficient, and departed down the hall with the sample as the three of them walked in the other direction back to the conference room.

"So, Doctor Rosen," she asked, smiling up at the tanned bearded face of the Bureau's consulting psychiatrist, "did I sleep well? Or did I have nightmares? What did my EEG tell you?"

"It was pretty interesting, Lara, but please just call me Sam. And I'd rather hear your own recollections first, if you don't mind."

"I don't remember a thing, Sam," Lara told him with the slightest pause. She smiled up at him with innocent green eyes. "I guess I must have been dreaming, but then all of a sudden I just woke up."

He smiled innocently back at her. Well, now, that's interesting, he thought, reading the tiny giveaway signs in her body language that he'd interpreted and parsed so thoroughly during the morning's interviews. This woman just told me a blatant baldfaced lie. She clearly made a snap decision that she's not gonna tell me jack shit. Well, I guess that makes sense. I'm not an old friend like TC, I'm a total stranger. And she obviously has a lot to protect, whatever the hell it is. I might do the same thing in her situation.

"Well, Lara, on the EEG, it seems as though you have two parts of your brain operating independently," Rosen answered aloud. "You were in a deep sleep cycle, and your body was sure locked into it, because you didn't move an inch. But your mind appeared to be in a very active waking cycle, like you were talking to some-one, or working intensely on a problem. I've only seen that once, with a Zen monk. You do any meditation? Study Zen? Anything like that?"

"A little, Sam," she replied, "as part of my martial arts training. Nothing very special, though."

Ah, now she's telling the truth, Rosen thought. She truly doesn't look on it as anything special. But it surely is. It has to be. He held the door for her as they en-tered the conference room.

A craggy-faced Army colonel stood spinning his green beret idly around his thumb as he studied the big topo map taped to the whiteboard.

"Lara Picard, Colonel Merton Shaundee," Demuzzio said as he followed them into the room. "Colonel Shaundee was kind enough to join us for a late lunch—that is, Lara, if you don't eat it all—and I thought we could talk about our idea for a trap. Mert and I worked out a concept while you were sleeping."

Lara nodded approval at Demuzzio, and walked around the conference table to shake the big soldier's hand.

They ate while the veteran FBI agent, a director of many special operations, spun out his ideas, alternately sketching on the whiteboard and tapping on the topographic map beside it. He asked Lara a number of questions, ostensibly seek-ing concurrence, but mixing in at random some of the questions that had been scripted by psychiatrist Sam Rosen.

Rosen sat across from Lara, where he could see her clearly, and clicked the tiny silent transmitter concealed in his left hand. The device put a corresponding mark and time hack on the digital tapes that were recording her expressions and body language from three different angles. He clicked the device once for each evasion, and twice for each answer he interpreted as an outright lie. He was doing a lot of clicking.

"Pisgah State Park," Lara said, washing down her sixth quarter-sandwich and reaching indelicately for another, "I grew up in New Hampshire, but I've never been to that park."

"It's pretty undeveloped, ma'am," Shaundee told her, "the state lets us close it off for war games. We run an anti-terrorist exercise there every other year. We're most of the way through this year's exercise, and we can easily make the rest of it a live-fire trap, as TC has so eloquently pointed out. DOD has signed off on this, at the highest levels. I'm not exactly sure how my old friend TC got the sign-off, and I guess he's not about to tell me, but we've got our forces committed."

Lara Picard looked at him, then at Demuzzio, and nodded.

Shaundee nodded his reassurance back. "My people have some hardware you just wouldn't believe. We can keep you safe from this *Warlock*, ma'am, and spring the trap. I'm sure of it."

Quantico Marine Corp Base, VA | Monday 1519 EDT

The Magician could almost taste a trap unfolding, reaching out for him, the green-tinged black blot pulsating, sending him its obscene siren song of invitation. He sat in the uppermost crotch of a tall oak tree, wrapped in his null-field cloak, blending into the dappled light through the leaves. He would be a ghost to anyone that should happen to look up.

His car was parked in a rest stop on the Interstate, a mile west. He'd walked around the small restroom building and disappeared, transposing through the tops of trees to the oak that looked down on the FBI building and its helipad. He scanned the roof. Yes, there was a way in.

Proximity to the Other was terrifying. The blot seemed to reach out toward him on his consciousness radar, seductive and powerful. The throbbing sense of evil was almost overwhelming this close, worse than at the Zoo. It played tricks with his mind. But he was a soldier, and clamped down on the fear. His resolve hardened as he prepared to descend into the icy passion of his Assassin persona and attack the enemy.

FBI Special Operations Center, Quantico, VA | Monday 1603 EDT

Sam Rosen watched Lara closely as Shaundee repeated his assurance.

"My people can protect you from this *Warlock*, ma'am. Even though TC's plan hangs you out there as bait, I'm sure we can protect you."

"Colonel, TC, bless you, I feel better already," Lara smiled at them, "this is a perfect setup. I couldn't ask for more."

She's being totally honest there, Rosen thought.

"So, we'll do it, Lara?"

"Yeah, TC, we'll do it!"

"You think *Warlock* can find you there?"

"He found me on Irving Street, didn't he?"

Demuzzio stared at her. "Yes he did, Lara. And I'm pretty uncomfortable about that. I still don't know how he pulled it off."

"TC, I'm telling you, he can sense me. There's no science to it, no rational expla-nation. He can just sense me! Like I'm a beacon, or something."

Rosen didn't click the transmitter when Lara compared herself to a beacon. That wasn't the exact truth, he sensed, but close enough. He nodded his agreement, silently answering Demuzzio's raised eyebrow, and then decided to verbalize the odd thoughts congealing in his mind. He would show Lara Picard some straightforward honesty and openness. Maybe she would change her mind about him, and reciprocate.

"You know, TC," he said, "a few years ago the idea of a mental beacon, or a consciousness beacon, would have made a laughingstock out of any serious scientist who proposed it. But now we know that the tools for investigating paranormal phenomena weren't adequate. Or maybe they were the wrong tools. There's a parallel to the evolution of analytical lab instruments. When I was a chemistry undergrad, we could identify a chemical at the part-per-million level. Now, we can get down to the part-per-billion level; even a part-per-trillion for some things. And think about some of the new diagnostic hardware in medicine. The techniques and the technology are getting more and more inferential, more and more subtle. Over the past few years, psionic contacts of various kinds have been demonstrated, with solid science. So, I don't think what Lara says is too far outside the realm of possibility."

Across the table, Lara smiled appreciatively at Sam Rosen's implied vote of confidence.

"And Lara's EEG," Rosen continued, "that was truly different. So right at the moment I've got an even more open mind on the subject. If she says her mind is a beacon, then it's a beacon. If she says Warlock will find her, then he'll find her. At this point, I'd put my money on it."

Chapter 30

"You have a very interesting background, Doctor O'Donnell," Special Agent Jack Socrates told him. They stood in the kitchen of the CIA safehouse on Argyle Road in Brooklyn, watching Joshua work at the large sketch he'd pieced together on the dining room table.

"Mmm? And how might that be, Agent Socrates?" Hamilton O'Donnell cocked a fuzzy gray eyebrow at him.

"You must have been born in your mid-twenties, sir. That's the first accessible record the Bureau or any other U.S. agency can find of you. Kenmare, in Ireland. South coast, I believe."

"Kenmare, yes. A lovely place, it is; Ring of Kerry to the west, Beare Peninsula to the south. I called it home for many a year. Still have the ould place on the Peninsula, I do. I was born there. Records were not particularly good in the ould days in the south country, I believe. And what is it, good sir, would be so interestin' about that?"

"Well, Doctor O'Donnell," the big agent smiled quizzically back at him, "if there aren't any records, that's one thing. But it seems to Agent Schmidt that there were records, and that they were deleted. With exquisite precision, he says. That's a real compliment, coming from Carl; he's probably the Bureau's best hacker."

"Mmm? So that's what he's been doin', in your little communications center upstairs? Hackin' away?" His gaze was non-committal, not irritated, merely inviting the agent to go on.

"Yes, sir. At least he was until he got his knuckles rapped. NSA came down on him like a ton of bricks, and when he blew them off, he got a personal phone call from our Director. Told him to cease and desist. You got a rabbi pretty high up in government somewhere, Doctor O'Donnell."

"And a troublesome thing that might be to you, Agent Socrates?"

"Well, sir, I want to do my job, which is to protect you and the boy, and this case is a total oddball. I'm just feeling a need for all the information I can get."

Ham looked at the big man sympathetically. A good man, he thought, a person who cares.

"Well, I can certainly tell you that an absence of records has absolutely nothin' to do with this case or your job, Agent Socrates. I'm thinkin' I must ask you to trust me on that." He smiled at the agent, and then smiled more beyond him, as he caught Joshua's attention lifting from the big diagram in the dining room. The boy's blue-green eyes appraised him, thoughtfully.

Ah, yes, me lad, he thought, ears keen as a wolf on your clever little head! And you haven't heard that one before, have you? That your poor ould uncle has lost some history? 'Tis a new datum for you to consider in your grand equations, there on that table. And what will you make of it, I wonder?

Global Consciousness Project, Princeton University, NJ | Monday 1606 EDT

Nathan Rodgers sighed his frustration. They'd been talking about this ever since noon, when Aaron got back from his expedition to the Zoo. Almost four hours of intermittent debate, and they were still nowhere. Maybe we're too close to it, he thought, too wrapped up in it. The forest and trees syndrome.

"All right," he finally said, "let's take it from the top one more time, keeping our respective hypotheses in mind, but acknowledging that there might be others, and see if we can winkle out any more ideas. If we can't, I think I want to get out of here for an hour or two, take Adrienne to dinner, walk around a little bit. Okay?"

"Good idea, Nathan," Aaron responded. "Now, taking it from the top, I gotta tell you I still like my battle hypothesis. Nothing that's happened today is inconsistent with that. Blue chased down Green. They fought in the house. Green escaped. Probably had some help. Then Blue chased Green into the Zoo. Some other kind of battle took place, and an ape got in the way, somehow. Green escaped again, had to be with more help, because there was a chopper ride to Quantico. The government's protecting Green there. That's what I think."

"Okay, Aaron, that makes sense, it hangs together, fits the facts," Nathan acknowledged, "but my rescue hypothesis does just as well, maybe better, because a battle doesn't explain why three humans weren't killed, just disabled. So, I'm thinking that Green was trying to position itself for pickup by Blue, but the government got there first and captured Green and is holding it—successfully so far—against rescue by Blue. Blue just wants to extract Green, not hurt any natives, so the agents got disabled instead of killed. The government wants to hang onto Green, for the obvious reasons, but Green isn't telling them bupkis about Blue. Because if Blue gets nabbed too, then the rescue doesn't happen."

"Guys, guys!" Adrienne interjected, laughing, "you men are too much! Battles and rescues! Listen to me, please! First of all, Blue is male and Green is female. Or at least those are the human equivalents. I know this, absolutely. I've got no idea how I know it, but I do. Definitely a him and a her. And they're trying to get together. I know this, too. Absolutely. When the government got involved, it just screwed things up. So, I still think this is a mating. He's trying to get together with her. She's trying to get together with him. And that encounter at the house? At the Zoo? Maybe they did get together, briefly. Maybe that was their child I sensed this morning."

Silence ensued for a good ten seconds, and then they all started to laugh simultaneously, realizing that they surely did need to take a breather and stand off from the problem. Otherwise, their hypotheses would run away from them and disappear into elsewhere, like the rabbit in Alice in Wonderland.

Flatbush Section of Brooklyn, NY | Monday 1609 EDT

Agent Jack Socrates caught Joshua's appraising look at his uncle. So, he thought, the kid didn't know his uncle's a cipher. That's interesting. I wonder what he'll say? But the boy disappointed him.

"Uncle Ham, I've spent all afternoon on this, since we got here," Joshua said, turning back to his work, "and some ideas are starting to come together."

The diagram, sketched out over many sheets taped to each other and the tabletop, bore a passing resemblance to a pit of intertwined snakes.

"This is the main evolutionary path, Uncle Ham, here in the middle, more or less. I can't make it any simpler, because of the adaptability of the human race. Cultural evolution happens alongside biological evolution, and they're intertwined. That's what the middle of this diagram shows, going out to the right."

"Ah, yes, me lad. I see that. And of course I agree. *Homo sapiens* is nothin' if not adaptable."

"And here are feedback loops in the DNA, retroviruses or snippets of something, and they carry some kind of genetic coding. These select out favorable characteristics in the gene pool, and make sure they get expressed in the present. And here are the feedforward loops, that adjust and adapt, and modify the coding and carry it into the future."

"Ah, yes. I see it. A variety of proclivities, cultural, affectin' the biological. Fascinatin', me lad, just fascinatin'."

"It is, Uncle Ham, it is!" Joshua exclaimed. "And it's not that nobody's thought of this before, I actually found a ton of literature on it." He gestured at the citations on the screen of his wireless laptop, and Hamilton O'Donnell looked them over.

"Umm. So I see: biohistory, evolutionary psychology, social Darwinism. Quite an array on the conjunction of biology and history. And now how do these concepts play into your magnificent drawing here, me lad?"

"Here, look at this, Uncle Ham. This branch is small bands of hunter-gatherers, migratory, who told stories around the fire. They developed more complex thoughts, and speech patterns. The physical development of a more complex palate to handle the speech patterns followed that. So there's a quantum leap, right there."

"Ah, yes. Punctuated equilibrium."

"And look here. Now people are settled in one place. They have an expanded food supply, so they can stay in one place and accumulate stuff. That physical development kicks off population growth. The gene pool expands. Written language develops. More complex thoughts and communications are possible."

Jack Socrates, a highly intelligent, well-read, broadly educated and articulate man, sighed softly as he looked down on the scrawled mess. He didn't understand any of it, but felt the same sense of awe as he had last week at the University concert hall. A visiting thirteen-year old girl pianist from Taiwan had shown them all how Chopin should really be played. Ah, well, prodigies were prodigies. He sighed again.

Global Consciousness Project, Princeton University, NJ | Monday 1616 EDT

"That's wonderful, Adrienne," Aaron told her, "very elegant. Logarithmic scaling for the signal strength brings those overloads back down into a range where they can be plotted? We lose much resolution? Or does it matter?"

Smiling at the speaker phone, Adrienne deprecated her achievement. "So simple, once it occurred to me, Aaron. All I did was to save the incoming data in two forms, the raw signal strength and the natural log of the signal strength, in separate files. If we get any more of those incredible spikes that blow out my algorithms, we can look at the log form. We lose a little resolution, and it will change the 15-minute average locations a bit, but it seems to work overall."

Nathan saw another Blue plot out close to Green at Quantico and picked up the thread of their previous discussion.

"Now, Adrienne, Aaron, Quantico is a Marine Corps base. There are some FBI facilities there, and Green is stationary. So doesn't it stand to reason that it... all right, Adrienne, all right, I'll accept your intuition about him and her... so *she* is stationary, and that probably means either she sought protection or the government's taken her into custody, right?"

Hearing guarded assent from both, Nathan continued. "Now I think it would be difficult to take a green glow—like you saw in the trees, Aaron—into any kind of custody or protection we might understand. So, that means Green has a physical manifestation. Something you can take custody of. And Blue... okay, Adrienne, *he*... got on airplanes, in Panama, and in Miami, so he also probably has a physical manifestation. The likeliest thing is that they've both got human bodies, either created or... somehow... adopted."

"Yes, sir, that's very logical," Adrienne interjected, "but if it's a rescue, like you believe, why didn't she go with him from the house on Irving Street, or from the Zoo? And if it's a battle, like you believe, Aaron, and she's being protected by the government, why aren't all the Marines in the world dropping on him right now? We know they must be able to sense each other. She has to know where he is, even if nobody's paying attention to our information. So both your hypotheses have holes in them. I still think this is a mating. Maybe it's playful. Maybe it's a mating game like humans play. Maybe that's a universal inclination." She sighed and smiled again at the speakerphone.

Flatbush Section of Brooklyn, NY | Monday 1627 EDT

"Well, that's a bit of alright, me lad, a theory of composite evolution worked out on a dinin' room table all on a Monday afternoon. Hamilton O'Donnell ruffled his nephew's hair affectionately. "But tell me more about this main line of your diagram, that stretches off to the right, in the middle. In particular, this cycle here is a feedback loop, I'm guessin'? For what?"

My uncle, Joshua thought wryly, has this uncanny ability to bypass questions for which I have good answers, and focus right on those for which I haven't.

"I think maybe, Uncle Ham," he answered, and then emphasized his uncertainty, "*maybe* this cycle is what takes developments in cultural evolution and codes them somehow into genomic modifications that can make changes in biological evolution downstream."

"Racial memory, young Joshua?" His bushy gray eyebrows danced in delight. "A little insider help and guidance for us poor Darwinian individuals?"

"That would be an aspect of it, for sure," the boy agreed, "but, Uncle Ham, it's a bigger feedback loop than that, and it's growing all the time. Accelerating growth, I think."

"Examples, young lad?"

"Oh, the development of a written language in a culture, for example. This might drive a downstream physiological change in the neural connections in the brain. More connections allow more abstract thought processes, like concepts, and symbols, and math."

"Umm, yes, me lad. But that example is from the distant past, thousands or maybe hundreds of thousands of years gone by. What have our genes done for us lately?"

"Here's where it gets iffy, Uncle Ham. I'm guessing at the loop without having any downstream results to look at; those haven't happened yet. But I think the genomic triggers—whatever they are—have been inserted for the next evolutionary development, or at least for the start of it."

"And what would that next development be, me lad?"

"If it stays within the communication sequence for evolution—first spoken language, then written language—then the next development logically would be a higher level of communication. That might involve quite different states of mind, more direct means of communication than spoken or written, access to group consciousness."

"And what makes you think some results like that have not already happened, me lad?" The old man wiggled quizzical bushy eyebrows again at his nephew. "There certainly is some history on such things...."

Global Consciousness Project, Princeton University, NJ | Monday 1638 EDT

"Green pattern is shifting, Doctor Rodgers," Adrienne Baxter noted, studying the bar graph of 1-minute signal strengths on her monitor. "See? The Richmond detector is dropping off, and the DC detectors are picking up. That means she's moving north, Doctor Rodgers. And it's too abrupt for her to be on foot. So she's either in a car or a helicopter."

"Well, Adrienne, she got from DC to Quantico in a chopper, we decided, didn't we? So it makes sense that she would be airborne again. The next 15-minute location plot will tell us that for sure, won't it?"

"Yep. The 1645 location will show displacement, and the 1700 will too. And the ones after that, too, if she keeps going past Washington. And Blue..." Adrienne continued, swiveling her chair to look at the other monitor, "...he hasn't started to move yet, but I'm betting he will, in the next couple of minutes. He'll be in pursuit, I'm sure." She hit the speed-dial on her phone.

"You think Green is moving out, Adrienne?" Aaron answered his phone without preamble, his voice a little garbled. "Scuse me, I got a mouthful of sandwich."

"Yes, Aaron. And we believe she's most likely in a helicopter. She may be going back to DC, we'll just have to wait and see. She's headed north, that's clear enough.

What kind of sandwich are you eating? You just made me realize I'm hungry."

"Oh, just some ham, turkey, cheddar. Nice wholesome grainy brown bread. Lettuce and tomato and sweet peppers. Hot mustard. I'm pretty self-contained down here, Adrienne. Everything is on one floor. If I get hungry, I'm only 30 ft away from the kitchen."

On one floor. Yes, it would have to be, Adrienne thought, for him to function efficiently. She tried to visualize what it would be like to be constrained to situations that would accept wheels. And he's so matter-of-fact about it, and he obviously doesn't let it limit him. I really admire that. The wellspring of affection she was developing for this man began bubbling up again under her ribcage. It moved further upward, displacing the growling hunger in her stomach, warming her heart. Her ears pinked a little, in resonance.

"How did you get hurt, Aaron?" The words were out of Adrienne's mouth before she realized it might be too personal a question.

"Huh? Hurt?" Aaron puzzled briefly, then connected. "Oh, it wasn't an injury, Adrienne. I was born with it. Congenital defect. They tried to do some repairs on the spinal column, and were actually pretty successful, for those days. I was somewhat normal as a young kid. But these days, motor nerve activity comes and goes. Sometimes I can walk almost unassisted. I'm sort of near the bottom of a bad cycle right now. And it's degenerative, I'm afraid. The older I get, the more I'm going to be in this wheelchair. But, it's just something you learn to live with, Adrienne, so I just keep pluggin' along."

"Oh, Aaron," she sighed, "you just keep pluggin' along. That's wonderful! I have to meet you!"

Light enveloped her in a warm cocoon as she conceded the inevitable. I've fallen in love, she thought, over the phone, with a man eating a ham sandwich. And given everything else going on, that doesn't seem strange at all.

Metropolitan Police Department HQ, Washington DC | 1645 EDT

Detective Lucien Safire, even though bone-tired from the long and stressful day running an investigation at the National Zoo, nonetheless conscientiously screened his phone messages. He listened intently to the follow-up message of one Doctor Aaron O'Meara, astrophysicist, while studying the graphics the man had left with him ten hours ago.

Well, it's wacky, he thought, but I guess that doesn't make any difference. The standing orders are clear that all material gets copied to the Bureau. So I'd best just ship it over.

He scrawled a brief description on a fax cover page, just a straight recitation of the facts, no judgment or opinion. He taped O'Meara's card to the cover page, and shuffled the graphics into their proper time sequence behind it. He set the papers in the fax machine, dialed the FBI number they'd given out, and watched the paper start to feed through.

"Good luck with this one, boys," he chuckled to the chugging machine. "Hope you got your X-Files Section cranked up and working good tonight."

Flatbush Section of Brooklyn, NY | Monday 1705 EDT

"No, no, leave your diagram right there, Joshua," Agent Jack Socrates told him, "the kitchen table will seat four. I'll set it up for when Carl gets back with the food. If this is a new theory of evolution in the making, I'm privileged to be here, and I don't want to perturb your brainstorm." The big agent smiled down at the small boy and the diagram covering most of the dining room table. "Besides, Lord knows what would happen to the human race if I spilled some sweet and sour sauce on a feedback loop." He walked out into the kitchen, and banged around finding plates and utensils for the Chinese food that would be delivered shortly.

"Now, me lad, now that friend Socrates has left us," Hamilton O'Donnell spoke softly to his nephew, "can you tell me more about what you see as this next evolutionary step? Enhanced communication? Group consciousness? And how does that relate to your mum? Can you show me on your diagram?"

"Not really, Uncle Ham, not directly. It's just when I look at this thing, and the symbolism I've chosen, I get a very strong feeling that she's a major development in the pattern. And there's a clear possibility—right here in my diagram—that evolution could go south, in a big way."

The boy tapped his pencil on the spot, a bifurcation of pathways. "New tools get into the wrong hands. Power gets turned the wrong way. Bad possibilities start to happen, the ones that Mom pointed out. It's scary, Uncle Ham."

Global Consciousness Project, Princeton University, NJ | Monday 1710 EDT

"Well, the 1700 position confirms it, Adrienne, she's moving out, at a pretty steady clip. Has to be a chopper, it's too fast for a car. Too slow for a jet, and anyway there's no indication of a stopover at National or Dulles. Or Andrews Air Force Base, for that matter," Nathan added thoughtfully.

The green locator circles and their crosshair coordinates marched steadily northeastward from Quantico. If the trend stayed steady, the next position would cross over into Delaware.

"And he's clearly following, but not as fast," Adrienne replied, "so he's got to be in a car, just outside of Baltimore."

On the other monitor, the blue locator circles and crosshair positions matched up well with I-95 on the underlying map.

"I agree." Aaron O'Meara's voice sounded thin and distant from the speakerphone. "And Blue's 1700 position is already past the Baltimore-Washington Airport, so he's evidently decided to pursue by car. Do you suppose this means he knows where she's headed? Or that he doesn't know, so he needs the flexibility of a car?"

"Now that's an excellent question, Aaron!" Nathan laughed. "And of course impossible to answer. How about if you ponder it and keep an eye on things while I take Adrienne out for a bite of dinner. We missed lunch and I think I just heard her stomach growling."

Chapter 31

In the Army Black Hawk helicopter slicing through the air over the Pennsylvania-New Jersey border, TC Demuzzio replayed the answers from Lara's debriefings in his mind. He was asking variants of the questions now; they were more oblique, conversational. He'd asked Colonel Shaundee to sit out of earshot, toward the cockpit, to give them privacy.

But she knows what I'm doing anyway, he thought ruefully. She's easily twice as smart as I am. She knows this confidential collegiality is a crock of shit.

Her wan face regarded him sadly, confirming it.

She knows I have to do it, Demuzzio's thoughts ran on, but she's mourning the loss of our openness. This really sucks. He forced a cheerful smile, slipped into his best Colombo act, and pursued the logical questions in spite of their mutual dismay. He had no choice, as he saw it.

"So, Lara, now let me just get this straight, because for tying up military resources, we gotta tell a helluva good story to the bean-counters, okay?"

She nodded wearily, resigned.

Demuzzio studied her, ordering the questions in his mind from the notes provided by psychiatrist Sam Rosen. Lara's first direct lie had been about the initial encounter with *Warlock* in the safehouse. Ditka reported she whipped something black at the intruder. In her debriefing, Lara said it was a black shift Lovelock had brought her, that she happened to have it in her hand when she ran downstairs. She just threw it at the intruder to distract him. But no black shift had been found at the scene. And in any case, Mary Lovelock, now out of her coma, clearly remembered bringing Lara a variety of spare clothing, but a black shift definitely wasn't in the mix.

"Now, if we could just tidy up a coupla loose ends here, Lara?" Demuzzio continued pleasantly, "The last thing Ditka reported over the radio? You threw this black dress, that Lovelock brought you, at the *Warlock*, right?"

"Right, TC."

"To distract him, right?"

"Right, I was unpacking the stuff, had the shift in my hand, TC. I just tossed it toward the island in the kitchen, thinking it might distract him, give Agent Ditka a better shot."

"And did it?"

"I don't know, TC. Ditka shoved me into the escape closet and slammed the door. He was still firing at the time."

Demuzzio cocked an eyebrow at her. "Forensics picked through all the debris in the safehouse, Lara, and they didn't find a black dress. Or even any pieces of black fabric."

I-95 West of Havre de Grace, MD | Monday 1728 EDT

Soft afternoon sunlight angled in the driver's-side window as John chased northeastward on I-95, following the witchy black blot on his consciousness radar. As he passed down the interstate north of Havre de Grace and sped across the long bridge into Delaware, an errant whisper entered his mind, persistent and edgy: 'Bridges are symbols of transitions, John'.

Ah, yes, my mom the artist once told me that, he recalled. His mind drifted back to happier times, and the whisper sharpened into a vision in his mind-space. The image of Duc Li smiled gently and contemplated the memory along with him....

He'd been fifteen years old. His three-year-old baby sister Jessica sat on his shoulders, clutching his curly hair for stability. They both watched with fascination over their mother's shoulder as she brushed the strokes onto the canvas. She worked quickly, inspired and absorbed.

The lower left part of the painting was a car's outside rear-view mirror. It held the brightness of a red setting sun just over the top of rocky escarpments, with a long bridge fading back to the shore. A hint of a curving approach to the bridge ran up the escarpment, tapering toward the sun on the horizon, the view framed by the mirror.

The right and upper parts of the painting held a different view—through a windshield—of that part of the bridge yet to be crossed. This view was cast in a dimmer light, fading with distance into an uncertain dusk. Shades of gray subdued the windshield and dashboard with an aura of bleakness. This part of the painting was devoid of color save for a pale and not quite round green moon.

The dimensions and perspectives of the painting were surrealistic, but somehow the parts cohered, and the painting became a powerful whole. It resonated within John's mind: a mystery, a message.

Jessica lost interest and signaled by tugging his earlobes: she wanted to continue her ride around the house. He patted her knee in response.

"That's beautiful, Mom. Is it the Golden Gate?"

"Thank you, John. No, this is a place I've never been." She turned to smile up at him, and tugged Jessica's socks up. "But it's some place I may be, I think, some day. Bridges are symbols of transition, John. Their images are—how do you say—evocative.

"Your father," she continued thoughtfully, "when he rescued me from the Pathet Lao prison, carried me across a bridge. A little footbridge. And then he blew it up behind us."

"Sounds like Dad," John laughed. His mother laughed with him, a tinkling sound, like a tiny waterfall.

"I guess that's why I like to paint bridges, John," she added, patting his cheek with her free hand. "Now would you mind dressing up Jess and taking her outside? Get her good and hungry for dinner, while I just finish up this last little bit?"

He remembered now, driving across the long bridge into Delaware, how he had played with Jessica that January afternoon. They rolled a snowman together in the fresh fallen snow outside Carlisle Barracks, Pennsylvania, until the fading light and growing cold drove them back indoors.

An anonymous buyer, a business foundation, had stumbled across the painting on exhibit in the Gettysburg public library that spring. His mother had been ecstatic over the ten-thousand dollar windfall, an extraordinarily generous offer in those days to an obscure artist. She accepted it immediately. John hugged her in congratulation when he heard, and held his dismay tightly within. It had been his favorite painting.

South of Albany VORTAC, NY | Monday 1731 EDT

"No black shift, Lara," TC Demuzzio repeated. "You have any ideas about that?"

Lara studied the agent's bland expression carefully. It's a trap, she thought; he's giving me his best poker face. Why is he doing this? What does he know? Why isn't he telling me? *What* isn't he telling me? Well, he got me, fair and square. But in for a penny, in for a pound; I've got to keep running with the story. I'm sorry TC, old friend. I know you have no real choice but to ask your questions. And I have no real choice but to lie to you.

"TC, I just don't know," Lara answered. "That's not something Forensics could miss. Even all shot up and mixed in with debris, it clearly wouldn't be part of any kitchen equipment or decoration. So *Warlock* must have picked it up, and taken it with him."

"And why would he do that, Lara?"

"Because he's nuts, TC. Maybe he's a cross-dresser, and it's a trophy. Or maybe he's a scent tracker, and he needs the dress to ferret me out. That actually makes a certain kind of weird sense to me. But how the hell can I really know?" She put an edge on the question, to let a little indignation show through.

Demuzzio regarded her calmly.

Lara regarded him with a reciprocal calmness, but only superficial. Internally, her intuition spiked and her mind wasn't calm at all. An insight suddenly coalesced: TC is withholding information. He knows I didn't throw a black dress, that's clear enough. But he knows something else he's not saying. What is it? He can't possibly know what a null field looks like. Ditka couldn't have seen it all that clearly, and he couldn't have identified it even if he had a clear view. And I'm pretty sure he didn't have time to describe it over the radio before he died. I can't even describe it in words myself, very well. The shootout lasted less than a minute. So the null field isn't it. What is it? Something to do with the agents? Yes, it must be. Her mind ran down that pathway, then up and down it again, but found no answers. So she remained silent, waiting him out.

"Okay, Lara," Demuzzio acknowledged, even though clearly dissatisfied, "I think we got most of the other loose ends at the safehouse tidied up. So now tell me about the Zoo. Tell me why the hell we got a dead ape, very messy, in the goddamn National Zoo. Here, here's a picture Forensics took."

Lara turned pale as she looked at the picture in the afternoon light coming through the porthole window. It showed a brutally dismembered ape. She thought for a moment she might be sick.

"So you ran past the ape compound, Lara," Demuzzio continued. "Did you leave anything there?"

She was astonished at his question. The null field fragments she'd tagged onto the apes wouldn't last more than several minutes. And they were not even from this dimension; Forensics couldn't possibly have detected them. I burned through the locks, she thought, but since the Beast was there too, they'll think *Warlock* did it. So what's TC onto? I might have lost a hair or two, but Forensics couldn't possibly pick those out of the dirt this fast. Then she remembered the sweatband. It had fallen off when she hung upside down above the big ape, tagging him with the chaos fragment as he lumbered beneath her.

"Oh, TC, now I remember! Yes! I tossed my sweatband into the compound when I ran by."

"Sweatband, sweatband..." Demuzzio thumbed through the pages of Forensics' initial report. "Yeah, got it here. Black fleece headband. That it?"

She nodded.

"Now, Lara, this strikes me as being one of the stranger things in a very strange morning. Why the hell would you do that?"

"I don't really know, TC." She fed him back his own puzzled look. "Just some kind of gut-level instinct, I guess. Like if a big dog is chasing you, you toss something on a bush, hoping he'll stop to smell it and buy you a few more minutes?"

"You telling me that *Warlock* is a smell-tracker, some kinda human bloodhound? That's the second time you said that, Lara. You serious?"

"I don't know if I'm serious about smell or not, TC. But it wouldn't surprise me. I just threw the sweatband in the cage on instinct, like I said."

"Well, it worked, I guess. He went in there. Sliced up the ape. That's gotta be a helluva sword. Or a battleax. Strong guy, too. Incredibly strong. But why didn't he take the sweatband, Lara, if he needs a scent to track you?"

Her eyebrow went up and she shrugged, but offered no answer.

"Well... doesn't matter, I guess. I believe you now, kiddo, that *Warlock* can track you somehow. The big question is how. While you were sleeping, we checked you over for any kind of implanted hardware, monitored for any kind of transmission pulse, did everything else we could think of, short of carving you up and picking through the pieces. We came up totally empty."

Lara merely raised an eyebrow again, inviting him to continue, subtly shifting his interrogation into more of a dialog between them.

"So I believe *Warlock* can track you, Lara, and I believe you can sense him. But there's no physical basis for it. So as much as I'm a skeptic about these things, it has to be mental, or psychic, or something totally outside my experience."

"Umm?" Her expression invited him to continue the dialog.

"And you've changed, Lara. That's very clear. You came back from total exhaustion to complete health in a few hours. And your brain... Sam Rosen said your EEG patterns were like you had two sections of your brain running independently at the same time. The only other time he saw that was a Zen master, he said. So now... you wanna tell your old friend TC about it?"

"Zen master? Now that's interesting, TC." Her eyes crinkled in a half-smile.

"Interesting? Look, kiddo, this is all very difficult for me to accept, but I ain't stupid. I put this Zen shit and your healing together, sort of, with your sense of *Warlock* coming after you, and there's only one place I can come out."

"Which is?"

"You're a new development, Lara. You, and probably *Warlock*, too, have come into talents the rest of us haven't got. So, you wanna tell your buddy TC about it?" he paused thoughtfully, re-emphasizing the psychological kicker, "old friend that I am?"

Lara considered his words, weighing her response. You *are* an old and dear friend, TC, she thought. And I love you and trust you implicitly, but this is just too dangerous a development to let out of the bag just yet. I'm sorry. I truly am. Lara Picard took TC Demuzzio's big hand in both her smaller ones, and returned the tired smile on his lined face, choosing her words.

"TC, you *are* an old friend. Believe me, if there were anything I could tell you about this, I would."

NJ Turnpike East of Princeton, NJ | Monday 1918 EDT

The Magician, accustomed to reading nuances in many kinds of tiny motions around him, sensed the vector change in the Other's transport. He ranged the green-tinged black blot on his consciousness radar, estimating distance and direction. A sharp direction change eastward, and slowing, he decided, over northern Massachusetts or southern Vermont. So the Other is going to ground in the hill country. And what's up there? Skiing in the winter. Hiking and lakes in the summer. A few farms still around. Some light industry, what little is left. Some state parks, other open land. So why create the trap there? He floated the question in his mind-space as he flipped open the powerful wireless laptop on the passenger seat.

The Other will seek to define the field of battle, thus to better control it, John Connard. Duc Li's image seemed thoughtful but bleak.

That makes sense, the Magician thought back. Pick a deserted area for the trap, one with minimum public attention, no civilians or bystanders to worry about. Create a free-fire zone and suck me into it. That's pretty much what I would do if the situation were reversed.

The Assassin's rage blazed unexpectedly into his mind-space at the thought of being trapped. He fought it under control, then backed away from its hungry vortex.

The image of Duc Li pondered the simmering rage somberly.

This is truly dangerous, John Connard. You have learned how to adapt the power of the primitive animal to your rational use. Your essential goodness and humanity have survived so far, but now your rapidly changing brain structure shifts the balance. You may destroy the Other only to replace it with something far worse.

Myself?

Yes. It is possible. I fear there may be more than one battle to be fought in your reality.

Conflicted emotions rolled into his mind-space, washing back over his nexus.

The emotions carried with them a fear of himself, of the much greater power he now held as an instrument of destruction. He desperately needed to use that power, but couldn't let himself be consumed by it. Ah, he thought, that explains the bleakness in my nexus; it isn't really diminished prospects for success in battle.

Yes, John Connard, you understand the problem, the delicate balance. To use the power, but not become it. A two-edged sword.

As his mind backed away from that conundrum to better study it, the Magician belatedly realized that the intensity of his focus on these issues had blocked out other subtle messages. Another presence had been in his mind for some time now, and on his consciousness radar: a light feathery golden glow, happy and curious, and very close by. It contrasted sharply with the distant menace of the black blot. The glow was also aware of him, mutuality in their contact.

Jessica's mind might have felt like that, he thought in wonderment, if she had lived. Keeping a fraction of his attention on the highway unwinding ahead of him, he gingerly rearranged elements in his mind-space, intuitively expanding the contact. The glow rippled responsively under the attention of his consciousness, a pleasurable sense, like the purr of a cat being stroked.

A vision drifted into his mind-space, fuzzy at first, but then sharpening into the image of a computer monitor, a big flat screen model, expensive, like Alex had in the office condo. Blue circles with cross-hairs marched from the lower left to the upper right of the screen, superimposed on... what was that, a map? It looked familiar. The realization came abruptly, shocking him.

"They're tracking me!" The scream roared out against the windshield. His hands flew into an attack reaction, fast, automatic, deadly. The Assassin slammed into place instantly, and a vortex of primal rage exploded out of his mind before he could suppress it.

Global Consciousness Project, Princeton University, NJ | Monday 1919

Eleven miles due west of the Assassin, the object of his sudden rage recoiled sharply, knocking over her chair and flying backwards to slam against the wall in a crouch, hands trembling defensively in front of her, face pale, mouth snarling. The shock resonated outward from an epicenter deep in a primitive part of her brain and was interpreted as an image of a roaring reptilian devil-beast. The image seemed to burn in the air in front of her. Her eyes saw the dripping bloody fangs. Her flared nostrils smelled the foul sulfurous breath of the carnivore. Adrenaline ran rampant through her body. Adrienne Baxter shook violently with terror, her body jammed tightly against the wall.

Special Forces Exercise, Pisgah State Park, NH | *Monday 1921 EDT*

"TC, please believe me," Lara repeated, still holding the big agent's hand, "if there were anything I could tell you, I would. Truly."

Demuzzio squinted his eyes at her as the Black Hawk banked to starboard and a golden evening sunbeam played over his face. The helicopter landed in what once had been a trap rock quarry.

Shaundee dropped out, holding his hand up for her. She took it and jumped down lightly, and they ran under the rotating blades with Demuzzio close behind. The aircraft turbines wound up its for its return flight.

"We have just enough light left for a quick walkover of the area, ma'am," the Colonel told her after the introductions to the reception crew were completed.

As they walked the flat-bottomed bowl that had been carved into the trap rock ridge, she began to smile. Not bad, she thought, not bad at all. In fact, she couldn't imagine a better layout for a trap. TC Demuzzio, a former infantry soldier himself, also began to smile as he worked out distances and angles for firing lines.

"How many men do you have here, Colonel?" she asked.

"Three hundred combatants, ma'am. Fifty-four support. Twelve referees for the exercises. Mostly Army. Fifth Special Forces Group out of Fort Campbell, First out of Fort Lewis. We also have a number of Marines and Navy Seals, a few Air Force and CIA and Delta Force people. Best of the best, ma'am."

A number of them were watching her, she sensed, drawing in her consciousness radar to focus on the immediate area. They're much more... delineated? She cast the question mark into her mind-space. They present much sharper images than the three agents that were at the safehouse: why is that?

Your talents are growing, your senses becoming more acute, especially under the pressure of impending battle. The three evolutionary segments of your brain are becoming less separate, more woven together. New neural pathways are forming. You are more sensitive.

Lara smelled the night air, picking out the different scents, discriminating, analyzing. Extraordinary acuity, she thought, even sharper than last night when I smelled each component of the spaghetti sauce.

And the sharper images are due in part to the collective focus of these minds on their goal. Her nexus sent an image into her mind-space of the hundreds of soldiers studying her from their camouflaged positions, marking her for their protection. Lara felt cocooned in safety and warmth by their energy, their singularity of purpose.

Garden State Parkway, East of Plainfield, NJ | Tuesday 1923 EDT

To use the power, John Connard, without becoming it. It puts you in a truly danger-ous place. So now you see. The image of Duc Li showed no expression, conveying the same absence of judgment that the real Duc Li's face had carried when he trained his favorite pupil in the martial arts.

John set that thought aside for the moment. He tried to re-establish contact with the golden glow, seeking to apologize. He painted disconsolate sorrow in his mind-space, and sent it off to the place on his consciousness radar from which the glow had so abruptly disappeared. Forgive me, I didn't mean it, it was a defensive reaction, you took me by surprise. He sent those thoughts repeatedly, putting the full force of his mind behind them, as the car flew northward.

Whoever it is, the Magician thought, is probably visualizing me as a friendly dog that suddenly turned into a rabid wolf with no warning at all and went for their throat. I guess I can't blame them. Shit! They'll probably stay hunkered down for a long while.

But ten minutes later, the golden glow re-appeared dimly and briefly on his con-sciousness radar, and then was gone. Its touch was tentative, fleeting, fearful. But it also carried undertones of courage and determination. The Magician was no less disconsolate about his uncontrolled reaction, but understood that his apology had been received, even if not accepted. As the contact faded, he sighed the dimen-sions of his sorrow into his mind-space: it was an accident.

Yes, John Connard, of course it was an accident. But I repeat, the power here is so much greater, and the shift required for its misuse is so much smaller, than any-thing you have dealt with before. The evolutionary layers of your brain are becoming closely interwoven. In you, and in the new Nova sapiens, they will be much more integrated. And part of what you now integrate is primitive and savage. It can easily upset the fragile balance you have achieved between the Magician and the Assassin. You are dangerous, John Connard, truly.

Forty minutes later, after an extended exchange with his nexus on the moral conflicts inherent to his integrating being, John turned the car eastward toward Nyack and drove down the long ramp of the escarpment onto the Tappan Zee Bridge. Conflicted or not, he was a soldier. He had a mission. For that mission, he needed the tools of war. He pushed a resolute message into his mind-space.

I will use this primal power, he instructed his nexus, but I will not become it. I will keep my balance. I will act from love. And you will help me.

As you will, John Connard. The image of Duc Li smiled at him, gentle and wise.

His mind-space became flooded with solace and support, and then, strangely, with a vision of Lara as the ultimate expression of love and hope. Clad in a white flowing gown, like a statue of some ancient Greek goddess, her hands rested on the hilt of a sword. It shimmered with the same light as her emerald eyes.

Abruptly, he remembered the poem Lara had written for him on the back of a napkin, while he dozed on the airplane back from their Grand Cayman trip:

"My moonbeam shadow ship is sinking,
disappearing;
I hear it dripping
droplets down:
a sound,
a sigh,
goodbye,
dreams die,
and hope is found."

She'd been thanking him, he knew, for helping her out from under the shadow-past of her suicidal husband Malcolm O'Donnell, for giving her hope for the future. But he could as easily have written it to her, for giving him hope. He'd saved the napkin, a scrap of paper, but a precious treasure forever, one of the few material possessions of his ascetic life. John smiled at Lara's shimmering image in his mind-space, thanking her in return for giving him hope.

Halfway across the long span of the bridge, he saw the full moon rising ahead and to his left. Framed in the rear-view mirror, the bridge stretched behind to the long escarpment bordering the Hudson, and the sun hung in the sky, just kissing the cliff as it set. The orb glowed red-gold in the mirror, hugely magnified by the evening haze.

At quarter past eight on Memorial Day evening, the Magician had already focused totally on the mission ahead. Staring straight down the bridge into the shades of gray in the growing dusk ahead, oblivious to the scene of transition, John Connard never saw his mother's painting come to life around him.

Chapter 32

The Chinese dinner had been better than passable. It actually bordered on tasty, thought Hamilton O'Donnell. He rubbed his belly and eased out a delicate belch of appreciation for the Szechuan beef. Then he walked over to the big table in the dining room to study Joshua's evolving work. The notebook papers taped, together on top of the table, showed a diagram of increasingly complexity.

"Ah, me lad, and what's this margin notation here, at 5:35 PM, marked with an asterisk and 'Mom'?" he asked. "Did she send you a message? Right before dinner? Tell you to eat all your veggies and clean your plate?"

"No, Uncle Ham, I sent her a message. I sensed her passing by, I'm pretty sure. I don't exactly know how or why. I sent her a hug, with my mind. And, you know, I think she got it!" He smiled at his uncle, the open delighted smile of a child.

"Well now, me lad, a truly fascinatin' concept that might be, a mental hug for your mum. And her acknowledgment of it, no less. How can that be? Telepathy? Has your research yielded a clue?"

"No, Uncle Ham, not really. All the concepts out there, in all sorts of literature, almost all of them uniformly peg such effects as being insensitive to distance. And yet Mom clearly moved into range, and clearly moved out again. So it's some sort of signal strength function, inverse with distance."

"Ah, yes, boy. Signal strength. But what of receptor sensitivity? Could that not be a factor on your end? And what of the—what shall we call it—the transmissivity of the medium between, to the signals being sent? And how about all those electromagnetic signals in the air, noise interferences. Could those not be factors also?"

"Sure, Uncle Ham, sure. They all could be factors, I guess," Joshua reflected, making another note on the diagram in his obscure shorthand, "but the trouble is, these are concepts from the physical world, not the psychic world... Unless you know something different?"

The boy's turquoise eyes seemed to darken with intensity as they regarded him. Loving eyes, thought Hamilton O'Donnell, but as laden with restless energy as the blue-green waves that batter the cliffs of my home. He would give another hint, then, to calm those waters.

"Well, lad, given the complexity of the organism, would not even the most punctuated of evolutionary equilibria have separate little stages and sequences embedded within them?"

Global Consciousness Project, Princeton University, NJ | Monday 1949 EDT

Adrienne had bundled herself in two fleece sweatshirts, but still shivered occasionally as she recapped her impressions of the psychic onslaught.

This approach is working, Nathan confirmed to himself. Making her relate it to me step-by-step, so I can write down the timeline, asking her questions, checking to make sure I get it all right, being a laboratory scientist. She knows the routine, so it's calming her down nicely. Absently, he noted the rounded hole in the gypsum wallboard. Her elbow had slammed into it as she sprang backward away from the awful thing in her mind. Maybe an icepack, as soon as we're done, he thought.

"Okay, Adrienne, a quick summary of the major points," he reviewed the sequence scrawled in the lab notebook. "Around 7:15 PM you got a sense of contact in your mind, much like Aaron described in Montrose Park last evening, and like you had in mid-morning today. By 7:18 you had exchanged some thoughts, calm and friendly. At 7:19, Blue looked through your eyes at the monitor, and then exploded with rage."

"Oh, Doctor Rodgers," Adrienne shivered as she spoke, "he was so friendly. I showed him what we were doing, I somehow sort of opened my mind right up and let him look through my eyes to see the monitor screen. And then he went berserk. Just berserk!"

"Adrienne, when you say berserk, exactly what did you sense, can you define it, describe it?"

"A beast. A monster. The worst of all nightmares. Primeval. A lizard or a dinosaur or something like that. Big bloody fangs, drooling. Reeking hot breath. I swear to God I can still smell it, Doctor Rodgers, and it stank." Her nose wrinkled reflexively. "It was like I'm petting this big friendly dog, and then all of a sudden he turns into this devil and goes for me. It happened instantaneously, as soon as he realized we were watching him."

"And then right afterwards, Adrienne, there was a strong reassertion of control, and a suppression of the beast, you said? Some sense of sorrow and contrition? An apology, wanting to resume contact?"

"Yes, sir. For the next ten minutes, I got this feeling non-stop. And I got the sense he felt horrified at what he did. And I don't think he was faking it, just to get back in my mind and try to kill me, or anything like that. I just don't think he's quite in full control, somehow."

"And so you didn't permit the contact, for those ten minutes?" Nathan continued annotating the timeline down the side of his notebook page. "How exactly do you not permit contact, Adrienne?"

"I don't really know." She paused to consider the question. "The closest analogy I guess would be turning down the volume of your radio when you don't want to listen to an ad or something."

"Do you think the volume could get turned up on the other end, so that you'd have to listen anyway?" That was a key question, at least for their personal sanity and safety, and Nathan's pencil fidgeted absently above the page as Adrienne considered it.

"I just don't know. I think maybe yes, because this being has enormous power. But he didn't force the contact, Doctor Rodgers. He was very respectful. Those later contacts were just like light taps on the door, not a battering ram. He didn't want to scare me any more than he already had. I got the sense he really cared about me."

Nathan scribbled madly in the notebook.

"And so, Adrienne, after ten minutes of him trying to apologize, you sent him a message? This was just before I came back into the Center?"

"Yes, sir. The strength of the contact faded, so I figured if he was going to go berserk again, the images wouldn't be quite so intense. I felt reasonably safe. I kept my message real short and sweet and broke the contact right after."

"You're a brave young woman, Adrienne. I'm not sure I could have done that. Reach out and pat a dog that almost took my head off." He looked at her keenly. "So, what message did you send?"

"Oh, I just said we meant no offense by tracking him. And I forgave him for his reaction, and..." Adrienne put her hand over her mouth in dismay, muffling her words, "and then I told him..."

"Told him what, Adrienne?"

The woman-child swallowed convulsively, "I told him never to let it happen again!" She put her hand over her mouth again, but the laughter started to leak out anyway.

Nathan Rodgers looked at his protégé in amazement. Her laughter was convulsive, but not hysterical. Even though the possible *lese majeste* worried him more than a little, he started laughing along with her.

Flatbush Section of Brooklyn, NY | Monday 2047 EDT

An hour later, Joshua was still pondering the mystery of the hints buried in their mind-dance when the computer search finally found what he'd been looking for.

A psychiatrist named Rosen and a neurobiologist named Roberts collaborated three years ago on research published in the journal *Neuropsychoanalysis*. The research tied the knowledge gained from modern sophisticated brain imaging equipment to the concepts of unconscious drives articulated in the past by Sigmund Freud. The writers pointed out that more recent applied psychology has downplayed psychoanalysis and marginalized Freud, focusing more on rational processes in consciousness. But their brain research corroborated, with almost eerie consistency, physical evidence of Freud's drives, rooted in the limbic system, below the level of the rational brain. Freud got it pretty much right, the article concluded, without much knowledge of brain structures or functions. The authors drew a persuasive parallel between Freud and Charles Darwin, who had gotten evolution pretty much right without knowing about genes.

"Uncle Ham!" Joshua exclaimed excitedly.

"Yes, me lad, what is it?"

"We have three brains!"

"Why yes, boy, I guess we do, from what little I know of the neurosciences. But sometimes I think yourself must have six or seven, the way you carry on. So, three? Why, piffle. A triflin' number, that. So what about three brains?"

"Evolution, Uncle Ham! The reptile brain, the early mammal brain, the human brain. These three brains develop and overlay in a fetus just like they did in evolution. And Mom..." he caught himself and held his tongue until his uncle walked close by, then spoke quietly so the agents wouldn't hear. "Mom said her senses got really acute. She said she could pick out all the smells, each of them, in the dinner last night. And she can sense emotions and danger, the enemy closing in on her. These sorts of things are in the primitive parts of the brain, below the rational level. And the energy I felt in her yesterday, that contact I could feel this afternoon... I think that's something very primitive and basic, too."

"And precisely what connection, me lad, do you make between your brain diagnosis and evolution?" He ruffled the boy's hair affectionately.

"This sudden leap in human evolution may not be anything fundamentally new, Uncle Ham. Maybe it's not a brand new brain structure or function, or anything like that. Maybe it's just a better connection of the three evolutionary parts. Or maybe it's a repair job, putting the parts together like they really were meant to be."

"Hmm?" His uncle invited explanation. "For what purpose, lad?"

"Well, if we're staying in the communications sequence, then maybe it's so we can read information fields better. Maybe even interact with them, somehow... look, Uncle Ham! Look here, on the diagram. See this loop? If it was really supposed to work this way, as a feed-forward control, then... then... when there's a genetic possibility, well, right here are the opportunistic retroviruses, just hanging around, waiting to do the job! I may be crazy, but I think it's possible!" Joshua tapped his pencil on the diagram as if to bring that possibility to the surface.

Global Consciousness Project, Princeton University, NJ | Monday 2058 EDT

"On the one hand a vicious beast, on the other a caring and respectful being," Nathan mused, "and did you get that sense of enormous power just from the beast side, or from both sides, Adrienne?"

"Both, I think, Doctor Rodgers. I don't think the beast is in control, but I sense that maybe it could be. She paused to let her mind run down a different path. "And I'm no longer so sure of my mating hypothesis. Or, if this is a mating, then maybe he's primitive, feral, like a tomcat. Or maybe it *is* an attack, like Aaron believes. I'm just not sure any more."

Nathan pondered her uncertainty for a moment.

"Or... if the ET is in a human host... then maybe the beast is on the human side, Adrienne, not the ET side? Wouldn't that make more sense? Wouldn't we be closer to our biological past than ETs, who are presumably much further evolved?"

A light broke across Adrienne's troubled countenance.

"Wow! Yes! That makes perfect sense! The ET sees the monitor, realizes we're tracking him, and the human side sees that as a threat! If it's a survival thing—which it could be—then that would explain the savage image, an instantaneous reaction from the animal mind. And the immediate apology, that could be the ET! Regaining control, putting the rational mind back in charge! I gotta talk to Sarah's dad!"

She rose out of the chair fluidly, with the quick recovery of youth, and rummaged an address book out of her purse.

Nathan was confused. "Sarah? You mean your roommate Sarah?"

"Yeah, Doctor Rodgers. Sarah's dad is Sam Rosen. He's a shrink. He does guest lectures here for Sarah's clinical psych seminars, takes us to dinner afterwards. We've had wonderful talks. He's really a super guy, a real Yoda. He works for the government, sees all kinds of really weird mental cases. He can tell us for sure, if anybody can."

Adrienne found a number in her address book and dialed it before Nathan could think through all the possibilities. He opened his mouth to speak, but then shut it.

Aw, hell, just trust her instincts, he told himself; what else do you have to go on?

Rosen Household, Alexandria, VA | Monday 2101 EDT

"Hey, Dad, pick up the phone, will you? Adie's got a question for you."

Psychiatrist Sam Rosen, whose thoughts had been dwelling unproductively on Lara Picard's strange developments, had a discomfiting premonition that the day's strangeness wasn't over yet. He reviewed what he knew of his daughter's roommate as he walked across the kitchen to pick up the phone.

Adrienne Baxter had been born the year after Sarah, adopted out of a Korean orphanage by an Army couple, and raised by her mom, a career Army nurse. Her adoptive father had died in the first Gulf War. No one, of course, knew who her real parents were, or where her incredible mind might have come from. She was a math major, psych minor, the inverse of Sarah.

Rosen regarded the girl as one of his family, almost. He was professionally fascinated by how her prodigy mind worked. She was equally fascinated by his casework on oddball psychiatric conditions. But she'd never called him at home before. The premonition washed over him again, more intense.

"Yo, Adrienne," he answered into his kitchen telephone, "what's up? You got boyfriend problems you need to talk to Doctor Sam about?" Sarah had found it amusing to get all her friends to call him Doctor Sam. For some reason it amused him too.

"No, sir, I just had a very strange experience, and I have a sort of hypothetical question for you. Is it possible for a sane and moral and healthy mind to have a savage reaction, and lash out, and then be immediately sorry for it afterwards, and really mean it?"

Oh-oh, Rosen thought, sounds like boyfriend problems to me. Young male, alpha, too much testosterone, overdeveloped emotions, underdeveloped control. Contrition's a good sign, though, means there's some moral basis present. Unless of course it's cyclical, a repeating abuse pattern.

"Sure, Adrienne, it happens all the time," he replied, "in a lot of different circumstances: young kids, before they develop a sense of consequences; during puberty, when all those hormones start getting restless; after puberty, especially in young men, if they haven't been in family situations that train them in how to control themselves."

"And how about in adults, I mean mature adults?"

"Oh, that happens too, sure. Especially in relationships where there's a cycle: abuse, then guilt, then making amends, then getting back in control, then more abuse. That's quite common, in fact. Is that what you're asking about? You doing a paper or something?"

"Oh, no sir, that's not it exactly either. How about one-time events?" Her voice sounded distant on the phone.

"Umm. A savage reaction followed by contrition? Survival reactions would be the best example of that, Adrienne. Policemen or soldiers under fire: they get shot at, fire back and accidentally kill an innocent person. It happens. I actually get involved in some of those cases, trying to parcel out what was survival reaction, what was operant conditioning, what was malicious intent."

"Malicious intent, Doctor Sam, tell me about that. Would that be a psychopath? Would that mean no sorrow afterwards?"

"Depends on which side you're looking at it from, Adrienne. Take a tiger for example. He sees you just as a meal. That's his context, and he sees nothing terrible about that, feels no guilt, no sorrow at all. He just licks his chops and belches. Psychopaths have that same sort of context. But what's normal and natural for a tiger isn't normal and natural for a human being. So, if you see sorrow, and it's real, not put on, then you wouldn't likely be looking at a psychopathic personality."

Silence greeted his analysis. He could hear her breathing, and waited patiently for her to think through her problem. But then another thought occurred to him, a more urgent one.

"Adrienne, if you're in some kind of dangerous or uncomfortable situation, we'd love to have you come down here for a visit. Get away from the situation for a while. You sure this is hypothetical, and not a boyfriend problem? You want to tell Doctor Sam about this experience that led you to call me at..." he checked the clock on the stove, "nine o'clock at night?"

There was another pause, a more dense silence, and he thought she might have put her hand over the receiver. Eventually she came back on the line.

"Doctor Sam, Sarah once told me if I ever needed to, I could trust you with anything." He heard her take a deep breath. "So, here's my situation... and I don't know if it's dangerous or not...."

It took all of Rosen's psychological training to discern that her experience hadn't been subjective. It hadn't been a waking dream in a fugue state. It was real mental contact from an outside source; an extraterrestrial source if what Adrienne told him was true. She obviously believed it, but he found it difficult to accept even with all the data supporting it.

Concepts about the nature of consciousness and how it tied into the physical brain tumbled around the psychiatrist's mind in confusion as they talked. Finally, the timing, the multiple coincidences, caused enough pieces of the mental mosaic to fall into place. Adrienne's experience and Lara Picard's were part of the same story!

The insight carried a blinding certainty. Sam Rosen slapped his hand on his forehead. His bare feet, which had been draped carelessly over a kitchen barstool, slapped down on the mosaic tile floor, and he yelped to his daughter.

"Sarah, hang up this phone, please, I'm going to pick up in my office!"

He trotted down the stairs to the lower level, and picked up the office phone beside his computer. Then he toggled on the high-speed Internet connection and tapped the URL she gave him onto the computer keyboard.

"Okay, Adrienne, your Global Consciousness Project, I'm looking at the website, and now... okay, I've got your tracking program display. Blue circles and crosshairs on a map, right? And I can toggle backward and forward in time through the data, from four AM Sunday morning to the present. Okay, I see that.

"And the other entity, Adrienne? The tracking program output for Green... hmm, okay, I've got it. Looks like it's been stationary in, what... southern New Hampshire... for the past few hours?"

"Yes, sir."

Right where it says Pisgah State Park on the underlying map, he noted. Bingo! A shiver started at the base of his spine and moved up, standing the hair on the back of his neck straight out. With an effort, he suppressed his alarm and keyed back to the blue traces. "And Blue is moving toward it, steadily. I can see that. So, it passed by your area and gave you that nasty reaction, and right now it's in... where? Connecticut?"

"Yes, sir."

"So it's pretty clear that Blue is chasing Green, Adrienne. Any idea why? Anything else you can tell me? Actually, why don't you go back, and start at the beginning," he invited, pulling a yellow notepad toward himself and clicking on the computer microphone so that his half of the conversation would be digitally recorded.

Much later, as Adrienne's story wound down, he looked at his notes, tapping the pencil on key points:

-The government knows about the ETs, they were told right from the start.

-Lara Picard is, or is carrying, an ET.

-TC had to know this right from the start, the sly old devil, and he never said a goddamn word.

-What's chasing her is another ET, something more incredible than any human super-agent.

-The real question is: what does it want?

"Well, Adrienne," Sam Rosen said slowly, considering how much information he could share with her, "to get back to your original question, if your perceptions about Blue's contrition are accurate, I'd guess he's ethical. Being tracked means that you could be hunted. And if you suddenly realize you're being hunted, that could certainly trigger a survival response. You could let the response out before it could be controlled. Could happen to anyone, because that sort of response comes out of the primitive part of the brain. Sometimes you can't clamp down on those reactions in time. They're the basic fight or flight responses, intrinsic to survival. I'm talking about the human side, not the ET side, of course," he added with a dry chuckle. "I haven't shrunk any ETs lately."

Rosen listened to Adrienne's profuse thanks for his time and insight. He sighed as he hung up the phone. *No, I can't tell Adrienne that just five hours ago I actually was with her green ET. That Green is—or is part of—one Lara Picard. If this all turns to shit, she may be better off not knowing those particulars. Especially if I'm wrong about Blue, and TC doesn't capture or kill him. The less she knows, the less she's at risk.*

And TC? He reached for the telephone, debating, thinking it through. *The Bureau Ops Desk could patch me in, wherever he is. But what's the point? TC obviously knows everything I just found out.* Rosen put the phone down and studied his computer monitor. The green circles on the screen sat, stable, on Pisgah State Park in southwest New Hampshire. *His old friend TC Demuzzio would be with Lara Picard, right in the center of those circles, implementing his plan, spinning his web, but controlling the information carefully; oh, so carefully.*

He switched URLs to study the blue circles, now tracking northward through central Connecticut, and felt the hair on the back of his neck stand up again.

Flatbush Section of Brooklyn, NY | Monday 2257 EDT

"So, me lad," Hamilton O'Donnell asked the key question, "what might we expect with better brain segment interconnectivity in our *Nova sapiens?* What else does your fertile imagination pull from this magnificent diagram?"

"Well, don't forget, Uncle Ham, Mom jumped like a cat, up from that ledge where we found her bike Sunday morning. Or maybe," he added thoughtfully, computing again the force required to vertically clear ten feet, "more like a raptor."

"Umm. So there may be physical manifestations of this interconnectivity? But your mum said it was only six feet, Joshua. Good high jumpers do that."

"Yeah, Uncle Ham, that's what she said. But that's bull. It was almost exactly ten feet. And you know it was!"

"Well, whatever the case, me lad, I can see no particular evolutionary advantage to good jumpin' in these modern times, unless the woman intends to take up basketball. Or politics. So what else would you infer from better connections, my young scientist?"

Joshua contemplated the diagram, and tapped his pencil on its genetic feedback loops as he spoke.

"Our intellect might be able to access racial memories encoded well below the rational brain. We might be able to read and maybe interact with a greater field of information than our present brains can perceive. Maybe we could access group consciousness, maybe a melding of some kind, those might be other possibilities."

"Ah, young man, we slip so adroitly from Freud to Jung, do we? Such philosophical dexterity! Me ould friend Carl, as I recall, presaged what you predict. He says every human being carries the two-million-year old soul of our species, and our kinship with the universe dwells within this soul. He claims we have moved away from it in modern times, but it calls us back. Possibly the improved interconnectivity you're suggestin' has evolved to remedy that, to bring us back."

The old man laughed out loud, patted his nephew on the back, and merrily continued the thought. "A genomic repair job, lovely concept! A mid-course correction for humanity's Ship of Fools! And about bloody time, some would say! But who's the skipper, my young philosopher? Who's the skipper of this ship?"

Chapter 33

The dashboard clock flicked over to the witching hour as the Magician left the car. He walked into the nearly deserted diner, just off Interstate 91 in Brattleboro, Vermont, carrying the laptop computer.

"Okay if I take a booth?" he asked.

The middle-aged waitress looked up from the newspaper, reflexively brushed off her apron and nodded at him, picking up a menu and a coffeepot.

"Thank you, Doris," he said, looking at the tag on her apron, "I don't need a menu. If I could get a six-egg omelet, ham and bacon and cheese and onion and anything else you want to throw in, and about a quart of orange juice, that would be perfect."

He flipped open the laptop and studied the topographic map of Pisgah State Park as he sipped the hot black coffee. Okay, the Magician thought, the good news is that I know the lay of this land intimately from war games a few years ago, and the Other can't possibly have anticipated that. The bad news is that she's somehow got Special Forces from this current exercise lined up and waiting for me. And it's certain to be live fire this time, not the lasers they use for the exercise.

His consciousness radar put the green-tinged black blot in the southern part of the park, where it flickered obscenely at him. That area had been a trap rock quarry, abandoned years ago, a half-bowl carved out of the hillside. Some of the old equipment and structures remained. They'd used it as a setting for skirmishes in their war games. Great place for a trap, he acknowledged. So I need to distract their attention, then get in and out fast, that's the only way it can possibly work.

The waitress brought his oversized omelet and put it down beside the computer.

"Ooh, that's pretty," she said, "what is it, a map?" She leaned over to peer at the screen.

"Yes, ma'am, it's a topographic map. I'm going hiking tomorrow, over in New Hampshire. Is this an airstrip, can you tell me?" He pointed at the tiny long rectangle on the flat bank of the river south of the oxbow, on the Vermont side.

"Yeah, honey, that's Brattleboro International," she chortled, "the name bein' three feet longer than the runway. Just a dirt strip, hon. Little Cessna be about the biggest thing ever set down there. Mainly it's just those tiny little things, like wings and an engine you sort of strap on, you know?"

"You mean an ultralight? Or a powered parachute?"

"Yeah, honey, them things. Never catch me in one a those. Wind picks up down this valley, blow you clear to Springfield, and you hafta walk back. My youngest cousin and three of his whack-a-doo buddies got a little airplane club down there, keep 'em in an old crop-duster hangar. They all crazy, if you ask me. One of 'em fetched up short of the runway and dropped in the river last weekend; nearly drownded."

Perfect, thought the Magician, nodding off Doris so he could eat his early breakfast. There's a high valley with a pond just north of the quarry. And it's a calm night, so we'll have good radiational cooling on the hillsides. Ground fog has to be forming right now. In another hour or so, if I remember right, it will start to spill down that depression into the quarry. I can come in right behind it. The inversion will keep them from hearing an engine that small, until it gets right overhead, and by that time I won't be in it. He worked out the details and contingencies for almost an hour as he stoked the furnace of his new metabolism with another omelet.

Good plan? He finally floated the question into his mind-space.

The image of Duc Li smiled confirmation. *Good plan.*

Well okay, then, the Magician decided, swallowing the last of his third omelet. Let's go steal an airplane.

Special Forces Exercise, Pisgah State Park, NH | Tuesday 0103 EDT

"So, how close is he, Lara?" TC Demuzzio looked at his charge, and she read the concern and frustration on the big agent's face.

Ah, TC, old friend, Lara thought, how very perceptive of you. I was just standing here, studying the map. You must have read it in my expression. So now you truly believe I can sense him.

"Several miles, TC, I guess. Maybe six or seven. West, and a little north, I think. He's getting ready."

Demuzzio nodded to Merton Shaundee. Take her at her word, the nod advised, silently. She watched the soldier's expression as he accepted it.

The three of them stood in the partially buried concrete structure that once housed the motors and gears of the rock conveyor system, but that now served as a command bunker for the periodic war game exercises. They studied the view outside on an array of monitors racked neatly against the long wall of the bunker. Lara marveled again at the technology. The entire command center could be set up or taken down in just two hours, for rapid response anywhere in the world.

"Your tax dollars at work ma'am," Shaundee noted. "Pretty impressive, isn't it? With four fixed cameras and eighteen mobile, we can pretty much look wherever we want to, so long as we've got line of sight. On top of the visual we've two bands of infrared, with anti-coincidence logic in case somebody's got one of those new temperature-controlled camouflage suits. We haven't had a single successful penetration of a perimeter this entire exercise. And the quarry here makes this a natural trap. We're gonna let this *Warlock* into the trap, ma'am, but he won't get out."

"I hope you're right, Colonel," Lara said softly. "And once he's in, you just blast away with everything you've got, don't take any chances, okay?"

The slightest of pauses made her look up at the tall soldier, who was looking toward TC Demuzzio.

"I hear you, ma'am," he said.

That wasn't the answer I was looking for, she thought. But then he's taking orders from TC, not me. A glance at Demuzzio didn't reveal anything; he continued studying the big topographic map of the park spread over the briefing table. Well, I'll damn well finish the Beast off myself if you military types can't bring yourselves to kill him. As she steeled herself to that necessity, the blue-tinged black blot on her consciousness radar thrummed somewhere behind her eyeballs, scorning her trap, telling her he was coming for her anyway. Suddenly her confidence slipped toward uncertainty.

I need more, she told her *ki*, more of an edge: a decoy, a distraction, some kind of confusion, like the fragments of the null field I pinned on the apes at the Zoo.

Her nexus considered that. *No, the null field interface is intact now in this reality, not fragmented.* The analogy formed in Lara's mind-space: a concept like the surface between air and water, but with no thickness or other dimension in this reality. She could use the field, intact or fragmented, but could not change its state.

There is another way. But it is dangerous.

Tell me. Show me.

You can make a simulacrum. Balance the null field with the energy field to make a shell around yourself, as you would in battle. Then dissociate the shell from your body. Project it where you will, as an image of yourself. Use your mind to animate the shell to make it behave as you would behave, to fight as you would fight.

I can do this?

Yes. Your fighting abilities are advancing quite rapidly now.

What's dangerous about it?

You leave yourself temporarily with less protection in this reality, because you cannot yet manage to fully shield your body and operate your remote image at the same

time. Also, to create a simulacrum, you give up part of yourself to another reality.
There is a limit to how many times this can be done before the null dimension exacts
payment.

Entropy?

Of a sort. That concept is close enough.

And I sense there are other variables?

Yes. If you invest the simulacrum with the primal energy of your primitive brain,
with the rage to make it fight, you will deplete your resources as rapidly as if you used
the energy yourself. The energy and null dimensions do not diminish when drawn
upon, but your ability to manage them effectively depends on your available psychic
energy.

Lara thought about that. It was good to know the risks, she decided, but clearly
they still should be taken. If she could use a simulacrum as a decoy to draw the
monster into the trap, while staying reasonably protected in the bunker...

Okay, she reflected into her mind-space, show me.

Best done in private to avoid confusion and consternation in your protectors.

"Gentlemen, I'm going outside," Lara announced to those protectors. "I need the
ladies room. And I'm getting pretty antsy, I need to move around a bit and blow
off some steam before the action starts."

Blodgett Airstrip, Vernon, VT | Tuesday 0110 EDT

The Magician drove south on Route 142 out of Brattleboro, alongside the cool
waters of the Connecticut River. The airstrip was exactly where the waitress said,
on a deserted river plain with no houses nearby. The old Quonset hut sat at the
south end of the strip, a shabby rusted half-cylinder in the moonlight. He parked
in a small pull-off overlooking the river's oxbow, and tuned his acute senses to the
quiet environment. No lights were visible in the distant houses across the river,
and nothing stirred except a dog barking faintly in the distance. A light humid
southerly breeze caressed his face as he ran down the slope to the flat terrace of
the airstrip. A quick check for an alarm system, a brief flash of blue energy shielded
by his body, and the Magician slipped inside the hut.

Wonderful, he thought, looking over his choices. This one; I've even flown this
type before. His mind flashed back through those training exercises, Special Forces
teams using various powered ultralights and unpowered parasails for night stalk-
ing. This assault would be no different. A trifle hillier terrain, but the engine had
enough power and the wings had enough lift for the elevations he would be flying
over.

He checked the fuel tank, pushed the ultralight out the hangar door, strapped himself in, and fired the engine. A few moments later, the small aircraft accelerated down the packed earth strip and lofted gracefully through the wispy fog rising from the river. The engine exhaust sound at ground level attenuated sharply as he broke through the inversion layer. No one woke to mark his passage.

The air aloft warmed perceptibly as the Magician gained altitude over the river west of Hinsdale and flew northeastward over wetlands to intersect Route 63. The wispy patches forming below told him that shortly there would be a real pea-souper of a ground fog rolling down the rills into the quarry. He smiled. Their visual would be useless and their infrared would get screwed up by his null field. His timing was superb. Luck flew with him.

He reviewed his strategy once again, ticking off the tactical options in his mind, one by one. Probably a couple of hundred Special Forces troops in position around that quarry, maybe more with the numbers they're training for terrorist operations these days. Ah, there, he thought, spotting a weakness in the plan. There—what if they don't all focus on the plane when it crashes, maybe that's not deceptive enough, even though it should take less than a minute to get in and kill the Other.

I need more of an edge, he told the image of Duc Li in his mind-space. I need to give them a better fake, make sure they're tied up tight.

There is a way, John Connard. But it is dangerous.

Show me. I really do need more of an edge, I can almost taste it.

You can recreate the simulacrum of the spider that you developed in the Harrier ride. This is a very realistic beast. You can dissociate the simulacrum from your immediate presence, project it where you will, operate it at a distance. His nexus flowed the symbolic instruction set across his mind-space and he saw immediately how it could be done. He marveled.

I can really do this?

Yes. Your talents have advanced quite rapidly in this area, and you have already practiced forming the image. It will be seen visually. You can imbue it with the proper energy level to show up on infrared detectors. A spider made large will strike a terrifying primitive chord in even the most seasoned soldier. It is an effective diversion.

So what's dangerous about it?

Until you gain more practice and such creations become a reflex, operating the spider simulacrum in a realistic manner requires considerable mental focus. Focus elsewhere leaves you temporarily less able to guard against the assault of the Other in this reality. You cannot yet manage to fight and direct the image at the same time.

Also, to manage such an image is to give up part of yourself to another reality. The null dimension eventually extracts payment. The nature of the payment floated symbolically across his mind space, an analog to entropy.

Those were acceptable tradeoffs, the Magician acknowledged. As he flew northward above Route 63, he recreated the Colombian spider out of his memory, and out of the materials of other dimensions. He made the spider smaller, made it larger, made it fly beside the ultralight, made it scuttle along the wing. He practiced making it move without actually looking at it.

A fearsome sight it would have been for anyone below who chanced to look upward through the developing fog into the moonlit sky. But the houses below were all dark, and the sound of the small engine kept isolated from the ground by the thickening inversion layer. Only a prowling coyote in the park noted the passage of the aircraft and its strange companion across the face of the full moon. It howled into the night.

Special Forces Exercise, Pisgah State Park, NH | Tuesday 0129 EDT

"What the fuck is she doing out there, Merton? She takes two minutes in the latrine and then goes wandering all over the goddamn quarry making these crazy motions. I know she said she'd come inside when *Warlock* got close, but she's been out there almost half an hour, and I'm getting pretty fucking antsy here myself." Demuzzio's tone shifted from querulous to angry.

"Shadow-dancing, my friend, she's shadow-dancing. Those are combat motions, synchronized to an imagined enemy. Beautiful to watch, isn't it? You told me she was black belt, but you didn't tell me how far along. What we're looking at is much, much more advanced than a simple kata." Shaundee shrugged his broad shoulders as he continued. "And, TC, you said we have to trust her instincts. So, I'd say that's what we do. She'll come inside when it's time. In the meantime, what the hell, leave her alone, she's just blowing off steam, like she said."

But releasing tension was not Lara's primary intent. The sweat dripping from her forehead reflected the intense psychic concentration of operating the simulacrum of herself she had created inside the old conveyor system control shack. The small shack stood on steel latticework stilts seventy feet above the center of the quarry floor. Only the superstructure of the old conveyor system towered higher. Out of sight of the soldiers, inside the boarded-over control shack, the simulacrum moved with her rhythms. Increasingly, as she spun and kicked in her shadow-dance, it seemed an extension of her body. She sensed the green aura growing around the flickering black nothingness dancing in parallel in the control shack. In her mind-space, she could see through its eyes, hear through its ears. It felt disconcerting to be in two places at the same time, but the shadow-dance helped her adjust.

On her consciousness radar, held in another corner of her mind-space, the Beast's approach was very linear, a steady direction, a constant velocity, no finesse. He's showing me his power, she thought, he's going to come straight down that stream-bed in the fog. It won't be long at all now. It's time to get inside. Lara ran lightly from the center of the quarry to its west edge and into the bunker.

"What the fuck were you doing out there, Lara," Demuzzio yelled at her at she ran inside, "and why did you climb up in that goddamn control shack?"

"I left my sweater up there, TC. Got it good and sweaty, and left it on the chair, and left the door cracked. *Warlock* will go for it, just like he went for the sweat-band in the ape compound. I'm betting on it. And when he does, Colonel, you better blast that shack into oblivion. You may not even see him, so I'll tell you when." She smiled grimly at the two astonished men, and at the patent disbelief on the faces of the other soldiers in the bunker.

"Lara, that's just absolutely crazy. Why in hell would he climb up into that shack?"

"I don't know why, really, TC, I just know he will. I'm certain about this. I think maybe his nature gives him no choice. They used to kill tigers that way, you know. Dig a pit, fill it with sharp stakes, cover it over with branches and tether a goat in the middle. The tiger knew something was up, but he just couldn't walk away from the goat."

"This isn't an animal," Shaundee objected, "this is a highly intelligent trained killer! And your sweatshirt isn't you!"

"He'll go for it, Colonel. I'm sure of that. It's his nature. I can feel it. You should reconfigure your firing zones and move troops up higher on the ridge if you need to, so nobody catches any crossfire. Now don't distract me with any more questions, please, I need to concentrate."

Lara ignored their incredulity and moved to a clear space in the back of the bunker. Closing her eyes, she dropped back into the shadow-dance. Her hands weaved gracefully and her feet took short steps back and forth in the confined space. She tuned partially out of her real location in the bunker and into her simulacrum in the control shack, making the creation amplify her small motions. It's like matched tuning forks, she marveled. Start one vibrating and another one across the room will pick it up and start going too. Only these vibrations form an image, like a hologram, that I can control, and amplify or diminish. God, it would be such a beautiful thing, if the situation weren't so deadly.

"A couple of minutes, gentlemen," she announced quietly, "just a couple of minutes, now, I think." As she spoke, Lara hardened her soul to the coming destruction. By recalling the memory of the three agents sacrificed, she absolved herself in advance for what she clearly had no choice but to do. The dilemma of the combat soldier, John once told her in a rare moment of shared retrospection on his past, is not the necessity of killing, but that it gets a little easier each time. She'd hugged him, and instinctively told him as long as he realized that he was okay. A movement in her shadow-dance now inexplicably mimicked that hug.

Merton Shaundee studied her motions for a moment, then shrugged and turned toward the monitor bank. He reconfigured his firing zones, speaking instructions quietly into the command channel, following the troop position changes on the three-dimensional graphic playing across the big command monitor screen.

Flatbush Section of Brooklyn, NY | Tuesday 0130 EDT

The boy twisted uneasily under the sheets, and nearly woke in the struggle to get his left hand untangled. In his dream state, the threads of evolution, past and present, came alive out of his diagram, and unwound past him as he stood at their point of convergence, in their field of light. He needed both his hands to feel the threads, to discern their texture and structure, to comprehend their meaning. He sighed and tossed again in his dream, almost waking, but then drifting back.

Hamilton O'Donnell stood silently in front of the dining room table downstairs. His gray eyes stared at the boy's diagram, but his vision turned inward. A bright thread of green and a bright thread of blue rose from his vision of the diagram's meaning and wound around him, enticingly. Green and blue, the emerald green of the woods and fields and the amethyst blue of the sea, were the very colors of the wild coast of the Beare Peninsula, his ancestral home. He loved those colors, so brilliant in the sun, so lush in the frequent Irish rain. He wanted to reach out his mental hands to the threads, touch them, embrace them, help them, but could not. He existed in a different time and a different place now, where Heisenberg's uncertainty ruled, where he dared not perturb the exquisite balance of probabilities. Instead, the old man just sighed, and used his physical hands to make the ancient Celtic sign for warding off evil spirits and bad outcomes.

In the bedroom on the floor above, Joshua smiled in his dream and reached out to touch the green thread lovingly as it twined around him. His hands began to move slightly over the white sheets, small economical motions, mirroring those of his mother's in her shadow-dance, over a hundred miles north.

Global Consciousness Project, Princeton University, NJ | Monday 0130 EDT

Aaron O'Meara fidgeted in the seat of his van, exercising what little motion he had in his legs, verifying that the circulation was still working after his three-hour drive northward from his home outside Washington. It had been a pleasant interlude, full of phone conversations with Adrienne and Nathan. He felt pangs of fear when Adrienne described her violent mental contact with the Blue ET, but then was reassured when she related Sam Rosen's evaluation. Blue seemed capable of violence, but also seemed to be a moral personality. Most of the three-hour drive had been taken up by fascinating speculations about the nature and meaning of their respective brief encounters with the consciousnesses of Blue and Green. He smiled now at Adrienne's tone as she mother-henned him again for driving up from DC with a dense fog chasing him up the Turnpike.

"Oh, it's not too bad yet, Adrienne," he went back to a smile as he answered her concern, "visibility is a good quarter-mile, I'd say. I'm coming up on the Princeton exit in a few minutes, I should be at your place before it really socks in. Put fresh coffee on, would you please? I have a feeling this may be a long night."

"Okay, Aaron, fresh coffee. Then, we can argue our different hypotheses right up to the point where the answer becomes clear. But what if we never get an answer? Wouldn't that be awful?"

"Never get an answer? Mmm. Oh, I don't know, Adrienne." He glanced down at the screen of the laptop strapped to the van's center console, watching the Blue circles homing in on Green. "That just reminds me of what Voltaire said about making metaphysical or theological judgments."

"What's that, Aaron?"

"Doubt isn't an agreeable state, but certainty is a ridiculous one."

Her charming laughter ran down the highway with him, seeming to guide his way and part the fog ahead.

Chapter 34

A bilious green haze flickering around cacophonous blackness beat at the Magician's consciousness, trying to cloud his mind and senses as he flew the ultralight steadily onward into the trap. It carried an almost physical pain along with the psychic, but he ignored it, focusing instead on the smaller blips on his consciousness radar. Soldiers, many of them, blanketed the perimeter of the quarry. Their blips flickered with the passion of the hunt, tinged with red, the color of blood, the color of war. Tiny tendrils ran from each to the green darkness in their center: radials of a web, the trap.

The thrumming beat of the blackness shifted then, as if acknowledging that the Magician's discipline was proof against the confusion it sought to induce. The pulsations phased into a semblance of music: eerie, a minor key in some unknown scale, seductive. A siren-song, it passed through the Magician's mental discipline, aimed at a deeper, more primitive level of his being. He sensed it as a female spider, summoning the male to copulation and dinner. He would be the dinner. The morbid appeal clutched him, almost overpowering. The Other felt his response, both psychic and physical, and mocked him. Your response, she implied, is a conditioned reflex over which you have no control, and against which you have no defense. Come to me. You are mine. Come to me.

Oh, I'll come to you, all right, the Magician thought. But I'm not yours, not tonight. Tonight I'm coming in with my own spider. He loosed the Assassin, and primal rage blew outward. He felt the Other recoil from its power. In the brief respite this provided him from psychic seduction, he cut the aircraft engine and transposed down to a scrub oak tree overlooking the quarry. The ultralight flew on, held to its carefully pre-calculated glide trajectory by the gravity field he projected on it. The spider simulacrum squatted on the aircraft in his place, an iridescent horror in the moonlight, twitching with the rage he had invested in it. The Assassin would remain with the spider for a brief time, his psychic power serving the same function as the spider's physical form, a decoy.

The lacework of soldiers on his consciousness radar suddenly flared more brightly with sensed purpose and small arms fire erupted from the hillsides. The ultralight's propeller disintegrated along with the front of the engine cowling, but the wings and fuselage were not hit.

Ah, now that's very interesting, the Magician thought as he transposed down to the quarry floor. They hit what they shoot at, so they want to capture me, not kill me. The implications of what fate the Other might envision for a captive made him shiver. His intuitive analogy probably was accurate, he thought: copulate, then be eaten. All of me. Body, mind and soul. Well, that's actually good—if they have to be careful to disable instead of kill, that gives me a huge and unexpected advantage.

He shook off the shiver and drew the chaos cloak from the null field tightly around him. Running across the quarry floor, he dropped into a shallow ditch created by years of storm water runoff, the elevated shack barely visible in the thickening fog ahead of him. He ignored, momentarily, the pulsating obscenity waiting there, and concentrated on his spider simulacrum. A viewpoint from its eyes played across his mind-space. Another part of him viewed the movements of the soldier blips. A dozen troops were closing in on the ultralight crash site in the trees. The Magician ran his spider simulacrum straight at the three nearest soldiers.

Special Forces Exercise, Pisgah State Park, NH | Tuesday 0133 EDT

"Jesus," came the yell over the loudspeaker in the bunker, "it's a fucking spider!" Simultaneously, the fuzzy shape on the infrared band became more highly resolved, and the command staff in the bunker got a look at what the soldiers were seeing, a hairy monster with glittering eyes and huge drooling fangs. The spider pulled itself clear of the wreckage and looked at them balefully, through the shaking helmet-mounted camera of the squad leader.

Lara sensed the evil in it, the primeval rage. "Shoot it," she screamed, "kill it for God's sake! Now! Do it now!" The rattle of gunfire sounded as the Beast charged. It covered thirty yards in a heartbeat, and they had a momentary vision of slavering jaws before the viewpoint shifted as the thing leaped over the falling squad leader's camera and disappeared into the trees at the south end of the quarry.

"Pursuit," Colonel Shaundee ordered over the command channel. "Target attempting to break out the south perimeter, in the tree line. Look sharp down there!"

"No," gasped Lara, "no, no! That's a decoy! He's in the quarry!"

"Sergeant Major!" snapped Shaundee.

"Nothing, sir... ah correction, the anticoincidence logic is picking up a track, it'll take a moment for the computer to confirm, Colonel."

Lara trembled, and sweat sprang out in beads on her forehead as she moved within the shadow-dance. The primitive rage outside the bunker beat at her mind unmercifully.

"Confirmed, sir. Second target in the quarry. Anticoincidence tracked it in from the north end of the quarry, right off the ridge, headed due south. Looks like it separated from the main target, somehow." A dotted red line diverged from the solid one on the command screen, as the computer responded to his command to display the graphic.

"Help me out, Ms. Picard," Shaundee demanded, "I can't commit to both targets, my troops will end up shooting each other."

"Unnggh," she grunted with effort, "the quarry! The one in the quarry! He'll be in the control shack any second."

"South sector, collapse back into your perimeter position," Shaundee instructed the command channel, "ignore the spider, it's a decoy. I say again, ignore the spider."

"Fog's getting thicker fast out there, Colonel," the Sergeant Major noted anxiously, "especially at ground level. It's gonna screw up the anticoincidence circuits pretty soon."

"Do the best you can," Shaundee ordered. "Ms. Picard, can you give us position on the target?"

"He's in the quarry, climbing into the control shack," she answered through gritted teeth. The effort to keep her simulacrum intact against the psychic assault waves projected by the Beast began taking its toll.

"All right! If he's inside the quarry, then we got him!" Agent TC Demuzzio exulted, "he can't get out!"

"Then how did he get in?" Lara gasped the question at him, and promptly flew back against the table as if blown by an explosion. She recovered as her hip slammed into it, and somersaulted neatly over the table to land in a crouch that blended smoothly into her shadow-dance. Her eyes perceived two realities simultaneously: the shocked faces of the command team in the bunker, and the flickering black nothingness of the Beast, surrounded by an eerie glow of harsh blue light.

"Anticoincidence says action in the control shack, Colonel," the Sergeant Major announced edgily, "and the west perimeter squad is picking up some light flashes through the fog in that direction. Nothing on infrared, all around."

"Is he in the shack? Lara, can you hear me, is he in that control shack," Shaundee yelled at her.

Through her simulacrum, Lara Picard fought the blue-haloed darkness, moving in her shadow dance, waiting for an opening that didn't come. Her skill was equal, possibly greater, but she was losing ground to his massive strength. She heard Shaundee's question dimly, like an echo through earmuffs.

"Yes," she gasped, "the shack, for God's sake, blow it to pieces. Incinerate the bastard!"

"Negative, Colonel," TC countermanded sharply, "you have your orders, and they stand. We're going take him alive if we can."

Lara grunted as if struck by a kick in the ribcage. "TC, you fool, you don't know what you've got here! If you're not going to kill him, then by God I will!" She screamed in agony and frustration as she danced, laterally and erratically, toward the steel bunker door. Primal rage flared from the lower regions of her brain, flooding her mind and soul with the awful power that would be needed.

Colonel Merton Shaundee moved to intercept her, but a shove of her hand lofted his two-hundred-pound-plus frame across the room into the lap of the Sergeant Major. The table collapsed, and the picture on the command screen went to white noise then blank blue as the laptop computer slid down onto the floor. The communications console slid off on top of it, yanking the connector out of its battery pack.

As she reached for the handle of the bunker door, a grimacing and distraught TC Demuzzio pulled the taser pistol from his belt and shot her in the thigh. The high voltage hammered the response from her voluntary muscles immediately, and her body dropped to the floor. Desperately, a part of her mind summoned more of the primal rage, to continue operating her simulacrum in battle. A gasping drool poured from her mouth, along with blood from a bitten cheek, as TC squatted beside her and put his big hand on her shoulder.

"That's right, Lara," he said, painfully, "I don't know what I've got out there. But I don't know what I've got in here either. Rosen says you've been holding back on me. So, I'm sorry, but I can't take any chances. I hope you can forgive me later on."

A small part of Lara sensed his genuine sorrow through the red haze of her rage, but then she had to give all her waning energy to her simulacrum. It was purely defensive now, fighting an end game. Reality condensed down to a single point, her simulacrum's view of its dancing duel with blue-tinged black death.

"All right, Merton," Demuzzio yelled, "chew off the shack roof with rifle fire and force him down to the ground. I'll be waiting to take him." He opened the bunker door and dragged out Lara's inert form by the back of her vest, yanking her up the steps into the arms of the burly agents stationed outside.

"Get her the fuck out of here, right now, to the ambulance down the road. Cuff her in it hands and feet. Keep her face down in case she pukes. And stay with the goddamn plan; don't talk to her when she comes to!"

The agents dumped Lara unceremoniously into the back seat of the idling SUV and roared off downhill. Demuzzio jacked another dart into the taser pistol in his right hand. He hefted the TEC-9 in his left hand, safety off, and ran toward the girder base of the control shack, now barely visible in the closing fog.

A part of Lara's mind fought on within her paralyzed body as they barreled down the gravel access road toward State Route 119 and the waiting ambulance. But without being able to move in the shadow-dance, the end of the battle was at hand. She felt her simulacrum falter again, and collapsed its reality just in the instant before the Beast struck a final killing blow. Alone and helpless and now barely conscious in the back seat of the fleeing vehicle, the tears of the betrayed ran down her cheeks to darken the upholstery underneath.

Special Forces Exercise, Pisgah State Park, NH | Tuesday 0133 EDT

The Assassin pressed his advantage as he felt the Other weaken, her blazing green aura condensing tightly down around the shifting black emptiness. Now, he thought, now! Primal rage funneled outward from the lower regions of his brain, tightly channeled into the plane of pure blue energy in his right hand. He slashed downward through what was suddenly no resistance at all, and tore a gaping hole in the steel-and-plank floor of the shack. He crouched down and stared at it stupidly as the planks fell toward the ground below.

Flatbush Section of Brooklyn, NY | Tuesday 0133 EDT

Joshua tossed fitfully in the upstairs bedroom of the safehouse as his dream-vision of intertwining blue and green threads grew more complex, less amenable to analysis. Other threads wound around them in convoluted patterns, forming the tapestry that his sleeping mind had chosen to represent as the meaning in his diagram. The rational part of his mind struggled with it, but the intuitive part saw the point clearly: the species can actively and consciously participate it its own evolution. Probability would govern, but within the framework of chance were opportunities for direction, for a level of self-determination. The outcome could be good, or it could be evil. The boy suddenly wondered if such distinctions existed, or meant anything. He tossed again in his sleep, discomfited by the question.

Downstairs, Hamilton O'Donnell leaned over the dining room table, studying the diagram that Joshua had pieced together like a huge puzzle, pondering the possibilities it offered. Heisenberg's uncertainty made intervention impermissible for him, but not for Joshua. "I pray for you, boy," he murmured, again making the ancient Celtic warding sign to protect against evil spirits and bad outcomes. "And please remember that in us humans God and Satan may be Siamese twins."

In his bed upstairs, Joshua moaned as the blue and green threads moved apart, and seized them, one in each hand, to restore their symmetrical twining. But they weren't totally subject to his metaphorical hands. In the main they were probability functions, moving through time and space, and through other dimensions he didn't understand. His hands did all they could, lovingly, and then released the threads. They flared around each other, scintillating. But then the green thread winked out.

"Mom!" the boy cried out in his sleep, and reached a shimmering thread from his own hand back into the green thread's prior existence, and tied the two of them together.

Downstairs, his uncle's vision remained inward as he leaned over the diagram, not seeing it. His frown of concentration changed into a smile of approval.

"Ah, such a good lad you are, young Joshua O'Donnell," he told the diagram on the table. "A reverse umbilical cord you send out to your mum in her time of need. A tiny bit of determinism amidst the probabilities."

He sighed and rubbed his eyes, still smiling. Soon, he thought, it might be time to wake the boy for a journey north.

Special Forces Exercise, Pisgah State Park, NH | Tuesday 0134 EDT

The Magician, his thoughts connecting like lightning, suddenly realized he'd been fighting a phantasm, a surrogate. The Other had made her own decoy! And she hadn't been destroyed, he sensed, she had simply gone elsewhere! As if to proclaim that realization, the corrugated metal roof of the shack blew apart under a fusillade of automatic weapons fire, filling the air around him with flying debris.

He looked down, through the gap in the floor. A soldier in civilian clothes and a vest approached, weapons in hand.

He looked up, through the remains of the disintegrated roof. The overhanging superstructure of the conveyor system was barely visible above him, the moonlight still holding its image visible against the enveloping fog: a way out.

Another fusillade ripped into the upper part of the walls, forcing him closer to the floor. "Nice invitation, my old friends," he murmured, "but not tonight. You want me down on the ground, well then... here you go!"

The spider simulacrum reformed instantly at his command, dropped through the floor, and scuttled down the girders. The soldier fired immediately with the weapon in his right hand, from a distance of less than ten meters. Something pinged off the steel tower.

Compressed air burst, the Magician thought; so it's a dart, a taser or tranquilizer. They want me alive. He sent the simulacrum scuttling toward the soldier for a diversion. Then he transposed to the superstructure a hundred feet over his head, just before the fog totally occluded it. He immediately transposed from there to the scrub oak which stuck up like a lonesome sentinel into clear air above the fog layer on the north rim of the quarry. As he looked back over the bowl of dense fog behind him, he heard in the distance the echoing chatter of an automatic pistol. The soldier had reflexively defended himself against the attacking spider.

The Magician's consciousness radar showed the small red blips of his former colleagues, but no longer their interlocking relationship with the green darkness. That obscenity had vanished from his mind, totally gone.

He pondered what that might mean as he transposed away from the scene of battle. He moved northward and westward, jumping to ridgelines that still remained visible, headed in an erratic retreat toward Route 63. The fog continued to build, as moist air behind the warm front moved northward and condensed in the cooler, higher terrain around him.

Special Forces Exercise, Pisgah State Park, NH | Tuesday 0135 EDT

Lara's tears dripped onto the backseat of the fleeing SUV, but as the vehicle jounced down the quarry road, she felt her mind accept events and turn inward, calming.

Yes, good! Focus your mind; you can drive the toxins of paralysis from your body. This urgent response came from her *ki*, a dim and small apparition, seen through haze, as if at the end of a smoky tunnel. The symbols flowing across her reduced mind-space were fuzzy, but she grasped the concepts immediately. There would be a serious metabolic price, and dehydration, but, yes, she could do it! And it wouldn't take long. She gathered the remnants of her strength, and turned her mind inward. A subtle emerald aura began to flicker around her body, just as the SUV swung left out of the quarry access road onto Route 119.

"Al, what's that smell," the burly driver asked his partner, "she puke or what?"

An awful smell, Lara agreed, her senses beginning to reassert their sharpness. The sweat was literally flooding out of her pores, eliminating biochemical metabolites, cleansing her system. Give me another couple of minutes, boys, she thought, and I might just tie you both up in one bloody package and leave you in the middle of the road as a fuck-you message to my former friend TC Demuzzio.

She sensed the agent in the passenger seat turn to inspect her, and kept her eyes closed and body inert as a big hand patted down her back and hip. The touch tickled her killing rage, and she bridled it with difficulty.

"Jesus, she's soaked," he told the driver, and sniffed his hand. "And she's sweating like a pig. You wanna pull over? I think maybe we should check her vitals."

"No, we got our orders. We'll get her to the ambulance, let the medics handle it. If it wasn't for this goddamn fog, we'd be there by now."

Ah, so TC had this all pre-staged, Lara realized. The crummy bastard! So it's a short ride to the ambulance, is it? Well, I'm almost ready, boys. Energy and will flooded back into her at that thought, and she levitated a fraction of an inch off the seat as a test. Not anywhere near full capability, she saw, but it would do.

The vehicle slowed, and coming around a curve, the flashing strobes of the ambulance scattered their pulsating glow through the fog. Lara's left eye cracked open and its emerald light resonated briefly with the strobe glow pulsing through the windshield. Then her hands shot up to the door, unlatched it and pushed it open. She hurdled out of the vehicle and over the guardrail in an instant, cloaked in the null field, flying cautiously in the fog, threading between the trees downhill toward the river. A screech of tires accompanied the sound of gravel thrown from the road's shoulder by the skidding tires. A bramble patch tore at her, shredding fabric and ripping skin as she flew down the hillside. She paused at the river, pulled off the torn shirt and tossed it into the brush on the far side. The noisy descent of the agents sounded behind her, but she was a wraith in the mist, gone from the sight of her keepers.

Global Consciousness Project, Princeton University, NJ | Monday 0136 EDT

Adrienne Baxter gasped as the blue and green traces for the 1-minute integrals spiked offscale for GCDs in Bennington, Vermont and Concord, New Hampshire and Amherst, Massachusetts. Detectors as far away as Albany and New York City and Boston also registered respectable hits.

"Holy cow, Dr. Rodgers," she yelled over to him, "look at this! These puppies were building up and building up for the past hour or so, and then, two minutes ago, wham! Jeez, they're into it now!"

"Holy cow is right, Adrienne," Nathan replied fervently. "Can you compress the scale so we can see the top of the spikes?"

"Yessir. Here, I've gone to logarithmic, and... wow! The signal strength is thirty or forty times what went on in the Zoo. They've picked up strength, that's pretty clear. And keep in mind what we're looking at is a couple of minutes behind. Lord knows what's happening now!"

On those very words, the monitor displays incremented with the next 1-minute integral. But the signals didn't pick up strength at all: Blue dropped sharply, and Green flatlined. Adrienne felt her face go pale. Nathan exhaled explosively. Neither said a word, staring mutely at the monitors. The phone rang.

"Adrienne," Aaron O'Meara asked quietly, "are you seeing what I'm seeing? Does it mean what I think?"

Adrienne trembled, recalling the savagery that had erupted from Blue in their brief contact a few hours ago. The tremble carried over into her voice.

"Oh, God, I hope not, Aaron. I hope not."

Another 1-minute integral flashed up on the displays, with a minor spike on Blue, but Green remained flatlined.

"Shit! Shit, shit, shit," Adrienne cried, "Goddamn it, it's not supposed to be this way, I know it's not! This is just wrong!"

"Adrienne, Nathan," Aaron announced, "I'll catch up with you later. I just made a decision; I'm not getting off at the Princeton exit. In fact I just passed it. I'm heading north to intercept Blue."

"Aaron, no! You can't! Are you crazy? We don't know what's going on here! He could be dangerous!" Adrienne yelled into the phone, her voice cracking.

"That's exactly the point, Adrienne, exactly the point," Aaron told her calmly. "We don't know, and Blue could be dangerous. And he knows where you are. And if he's eliminated Green, then maybe he won't want to leave any traces, and maybe he'll be headed down this way, and maybe you'll be next on his list. I can't take that chance, I have to intercept him if I can."

Nathan and Adrienne stared at each other, aghast. He spoke first.

"Aaron, our elimination may or may not be a possibility, but you going north doesn't make any sense. First, you probably can't intercept him, unless he wants to be intercepted. And second, how could you possibly stop him, anyway?"

"Oh, I can intercept him all right, Nathan. With you folks as spotters I can easily get within a mile, and he had to be ten miles away when Adrienne contacted him. And stop him? Well, from what your friend Rosen said, Adrienne, Blue has a moral component. So I can probably jawbone with him, with his good side. And

I'm a pretty good jawboner, actually. Mom always said I could talk the ears off an elephant."

"Aaron, please! Take the next exit! You can loop back to Princeton from the north," Adrienne demanded anxiously. "It's too dangerous. What if you find Blue and he decides to eliminate you?"

Aaron smiled into the fog as he drove northward, and spoke softly back. "Well, then, that gives you some advance warning, doesn't it? You can run and hide, and get police protection, or something. Or you could shoot down to DC, maybe, and get some military or government protection."

Adrienne sat back in her chair, stunned. He would buy us time. Aaron would risk his life to buy us time! And he's never even met me! She basked in the warmth of his caring, reveling in it, only dimly aware of the practical interception logistics he was calmly discussing with Nathan.

"Repeat that again, Aaron, would you? Your cell phone's breaking up," Nathan yelled into the handset.

"Gotta... recharge... this thing... talk... later... later," the garbled reply came back.

"I love you, Aaron," Adrienne told him, suddenly desperate this man she'd never met—and now might never meet—know that unequivocally, before communication was lost, maybe forever. Bursts of garble and static interspersed the silence of no transmission, as she waited with the handset pressed hard to her ear. Then the reply came, in a clear voice, no static at all.

"I love you, too, Adrienne."

Adrienne Baxter hung up the handset with a soft smile, uncertain whether his reply had come via erratic cell phone relays or some means entirely different, but not caring in the slightest.

Chapter 35

The profane cries of dismay from her FBI keepers faded into the enveloping mist as Lara's flight path threaded downhill, toward the sound of water over rocks. This has got to be that stream the chopper flew over on the way in, she thought. That means it's flowing west and has to join the Connecticut River. And that means I can find Interstate-91, south of here somewhere. So, I'll put myself beyond your reach, Demuzzio, you miserable schmuck.

Betrayal ate at her. She realized that the man only had done what he thought he should, but paradoxically that just fueled her anger more. Now, clearly, she would have to set her own trap, without external help. Ham I can trust, she thought, and he can find a way to get John back. And John will know exactly what to do, how best to trap and kill this Beast.

Staying just a few feet above the stream's surface, Lara flew over some small rapids, and felt its cool splashes of foam. A bridge abutment loomed out of the mist.

"Okay," she muttered, "that bridge means a road, let's just check and see where I am in this damn fog, maybe I can pop out of it." She flared vertically upward, and immediately started to feel the resurgent cacophony of the Beast in her mind, a blue-tinged blackness pounding in her consciousness radar. Well north of her, past the Pisgah quarry, he was still hunting. She could almost taste the malevolence; it rolled over her in painful waves as she broke out of the fog at five hundred feet.

"So you didn't get him, did you, TC, you stupid schmuck," Lara screamed her frustration at the full moon. "All that planning, all those resources, all that firepower, and you didn't get him. You idiot! You goddamned idiot!"

Agony at the piercing sensations of the Beast in her mind drove Lara back down, into the mist, into a welcome diminishing of the throbbing blackness. She flew cautiously, slowly downward, finding the stream again by intuition rather than sight, and flew along two feet above its surface until it spilled into a bigger river, the Connecticut.

Now, she thought, now I've got more room for error. A wider river, I can go faster. She let her intuition guide her, seeing it as a sort of safety line pulling her along the proper path. To verify it, she flared up through the fog and down again to the river's surface several times.

That brought her to the clear realization that the pulsating sensations of the Beast were related to her altitude. The conclusion was inescapable, the deeper she was into the fog, the lower the level of that intrusive blue-tinged blackness in her mind. Why would that be? She directed the inquiry to her *ki*, in her mind-space.

Water is the essence of life. Microtubules in your brain's nerve cells contain water molecules that resonate with your psychic frequency. Fog is water droplets, very small. When it surrounds you, it shields you by making you seem more diffuse.

Symbology floated across her mind-space but was of little help, it was too arcane. The concept was clear, though: the thicker the fog, the more the shielding. She objected. After all, she had been able to sense the monster at a great distance.

This kind of sensing is a near-field effect. You also possess a far-field effect, which is an entirely different mechanism of sensing, non-local. The two can overlap. You have no metaphor developed enough to separate the two effects in your mind, so you see them both as one effect on your consciousness radar. You are much more sensitized to the near field at the moment, because of your contact, your recent battles.

Lara drew a parallel to what she knew of mathematical algorithms that modeled dispersion of pollutants in air or water, near a source and far away from a source. The concepts coincided, roughly, with the symbols in her mind-space.

Yes. The near-field effect follows more the traditional physics of this reality, which is why the signal can be attenuated. The far-field effect is of a different reality, it operates independent of distance, obeying only the premises of event simultaneity. The ability to distinguish the two effects will increase as your brain segments integrate.

Thought? Telepathy? Lara shoved a dozen questions into her mind-space, helter-skelter. What's the means of transmission?

Greater consciousness.

Oh! And you're part of it, aren't you? That greater consciousness? You're not just my own consciousness, with expanded awareness?

The answer floated into her mind space, slowly, indecisively. *In a way, Lara Picard. In the same way as I am a part of you.* Her *ki* smiled at her, a motherly smile, full of warmth and compassion. But troubled.

State Route 63, North of Hinsdale, NH | *Tuesday 0143 EDT*

The fog continued to wrap the Magician in its soft amorphous grasp, and he realized transposition was no longer an option. The level of fog had risen past the ridgeline, and even from its tallest tree he couldn't see any landmarks. There were no visual targets to which he could transpose.

The Other had suddenly been reborn into his awareness minutes ago, a green flaring of painful blackness on his consciousness radar. He felt her contemplation, baleful and angered; she was in pain. The Assassin reacted instinctively and instantly to her appearance in his mind, lashing out with waves of psychic destruction. He felt the recoil, and her backlash nearly knocked him from his tree perch. But then the strength of her presence in his consciousness dropped down just as suddenly as it had risen. Shortly after, cyclical waves of intense presence and then diminishment registered on his consciousness radar. The cycles made it difficult to judge, but he thought the thing moved south, away from him, fleeing.

Good, the Magician thought, climbing down the tree until he could see enough of the ground surface to transpose down. She's hurt, and I don't know why, but she's lost her Army support. She's just trying to get away. She's weakened, probably. So all I have to do is catch her before she can set up another trap, and it's all over.

He pulled a chaos cloak from the null field lightly around him. The questions ran through his mind as he ran south on Route 63. How could she disappear off my consciousness radar like that? Does that mean she can hide from me? Could I get ambushed? And how the hell did she do that simulation? I thought you told me I wouldn't be able to do that without a lot more practice and a higher skill level!

The image of Duc Li contemplated him in his mind-space, the usually bland face ridged with lines of concern and puzzlement.

The host selected by the Other must have a remarkable natural talent for creating deceptive imagery, John Connard, greater even than your Magician's talent.

More time to practice, too, while I traveled from South America?

Possibly. In any case, it is a demonstration of a present skill level significantly higher than yours, and another reason to end this quickly, before she becomes even more skillful. I judge that you still have the greater power; you can kill the Other if you can see through her deception.

The Other is hurt, weakened. If I could find her now, it would be all over pretty quickly, I think. But if she can hide from me, the advantage may go back to her. How did she drop entirely out of my mind?

Her mind may have been overwhelmed by the force of your attack, or possibly she was disabled by her own people, or possibly both.

A traitor in the ranks of her Army support? So she doesn't have total control? Somebody exposed her for what she is? Or her behavior gave it away? Which would explain why none of the troops are with her now, so that's plausible. But why is her presence cycling up and down on my consciousness radar? How is she concealing herself? Can she shroud her signal entirely? That would be troublesome, to say the least.

It appears that fog is obscuring the signal.
What! How can that be?
Water is the basis for life on your planet. Quantum coherence exists in molecules of water, inside cellular structures of nerves in your brain. This physiology is the basis for your sensing ability.
So, fog being small water droplets, it suppresses what? The signal generated? The receiving ability?
Both, in a sense. The quantum coherence generates a hologram of you, which resonates within a larger matrix. This resonance is damped by the fog.

Symbology floated across John's mind-space, connoting similarities to transmissions of certain wavelengths through the atmosphere. He intuited that a fog as dense as this one indeed would be a significant damper, although the mechanics involved were beyond his grasp. But it didn't explain why he previously could sense her at a greater distance. The riddle floated into his mind-space.

Your mind is presently too constrained by your schooling in the sciences and mathematics of this physical reality. It will take time to achieve the mental and psychological release required to step past these constraints, and to integrate your brain segments. That is probably several days away yet. For now, it would be best just to accept what is.

Several days. He would be successful by then, he thought, or be dead.

Connecticut River at East Northfield Station, MA | Tuesday 0159 EDT

Lara flew down the Connecticut River, two feet above the surface, and passed from New Hampshire into Massachusetts unseen in the fog. The last burst of rejected metabolites exuded from her skin, and she wrinkled her nose in distaste. Suddenly she couldn't stand it. Slowing her flight, she dropped into the water to rinse off the smell of betrayal.

"Hoo-wee!" Lara gasped as the cold water shocked her. She flew out of the water and then dipped back in, rolling around to let the river wash her everywhere. Like a porpoise, she dipped in and out, still moving down-river, learning that she could fly as well underwater as through the air, if a bit more slowly.

Belatedly, the realization caught up with her: when I'm underwater, the signal is totally gone! Not just damped down, totally gone, the near-field effect anyway. She excitedly asked her *ki*, in her mind-space.

That is true. Rain or fog will attenuate the near-field signals, but immersion in liquid water will damp them out entirely.

Why didn't you tell me before?

There is little practical utility in it. You cannot stay underwater for long without equipment.

But it's a potential escape mechanism! It's good to know! You should have told me!

I am you, Lara Picard, I need not tell you things you already know.

Lara considered that for a moment. It was true; at some very instinctive level, she had somehow known exactly what water would do. Early primates had probably jumped into a river to avoid a big predator. They had certainly used streams to avoid leaving a scent trail for animals tracking them.

With the residual effects of the taser purged from her system and the sharpness of her perceptions returning, Lara studied the muted image of the Beast on her consciousness radar. She periodically flew upward into thinner fog to gauge his location better. Nine or ten miles due north, she finally estimated, and clearly following her. Not gaining, particularly, but she wasn't pulling away much, either.

"I've got to pick up more ground," Lara muttered to the wavelets beneath her flying form, "I need distance, time to get to Ham."

The lonesome sound of a train whistle gave her the answer, just as the diffuse glow of its headlamp appeared through the fog. She angled off instantly to the right, toward the west bank of the river, and saw the train coming in from the southwest.

Okay, she thought, that's a decent possibility. If I follow the tracks, I'll still have a southward vector, away from the beast. And Interstate 91 can't be too far west, so I'll just zip down these tracks and hitch a ride. That'll be faster than flying down the river; I won't have to watch where I'm going. And it'll conserve my strength. If he catches up, I'm going to need all of it.

As the train passed an embankment on the river's edge and followed the curved tracks northward, Lara Picard flew back along the way it had come, heading south and west. With the shiny surface of the steel rails as a better guide through the fog, she picked up speed until her eyes began to tear.

An owl, perched in a dead oak above the tracks, sensed the fleeting wraith and unfurled his wings in momentary alarm, but then settled back with a hoot of defiance at this odd disturbance to his nightly hunt.

State Route 63, South of Hinsdale, NH | *Tuesday 0231 EDT*

The Magician passed unnoted through the tiny hamlet of Hinsdale, all its residents tucked in and sleeping. He saw the sign for the boat ramp, and angled immediately down the small road. It had to be the same boat launch area he'd flown the ultralight over. So his car would be close by, a few hundred meters uphill from the west bank of the river.

Loping like some graceful big cat, he ran down the road and off the boat ramp into the chill waters of the Connecticut River. With no break in his body's rhythm, and ignoring the disorienting effect of limited visibility and the ambiguous boundary between the water surface and the dense fog, John Connard swam strongly westward. Within a few minutes he struck a rocky shore and climbed up the rip-rap near the north end of the air strip.

Now, twelve minutes later, he was toweled off, in dry clothing, sitting in the car, and studying the road map on his laptop computer. Effortlessly, his mind analyzed the sequence of distances and directions where his consciousness radar had placed the Other over the past hour, and referenced those to his own location on the road map. Time markers and extrapolated positions flowed easily into his mind-space, and he mentally superimposed them onto the laptop screen.

"So, she came west on 119 out of the quarry, and then south on 63 down into Massachusetts through Northfield," he muttered to the laptop. "And now she's headed more westerly, so that's got to be Route 10, because she crossed the river. Which means she's got wheels, and picked up ground on me."

Fifteen to eighteen miles an hour had been her average speed headed south, he estimated, but now, headed southwest, it seemed like she'd picked up speed. She would intersect Interstate 91 in a few minutes. Then, the Magician thought, almost certainly she would take it south, away from him.

"Fog's got to be thinner away from the river," he muttered as he started the car, "so I'm better off going back north into Brattleboro and picking up the Interstate there." His mind chafed at the thought of driving in a direction away from his quarry, even for a short time, but the back-scattered glow of his headlights off the dense fog confirmed it as the prudent decision. He turned the car northward.

Later, with two large coffees and a pile of pastries from the diner in Brattleboro, his decision had been made moot: the fog was now uniformly dense everywhere. John pounded the steering wheel in frustration. Safe speeds were only twenty to thirty miles per hour, the radio said. It would be a long chase. Eating pastry and drinking black coffee, John Connard pressed the limits of visibility as he drove southward on Interstate 91 in the fog. The meteorological obstruction to his vision paralleled the psychic obstruction to his spirit, the two riding in tandem with the Magician down the highway.

Interstate 91 Rest Stop at Bernardston, MA | Tuesday 0240 EDT

"I can't thank you enough for picking me up, Wally," Lara smiled at the burly bearded trucker. The man tried to focus on the fog-shrouded Interstate, but his eyes kept flicking to the chilled nipples pressing through her sports bra. He sought to conceal his admiration of her fine shape, but was losing the battle.

Ah, men, Lara thought. Nipples. Well, what the hell, it's leverage, and I need the ride. She patted the shirt on the console between them.

"Mind if I put your sweatshirt on, Wally? I think I'm pretty much dried off now." She bent her head into the heat streaming from the dashboard vent of the small box truck and ruffled her hands through her short hair one last time. The diffuse light reflected back through the windshield by the fog played over the toned muscles of her shoulders as she leaned forward.

"Sure. Here ya go," he croaked from a suddenly dry throat, handing her the shirt. The right tires of the truck caught the rumble strip briefly as Lara stretched forward to pull the shirt over her head. She heard him sigh as the view was covered over and he went back to watching the road unwind through the fog.

"So, tell me again, Lara," the trucker asked, "you swam the river from Northfield and ran down the railroad tracks, which must be five miles, at least, and you think your rotten ex-husband is *still* gonna be on your tail?"

"Oh, yeah, Wally," she replied, "definitely. He's very smart, very resourceful. I've got to get as far away as I can, as fast as I can, until I can get to a safe place with some protection. I need to call my uncle, he'll help me work it out. May I use your car phone?"

Wallace Lockerby unclipped the phone from the dashboard and handed it to her.

Lara smiled at him again and dialed Hamilton O'Donnell's cell phone number, hoping he'd kept it with him as he promised. She exhaled with relief as his familiar Irish lilt answered almost immediately.

"Ham," she said quietly into the phone, "I need your help. I'm in a truck, southbound on I-91 in northern Massachusetts. Coming into the... Greenfield area, it looks like. Where are you now? Is Josh with you?"

She listened intently, amazed as always at the man's rapid grasp of nuances and his extraordinary intuition for situations.

"Yeah," she answered finally, "definitely overseas. Thank you for that idea. I really do think I'm better off getting out of the country, into a protected place, since I can't count on my former friends to help out any more. And I need John back, desperately. Can you make that all happen?"

She listened intently again, then addressed Lockerby.

"You said you're making a delivery in New Haven, Wally? Do you know where Tweed New Haven Airport is? Can you drop me there?"

He nodded yes, astonished.

"Okay, Ham," Lara spoke into the cell phone. "We're doing about 30 miles an hour in this miserable fog, so we're maybe two-and-a-half or three hours from New Haven, I guess, unless the weather clears up. But Wally says the radio's reporting the whole east coast is socked in and probably will be until after sunrise. If you and Josh leave now, it'll take you about the same amount of time to make New Haven from New York, I think."

She listened again, and smiled.

"You can do that? And you've got the passports? Oh, Ham, you're incredible. And the fog won't matter, then, will it? The plane will be all warmed up and pre-flighted and we'll just be on our way to Cork and Kenmare? That's great! See you in New Haven."

She clicked off the phone and handed it back to Lockerby.

"Wally," she told him, smiling, "everybody should have an uncle like that. That man is just pure magic. Better even than a fairy godmother. We're going to his family home in Ireland. Right from the airport in New Haven."

Her relief must have been palpable. Lockerby smiled along with her as they drove slowly southward in the dense fog.

Global Consciousness Project, Princeton University, NJ | Monday 0242 EDT

Adrienne would rarely raise her voice to any senior she respected, but she raised it now to Nathan Rodgers. It wasn't that he was wrong; it was just that so much uncertainty made it impossible to judge the risk.

"Adrienne, you'll be okay here by yourself," he said, totally misjudging the reason for her objection. "Campus Security is right down the street, and there's a town police substation a half-mile off campus."

"Nathan! I'm not worried about me; I'm worried about you!" She was too upset to realize she had finally breached her self-imposed etiquette by calling her boss by his first name.

Nathan Rodgers smiled approvingly at the informality. It was long overdue, he thought.

"Adrienne, I'll be okay. And it truly makes sense for me to follow Aaron north and help him out. I can get around much more easily than he can, at least on foot. And with two of us, we can converge on a location and maybe identify the signal source much faster than one person. It just gives us a whole lot more flexibility. And if Blue decides to go after one of us, well then, we've probably got additional time to warn you." Nathan reflected more on his thought process. "And besides, now that we're picking up Green again, maybe it wasn't a battle after all. So maybe it's safer now."

Ah, shit, he's right, Adrienne admitted to herself as his logic beat down her emotions. She took in a deep breath, and her shoulders dropped in acquiescence as she let it out.

"Okay. But be careful, okay? Please, Nathan? Promise?" She ran over and hugged him tightly and kissed him on the cheek, another breach of etiquette. But in the months of their collaboration she'd grown to respect and love this man, who in many ways had become the father she'd never gotten to know.

Nathan hugged her back, then held her shoulders and smiled into her eyes.

"I promise, Adrienne. I promise. And I'll stay in phone contact regularly, just like Aaron." Then he turned, picked up his jacket and laptop computer, and left the GCP Center, walking purposefully across the fog-shrouded campus parking lot to his car.

Adrienne pulled up the bottom of her sweatshirt and rubbed it over her wet eyes, sighing. Then she walked over to her monitoring station. Back to business, she thought. Keep my mind busy. That's the best thing I can do. Support these guys with all the smarts I've got. She moved the monitors closer together and sat down in the chair to consider them. On the left screen, overlapping 15-minute blue location circles tracked away from the New Hampshire woods where Blue and Green had come together so dramatically an hour ago. On the right screen, a green circle for the time period right after the encounter was missing, but the subsequent circles also tracked away from that place, headed south.

Adrienne tapped a pencil absently against her chin as she mentally reviewed the recent events. No, I don't believe that New Hampshire event was the endpoint, she thought. Something else is going to happen. Yes. She definitely sensed something else, but what, and when, and for God's sake, why? What does it all mean? Her hands moved slowly toward the keyboard, preparing to search for answers. Then they moved back, and she hugged herself against the shivering induced by her questions.

Chapter 36

Hamilton O'Donnell clicked off his cell phone and breathed a sigh of relief that Lara Picard was safe. His vision blurred with dampness and his forefinger trembled a little as he traced it along the conditional probability sequences in Joshua's diagram. If A happens, then B's chances are improved from fair to good. If A doesn't happen, B's chances are truly a longshot. He sighed at the inescapable rigors of evolution. Probability was such a necessary evil.

"Ah, Doctor O'Donnell, I thought I heard voices." Agent Jack Socrates smiled as he walked into the dining room. "Can't sleep until you figure out what the boy has done here? Well, good luck. It's way beyond me, that's for sure."

The man's dangerous, Ham thought, he moves way too quietly for someone that large. If he overheard the phone conversation... well, it doesn't really matter at this point, does it?

"Ah, Agent Socrates! Yes, the boy's concepts are quite subtle. Quite difficult to understand. Here, take a break from your guard rounds, make yourself comfortable. Let me use you as a soundin' board while I talk my way through some of this for just a few minutes?" He waved at a chair, and smiled invitingly.

The big agent sat down and rested his chin on his hand, staring at the diagram on the table in front of him, then looked up expectantly.

"Agent Socrates," Ham began, his voice a soft soothing that immediately insinuated itself at an elemental level of the agent's consciousness, "do you believe in altered states of reality?"

The agent nodded his head, keeping time with the metronomic pacing of the words. A friendly numbing warmth enveloped him and his head nodded down onto the tabletop with a comfortable snore. Ham patted him on the shoulder affectionately and walked lightly upstairs to place Agent Carl Schmidt into the same altered state. Then he woke the boy.

"Brush your teeth and pee, me lad, and it's off we go to meet your mum. Flyin' off to Ireland, we are, possibly."

Joshua yawned at his uncle blearily, pulled reluctantly out of his dream. Then he grinned up at the old man.

"Possibly, Uncle Ham? You mean you don't know?

"Life is all possibilities, me lad. Some of them are beyond your poor ould uncle to know. Hurry now, I've called a cab."

"Our FBI friends are not taking us?"

"Ah, no, lad. Just you and meself. On our own now, we are. The Bureau is... umm... no longer involved. It appears your mum has dismissed them. Hurry now, I have your diagram and computer and bag all waitin' by the front door."

Joshua did as his uncle instructed, pulling on his clothes and running directly downstairs to the open front door, the sleeping agents never coming into his field of view.

"Uncle Ham," he said as the cab pulled away from the curb, "when you woke me up, I was dreaming, and it felt like I was actually working in the dream. I was an artist, weaving a tapestry, or part of it. It seemed very real, or at least that what I was doing could have some kind of expression in reality. What do you suppose that means?"

"Ah, young one, a dream-workin' is it? In my Gaelic pagan heritage those myths go far back in time, very far back. And come to think of it, they are not limited to the Gaelic culture, nor to any other, particularly. They are universal. Which, possibly, means they are not myths at all."

"Possibly?" Joshua peered at his uncle intently, half-grinning, half-frowning.

"Possibly," the old man affirmed.

Global Consciousness Project, Princeton University, NJ | Tuesday 0250 EDT

Adrienne's fingers paused over the keyboard. A multitude of possibilities flew around in her mind. Some were good. Some were bad. But one of them was going to become reality. Something big, good or bad, a deep-down certainty told her. She sighed and pushed back in her chair as the phone rang.

"Yo, Adrienne," Sam Rosen greeted her, "I've been staying up, watching your Blue and Green activities, you got a minute to talk?"

"Oh, sure, Doctor Rosen, I'm just trying to figure out what to do next, and I wasn't really getting anywhere. Heck of a show, wasn't it?"

"What do you think that crazy interaction means, Adrienne? Green had me worried for a while, disappearing like that. She hurt, do you suppose? Unconscious? Hibernating? How does this event affect your three hypotheses?"

"Doctor Sam, when Aaron first saw Green drop off, he thought it confirmed his battle hypothesis, and that she lost the fight and got wiped out. But now he's not so sure."

"Okay, remind me again, Adrienne; Aaron is your astrophysicist contact at

Goddard, the one who's keeping the government plugged in, right?"

"Yes sir, Aaron O'Meara, he's relaying everything we figure out back to Goddard."

"You mean Aaron is with you guys? He drove up there in this fog? The whole east coast north of Virginia is socked in."

"Well, he was coming here, and he was right at our exit on the Turnpike, but when he saw what happened to Green at one-thirty, he just kept on going north. Right now, he's creeping along in the fog, a little north of New York City, I think. He wants to try to intercept them, or at least be there when they come together again."

"Is he getting direction from Goddard, or somebody else in government, do you know, Adrienne?"

"Oh, no, sir, he hasn't heard anything back from them. The information has been all one way, just emails, with an acknowledgment receipt. The reason he went north was to protect me." Her voice softened at the recollection. "When this is all over, whatever it is, he wants to have a talk with Blue, to make sure his good side is in control, that he won't come after us."

Rosen Household, Alexandria, VA | Tuesday 0255 EDT

Sam Rosen, sitting in his home office in Virginia, had difficulty sequencing his rampant thoughts. He ran a hand nervously through his thinning hair.

"Adrienne, Aaron knows that could be dangerous, right? You've told him about your mental interaction with Blue, the vicious response you got?"

"Oh, yes, he knows. He said that if the creature is really nasty and kills him, that would give me some warning, and buy time to escape, or get protection."

Whoa! Things are definitely not adding up here, Rosen thought. His grip on the phone tightened as Adrienne's answers belatedly sunk in. One Lone Ranger government scientist was headed north in a fog to talk to an ET that could be savage and deadly? Where was his protection? Where were the police, the Bureau, the Army troops? What the hell was TC thinking? He took a calming breath, and a roundabout approach.

"Adrienne, do you know if Aaron arranged any kind of support, any police or military? Does he have any help?"

"No, sir, I don't think so. I can ask, when he calls in, but I don't think so. Once Green came back online, we weren't nearly as worried. Of course, Nathan is still concerned a bit, so he left a few minutes ago. He's going to try to catch up with Aaron before Blue and Green converge again; to see if he can help."

The psychiatrist was nonplussed. Now it's the Lone Ranger and Tonto? He ran his hand through his hair again and massaged the tension in his neck.

"Adrienne, let me be sure I understand this. Green is in northern Massachusetts. Blue is in… southern Vermont, it looks like. And they're both headed south, probably on Interstate 91. Aaron O'Meara is past New York City, headed north on Interstate 95 to intercept them. Nathan Rodgers is behind him, maybe an hour or so, depending on the fog. And you're in the Global Consciousness Project Data Center in New Jersey, keeping track of all this. Is that accurate? You're going to do the tracking, help position Aaron and Nathan for an intercept?"

"Yes, sir, that's about it."

"So do you know, Adrienne, how much the government is involved in any of this? Or is all you know just that you've kept them aware and updated, through emails to Aaron's outfit at Goddard?"

"Well, sir, we assume the government is involved with Green, because she was at a Marine Corps base and moving around by helicopter. I guess we don't know much that's happening outside our little group, but everything we know, plus what opinions we've developed, have been sent along to Goddard. Aaron's been very good about that. So the government knows everything we know."

"But you never got anything back, Adrienne? No phone calls, no emails asking for more information?"

"No sir, but our emails were acknowledged. We talked about doing something more, like maybe calling a different agency, but Aaron says his boss at Goddard is one of the sanest people in government. And besides, who else would you call for something like this?"

Her voice seemed a little defensive to the psychiatrist.

"Well, anyway, that's what we did, Doctor Sam," she continued. "Were we wrong, do you think?"

"Umm. No, Adrienne, I probably would have done exactly the same thing in your situation."

But of course I'm in a totally different situation, aren't I, Rosen realized. And all of a sudden I've got the big decision. Lara Picard probably *is* in real danger of some sort, even if I'm not sure what. With local ground control, those Special Forces choppers can fly in almost any kind of weather, but Green is moving at car speed for a foggy highway, not helicopter speed. And Blue is on her tail, moving at car speed too. Maybe the trap worked just fine, and maybe I'm totally misinterpreting all this, but probably it didn't work. Sure looks like Blue and Green are on the loose, driving down Interstate 91.

And what's worse, he thought, as his methodical mind unraveled earlier preconceptions, I automatically assumed TC knew all about this ET thing, but maybe he doesn't. A lot of key communications get lost in government channels. Maybe the guy at Goddard thinks poor Aaron O'Meara has gone round the bend and is dropping all his emails in the trash basket. Or maybe he's shooting them over to the Bureau or the Pentagon and they're dying of laughter over there. So maybe TC doesn't know anything about this ET connection. Maybe he still thinks he's trying to trap a human superspy, this *Warlock.*

His long pause unsettled Adrienne. "Doctor Sam? Are you still there?"

"Yes, Adrienne, sorry, I'm just trying to think through some of this logically. To answer your question again: yes, I think you did the right thing. You passed along all the information. So don't worry about it," he added comfortingly, "you've done everything you should have. And listen, I've got to go now, but you call me at this number if anything bad happens, or if you need help. Okay?" He gave her the number of the cell phone in his hand.

"Okay, sir, I will. Thank you. Bye."

Well, the fog over the East Coast is fucking apropos, Rosen thought as he put down the cell phone. We're probably all in some kind of fog; nobody knows what the hell is really going on here. He picked up his office phone and dialed the Bureau's duty officer.

"This is Sam Rosen," he barked his identifier code at the agent who answered, "patch me into TC Demuzzio, please. This is a Category 5 situation. Patch me in right now!"

I-278 to LaGuardia Airport, Queens, NY | Tuesday 0321 EDT

Joshua watched his uncle, across from him on the seat of the cab, make calls on his cell phone. He focused all his mental resources on his uncle's words, but to no avail. Most likely they were some dialect of Gaelic, based on intonation and cadence, but few of the words were ones that he recognized. One thing seemed clear, though: his uncle was giving instructions to the party on the other end of the call. Hamilton O'Donnell caught his nephew's gaze and winked at him, without interrupting his stream of instructions.

Finally he hung up. "Ah, Joshua, me lad, 'tis a fog here that would do justice to me ould homestead on Coulagh Bay. Requires consideration of several contingencies, all taken care of, I hope." He patted the cell phone and slipped it back in his shirt pocket. "Now where did we leave off in our little metaphysical peregrination of last evenin', umm?"

Joshua considered the man carefully. My uncle really does look like a lepre-chaun on some days, he realized. And he sure acts like one when he evades a question before I can even ask it. So that's probably all the explanation I'm going to get about the language he was using, or what he was arranging just now. Nothing. Zippo. So why bother? I'll take him up on the mind-dance offer. Even though he remembers exactly where we left off, and probably why.

"We left off at genomic repair jobs, Uncle Ham; course corrections for evolu-tionary development. You liked the idea."

"Oh yes, lad, thank you, I recall now. Our genome is busily evolvin' a better interconnection between the three brains in our poor ould noggins? Would that be right?"

"As I recall," Joshua agreed, affecting a reciprocal nonchalance.

"And your dreams, me lad, that you had after our little discussion, after you went to sleep, your dreams of threads and weavin', and a tapestry, and your dream-wor-kin' of that tapestry... hmm?" His voice trailed off invitingly.

The boy played his mind back through their midnight conversation, the thoughts he'd had while falling asleep, and the beginnings of the dream. Looked at retrospectively, they sequenced into each other seamlessly. The threads and the weaving and the tapestry were metaphors for the concepts in his diagram, dream-constructs that his mind could better understand, but their point was obvious.

"Oh!" he exclaimed, laughing.

"Oh?" prompted his uncle.

"Uncle Ham, I believe maybe we're in charge of our own course corrections. I think maybe the human race can intervene in our own evolution. Maybe pretty directly."

"Well, of course, me lad; that's hardly a secret. Advances in the biological sci-ences make it inevitable, do they not? Mappin' the human genome. Understandin' it. Manipulatin' genetic structure is not so very far away. Medicine seems about to make a quantum leap."

The boy rejected his uncle's red herring, bluntly. "No, Uncle Ham, you know I don't mean anything mechanistic. You saw my diagram. You know what I'm talk-ing about."

"Ah, yes, boy, guess I do. Consciousness affectin' evolutionary development, is that it?"

"Group consciousness, racial consciousness, greater consciousness, whatever it is, however it develops, Uncle Ham; that's what's in charge of the feedback loops and the feed-forward loops in my diagram!"

"And this consciousness, boy, what would it look like, taste like, smell like?

What would be its characteristics, do you think? Would it be intelligent?"

"Yeah!"

"Would it learn?"

"Sure! Trial-and-error, Uncle Ham. Darwin."

"Would it evolve?"

"Oh, yes! Definitely! To deal with our increasing complexity."

"Would it interact with us?"

"Oh, yeah, Uncle Ham! It has to!"

"So it's participatory?"

"Gotta be!"

"Ah, yes, boy. So said me ould friend Edgar Mitchell."

The taxi turned at that moment under the arc lights in front of a private commercial airplane hangar at the outskirts of LaGuardia Airport. The brightness masked the turquoise aura flaring around Joshua O'Donnell, a glow that reflected palpable excitement at his moment of *satori*.

"It's wonderful, Uncle Ham! It's wonderful!"

"And dangerous, Joshua?"

Recognition clicked over in the boy's mind.

"Yeah, Uncle Ham. Of course you're right," he replied, his aura dimming down, "wonderful, but dangerous too."

Special Forces Exercise, Pisgah State Park, NH | Tuesday 0322 EDT

FBI Special Agent TC Demuzzio was having a bad morning. The trap had failed. Both Lara and *Warlock* had vanished without a trace. Visibility had degraded to near-zero in the quarry, and reportedly over the entire surrounding area. The Special Forces search teams, hampered by the fog, reported no sightings on visual or infrared. Any pursuit was effectively cut off.

To add to the insult, Demuzzio was bent over a table with an Army medic carefully picking slivers of wood and metal from his buttocks. He'd stumbled backward and sat down hard in debris from the blown-away control shack when the phantom spider had charged him. Colonel Merton Shaundee might have found this humorous, had he not himself been nursing bruises from being flung carelessly across the room by a woman half his weight. The two men were trading ideas on possible next steps when the signal came in on the command channel. The Sergeant Major took the call, glanced at Demuzzio's twisted grimace, shrugged, and passed him the handset.

"Agent Demuzzio, it's your HQ duty officer, says he's got a Cat 5 from a Doctor

Sam Rosen, with the right authentication, suggests you take it, even if you are... indisposed."

"Now what the fuck?" Demuzzio barked into the handset. "Yeah, yeah, patch him through," he added, with a discomfiting sense that the bad morning was about to turn worse.

"TC, this is Sam Rosen," the tinny voice sounded, "are you by any chance no longer in control of our subject?"

"Aargh!" Demuzzio grunted partly in frustration and partly because of the extraction of a particularly long sliver, "how the fuck would you know that, Sam?"

"And you don't have *Warlock* either, I take it?"

"Yeah, doc, that's right," Demuzzio replied, dangerously subdued, "and you fucking well better tell me how you know this! Right now! Has Lara called you?"

"No, TC, she hasn't. Just answer one more thing, and I'll tell you all I know. Did you get any calls or emails or any kind of information from anybody at Goddard Space Flight Center or the Pentagon about an event on Sunday morning that possibly could have been... ah... could have involved... umm... extraterrestrial visitors?"

"Owww! Shit, doc that hurt! For crissakes shoot some more fucking Novocaine in there," Demuzzio yelled as another long sliver came out.

"TC, what did you say? Novocaine? I'm not following."

"No, not you, Sam. I'm getting some first aid here. Without enough freakin' anesthetic. Extraterrestrials? ETs? No. Nobody's told me shit about ETs, Sam. Not Goddard. Not the Pentagon. Not the Bureau." The agent's eyes blinked at the sting of the Novacaine needle. Well, he thought, why not? Why the hell not? Nothing else makes any sense. "All right, Sam. Tell me your goddamn ET story."

"Okay, TC. You better sit down and make yourself comfortable, this could take more than a few minutes. And you should record it too, I suppose. Is this a secure line?"

Demuzzio grimaced at the thought of sitting down. "Yeah, yeah. Line's secure. All the duty desk calls are recorded automatically. I've got Colonel Shaundee and his command crew here, I'm gonna put you on the squawk box. I'm reminding everybody this is a top secret classification. Go ahead, Sam, lay it on us. And it fucking well better be good."

The psychiatrist spoke to them slowly, with proper care and precision in his scientific language, about recent revelations from one Adrienne Baxter at the Global Consciousness Project in Princeton, New Jersey. He started with the event first noted by the SDI exercise team at Goddard, and worked forward in time. Demuzzio interrupted him only once, with a request to repeat the URLs for the ET tracking outputs on the Project's website.

Twenty minutes later, he concluded with his opinion that the so-called Green ET was attached to or in the persona of one Lara Picard, presently in north central Massachusetts. Based on the time-sequenced location plots from the Global Consciousness Project website, she was headed south, most probably in a vehicle on Interstate-91, speed limited by the poor visibility that blanketed the northeast coastal states. The so-called Blue ET, attached to or in the persona of one *Warlock*, or some other high-capability soldier or agent, was just now entering Massachusetts. He appeared to be following her on the same highway, about twenty minutes behind.

Dead silence greeted the end of Sam Rosen's exposition. Finally, he said, "That's it, TC. That's my briefing. That's all I know at this point."

"Thank you, Doctor Rosen," TC Demuzzio said, unconsciously adopting the psychiatrist's formality for the record, "good briefing. Very good." Then he started laughing, a choking, braying, quasi-hysterical release, laden with invective, ending with a sob. "Ah, God help me, Sam. An ET. Yeah, it fits. It's the only fucking thing that fits. No wonder she couldn't tell me."

"You okay, TC?" Rosen asked him quietly.

"Ah, shit, Sam. I've known that girl for years. She's a wonderful person. A great mom. She came to us for help, and I fucked it up. Oh, Lord Jesus, I fucked it up." He sobbed again. Merton Shaundee squeezed his shoulder in sympathy.

I-95 East of Mount Vernon, NY | Tuesday 0346 EDT

"Much is foretold in fable and myth, me lad." An elliptical answer, Joshua thought, to his questions about global consciousness, racial memory and the remarkable persistence of similar archetypes down through various cultures.

The boy stared out over the long hood of his uncle's Edsel convertible into fog-shrouded Interstate 95 outside of New York City. His earlier question about how the Edsel had come to be moved from Georgetown to a private aircraft hangar at LaGuardia had been met with a chuckle and a statement that good planning was a necessary ingredient for success. Hell of a mind-dance to start the morning off, the boy thought. My uncle is being particularly obscure.

"Joshua, me lad," the old man continued cheerfully, "in some of the Eastern religions, as well as in me poor Gaelic heritage, dream-workin's are seen as a means to desired outcomes, to fulfillment. A tapestry is but the image your mind creates to better define what it seeks."

The boy pulled his legs up onto the seat of the Edsel, and squirmed into a lotus position within the seatbelt. His eyes closed as he quieted his mind and returned to meditation. His consciousness chased back into the dream, trying to illuminate it with the new hints from his uncle. Threads. Tapestries. Energies moving toward fulfillment. Participatory energies.

All of us are just evolutionary possibilities, Joshua speculated, and thus subject to the laws of chance. But within that framework, we can touch probability, influence our evolution. Tentatively, he stepped back into the flowing energy of his metaphorical dream tapestry. Lovingly, he reached inward toward its intertwining blue and green threads. Those two threads clearly were the key. He would touch their probabilities, engage their energies.

Special Forces Exercise, Pisgah State Park, NH | Tuesday 0347 EDT

"Listen, TC, we can track them now, using this website. We can scramble the choppers. We can pick up the website off a satellite uplink while we're airborne. We can intercept these ETs, either or both. We can land assault teams on the ground *toute suite* when the fog clears." Colonel Merton Shaundee squeezed the quivering shoulder of Agent TC Demuzzio as he made each point.

"I can see there's a personal element here, TC," the colonel continued, "but you had to make a choice, and Lara didn't tell you what was going on, so you did what you thought was the right thing at the time. Snap out of it, man! We can retrieve this situation now. Right now! We've got ourselves a modified mission, that's all, just a straightforward snatch-and-grab of a tracked target. We practice those all the time."

"Yeah, Merton. Yeah. Thanks," Demuzzio replied gruffly. He patted the big hand on his shoulder as he stood up, and wiped his shirt sleeve down over his face. "See if you can get our chopper back in here, will you? And Sergeant Major, gimme back that goddamn phone. I gotta find out who fucked up the info flow. I'm gonna have their balls for breakfast." Demuzzio felt the anger building inside him.

"Fax coming in on that now, sir, I believe," the soldier said, squinting at the screen. "Looks like a detective's report from Washington Metro PD. You want hard copy?"

Demuzzio strode to the computer and read over the soldier's shoulder. Late Monday morning, while they'd been watching Lara Picard sleep, one Aaron O'Meara of Goddard Space Flight Center had driven up to the west entrance of the National Zoo. He'd told one Detective Lucien Safire a strange tale, and passed him some printouts of what he purported to be alien presences, moving around Washington, converging on the Zoo just before dawn.

Oddly enough, Metro hadn't blown O'Meara off. Later in the day, the detective had written his report and included the printouts. All were dutifully compiled and delivered to the Bureau last night. And there they sat for a while. Well, shit, I guess I understand that, Demuzzio thought. Who the hell is gonna stick a priority flag on something like this. His anger faded to resignation. Goddamn bureaucracies have no imagination and can't move fast enough, that's always been our problem.

Demuzzio studied the location plots as they came out of the printer. Yup, there was Lara, green crosshairs moving out of her house near Montrose Park, working her way through Rock Creek Park up toward the Bureau's safehouse on Irving Street. He walked over to the computer showing the green location plots from the website. He toggled back to the proper time periods, and saw that the plots matched those he held in his hand. He toggled the blue location plots, going back to the very beginning and letting them play forward: Colombia, Panama, Miami, DC.

"Hey, Merton," he shouted excitedly, "we got us a lead. If this Blue ET or *Warlock* or whoever... if he came in on commercial flights, we can isolate him based on the passenger manifests, get a handle on who he is. Maybe get a picture from an airport security camera. Merton? Merton, you hear what I'm saying?"

Shaundee, bent over another computer monitor with his Sergeant Major, let out a long sigh. "We don't need to, TC. We know who he is. Human blood from the ape compound at the Zoo came back with a quick DNA hit. The ID just came in." Perplexity and dismay ran in countercurrents across the big soldier's face.

Demuzzio ran across the room, and stared at the picture on the computer monitor. An exotic face looked out at him, smiling faintly. The deepest blue eyes he'd ever seen eerily complemented the coppery face. The soldier's name, rank and serial number were printed across the bottom of the picture. Connard. Captain John Connard. It carried a connotation of some sort, he thought. But it wouldn't come out of his memory. He tapped at the green beret on the soldier's head.

"This one of yours, Merton?"

"Yes, TC. Used to be. John got brevetted to major and retired, real early. Almost always that means they've gone to black ops, CIA or some government group we don't even know about."

"And you know what else it means, don't you, Colonel?" The Sergeant Major's shoulders drooped. "This being the soldier we all called the Magician?"

Merton Shaundee ran his big hand across his stubbly hair. He looked at his old friend TC Demuzzio. "It means we're fucked, TC. The Magician was the best there ever was, in our business. Maybe the best there ever will be. And if he's tied up with an ET, and can toss people around and shake off taser shock like Lara Picard... it means we're fucked."

Chapter 37

The highway ribboned out in the diffused glare of the truck's headlights. Wallace Lockerby pressed as fast as he dared southward through the fog, averaging somewhat under thirty miles an hour. He stole a glance at the sleeping hitchhiker beside him.

Gawdallmighty she's beautiful, he thought. And eat! Jeeze, she just about inhaled those roast beef sandwiches Mary made me. And that story she told... should I believe that?

It had seemed perfectly plausible when she first told it, her green eyes flashing strangely. Maybe she's some kinda witch, and laid a spell on me, he thought humorously. Well, that's okay; that way Mary will have to forgive me for what I'm thinking right now. He squirmed uncomfortably at the pressure of the erection caught sideways in his underpants, and surreptitiously adjusted himself.

But Lara Picard wasn't asleep, even though her eyes were closed. She smiled in her meditation as the emanations from Lockerby's consciousness diffused through the heightening awareness in her mind-space, displaying as conflicted bubbles of desire and protectiveness. You're a nice man, Wally, she acknowledged; I'll make sure that Ham rewards you handsomely for your kindness once we get to the airport. Then her mind retreated to the deeper level of communing with her *ki*, fretting about the pace of her escape.

You cannot control the fog. But neither can the Beast. He cannot gain ground very quickly. You are safe for the moment. Use this time to reflect, to plan, to gain enlightenment. Consider the null dimension, the great emptiness, in which there is nothing and everything. You have great facility with the null. Draw from it, learn from it. It may hold the answer to winning this battle, to banishing the monster back to the depths from which it arose.

The very same depths from which I also arose, Lara thought the irony back into her mind-space.

That is true of all creatures who live and evolve. But transcendence from the depths rewards those who move forward. Reversion to the depths punishes those who do not.

Lara stirred in the truck seat as her previous enlightenment enticed her. The beast in myself is moving up closer to the surface, isn't it? That primitive part of me that demands survival above all else is coming out of its cave, isn't it? She floated the questions across her mind-space.

Indeed. The change triggered in you, the closer alliance of the three evolutionary segments of your brain, brings the unique characteristics of each of those segments more into your active consciousness.

So I could revert, move backward, easily. My own beast is stirring, nervous and hungry. If I reach down I can feel it, that primal power. Each time I draw from it, it grows more dangerous. If its claws sink too deep, my beast can take me over. That's a possibility, isn't it?

We are all just possibilities, Lara Picard.

I-91 South of Northampton, MA | Tuesday 0349 EDT

John pressed southward through the fog, driving faster than he should, counting on his lightning reflexes to keep him safe, marginally closing the gap to his quarry. The green-hued blackness of the Other pulsated on his consciousness radar, damped down by the fog. She was, he estimated, twenty miles further south on Interstate 91. He took another sip of coffee and pressed the accelerator down a tiny incremental amount. His fingers drummed against the steering wheel in frustration. That part of his consciousness not watching the road retreated into his mind-space and communed with his nexus. He twisted uncomfortably in the seat of the car as the parameters of the coming battle twisted around in his mind. To win, his beast must be released once again, with all his new and phenomenal powers at its disposal.

Yes, that is discomforting. The increasing linkage of the segments of your brain has brought your primal beast much closer to the surface. But you must deal with it. You must control the power, and transcend it. You must go forward and not backward. Your species depends on that.

I could easily go backward, John thought into his mind-space. I did it not six hours ago, with that consciousness tracking me in New Jersey. And I even know my beast, don't I? I created him the day I saw my baby sister lying in the morgue. His name is the Assassin.

The image of Duc Li nodded agreement, and John Connard's spirit winced at the enlightenment: I've been running along the edge for awhile now, and my beast awaits me there in the depths if I fall off.

He framed the insight more clearly in his mind-space: the edge was the moral edge presented by their program to terrorize the drug trade and systematically remove its leadership. The insight floated in front of him: I might have gone off that edge, were it not for Alex, and later, for Lara and Josh. In fact I probably did go off the edge that time in Burma, but the thought of Lara pulled me back. That's true, isn't it?

Ah, yes. Love is protection from the beast.

John smiled at that, but its significance was lost in a new dilemma. He edged it into his mind-space. Each time I call up the beast now, I give it exponentially more power. And yet I will need the Assassin once more, won't I? Now I see that may drive me backward one final time, past all hope of transcendence. I may kill the Other, but then become the monster that it is. It's definitely possible, isn't it?

The Magician pondered the darkness of that possibility.

The Assassin paced nervously within, a caged beast.

His nexus answered for them all.

All beings are just possibilities, John Connard.

I-91 South of Holyoke, MA | Tuesday 0359 EDT

Wallace Lockerby saw the repeated shivering twitch running up Lara's left leg. He pulled a fleece jacket from behind his seat and draped it over her clumsily, not taking his eyes off the road.

"I'm not cold, Wally, I'm scared. But thanks." Lara tucked her feet underneath her and the jacket around her. "Can you go any faster?"

"Mebbe so. Mebbe so," he muttered, nudging the gas pedal down a tiny bit against his better judgment. Lara watched the speedometer creep from 28 to 30, and had to agree with Wally: any faster would be way too dangerous in a fog this dense. The race to the airport in New Haven was going to be close. She closed her eyes again and returned to her contemplation of the null dimension, and the ways in which her mind might craft from it a weapon of greater subtlety and finesse. It seemed unlikely she could overcome the Beast with raw power. From her experience at the Washington safehouse and the New Hampshire quarry, he was incredibly strong and resilient, and could take more of a pounding than she could give. She would have to deceive and entrap, and this time do a better job at it. *Aikido*, she thought, turn his own strength to destroy him. Her *ki* responded, scrolling symbols of possibilities across her mind-space. All but one of them depended on the development of future skills, days of training away.

This one, then. At your present development level, this is the only one. But you will have to be in close proximity to an electrical energy field in this reality.

Power lines? An electrical substation?

Either will suffice. Or a radio tower. A microwave dish. A power transformer or generator.

Show me.

The symbology her *ki* played into her mind-space escaped her, but the diagram was clear enough. It would indeed make a subtle and elegant trap. She could let the Beast wear her down with his greater strength, absorbing all she could throw at him, bleeding down her access to the energy field, like he'd done in the quarry. Then, when he was poised for the killing stroke, she could stream electricity back along the channel his energy came from, into his physical body. Electricity was a lower frequency energy, primitive by comparison to the energy field they were using. The Beast would never see it coming, or if he did, it would be too late. An internal electric chair: fry him from inside out, she thought, that's great!

He may be able to negate such a primitive attack by manipulating his null field.

Show me.

Observe how it could happen within yourself.

Ah! Okay, but don't I see another inside-out possibility here? She squinted at the diagram in her mind-space. Couldn't I slip my own null field in along with the electricity, camouflage it?

Yes. Electricity as a carrier, your null as the poison. And on delivery of your poison, his mind will be cast into emptiness, at least momentarily. If that works, you will be able to destroy him easily. Very elegant, Lara Picard.

If. She saw how the trap could work, but there were enormous tactical difficulties. She would have to choreograph her fight to retreat to just the right place at just the right time. And in the fog she might not see the battleground well enough to locate possible sources of electricity. And her retreat would have to be acted with great skill: the Beast would be wary of a trap. That was the greatest difficulty.

Lara sighed, and her knuckles whitened as they closed over the jacket tucked around her. It would be much better to escape to Ireland, to buy time to train her mind and become more dangerous, to get her best friend and lover John Connard to help set a better trap, one that would be absolutely sure to work. But if that possibility wasn't to be, at least now she had an alternative. It was subtle and complex, and tactically difficult. But it was an alternative, nonetheless. And in her mind-space were no others.

I-91 North of Holyoke, MA | Tuesday 0401 EDT

Twenty miles north up Interstate 91, John chafed at how slowly he was closing the gap. The dense fog made him feel as if he were swimming through molasses. Frustration urged him to move faster, but caution urged him to slow down. He compromised, and held his speed to just above thirty.

Although damped by the fog, the pulsations of the Other beat at his mind relentlessly, an eerie counterpoint to the drone of the tires. That mind was active and planning, trying to ferret out some advantage; John could almost taste it. He forced the thing off into a distant corner of his mind-space, where it would not interfere with his own thoughts or preparations. There were several things to be clarified. The Magician floated them out for consideration. His nexus contemplated them judiciously.

Yes, the Other has taken full advantage of the astonishing latent capabilities of its human host. The host's native ability to deceive is enormous. The simulacrum in the quarry was indistinguishable from the Other.

So why can't I do the same thing? I can do a pretty good spider, but I can't do myself? That doesn't make any sense. The Other's simulacrum was just a haze, a vaguely female body cloaked in a null-field, with that green energy and aura around her. It hardly had any detail. That seems simple enough to do. And I really like the idea. Fight remotely, and if you lose, hey, you just disappear. Like some of those new virtual reality games.

With an external simulacrum, a spider or any other physical object, you merely project a conceptual image. With a simulacrum of yourself, you pass an actual portion of your being, your outer shell, through null space to another location. Thus your being exists simultaneously in two realities. It is beyond you, for now.

The metaphors flooded into the Magician's mind-space to illustrate the concept. It was like a lobster shedding its shell, and yet being able to animate the shell for defense as it moved itself away unprotected. Simultaneity in dual realities presented him with no conceptual difficulty, he'd gotten past that in quantum mechanics. But when he saw in his mind-space the metaphor for the level of talent required, he whistled through his teeth.

Yes, John Connard, even your Magician's mind will not integrate brain segments to that level of control for several days.

So, basically, the Other's host is getting more capable, more dangerous, much faster than I am?

More capable in some ways, but not in others. Yesterday, the Other had a greater capacity for absorbing chaos from the null field and transferring it into this reality. What she threw at you in the house in Washington was impressive, nearly fatal. But your own ability with the null has increased markedly with our meditation and practice on the drive north last night, so it was not as much a weakness in the battle at the quarry.

The Magician sensed the accuracy of that assessment; his ability to manipulate the null field had indeed grown. But the Other's simulacrum, that's a new development, a new weapon, he objected.

True, but that weapon is no longer a surprise, so it has lost much of its edge. And the Other's host, I judge, will never be able to wield such raw power from the energy dimension as you. Nor will she have as much control as you over dimensions that you better comprehend.

Such as?

Gravity. She may be limited to control of gravity with respect to herself, rather than to imposing it on other objects. Not that she can't do it, she just doesn't think of it in the same way you do. Her mind probably has different training than yours, less exposure to physical sciences and engineering, possibly.

So I still should catch the Other as soon as possible? While I still may have an edge?

Yes. The edge is slight, but your control of energy and gravity still tilts the balance in your favor, I believe. The more time that passes, the more deadly the Other will become. We must strike, soon.

I-91 South of Hartford, CT | Tuesday 0442 EDT

This is going to be close, Lara thought as she extrapolated her position and her pursuer's position forward in time. It's going to be very close. Ten minutes difference, no more, maybe as little as five. I might have to call Ham, advise him to have that jet sitting on the end of the runway with the door open.

And Hamilton O'Donnell would be just the one to do that sort of thing, wouldn't he? She smiled as she realized how completely she had come to trust the little man and his astonishing abilities over their eight-year friendship, and how incredibly well he understood and related to Josh.

Just last Saturday night, she remembered, right before her fateful Sunday dawn bike ride... no... no, that's wrong, she corrected, wondering if the fog somehow was occluding her memory as well as her vision. No, it was two Saturdays ago, because John was there at dinner. We were having fresh strawberries for dessert, the first local crop, debating the significance of recurrent symbols in philosophy and religion. Ham told Josh I was love and compassion, moving toward enlightenment.

Ah! I wonder if this memory is a message for me. Maybe it's one of those threads I sense weaving around me. It sure seems like one is tugging at me. If I truly am love and compassion, and moving toward enlightenment, how then can I kill this Beast? Maybe I can change him. What is it that Ham says? God and the devil are Siamese twins? Something like that. Maybe this is a perception issue?

The response from her *ki* was immediate and harsh. The evilly pulsating blue-tinged blackness sprang abruptly to the forefront of Lara's mind-space.

There! Look at it! Is that thing love and compassion? Will that thing return love and compassion? No! That thing doesn't love, it hates. It has no compassion, only ruthless pursuit of its own power. That thing is the ultimate reversion to darkness, to the monster within. Put thoughts of love and compassion out of your mind, they will not sway the Beast. They will weaken you, make you less decisive in battle, and we will be destroyed, the hopes of a new and better humanity along with us. Observe! Please, observe....

A collage of images flooded across Lara's mind-space, graphic displays from all the evil things she had ever imagined. They came spiraling at her out of that pulsating blue blackness: Nazi death camps, genocidal wars, killing and rape and torture and unspeakable depravity and squalor, loss of art and music and beauty. The agony and destruction the Beast could cause would make the worst of the Taliban look like saints. If the Beast won, there would be a screaming unstoppable jihad to hell.

Lara's mind recoiled in horror. She tucked tighter into the fetal position in the passenger seat of the truck, and clutched Lockerby's jacket as if it were a lifeline. Slowly, her focus returned, and resolve along with it. Thoughts of love and compassion were shoved aside. She would do what had to be done, what her martial arts trainers had taught her, what TC had taught her, what her lover John Connard had taught her. When you're attacked, they had all drummed into her, it's survival time.

You strike hard, decisively.

You take them down, completely.

You show no mercy.

You kill. If they're dead, they can't hurt you.

I-91 North of Hartford, CT | Tuesday 0443 EDT

The edge may shift from us to the Other. The Magician parsed that thought into its underlying implications, and didn't like them. He was acutely aware of the value of deception and subterfuge in war. His nickname, in fact, derived from his skills in those areas.

So I've got a slight edge right now, he thought, just from raw power. But tomorrow? Who knows? She's already way ahead in constructing a false image, so she may be smarter. She may be more devious. She may even be a better magician.

He pressed down a tiny bit more on the gas pedal as he squinted into the fog. The roiling patterns of mist in the car's fog lights developed a harmonic with the sound of the tires. It tugged on distant memories as he rolled down the highway.

"Ah. Yes. Now I remember," he murmured to the fog outside, "where I've seen you before, my troublesome mist. You're another one of Mom's surrealisms. Her last painting, I think, before she died."

Wisps of fog danced in the lights ahead of the car, as if in response to his words. He still had that artwork, rolled up in a hermetic tube, stored somewhere in Alex Shaughnessy's Georgetown office. He loved the painting, but found it difficult to look at. A gnarled old tree on a ragged cliff, fog shrouded off into darkness behind it. It seemed to presage death: his father's, his mother's, his sister's, possibly his own. Bleakness imbued the painting's beauty, or maybe vice-versa.

We actually talked about that painting, John remembered, all four of us at dinner... when was it... a week ago, maybe? His recollection seemed momentarily as occluded as the highway, then cleared.

Yes! Saturday before last. At dinner. Josh and Ham were arguing about the origin and meaning of recurrent symbols in art and philosophy, and I told them about the painting. I told them about the tree, and the fog shrouding off into darkness, and the feelings the painting generated, and the images it conveyed.

Lara and Josh wanted to see it immediately. Ham got me off the hook; he said something like... each of us must eat the apple from the tree of knowledge of good and evil... each of us must fall into darkness to come out the other side. That sounded so tuned into the painting that it scared me.

And then Ham told them I was the voice of truth, moving toward enlightenment. Lara giggled, until she saw my face, and then her compassion just flooded over me. Joshua just stared at me, and he stopped arguing with his uncle for once and nodded along with him.

The dissociated memories flying through John's mind crossed a sensitive synapse somewhere, and an errant idea presented itself: I wonder if that dinner signified my bite of the apple. I wonder if this memory is a message for me. I wonder if it's one of those threads I sense dancing around me. One of them seems to be tugging at me. If I really am the voice of truth, and moving toward enlightenment, can I then speak for the Other? Can my truth transform her? What is it Ham likes to say? God and the devil are Siamese twins? So which am I, and which is the Other? Or maybe I don't know the truth well enough yet to speak it?

The response from his nexus to these wandering thoughts was prompt and blunt. The evilly pulsating green-tinged blackness flew into the forefront of his mind-space.

There! Look at it! Does the Other *represent truth? Will it ever say anything true? No! The* Other *has only lies and deception, in ruthless pursuit of its own power. The* Other *is the ultimate reversion to darkness, to the most expedient means to an end. So put sympathy out of your mind, John Connard. The* Other *will use it to weaken you, make you less certain of your own fundamental truth and goodness in the coming battle. Then we will be destroyed, you and I, and a terrible new species will take over your planet, and issue forth to scourge the gentler races in this galaxy. The power your species will develop is incredible. Observe, John Connard, observe…*

The pulsating green blackness superimposed itself on his mother's painting. It nestled obscenely in the gnarled tree and transfigured into a wasted planet. Graphic images of horror spiraled outward from it. They portrayed all too vividly the agony and destruction of unfettered new human beasts released on the Earth, and later, on a screaming jihad of rage and destruction across the galaxy. It would go on a long, long time before civilizations could band together to stop it. While it lasted, there would be genocidal wars and killing and rape and torture and depravity and squalor. The art and music and beauty of many cultures would be destroyed, some so completely as to never return. John's mind recoiled in horror.

He winced as the last images twisted outward from his mother's obscenely degraded painting, and felt trickling drops of sweat soak his shirt.

If the Other won, the Earth would lose. Many other civilizations would be destroyed. He could not let that happen.

John Connard hardened his resolve.

The Magician marshaled his skills.

The Assassin sharpened his blade.

They drove together through the fog, southward.

Chapter 38

"Adrienne, I took the liberty of calling some of my contacts at the FBI," Sam Rosen spoke gently as she answered his phone call, "and I've been talking with them for the past hour or so. I don't know exactly how to tell you this, but all of the material your friend Aaron O'Meara sent to the government got hung up in transit, and they're just now realizing what's going on."

"Omigod, you're not serious. Tell me you're not serious! Aaron's not in trouble, is he, Doctor Sam?"

"No, Adrienne. Nobody's in trouble. Aaron sent everything to Goddard. Goddard passed it along to the Pentagon. The Pentagon passed it along to the FBI. But the information just didn't connect up with the right people. Maybe somebody made some bad judgments along the way, but it wasn't Aaron. And it wasn't you or Nathan Rodgers, either."

"So what's happening now, sir?"

"Ah... you know, dear, I probably can't talk to you about that, at least at the moment. There's a security cap on things. When we hit a quiet moment, I'll ask the agent in charge of the investigation what can be disclosed and what can't."

"Doctor Sam, that's bullshit," Adrienne replied firmly. "I want to be involved. I need to be involved. I developed the tracking software. I've been in this since it started Sunday morning. I've been thinking about it for... almost two days, now. I've got some opinions, and a whole lot to contribute. And so does Aaron, and so does Nathan."

"Umm. Yeah. Good point, Adrienne." Rosen weighed TC Demuzzio's predilections on need-to-know against his own judgment, and compromised. "Well, okay, let me tell you that at this point, a team of Bureau people and a group of military Special Operations folks are involved. They're using your website to track Blue and Green. They're just observing, at the moment. They may or may not attempt an intercept. They probably will if it looks like Green is at risk, or like there's going to be some kind of danger to the public."

"Umm, I guess that's reasonable," she replied, "but what makes them think Green is at risk? Do they just like Aaron's battle hypothesis better, since they're military? Or have they actually seen something that would lead them in that direction?"

Shit, she zeroes right in on it, doesn't she, Rosen thought. But there's no way I can tell her about Lara Picard and the trap in New Hampshire, and everything that led up to it, or the fiasco that followed. That's definitely need-to-know. TC has to make that decision.

Rosen sidestepped the question. "I think they probably don't know what to make of the situation, Adrienne. The agent in charge is Thomas Charles Demuzzio. TC and I are old friends, actually. He'll probably want to talk to you. I should warn you that he gets a little... ah... abrupt, at times, Adrienne. He can be sort of heavy-handed. He's playing catch-up here, under a lot of pressure. So if he aggravates you, my dear, just keep in mind that he's a good man, with a heart of gold, okay?"

"Oh, sure. No problem. If he's an old friend of yours, I'm sure he's fine," her voice trailed off as she dismissed that subject to consider a more pressing one.

"Hey, Doctor Sam! I just had an idea about our earlier conversation. You told me how different kinds of consciousness are tied into different parts of the brain, when we were talking about Blue's mental attack on me, remember?"

"Sure I remember," Rosen responded, "his nasty reaction maybe coming out of a primitive part of the brain?"

"Yes, sir. And then you made an analogy, remember, the three brain segments being like three different computers? And even though they could communicate at some level, they each had their own kind of consciousness and intelligence, and perception of time and space, and they served different functions? They all had their own programs?"

"Yeah, Adrienne, I remember."

"Doctor Sam, I work with computers a lot."

"So I understand," he replied dryly. Compared to her, he thought, I'm just a savage sitting in front of a monitor with a stone knife in my teeth, tapping it on the keyboard.

"And I'm always sort of futzing around, in the Psych Department here, with computer simulations of how the mind works."

"Umm. Guess I knew that too, Adrienne, from conversations with Sarah. So?"

"So, this odd flash just came to me. Humans are getting computers to talk together better all the time. What if the ETs are getting our three brains to talk together better? What if their separate functions are becoming more unified? What would that mean to our consciousness? Wouldn't it become more unified, along with our physical brains?"

"My goodness, Adrienne, what an interesting thought! But I'm probably the last one you should ask. You need to talk to a research neuropsychologist," he smiled and added, "preferably one who moonlights as a philosopher. Or possibly a medium; nobody really knows diddly-bop about the true nature of consciousness."

I-95 West of Fairfield, CT | Tuesday 0451 EDT

Joshua sat in the lotus position, rocking gently with the motions of the Edsel, his mind easily engaging the flowing energy of his metaphorical dream tapestry. This tapestry is a picture of the evolution that has been, he reaffirmed, but it's also a picture of what is and what could be. Actualities and possibilities floated through the tapestry in response, intertwining.

The boy tried to move his viewpoint progressively backward from the picture, and suddenly understood he could never back out far enough to see the whole tapestry. He would always be embedded in it. Relativity was inescapable, its hook strong in his consciousness.

But he was far enough away to sense, underlying his tapestry, a mathematical field. It played across his mind as a holographic matrix, expressing probabilities across multiple dimensions. The matrix formed the framework of the tapestry, the warp for the constantly interweaving weft of the threads of evolution. Joshua laughed at the beauty of it, so complex but so simple. Then he drove his viewpoint back down to his immediate concern: that small part of his tapestry within which the green and blue threads of his mother and her lover John Connard were weaving their own possibilities, in both present and future.

Joshua let those threads run across and through his fingers, sensing their energy and moods, admiring the intermittent coruscations of emerald and amethyst light when their possibilities intersected. He twined his own thread in around them, his bright turquoise filament glowing with its own possibilities.

The framework adjusted its probabilities by tiny increments in response as he manipulated the weft of the blue and green threads. He tugged at them, aligning them better within the matrix, investing them with his own sense of what their possibilities should become in this reality.

Sensing he could do no more, he slid away from his dream, up through darkness toward morning. When he arrived back in the Edsel, he unfolded his upturned hands from his lap and stretched fluidly out of the lotus position. He yawned and smiled at his uncle.

"Well...?" Hamilton O'Donnell prompted him.

"We're all just evolutionary possibilities, Uncle Ham. My tapestry metaphor shows our possibilities as genetic threads weaving in and out of a probability matrix, some sort of mathematical field. It actually sort of looks like a hologram, coherent resonances interacting."

The boy hiccupped, as if his nine-year old mouth didn't believe the complexity of the concepts that just came out of it. He grinned at his uncle owlishly. "We're all subject to the field, but within it... within it, Uncle Ham, we can touch the probabilities a little, influence our evolution, shade our chances. I think I just did that, in my meditation. I don't know exactly what I did, or how or why, but I think I've affected chance."

"Ah, another dream-workin', young lad? Affectin' chance? Well, isn't that just the bee's knees and the thrush's ankles! My old friend Louis Pasteur famously said that chance favors a prepared mind. So was it your own mind you were preparin' in your dream-workin', or someone else's?"

Joshua contemplated that for a moment, marshaling his impressions of the meditation.

"A dream-working? Well, if you like, Uncle Ham. But I don't really know whose mind I was preparing, or even if I was. I just wrapped my thread around Mom's thread, and John's. It was intuitive; it seemed like the right thing to do, because I love them. And the tapestry is just a metaphor, I think. It's my mind creating a context I can understand. It's more of a rationally created thing than a dream."

"Umm. Yes, me lad, of course fabric and weavin' is a pretty universal metaphor, at least the basic concepts, and can be rationally derived. But I believe you dreamt of the threads last night, and the night before that, did you not? So therefore your facile mind has just this moment overlaid the mathematical structure on it?"

"Umm," the boy responded, "you may be right...."

"Well, the dream always must come first, Joshua. Without it, rationality has no toehold. But tell me more about affectin' evolutionary probabilities, shadin' our chances, as you put it. Now *that* is a fascinatin' concept."

"Your old friend Heisenberg wins again, Uncle Ham. I tried to back out of my tapestry, get far enough away so I wouldn't affect anything. But I couldn't. We're all part of the tapestry. So we will always affect the experiment, and be affected by it. So uncertainty will always be present." Joshua smiled at his uncle hopefully. "Is that good or bad?"

"Good or bad? Ah well, Joshua, who is to say? It is what it is. Or perhaps it is what we make it. I say that with some uncertainty, of course."

Global Consciousness Project, Princeton University, NJ | Tuesday 0510 EDT

"Yes sir, that's right. That's exactly how it works. There's a 95 percent certainty that the signal source, Blue or Green, is inside the circle. When the signal gets stronger, the circles tend to tighten down, get smaller, that's a more precise location. Of course, it's an average location over a 15-minute period, so if the signal is moving during that period, that makes the circles bigger." Adrienne Baxter frowned. This was the third time she'd repeated the same explanation to Special Agent TC Demuzzio. By the rhythmic beating sound behind his voice, she surmised he was airborne, in a helicopter, so maybe he wasn't hearing her clearly.

"Miz Baxter," the voice came back, as if her thought had been verbalized, "believe I've got it now. Sorry if I've been dense."

"Adrienne," Rosen intervened in the conference call, hoping to expedite TC's next inquiry, "what you're telling us is that the crosshairs in the circle can't be relied on as a precise location at any given moment, can they? Just a high probability, and a good point to start from if you wanted to do a search, is that right?"

"Thanks, Doc," Demuzzio added dryly, "that's my next question."

"That's right, Doctor Sam," Adrienne answered. "Maybe out in the cornfields in Iowa, with nothing else around, they'd be a pretty good locator. But that's not true here, with a lot of people and buildings and stuff. We can't solve out the average location until we get the last 1-minute datum for the 15-minute period. So the information is always a little out-dated if the source is moving. A fast runner, for example, could be over a mile away from the average location."

"So why the hell did you do it that way?" Demuzzio sounded peeved that the tracking tool wasn't going to be adequate for his purposes. "Can't you use the 1-minute data?"

"Oh, sure, Mr. Demuzzio, I could have programmed it that way, but it's a question of computer resources. It was a tradeoff. We don't have any supercomputers here, just run-of-the-mill PCs. And a 15-minute average location seemed plenty good enough for our purposes."

"Could you re-program to work off the 1-minute data, Miz Baxter?" The beat of the helicopter rotors in the background seemed to add urgency to his voice. "So we can get a location to the nearest minute?"

"Oh, sure, sir." She paused while chains of both logic and intuition flashed through her mind; then she lied. "But it will take some time."

It won't take any time at all, Adrienne thought. In fact it's already done; all I have to do is re-code the output display algorithm. But I'm just not sure whether we ought to be intervening and trying to capture these ETs, or whether we should just let this event play out. And if we do intervene, well, frankly, I'm not real sure you're the right person to do it.

"How much time do you think, Miz Baxter?"

Adrienne studied the positions of the blue and green icons on her monitors, and mentally extrapolated their steady movements. Within thirty minutes—if Green stayed on Interstate 91 and held her speed—she would be approaching the coast of Connecticut in New Haven. Then she would have to turn east or west on Interstate 95, either toward New London, or toward New York, if she stayed on the highways. Blue would catch up a few minutes after that, or possibly even in New Haven, if he accelerated a bit. So, she calculated, add another half an hour, for whatever was going to happen. And add in some margin for uncertainties. Adrienne bit her lip, and made her decision.

"A couple of hours, I guess, Mr. Demuzzio," she answered.

"Okay. Speed it up all you can, please," Demuzzio demanded. "We gotta presume a national security problem here, until we know different. You understand me?"

"Yes, sir, I do," Adrienne said softly.

"Okay. I'm gonna send a couple agents down there to keep you protected, Miz Baxter, just in case these ETs are hostile and somehow show up to visit you. You sit tight and keep programming, fast as you can. I'll check in periodically. Demuzzio out."

"Adrienne?" Sam Rosen asked gently after the click and the helicopter background noise dropped off line.

"Yes, sir?"

Rosen paused, obviously choosing his words.

"Work as hard as you're able to, dear, to give TC just exactly what he should have."

Adrienne gave a wry little laugh, acknowledging his subtlety.

"Yes, Doctor Sam, I understand. I will."

113 km Northeast of Kennedy VORTAC | Tuesday 0531 EDT

In the lead Black Hawk helicopter, TC Demuzzio held up his hand to forestall the printouts Merton Shaundee was handing him, and punched his cell phone for the command center now being set up at the FBI New York office.

"I want three agents down at Princeton," Demuzzio barked into the phone, passing along the address and naming Adrienne Baxter as the subject of their coverage. "Right now. Two male, one female, and they stay on this kid like glue wherever she goes. But be polite, very polite, and don't interfere with what she's doing. You got that? All right, make it happen!"

Demuzzio clicked off and held out his hand to Shaundee for the printouts. They were grainy stills, obviously cropped from surveillance cameras.

"This our boy? Where?" He stared at the printouts.

"The first one is entry at Miami International, TC, at the Customs checkpoint. He came in on American 1524 out of Panama, around 2000 hours Sunday evening. He used a civilian passport under his own name, had an open ticket for first class. The second one is the concourse at DC National. He came in on American 59 non-stop out of Miami; it landed just before midnight. Still his own name, first class, booked right through from Panama." He paused to consult other notes. "The Air Force guys at the Pentagon confirm that the blue tracking plots from our friends at Princeton lie almost right on top of the recorded flight paths for these aircraft."

So you're the Magician, Demuzzio thought, looking from one fuzzy airport surveillance printout to the other, and then at the Army's much clearer file photo of that exotic, dangerous face. And you're a war hero, Captain John Connard, now turned into some kind of high-level spook.

The big agent tapped his fingernail on the name, rank and serial number printed beneath the face on the photograph. Connard. John Connard. The memory that had been edging around the back of his mind exploded to the forefront.

Ah, sweet Jesus, he thought. Now I remember! Even though we've never met, I remember now. Lara talked about you, soldier, sometime late last year, maybe at our annual inter-agency pow-wow. She mentioned your name, very fondly. So! You're her lover, John Connard. Or at least you were. And now... now you're trying to kill her? So what in all the blue hells is going on here? He considered that riddle for a moment, then hit his cell phone speed dial for the command center.

"This is Demuzzio," he barked. "Find out where the hell John Connard lives, and toss the place. And I want a crew to look over Lara Picard's house in DC. It's on Phoenix Court, off R Street, northwest, near Montrose Park." He listened for a brief moment, and then cut his questioner off. "Don't worry about it. We got a felony at the Zoo, we got positive genetic ID on him there, we got plenty enough dots connected, plenty of probable cause. We got national security on top of that. Go to the Director if you need to, but get it done. And don't make a mess in Lara's house. I want you in and out clean and fast. Just a look around. Pick up any photos of the two of 'em together. Take pictures of anything odd in the house." He listened again, and snapped, "no, I don't know what *odd* is. Use your judgment. Just take a lot of pictures."

Demuzzio looked again at the face in the file photo, the formidable talent the Army had nicknamed The Magician. I wish I'd met you, boy, he thought. I wish I knew how your mind works. I wish I could guess what an alien mind would do to yours, how much control it would have. I wish I knew what it means that you've been careful not to hurt anybody, except an ape where maybe you had no choice. I wish I had the slightest clue as to what the fuck is going on here.

The big agent sighed, and squinted as a beam from the rising sun shot through a break in the cloud deck into the Black Hawk. He saw the two troop-carrying choppers holding station on their port side. An hour or so after sunrise, the forecasters said, and the dense fog beneath them should start to dissipate. He looked down into the thick murk, and saw just a few hills and radio towers sticking up through it. Then he looked across at the laptop secured to the fold-down table. The blue cross-haired circles were moving inexorably after the green, and slowly catching up. It looked like they would coincide around New Haven. The choppers would arrive overhead at the same time. But what would they do then?

I-95 East of Milford, CT | Tuesday 0538 EDT

"Evolutionary uncertainty, me lad?" Hamilton O'Donnell repeated his nephew's question as the lane markers on the highway unfurled hypnotically out of the fog ahead of the Edsel. "Hah! How could we ever become certain, given all the complexities and variables attendin' our human condition?"

Joshua's eyes opened wide with the challenge of that question.

"Maybe we can test against those complexities and variables, Uncle Ham, if we know enough. Maybe we can determine what will work and what won't, in terms of successful evolution, within reasonable bounds of uncertainty."

"A test, eh? And what would be the nature of the test, me lad?"

"I don't know; multiple tests, probably, but I'd have to think about them for a long, long time before I could even begin to give you an answer."

"Mmm. Joshua, me lad, me young philosopher... in India, many years ago, the people used to catch monkeys. Do you know how they did it?"

"No, Uncle Ham, I don't think your teachings ever covered that."

"They would hollow out a gourd, me lad. Cut a small hole in one end, a smaller hole in the other, and let it cure and harden in the sun. They'd pass a rope through the smaller hole, with a knot to secure it inside the gourd, and tie the other end of the rope to a stake. Then they'd put some of the monkeys' favorite nuts inside the gourd. A monkey would smell the nuts, and reach his hand inside and grab them. But the hole was barely big enough for the monkey to work his hand in, and when he closed his fist around the nuts, he couldn't pull it out of the gourd. And the monkey would get frustrated and upset, and go running around on the end of the rope, trapped. So the Indians could just walk up and grab him, and cart him off to make monkey soup. Or monkeyburgers. Whatever."

"Monkey trap," said Joshua thoughtfully. "This really worked? But Uncle Ham, why wouldn't the monkey just let go of the nuts, and pull his hand out and run away? Or just turn the gourd upside down and pour out the nuts?"

"Well, y'see, me lad, here's the way of it: monkeys know what monkeys know. They have genetic instincts, plus some learned knowledge, conspirin' against them. Turns out 'tis a rare monkey who will let go of the nuts, or look outside his own context far enough to simply turn the gourd and shake out the nuts."

"An evolutionary breakpoint? The smarter monkeys survive?" Joshua smiled at his uncle.

"Well... yes, young man, but smarter in a broader sense than merely more intelligent. Wisdom takes many forms."

"Mmm. Okay, Uncle Ham, I catch your drift. I like it. A monkey trap. A lot of variables, but only one decision. A make-or-break test. But human beings are more complex, aren't they?"

"Ah, indeed they are, Joshua. Indeed they are. So what would you put inside the gourd to trap a human bein', me lad?"

Hamilton O'Donnell got the answer he both hoped for and feared.

"Power, Uncle Ham." The boy spoke softly. "Power."

Chapter 39

The tires screamed and the small panel truck tilted crazily as Wallace Lockerby yanked the wheel to the right in reaction to the flaring brake lights and sudden metallic crunching sounds of the pileup ahead. For a brief moment Lara stared at the pyramid of sand drums protecting the exit ramp abutment, but then Lockerby regained control, and pulled more to the right. The truck cleared the drums by inches and fishtailed down an exit ramp that curled back under the highway.

"Shit! You okay? Damn! I knew I was going too fast."

"Yes. I'm fine, Wally. Nice reaction!" Lara exhaled, and looked above them at the mess on the highway. She saw that the highway beyond the pileup was clear.

"Wally, slow down, slow down! There's a gap in the guard rail—you can cross over the grass strip and get back on the entrance ramp. The highway looks clear further south." With the pounding pulsations in her head, she didn't need to consult her consciousness radar to know that her pursuer had gained ground and wasn't more than a few minutes behind. But if they could get back on the highway with the pileup as a barrier behind them... that might extend their lead enough to reach the airport.

"Shit, Lara, I gotta call this in. The State Police gotta get down here."

As if to punctuate his opinion, a fire lit up the highway behind them. He caught it in his rear-view mirror as he turned the truck left onto the grass strip, and breathed a silent oath. With the truck stopped athwart the median, he reached for the phone clipped to the dashboard.

"Sorry, Wally," Lara apologized, "I just haven't time for this." She waved a chaos field over the burly trucker and he collapsed against the truck door. She jammed the shift lever into park, then ran around and pulled him out, lifting him easily and laying him gently into the protected area between the guard rails. In a fraction of a second, she ran through possible outcomes for the man, then waved a stronger chaos field over him. The less he remembered, the better off he would be.

Climbing into the driver's seat, Lara swung the truck left and barreled up the entrance ramp onto the highway. The pulsations in her mind beat at her, so strong she could barely think.

The Beast is as disadvantaged as you. Your resonance is pounding in his skull too.

And this is not an unequal match. He may have more strength, but you have more finesse. The answer still lies in the null, and concealing within it the means of his destruction.

The accident on the highway behind her hadn't slowed up the Beast at all, Lara realized. Even though she held the small truck at a truly reckless speed, he was pulling inexorably closer. The pounding malevolence in her mind seemed to increase proportionately with that thought. She might not make the airport.

But I'm going to be coming into the harbor area shortly, Lara reminded herself. And it's heavily industrialized. There are bound to be multiple electrical energy sources there: power lines, substations, transformers. If this is the only chance I'm going to get, I'd better make it good! The conscious part of her mind processed possible energy sources, while the unconscious part sought the null field and communed with its nothingness, looking for an edge.

I-91 New Haven, CT | Tuesday 0545 EDT

The pounding pulsations in John's skull resonated out of the green-hued black blot on the radar screen in his mind-space. Insidious, they seemed to wrap around his consciousness like a python, and meld to his own body's heartbeat. The squeezing sensation felt almost physical. He was getting very close now, and the pulsations increasingly ate at his focus, sapping his will. No doubt that was their purpose. He clamped down on them with iron control.

Good! Do not let her psychic assault conceal her physical trap.

Only good reflexes and luck had saved him from plowing into the accident two miles back. There had been just enough clearance between the pileup and the median to slip unscathed past the mess that the Other must have created.

So there's more than one kind of trap to look out for, isn't there? He directed the thoughts into his mind-space. She's smart and devious and resourceful and vicious, maybe more so than I am.

Yes, John Connard, you are evenly matched. You have more strength. But she has more finesse, more skill, especially with the null dimension. Her trap likely lies in the null and its manifold possibilities. I cannot guess what form it will take, and you may have to enter it to destroy her. But you must destroy her.

My own survival? And yours?

Reasonable secondary objectives.

A soldier's answer, John Connard understood. Bleak amusement echoed back.

The conscious part of his mind continued to monitor his berserk speed down the highway, closing rapidly now on the black blot ahead of him. The blot acknowledged imminent contact, and beckoned him obscenely: another derisive dare. She clearly planned a trap; the Magician could almost taste it now. But was there also a sense of desperation underlying the evil beckoning? Or was this simply another deception, a part of the trap?

The Assassin emerged, elemental rage flickering at the edges of sanity. Human hands gripped the steering wheel, knuckles dead white with pressure, but there was little else human in the car. The tires screamed over the curving ramp from Interstate 91 onto Interstate 95, the turn eastward toward New London. His mind-space exploded with overloaded signals, and his consciousness radar flared out into shards of painful static. But he no longer had any need for mental radar. The only vehicle ahead of him, a small truck, sped up the bridge. It contained his elusive quarry. But this time the surprise would be his. He turned off his headlights.

Gravity field, now! That dimension leapt to the Assassin's bidding, and the car rocketed forward with impossible acceleration, under the control of forces far greater than the horsepower of its engine. In the instant it blew past the truck at the peak of the bridge, the Assassin shifted the field's directional tensors laterally and upward. He sensed the gathering of an enormous chaos field to be thrown at him, but his gravity strike was first, and unexpected. The truck slammed hard into the bridge wall and spun upward and over it, crushed metal in a mist of gasoline droplets that immediately whooshed into a fireball. The Assassin laughed madly as he fishtailed on the downslope of the bridge. The truck had dropped out of his view, but he heard the impact behind and to his right. A second explosion followed, with a horrendous fireball. The Assassin smiled a wicked smile, and re-treated laughing and snarling into the cave levels of John Connard's mind.

The Magician fought the skidding car onto the exit ramp at the bottom of the bridge. A picture of fire and destruction presented itself in his rear-view mirror. The truck had plunged into what looked like a petroleum depot. That would ex-plain the secondary explosion and fireball, he realized.

He accelerated down the ramp, screaming around corners, working his way back toward the point of impact, turning left on the city street paralleling the el-evated bridge. His consciousness radar was fragmented and useless, but the pound-ing presence in his mind was totally gone. A cautious tranquility settled over him; that of a soldier moving in on a battleground no longer contested. Unlikely the Other survived that, he thought. And I sure don't sense her anymore.

Upper New Haven Harbor, CT | Tuesday 0546 EDT

Lara had spun through space, momentarily disoriented from her skull's impact with the side window, but otherwise cocooned safely by the truck's airbag. When the bag deflated, she instinctively slammed open the door and flew out, plunging directly downward. She gulped air just before she clove the surface of the murky waters of New Haven Harbor, not ten feet off the seawall bordering a petroleum terminal. Her flaming panel truck arced almost lazily overhead. She never saw it slam into the parked tanker, and the concussion from the second explosion was damped out by the water over her.

Underwater, Lara's lips curled into an animal snarl of frustration. She'd had enormous chaos snatched from the null field, ready at her fingertips, ready to lash her enemy, but he had somehow struck first. Stupid, stupid, stupid, she raged as her outstretched hands plunged into the silt and ooze at the bottom of the harbor.

There is no time for recrimination. Go north. Quickly, now. Stay underwater as long as you can. She sensed the concepts from her nexus, her *ki*, even though her mind-space could provide only fragments of pictures. She had a sense of internal forces turning and leveling, pointing her north.

The icy water shocked Lara back into full sensibility. It was cold, but a safe place to be for the moment; no obscene pulsations pounded her skull. The water shielded her from contact, just as it had in New Hampshire. North, she surmised, must be directly away from the seawall, back across the harbor to the industrial side. She knifed through the water, determined to put as much distance as possible between herself and her pursuer before coming up to breathe. A few hundred yards offshore her air ran out. She porpoised out of the water, emptying her lungs and gasping in as much of the damp sea air as they could hold. As soon as she surfaced, the madness of the Beast permeated her senses as if she had flown into a slaughterhouse. She dove back underwater, not knowing his distance or direction, but knowing for certain that the rabid monster was still out there, still very close, and still hunting.

Well, you'll have to come and get me, you miserable bastard, she thought. You showed me your surprise, but I haven't showed you mine yet!

In her brief surfacing, Lara had seen the power lines crossing the harbor, and angled her direction to follow them northward. Fog still obscured the far shoreline, but there would be sources of electrical power there for her trap, she was certain.

Upper New Haven Harbor, CT | Tuesday 0547 EDT

As sirens sounded in the distance, the Magician drove slowly past the flaming wreckage and the elevated bridge from which it had plunged, moving northwestward into the streets of the city. Was the Other truly destroyed? He stared at the flames in his rear-view mirror, and off into the fog over the dark waters of the harbor. Cautious hope was shattered when the pounding in his skull swept back in with a vengeance. The wave of blackness almost ran him into a parked truck. Then it disappeared.

The Magician stopped the car and grabbed his head. "Where the hell is she?"

The Other has survived. She is in the water, it appears. The near-field signal is damped out. The water is shielding it, except when she came up for air. That is clever; and it probably means she is uninjured.

I couldn't pick out her location, my consciousness radar is still fragmented! Where the hell is she?

Your radar screen will re-gather, and re-cohere. The strength of your gravity wave perturbed the interface between dimensions, just as the strength of the Other's chaos field did in Washington. A few minutes, John Connard. The perturbations will die out as the interface equilibrates. Your radar will return soon.

The Magician accelerated across a low swing bridge that paralleled the elevated highway, and pulled over beside a railroad spur. The sky above lightened perceptibly, the fog starting to thin. His soldier's ears picked the vibrations of circling choppers out of the background noise.

Just then, the Other came fully out of the water. The pounding in his skull resumed with a vengeance, but now it was tied to a location that his radar screen began to shakily assemble in his mind-space. She was a few hundred meters to his right, to the northeast, he estimated, and moving north. The fog offered him nothing. He couldn't see well enough for transposing to be effective. He'd have to pursue in the car until visibility improved. And then he'd have to be careful, he reminded the Assassin. In this industrial area, workers would be showing up for an early shift.

The choppers were clearly tracking one or both of them, the Magician's thoughts ran on; there was no other reason for their continued presence. Had they somehow come to realize the Other was the enemy, and not him? Or were they supporting her for another trap? He could sense the presence and focus of the troops, but not their intent: the heavy pounding in his skull obscured such subtle discernments.

Upper New Haven Harbor, CT | Tuesday 0548 EDT

The renewed evil pulsations of the Beast chased Lara as she followed the high voltage lines northward across the harbor. She suppressed the pounding in her skull with an effort of will, and concentrated on the power lines, above to her left.

They presented a diffuse vibration in her mind-space: not heat, more of a zone of disturbance in the magnetic field. She sensed the zone clearly, even through the pounding mental onslaught caused by the Beast.

Why didn't I sense power lines before? She framed the question in her mind-space.

You weren't looking before. Sensitivity to magnetic fields is in a vestigial part of your brain, the pineal body. For many of our evolutionary predecessors, simpler organisms, if a thing was not observed, it did not exist.

Lara's consideration of that thought, and its embedded possibilities for clever deception, almost caused her to fly into a steel bulkhead wall beneath the power lines. She saw it loom out of the fog, and flared over it to a running landing on solid ground.

"Oh, how great," she exclaimed, "how absolutely stupendously great! Finally a break! A power plant, by God! There's lots of energy sources here, lots of possibilities for my trap." Hope blossomed in her mind, damping down the insistent pounding that told her the Beast wasn't far behind. She extended her senses to isolate the centers of power, and flew left around the corner of the building to find a door or window for entry.

As she searched, the belated recognition came that the nature of the Beast was different now. The black blot on her consciousness radar still was tinged with blue, but the blue had shaded darker. The pulsations carried with them some ill-concealed weariness, some sense of desperation. She understood, at some elemental level, that the Beast was tiring, losing energy. Forming and controlling a gravity wave to pick up a truck and fling it off a bridge had taken a huge toll. On the other hand, she had spent relatively little energy. The Beast might still have more raw strength, but they were much closer to equal now. And she clearly had a novel application of the null field that he couldn't possibly foresee. More hope blossomed in her mind. The sound of the helicopters above the fog added to it.

That has to be TC and Shaundee and the troops, she thought. It's definitely more than one chopper, and they're just hanging above the fog layer. The clever devil! He must have planted another transponder on me, in my shoe while I slept at Quantico. That's okay, TC. You can be a backup, if it comes to that.

The battle has yet to be won. Her *ki* cautioned Lara soberly.

Yeah, I know. But the Beast is fading. I can sense it. That means I can let him wear me down, but still have something left at the end to spring the trap. The blossoming hope shaded possible into probable in her mind. She was going to win this battle! Teeth bared in a snarling smile, Lara Picard laughed right in the indiscernible face of the monster she knew would be coming for her in a few moments.

Upper New Haven Harbor, CT | Tuesday 0549 EDT

John swung right, onto a city street headed due north, paralleling the green-tinged black blot on his consciousness radar. Just a few hundred meters separated them. He glanced to his right, and saw nothing but fog and dilapidated industrial buildings. He glanced down at his speedometer. She'd come across the harbor, in and out of the water. He hadn't heard a boat. So she had to be flying over the water's surface now, as fast as she could in the fog.

Yes, she is evidently a flyer, not a transposer.

Does she know I transpose? Can she do it?

Probably. She understands the capability, but it is less natural to her, as flying is less natural to you.

Why is she flying north, up a neck of the harbor? She's moving toward land, where the fog will break up eventually and she'll lose some advantage. Why doesn't she fly south, over the harbor? That's open water, and then Long Island Sound. She could fly to Long Island in... half an hour, maybe less. I wouldn't be able to follow her since I can't see to transpose. There are no bridges across; if I drove south to New York it would take hours. She probably could pick up a lot of time on me. So why is she headed north?

Uncertain. Possibly she became disoriented in the fog, and is not familiar with the area. Or possibly she suspects you could commandeer another aircraft, or a boat, and catch up easily. She would be quite vulnerable over open water.

Possibilities tumbled around in John's mind-space, as if blown by the rotors of the helicopters in the vaguely brightening sky overhead. The blot on his consciousness radar abruptly slowed and stopped, off to his right. He spun the car into a tight turn into a factory area, barreled down between tall conical piles of some kind of scrap material, and slammed on the brakes at a docking area by the water. An errant breeze, a warmer downdraft from one of the circling choppers, momentarily improved visibility. Across a channel to the east, he got his first visual sighting of the Other. The flittering black form, its evil emerald glow around it, slithered into an access door on the side of an old power plant.

No, John thought, as the pounding in his skull increased. No, she isn't disoriented at all. She's a superb tactician. And not fleeing across the Sound is choice, not accident.

This is another trap. The soldier knew it. The Magician tasted it. But the Assassin cared nothing for a trap. The rage started to build.

107 km Northeast of Kennedy VORTAC | Tuesday 0550 EDT

"No, keep them the fuck out of the loop," Agent TC Demuzzio ordered Colonel Merton Shaundee, "Tell the New Haven PD we're just orbiting, waiting for the fog to clear at the Coast Guard Station. Pass it along through Tweed tower. Say it's a training mission, classified, an anti-terrorist exercise. We may need 'em later, but not just yet."

Shaundee leaned forward to relay those instructions to the Black Hawk copilot.

Demuzzio looked out at the impenetrable layer below him and marveled at just how complicated the situation had become. A densely populated city was waking up after a holiday weekend, school buses were warming up, early shifts were leaving for work, and all this in a fog as heavy as anything seen over the northeast in decades.

Three helicopters full of armed troops circled above the city, containing the best and the brightest, not to say deadliest, fighting force on the face of the earth. The soldiers were about to take military action, if they could, to capture or possibly kill two American citizens that by logic and inference contained extraterrestrial beings. And his information on their position could be minutes off, unless he got lucky and they stayed put.

The big agent dropped his head in his hands and massaged his stubbly face as he contemplated the orders he might have to give. Soldiers operating on US soil, even supporting a legitimate police action, was constitutionally gray. It was inconceivable that even the broad authority he'd been given, and duly recorded, would cover some of the orders he might have to give. And yet he would give those orders anyway. If it all turned to shit, he'd be the one holding the bedpan. Along with his old friend Colonel Merton Shaundee.

"No, sir," the pilot told Shaundee, "we can't get any lower. See that double vortex in the fog? That's the steam plume from the power plant. The nav maps put the plant stacks at three hundred feet, and show transmission lines and structures lower down. It's just too tight an area to descend in the fog, even with infrared, sir, unless we had a transponder down there in a confirmed open area. We'll just have to hang on station here until it starts to break up, sir. Shouldn't be long now, with the sun up. Half an hour, maybe less."

"Strings?" Shaundee asked him.

"No, sir. The fog is still too thick. Our altitude is too high, and the nav info isn't precise enough. We could end up dropping troops into the power lines."

Shaundee looked over at Demuzzio and cocked an eyebrow. The agent shook his head: no heroics at this point, not even if one of those soldiers was foolish enough to volunteer taking a landing transponder down. For all they knew, their quarry might depart this area in a hurry, and then they'd be further behind. He sighed in frustration and pressed his hands to his crew-cut head again, as if to squeeze some clarity out of the mental popcorn inside.

I-95 / I-91 New Haven, CT | Tuesday 0551 EDT

"No, Uncle Ham, no! We have to turn around! Take the first exit you can!" Their Edsel was just crossing the crest of the bridge, staying well to the left to avoid the flashing lights of the state trooper in the right hand lane beside a damaged railing.

Hamilton O'Donnell glanced quickly at his nephew. *"Airport's ahead of us, me lad."*

"But Mom's behind us now! And John, too, I think. I can sense their threads. They're heading into trouble!"

And well they may be, laddie, but the question here is, do you need to join them in their troubles? Or do we await the outcome at the airport, at some safe distance? He turned that infinitely complex question over in his mind, but then submitted to instinct and turned the car smartly onto the exit ramp at the base of the bridge. *Well, if you're determined to join them, he thought, perhaps your uncle might be permitted to prepare you a bit. Yes, I believe that would not be... inappropriate. Even with due regard for me ould friend Werner Karl Heisenberg's feelin's on such matters....*

"Joshua, me lad," he resumed their mind-dance as he turned the car left under the bridge to find an on-ramp and reverse direction, "in the tarot deck, the Universe card sets the final seal on that series of fables. It depicts a dragon. In some portrayals, the dragon is eatin' its tail; in others it is uncoilin'. In either case it represents an openin' of its eyes to hidden truths."

"Entrance ramp coming up on the left, Uncle Ham," Joshua advised him, preoccupied, not easily drawn into the mind-dance.

"Umm. Got it. Did you hear what I said, Joshua?"

"Yes, Uncle Ham. The Universe card. Hidden truths? Tell me about them. But hurry up across the bridge. Please!"

"Shapes arise from above the dragon's eyes on the Universe card, me lad. They symbolize the discernment of these hidden truths, the enlightenment at the end of its fable."

The boy abruptly snapped his attention off the ramp's convergence with the bridge highway and onto his uncle's profile.

Ah, he has connected, the old man thought. He nodded his head and continued. "The dragon on the card breathes fire, me lad. Fire for a dragon is breath. The Latin for breath is *spiritus*. From that root spring English words such as spirit, and inspiration. Are you catching my drift, as your generation likes to ask?"

"I think so, Uncle Ham. Bear to the right here." Now that's of note, his uncle thought. The boy didn't even take his eyes off me to glance at the road.

"For us, my young philosopher," he continued as he steered the car to the right, "for us poor puny humans, the dragon's breath might be danger and destruction. Or, alternatively, it might be seen as burnin' away illusions, a cleansin'. Very different possibilities, me lad. And you just told me this fine foggy mornin' that we are all mere possibilities, did you not?"

"Bear to the right here again, Uncle Ham, quick," the boy said, unblinking eyes still on his uncle.

They rolled down a long exit ramp off the highway. It curved onto a city street. Joshua glanced up at it through the windshield, weighing and computing. "Straight through to that second light, Uncle Ham. Then turn... left."

"We poor humans tend see our enemies in terms of ourselves, me lad, the worst part of ourselves, some ravenin' beast. But the dragon that most truly invites destruction comes from within us, not from outside. External dragons are illusion. *Comprenez-vous?*"

"Turn right, here, Uncle Ham. I do understand, sort of. Illusion and perception. Perspectives and points of view. So many variables. It has to be difficult to uncover the hidden truth sometimes. But the answer always is inside us, you're saying."

"Ah, me lad, yes, bless your heart, there you have it. What if we choose not to perceive others, or the world, or even ourselves, as the enemy? Then we become more careful, do we not? We check our beliefs. We verify our perceptions. We admit to the possibility of illusion. We consider whether our battle might better be made one of liberation and love. We make sure that our battle truly needs to be one of conquest and destruction. And only then do we choose, Joshua. Only then do we choose."

"Turn right, here, Uncle Ham," Joshua said, his voice suddenly uncertain, edgy with concern.

The Edsel pulled to a stop in front of a security gate. Behind it, an old power plant loomed through the fog, vaguely reminiscent of a gothic castle. As the fog layer lightened slightly in response to the rising sun above it, the castle's lights shaded eerily into the fog. It became impossible to discern where solidity ended and air began. They got out of the car and stared at the plant through the chain link fence.

Joshua rattled the gate, and looked at its ten-foot height and rolled razor wire on top. "I have to get in! Uncle Ham, I have to get in! Can you give me a boost?"

"Ah, well, that wouldn't seem to be a good idea, me lad. Why don't we see if we can't talk our way in?" He walked over to the speaker box on the post and pushed its button. There was no answer. He pushed it again.

"Uncle Ham! I have to get in!" Joshua said emphatically, almost screaming. His uncle ran a hand down over the keypad below the speaker. Inexplicably, the gate began to crank open.

They got back in the car and drove quickly onto the power plant grounds. Behind them, the gate went to the full open position and held there. Hamilton O'Donnell shrugged noncommittally in silent answer to his nephew's look. More important questions were at hand than manipulation of electronics.

"And what reaction might you have to our little discussion, me lad? About the Universe card, the end point in the tarot, if I might enquire?"

"Like you told me Sunday night, Uncle Ham, the tarot teaches choices." The edge of hysteria left the boy as they entered the gate, but his voice still shook with tension. Joshua paused as they climbed out of the car in front of the plant entrance, obviously forcing a calmness he didn't feel. "I believe that's exactly right. It fits my diagram. So the monkey can choose. It can choose to hang onto the nuts, with its hand stuck in the gourd, and become monkey soup. Or it can choose to let go, and escape the trap. Choices, Uncle Ham. Possibilities and choices."

Flickers of blue and green light shot from the upper windows of the tall old building to greet the boy's answer, but were lost in the fog.

Chapter 40

Inside the generating station, Lara flew across an old and gutted turbine hall toward the newer part of the plant. That part held an abundance of live electric equipment for her trap. The plant shift mechanic exiting the control room to check on the security alarm had a brief frozen moment of amazement before a wave of blackness enveloped him. His coffee mug dropped from nerveless fingers and he collapsed on top of it. Wasting no time, Lara lifted him one-handed in a gravity embrace and impelled him back to the control room. The plant shift operator there had not even a chance to swivel around in his chair before a tossed chaos field overtook him too.

She flung herself into a frenetic reconnaissance of the superstructure and catwalks around the big boilers. She memorized the layout, cataloging equipment where instinct said the voltage would be high enough for her purposes. She picked the concealed areas from which her three simulacra would emerge, and held those illusions there, quiescent markers, baleful entities of emptiness limned by green flames.

Time seemed to stand still as she flitted through lines of retreat on her carefully chosen battleground. Then she was done; the trap was set. She flew out onto the generator deck to greet the Beast, just as he appeared at the far end of the old turbine hall.

They surveyed each other across the length of the long open structure, easily a hundred meters. Like her, he wore the formless chaos cloak of the null dimension. The Beast's energy aura was a deep, deep blue, an amethyst, she saw, almost beautiful. But surrounding that shifting black emptiness the color became obscene: a flickering precursor of hate and destruction, an incarnation of the evil that pulsed in her mind.

As he stood there regarding her, the Beast's pulsations took on a sardonic overtone. *Got you now, bitch, you've run out of time, and places to run to,* they said. The message had a crystalline clarity to it, a hard edge, unforgiving and sharp. Lara reached down into her lower levels of consciousness for the only possible response to that intimidation; she arrowed the elemental rage of her own beast at him. His evil image in her mind did not flinch, and his overtone did not change, except possibly to signal amusement at her puny capability. But she picked up visually, even from that distance, tiny telltale shiftings. They validated her intuition: the Beast was indeed tired, his resources depleted, his intimidation a boastful sham. He was far from unbeatable now.

Her second message, sardonically overtoned to match his, pulsed back at him, fueled by elemental rage. *Nice try, asshole, except you're the one who's run out of time*, it said. But her rage was carefully modulated. She would not disclose its full strength just yet. She still had a trap to spring.

As they studied each other, Lara realized, time had become dilated, nearly non-existent. Only fractions of a millisecond were passing.

Anglick Generating Station, New Haven, CT | Tuesday 0552 EDT

The Magician examined the Other across the length of the long structure, analyzing the battleground. The turbine hall was more than a hundred meters long, a relic of the days when electrical generating equipment had been bigger and bulkier. The old steam turbines had been removed, and only pedestals and holes in the floor remained. The roof arced high overhead. Holes in the floor showed a sheer drop down to demolished steam condenser boxes below ground level, all broken and jagged metal, with pipes upturned like a graveyard of rusty bayonets. The Magician tried to visualize what her trap would be, while the Assassin pulsed impatiently within, his elemental rage building.

The distant apparition was almost like a painting, like something his mother might have done. Exacting details, applied to a representation almost entirely symbolic. The Other's energy aura flickered a brilliant emerald green, he saw, a painfully pure tone. It would be beautiful on a good human being. But on one who had been turned to darkness, when it surrounded that shifting black nothingness, the color became disgusting. The aura signaled not beauty, but hate and destruction in the seduced mind of its human host.

The Assassin's rage cast his challenge, and it flowed sinuously across the distance between them. It carried an overtone of derisive dismissal of whatever defenses she could possibly mount. *You're mine now, you're dead meat, your time is up*, that challenge said, a statement designed to intimidate and weaken.

But as the Other stood there regarding him across the length of the turbine hall, her evil pulsations reflected back the overtones of an unexpected and equally scornful response. *No, asshole, you're the one who's run out of time*, it said. Her message also carried an amused overtone that he was a country bumpkin who had stupidly stumbled into her trap; she clearly intended not only to undermine his confidence, but also to get him to watch out for too many possibilities. Clever, the Magician realized. If he bought into that message, it could either infuriate him into precipitous action, or slow him into a fatal misstep.

Under the pressure of that moment, John felt the physiological barriers between brain segments drop below some unseen threshold. His personae began to converse and coalesce.

She knows we are tired, the Magician thought, *she picked that up somehow.*

Yes, but she gave herself away, the Assassin gloated in riposte. *She showed her strength, and it is less than ours. She is weaker, we are stronger.*

That is not certain, the Magician cautioned, *she might not have disclosed her full strength.*

Only fractions of a millisecond had elapsed, the Magician and Assassin realized simultaneously. The thought that immediately followed came directly out of John Connard's experience as a soldier: speed is a weapon, especially the speed at which overwhelming force can be applied. Instantly upon that thought, and without recourse to either the Magician or the soldier, the Assassin transposed straight for their enemy at the far end of the long hall. He held in front of him a massive shield of chaos, all he was capable of drawing from the null dimension, surely enough to swamp the puny thing that dared defy him.

Anglick Generating Station, New Haven, CT | Tuesday 0553 EDT

Lara sensed the intent to attack before it happened, and was twenty feet in the air overhead when the Beast snapped into the place she had just vacated. The wave of chaos preceding him like a bow wave would certainly have dropped her like a rock. Instead, the black nothingness wrapped itself around the end of a turbine generator, where it dissipated the thick red paint and a few millimeters of the underlying steel into nothingness. She was shocked at the intensity of the field; it was many times over what she had been able to throw at him in the Irving Street safehouse. Her mind-space fragmented, and her consciousness radar burned out from the distortion of the dimensional interface.

Lara watched the Beast's amethyst aura dim and drop to a deeper shade as he crouched beneath her. She sensed a further depletion of his resources. Two big swings and two big misses, she thought, a huge gravity wave and an even huger chaos field. So you're tired, aren't you, asshole? Now just play along with me here, and we'll see if we can't get you to punch yourself out some more on my doubles. She unleashed the elemental rage at her primitive core, her own beast, and slashed downward with her right hand, a dazzling scimitar of pure green light, a screaming primal *kiai*, enough energy behind it to behead a granite statue.

The Beast reacted instantly, sweeping up a block with his left hand, a plane of blue light. Coruscations of energy erupted from the contact, sparkling off into the air, spattering with explosive snaps upon contact with concrete or steel. He followed the block with a counter thrust of his right hand, a lance of blue flame to her midsection. Dancing in the air above him, she knocked it aside with a sweep of her left foot, and kicked downward with her right foot, green flame lancing outward. His head jerked sideways, but the energy lance caught his shoulder. The blow fizzled on contact with the chaos field cloaking the Beast's body; but nonetheless the force of it knocked him backwards away from her. He rolled out of his somersaulting turn with automatic defensive motions, blue planes of light flickering angrily around his weaving hands.

"First blood, asshole!" A snarling smile crossed Lara's lips as she grunted those words to herself, but she suppressed the full depth of her primal rage and its crying need for all-out attack. No, he was still too strong, too formidable, for a direct attack. And he had been very well trained in the martial arts. Those defensive motions carried a familiar style, probably the same techniques that John had trained in, and subsequently trained her in. Well, that style was common enough. This was both good and bad, the attacks and defenses would be recognizable to her, but probably also to the Beast.

Lara clamped down hard on her rage, and forced her mind back into the rational: adherence to the plan, the trap. That's it, girl, cool off! Get him to wear himself down some more. She spun in the air and flew up into the maze of catwalks and equipment around the big steam boilers. His roar of rage resonated in her mind as he transposed to the catwalk in front of her trajectory. But she had anticipated that, and changed her vector in mid-flight: she flew instead underneath him, one level down, weaving agilely through the constricted area to where her first simulacrum awaited.

Anglick Generating Station, New Haven, CT | Tuesday 0553 EDT

The Magician struggled to bring the Assassin back under control, to reset his hard rational edge onto the Assassin's rage before its mindlessness got them killed and their mission failed. The belated realization that he had just entered a trap finally made the Assassin relinquish control, retreating into its cave. Its eyes, ancient and cold and reptilian, looked out from the cave warily, awaiting opportunity.

"Definitely a trap," the Magician muttered to himself, "somewhere in this place." He would have to be careful. She hadn't much time to set it up, but she surely picked it well. She could flit around in this maze much better than he could transpose limited by line-of-sight. She would fight again with a simulacrum, he believed. She would try to keep herself protected from damage while she wore him down. He weighed that possibility as he dropped to the level below. The pounding in his skull would make it difficult to tell her apart from her simulacrum. And she was carefully not revealing her full strength; she wanted him to underestimate her. Clever bitch! Still, he should have enough left. He had years and years of Special Forces conditioning in deprivation and living on the edge of exhaustion. He thought it unlikely he would crumble first, even in his depleted state. The thought cheered him so much he was almost too late in reacting to the burst of energy that speared toward his side.

The Magician reacted belatedly, but still with a speed beyond comprehension, a speed far greater than he'd seen or imagined even when sparring with his sensei Duc Li. The shaft of green energy was knocked away by his block, but his counterstrike was blocked too. He sparred across the catwalk with the Other, a flashing dance of death, strike and block and counterstrike. The steel of the catwalk structure was sheared through in several places, and crumbling about them. It abruptly collapsed beneath him, and his last shearing strike went wild, nicking a steam line. A deadly plume of superheated vapor under six hundred pounds of pressure screamed into the face of the Other. He saw as he fell that it blew right through her. Simulacrum! Instinctively, the Magician slashed downward with defensive energy planes from his feet as he dropped, knowing that the Other would be waiting.

And she was. The blades of blue energy took her full in the chest and sent her spinning completely off the catwalk into empty air. Her simulacrum winked out above him. First blood for me, bitch, he snarled.

The Other spun gracefully in the air below and flew back into the lower levels of the boiler superstructure, but more slowly than she could have. Could be faking it, the Magician thought, but she's probably really hurt; I made solid contact. That means she won't be able to take the pounding, if I can just get her cornered.

From not very deep in his mind, the Assassin's reptilian eyes shone its rage outward at the thought of pounding his quarry into oblivion, and the Magician transposed downward to the lower catwalk where that quarry had disappeared.

Anglick Generating Station, New Haven, CT | Tuesday 0554 EDT

Good God, he's strong! Lara coughed the thought out as she gasped in air to replace that kicked out of her lungs. If the null field of her chaos cloak hadn't been so effective, and those energy blades had penetrated more, she would have been totally eviscerated. As it was, she would have massive bruises on her ribcage.

Lara sensed, without looking behind her, the Beast's appearance on the lower catwalk, and veered to the right, putting the massive structure of the boiler between them. She turned upward, toward the place where she had concealed her second simulacrum, and knew the Beast followed. I'll let him get punched out on another double, she thought, and wear him down some more before we engage directly. As he transposed upward to her hiding place on the upper catwalk, she released the simulacrum behind him and attacked with it. The weakened aura around the Beast flared back into an intense amethyst blue as he reacted to the ambush and engaged her surrogate.

Lara moved and twitched, puppeteering the simulacrum to her bidding, striking and counterstriking with brilliant planes of emerald energy. The contacts were greeted with grunts of absorption, the misses sheared off steel and concrete. She felt her control over the simulacrum fading under the pounding, and she also sensed the loss of energy it was costing her, but his loss was significantly greater. Aikido, she reaffirmed. Cause the opponent's own strength to turn on him. It was working!

Then he did something totally unexpected. He cast a gravity field on the simulacrum. Lara recognized it only from the loose guard rail exploding outward from behind the sparring forms; it had no effect at all on her doppelganger. As of course it wouldn't, her simulacrum had no mass, no real substance in this reality; it was merely energy confined and wrapped into a material shape. Ah, very clever, she thought, you've diagnosed it, you've figured out how to tell what's real and what's not.

With a casual, almost dismissive backhanded chop, the Beast swept the spent simulacrum out of existence and turned to stare at her, at the far end of the catwalk. She stared back for a fraction of an instant and vanished, fleeing to the uppermost level where her third and last simulacrum was waiting. I've just got to work him a little bit more, I think, and then he'll drop into my trap like a meteor into a black hole.

Anglick Generating Station, New Haven, CT | Tuesday 0554 EDT

The Assassin raged at the deception, but the Magician shrugged it off and stayed in control. Ah, we're making progress now, my friend, he told the Assassin. The Other's trap was ad-lib, set up to cause me to spend resources at a faster rate than her, that's all. This is a simple equation. All I have to do is be a little smarter, conserve my strength. Use some mind games, undermine her will. We will outlast her, grind her down. Be patient, my beast. The Assassin blinked its reptilian eyes in acknowledgment, harnessed.

Patience, John Connard, patience. Become the thing you wish to understand. He remembered that instruction from Duc Li, a bit of Taoist wisdom to enlighten a brash young Special Forces trainee. Ah, I've been too quick, he realized, too intent on application of overwhelming force, too eager to get it over. I need to anticipate better. This battle may go on awhile. He forced himself into a leisurely pace over to the catwalk from which she'd departed, and looked upward. The Other, or a double, was standing on the catwalk around the other boiler, and looked down on him from five stories above.

The Magician transposed to the upper catwalk, casting a gravity field as he arrived, and when there was no effect from gravity, he followed that with a chaos field before the thing could react. The simulacrum dissipated into nothingness.

He spun around, wary of another ambush, but there was none. She's playing with me, sapping my strength, trying to buy time. Maybe she's waiting for those choppers to land, after all. Well, how about a little mind-game, bitch, he thought. Maybe that will smoke you out.

The Magician walked to the spot where the simulacrum had been and projected a crude replica. Along with it he projected an interpretation of his Assassin as a primitive reptile, a raptor. The Assassin held the inert body of the replica in prehensile claws and bit into it. Blood and gore splattered the catwalk, actually shocking the Magician at the reality of the intimidation he'd created. Maybe that will smoke her out, he hoped. But as he let the Assassin crunch realistically into his artful creation of muscle and bone, a huge blow to his back knocked him over the railing into the air.

Anglick Generating Station, New Haven, CT | Tuesday 0555 EDT

Maybe I can't lift a truck with gravity, asshole, but I sure can give a fire extinguisher some good velocity! Maybe I got lucky and broke your back. Lara hung in the hot air at the very top of the building and watched the Beast fall, hoping. But just before he reached the floor, his aura flared and he vanished.

"Shit! So now it's time to unleash my own beast. We'll see who crunches who now!" With a bloodcurdling scream echoing off the pounding in her head, she loosed her primal rage and launched herself downward to the plant floor.

The Beast crouched by a steel column, waiting for her. He hunched over, hurt; his aura was dimmer and darker, almost purple. It made the shifting nothingness of his chaos cloak even more sinister. The air crackled as planes of dark blue light leapt from his hands. There could be no quarter for this Beast, she thought, nor would he offer any to her. Bright emerald planes of light flared from her hands as she circled her enemy.

More air ionized, but amid the ozone smell of lightning and scorched metal, her sensitive nose twitched as it picked out other smells. It's part of this evolutionary development, the back of her mind realized. And I just felt the barriers between my brain segments drop another notch; I'm reconnecting with the survival senses of my primeval ancestors. The smells were hauntingly familiar, but what did they mean? Were they important here? Now? The mystery disturbed her, but she pushed it away; more important survival matters were at hand.

He's not moving. I wonder just how badly he's hurt. Immediately on that thought, she danced into the air. A gravity wave rolled beneath her and crushed a tool cart into the side of a boiler. Ah! Playing possum! Not hurt too badly, just tired and depleted. Well, there goes another missed shot, asshole! She slashed energy planes at him with her feet as she flew overhead to the first catwalk. The resistance they met at his null field told her intuition that he was nearly ready for the trap. She attacked again, playing her rage like an instrument, but keeping the full extent of its power concealed.

Thrust and parry. Strike and counterstrike. She drove screaming blades of energy at him. She tore fields of nothingness from the null dimension and cast them at him. She sent loose objects hurtling toward him on gravity waves. She gave full play to her primal rage, save for a last little bit.

The air thickened with dust and debris, and with the increasingly dense condensation from the screaming steam leak aloft. The smell of lightning grew as their efforts intensified, mixed with other, more subtle odors of battle that nibbled away at her consciousness with a haunting familiarity.

The Beast was wearing her down. As tired and depleted as he was, he was wearing her down. Lara Picard backed away toward the electrical generator end of the active turbine, fighting, slashing him with planes of energy, feeling their impact. She sensed the fire extinguisher flying at the side of her head, and ducked, letting it make just enough of a grazing contact to be persuasive. Pretending to be stunned, she reached out as if to catch herself on the big machine, and was slammed back against it, pinned there helplessly by his massive gravity wave. The wave was pulsating, unstable, so in his battered condition he probably couldn't hold it long, she thought. Other than that, her situation was exactly as planned. From not very deep in her mind, the carefully concealed remnant of rage in her own beast smoldered and snarled impatiently as it waited to spring the trap.

Anglick Generating Station, New Haven, CT | Tuesday 0555 EDT

A hurt and depleted John Connard held the Other against the steel housing of the generator with an inescapable gravity field, but his control of the field was marginal. Incredible strength, he thought. I wore her down, but she faded only a little faster than me, and she was smarter, too. So I got lucky. He stared at the cloaked form that his gravity field held crucified helplessly against the generator housing. A deep green aura flared around the nothingness of her chaos cloak, and pulsated in resonance with the pounding in his head. That pounding now contained terror as well as defiance, he sensed. The Magician raised his left hand to stabilize the gravity field as best he could, then flared a plane of blue light from his right hand for the killing stroke.

Then he stopped. Something was not quite right, and it tugged at him. Nothing is ever exactly quite right in combat, he thought. But I'm used to that. No, this is something that's more subtle. Much more subtle; it's something to do with perception. Ah, yes: perception is subject to illusion.

That's why, even with the drug lords, the scum of the earth, the Magician always insists on seeing clearly. He decides for himself on the target, and studies until he knows him, his life, his habits, his redeeming qualities if he has any. Alex told me one time that the Magician did that out of love. Even though I'm killing, I'm really just culling the herd, removing the misfits, so that on a larger stage I'm acting out of love for humanity.

So by the Magician's own moral code I must know this thing I'm about to kill. He wrapped nullity around the blade of energy, to strip the chaos cloak away from the Other's face.

No! Kill it! The Assassin raged, a burning red flame in his mind. *Kill it now!* The Magician's hand trembled, barely controlling the Assassin's killing thrust. His mindspace was white static, and there was no voice of his nexus Duc Li to consult. There was no Alex Shaughnessy with whom to reflect on his moral dilemma. This decision would be his, and his alone.

John Connard sobbed in moral agony, and the pounding in his skull escalated as if in resonance. The Assassin was probably right. But the Magician had to know. He subdued the Assassin and extended his strangely configured hand toward the cloaked face of the Other.

Anglick Generating Station, New Haven, CT | Tuesday 0555 EDT

Even through the haze of the gravity force pinning her against the generator, and even through the pounding of the Beast's evil gloating pulsations in her head, Lara Picard could sense the electromagnetic fields of the massive generator spinning underneath her. Weeping with the agony of the effort, she made herself part of that circuit, channeling a portion of its electricity through the null dimension of her chaos cloak, between her crucified arms. The diverted electrical field ran across the surface of the cloak, from her right hand to her left, but was isolated from her physical body. The field's potential sought a path to ground but found none, and thus remained concealed in deadly ambush. In this reality, she understood, electricity is a lower frequency energy. Unlike the planes of ionizing light abstracted from the energy dimension, it gives little hint of its deadly presence.

So, her trap was set. The instant his killing energy strike hit her chaos cloak, the electricity flowing over it would have a direct path to ground, straight through his body. Lara strained to see through the bloody haze in her eyes, their capillaries bursting from the gravity field. She held her trap steady, silently begging him to get on with it.

He did. And even though she had planned this very outcome, she watched in terror as the shadowy form extruded a plane of pure blue energy from his right hand. It reached inexorably toward her throat, hesitated, and then, obscenely, reached for her face. He was going to stab through her mouth, into her brain! Lara Picard drew on the last of her reserves, powering them with that primal survival rage of a cornered animal. She shifted the electrical pathway slightly to compensate for his intended point of contact, and felt its tickling vibration run across her cheeks and mouth, on the outside of her null field.

A flash, a blackness in her vision, and then so sudden a release from gravity that Lara went sprawling forward over the hard concrete floor. Gasping in air, clamping down on the urge to void or vomit or both, she pushed up onto her hands and knees, scarcely willing to believe that the pounding in her skull was gone. She willed some sense of orientation to return. It did, slowly, and along with it she felt the erratic return of her control over other dimensions. Her chaos cloak closed protectively back around her, and an aura of green energy took shape dimly outside it. She formed an energy plane, weak and tentative but still deadly, with her right hand. Well, she decided, she was still a functional fighter, sort of. And she sensed her ability to fly would return shortly. That's good, she thought; I need to be gone and on my way to Ireland with Ham and Josh before those helicopters land.

"But first things first," she muttered, remembering John's soldierly practical instructions to her about deadly combat, "let's make sure the Beast is dead." Standing up shakily, she limped over to his inert form.

Global Consciousness Project, Princeton University, NJ | Tuesday 0556 EDT

Three FBI agents guarded Adrienne Baxter inside the Global Consciousness Project computer room, one at the door, one across the room. The third, a female agent, sat beside her at the computer console, sticking to her, as TC Demuzzio had ordered, like glue. The three of them were very polite, Adrienne acknowledged, even friendly, but it still was aggravating to operate in a fishbowl. She worked in desultory fashion at re-coding her 15-minute average location displays into the 1-minute locators Demuzzio had instructed, hoping she was faking it effectively. Mainly she watched the bar graphs as they changed, minute-by-minute. She could infer easily enough from them what was going on.

Blue had caught up with Green; that much was certain. Huge spikes in the data occurred around 0545. The effect could be seen to varying degrees on all the GCDs from Maine to Ohio to North Carolina. From their strengths and distances, Adrienne mentally interpolated the epicenter to be near the mouth of the Quinnipiac River. Her re-coded algorithm would give her a more precise displayed solution, with crosshairs and probability circles updated on a 1-minute basis, just what the FBI agent wanted. That display was only a keystroke away, but she continued to withhold the stroke. A strong intuition told her to let this play out, without the intervention of one TC Demuzzio and his soldiers.

Although she believed her intuition was right, another part of her mind squirmed helplessly with concern for Aaron and Nathan. What if they stumbled into some kind of psychic crossfire? Aaron was surely approaching the scene, and Nathan at last report wasn't very far behind. She glanced at the clock on the bottom of the computer screen. That was only ten minutes ago, just as the agents had arrived.

Time dilated for Adrienne, becoming very subjective. Minutes felt like hours. She felt stretched and flattened, as if her body had become a sheet of rubber being pulled in different directions. Her delicate fingers trembled indecisively over the keyboard, but made no stroke.

Chapter 41

Nothingness. Complete and total blankness. John Connard was nowhere and nowhen. His consciousness must exist, though, in some form, he was sure of that. He tried to push outward, imagining metaphorical hands pressing against unseen barriers, a baby in a womb. There was nothing physical to press against in this sort of womb, but the movement created dimly sensed vibrations. They whispered around him, seeking resonance, wanting to build into a song. As he opened his consciousness, they took on a threadlike form, vibrating with different harmonics, weaving around each other. They were definitely singing, he thought, and he recognized their melodies.

John smiled at the threads as he accepted his father, or his father's memory, into the music. As in the caves, it carried concern and amusement, mixed in equal measure. His mother, or his mother's memory, slid in, resonating in harmony, all kaleidoscopic art and beauty. His baby sister Jessica, or her memory, contributed the counterpoint of a child's pure unconditional love. The threads of their songs wove in with his own. The quiet spiritual thread-melodies of his mentors Duc Li and Alex Shaughnessy played in the background. He contemplated the music they all made together.

All of it, John understood, was the past. But he was in the present, in an instant of no time, the null dimension. He was nothing, and everything, both at once. He was the physical or spiritual composite of their threads, their songs. And those songs still played forward somehow, into the future, didn't they? But his own threads into the future were tangled. He saw that he needed to smooth them out; otherwise his song would be a discordant mess. He called to the Magician to interpret the metaphor, to guide his actions into the future.

But the Magician clearly had more pressing business, and John Connard had to step back to let it unfold. Ah, so that's what happened, the Magician thought, running mind-images backward in time. That was her trap all along! So prosaic I couldn't even see it. She hung the electrical outlet right there and I stuck my finger right into it, didn't I? Electricity! So primitive, yet so simple, so elegant. And so well concealed! So who's the real Magician here? He laughed at the absurdity of being beaten at his own game.

But then, he wondered belatedly, why am I not dead? Clearly, he wasn't. He looked down on his own inert body on the floor below. It still pulsed with life. How could that be? A chaos cloak still enveloped the body, and a deep blue aura still flickered dimly around it. And how could that be? Yet his body definitely lay down there, and he floated up here, three or four meters above it. He panned back through his mind images, more slowly. Ah, that's it, then. I had a second null field imposed on top of the energy plane, so I could strip the chaos mask off her face. Most of the electricity went over me as a surface effect, not through me. The Magician smiled. If he had simply thrust the energy plane through her throat, as the Assassin demanded, he would have been fried from the inside out. He sent that graphic image to the beast lurking within him, a chiding reminder against thoughtless precipitous action.

The Other limped into the picture below and stood over his body, a plane of green energy hanging down from her right hand, tired and wavering but still quite deadly. Ah, it's time to go back to my body, John thought, before this thing cuts the threads to my future.

Anglick Generating Station, New Haven, CT | Tuesday 0557 EDT

"Shit," Lara muttered, flipping over the Beast's limp body with her toe, "he's still alive." A chaos cloak still encased him, obscuring his face. A dimly flickering blue aura extruded from the cloak, almost lost in the floating fine particulate dust and steam mist caused by their battle.

"How the hell did he survive that jolt of electricity? I felt it go right into him." Well, it didn't really matter; she decided. The Beast was inert and helpless now; the pounding pulsations in her skull had disappeared. The plane of green energy pulsed and brightened in her right hand. She steeled herself to the necessity.

I've done it before, she reminded herself. I've killed a human being. I broke the neck of that crackhead hitman the Castagnas sent after me in San Diego. I didn't feel bad about that. In fact, I really wanted to stand him upright and break his neck again. I killed a man then, I can do it now. The plane of green energy pulsed and brightened more. Helpless as he was, she still had to kill this Beast. A cold and righteous delight in her power over this thing, in her ability to rid the earth of this abomination, slid into her mind and suffused her being. She stepped into the power, exulted in it. She drew in a deep breath and drew back her hand for the killing stroke.

But still, she thought, hesitating, something is not quite right. Something tugged at her, whatever it was. She knew from extensive courtroom experience that almost never is everything quite right in a case. As a prosecutor, you learn to live with those uncertainties. But no, this uncertainty is more subtle. For one thing, the events when taken together seem like too much of a set piece. In fact, the intuition flashed on her, something is very, very scripted about them. Something to do with perception. And perception is subject to illusion, almost always.

The best lawyers make juries see what they want them to see. They filter, they slant, they interpret. They object to counter-interpretations. In jurors' minds they turn possibilities into probabilities, and probabilities into certainties. They withhold key pieces of the puzzle, if they can. Sometimes they're so good at it they even mislead themselves. This whole event has that sort of feel to it, doesn't it?

And then there are the smells, mixed in with the ozone, familiar smells, somehow. Do those need to be considered? They have some meaning, but it's escaping me.

As her killing hand paused at the top of its arc, Lara's memory abruptly flashed back to her former friend and mentor TC Demuzzio, consoling her yesterday morning, in the Black Hawk ride from the Naval Observatory down to Quantico. "Three good people dead, TC," she'd mourned, tears running down her face for the agents who had defended her. TC had blinked at her, and lowered his eyes. "I'm sorry, Lara," he'd said.

Lara replayed that scene in her mind-space, now, in slow motion and in exquisite detail of sights and smells and nuances. She recalled TC's noncommittal answer: *I'm sorry, Lara.* Shafts of morning sunlight had slanted through the helicopter window, playing across the lines of hard experience and harder decisions on the agent's face. Those lines twitched where they shouldn't have, and his eye focus shifted and their pupils changed, ever so slightly. Telltale pheromones also should have alerted her. In retrospect, she understood perfectly: her good friend TC Demuzzio had lied to her. Misled her, at least. Those agents weren't dead! The Beast hadn't killed them! She confirmed that now: tiny nuanced giveaways in TC's expressions that replayed with exquisite clarity in her mind's eye.

The Beast wanted to kill Lara Picard, that was quite clear, but not necessarily anyone else. Was this a pragmatic consideration for the Beast, or a moral one? It would make a big difference. If moral, then compassion or morality or something existed there, inside that awful thing, didn't it? She had no choice; she had to find out. If I see his face, she thought, then I'll know. Lara lowered her blade of emerald energy, and edged it with nullity; this, she intuited, would strip the chaos cloak away from the Beast's face.

The fragments in Lara's mind-space started to re-cohere at that very moment.

Her nexus, her *ki*, screamed at her with overwhelming demand: *No! Kill it!* A burning red flame of primal rage pervaded her entire being. *It will kill you, and your son. It will subvert the entire new human race! You must kill it now, Lara Picard! You must! It is deadly, still deadly!*

Exultant power flooded into her along with the primal rage, a demanding imperative that she kill, and kill now. Lara trembled in indecision, then sobbed in moral agony. *I will not do that! Not without knowing!* She threw her rejection into her mind-space, a shield to hold the rage and power at bay, if just for an instant. With a chaos-encased plane of pure emerald light, she stripped the null field off the face of the Beast.

Reality shimmered, like some cosmic gong had sounded. She remembered with perfect clarity when that exact sensation had happened before.

When they had first met.

When she'd first touched his hand, three and a half years ago, standing there in her kitchen.

"John!" She screamed his name, and stepped out of her own chaos cloak to fall beside her lover, to kiss, to heal, to resurrect, to pull him back from wherever she'd sent him.

Only the briefest premonition of a resurgent pounding in her skull preceded the instantaneous physical and metaphysical forces that exploded out of his body, and blasted her away from him, out and away into blackness and oblivion.

Anglick Generating Station, New Haven, CT | Tuesday 0558 EDT

The Magician left the contemplative peace of the null dimension, the ultimate *eye of the storm*, and slid back into his body. It felt strange, foreign. He wriggled a bit, like fitting himself into a wetsuit. Hard floor and pain, he thought, and strange but familiar odors. His practiced discipline evaluated the pain as unimportant, and shunted it off for future evaluation; the smells were what interested him. Those smells were like little harmonics, riding the great waves of odors from ionized air and scorched metal. His nostrils flared reflexively as he tried to decode their subtle messages. The Magician played with the riddle as John Connard's physical body rose toward awareness.

With vision and hearing not quite fully restored, he sensed a vague form over him, screaming something, descending fast, a crackling wave of green fire beside it. The Assassin in him reacted reflexively, throwing out all the defenses it could grasp. A mish-mash of gravity, null and energy slammed the descending figure away from him, and spun it a hundred feet into the air above. John lurched to his feet, stumbling sideways momentarily as his vision and hearing and mental faculties snapped in. The Magician held up his left hand, and with a gravity wave held the Other in position where he had thrown her, at the top of the arc. The inert body hung suspended in mid-air, rotating slowly in the condensing steam shroud under the roof of the turbine hall. He transposed to a sheared-off catwalk just underneath it, steadying his still-wobbly legs against the remaining guard rail in the wreckage of steel. He nudged the gravity field to bring the suspended form toward him.

John's mind-space began to re-form then, slowly regathering itself. No pounding in his skull obtruded on his consciousness, and his perceptions, it seemed, had widened from his sojourn in the null dimension. He could sense more clearly the consciousnesses and focused intent of the soldiers in the hovering helicopters above. He sensed two minds in the power plant below him, peacefully resting. Interesting, he thought. The Other didn't simply kill them. Now why is that?

As he asked that question, fragments of the image of his nexus Duc Li began to cohere, to reassemble themselves inside his mind-space.

Anglick Generating Station, New Haven, CT | Tuesday 0558 EDT

Emptiness. Nothing. Lara Picard existed, she was certain, or at least her consciousness did, because she had cognitive thought. But the thought had nothing to tie into, no reference point, no horizon, no anchor. There was only the total absence of anything external to her thought. Then she moved, and stretched out a metaphorical hand into the emptiness. The movement created tiny musical vibrations; they surrounded her, whispering, weaving into a song. Lara smiled as she recognized them. She drew her hand along the vibrations, and they took on a threadlike form, as they had when she had first dreamed them, lying on the cot in the protected quarters at Quantico. They twisted again as she reached out and touched them, helical spirals, representations of DNA and its manifold possibilities for evolution.

The singing helical threads tingled and pleasured Lara's metaphorical hands, like the vibration of a purring kitten. Her father's music played into the threads, deep and strong like the granite bedrock under his New Hampshire farm. Her mother's music merged in with those threads, the calmness and serenity of a quiet lake. Joshua's music played out from her own in a rich and complex counterpoint. But that music, she understood, comprised the past. She was in the present, in an instant of no time, the null dimension. She existed as nothing now, except possibilities.

But all music plays forward, into the future, doesn't it? She found John Connard's bright thread, and wove hers around it, hopefully. From her present instant of no-time, she guided that possibility into the future. One of the outcomes, she saw, could be a symphony of surpassing beauty and grace: a new child, a new era. But that was only one possibility of many. John himself would determine which one would occur.

With that thought as an anchor, she sent her senses outward from the null, and looked down on her body. It hung in a haze of steam and dust beneath her, twisting slowly. The dim figure below on the catwalk held it suspended above him in a gravity field, directed by his outstretched left hand. Am I dead, she wondered? Did John kill me? She watched blood trickle out of the corner of her mouth as her body rotated slowly. No, she thought, I'm not. Life exists in that body. I can sense it. But pain and sorrow, along with life. She focused her intention on the sorrow.

Ah, so that's what happened, she thought, running mind-images backward in time. John never had time to recognize me. He was only coming into consciousness, and he just reacted with those wonderful animal reflexes. And he still doesn't know it's me! I have to get back! Panic suddenly flooded her as she realized she did not know how exactly to leave the null and return to her body. The threads of the past and future that weaved through the null danced excitedly around her. Their music conveyed an evolutionary imperative of great urgency. She must leave this present infinite instant, her no-time, and leave it now!

One single bright twisting thread reached toward her: a life preserver, or an umbilical cord. Its beautiful turquoise coloring and the complexity of its music told her it was Joshua. As his thread embraced her, Lara's consciousness spun out of the null dimension, and started its journey back into her body. That body now drifted slowly downward toward the shimmering entity on the wrecked catwalk. It was drawn inexorably toward her lover John Connard, who hadn't recognized her, and whose right hand held a deadly plane of crackling blue light.

Anglick Generating Station, New Haven, CT | Tuesday 0558 EDT

Following reflected flashes of blue and green light, Joshua ran up the stairs from the entry door and out onto the turbine hall floor. He froze in the precise spot where the Magician had stood just a few moments ago.

The far end of the hall showed a scene of chaos and destruction. Steam screamed out of a pipe in a high-pitched squeal, and hung near the tall ceiling in a mist. Dust and debris circulated upward into the mist, drawn by the exhaust fans that had kicked on. Sparks flew from equipment as it failed and short-circuited, creating a random pattern of electrical discharges. High above, near the ceiling, a human form floated in the haze. It began to move slowly downward, toward a second, shrouded figure beckoning it from the end of a wrecked catwalk. The infinite possibilities implied in the present moment struck the boy's mind like an anvil, and his knees buckled.

Hamilton O'Donnell caught up with his nephew and grabbed his shoulder to steady him. Joshua started to move forward, but the hand on his shoulder cautioned him.

"Careful here, boy. Careful. This is a delicate time, a dangerous one."

Joshua froze, sensing the danger. There were too many possibilities; a misstep could be catastrophic. That was his mother, floating in the haze, and he sensed the danger around her. He would help, but only with the greatest finesse.

Time slowed for Joshua O'Donnell as a vision of his evolutionary diagram spun in his mind, the bright threads of its possibilities shifting like dunes in a sandstorm. He saw that he stood on a nexus, a present moment through which the threads in his diagram danced from the past into the future. Those threads were possibilities, and far too many combinations existed for him to analyze. But the threads existed within a topological space, a matrix, a structure containing certain invariants, reliable stable referents in the shifting sands of probability. One of those invariants was love; he anchored himself on it, and reached his consciousness out toward his mother.

Ah, yes, my young friend, Hamilton O'Donnell told himself. That's the ticket. The very thing. Gently. With love. This is a convergence of key possibilities, a reconciliation of dualities, just as you intuit. The High Priestess and the Magician, coming together at last. The third eye, then they both will see. Together. The Universe card, the completion of the tarot sequence. And its choices, boy: its terrible and wonderful choices.

Your thread and its music may help. But I think you can help only within the topology of one side, boy, that of your mother. So you may help her back into her body, but she has already chosen to escape the monkey trap. She has already secured her soul.

The Magician and the Assassin, lad, they are beyond your reach. John Connard must help himself. He is a good man, and may escape the trap, but his way is more difficult. His soul is more troubled. And he has yet to choose. He has not yet come to the Universe card. His outcome is still uncertain. With him, we cannot intervene, boy. We can only hope.

Anglick Generating Station, New Haven, CT | Tuesday 0559 EDT

Tiny familiar smells, somehow distinguishable from those of ozone and scorched metal, still troubled the Magician with their mystery. His nostrils flared out reflexively, trying to pick out the subtle messages in the air currents wafting toward him from the floating body of the Other. He would bring it closer, and investigate.

No, John Connard, no! You made that mistake once, and were trapped and nearly killed. Kill this thing now! The image of his nexus Duc Li snapped into full coherence in his mind space, screaming that urgent demand.

The Assassin's rage welled up in immediate support, voracious and hungry for the kill. His left hand adjusted the gravity field slightly and slid the floating form faster toward him. It faced away, out into the mist from the screaming steam leak. The Assassin's right hand flared into a plane of pure blue energy, twitching uncontrollably with the memories of those who had paid with their heads for his baby sister's murder. An exultant sense of power flooded into his being along with the rage, accompanied by the demanding imperative that he finish the Other. As the form slid closer, he saw she was totally defenseless. The power and rage thickened around him like congealing blood, exulting more.

But the Magician forced himself to stand off a distance from the Assassin's rage. He became calm, and questioning. His uncertainty about perceptions and illusion remained. In fact, he realized, those uncertainties had been magnified by his contemplative time in the null dimension. The intuition that all was not as it seemed here, that there were subtleties lurking just beyond his comprehension, became even stronger. Why had she disabled the two power plant workers, put them to sleep, rather than kill them outright? That implied a certain morality: avoidance of unnecessary collateral damage. But morality was inconsistent with the Other as the pure embodiment of evil, was it not? A big question, the Magician thought. And *by our own moral code,* he reminded the Assassin, *we must know this thing we are about to kill.*

The inert form of the Other slid down the gravity field closer to John Connard. Tattered remnants of a chaos cloak chased themselves around her body, uncertain residual fragments of the null dimension, cut off and weak and homeless. Her green aura flickered sickly, all but gone now. Her tattered and shredded clothing exposed burned and bruised flesh underneath. He wondered absently how he looked, and that thought was enough to unleash the Assassin, to trigger his rage again. The plane of blue light crackling from his right hand flared as brightly as an electric arc. He trembled in the striking position as he guided the body closer. The

Assassin snarled within, gleeful, impatient. One stroke, and her head and body would fall separately to oblivion. And the world would be safe.

Or would it? That world would still have him in it. The Magician. The Assassin. And they would be very, very much enhanced. Would the three of them meld, in time, to become the same kind of monster as this Other? Was that in fact what he feared so much about the Other? I have to know, the Magician told the Assassin. I have to look upon the Other, to see if she portends what I might become. I have to see its face before I kill it.

Glowing threads sang in the Magician's mind as he reduced the plane of blue light in his hand and reached out to turn the body to face him.

No! The Assassin screamed, and the energy flared again from his hand.

No! Kill it! You must kill it now! You must! It is still deadly! It will trick you! It will kill all you love! It will drive the human race into soulless evil! The image of Duc Li added to the overriding insistence in his mind.

The Magician gasped with effort. It would be so easy, so pleasurable, to slide into the rage that sought to envelope him. To use the power, to dominate, to kill; to accept without question or caring that which lay smoldering in his deepest self, the most primitive level of his being, a level now so intimately integrated with his higher selves.

The threads in his mind sang to him again, one last redeeming time, and John fought for control. He got it, barely, and the blade of blue energy in his hand flickered off. He rotated the body of the Other in the gravity field, and her battered face turned into full view.

Reality shimmered, like some cosmic gong had sounded. John remembered with perfect clarity when that exact sensation had happened before.

When he had first met his lover Lara Picard.

When she'd first touched his hand, three and a half years ago, standing there in the kitchen of her house next to Montrose Park.

Understanding came in a flash, and with absolute clarity: the Magician, the master of deception, had himself been deceived, strung along. He saw the nature of the deception, how subtle, how masterful. He saw how carefully the truth had been tailored, shifted ever so slightly. His nexus had played him like a violin, collaborating with his Assassin, binding him to its distorted reality. He saw it all in an instant, though he didn't see why.

But John Connard didn't care why. He blasted both the screaming Assassin and the suddenly quiet and contemplative false image of Duc Li entirely out of his mind-space. He felt the gap where their existence had ceased, and felt the simultaneous disappearance of his power and control over other dimensions. He caught his love gently in his arms. The fluttering remnants of her chaos cloak snapped out of existence, and she murmured his name as she curled her bloodied arms tightly around his neck.

The sheared end of the wrecked catwalk groaned once under the added weight, and collapsed underneath them. The lovers fell into space, holding each other. A hundred feet below, a field of jagged corroded condenser pipes pointed straight up, awaiting their arrival.

Chapter 42

Two bruised and bloody bodies, entwined in a desperate embrace, fall though space, rotating around each other. Time slows into frozen frames, as in a time-lapse camera. Rotation. Click. Frame. The brick walls of the old plant slide by their entwined bodies. Rotation. Click. Frame. The steam and debris-filled nave ceiling of the old turbine hall swings into view. Rotation. Click. Frame. The gap in the turbine hall floor spins into sight, its opening a fatal passage to the jagged field of upended condenser pipes below. Rotation. Click. Frame. That field of jagged pipes is coming up all too fast. Rotation. Click. Frame.

John Connard desperately seeks the power to transpose, to carry his love off to the catwalks they are falling past. Lara Picard desperately seeks the power to fly, to lift her love to safety. But those powers have been replaced by emptiness, and the emptiness holds no hope. Rotation. Click. Frame. A loud noise, a yell, sounds from the other end of the long turbine hall. Then another, of commanding force and tone. Rotation. Click. Frame...

"Mom!" Joshua O'Donnell screamed as the high catwalk collapsed and the two entwined forms fell through the haze at the far end of the turbine hall. He started forward, hands outstretched as if to catch them. Power ramped up rapidly in those small hands, and reality shimmered in front of them.

His uncle reacted instantly, catching the boy's shoulder and shunting away the power. He made a stentorian authoritative demand that resonated through the murky air to the end of the hall: "The Covenants!"

The two forms fell, wrapped around each other, toward the opening in the turbine hall floor, almost to the deadly bed of jagged pipes in the condenser bay below. But then... then... they winked out of existence. The pop was audible even at the other end of the long turbine hall.

"Is Mom okay?" Joshua gasped. "And John? Is John okay? That was him, wasn't it? Wasn't it, Uncle Ham? Are they okay?"

"Ah. Yes, me lad," the old man exhaled, "I believe they are." He paused as if to consult some internal barometer, and exhaled again. "I believe that they actually are doin' quite well, given their experiences."

"Quite well," Joshua repeated tremulously. He held the truth of his uncle's statement to the core of his being and burst into tears.

Hamilton O'Donnell picked up Joshua in a bear hug and felt the boy's tears of relief trickle inside his collar. He walked slowly back off the turbine deck toward the stairs, carrying his trembling nephew, brushing away tears of his own.

Northwest Washington, DC | Tuesday 0601 EDT

A sense of envelopment is followed by a sense of displacement. The vision of a bed of jagged corroded pipes is replaced by the vision of a more prosaic bed. Rotation. Click. Frame. Downward velocity is amended, gentled to just a slight drop. Rotation. Click. Frame....

Two bruised and bloody bodies materialized with a pop of displaced air and dropped onto the down comforter on the big air bed in Lara Picard's house on Phoenix Court, in Washington, DC. John and Lara grunted as they hit the bed, their expectation being contact with something far worse.

Their impressions had all the crystalline clarity imparted by the frozen view-frames of incipient trauma, but that clarity fuzzed and faded in mere seconds of time under the softness of the bed beneath them. The heat of their adrenaline was flooded by a cool soothing forgetfulness as autonomic endorphins and sleep chemicals from the primitive depths of their brains ran outward in a massive flood. John barely had time to mutter "Wow, what a dream!" into her tangled hair. Lara barely had time to murmur a "Mmmffff!" of agreement into the hollow of his neck. Then both consciousnesses dropped into an emptiness greater than that created by any sedative or narcotic known to medical science. They lay inert on the comforter, totally naked, cut and burned and bloodied, but wrapped in each other's arms. Smiling.

Anglick Generating Station, New Haven, CT | Tuesday 0601 EDT

"Quite well," Joshua repeated again, wiping his eyes and heaving a gigantic sigh. Curiosity immediately followed his recovered breath. "And where, exactly, are they doing quite well, Uncle Ham?"

"Ah, well, young man, it would appear to be the house."

"Our house in Washington?"

"The very one."

"The house that's three hundred miles from here?"

"Umm. Somewhat less, boy, as the crow flies, I believe."

"And how about as they flew, Uncle Ham? About how far would it be as they flew?"

Hamilton O'Donnell furrowed his brow and rubbed sweat backwards off his bald pate. He eased the boy out of his embrace and set him down on the stairwell landing. "Well, now, y'see, me lad, that's a bit of a mystery, isn't it? A question of relevance of concept, I s'pose. You can't use a ruler to measure a sound."

"But..."

"Aye, laddie, you have questions, of course. But your mum and John are safe and sound, and we need to be goin', we do. At this very moment. Before matters become more... complex." His hand on the boy's shoulder turned him back toward the stairs they'd run up, and they walked swiftly down to the ground level entrance.

"And do we need to be going to Washington, now, or Ireland, Uncle Ham? Or somewhere else entirely?" The boy's reddened eyes studied his uncle intently as they strode out toward the parking area where they'd left the Edsel.

"Ah, Washington for now, boy. For now. And then we'll see."

Joshua continued studying his uncle as they walked.

"Mom and John... they didn't recognize each other until just now, did they, Uncle Ham? They actually were trying to kill each other, weren't they? This was dangerous, wasn't it?"

"Life is dangerous, young man. Life is dangerous."

"Still?"

"Oh, less dangerous at this very moment, I suppose. But the danger will return. It always does, in one form or another." The old man cast a wary eye on the fog as spoke. Then he analyzed the sounds of the helicopters overhead and relaxed slightly. They still had a few minutes yet.

Northwest Washington, DC | Tuesday 0601 EDT

The FBI agent dispatched earlier by TC Demuzzio stepped lightly upstairs in the Picard home on Phoenix Court. He froze in place at the thump from a room down the hall. Nobody was supposed to be home. A cat or a dog, maybe? He debated his options as he listened for other sounds. His was an illegal entry, even if ordered by higher authority. What the hell, he decided, he could bluff it out if confronted. He had his orders, duly recorded. Let TC Demuzzio and the brass take the heat for a fuckup. After a minute of no other noises, he cracked the room door and peered inside. Two bodies lay on top of the bed, naked and bloody. Jesus, were they dead? He padded silently over on the thick carpet.

No, they were breathing, in the relaxed rhythms of deep sleep. The cuts and scrapes and bleeding looked superficial. But they must be painful. He wondered if they were drugged. Probably had to be, the way they were smiling. Well, I guess it doesn't matter, he realized. These sure as hell are the people in the ID pictures, no question about it.

The agent palmed the small digital camera, switched off the flash, and photographed their sleeping forms, with close-ups of their faces. Then, doubting if even Gabriel's horn of the second coming would rouse them, he took out his Swiss Army knife and pulled out the scissors attachment. Small snippets of their hair, wrapped in tissue, went into separate pockets.

The agent padded silently out of the bedroom, eased the door shut behind him, walked downstairs and out into the brightening morning. He climbed into the nondescript sedan parked at the corner of Phoenix Court and R Street and informed his partner of the developments.

"Get TC on the horn! Oh, my, is that man gonna shit bricks! The suspects he thinks he's closing in on in New Haven are right here in DC. Looks like they been having themselves a pretty fine S & M session, and they're sure as shit zonked on something. He musta got some pretty bad intel to place them in New Haven. Man, what a fuckup! Wish I could be there to see old TC's face. And hear him cussin'. The man's gonna invent a whole new vocabulary!"

The agent busied himself by putting the hair samples in separate plastic bags and downloading the camera images into the laptop computer. The phone call clicked through its high-security relays, seeking one TC Demuzzio, presently airborne in an Army Black Hawk helicopter above the thinning fog layer over New Haven Harbor.

Global Consciousness Project, Princeton University, NJ | Tuesday 0602 EDT

"Aaron, be careful! For God's sake, be careful!" Adrienne Baxter screamed her concern into the phone, a white-knuckled grip on the handset. The off-scale spikes of the past two minutes on all GCDs within a hundred miles of New Haven implied some enormous psychic energies were being deployed.

"Yes, Adrienne, of course I'll be careful," Aaron O'Meara answered as he slowed and turned into the driveway of the power plant they agreed on as the probable epicenter for the signals. "And I'll keep up a running narrative of what I'm seeing. You recording all this?"

Adrienne looked at the FBI agents protecting her. They nodded.

"Yes, Aaron, you're on tape. We don't have a phone patch for you to the helicopters yet, but they're working on it, and should have one in a few minutes. They want a description from you of where the buildings and the power lines are."

"Hmm. Yeah, I hear the choppers, Adrienne. But I can't see them. The fog looks like it might be thinning out, but maybe that's just the sun getting higher in the sky. No, I can't see the choppers at all. I can barely see the power lines. I can't see the top of the stacks, either, so I really can't guess how tall they are."

"Okay, Aaron, are you on the plant property now?"

"Yeah. There's a few cars in a parking area in front of the entrance, I'm heading toward it. Passing under some power lines now... Adrienne, Adrienne, you're not gonna believe this. There's that Edsel! And there are those two... I saw... Phoenix Place... Washing..." Aaron's voice faded off into an incoherent crackling.

"Aaron. Aaron! Talk to me!" But nothing came out of the phone except static, and after several moments that cut off into the dead silence of a dropped connection. Adrienne screamed and bit her knuckles as the 1-minute integrals on her monitors simultaneously flatlined. Both blue and green traces were gone from her screen. Nothing. Not a single detector registered above the baseline. Then logic hit her, and she relaxed. The data were more than a minute old, and their signals actually had flatlined before Aaron turned into the plant driveway. So none of the psychic energy implied by those monstrously high signal peaks could have affected Aaron. He simply drove into an area under some power lines where the phone reception was lousy, that's all.

But maybe not, Adrienne thought. He had seen something, certainly. An edzel, he called it, whatever that was. And two of something else. The female FBI agent, who had been quietly relaying Adrienne's half of the conversation to TC Demuzzio in the command chopper, took the phone away from her mouth.

"Agent Demuzzio has been holding off on involving the local police, Ms. Baxter," she relayed, "but now he wants to know if you think Dr. O'Meara is in any danger. He's asking if you think we should send in the New Haven PD on the ground. He doesn't want to get local PD involved if he doesn't have to, he says, but his military can't land yet, the fog is still too thick."

Adrienne paused, and looked again at the flatlined monitor screens. Why? The party had ended, obviously. Blue and Green had done whatever they were supposed to do, whether fight, or rescue, or mate. So there was no longer any danger zone for Aaron, and no more worries that maybe Blue would come to visit them with a grudge. Aaron probably just entered a dead zone for his cell phone, she thought. She was being paranoid.

Then the latest 1-minute integral updated onto the screen, and many of the GCDs spiked back up. They were not nearly as strong as before, and neither green nor blue by her coding, something totally new.

"Yes! Tell him yes," Adrienne Baxter said to the agent, as calmly as she could manage over the growing lump in her throat. "Police on the ground is probably a good idea. And tell Mister Demuzzio we've gone active again at that same location."

Anglick Generating Station, New Haven, CT | Tuesday 0602 EDT

"Shit!" Aaron heard Adrienne exclaim, and the rest of her statement faded off into crackling interference. But he wouldn't have been able to speak coherently anyway, he thought, given the situation.

Aaron pulled in beside the Edsel, and leaned out his window to greet the Irishman he'd last seen on Phoenix Court in Washington, DC. The boy with the curious probing eyes had been there, too, Aaron remembered; the two of them had been putting tennis gear into the back of the Edsel.

"Ah, well now, laddie, I must apologize, y'see," the Irishman said as he smiled at him.

The lilt and brogue were just as Aaron remembered, but the greeting confused him.

"Apologize?"

"Faith, and 'tis terrible directions, I've been givin' ye, no? For your poor self to end up here, a good three hundred miles north of your mark?" The Irishman laughed and raised his arms in a shrug of contrition to the foggy skies. As he brought them down, Aaron felt an enveloping warmth in his mind and passed into blackness.

Hamilton O'Donnell reached in the window, jammed the transmission into park and cut the ignition. He opened the driver's door, unlatched the seatbelt, and let Aaron slump gently into his arms.

"Come, lad, help me here," he told Joshua. "Pop the back hatch. We must be quick about this. Such opportunities are not to be missed, and we have precious little time." He cast a measuring eye upwards toward the sound of the circling helicopters. The sound of one of the rotors changed in pitch, ever so slightly, as if acknowledging the need for haste.

"Opportunities, Uncle Ham?" Joshua raised the rear hatch of the van obediently.

"Aye, lad," he replied, tucking Aaron's inert form into the fetal position on the rug in the back of the van behind the wheelchair apparatus. "An opportunity for you to do a spot of doctorin'. An opportunity for this fine laddie to do a spot of healin'. An opportunity for a bit of species development, furtherin' a nice genetic line."

He pulled Aaron's shirttails out. "Place your palms on his back, me lad, right above the belt, either side of the spine. Yes, yes! There! The very thing!"

"I don't know what's wrong with him, Uncle Ham," Joshua objected.

"Ah, but you do, boy. You do. Just feel it. Quickly, now, before this reality settles down too much. We have only a brief time to remain undetected." The old man put his left hand on the back of Aaron's neck, and his right hand on Joshua's neck. The power that he had shunted off a minute ago rolled back through the boy's hands.

"Spinal cord. Sheath. Nerve bundles. Atrophied muscles. I see them, Uncle Ham. I see the problems," the boy said wonderingly.

"Well then, me lad, fix them!"

"But I don't know how!"

"Nonsense, boy. You are a Magician, a Mercury, a *kahuna*, a healer. You know exactly how. Now just do it!"

And he did know how, Joshua realized. Something very ancient was telling him. Time dilated and slowed, and he carefully set the healing process in place, then enabled it.

Reproductive problems? Any genetic predisposition affecting offspring? The thought-questions were his uncle's, clearly, but seemed to come from a great distance, or from the depths of a well. Or maybe from the top of the well, and he was at the bottom, Joshua thought; it was impossible to tell, there were no referents. Joshua let the music of the man's genetic threads slide though his hands. No, he thought, no significant hereditary defects there. The man's condition was an accident of gestation. He saw a minor reproductive problem, related to the nerve condition, and fixed that, too.

"Ah, yes! Then come on out, me young *kahuna*," his uncle told him out loud, "'tis time to be gone. Past time. Hurry!" He slammed the van's hatch door, and half-dragged his dazed nephew into the Edsel. The old car sped out of the plant gate and slewed left on Grand Avenue. Ah, excellent timing, he smiled. Truly excellent! He slowed to a sedate pace approaching the intersection with East Street, so not to attract the attention of the New Haven Police cars that roared by them in the opposite direction. Those cars spun into the power plant driveway, sirens screaming, tires squealing, while the old Edsel drove casually away, following the signs for Interstate-95 South and the long trip home.

Anglick Generating Station, New Haven, CT | *Tuesday 0610 EDT*

"Taking it down, now, sir," the copilot advised TC Demuzzio. "We can make out a good LZ north of the building, no wires. We'll set down there. The other aircraft will drop troops and then go to the airport to get refueled. We'll be on the ground in a minute."

Yeah, we will, Demuzzio thought, but for what purpose? The detectors blipped up again, a little, but now they're all flatlined. And if the transmitted pictures on this laptop screen are any indication, Lara Picard and her lover John Connard are at this moment sleeping comfortably in a bed three hundred miles southwest of here. No question it's them. And the hair samples will lock down the DNA identification. So what the hell will we look for when we get down on the ground?

The big agent sighed in frustration and tapped the laptop computer with his fingernails while his unproductive thoughts ran on. Other big questions: how did they, or at least she, get from New Hampshire to Washington between 0130 and 0600 this morning? How did they come by all those scrapes and cuts and burns? And if those two birds are in DC, then what in seven blue hells were we chasing down Interstate-91 in the fog?

TC Demuzzio shook his grizzled head, unsnapped his harness, and followed Shaundee and his troops out of the Black Hawk as it landed. He already had the sinking sense of a blown mission, but they had no choice except to play it out.

"Let's stick to the game plan, Merton. Assault teams. Careful entry. Clear every square inch of this place. And tell them not to disturb evidence if they find any. You deploy the troops. I gotta go spin my story for the locals, take jurisdiction." Demuzzio trotted toward the New Haven PD command car, authoritatively holding out his ID, assessing the police shift supervisor's raised eyebrow and tailoring his spin appropriately.

"Sergeant... Jackson," Demuzzio peered at the name tag and police rank and offered his hand, "thanks for responding so fast. What we got here is possible terrorist sabotage on the electrical grid. The Bureau is taking jurisdiction, at least until we sort out whether this is a real attempt or not." He cited the section of the US Code giving him precedence, and saw the sergeant nod in acknowledgment as the soldiers dropped out of the choppers.

"And how might we assist the Bureau this morning, Agent Demuzzio?"

"Anybody in or out since you got here, Sergeant?"

"No, sir. That would be about... six minutes ago."

"Well, then, if you would just put one car on the gate, and stay here yourself for coordination, I think that's all we need from PD at the moment. You can send the rest of them back on duty. And thanks."

"Always a pleasure to help the Bureau, Agent Demuzzio," Jackson replied.

"Those all Special Forces boys? I take it you won't be needing our SWAT, or the bomb squad, or the Fire Department? You want us to put any of those functions on standby?"

"No, Sergeant, I don't think so," the big agent said slowly, "we've already tied up some huge federal resources, and this may turn out to be a false alarm. No point in spending the City's money, too."

Demuzzio motioned Jackson to follow, and walked down to inspect the van parked against a dividing wall. It had Maryland plates, with a handicap symbol. It had to be the Goddard guy. O'Meara. The keys were in the ignition, but nobody was in the driver's seat. So where was he? Demuzzio stuck his head in the window and looked around. Was that him? Curled up in the back? Yes! Jesus, what next? He pulled open the rear hatch just as Jackson's radio announced the arrival of one Nathan Rodgers at the gate, requesting to talk to an FBI agent named Demuzzio. Jackson cocked an eye at him.

Sure, sure, send him down, Demuzzio thought, nodding okay as he opened the hatch. Why not? Why the fuck not? Maybe he can tell us why a crippled astro-physicist is curled up in the back of his car having himself such a fine snooze, when he just got here a few minutes ago. And why has he got that fucking goofy smile on his face? It was, he reflected, exactly like the smiles on the electronic images of Lara Picard and John Connard, sleeping on a big bed three hundred miles to the south.

I-95 West of New Haven, CT | Tuesday 0611 EDT

The fog started to lift and burn off as Hamilton O'Donnell piloted the Edsel southward, away from the power plant. He stopped along the access road beside the long straight section of sand that formed the west shore of the Harbor, and put the convertible top down.

"Ah, Joshua, 'tis shapin' up to be a lovely sunny mornin', I'm thinkin'," he said and smiled at the boy. "So let us proceed home well illuminated." He opened the trunk and removed the custom-made tonneau cover, clipping it carefully over the retracted soft-top. Then he pulled a mesh bag full of baseball caps from the trunk and tossed it on the front seat.

The invitation to shield his eyes from the brightening sun pulled Joshua out of the dazed contemplation of his repair job on a damaged spinal cord. He rolled the bag over in his hands, and picked out a Red Sox cap.

"Umm. You owe me some illumination, Uncle Ham," he said as the car ran up the entrance ramp onto the highway, "and possibly you could start with The

Covenants. That command you yelled out to save Mom and John.'"

"Indeed I do, me lad, and indeed I could. Start there. The Covenants. Yes, that might be a good place to start. 'Course 'twere more a reminder than a command...'" His voice tailed off into contemplation. "But first, me lad, if you'll permit, I must tidy up a few loose ends." He thumbed a number into his cell phone without taking his eyes off the road, and began speaking rapidly and authoritatively in that dialect Joshua thought might have been a derivative of Gaelic. The conversation went on for some time, lasting from I-95 to the Merritt Parkway and down through Greenwich. As they passed into New York, the fog lifted entirely, and the morning sun warmed the back of their necks.

Finally, Hamilton O'Donnell clicked off, and held up one finger to his nephew.

"Just one more call, laddie buck," he said, smiling. "Incomin'. I have to stand by for it. Shouldn't be long now."

He was right. Thirty seconds later the phone chirped.

"Ah, yes, darlin', of course I'll hold for the dear man."

Joshua O'Donnell's ears sharpened. This conversation might not be in Gaelic, he thought.

"A grand day to ye, sir. And a grand one it is, up here in the north country."

His uncle's tone had changed, Joshua noted. No longer commanding and instructive, it was more like he was talking to a friend. Then there was a long pause, with his expression becoming first thoughtful, then appreciative.

"Yes, sir. That's the gist of it. Your perception is entirely accurate."

A longer pause, and then his uncle's expression became a smile of approval.

"Why, yes. Thank you, sir. That would be most helpful. Yes. It would avoid widespread concern over nothin'."

His tone now sounded more like that of a successful supplicant, Joshua thought. So it might be a friend, but definitely someone with more authority than his uncle, or at least someone with the sort of moral authority his uncle respected.

"Yes, sir, I will, sir. Thank you. And you have a nice day too, Mr. President." Hamilton O'Donnell clicked off the cell phone, put it back in his shirt pocket, and smiled broadly at his nephew.

"Well, me lad, that's that. Some minor dangers eliminated, or at least forestalled a bit. All in all, a good mornin's work, I'd say. And now, me lad, what was your first question? And change your hat, for God's sake, boy! Here, put on this Yankees cap. For God's sake! Don't you realize we just crossed over into New York?"

"Protective coloration, Uncle Ham?" The boy delved into the mesh bag and pulled out the designated cap as he considered what his first question should be now. The Covenants? The President? One of the several hundred other imponderables his analysis had identified during the hour his uncle had been on the phone? He adjusted the cap and pulled it securely down on his head so it wouldn't be blown off in the wind of their passage.

"Protective coloration. Why yes, indeed, me lad. Hit it on the head you have! That would certainly be the next logical development in our little fable, would it not?"

The boy's jaw dropped as he realized how many of his imponderables that semi-rhetorical question had instantly resolved.

His uncle rooted around in the mesh bag for another Yankees cap, and slapped it over his own bald head, putting it on backwards. "Might as well have some protective coloration meself," he chuckled, "probably wouldn't hurt."

The fuzzy side-hair and twinkling eyes and quizzical cocked gray eyebrows so absurdly parked under the backwards cap made the boy burst into helpless laughter. Tears of relief and joy mingled with those of his nine-year-old humor. After several minutes, he clutched his aching sides and unsuccessfully tried to stop. It was going to be an exhausting mind-dance all the way back to Washington, Joshua O'Donnell realized, exhausting but wonderful. The thought sent him into additional paroxysms of laughter.

Northwest Washington, DC | Tuesday 0711 EDT

Lara woke first, her mind a kaleidoscope of fractured images and strange memories. They sank quietly into an enveloping mental warmth, like an ice cube disappears into hot coffee, before she could examine them. Those memories didn't matter, she thought. Only the warmth mattered. She stretched fully on the big bed and contemplated how wonderful she felt, her right side snuggled against John, the rippled green light of the morning sun through the trees playing into the bedroom. She turned and kissed his ear, and a wave of passion engulfed her as she threw her leg over him and pressed her crotch into the hard muscle and bone of his hip. He smiled in his sleep.

Lara rose up on her elbow and looked down over his naked back and legs. Hmm? Patches of blood were crusted over him, over her, all over the down comforter.

"Where the hell did that come from? John, you okay?" It was a curiously soft question, more rhetorical than anything else, of little concern to the glowing warmth in her mind. That warmth whispered to her that she was just fine, John was just fine, they were together. And other questions were irrelevant.

Lara ran her hand down the length of his back, flaking off little crusts of blood, making small circular motions on his buttocks.

"Mmmfff," he said, into the pillow.

"What a great ass you have, John Connard," she whispered in his ear.

John smiled into his pillow as he slowly woke up. Images of strange things that had been flitting through his mind faded, and disappeared into the realization of just how good he felt. Got to be illegal, he thought, to feel this good. He struggled to define the feeling, as her hands stroked his back and butt. A wholeness, that's what it is, a nice warm cozy wholeness. And Lara feels the same way, I can sense that in her touch. Passion enveloped him. He felt himself come erect, and rolled onto his side to take her in his arms.

Congealed blood plucked at John's skin as the comforter came unstuck from his torso. He looked down in confusion. The defensive reaction, the sudden snapping into full combat acuity that should have happened did not. Almost as soon as he saw the dried blood, the warmth in his mind dismissed it. An academic curiosity only, it whispered to him. He was just fine. Lara was just fine. They were together. They were whole.

"Yycchh," Lara exclaimed, looking at the mess he'd uncovered, "John, you need a shower. I need a shower. And this comforter needs to go in the wash."

He smiled slowly at her, nodding slyly downward to a higher priority for them both, and reached out his arms.

She leaned past him and grabbed fist-fulls of the comforter. Then she flipped her body off the bed and pulled, rolling him across and dumping him unceremoniously on the floor at her feet. She didn't wonder for even an instant at her ability to so adroitly move a mass fifty percent greater than hers. It was just so natural. She yanked the blanket from around him and wadded it up in her arms, smiling down at him.

"I love you, Lara Picard." John smiled back at her, then grabbed her ankle and kissed it, kissing his way up her calf, admiring the dew forming on her labia above him. He didn't wonder for even an instant at his ability to see something that at this point actually was still internal to her body. It was just so natural.

"Well, I need a shower," Lara said firmly, stepping out of his grasp and dropping the comforter on his face. "Catch me if you can, big boy!" From a standing start, with no visible effort, Lara somersaulted neatly over the bed without touching it, and ran into the bathroom.

In the steaming shower, his hands caressed her. God, I'm a lucky woman, she thought, as his lips and tongue moved down her neck, pausing on a nipple, working in a slow arc down past her hip bone. She grabbed his head, pulling him upright to whisper agonizing need into his ear.

"Now, I want you now," she husked, parting her legs and pushing up onto her toes to welcome him.

God, I'm a lucky man, he thought, to have a woman like this, all passion and love and goodness. His amethyst eyes smiled into her emerald ones. Star-shaped patterns flared and glistened in the depths of their eyes and refracted outward off the water droplets in the shower, tiny shards of blue and green light. Two wet throbbing bodies slid together and moaned with pleasure. Hot water and steam enveloped them. The internal warmth of their wholeness embraced not only their bodies, but their minds and spirits as they spiraled into orgasm. The moment seemed to go on and on and on, as if the enveloping sense of passion and pleasure and love and wholeness had an independent existence all its own, and wouldn't let them go.

A short time later, scrubbed and clean and brushed and shaved and flossed and tucked between fresh sheets with the French doors open to the warming spring air, they made love again. Their passion and pleasure and love and wholeness continued, and expanded outward, waves from an epicenter. Locked in an embrace as much spiritual as physical, they fell into the deep sleep of perfect contentment.

Chapter 43

Nathan Rodgers sat in the warm hazy sun on the van's tailgate, his hand lightly resting on the shoulder of Aaron O'Meara, whose sleeping form had remained remarkably inert, curled in the fetal position. Except for an occasional spasm of the lower back breaking the slow rhythms of his breathing, Aaron hadn't budged since Nathan had arrived at the power plant, an hour and a half ago. The Army medic had been concerned about the inability to rouse him, but after checking his vitals periodically, said he just seemed heavily sedated, in no imminent danger. And Adrienne Baxter had been quite emphatic, convincing even a skeptical TC Demuzzio to let Aaron recover naturally, whatever naturally meant at this point.

Nathan wondered for the seventh time that morning about the certainty in Adrienne's voice, the intuition she couldn't explain. She claimed that everything had worked out, and that it would work out with Aaron, too. Fundamentally, they were all riding on that, instead of sending Aaron off to the hospital. Surreal, Nathan thought, how a young woman not far out of childhood could take charge of their actions.

At the other end of the spectrum, Special Agent in Charge TC Demuzzio was feeling more like events were in charge of him. He glanced across the access drive to the van where Aaron O'Meara still slept. *An hour and a half since we landed,* he thought, *and the only person who might have seen any part of what happened is still out like a light. The troops have turned this place upside down and inside out. And all we've got are Picard's and Connard's bloody clothing, right down to their shoes and socks, impaled on some rusty pipes. Their naked bodies are three hundred miles away, lying in Lara's bedroom in Washington, bloodied and bruised but sleeping like babies. And they've got the same goddamn stupid satisfied smiles on their faces as this O'Meara character.*

Demuzzio ran his hands over his grizzled head and sighed in frustration. He was losing it. He'd yelled at the sleepy plant operators. How the hell could they remember nothing when their plant was a fucking shambles? He'd yelled at Nathan Rodgers, accusing him of running some kind of elaborate scam, to get them to chase two signals down Interstate 91 when the purported sources of those signals were actually in Washington and not here. Unless you believe in teleportation, which, he had to admit, seemed more and more likely. Probably a good thing that Rodgers had yelled back at him, telling him with exquisite logic and sarcasm exactly how much less plausible a scam was than teleportation. At least that had snapped him back into some semblance of sanity. But teleportation? Fuck it, beam me up, Scotty, he thought sourly, I'm not getting anywhere down here.

His cell phone rang, and he clicked it on and barked with barely controlled frustration. "Demuzzio!"

He listened intently, running his hand over his head some more.

"They're gone, huh? And of course you have no idea where they went, do you?" A rhetorical question, he knew what the answer would be from agents Socrates and Schmidt—they'd probably been sleeping just as soundly as O'Meara. No point chewing them out, the situation obviously was beyond their control. But that just deepened the mystery, adding another layer of frustration. So now it was Hamilton O'Donnell and his nephew Joshua who had disappeared, too, out from under the noses of two very good, seasoned agents, who never in their careers had fallen asleep on the job, but who had just woken from a nice nap of four-plus hours. So did their two wards teleport, too? Or did they just walk away? He rubbed his head some more.

"Naw," he paused to think and then answered Jack Socrates' question, "no APB. Not yet anyway. I'll think about it. Seems like maybe the danger is over. Head back to DC, Jack, you and Carl both. I'll call if I need you."

The big agent kept rubbing his head, looking up at the brightening sky for answers. None were forthcoming. When he looked back down, O'Meara was sitting up in the back of the van, and woozily resting against Rodgers.

"Merton," he announced as he strode past Colonel Shaundee toward O'Meara, "maybe you should just shoot me now. Fucking shoot me, will ya? Save the government some trouble, shoot me now. Before I shoot somebody myself. And these two turkeys over here are prime candidates."

Shaundee smiled and followed him.

"Aaron O'Meara," Demuzzio shouted at him, "you got ten seconds to tell me what went on here, and why the fuck I shouldn't arrest you for interfering with a federal investigation!" The tirade brought out a goofy smile, but the eyes behind it seemed alert enough, he thought.

"You must be... Demuzzio?" Aaron's voice crackled hoarsely, huskily, as if it were an old piece of machinery groaning into use. "I don't really remember, Agent Demuzzio. I drove into this plant. The gate was open. I remember that. And I must have parked down here, but I don't remember that. The next thing I know,

Nathan's waking me up..." His voice trailed off uncertainly, and he added, "and that's all I remember. I'm sorry."

"O'Meara, you better fucking well start remembering," Demuzzio's tone started to curdle the air, "because if you don't, I'm gonna haul your sorry ass off as a material witness under a national security writ, and you ain't gonna see the light of day or a fucking lawyer or anything else until you tell us what went on here!"

Aaron shrugged at him helplessly.

"And I'm gonna haul your two buddies off, too. Rodgers here, and who is that kid... Baxter, Adrienne Baxter. You people are all gonna sit in a fucking federal detention lockup until you tell me what you know. So goddammit, you better start remembering, or you're fucked! And if you people have been scamming us somehow," he added more irately, "you're double-fucked. We'll throw away the goddamn key!"

Aaron shot upright and grabbed the big agent's jacket in hands made enormously strong by years in a wheelchair.

"Listen to me, you shithead! You do anything to Adrienne, I'll rip off your head and stick it up your ass where it belongs. I'm telling you I don't remember!" Aaron was adamant. "If it comes back to me I'll tell you. But right now, I don't remember a goddamn thing! And that's the truth!"

Ah, thought Demuzzio, well, yes, that reaction would seem to be truthful. I can see it in his face. But lookee here, maybe this has been a scam, after all. His voice went cold.

"I heard you were supposed to be disabled, O'Meara. You can't walk. You get around in a wheelchair. Or did you forget that, too?"

No, he hadn't forgotten that, Demuzzio realized, as he watched the shock of discovery run across the man's face. He just hadn't realized he was standing up. Therefore, he'd been fixed. Lying there in the back of the van, the man's defect had somehow been fixed. Well, once you step off the slippery slope of logic and concede teleportation, then it's not really much of a jump to miraculous healing, is it? If Demuzzio was any judge—and he was—of how people reacted to the sort of psychological pressure he'd just applied, then Aaron O'Meara was not faking it. He truly did not remember what went on after he'd entered the plant, nor did he know what had happened that could have made him able to walk.

Aaron's grip on Demuzzio's lapels tightened as his knees buckled slightly, then loosened a bit as he straightened and locked his legs.

"I can stand," Aaron said wonderingly. His flare of temper forgotten, he looked up at the big agent in amazement. "I took a step!"

"Yes, you did," Demuzzio conceded sourly. "Rodgers, here, grab your buddy, take him for a walk out to that phone pole and back. Let's see what we got here." Aaron leaned on Nathan as they made their way slowly out to the pole, fifty feet away.

"Jesus, Mert," Demuzzio observed, rubbing his head more forcefully, "we got a cripple walking, but not remembering. We got two of the Bureau's best field agents taking a snooze on guard duty, while the boy and the old man they were guarding have gone missing. We got a wrecked power plant and two operators who don't know jack shit about how it happened. We got clothes here belonging to Picard and Connard, but those two are laying in bed down in DC, naked as jaybirds. We got a global consciousness network that tracks ETs, only now they've suddenly disappeared. We got forty of your best soldiers trying to dig two people out of the plant when they're not even in there. Did I leave anything out?"

"Yeah, TC," Merton Shaundee said softly, acknowledging what he'd just heard in his communications earpiece, "you did. You left out one last thing. Your phone's gonna ring. Sorry."

It did, and Demuzzio listened glumly to the stand-down order. It came from the top—the very top, apparently, no chance of appeal. The order said cease operations, pack up and go home forthwith. No arrests were to be made, no detentions, no more questioning of witnesses, no contact or communications with the press or anyone else. Officially, this had been just an exercise, an unannounced assessment of anti-terrorist capabilities. The PR people would handle any fallout. There would be a debriefing within two days. He should keep himself available on two-hour notice, in or near Washington. Other than that... have a nice day.

"Yes, sir," Demuzzio acknowledged, and clicked off the cell phone.

"Aww, shit! You, too, Merton?"

"Yeah, TC. I got the word just before you did. I gotta pack my boys up and re-fuel and get back to Pisgah *toute suite.* I'm sorry."

"Shit, Mert. This isn't reality. This is fucking science fiction!"

"No argument from me, TC. No argument from me."

The two old friends stared at each other, then at Aaron O'Meara. He walked slowly and tentatively back toward them, Nathan Rodgers by his side but no longer supporting him.

"Over a beer someday, Mert?"

"Yeah, TC. Someday. A beer. Definitely. Probably a shot and a beer."

They stared at each other some more, and finally started laughing. Big belly-wrenching, rib-cracking laughter. There was nothing else they could do.

I-287 at Tappan Zee Bridge, Nyack, NY | Tuesday 0718 EDT

"Uncle Ham, this bridge sort of reminds me of that painting in your office at the University," Joshua observed, "maybe looked at from a different angle."

"Mmm, Joshua, I see. You have a good eye, me lad. And well, isn't life all perspectives and angles? Different ways of looking at things, *n'est-ce pas?*"

And I will give his mother's painting back to John as a wedding present, I think, Ham noted to himself.

"The monkey trap, Uncle Ham. It's a *gom jabbar*, isn't it? It's a test that separates humans from animals, isn't it?"

Ah, so you remember that wonderful story, do you, my young friend? "Well, yes, me lad," he replied, "I suppose it is. I mean aside from the obvious difference of keepin' your hand inside the *gom jabbar* versus takin' it out of the monkey trap empty, the intent would be the same. And of course the bait in the monkey trap, the ultimate power to control, is a more subtle diagnostic than simple life or death. First to recognize the bait—and power comes in many guises—and then to decline it in favor of love... Ah, yes, that would be a good test, I would say—a test of the ability to love, to unite, to become whole, a key ability for any species if it is to move forward without destroyin' itself in the evolutionary process."

"But two organisms, Uncle Ham? Determining the fate of an entire species based on just two organisms? Is that realistic?"

"If the best of the best cannot pass the test, young man, then there is no chance the rest will pass. The species must wait another cycle."

"And you? Are you the gatekeeper, Uncle Ham?"

"Gatekeeper? No, me lad, no, no! Not a bit of Saint Peter in me! I am but a simple monitor, a timekeeper. I observe. I await the cycles, the punctuated equilibrium of the genetic clock, the time of convergence of the species toward enlightenment. When I judge that time to be right, I merely announce it. The rest is out of my hands."

"But such a time always comes, doesn't it, Uncle Ham? Sooner or later? Species cycle forward toward self-realization, don't they? It's all configured, isn't it? Just like my diagram on the table in Brooklyn. Just like the threads I can feel in my mind. The topology has invariants, and the probabilities of genetics, of evolutionary outcomes, they just cycle around those invariants, don't they?"

"Ah, well... yes, me lad, I would say that is an accurate assessment, so far as I understand these things."

"So the structure exists, Uncle Ham, but we develop within it, at least on a species basis, is that it? For individuals, random chance and free will are... accessible?

We can make choices..." Joshua paused thoughtfully, "...and if enough of us make bad choices, that sets us back as a species, doesn't it? A holocaust, or something. So that maybe then we have to wait for the next cycle?"

"Mmm. Choices, boy, yes, they are very important. Choices are portrayed in the Christian Bible, in the Qu'ran, in the Talmud. They exist in Eastern religions and philosophies, in Celtic myths, in oral traditions. They cross many cultures and ages."

Their mind-dance continued as they drove down the highway toward home. Passing through New Jersey east of Philadelphia, they changed baseball hats, then changed them again in the Baltimore tunnel. Protective coloration.

Northwest Washington, DC | Tuesday 1117 EDT

Lara woke first, with a thought in her mind, origin unknown, but clear enough: Josh and Ham would be arriving. She and John had a few minutes yet. She made a delicate trace with her forefinger down the center of her sleeping lover's back. Once more, for good luck, she thought. A few minutes would be plenty of time, as ready as she felt herself to be, the heat and pressure building outward from her core. And Lord knows he's always ready when he wakes up. Lara eased her hand across the hard bone and muscle of his hip and confirmed that other hardness. Oh yes, he's ready.

She smiled at his peaceful happy face, nuzzled it, and whispered in his ear. "Roll over, big boy, I've got a little brunch sandwich for you."

John Connard woke with hunger on his mind. He'd actually been dreaming of the four of them sitting down to a late brunch, but the tickle down his back and the surreptitious check under his stomach built another kind of hunger. The message whispered into his ear certainly left no doubt.

He smiled and obediently rolled over. "And I have for you, my love," he told her, "a little breakfast sausage. To tuck into your sandwich."

"More like a salami, lover," she grinned as she wriggled a little and eased down onto him. She pulsed her kegels rhythmically. "Ahh. Yes! Definitely feels like a salami. Not a sausage at all." Her hands clenched his shoulders with the same sudden urgency as her vaginal muscles clenched his engorged penis.

God, what a beautiful woman, he thought, looking up at her smiling face as she crouched over him, impaled. John's right hand ran down to where their bodies joined, and he drew his fingernails slowly upward across her hard flat belly to the soft underside of her left breast, and drew circles around its hardened nipple. He raised his head and took her right nipple in his mouth, hardening it to match its mate.

Her motions quickened, and he dropped his hands to her hips and raised up to press deeper into her, wanting to be closer, wanting to be one.

I-395 Entering Washington, DC | Tuesday 1119 EDT

In the antique Edsel a few miles to the southeast, Joshua smiled joyfully in his mind-dance. A brilliant new indigo-colored thread, or its possibility, had begun to unfold in his present reality. He was going to have a baby sister!

The addition of this new thread into the background of his consciousness brought the boy back full circle to his fuzzy memories of events at the power plant. He had magicianed a man back to health, and discovered in the process many strange things. Bodies were malleable, from within. Damage could be repaired, from within. All the mechanisms needed were present within cellular structures. The only other thing required was focusing the intent of greater consciousness. The chain of inferences being sifted and sorted in the back of his mind for the past six hours suddenly rearranged themselves in a blinding enlightenment.

"Uncle Ham!"

"Yes, boy?"

"I figured it out, I think!"

"Umm? And which of our many puzzles would that be, now, me lad?"

"The Magician. The Healer. What you showed me with that guy in New Haven, at the power plant, to fix his spinal cord problem. We didn't really do that for him. We just opened the conduit and focused the intent so he could heal himself."

"Ah, focused intent, 'tis it? That sort of thing, me lad, certainly is rife in fable and myth. But there is little documented analog in modern science or medicine for what you are assertin' so blithely."

"Oh, Uncle Ham! So what? Aren't you the one who just told me that all is foretold in fable and myth?"

"Mmm. Possibly, boy, possibly. It sounds like somethin' I might say to a young and impressionable mind. But then, I say a lot of things, most of which you should not take too seriously."

Joshua looked at his uncle in disbelief, then blew him a loud raspberry. "To paraphrase something else you told me, Uncle Ham?"

"Yes, boy?"

"Mysticism and science are Siamese twins."

"Mmm. *Touché*, me lad. Is there more to your enlightenment? Do go on."

"Another thing, Uncle Ham, is how the monkey trap must work. It's a species *gom jabbar*, it tests whether we're ready. So it re-integrates the brain segments in the two test organisms, then it sees what happens. Feeds in some disinformation. Sees how the organisms handle the complexities of the kind of power the species will develop. Sees how well they fall back on fundamental truths. Sees how well they can open their conduits to greater consciousness. How effectively they use it to make hard choices."

"Mmm. Fascinatin', me lad. Fascinatin'."

Joshua stepped out of the mind-dance momentarily, with a direct question.

"They passed the test, didn't they, Uncle Ham. Mom and John."

Hamilton O'Donnell sighed at his greatest hopes and worst fears, the very same as those of all parents: children growing up, and moving on.

"Yes, Joshua, they did."

The boy grinned at him. "I knew it."

"But let me caution you that they will remember none of the actual test, boy. The Covenants are quite clear on that. It is for their own protection."

Joshua contemplated that. "But what about their powers, their access to other dimensions, the energies I felt flowing around Mom? I can still feel in my mind how different their threads are now," he asked hopefully.

"Cellular integration of brain segments cannot be reversed, 'tis too dangerous to go retrograde. So their powers remain, me lad. That also is for their protection. There is danger yet to come."

Joshua contemplated that statement as the Edsel transited lower Washington. This city is seat of a lot of power, which means a lot of danger. My uncle is right. The danger may have abated for now, but it's far from over. I can even see how some of the possibilities might play out. More of them are dangerous than not. Many more. But that's a problem for another time, and another place, isn't it?

As the Edsel turned off R Street onto Phoenix Court, Joshua sent a wave of love and greeting ahead of him down the street to his mother and John and the indigo thread of possibility they had just created, and felt theirs reflected back in return.

Global Consciousness Project, Princeton University, NJ | *Tuesday 1120 EDT*

Adrienne puttered around the Global Consciousness Project data center awaiting the return of Nathan and her first meeting with Aaron. Her young mind felt suffused with the love that lay just under the spoken words of their phone calls. Interesting how a mostly technical discussion of how to document the happenings of the past few days could carry such emotional undertones. Or maybe, she thought, the telephone equipment merely produced a focal point for some other kind of communication, something much more subtle.

I'm so tired I can barely stand up, her thoughts ran on, but I've got to keep moving around. My mind is at warp eight, it'll blow up if I try to sit still. I'm in love with a man I've never met, for crying out loud! There's so much to do, so much to learn about each other. What do I say when he rolls in the door? Should I hold the door, since it opens out? No, Nathan will do that, probably. I should hug Aaron, I guess, because of what we've been through. But can I kiss him? I'd better brush my teeth! Can I tell him right off I don't care that he's in a wheelchair, that I love him anyway? Oh, gosh! Would that offend him? Should I wait and see how to be more delicate about it?

She thought back to their last conference call. Ten minutes out, Nathan said, and Aaron was right behind him. They would all go to lunch, Aaron had chimed in, and try not to get too blasted. His cheerful voice suffused her mind. It's got to be a chore for him to get into his wheelchair and get out of that van. Maybe I should go out to the parking lot and meet them there, and we can leave for the restaurant right away. That way he only has to get out once. Jeez, what should I do here? She nibbled her lower lip nervously and looked at the clock.

She clapped her hands on her young head, and looked up at the ceiling for inspiration. The fluorescent lights flickered. When she turned around at a creak of the door, Nathan and a handsome freckled young man with an abundance of curly red hair stood in the doorway looking at her.

"Adrienne Baxter, say hello to Aaron O'Meara," Nathan intoned in his most paternalistic manner.

"Aaron?" The words of the question intended to follow got lost in an inarticulate croak. All she could do was point at his legs.

"Adrienne! Hello! You're even more beautiful than Nathan said... if that's at all possible!"

His Irish blarney, she thought fleetingly, is going to be such fun! She opened her arms and started across the room, still trying to get words past the croak in her throat.

Aaron unhooked his arm from Nathan's shoulders and started across the floor, but tripped on his feet and went sprawling into her. She tried to catch him up, but they both tumbled to the floor.

"Ach, Adrienne, I'm sorry! It's my new feet, still in training—a difficult adjustment," he grinned up at her and opened his arms. "Hello, love!"

"Hello, love," she echoed softly. She leaned down and kissed him full on the lips, folding into his arms like she'd always been there.

Reality shimmered, like some cosmic gong had sounded. Nathan Rodgers looked down at them smiling. He thought for a moment that their bodies had sort of flickered with light, but put that transient impression down to the moisture in his eyes, and blinked it away.

Chapter 44

The sun played full on the earth below, dayside noon. Three images communed, drifting in space in the plane of the ecliptic, forty thousand kilometers above the central Bahama Islands in the Caribbean. The energies the images controlled kept them in their chosen human forms, but starlight shone straight through them. The international space station hove into view far below. It moved busily across the face of the planet, blissfully unaware of the strange energies communing above.

"Congratulations," the image of Lara Picard said, smiling at the image of Hamilton O'Donnell, "you configured it well. The test played cleanly and seamlessly in the consciousnesses of your two subjects."

"And each of the many support consciousnesses played their parts flawlessly," the image of John Connard added, "which also is a high tribute to your configuration. Every single one played out within the error bands you predicted for their evolved states of intelligence and morality."

The Ham-image made a slight bow of appreciation, but held his silence.

"A good clean test," the Lara-image continued, "except for the boy. But then, there always are outliers in any experiment, *n'est-ce pas?*" She looked at him shrewdly, evaluating.

The Ham-image smiled back at her, inscrutably, and elected just to shrug his acceptance of her rhetorical question.

"Well, one outlier isn't bad, and certainly isn't any reason to invalidate a test," the John-image said judiciously. "We therefore certify that the tests were properly made and The Covenants observed."

"And our thanks for rescuing the test organisms," the Lara-image said with a tone of formality, "when they fell from the catwalk. You correctly perceived we were disengaging and could not easily see the danger; you correctly invoked the command, an acceptable intervention. We wish no avoidable harm to any test subjects."

"Ah, 'twas no problem. Me ould colleague Werner prepared me for such eventualities within experiments," the Ham-image replied.

"Well, you know the formula, old friend," the John-image smiled at him. "So now you must state it for the record."

The Ham-image didn't hesitate. "I, known as Alexander Hamilton Shaughnessy O'Donnell, monitor for the species *Homo sapiens* and *Nova sapiens* of this planet Earth, solemnly swear that my monitoring activities and this test configuration have been done in full conformance with The Covenants, with no interventions, save the acceptable one just noted."

"All right, then," the Lara-image said, "for the record, the hold on the evolutionary development of this dangerous species is hereby released. The control loops may be disengaged. The transition pregnancy may proceed." She smiled slyly. "If it hasn't already."

"But the test consciousnesses must retain no memory of the test itself. The sequencing must be completely uninstalled from their minds," the John-image added.

"Yes, of course. I've already done that," the Ham-image replied.

"And the support players—those whose consciousnesses were tapped for this test—they must be carefully re-set as closely as possible to their origin state." The Lara-image looked at him, evaluating again. "Can you do this, old friend, or will you require our assistance?"

"Ah, yes, that is within my capabilities, thank you, and I will start as soon as we're finished here."

"And the boy," the John-image said thoughtfully, "the boy is an outlier. He may grow beyond you, given time. He might go his own way; he must be allowed to do that. You may help him, but only within the constraints of The Covenants. And be very careful. Damage and destruction come all too easily at delicate junctures like this. Other macroshifts have taken destructive turns, galactic pursuits of senseless rage. Remember our own terrible history, and that our purpose is to refine, not destroy. You are a gardener for that planet below, and a midwife to its new beings."

The Ham-image snapped into the uniform of a colonial British soldier. He saluted smartly, palm out, and exclaimed, "Yas, sah!"

"Fare well, old friend." The Lara-image smiled, reaching out to touch his insubstantial cheek. "Return to your gardening. We will see you again, perhaps, in another turn of the cycle."

He smiled back at her, and at the John-image. Then his form elongated into a vortex of energy and spun downward, returning to the surface of the planet that he had called home for a long, long time.

Northwest Washington, DC | Tuesday 1201 EDT

"Mom!" The boy charged into the kitchen and tackled his mother's waist, hugging her hard with his surprisingly strong young arms, almost lifting her off the floor.

"Ooomph! And hello to you too, Joshua O'Donnell!" Lara hugged her son's shoulders just as hard, squeezing the breath out of him, bending down to ruffle his thick black hair, kissing the top of his head.

"Oh, Mom! I'm so happy to see you!" He pressed his face into her blouse, smelling the unique scent of her skin through the freshly laundered cotton. "I'm just so happy to see you," he repeated, looking up at her with moist eyes.

"And you too, John," the boy said, releasing his mother and giving John Connard an equally substantial hug. "I'm so happy to see you, too! And thank you!"

John Connard smiled down at him, cocking a quizzical eyebrow at Lara. "And we're certainly happy to see you, too, Josh," John told him, giving the boy a return squeeze.

"Yes, we are," Lara said, moving over and throwing her arms around both of them, "it feels good to be all together again."

The three of them stood there, in the kitchen, for the moment a frozen tableau in time, an essence of harmony and love, very much like a seasoned version of the tableau created when the three of them first came together in that very spot, three and a half years ago. But now their frequencies and resonances and melodies were all weaving together, much more like a completed symphony. They all recognized it, and smiled at each other. Then the moment passed.

"Where's your Uncle Ham, bub?" Lara gave Joshua's head another ruffle.

"Oh, he'll be along in a few minutes, Mom. He said he had a few loose ends to tidy up."

John laughed. "Ha! I should think so. I get the sense there were a ton of loose ends flying around this morning." His brow furrowed. "I just wish I could remember what they are."

"Yeah, me, too," Lara added, "I've got a brain full of fuzz this morning." She reached over and stroked John's cheek. "See what you've done to me, lover?"

Joshua laughed and hugged them both one last time. Well, there's a good reason for that mental fuzz, he thought, but I'm not the one to tell you. So let's get you back on track here, before you start asking too many worrisome questions. "I'm starved, Mom! What can I do to move food closer to the table?"

"Well, set the table, Josh," she laughed, "then dice up this onion. John is going to be making his famous Connard omeletto for us. He claims it's still legal, even if it is past noon."

Interesting, Joshua thought, as he caught the tossed onion. She didn't pick that onion up in her hand to toss it to me. She just flicked at it with her finger, but her finger didn't touch it. And what's more interesting than that, she did it so naturally she didn't even notice. And neither did John.

The boy set four places at the table, then peeled and diced the onion. He observed his mother and John move around the kitchen. Their motions were complementary, almost choreographed, never in each other's way. It seemed almost as if one mind was controlling two bodies, until John bent down to get some vegetables out of the bottom refrigerator bin. Then his mother snatched up his tee shirt and nibbled him on the ribcage. John twitched up, and bumped his head on the refrigerator door shelf. That broke the pattern, and the boy actually felt relieved.

With the vegetables stir-frying in the wok, and the big seasoned skillet heated and just about ready to receive the omeletto mix, Lara rapped smartly on the pantry panel. She and Ham had installed that panel in the wall between the two kitchens of the duplex years ago, so they could pass dishes and recipes through more easily. Lara yelled her message through the panel into the other house. "C'mon, Ham! Brunch-time is almost here!"

"Be there in a minute, my friends," the yell came back, "it's me reentry orbit I must compute first."

John smiled. Lara laughed. Joshua looked thoughtful.

In the adjacent duplex, in the small room behind his kitchen that he used for a home office, Hamilton O'Donnell's body floated comfortably in the lotus position six inches above an office chair. His wide-open gray eyes carried a silvery-white star sapphire pattern in their depths, a reflection of the energies he directed. As his split consciousness departed the communion above the planet and reintegrated fully into his physical body in this reality, the bright star-shine faded in his eyes. But it didn't fade to nothing, just down to what his many friends described as his wonderful Irish twinkle. As he sank slowly onto the seat of the chair, a very satisfied smile formed below those twinkling gray eyes.

Plane of the Ecliptic above Central Bahamas | *Tuesday 1202 EDT*

"How do you think he finessed the test?" The Lara-image smiled fondly at the last traces of the departing energy vortex.

"Ah. Not *if*, but *how*? An interesting question," the John-image replied, "since there was no trace of any level of intervention in their memories or genetic structure. Our hosts were exactly what they appeared to be, two organisms on the cusp of change, arriving there themselves, quite naturally. Of course, considerable selective breeding occurred in their past, but that is not outside The Covenants."

"The boy, then, during the course of the test? It seemed more than just matura-
tion under pressure," she queried.

"That's the most likely," he agreed, "but if so the boy did it by himself. He wasn't
engineered by our old friend, that much is clear."

"Mmm. No, our old friend is more an artist than an engineer. His hand is more
subtle, I think." She laughed merrily. "So he finessed it, putting the boy in the right
place at the right time, with the right amount of mind-sculpting, all without perturbing The Covenants. Oh, that's quite elegant."

"Though he probably didn't need to." The John-image laughed back. "These
were high-caliber candidate organisms, and likely would have passed the test
anyway."

"True, but it is a useful piece of information in validating our decision."

"How so?"

"If our old friend is willing to skate so close to The Covenants to give his candidates a little edge, then he must truly love this species. We must respect that."

"Love can cloud judgment."

"And love can also see clearly, my dear." She smiled a brilliant smile at him,
emerald eyes glimmering like the stars that shone through her constructed image.
"In any case, our decision is made. This species will proceed, danger or not, and we
will hope for the best."

"And we have many memories to comfort us in our long journey home, don't
we, my love?" He smiled brilliantly back at her, amethyst eyes blazing with an
ancient and amused light in acknowledgment of her shifting thoughts.

"Ah, yes. I see that we do," she said softly, shifting her image so that water from
the shower dripped off her naked body. "Well then," she dropped her non-existent
towel on a non-existent floor and whooped, "catch me if you can, big boy!"

Vortices of light and energy chased each other to elsewhere and elsewhen, brilliantly green and blue, their components complex and entangled, but ultimately
one.

Goddard Space Flight Center, Greenbelt, MD | Tuesday 1202 EDT

The SDI exercise at Goddard Space Flight Center had just broken for lunch, but
Amy McLaughlin stayed in the X-Room for the moment. The exercise segment
was over, but her keen competitive spirit liked to play through the sequences
again, even when they were taking a break, to see how performance could have
been improved. Her restless fingers tapped the keyboard, adjusting the gimbaled

sensors on the satellite array so they would pick up the simulated missile launch from a ship in the Atlantic south of Bermuda. She watched the replay as the missile's controls were successfully fried by the team's simulated microwave bursts. No question about it, they were getting better and better as the exercise progressed. When Aaron O'Meara got back to his shift tomorrow night, she would show him who the new champion zapper was!

McLaughlin smiled at the thought, her hands toying idly with the joystick controls, her mind wondering where Aaron was and what he was doing. His cynicism about government would no doubt be vindicated when he heard that all his emails, faithfully forwarded by Ed Edwards to the Pentagon situation room, had fallen on deaf ears. There hadn't been a whimper of any response to Goddard, no inquiry, no thank you, not even a go-away-and-don't-bother-us-feedback. The Pentagon had put the initial event down to a high-speed meteorite slamming into an asteroid, with chunks burning up in the atmosphere, just like she'd said. And they must have put down Aaron's subsequent pursuit of purported consciousness signals as just a bunch of wacko nonsense. She did, too, and she planned on telling him exactly that when he showed up for tomorrow's exercise segment.

"Greater consciousness," she muttered, "ha! ETs! Gimme a break!"

But then, as the sensors on the satellite traversed westward from Bermuda and turned northward up the east coast, all breath left her lungs in a whoosh of shock. Her professional decorum deserting her, she yelled at Jack Walton, the tactical tracking technician. He was spending his lunch break looking at the sports section and sipping a Coke.

"Omigod! Jack, get in the Tac seat. Get the tracking on! Hurry!"

Walton had good reflexes and excellent instincts, and his hands were moving over the control board even as he slammed into his chair. The sensor array stopped its traverse and focused on the incredible scene. Two objects of some kind were boiling up out of the atmosphere. Their point of origin was slightly south and west of Goddard, somewhere in DC. They had very high kinetic energy; it boiled the air around them. They clearly were accelerating. Then they started to spiral around each other.

"History! Omigod! Plot it, for God's sake, Jack, plot it!"

"History plotting, coming up, a few seconds," the technician muttered, fingers flying. "Recording all. Going into Tac Computer and mainframe both. Full online archival engaged."

Edwin Edwards, SDI exercise controller, ran in the door when he heard the yelling. He slammed to a stop and watched with his mouth wide open as the big display screen phased in. The satellite sensors, struggling gallantly on their gimbals, barely managed to track the outbound trajectories. As the objects cleared the lower atmosphere and climbed into the ionosphere, they displayed stranded flaming interwoven spirals, erratic, disjointed, impossible motions. Then, further out, in deeper space, they came together in a flash of blue-green lightning, and in one stunning center of brilliance lined out in a straight path, just south of the plane of the ecliptic. The three people present in the X-Room watched, fascinated, as that brilliance appeared to gather its light back inward. It folded itself into a tiny blackness and disappeared, several hundred thousand kilometers distant.

Jack Walton, the tactical tracking technician variously known as T-Cubed as well as Tac, made the first coherent statement, just like he had on Sunday morning two days ago.

"I believe this is pretty close to the reverse of what we saw Sunday morning, Amy."

"Aw, shit, Jack. Don't tell me that!" Her voice trembled with its adrenaline burden.

"Yup. 'Course it came outta DC, so could be it's some high-energy bullshit from the Senate and House." Jack Walton was a Libertarian.

"They're not in session 'til tomorrow, Jack," Edwards noted absently, regaining his breath.

"Well then, Amy," Walton said, "you're gonna have to explain to Aaron how those meteors of yours, that they could never find on the ground Sunday morning, just jumped right up two days later and hauled ass off into space." He used the napkin that the Coke had been sitting on to wipe a sudden sweat off his brow.

"Hmm, Amy," Edwards agreed, "I believe I'd like to be here when you explain this to Aaron. I'll bring the crow to the party. You prefer it medium, or well-done?" He collapsed in the controller's seat, ceding control to a laughter more than slightly edged with hysteria.

Northwest Washington, DC | Tuesday 1202 EDT

Not very far from Goddard, Hamilton O'Donnell sank down slowly into the cushion of his office chair, his eyes twinkling. Yes, he thought, it had been quite elegant. Probably unnecessary, but you never know. And as for skating on the edge? Ha! The old Georgetown University graduate smiled at the bronze plaque on his desk, the one that the head of the Jesuit order had given him years ago. It read *'Jesuit's Rule: Better to ask forgiveness than permission.'*

"Well, now, let us see what fable and myth have to say about this happy outcome," he murmured. He shuffled the deck of tarot cards expertly, three times, then cut to the middle of the deck and turned up a card. The Fool.

"Perfect! The zero card. The null. The beginning of the story. Calls for a toast, this does!"

The renewed banging on the pantry panel brought him out of his contemplative happiness. He yelled he was coming and gathered an ice bucket and bottle of Asti from his refrigerator on the way to the other half of the duplex for brunch.

Three of them sat down at Lara's kitchen nook table while John flipped his huge omeletto. Joshua's cocked eyebrow wanted to know if his uncle had seen that no spatula was in use. Neither John nor Lara appeared to notice anything out of the ordinary as the concoction rose a foot above the skillet and flipped itself over, intact. Ham's slight nod acknowledged to Joshua that yes, they might have to work on this a bit. Joshua tugged down the brim of a non-existent baseball cap to remind his uncle of his own allegory on protective coloration. The old man burst out laughing, and tousled the boy's hair, his gray eyes twinkling. The action was a silent message back to the boy: a minor problem, Joshua, easily solved. Not to worry.

Downtown Washington, DC | Tuesday 1205 EDT

It had been a long, long day for Special Agent Thomas Charles Demuzzio. He rubbed his hand over his grizzled face one more time as he walked out of the Bureau's headquarters building in downtown Washington and reflected on his morning: a lift on the Black Hawk from the power plant to Tweed Airport in New Haven, a puddle-jumper to New York, a commuter jet to Washington.

Not enough time on any of those flights to grab a decent nap. No way he could wriggle enough in any of the airplane seats to get some relief from the soreness in his thighs and butt, which still stung from extraction of the slivers. Well, he thought, at least I didn't get my sore ass chewed out more by the boss when I got here. His management chain had in fact gone out of their way to be very sympathetic and understanding. But they were also very firm. It's a national security issue, TC. Strict need-to-know, and you're out of the loop now. In fact, the Bureau is out of the loop. Go home, TC. Get some sleep. We'll call you for the debriefing session, a couple of days, probably.

Demuzzio had stopped by his cubbyhole office on the way out of the building and picked up his backup digital recorder. He declined the offer of a ride, deciding to walk the three miles or so to the government agency heliport in southeast DC where he'd left his car parked.

That should work some of the soreness out of my legs and butt, he thought.

I'll enjoy the warm spring air and the sun on my face, and maybe sweat a little of the tension out of my system. In the hour or so it takes me to walk it, I'll gather my thoughts, and record them while they're still fresh in my mind. Some of these memories of the past two days seem to be getting pretty elusive. Then, when I get home, I'll put some Epsom salts in the hot tub and three or four nice icy Heinekens in my belly, and I'll put this whole fucking crazy case out of my mind for a few days. TC Demuzzio was always one to have a plan, and this seemed like a pretty good one.

His dry and succinct recitation of the facts as he knew them took him only half-way to the heliport. He paused to look at the time left on the recorder's memory chip, and saw plenty of capacity left. He wondered if he should bother adding the non-factual material: impressions, inferences, intuitions, assessments. A lazy insidious voice spoke to him from far back in his mind. *Aw, shit, let it go, TC, let it go. What the hell, they're gonna suppress this whole thing anyway. So don't waste your time on it. Think of how good that hot tub is gonna feel on your sore ass; think of the contrast of heat on your outside with cold beer hitting your inside. Ummm. You've had enough misery for one day, buddy, more than enough. Let it go. Let it go....*

Tempting thoughts these were, a siren's song flirting with his mind. But TC Demuzzio was a stubborn, disciplined man who never willingly gave up on a case. He forced his mind to spit out the questions, assess the possibilities, speculate on the reasons.

They were all there, in the back of his mind, in spite of the whispering enticement to forget them, and out they came. He dictated non-stop, stream-of-consciousness impressions, inferences, intuitions, and assessments. The verbal purging persisted until he reached his car, and then he continued it for most of the twenty-minute ride to his house in Clinton, Maryland, south of Andrews Air Force Base. He only stopped when his recorder beeped at him saying its memory was full. He'd put down enough information, he thought, and walked satisfied into his small bungalow. Tossing the recorder on the kitchen table, he went straight out the back door onto the sheltered deck. He took the cover off the hot tub and cranked up the heater.

Seven minutes later the agent eased his big naked frame gingerly into the steaming tub. He pulled the small cooler full of icy bottles close to his right hand so he wouldn't have to reach too far. Then, finally, as the cold beer sank into his belly and his body slid deeper into the hot jetting water, he succumbed to the soft voice and let memories of the past two days slide away, out of his mind.

Twenty feet behind TC Demuzzio's steamy relaxing face, the little recorder sat on his kitchen table. Its *Memory Full* message blinked periodically. The recorder was a machine, and had no consciousness. Its message lay outside the purview of Hamilton O'Donnell.

Northwest Washington, DC | Tuesday 1323 EDT

The merry crew of four cleaned up the dishes from their extended brunch, and Hamilton O'Donnell pulled the celebratory champagne out of its ice bucket.

"Just gettin' up when Joshua and I arrived, were you two?" he asked. "And how did you sleep? You both look quite rested. Quite content. Quite... together."

"I feel absolutely wonderful," Lara said, "but I had some weird dreams, I think. I just can't remember them."

"Me too," John added, "but I have a vague recollection of dreaming about a tapestry, about weaving of some kind. Probably a memory of something I saw in Afghanistan, or some place where they do that sort of thing."

"Oh! Yes! That was it! Now I remember," Lara exclaimed, "and there was a new thread, John. You and I were weaving a new thread into the tapestry, my love." She frowned. "Only maybe it wasn't exactly a tapestry, maybe it was more of a symphony. We wove melodies, I think."

John finished wiping down the big omeletto skillet and sat down beside her. He squinted into the middle distance, struggling to pull up the elusive memory.

"And we had help, somehow, Lara. Didn't we? There was another hand, wasn't there, helping out the threads, or the melodies?"

"Yes, but the hand was hiding, I think. I can't remember actually seeing it."

"Yes! We had the same dream then!" Certainty laced John's voice. He and Lara grinned at each other daftly, and burst out laughing. Joshua joined them.

"Well, of course you did," Ham told them with supreme certainty. "You two are *anaim cairde*, soulmates. You very often dream the same dream." He popped the champagne cork, poured into four glasses, and picked up his. "Here's to tapestries and symphonies, my friends," he toasted, "old and new, finished and begun, human and divine."

Light reflecting off the facets of the champagne glasses seemed to twinkle a silvery white star-cross deep in his old gray eyes. An emerald star-cross glittered in Lara's eyes, an amethyst in John's. Sunlight reflecting off the birdfeeder in the trees outside the kitchen splintered around in the cut crystal glasses and came to rest in Joshua's eyes. A deep turquoise star-cross flared brilliantly there, merging the colors of the green trees outside with the blue sky above, merging them into the color of the waters that battered the wild Irish coast of his ancestors. The boy's mind turned fluid, like the waters. A no-mind; open, receptive.

Into that mind the splintered light carried a sharp sense of displacement, and a vision of extraordinary clarity.

A path, carved in the side of a cliff along that wild coast.

He had walked that path, once.

Walked in danger and darkness and pain. Eons ago.

Walked carefully. A shepherd, caring for his charges.

The waters below had been troubled then.

They were troubled now.

The message was crystalline in his new consciousness.

Danger and pain would be the other shepherds of this new species.

But he would hold the torch of hope against the darkness.

Out of some deep racial memory, urgent and demanding, the vision beckoned young Joshua O'Donnell.

On that path, he knew, he would one day walk again.

-End-

Author Bio

Lee Denning is the pen name of a father-daughter writing team. Denning Powell has been a soldier, scientist, engineer and entrepreneur. Leanne Powell Myasnik is a psychologist, poet and mystic. He lives on the East Coast, she on the West. They correspond and swap tales. With love. And hilarity.

Monkey Trap is their first book of a planned trilogy about the emergence of *Nova Sapiens*. *Hiding Hand* is in progress. *Splintered Light* is being structured. They're working hard and having a blast.

Don't miss any of these
other suspense novels

➢ Fire Owl
(1-931201-85-4, $16.95 US)

➢ Strange Valley
(1-931201-23-4, $15.50 US)

➢ Then is the Power
(1-931201-86-2, $19.50 US)

Twilight Times Books
Kingsport, Tennessee

Order Form

If not available from your local bookstore or favorite online bookstore, send this coupon and a check or money order for the retail price plus $3.50 s&h to Twilight Times Books, Dept. FD904 POB 3340 Kingsport TN 37664. Delivery may take up to four weeks.

Name: _____

Address: _____

_____

Email: _____

I have enclosed a check or money order in the amount of $_____

for _____ .

If you enjoyed this book, please post a review
at your favorite online bookstore.

Twilight Times Books
P O Box 3340
Kingsport, TN 37664
Phone/Fax: 423-323-0183
www.twilighttimesbooks.com/